WHEN DARKNESS FALLS . . .

A shift of wind, an updraft, something, had created a lull in the storm and everything was changing again. The horsecar was almost gone. The outline of a Fifth Avenue MTA bus was materializing in its place. And he became afraid again, realizing only then that he did not belong in that lost world. If there really was such a world. If he was not, in fact, going out of his mind.

That, at least, was what happened one time. One of the first times. Back just after Thanksgiving. But it was always different. The street scene always varied from one time to the next, as it did between any two ordinary strolls through midtown Manhattan. Yet three things were always the same. Jonathan Corbin was seeing, living, a time long past and dead. And there was always the snowstorm. And when the blizzard was at its worst and the night at its blackest, he would see the bareheaded woman running from him. The woman he would murder . . .

Books by John R. Maxim

Novels
PLATFORMS
ABEL BAKER CHARLEY
TIME OUT OF MIND
THE BANNERMAN SOLUTION
THE BANNERMAN EFFECT
BANNERMAN'S LAW
A MATTER OF HONOR

Non-Fiction
DARK STAR

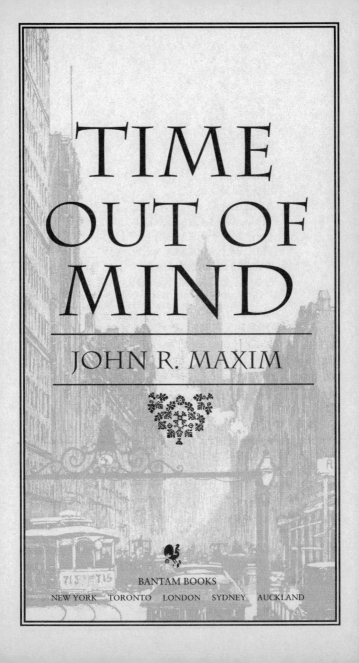

TIME
OUT OF
MIND

JOHN R. MAXIM

BANTAM BOOKS

NEW YORK   TORONTO   LONDON   SYDNEY   AUCKLAND

This edition contains the complete text
of the original hardcover edition.
NOT ONE WORD HAS BEEN OMITTED.

TIME OUT OF MIND

A Bantam Book / published by arrangement with the author

PUBLISHING HISTORY
Houghton Mifflin edition published 1986
Bantam edition / March 1994

ISBN 0-553-56039-5

Published simultaneously in the United States and Canada

Bantam Books are published by Bantam Books, a division of Bantam
Doubleday Dell Publishing Group, Inc. Its trademark, consisting of the words
"Bantam Books" and the portrayal of a rooster, is Registered in U.S. Patent and
Trademark Office and in other countries. Marca Registrada. Bantam Books,
1540 Broadway, New York, New York 10036.

PRINTED IN THE UNITED STATES OF AMERICA

OPM   0 9 8 7 6 5 4 3 2 1

FOR IRWIN SHAW
. . . who always had time.

I'll be with her again, in this life or next,
I'll go back to the past if I must.
I'll be with her again in time out of mind,
Where who hate us ne'er were, or are dust.
　　　—*C. G. Sterling, "Outback"*

Make no mistake. The genes we're born with carry memory. They carry knowledge we've never learned, talents we've never studied, even fears of things that have never frightened us. . . . But someone, some time, in our blood lines, had these memories. Yes, you might say that all of us are haunted to some degree. You might very well say that.

ONE

 E DID NOT HAVE THE LOOK OF A MAN WHO frightened easily. But what made him afraid, in a way no bar bully or snarling dog could, was snow. Ordinary snow. The kind that dusts and occasionally blitzes New York City between November and April. Jonathan Corbin saw things in the snow. Things that could not have been there. Things that could not have been living.

He'd moved to New York just last September. From Chicago. That was what made all this so absurd. Chicago got twice as much snow as New York. All his life he'd lived through midwestern winters harsher than anything seen in the East. And he'd liked the snow there. The heavier the better. Snow was beautiful as long as you didn't get stuck in it on a highway at night. Two or three inches of fresh snow could cleanse and soften even the meanest city streets. But with two months remaining of his first winter in New York, all that had changed. Now the first few flakes from any passing cloud had come to seem like living creatures. Malevolent, probing things. Like scouts for an advancing army. They would float slowly past the window of his office, sometimes stuttering along the glass as if to make certain he was there, catching a rising current to come back for a second look.

On this Friday late in February, the first random crystals appeared an hour before noon. Jonathan Corbin saw them, not through the office windows at his back, but in his secretary's troubled eyes as she stared past his shoulder. He did not turn. He sat frozen until she closed her book and stepped wordlessly from the room, shutting the door behind her.

Corbin buzzed her extension minutes later. In a carefully measured tone he instructed her to cancel the luncheon meeting he'd scheduled at the Plaza Hotel and said he'd take no calls. Not from anyone.

Four hours passed. It was after three when Jonathan Corbin allowed himself to hope that he might make it through this day after all. From his window, where he'd been standing almost constantly, he looked down on Sixth Avenue, four floors below. The snow was still not sticking. Only a wet gauzy layer clung to the tops of cars. The stored-up heat of Manhattan swallowed all others as they touched. Maybe, Corbin told himself, nothing would happen this time. He dug his fingers into the thigh of one leg to halt the trembling, which came in spasms. It would not happen this time. It could not. The snow was going to stop.

He pushed the draperies aside for a better look, and his eyes fell upon his own reflection in the double-paned glass. What he saw disgusted him. A grown man quaking. Cowering at the sight of a little wet snow. Hiding out in this room like a whipped dog. Angrily, he turned from that image and forced himself back to his desk. Anger, he knew, was a good sign. It always came when the fear began to recede and his fury at himself became stronger than the terror. He'd be fine now. As long as the forecast turned out to be right. As long as there was no more snow.

He wished that he'd kept that lunch date. It was important. Weeks in the planning. He could have handled it. They'd have noticed that he didn't look good, that he was pale and sweating and barely touched his food, but he could have bluffed his way through. As long as the snow didn't start to pile up outside. As long as he didn't start to see people who were no longer alive strolling past the windows of the Edwardian Room.

But that wasn't going to happen. Not this time. The forecast was accurate after all. Light snow. Flurries. Rain toward evening, possibly heavy at times. The weather page of the *New York Times* had promised that the main storm would pass well to the south. The weather bureau agreed each time Corbin called. He began to forgive himself at last for not checking the forecast before he left his house in Connecticut. He'd overslept and had to rush, unshowered, for his train. The morning sky had been more clear than clouded, and he'd smelled no moisture in it. Temperature in the low forties. Still, he should have checked.

But maybe, he thought, it was just as well he hadn't. Corbin knew that if he'd flipped on the marine weather station he kept mounted by his back door, and its tinny voice had even mentioned snow, he might never have left the house. He might not have even looked out a window until bright sunshine had baked a sealing crust onto whatever had fallen. And he'd end up losing his job. This time or the next, the terror he could not bring himself to explain would get him fired. They would have no choice. If he had a drinking problem, a drug problem, if he was depressed or a casualty of executive stress, if he had any kind of problem that they could at least begin to understand, they would try to help him. The Network was decent enough that way. Like they were with his boss, Bill Stafford, who was afraid to fly. They got Bill to enroll in one of those anonymous nervous flyers classes, and even when he flunked out a second time they just gave up and started booking him on trains for trips he couldn't avoid. Corbin had heard of other Network people who'd been put through detoxification or counseling programs of one kind or another. But what do you do with somebody who's afraid of snow? Demote him to some Sunbelt affiliate? Ship him back where you got him? Back to the Chicago station? For all Corbin knew, Chicago's snow would have changed, too, and twice as much snow would end up driving him out of his mind twice as fast.

March. A few more days to February and then March. If he could only get through March.

Corbin blinked. The room was suddenly darker. He spun out of his chair and again stepped to the window. The whole of Sixth Avenue seemed to be in deeper shadow. And the snow had thickened. It fell more purposefully now. A light veil was forming over untrod sections of the sidewalks on the branches of young elms whose buds had just begun to swell. And the sky. It was lowering even as he watched, swallowing lighter shades of gray as it eased downward, digesting the tops of taller buildings. Across the street, the Warwick Hotel was already in soft focus, and to his right he saw that all the upper floors of the rival ABC television building had vanished. The people! It suddenly struck Corbin that there were people up there. A part of his mind saw them screaming and crying as they began to realize that the city they knew was fading away and that something long dead was coming to life in its place.

"Oh, God," he whispered. Jonathan Corbin pressed both palms against his temples as if to squeeze away that image. "Oh, God, don't let me be going insane."

Corbin knew there would be no panic at ABC. No screaming. At worst there would be a little worry about what the subways would be like and whether their bosses would let them out early. Or they'd be wishing they'd brought overshoes and umbrellas. Some would be happy because ski conditions would be great this weekend. Or because they thought snow was pretty. Some would like it, some would grumble about the inconvenience. But they wouldn't be afraid. Because they wouldn't see the things that Jonathan Corbin would.

Then don't look, damn it. You don't have to go out. You can sleep here on your office couch. You don't even have to look out this stupid window.

Corbin snatched at the cord of his drapes and yanked, too hard. He'd found the wrong cord and it snapped away in his hand, dragging a potted plant to the floor with it. Outside he heard his secretary's chair slide backward at the sound of the breakage. Corbin stepped to the door and listened, hoping that Sandy would stay away, that she wouldn't knock. He waited there until he heard the chair again. He could not see the worried shake of her head or her hand reaching for her telephone.

Once again, Corbin was drawn to the window. The snow was coming faster still and at a driven slant. A new wind had risen from the south. It came in waves. Gusting. Its great breaths swatted umbrellas aside and slapped at the hems of topcoats. Within minutes all the city he could see had faded to a whitish blur. It was no longer solid.

Too late now even to run. Grand Central Station was twenty minutes away on foot. There would be no cabs. Corbin knew that he would get no farther than a block, to Fifth Avenue at best, before the city began to change.

His first sensation would be that it was shrinking. It would be as if all of Manhattan were made of modeling clay and some giant hand was slowly pressing down on it. Buildings would become squat at their bases and they would ooze closer together, narrowing the streets and sidewalks. This giant pressing hand would distort the features of the buildings, breaking up clean lines, creating bulges and ridges and a sense of massiveness rather than height. Then the hand would lift and the tops of the buildings would be gone. Not hidden in cloud. Just gone. Faded away. And among the home-bound office workers he would see people dressed in clothing that was no longer worn and pass buildings that were not there in sunlight. Corbin would be on the street and he'd notice that the midtown trucks and buses were becoming translucent, and through them he would begin to see other shapes.

He'd see wagons drawn by horses. Not just the Central Park kind that tourists hire during the warmer months, but every size and shape of unmechanized vehicle. On Fifth Avenue, Corbin would see little horse-drawn trolleys that had not appeared on New York streets for . . . Corbin didn't know. Eighty years? A hundred years? He'd see ponderous freight wagons, brewery wagons piled high with kegs, sleek black broughams and landaus with liveried drivers sitting erect at the reins, fully exposed to the weather. And they'd be moving. Living. He'd see the breath coming from the horses' nostrils and the steam rising from their flanks. He would actually smell their manure, mounds of it, everywhere, being churned into a repulsive brown slush by passing hooves and wheels. The people on foot would be mostly men. Few women anywhere except in carriages, holding buffalo robes across their laps. The men, the business types at least, would nearly all be dressed in black. Fur-lined inverness coats, or ulsters, or flaring Prince Alberts that reached well past their knees. Most carried walking sticks. All of them wore hats, either high silk or derbies. Nearly all were mustached or bearded. And they would see him.

They would not seem afraid, or at all surprised, or even especially interested that he was among them. But they would see him. A tall policeman would pass, acknowledging him with a nod and a touch of his truncheon to the brim of his helmet. The helmet was the sort British bobbies wore, except that his seemed not so high and was a lighter shade. There were two women, Corbin recalled, the last time he saw the policeman. They were following close behind him as if determined to stay under his protection as long as possible. The two women, girls really, were escorted by a third woman, who appeared to be in her thirties. A chaperone, Corbin realized. The two younger women modestly dropped their eyes as he passed, but the older one glowered at Corbin as if he'd committed a breach of etiquette by even noticing the girls in her charge. Corbin was struck by the tiny steps they took. Quick mincing steps that seemed to cover only inches. It occurred to him that all three were out of breath but trying to avoid the appearance of breathing hard. It was their corsets, he realized. Contraptions of wire and whalebone cruelly choked their waists and stiffened their spines, making exertion almost impossible. Knowing that, thinking that, Corbin felt an unaccountable sense of embarrassment, as if he had committed another, graver breach. What was it? The corsets? Yes. He should not have reflected upon their undergarments. Not even to himself. Corbin felt curiously protective of these women. It was clear that they could never have begun to defend themselves against any form of assault, nor could they have reacted to any minor emergency that might require quick physical movement. Small wonder, he thought, that these creatures swoon as often as they do. It's a marvel that they even manage to cross a busy street without more of them being knocked down by one of those maniacs who drive hacks these days.

Still vaguely ashamed of allowing his thoughts to penetrate their outer clothing, Corbin watched as they struggled to board the rear platform of a two-horse omnibus. He felt an urge to go and stop them, to offer to engage a hack to take them home. They certainly dressed as if they had the means to pay for a cab. They must have gone abroad without sufficient funds, not sufficient, at all events, to meet the larcenous demands made by New York's hack drivers every time an unpropitious turn of weather turned them into grasping auctioneers. Corbin made no move toward the ladies, however. The risk of embarrassing them was great and, worse, his motives might well be misunderstood. Still, he regretted that they must endure the discomfort of a tightly packed horsecar whose only protection against the cold would be a host of steaming bodies and four inches of filthy straw on the floor. But at least the conductor, Corbin saw, seemed like the sort who would do well by them. He'd stepped to the street to offer an arm and to hold back those who would crowd past the three women. They declined the arm, as the conductor might have expected. They would need both hands to carefully raise their skirts high enough to step onto the platform but not so high as to permit the display of an ankle. Two men promptly offered their seats. The conductor glared at a third, in a laborer's peacoat and wool cap, until he, too, surrendered his seat to the chaperone, who was the last to board. Satisfied, Corbin adjusted his hat and turned into the wind.

He hadn't waited to watch them take their seats. But now he found himself wondering how they would manage it. All three wore bustles and panniers and enough heavy fabric to clothe half a dozen of the women who worked in his office . . . in *his* office. As he held that thought, Corbin spun around and focused once more upon the omnibus. It was fading. A shift of wind, an updraft, something, had created a lull in the storm and everything was changing again. The horsecar was almost gone. The outline of a Fifth Avenue MTA bus was materializing in its place. And he became afraid again, realizing only then that he did not belong in the world of these women and the policeman. If there really was such a world. If he was not, in fact, going out of his mind. Hadn't he just straightened his hat against the wind? He wasn't wearing a hat. What's going on here? What the hell is happening? Corbin staggered forward in the direction of Grand Central. Soon he was running.

That, at least, was what had happened one time. One of the first times. Back just after Thanksgiving. But it was always different. The street scene always varied from one time to the next, as it did between any two ordinary strolls through midtown Manhattan. Yet three things were always the same. Jonathan Corbin was see-ing, living, a time long past and dead. And there was always the snowstorm. And when the blizzard was at its worst and the night at its blackest, he would see the bareheaded woman running from him. The woman he would murder.

He would be on a corner, he wasn't sure where, leaning into a wind of astonishing force and sleet that threatened to seal his eyes. It was useless, he knew, to move in that direction. The woman would not have gone there. Wind or no wind, she would have gone the other way. Corbin, in fact, knew exactly when and where he would see her, yet he felt compelled each time to act out a search, as if he were living these moments for the first time. He would turn, toward the north, he thought, and on the sidewalk before him he would see a half-buried clump that looked like a dead raven. It was a hat. Her hat. A narrow, tapering toque of cloth and feathers from Lord & Taylor's Broadway store. As the woman had reached this corner, the full force of the gale had torn the useless ornament from her head.

Now the same wind would shove at Corbin's back, pushing him forward in the direction she must have taken. He lurched on, digging his heels into packed snow and ice for purchase, finally reaching the next corner, where he paused in the doorway of an apothecary.

She'd turned right, he was sure, from this corner. Her reason for turning right caused a churning of hurt and anger in Corbin's stomach, although as yet he had not the slightest idea why. But he knew that he must hurry. Corbin pulled a collar up against his cheek, mildly startled by the scratch of black lamb's-wool trim he hadn't known was there, then plunged forward across the north-south avenue that was funneling the winds into hurricane force. Twice he fell, tripping over a tangle of fallen telegraph wires that sagged everywhere over roadway and sidewalk alike. He could scarcely believe that the woman would have tried this crossing, but he understood that she would have had no choice. How desperate she was! How depraved she was by a sin that would lead her to ever greater shame and condemnation. Corbin drove himself on. A snowbank blocked him on the far side. He stepped into it and cried out. There was someone in there. Beneath the snow. Corbin's gloved hand locked fingers with another that was stiff and unyielding. A large hand. Gasping, Corbin threw himself backward, but the other gloved hand stayed entwined in his own, only for an instant, but long enough that his momentum pulled the upper torso of the hidden body free. A frozen face stared past him through half-open eyes.

Corbin knew the face. George. His name was George, but any other knowledge of him stayed just out of Corbin's reach. The corpse was a big man. Corbin's size. Thickly mustached. His dead eyes were wincing as if in pain, and his mouth gaped open to receive a breath that never came. George was dead. He'd fallen here. Hours ago. There was no connection, Corbin knew, between the man in the snowbank and the woman somewhere up ahead. He was sure of that. But for that reason a part of Corbin wondered why this man was here in this dream, this nightmare. And why was another part of him sorry at this man's death? Who was George? Not a friend, he felt sure. Not a close one at least. A business acquaintance perhaps. Or a neighbor. Corbin eased him back into the shelter of the snowbank and gently covered his face. He clasped the dead man's hand for a moment, as if in apology for leaving him, then crawled over him toward the lee of the nearest building.

He was now on a very long and narrow side street with a downward slope. By a trick of the wind the walks of the side he was on were swept almost clear of snow. Yet on the windward side, to his left, first-floor doors and windows were fully covered by drifts, some to a height of ten feet or more. A huge building was there. A single massive structure that looked like the wall of a great white canyon. Its windows, ledges, and cornices were obscured by a troweling of packed snow and ice all the way to the ragged line of its roof, which must have been eight or ten stories above the ground. This building seemed to go on for the entire block. Corbin felt another stab of anger as he looked at it, but he forced his attention back down along the dark and snowless windbreak where he stood. It was then that he would see her. She would be some fifty yards ahead of him, moving haltingly, and almost invisible but for the light she reflected from an occasional uncurtained window. There were gas lamps at intervals along the street but none were lit. No lamplighter would make his rounds tonight.

She would move a few steps, then pause and turn toward the building across the street, then move on again. Corbin could see that she was baffled by the drifts that began in the middle of the roadway and rose up against all the building's entrances. She stopped again. Both hands came up to warm her frozen ears as she searched in vain for a crossing she could manage in the heavy floor-length coat she wore. It was then that she saw Corbin's shape closing in upon her. She screamed. It struck him that it was a cry more of hatred, of vexation, than of fear. He saw a flash of teeth as she gathered up her frozen skirts and turned from him, running.

This was Corbin's first clear look at the woman. She was young, no more than twenty-four, he thought. In daylight he would remember her as pretty, almost beautiful. But now she seemed ugly, hateful. Corbin was moving again. In his right hand he noticed the glint of a polished ebony cane. It flicked forward in rhythm with his pace. He could feel the cane's carved silver knob against his palm. And he saw his sleeve. More lamb's wool at the cuff. The rest was a soft gray plaid unlike any coat Corbin owned. When he looked up again, he saw that he had halved the distance between himself and the woman.

She was becoming frantic. And exhausted. She staggered against a high iron fence in the light of a brownstone's parlor window. A man came briefly to the window, pausing only long enough to steam it with his breath, then he turned away.

"Sir, please," he heard her call. "Sir, please help me."

Corbin knew it was useless. She would not be heard against the whistling wind. And if she tried to climb the steps leading to the door and if her knock were not promptly answered, she would be trapped.

The woman seemed to realize that as well. Again she ran.

There was another wide avenue like the last. But this one, Corbin saw, had some monstrous unlit structure above it which straddled the roadway like a giant spider. A railroad. Yes, that's what it was. An elevated railroad and a large terminus. He thought he heard a wail of despair as she peered through the blast of wind at the lifeless building above her. There would be no help there, either. The trains had long since stopped running, unable to make the slightest grade on icy tracks. The terminus and platform would be another trap at best. Corbin watched her stumble on toward one of the steel columns that supported the elevated. She fell to her knees as she reached it and held on, chest heaving, gathering her strength for a dash to the column's opposite number on the other side. Suddenly she straightened. She had seen something. She raised a hand to shield her eyes against the ripping sleet.

"Police!" she screamed. "I need you! Police!"

But the sound went nowhere. Even Corbin could barely hear it. The wind seized her words and shredded their sounds and threw them back past her face. The woman pushed heavily to her feet and lunged in the direction of whatever salvation she saw, but the wind did to her skirts what it had done to her plea. Her feet were slashed from under her. On hands and knees, she shot a desperate glance toward Corbin's advancing form, then turned, crawling her way across the avenue.

Corbin, or the part of him that remained Jonathan Corbin, began to feel a stirring of pity for her. He wanted to tell her that she needn't scream, that she needn't run. But another part of him knew that was wrong. It was right that she should suffer. It was right that she be punished for the terrible wrong she had done him. Corbin placed one hand upon the thick fur hat that he wore and leaned into this new avenue, crossing at an upwind bias as one would attempt to swim a rapids. A short block into the wind he saw through squinting eyes the aid the woman had sought but had not had the strength to reach. Two uniformed policemen were struggling to raise a fallen horse. On the open seat of the delivery wagon to which the beast was harnessed, Corbin saw the dead or senseless body of the driver. He was hunched forward. Frozen. The loose end of a long scarf streamed out in the wind and slapped unheeded at his face. Corbin hesitated. He thought he should offer assistance. But no, he decided. The driver was either beyond his help or already in the good hands of the two patrolmen. And the woman had reached the shelter of the building line and was now regaining her feet. If he let her go to find new sanctuary, what stories would she tell? What new humiliations would she bring upon his name? Corbin turned after her.

They were near the end of a second long street when Corbin was again close upon her. There was a house. A huge house. A mansion of brick and stone set well back from the sidewalk behind a high spiked fence of wrought iron. The gates of the fence were fully open upon a driveway and garden well lit with electric lamps. The curved driveway led to a porte cochere big enough to accept the largest barouche or coach and four. She stopped there, shivering, staring at this house. Corbin could almost hear her thoughts. Another windswept avenue lay ahead of her, this one even more open and exposed than the last. He knew that she could not bear to attempt another crossing. She would not have the strength. But this great house. Surely she could find refuge here. The servants would take her in. She could ask them to say nothing to their mistress. Only to let her warm herself in the kitchen. She could sit in a chair until morning. Their mistress need not know that she had forced herself upon this house uninvited and in such a state. But it was no use. They would surely tell her. Or worse, they would sell this intelligence to that dreadful Colonel Mann for a silver dollar and within a week her humiliation would be made public in his newspaper.

The woman, Corbin knew, could not bear that. She would not seek shelter there. It would mean the end of all she valued. With an anguished waving of her arms she turned from the warmth of those lights and plunged insanely back into the storm.

Across from the mansion, at the edge of a great open square, was another building in the early stages of construction. All around it were piles of bricks and lumber under wind-whipped tarpaulins. The storm made small mountains of these and filled in the passes between them. It was in this direction that the woman ran. There was no light there. Only the distant glow of the mansion's arc lights. But it was enough that when she turned at last to face him he could see the full measure of the mocking contempt in which she held him. There was a smear across her mouth that looked like blood. Her hair, once piled high and teased into ringlets at her brow, was now a fallen, frozen reddish mass. He knew all the more clearly why she had turned from those gates. Vanity. Shame. The fear of being whispered about in drawing rooms, of her name being stricken from guest lists, of heads in passing carriages turning away from the woman who had the coarseness of manner to appear at the door of Alice Vanderbilt in such a state of dishabille. If only they knew, Corbin thought. If only they knew the true depths of her shame.

He stopped in front of her. He saw his walking stick rise until its silver tip was level with her breastbone. She backed away, her lips curling into a sneer. A word. She spoke a word. *Children* is what Corbin thought she said. Only that. Inflected upward at the end as if spoken as a warning. Corbin advanced upon her, his cane held poised, steering her backward into the construction site, into the farthest and deepest drifts. Against one of these she fell. She reached both arms behind her to break her fall and these plunged into the soft snow almost to her shoulders. She did not try to rise.

"Be done with it," the young woman spat at the figure standing over her. "Beat me, children." That word again.

Corbin saw the tip of his cane find a place between her breasts. There was something hard there, a wire form beneath her clothing. The cane did not seem to hurt her as he pushed down upon it, pressing her more deeply into the bank of snow. Her head was buried past the level of her ears. The lighter edges of the imprint she made crumbled in against her cheeks. The woman was struggling at last, spitting, biting uselessly at his cane, but the effort left her arms impacted behind her all the more. She tried to kick at him. Corbin saw his own right foot rise and then come down across the buttons of her coat at a point between her knees. She was pinioned. Helpless. Unable to move at all.

All at once, Corbin felt ashamed. One does not treat a woman in this manner. Not for any reason. If only she would say something. Some small spoken kindness. Anything that might serve to take away a hurt he keenly felt but whose source he could not remember. He would let her go if she would ask his forgiveness. Or even if she would cry. He would let her go as far away as possible. Away from him. And take the humiliation with her.

What humiliation?

Whatever it was, she must have known the answer. Or perhaps Corbin said it aloud without realizing it. Because then she said, "He'll be twice the man you are."

"And the other?" Corbin heard himself ask. His voice was flat and cold.

"I warn you." She coughed.

He pressed harder with his cane. "And the other?" he repeated. "What sort of man is he?"

"Twice." She raised her face and shouted. "Twice as well. Twice and more. Twice in all ways, damn you, sir."

Nothing more was said for several minutes. She lay quiet and still. As still as the dead man named George except for the shallow rise and fall of her bosom.

"I cannot feel anything," she whispered sleepily.

"No," he answered, "I fear that you cannot."

And Corbin held her there until his own feet were numb and the snow stopped melting on her face.

TWO

 HE SLENDER, HONEY-HAIRED ENGLISHWOMAN HAD been in a windowless conference room for four hours when she was called to the telephone and heard the worried voice of Jonathan Corbin's secretary. She frowned. She knew at once that it must be snowing outside.

Gwen Leamas listened, her frown deepening. "It's been since before noon," Sandy Bauer told her. "There's already going to be trouble because he bagged his lunch date with the people from the Masters golf tournament. And now I hear things breaking in there."

"Why didn't you call me before this?" she whispered.

"Because it was hardly snowing," Sandy told her. "I stayed and had a sandwich at my desk just in case. It only started really coming down a few minutes ago."

"You're a love," Gwen said. "I'll be there in two minutes."

She made her apologies to Bill Stafford, citing a minor but urgent personal matter. Their meeting, held to discuss the format of a new magazine show, was essentially over anyway. Stafford, who adored his wife but loved to watch and listen to Gwen Leamas, was visibly disappointed. He liked to say she gave the dump some class. She'd already thoroughly charmed the new show's prospective host, an otherwise difficult columnist named Hobbs.

Sandy Bauer breathed deep relief at the sound of the jingling chain jewelry and the *whoosh* of leather pants that signaled the approach of Mr. Corbin's girlfriend. Used to be, anyway. If the office talk was right, they had lived together for a couple of years in Chicago until she left six months before he did and came here. Sandy knew for a fact that Mr. Corbin had lived at her place while he looked for a place of his own. But whatever was between them seemed to fade away as soon as Mr. Corbin found that crazy old house of his in Connecticut.

Gwen stopped at Sandy Bauer's typewriter, glancing at Corbin's closed door and placing her hand over the several bracelets she wore to silence them.

"Has he not been out at all?" she asked in the soft precise accent that Sandy sometimes tried to imitate.

"Not since he saw it was snowing." She cocked her head toward the phone console on her desk. "I've been saying he's in a meeting, but it's only a matter of time before Stafford or someone else I can't stop decides to walk in on him."

Gwen nodded, looking down to check the watch she wore looped over a silver belt. Stafford would be busy a while longer, she knew. Another hour of swapping stories with those left in the room and then drinks with Mr. Hobbs at "21" or the Algonquin. Still, "I'm going to try to take him out of here," she said quietly.

"Do you think you can keep everyone at bay a bit longer?"

Sandy nodded. "Miss Leamas, are you going to . . ." Corbin's secretary bit her lip. "If all you're going to do is put him on his train, I'd just as soon take him to my place and let him stay there."

Gwen Leamas met her eyes. "I'll take care of him," she said evenly. And then she softened. "That was very nice of you, Sandy. Very nice indeed."

The younger girl smiled, pleased with herself that she had the nerve to ask and relieved that she got away with it. As for being nice, though, Sandy didn't know how nice she'd be if Mr. Corbin ever looked at her the way he still looked at Gwen Leamas sometimes. Not that I'm jealous, Sandy thought. What's to be jealous about a model's cheekbones and huge brown eyes that can look smart and nice at the same time, and good boobs, and also a skinny body, which is especially aggravating since I know for a fact she's a cheeseburger freak.

Gwen answered the secretary's smile with one that she hoped was reassuring but hesitated with her hand on Corbin's door. It crossed her mind to ask Sandy to say nothing of Jonathan's emotional state or about them leaving together. But the request, she decided, would be gratuitous and probably offensive. Jonathan Corbin was Sandy's boss, but she clearly liked him in the bargain. To say the least. In any case, there would be no gossip. Gwen settled for a wink, then took a breath and stepped through Corbin's office door.

Corbin stiffened as she entered but did not turn from the window. The draperies at his right hand were swinging slightly, as if just released. She could see a large wrinkled area where his fist had been clutching them. Jonathan was posing now, she realized, trying to look like an executive pondering a problem while gazing thoughtfully out a window. Yet she felt sure that his eyes were tightly closed.

"It's Gwen, Jonathan." At her words she saw his shoulders sag and heard his lungs expel the air they'd been holding. His head shook slowly but he did not turn.

"These things you see," she asked gently, "are they out there now?"

"No." The word croaked from a dry and tight throat. Corbin coughed and swallowed. "Not from here. I never see them from here."

"From the street then. You see them when you're down on the street?"

Corbin hugged himself and nodded.

She touched her fingertips against the door to see that it was securely closed, then stepped to his side. Gwen barely glanced at the gray-white blur outside the window. Raising her hands to both his shoulders, she turned him, Corbin resisting at first, until he faced her. Only then did Corbin open his eyes. Leaning closer, she placed her palms against his cheeks and kissed him lightly on the lips.

"Jonathan?"

"Yes."

"Will you show me this time?"

"No." He tried to pull away.

"Do you ever see them when someone is with you?"

"Yes," he answered, then blinked. In truth he wasn't sure. He'd seen them when there were other living people around. Always. But with someone he knew? Someone whose hand he could hold and maybe keep from slipping back into another time? "I don't know," he added distantly.

"Let's try, Jonathan."

"No."

"You can't just bury yourself here all weekend like

some den animal. What will you do for food if the snow doesn't stop?"

Corbin had already thought about the coffee and candy machines near the freight elevator, and the partially uneaten lunches that were often abandoned in the refrigerator of the office kitchen. He shook his head miserably. "Gwen, you just don't know what it's like."

"Then tell me, Jonathan. What is out there that a man who's never shown the smallest spark of timidity would fear? Are there monsters? Do these people you see try to harm you?"

"No, nothing like that." A hand he could hold, he repeated to himself. Except it wouldn't work. It's supposed to be ghosts who fade while what's real and alive stays that way. But out there it's the living who fade. The flesh and blood.

"Then if you really do see the things you've told me about, Jonathan, I should think it would be bloody fascinating. My God, it's like time travel."

"Time travel?" he snapped. An angry spark lit his eyes, as if she'd just said something dangerously foolish.

Gwen Leamas said nothing, satisfied at least that she'd managed to stir a little life into him.

"What if your time travel isn't a round trip, Gwen? What if one of these times I can't get back?"

Gwen wet her lips. "You think this is real then, don't you?"

"No, damn it." Corbin turned away from her helplessly. "I know," he said softly, "that I don't really go back in time. No matter how real it seems, I know that I'm only going there in my mind. But if I can go there in my mind, I can get stuck there in my mind."

"That's what you're so frightened of?"

"That's a big part of it, yes."

"What's the rest of it?"

Corbin raised a hand to her face and brushed back

a long curl that fell across one eye. He sighed deeply, his lips moving tentatively, reluctant to form the words.

"The same thing you're afraid of," he answered finally.

"Which is what, Jonathan?" she pressed.

"That I'm flat out going nuts."

Gwen took his hands and squeezed them. "I know you, Jonathan," she said firmly. "Better than anyone, I'll be bound. There was nothing at all odd about you until weeks after you moved to New York. Whatever change came over you began the moment you laid eyes on that ridiculous house of yours and then all the more when the weather turned wintry. In Chicago we've walked blithely through snow that was deeper by half than anything New York ever gets and it never bothered you one whit. It seems to me, then, that the cause of your difficulty is out there on those streets as much as it's in your mind and that there is a perfectly sensible explanation to be found. But it must be sought and faced, Jonathan. I will not have a man I . . . respect . . . hiding from it."

She backed away from Corbin and reached for the tan trench coat he kept on a hook behind his door. She held it outstretched and open, but Corbin made no move to take it.

"Tomorrow," he said quietly. "I'll call you tomorrow. We'll talk."

"We'll talk today." She shook the coat impatiently. "I'm going to plunk you into a hot bath at my flat with a good stiff drink or two in you and then we're going to thrash this out."

"Gwen . . ." Corbin shook his head again but his refusal seemed less definite this time.

"One block," she insisted. "It's just one short block to the subway entrance on this end and scarcely a hundred paces to my front door on the other."

His eyes narrowed slightly and darted twice to the

street below. She could almost see the circuits opening and closing as his brain calculated the speed and distance. One short block. Perhaps eighty yards from the Burlington Building's doors to the BMT entrance at Fifty-fifth Street. Under a minute on foot. Twenty seconds if they ran. Then safety. There would be no falling snow, no ectoplasmic buildings materializing through it, no dead people. Only crowds and noise and dirt.

"Come on, Jonathan." She threw the trench coat over his shoulders and was steering him through his office door before the glaze that covered his eyes could clear. Sandy Bauer was ready with Gwen's coat. She led them both down a short corridor that led through an empty mailroom and out the back way to the elevator banks. There was a reception desk at the far end. As Gwen pushed the Down button, Sandy walked, chatting, toward the receptionist, blocking her view of the trembling Jonathan Corbin and the look of panic that was building on his face.

THREE

 N THE FOURTH FLOOR OF THE WARWICK HOTEL, IN a room directly facing Corbin's office, a thickset man of about fifty rose from his chair at the open window and slammed it shut over a half inch of snow that had collected on the sill. He twisted the 200-millimeter lens off the Nikon he held and set the pieces into a padded camera bag. He logged the time and date in his notebook and buttoned the topcoat he had not removed since taking his position five hours earlier.

Using the fire stairs, Raymond Lesko took less than a minute to reach a new position at the corner entrance to the Warwick Bar. From there, as long as the Sixth Avenue buses stayed out of his field of vision, he could watch the entire plaza of the Burlington Building and all its exits. Unless Corbin grabbed a cab, and fat chance of that, thought Lesko, he would have to pass this corner on his way to Grand Central Station.

Two or three incoming bar patrons eyed Lesko uneasily as they shouldered past him. He ignored them, being long accustomed to people looking at him that way. Lesko had a wrestler's body and the intimidating eyes of an aroused bouncer even when he wasn't mad at anyone. He had a tight, cruel mouth that concealed perfect teeth of which Lesko was proud. But even the perfect teeth frightened people when he showed them. Sometimes that made him sad, especially when he meant to be friendly, but more often it turned out to be useful.

Raymond Lesko's mind, however, was not on his appearance. It was on Jonathan Corbin and the paying job at hand. A hunch had warned him that something would be different about today, but even so he came close to losing Corbin. The snow was what was different. What Lesko was hearing about Corbin was right. The guy's a wacko when it snows. Not that he's any tower of mental health when it's balmy. Here's your basic eligible bachelor who has all of New York and its women to play in after work but all he does is bust out of those doors at five o'clock and runs with his head down for his Connecticut train. Same way he runs for the office in the morning. Head down. Not even looking sideways. Like a guy who's scared to death of this whole town. Which is why it's such a pain in the ass to get a decent picture of him except through his office window.

Lesko checked his watch. Where the hell is he? Damn. Lesko realized he'd been looking for Corbin's trench coat, Corbin all by himself in his head-down run. But the Leamas woman left with him. Lesko stood as tall as he could and scanned the Burlington's doors, nearest to farthest. There they were. He'd almost missed them but there they were, just clear of the last revolving doors and heading the wrong way, north, running like a pack of dogs were on their heels. With a curse, Lesko stepped into the storm and followed.

Even with the driving snow and the trucks that strobed across Raymond Lesko's field of view, he was able to lock on Corbin easily. Corbin stood out from the others who rushed toward shelter along the same sidewalk. There was a special frenzy to his movements. The head wasn't down this time. He was glancing around wildly as the woman steered him. Did he suspect he had a tail? Lesko wondered. He decided not. Corbin wasn't looking at people and things so much as he was looking through them. Now he's looking up. And flinching. What do you see, Corbin? What do you see, right this second, in the wind above Sixth Avenue? And the woman, yelling into your ear. She's asking you the same thing, isn't she?

A packed northbound bus hissed to a stop, blocking Corbin and Gwen Leamas from Lesko's sight. When it passed, the two had vanished. Shit! Where'd you go, Corbin? You didn't slip into that bus, did you? No. Not without a shoehorn and a pot of grease, you didn't. Down that subway, then. Ah, yes. The subway.

Lesko did not follow. Instead he pulled his notebook from an inside pocket and, sheltering its pages with his body, peeled back to the penciled address of Gwen Leamas—145 East 77th Street. He nodded. Yes. That would explain the BMT subway. A short ride to the East Side and then a switch to the Lexington Avenue line would have them at her address in fifteen, maybe twenty minutes. Lesko stepped into the roadway at Fifty-fifth Street and waded through the eastbound crawl until he reached the first of those taxis whose Off Duty signs flick on at the first sign of inclement weather. Lesko slammed a fist down on its hood and, having won the driver's attention, waved a gold shield and ID card in front of the wipers.

"What, you can't read, pal?" The driver rapped his

knuckles against the roof. "That light out there says I'm off duty."

Lesko showed his teeth. "We should all be so lucky. Open it."

The driver angrily slapped at a lever that popped up the door locks and Lesko climbed in, pocketing his ID before the driver could ask for a closer look at it.

"You're on this big case, right?" the driver snorted. "Cops are always on this big case when they don't feel like taking the subway."

Lesko glanced at the hack license on the dashboard. Marvin Posey. A wimpish name, Lesko thought, for such a surly little bastard.

"Marvin," he said, "I must get quickly to Seventy-seventh Street between Lexington and Third. I would like you to fly there on the wings of your civic duty."

"What?" The driver's expression dulled.

"Get this fucking thing moving."

Lesko soon realized that, surly or not, Marvin Posey knew his job. He pushed through a red light and a line of pedestrians onto Sixth Avenue, bullied and honked his way to Central Park, ran another light at the Seventy-second Street exit, and was turning north on Third Avenue in ten minutes flat.

As the cab crunched into the unplowed snow of East Seventy-seventh Street, Lesko leaned forward to choose a spot from which he could watch both number 145 on his right and the Lexington Avenue subway exit straight ahead.

"Pull in right here." He pointed.

"That's a hydrant. Good citizens don't block hydrants."

"Behave yourself, Marvin." Lesko had counted at least six moving violations since he climbed into the cab. Which was fine. Anything to help Marvin find inner peace. The cab stopped and Lesko stepped partially out of it just in time to see Jonathan Corbin emerging from the subway steps a quarter block ahead of him.

It was a changed Jonathan Corbin, Lesko noted with interest. Now it was Corbin who was standing up straight and strong and assisting the Leamas girl instead of the other way around. The sleet was smacking him in the face just as hard but he didn't look like it bothered him. What happened? Could the Lexington Avenue subway have curative powers? Or, Lesko wondered, was it the calming attentions of Miss Leamas? Or do Corbin's devils only hang out down in the high-rent district?

Lesko watched closely as Corbin and Gwen Leamas crossed Seventy-seventh Street and waded along the uncleared sidewalk toward number 145. He could see Corbin's face clearly. The expression he saw was not the look of a man who had just spent four hours biting his drapes. The guy's suddenly happy, thought Lesko. Not relieved, not recovered. Happy. Like everything's been just fine all along. You could ask what's not to be happy about being snowbound for a weekend with his tasty English squeeze. But you could also ask why midtown snow scares him shitless and uptown snow doesn't. For that matter, you could also ask why Raymond Lesko is getting top dollar to bird-dog some stiff whose worst enemy seems to be himself. Ask that question and you already have a big part of the answer. Jonathan Corbin's worst enemy is not Jonathan Corbin after all.

It was during the underground crosstown ride to the Lexington Avenue subway, where they transferred to the northbound IRT local, that Gwen Leamas began to notice a subtle change in Jonathan Corbin.

The most welcome change was that he'd begun to relax. On that first short jog to the BMT station at Fifty-fifth Street, Jonathan had almost bolted. It was

more than panic. She'd seen him look upward, not so
much at the snow or sky but at the air space above
Sixth Avenue, as if some great beast had begun materializing there. She could tell that by his eyes. They were
focused, she felt, not on the buildings at the end of his
line of sight but on some midpoint where there was
nothing at all. What is it? she'd shouted into his ear.
What do you see? His answering look was almost one
of accusation. Of betrayal. See? It's happening. Even
with you here, it's happening. She dragged him forward.

The sanctuary of the subway entrance, however,
made all the difference. He'd seized the stairway hand-
rail as if it was a lifeline, and his body sagged in relief
as he staggered down below the street. There was a
long backward glance at whatever floating thing had
frightened him, but the fear was now replaced by . . .
she wasn't sure. Recognition, perhaps. The beginnings
of recognition. There would be time to ask him later.

On the first of the two trains they took, she could
almost feel Jonathan's pulse returning to its normal
rate. The veins at his temples were quiet. His hands,
although restless, were no longer knotted into fists.
He'd stopped trying to scan every face in the car and
now sat back reading, with an odd sort of thorough-
ness, the chain of advertisements that lined the inside
crown. Gwen had a sense that the ads served as proof
to Jonathan of where he was. About half the ads were
in Spanish, reflecting the mix of riders. Gwen looked
around. Half Spanish, most of the other half black,
leaving only a minority of middle-class white types in
their car. More than usual, actually. Today there were
even a few affluent looking WASPs who would normally have avoided subways but who must have de-
spaired of finding rides on the surface.

A single such woman appeared, working her way
through the car. She chanced to stop near Corbin's seat

when she saw no use in searching further for one of her own. She was in her mid-thirties, Gwen Leamas guessed, and expensively dressed. Her long, hooded coat, trimmed in fur, had a Bergdorf Goodman look about it. At her throat she wore a choker whose center-piece was a large amethyst in an antique setting. Her blandly attractive face was pinched into an expression of aggrieved martyrdom at her own discomfort and at being forced into close association with people who could not otherwise approach the world she lived in. She looked as though she was trying to breathe in as little of their exhaled air as possible and to touch her surroundings not at all. The train rocked sharply as it passed over a section of rutted ties, and the woman, whose name, Gwen decided, was Alicia Poindexter or some damn thing, reached reluctantly for the support of a metal post. She gripped it with only the fingertips of a gloved hand.

Corbin, suddenly, was on his feet. He bowed in the woman's direction and indicated his seat with a courtly wave of his hand. Gwen knew that the woman had stopped near them, not in hopes of being offered a seat, but because of all those in the car she and Jonathan came closest to being acceptable company. The woman hesitated, staring appraisingly at Jonathan, but only for a moment. Another woman, darker and heavier, was pushing into position for a dash at the vacant seat in the event Bergdorf Goodman waited so much as another heartbeat. The woman in the long coat stepped forward, turned, and lowered herself daintily into the seat Corbin surrendered. She thanked him with an un-smiling flicker of eye contact and a tiny nod, thereafter keeping her eyes fixed on the Gucci purse she held securely in her lap.

Bloody hell, thought Gwen Leamas. Here's a man not ten minutes after being scared half out of his wits and now he's playing the subway gallant for some uptown twit who's mortified to be in the company of people who work for a living.

She didn't mention it, either then or on the final leg of their trip to her flat. Corbin was calm, even detached, and that was all that mattered for the moment. Gwen allowed herself to hope that she would not have to physically pry him out of the train that was now gliding to a stop. She stood up and took his hand tightly.

But Corbin did not resist. Nor did he hesitate except to stand back politely as other passengers shouldered past him and onto the platform. Gwen tugged at him and he followed. His pace remained unhurried as they passed through the turnstile and strolled toward the natural light spilling down from the street ahead of them. She wasn't sure whether to be relieved or troubled by this new turn in Corbin's behavior. He didn't even seem to notice the sound of the wind, which could be heard above the receding roar of the train. Or the scattered flakes that were already being sucked toward them well short of the ascending stairs. Keep it up, Jonathan, she prayed, electing to count her blessings. Wherever your mind has wandered to, by all means leave it there until we've dragged ourselves through the last few yards of this mess.

The storm, though Gwen had not thought it possible, had worsened. The stairs were covered, their risers obscured by drifting snow except for a path stamped into the center. Looking up, it was she who gasped at the swirling arctic mass that awaited them. It looked, she thought, like a great maniacal swarm of white bees. Living things. Christ—she caught herself—now he's got me doing it.

"Let's go, Corbin." Gwen Leamas squeezed his hand and began climbing, one untrustworthy stair at a time, into a storm that seemed to turn, snapping and growling at them as they rose to confront it.

"Good God," she muttered as she half stumbled onto the Seventy-seventh Street surface. A jet of sleet slapped color into her cheeks and lashed at her legs as she tried to grind her heels into a glaze of wind-polished ice.

"Permit me," she heard Corbin say.

Permit me? She blinked at him through eyelashes already weighted with bits of clinging ice.

"If I may," he added, as one strong hand took her arm and the other circled her waist. It was this serenely decorous Jonathan Corbin who steadied her, guided her, across Seventy-seventh Street and on toward the steps of the brownstone that waited some hundred paces into the storm.

She'd sort all this out later, Gwen Leamas thought as she squeezed off her boots inside the door of her second-floor flat. Her encrusted coat was already melting on the carpet runner where she had dropped it. She turned toward Corbin, who had not moved since entering, and, with fingers still numb and tingling, began working the buttons of his trench coat. His eyes now had a vague confusion about them, in contrast to the assured calm she'd seen only minutes earlier. She stepped behind him and peeled the coat down over his arms, shook it, and draped it on the floor next to her own. Gwen then took his suit jacket and hung it on a closet knob.

"A hot bath," she reminded him, easing him forward through the high-ceilinged living room. "A hot bath while sipping a very large Scotch and then a bite of supper sitting in front of a great blazing fire. Somewhere in all that we're going to cook this storm right out of your system."

Corbin managed a small smile as he allowed himself to be led into a square old-fashioned bathroom where an oversized tub squatted heavily on clawed feet.

Gwen called it her candlelight-and-wine-for-two tub. But this time it would be all for Jonathan. She turned both taps on full and waited for the usual belch of rust to clear before dropping a rubber plug into the drain. Gwen straightened and turned, invitingly pushing open the shower curtain. Corbin seemed hesitant, as if unsure of what he was expected to do next.

"The usual course is to undress," she observed, "unless one's clothing needs a good soak as well."

If she had not known Jonathan Corbin so long and so intimately, she would have sworn that she saw the beginnings of a blush. She watched him as he undid his necktie and carefully folded it across a varnished wicker hamper. Next he pulled off his shoes and took pains to place them neatly under a makeup stool. Gwen realized he was stalling but could not think why. The sight of Jonathan's undraped physique was hardly new to her. They'd shared this very tub several times during his first weeks in New York. Now, as she watched, he opened his cuffs and slowly worked the three top buttons of his shirt. Again Corbin hesitated. He stood, eyes averted, fidgeting with the third button, as if reluctant to proceed further while she was in the room. Gwen reached to shut off the taps. In that moment, Corbin made a half turn and, gripping the collar of his shirt, pulled it sweater fashion over his head.

"Why did you do that?" Gwen asked.

It was a small thing, she knew, but it was the latest in a series of small peculiarities in his behavior. How many times had she seen him remove his shirt? Hundreds, certainly. But she'd never once seen him pull it off over his head. Not Jonathan or any other man.

Her question seemed to confuse him. He followed her eyes to the shirt, which he held with one hand against his chest. With his other hand he touched his fingers to the row of still unopened buttons. With a self-conscious shrug, Corbin spread the shirt further over his bare chest, looked uncomfortably at Gwen, and waited.

"Do I gather you'd prefer privacy," she asked, "or is it just that you don't want me to know your technique for removing trousers?"

Corbin's lips moved but he said nothing.

"You do remember me, don't you?"

Still no answer. Just a look of desperate sadness that told her he knew perfectly well how strangely he was behaving and how much his actions must be troubling her.

"I'll bring you your drink," she said, forcing a smile. She closed the bathroom door behind her.

"You do remember me, don't you?" she'd asked. Corbin brooded over the question as the hot water eased the spring-taut muscles of his neck and shoulders. The double Scotch, nearly gone, had passed quickly through his empty stomach and was mercifully dulling the edges of his thoughts. Yes, he had remembered her. Of course he remembered Gwen. But there had been times, mostly brief flickering moments, when he remembered her as someone else. A woman he knew but did not know. Margaret. A woman called Margaret.

See, he thought. She even has a name. How unreal could she be if he knew her name, remembered her face, could hear the way she spoke and laughed, and could almost feel the soft texture of her skin. Margaret. Lovely Margaret. Beloved Margaret. A marvelous young lady. Very much a lady. One who could make him the happiest and most miserable of men all at the same time. Margaret.

Margaret? Margaret, damn it, who are you?

There had been moments on the subway when he thought he was with her. He'd been sitting with her when he rose to give his seat to another lady of . . . quality? Another lady of quality. And breeding.

There. There was another thing. An expression he'd never used, or even thought, in his entire life. Nor was he in the habit of surrendering subway seats to women, either, unless they seemed old or weak or were carrying babies. But this time it seemed natural, proper. And looking back, he wasn't sure how much quality and breeding that woman had anyway. She reeked of money all right, but she was behaving like a jerk. None of that, however, had even crossed his mind at the time. He was happy, he was with Margaret, and they were going to the house, the brownstone, where Margaret lived. Except this wasn't it. He seemed to realize that only as he stepped through Gwen's front door and recognized the place. And he knew that Gwen had seen his confusion. Or his disappointment. It wasn't Margaret's place and Gwen Leamas wasn't Margaret. But she *had* been, by God. Just moments before. The woman he helped. The woman he walked with, his arm around her tiny waist, from the corner to this house. That was Margaret.

Corbin picked up his glass and drained it, then made a face at the taste. Scotch. He'd have preferred hot rum on a day like this. Or maybe a bumper of mulled wine sprinkled with pepper. One or the other. These were the drinks his taste buds expected, even if he'd never so much as tasted either one in his entire life. Corbin wasn't even sure what a bumper was.

Then there was that business about the shirt. Corbin couldn't say why he was suddenly bashful about undressing in front of Gwen, but he knew about the shirt. He only opened the three top buttons because he thought three buttons were all it had. The rest of the shirt was supposed to be solid. Even stiff. Heavily starched. And he pulled it off over his head because that's how a shirt has to be removed when it only opens halfway down and because that's the way he always takes off his dress shirts. Except Corbin knew he never had. Not ever.

The double Scotch and the heat of the water were working together now. On his mind as well as his body. His anxiety began to soften into a sort of floating detachment. It was a more merciful state of mind because it permitted thoughts that he would not otherwise have allowed himself to entertain. And words he would not otherwise have considered if applied to himself.

Such as *possession,* he thought, or *haunting.* Such as here's old Jonathan Corbin trying to live his life while somebody else is trying to take it over. A dead man. A ghost. A ghost who starts seeing other ghosts the minute he gets access to Jonathan Corbin's eyes. A ghost who kills when he gets hold of Jonathan Corbin's arms and legs. A ghost who loves when he takes over Jonathan Corbin's heart. A ghost who loves Margaret.

"Who are you, ghost?" Corbin whispered into the steam rising off his chest. "And why do you only come out when it snows?"

But that, Corbin knew, was not exactly right, either. He began to wonder if the ghost had always been there. Just out of sight. During all the times of his life when he did things that made no real sense to him afterward. Maybe even like buying that place in Connecticut. Was that you, ghost? Is it me who feels so good up there? Or is it really you?

And Gwen. Look what I'm doing to Gwen. There's the kind of woman you meet once in a lifetime and I could only let her get just so close. I used to think there was something wrong with me. Something missing. But it isn't something missing. It's something extra. It's you, you bastard. It's you standing at my ear every time I begin to care about someone, saying not this one. This isn't the one. The one you have to wait for is about five feet two, she has wide green eyes with little gold flecks in them, a mouth that always has a little smile, and light brown hair that goes down past a waist you could fit both hands around. I know her now. Margaret. I've seen her. I've even talked to her. But who are you, God damn it?

Who the hell *are* you?

Corbin did not know that he screamed the question until he heard it echo off the tiles.

FOUR

S THE TAXI PLOWED TO A STOP OUTSIDE THE Lexington Avenue entrance to Grand Central Terminal, Raymond Lesko dropped a ten-dollar bill into the lap of a surprised Marvin Posey, who had fully expected to be stiffed. The cab company, Lesko was sure, would see no part of the money since the off-duty light had been left on and the meter off for the entire ride. But the ten spot would make the driver less likely to log the trip. Lesko heard the door locks snap shut behind him as he climbed a mound of shoveled snow and stamped into the terminal building.

Inside, the former New York City policeman checked his watch. Half past four. He was ninety minutes early for his meeting with the secretive little man who was funding this particular activity. However, passing that time in one of the station's various bars seemed preferable to sitting in the back of a taxi enduring Posey's prolonged sulk. Lesko bought a copy of the *New York Post* from a vendor who'd moved his stand out of the storm and proceeded toward the Oyster Bar on the lower level.

The bar, he noted gratefully, was still half empty. This meant that the inevitable series of frozen switches and stalled trains had either not yet begun or had not been posted. Within an hour the Oyster Bar would be jammed with sullen commuters. Many would not reach their homes at all that night.

Choosing a stool at one end, Raymond Lesko ordered a Heineken and nursed it as he reviewed his notebook, leaving an account of his expenses until last. This completed, he unfolded his *New York Post,* whose four-inch headline shouted the single word BLIZZARD, and then flipped to the sports pages, where he began a hopeful assessment of the play-off chances of the New York Knickerbockers. Only forty-five minutes and two Heinekens had passed when he felt a presence at his right shoulder.

"Good afternoon, Mr. Dancer," he said without turning.

How long the smaller man had been watching him, even following him, Lesko did not know. It was the habit of Mr. Dancer, who apparently had no first name, to arrive early for their meetings. He would wait unseen for Lesko's appearance and then choose a place of conversation where, Lesko presumed, there would have been no opportunity for prearranged eavesdropping.

"There is a satisfactory table in the corner," came the tight little voice. Lesko heard a note of irritation in it. Good, he thought. Let the little bastard wonder if I've been watching him as long as he's been watching me. He picked up his beer and newspaper and turned to join Dancer, who was already seated, an attaché case partly open on the table in front of him.

"May I be assured, Mr. Lesko," he began, offering no greeting, "that I have not been under your surveillance?"

"You hire a detective, you hire his instincts," Lesko replied offhandedly. "But no, I haven't been tailing you." He didn't add that if he ever did, this turkey would never know it.

"You understand that any such attempt would be in serious violation of our working arrangement? That it would be grounds for immediate and uncompensated dismissal?"

"I've answered your question, Mr. Dancer." At least all I'm going to, Lesko thought. The simple truth about knowing you were behind me is that you sponge on enough Aramis to have every fairy within fifty yards sniffing at your ass.

Dancer grunted, indicating acceptance of Lesko's reply at some level, and began fingering a device inside his attaché case that made soft clicking sounds. Lesko knew what it was. He was being scanned for recording devices and very likely being recorded himself. He used the time to study the man who sat across from him. It was, Lesko knew, a basically unrewarding exercise, since barely a hair on Dancer's head changed from one meeting to the next. He wore a dark blue, expensively tailored three-piece suit. Dancer must have had six more just like it, plus perhaps a ledger-lined blue pinstripe for his wilder moments. His shirts were invariably white and well starched, probably from either Brooks Brothers or Sulka. His ties were always a solid maroon, except for one lapse when he wore a recognizable club tie. He wore untasseled loafers by Bally of Switzerland on feet that were exceptionally small, even for a man of Dancer's unexceptional height. His body was squash-court lean, maybe tennis-court lean, thought Raymond Lesko, noting the callus on the inside of Dancer's right thumb. On the wrist above it,

Dancer wore a gold Patek Philippe watch with a black face, blank, no numerals, which seemed an admirable fit to his personality. His hair was freshly trimmed, probably twice a week by one of those barbers who make office calls. Lesko guessed his age at thirty-eight, although he could possibly have been ten years older.

"Are you drinking anything?" Lesko asked, although he perfectly well knew the answer.

"A Perrier, please. Two slices of lime."

Lesko mentally rolled his eyes as he signaled the waitress. The little twerp even drinks designer water.

"Your report, if you please." Dancer moved his case to one side of the table, having propped the lid from inside so that it remained open a half inch. Lesko pretended not to notice. He opened his notebook to a paper-clipped page well short of his most recent entry.

"I have a pretty good fix on the subject's history. How deep do you want to hear it?"

"All of it," Dancer told him. "Assume I know nothing."

The ex-cop waited while the Perrier and another beer were set on the table along with a bowl of fresh peanuts.

"The subject's full name is Jonathan T Corbin. He was born—"

"What does the *T* stand for?"

"Nothing. Just an initial on his birth certificate. No period after it, as in Harry S Truman. If it ever stood for anything, nobody who's alive seems to know what it was. Anyway, Jonathan T Corbin was born in Evanston, Illinois, on the twenty-fifth of December, 1944. A Christmas baby."

"You're certain?" Dancer stiffened slightly.

"About which part?"

"Never mind. Please continue."

"Parents," Lesko read, turning his notebook up toward an overhead light, "were the former Agnes Ann

Haywood of Wilmette, Illinois, and Captain Whitney Corbin. The father never saw him. He was an Army Air Corps pilot, reported missing in action in Europe on November sixth, 1944. Later confirmed killed."

"Positive identification?"

"Enough for the army. There were civilian eyewitnesses to a crash and burn just outside of Antwerp. The local Resistance ended up with his dog tags and turned them over to American Intelligence a month or so later." But a funny question, Lesko mused. Why should Dancer care about being sure the Corbin guy's father bought the farm?

"Do you have a marriage date for the parents?"

And there's another one, he thought. But as a matter of fact, he did. "The parents were married by a Cook County Justice of the Peace on June thirtieth, 1944. The baby was already three months in the oven. The captain had been home between tours in March of the same year, which is obviously when Jonathan T Corbin was conceived. I don't know how the father pulled it off in time of war, maybe because he won a few medals, but he wrangled a compassionate leave and the army sent him home long enough to get married and also to do a short war-bond tour around Evanston and some other Chicago suburbs so it shouldn't be a total loss. After about ten days they shipped him back to his fighter escort base in Bury St. Edmunds. That's in England. East Anglia."

"Thank you so much, Mr. Lesko." Dancer pursed his lips in an expression meant to assure the ex-cop that he had a passing knowledge of English geography. "Kindly continue."

"That's it for the father. He won one more medal for shooting up a troop train and another one for getting killed. The University of Notre Dame, where he went, put up a plaque in their trophy case with some of his medals and a baseball MVP he won there in the early forties. As for the mother, Agnes Haywood Corbin stayed home with her own parents, had the baby, and after about two years she got married again to a lawyer named George Satterthwaite. Satterthwaite bought a house in Winnetka and the two of them raised the kid."

"As a Satterthwaite?"

"Funny you should ask," Raymond Lesko answered, this time saying it out loud. "The records were a little confusing at first. What happened was that Satterthwaite adopted the kid and then filed for a legal name change. Judges won't usually let a stepfather do that, but Satterthwaite knew his way around the courts and he found one who would. It turned out to be a waste of time because the kid changed it back to Corbin, Jonathan T, just before he started high school. The second petition for a name change said he wanted to keep his blood identity and, besides, Jonathan Satterthwaite was too much of a mouthful. Try saying it fast after you've had too many Perriers."

Dancer waved off the suggestion with an impatient flick of his fingers. In his eyes, and in the nervous tapping of his knuckles, Lesko saw a curious mixture of excitement and annoyance. It was the body-language equivalent of a slap to the side of one's head when he learns something he should have known all along. As in, So that's where the goddamned kid was. Lost in a bunch of legal papers and some lawyer's ego trip. Lesko had the clear impression that he'd just earned his fee.

"Anyway," he continued, "the kid finished high school and then followed his real father to Notre Dame. Father's footsteps all the way. Good grades, played most of the same sports. Made cocaptain of the baseball team. He wasn't the star his old man was, but Corbin's thing was really boxing. Real good record as an intercollegiate light-heavy. He was going out for the

1968 Olympic trials until mononucleosis knocked him on his ass. Otherwise, never knocked out, never off his feet. He still puts on the gloves over at the New York AC. This guy's no pansy even if his head's not always on straight."

Dancer's eyebrows ticked upward. "You found a history of that?"

"Of what?"

"Irrational behavior. Compulsiveness. Paranoia."

Lesko studied the smaller man. "Who said anything about that?"

"Have you or have you not?"

Lesko hadn't. Not really. Not in Corbin's past, anyway. Well, maybe one little thing. "I talked to one of his teachers who remembers him getting counseling for what they call an identity crisis these days, but the problem doesn't seem to have been serious. The teacher wouldn't have even mentioned it except I told him I was doing a government security check."

"Go on."

"That's mostly it." But what the hell, thought Lesko, let's see what happens if I let out a little more line. "Except I'm not surprised if the kid had problems. As far back as I can trace it, the guy's family had a real cloud over it."

Something happened on Dancer's face. A subtle change. It struck the ex-cop that Dancer was suddenly far more interested in what Lesko knew than in the facts themselves.

"What are you saying?" Dancer asked finally.

Lesko leaned forward on his elbows. "Jonathan Corbin is an only child. A son. His father, Whitney Corbin, also an only son, dies violently before Corbin is born."

"Wars have a way of producing violent deaths, Mr. Lesko."

"His grandfather," continued Lesko, ignoring the

interruption, "was again an only child. A son. The grandfather, also named Jonathan T Corbin, gets killed by a Chicago hit-and-run driver in March of 1944. Same year as the father. He also gets run down at the height of wartime gas rationing when there's only a handful of private cars driving around in all of Chicago. The grandfather, by the way, was another ball player. Except this guy made it to the majors. He pitched for the White Sox during the 1907 and 1908 seasons. A spitballer. But then they outlawed it after the 1908 season and he eventually retired. Too bad. This guy actually played on the same team as Tinker to Evers to Chance. You know. The double-play combination. There was even a poem about them."

"You were driving toward some point, Mr. Lesko."

"Sorry. Just want you to know that when I dig, I dig deep."

"Noted."

"Next there's the great-grandfather, Hiram Forsythe Corbin, who died in a railroad accident in 1888, also without living siblings and also before the birth of his son, Jonathan T Corbin the first. If that's not coincidence enough, the first Jonathan T was also a Christmas baby, born December twenty-fifth, 1888." Lesko looked for the stiffening he'd seen at the last mention of Christmas babies and he saw it. Lesko knew that he was on to something and that whatever it was was already in his notebook. But in pieces. He stared hard at the page he was on.

"You know what's interesting?" he said. "These Corbins are big on holding on to family names. For example, the late Captain Whitney Corbin's first name was his grandmother's maiden name. But nobody seemed to care about naming anyone after old Hiram Forsythe."

"Mr. Lesko"—Dancer reached across the table and touched his fingertips to the notebook—"I'm sure this is all very fascinating. My immediate interest, however, is in the living."

"If it's living Corbins you're interested in, Mr. Dancer, you're following a one-horse race. The only Corbin on record to make it past sixty was old Hiram's widow, who lived to be . . ." Raymond Lesko wet a finger and began peeling to an earlier page. Again Dancer reached his hand to the notebook.

"While I think of it, Mr. Lesko, I'll want those original notes."

The ex-cop's brow lifted. He folded his hands over the cowhide notebook, leaving one finger to mark its place, and showed his perfect teeth. "I don't think so, Mr. Dancer."

"I want them, Mr. Lesko. I believe I've paid for them."

"You paid for information, which is what I'm feeding into that little tape recorder in your briefcase. The notebook is my property."

"I don't choose to get into a discussion with you, Mr. Lesko." The little man held out his palm. "I'll take it now."

"Behave yourself, Mr. Dancer." Raymond Lesko's eyes turned hard.

Corbin had told her everything. All that he could. All that he knew. Gwen had helped him from the tub and wrapped him in a white terry robe and laid him down on the shag rug in front of the fire she'd built in her living room. There she sat astride his back, her fingers gently kneading the muscles of his shoulders as he talked, encouraging him, listening, trying hard to understand. She'd put on a loose nightdress that now rode up high on her thighs and she'd brushed out her hair. The room's only light came from the remains of three birch logs. The fire's warmth, her body's warmth, made the snow seem far away.

He could not speak at first. He would try a few words but then a catch would form in his throat and he would hold his breath until it left him. Gwen was patient. She reached for his third double Scotch of the evening, brought it to his lips, and waited.

Hardest of all for Corbin was knowing where to begin. He told her first of the woman he'd stalked through the snow, of the things he'd seen and heard that night, of the elevated railway station in which she'd tried to find refuge, the same elevated railroad that had begun to materialize again as he and Gwen ran for the BMT subway that afternoon. He told her of the first time it snowed, the first time the city began to change. It was three months earlier. November. He'd stayed late in the city, a sales department meeting followed by drinks at the Warwick Bar. The next morning, that time at least, he was able to tell himself it was the work of an overtired imagination and one Scotch too many. His brain had merely replayed a street scene from some forgotten movie. *Gaslight. The Magnificent Ambersons*. But then it snowed again. And again.

"Tell me about Connecticut," she whispered. "It began there, didn't it?"

It did. And it didn't. It began, he thought, with the other woman. Margaret. It was true that the name had only just come to him, and that she'd only just begun to take shape and form, but it seemed that she had been there all his life. She was there when he was a boy. He would have a boy's troubled dreams and nighttime fears and at the end of the worst of them he would feel her holding him, rocking him, in her slender arms. She was there when he was in college but she was different by then. Where before she'd been a wraithlike but comforting mother or aunt, she was now a young woman, his own age or close to it, and she was everything a young woman should be. Loving, giving, bright, and gay. Jonathan had known many girls while he was in college. A few were special to him. But none who even began to be so wonderful as this woman whose name he did not know.

Margaret. Her name is Margaret.

Looking back, Corbin realized that he might never have come to New York if it were not for Margaret. He would have stayed in Chicago because Gwen would have stayed. She would not have left him after two good years of living together. Two very good years. We should think about getting married, Gwen had said. Just think about it. Jonathan had said yes. Yes, we should think about it. And more time passed.

"If I'm going to have babies," Gwen said, "one at least, it should be soon."

"Sure." Corbin smiled. He liked that idea, having a child with Gwen. A son. Especially a son. "We'll have to start thinking about that."

"We've *been* thinking about it."

"Soon. We'll decide something soon."

"You like to dream about it, Jonathan, but you always start to squirm when we talk about actually making it happen. Do you want children or don't you?"

"I do. Very much."

"But not if marriage is part of the bargain, I take it. What is it, Jonathan? Perhaps you think I'd be an unfit mother. Perhaps I've tarnished myself forever by living in sin with you."

"Oh, for Pete's sake, Gwen."

"Jonathan, do you want to marry me or not?"

"Gwen"—he took her hands—"I love you. I do. But I can't. I mean, I just need a little time."

She had pressed him for a decision he could not bring himself to make. And for reasons he couldn't bring himself to say aloud. They were too stupid. Childish. How could he tell her of this fantasy woman that he could not push out of his mind? It would sound so dumb. And it would have hurt her. But Gwen, being

Gwen, would have been willing to deal with it. She would have pointed out to him that all men probably have fantasy lovers at one time or another. Women, too. Nothing wrong with that.

But there was another ghost. A man. Not the man he became when it snowed but someone else. This one was tall, taller than Corbin, and very thin. He was dressed like an undertaker. Like the green-eyed woman, this one had lived in a distant corner of his mind for as long as he could remember. Unlike the woman, this man hated him. He hated Corbin, and if Corbin had had a wife and children, he would have hated them, too. Enough to kill them. All of them.

This was still another thing that caused Corbin to maintain a distance between Gwen and himself. It was not so much that Corbin feared the hatred of the man in black. To fear him would be to acknowledge that he was real. And to do that would be to acknowledge what Corbin had long begun to suspect, that in the same dark corner of his mind where this man lived, a certain madness had taken root and was growing by degrees. He could not ask Gwen to share that. Corbin would fight it by himself. One on one. The way he used to do in the boxing ring. Except in the ring you didn't have far to look for the enemy. He was right there and he couldn't hide.

Gwen stayed with Corbin. They enjoyed each other almost as much as ever, but a cloud had formed. A few months later a job opened up in New York. Gwen was perfect for it. Her salary would nearly double. Her boss, reluctantly, said she'd be crazy to pass it up. Gwen asked for a month to decide. She was given ten days. On the ninth day she took Corbin out to dinner.

"I have to ask you again, Jonathan." Her hand was in his across the table. "Do you want to marry me or not?"

"The job, right?" Corbin dropped his eyes. "You're really thinking about taking it?"

"I'd be a full producer. Of course I'm thinking about it."

"I do *want* to marry you, sweetheart."

"But?"

"I still need some time."

"Perhaps you need some time by yourself."

"Maybe. Maybe I do."

Corbin didn't mean that the way Gwen heard it. What he meant was that if he could be alone for a while, just a while within himself and with no distractions, the ghosts might take another step or two out of the shadows. He'd either know who they were, or he'd know they weren't real. What Gwen heard was, I care about you, but not quite as much as you'd like me to. And I'm not sure I need you.

"I'll miss you, Jonathan." Gwen was gone a week later.

By the second week after that, Corbin realized he'd made a disastrous mistake. So great was his sense of loss that it crowded out both his angel and his devil. They did not come further out. They were gone entirely. He called Gwen every day on the network WATS line and again most evenings to say goodnight. He flew in for weekends with her as often as he could. Gwen remained loving and caring but a touch more guarded than before.

Suddenly, in mid-August, another job opened at network headquarters. Ben Tyler, the senior producer for sports programming, had suffered a massive heart attack while playing tennis in the Hamptons. Doctors gave him a better-than-even chance for survival but almost no chance of returning full time for at least a year. The network asked Corbin to fill in, beginning immediately. He leaped at the opportunity. Gwen pretended to be surprised when he called her with the news. But his new boss, Bill Stafford, had already told him how hard Gwen had pushed for him.

He moved to New York over Labor Day weekend. The network needed him there in time for the fall football season. Gwen flew to Chicago to help him pack. They made love on the floor among cardboard boxes after Corbin told her what an ass he'd been and thanked her for being so patient with him.

"Was it . . . Is it another woman, Jonathan?"

Corbin shook his head and kissed her.

"If it is, Jonathan, I want to know. I'll try to give you room to work it out but I won't be made a fool of."

"There is no other woman." He looked into her eyes. "There's never been another woman." It was not exactly a lie.

After Corbin's first weeks in New York, he allowed himself to believe that he was winning. The woman with the gold-flecked eyes and the man in black had retreated to their dark corners. He was too busy to think about them. The job was going even better than he'd hoped. He had moved into Gwen's apartment in the East Seventies but only, she insisted, until he could find a proper place of his own. One breakup was enough, thank you. Their feelings had some more settling to do before they decided on any longer-term arrangements.

Meanwhile, Corbin and Gwen, who saw little of each other during their business days, were spending virtually all their free time together. Most evenings and weekends they'd spend hunting down apartments and negotiating bribes with rental agents. Otherwise they'd shop, explore restaurants and museums, see Broadway shows and cabarets, happily sampling all the pleasures of the city in autumn. In late October, on a Thursday, Corbin placed a deposit on a one-bedroom in a high-rise near the East River just above the Queensboro

Bridge. It would be available in three weeks' time. Wouldn't it be fun, Gwen suggested, to celebrate by getting out of the city for the weekend? The leaves up in Connecticut were just at their peak of color and she knew of a lovely old inn in Greenwich that was easily reached by a New Haven Railroad train and taxi. The inn was called the Homestead. It was a marvelous old Victorian house, she told him, formerly a private estate bearing the same name, and totally restored with genuine period furnishings. Which gave her another idea. Let's do it right, she said. You go and buy a straw boater and a pair of white duck trousers. I have a long, frilly, light blue tea dress and perhaps I can find a parasol someplace. We can play croquet on the lawn and take quiet walks along country lanes and push each other into leaf piles.

"The Homestead?" Corbin asked. His face had an odd and dreamy look about it.

"Do you know it?" She was dialing Greenwich information and did not see his expression.

"No." He blinked. "No, I've never been to Greenwich." The Homestead, he thought. A common name. You'd find an inn or restaurant called the Homestead almost anyplace you went. But Corbin wondered if this one was painted white with black shutters, and had a widow's walk on top, and whether it sat high on a knoll above a steep open lawn, and had a full-length veranda and a circular driveway that approached from the right.

Two more weeks would pass before Gwen had cause to regret that she'd ever heard of the Homestead. But the weekend they had there together was perfect. Utterly, ecstatically perfect. The room they shared was a delightful confection of Victoriana. There was a heavy mahogany sleigh bed, Tiffany lamps, stenciled wallpaper, an ancient bouquet of artificial flowers under glass, and a ponderous dresser of walnut burl topped with pink marble. Although modern baths had been discreetly added, their room contained an antique washstand whose pitcher was filled with lilac-scented water. The dining room on the main floor had once been an attached barn. They sat on Windsor chairs under a high ceiling whose original chestnut beams had recently been exposed.

The menu, though excellent, disappointed Corbin at first glance. He'd had his heart set on canvasback duck, but it was not listed. And he thought a maraschino sorbet should have been added between courses. And terrapin. How could a proper menu not include Maryland terrapin. But no matter. There was a wonderful mussel bisque that he could almost taste from the menu although he could not specifically recall ever having it. And a good selection of game foods—quail, pheasant, venison, and partridge. But no woodcock. There should have been woodcock.

After dinner, Corbin and Gwen stepped outside to the open section of the porch, each with a cognac in hand. As Corbin, with one arm around Gwen's waist, looked down over the sloping lawn toward the road below, an urge to take her by the hand and sneak off for a moonlight swim flitted across his mind. There was a small hidden cove, he thought, or imagined, just through those trees down to the right. Smiling to himself, he shook off the notion. Even if there was such a cove, and he had no reason to believe there was, it was late October. The water would be more bracing than he bargained for. The very thought of it gave him a chill, and he remembered the warmth and coziness of their room. Gwen read his mind.

"I've never made love in a sleigh bed." She squeezed him.

Saturday morning brought a late breakfast in bed, another turn at lovemaking, and then a long cool walk past the impressive homes of the Belle Haven section of Greenwich. Along the way, Corbin thought of that secret cove again and the path that led to it. But there was no path, only the macadam driveway of a sprawling Tudor house. As they returned to the Homestead, Corbin had his first daylight look at the inn. It was, in fact, much as he had envisioned it when he first heard Gwen say the name. Except it was painted brown, not white with black shutters. And there was a sort of rotunda porch built on one corner. And there were outbuildings that did not appear in the picture he'd seen in his mind. But the widow's walk was there, and it was high on a knoll, and there was a circular driveway approaching from the right. Corbin, however, did not dwell on these similarities. He knew they could have applied to a thousand other buildings. And anyway he didn't care. He was having too nice a time with Gwen.

After a salad lunch there was croquet. Gwen changed, as promised, into her old-fashioned blue summer dress with a carved onyx brooch at her throat. And Corbin, to her delight, had bought not only a straw hat and a pair of white duck trousers for the occasion but also a white linen blazer with wide brown vertical stripes. Several of the other guests applauded when they appeared on the croquet court and Gwen, given an audience, decided to play the dainty Victorian maiden for all it was worth. She insisted that he stand with his arms around her from behind to help her hold and swing the mallet, then pretended to be shocked when he took that liberty. That scene played, she proceded to trounce him, cheating shamelessly and brushing aside any protest with the reminder that she was only a mere girl and he was so strong. Corbin loved it. All of it. Every minute of that day and the next. On the Sunday evening train ride to New York he told Gwen Leamas that it was easily the happiest and most loving weekend of his life and that Greenwich, what he saw of it, was the most beautiful place he'd ever seen.

On the next day, Monday, Gwen was asked if she could fly to London right away as part of a group going there to negotiate the rights to several Thames Television properties. She could scarcely refuse. The business sessions and the obligatory entertaining would last well into the following weekend. After that, although she did not want to be away from Jonathan, she would have at least several days in which to visit a few favorite relatives and carouse a bit with some old chums from school. Corbin rode with her to the airport and walked with her to the gate. His voice broke a bit when he said goodbye. He said he must be getting a cold. I love you, too, she answered.

Corbin had told himself that this was a great chance to catch up on his reading. Maybe play some racquetball. Maybe see a couple of those blood-and-guts movies that Gwen never wants to sit through. He'd halfway convinced himself that he would enjoy the period of privacy. A nice break. But he was back at her apartment for less than an hour when he realized for the second time in a year how hollow a place can be when the person who means everything to you isn't there anymore. He wished she hadn't gone. He wished they'd never left the Homestead.

By Friday Corbin couldn't bear the thought of a whole weekend alone in her apartment. When he left the Burlington Building at the day's end he found himself falling into the stream of men and women who were walking in the direction of Grand Central. Why not, he thought. There was no use going back to the Homestead. It wouldn't be the same, but what would be the harm in seeing a little more of Greenwich. He could take a late train back. Or, if he chose, he could stay over. Whatever felt good.

Corbin stayed over. And it did feel good. He didn't

know why exactly, but it was better than feeling lonely, so he was not about to look for reasons. It was certainly a pretty town, full of attractive people who kept themselves looking fit. Nice homes. Nice yards. Women in tennis dresses. The leaves all red and gold like Japanese jewelry. After a morning of walking and breathing the crisp clean air he decided on lunch at a large hotel he seemed to remember down along the shore of Long Island Sound. It wasn't there. He must have been thinking of someplace else. But no matter. There were plenty of nice places to stop. On his way to the nearest of them he passed the storefront office of a real estate firm. In the window he saw about a dozen snapshots of homes that were offered for sale. Corbin stopped and looked. Two of the houses looked rather like the Homestead. Victorians. But on a smaller scale. Corbin turned away and had his lunch. That afternoon he returned to the city.

Sunday passed, then three workdays. On Wednesday evening, he once again took the train to Greenwich. He knew that the trip didn't make much sense, spending a solitary two or three hours there and then catching a late train back. But it couldn't hurt. And he liked it there. He went again on Thursday night. Gwen called from London on Friday to ask how he was getting on. Fine, he said. Hurry back. One more week, she told him. Love you. On Friday evening he packed a bag for the weekend.

The real estate agent, a fortyish woman named Marge, was friendly and helpful, but she didn't really have the feeling that she had a live one in Jonathan Corbin. He wanted to look at Victorians and she'd shown him six. The last two were closer to a Federal style and Corbin didn't even want to look inside. They weren't right. What is? she asked. I'm not sure. But you'll know it when you see it? I think so. Right.

Just above the Post Road, not far from Greenwich

Avenue, a heavily overgrown piece of property caught Corbin's eye. On it stood a house that he could barely see because it was largely hidden by two old and neglected willows. He asked Marge to turn around.

"That one?"

"I think so."

She pulled into the gravel driveway, past a For Sale sign that had fallen over.

"Isn't this one listed with you?" he asked.

"It's listed with everyone. Has been for almost two years. I have to tell you it's not in real good shape. The property will eventually go to someone who just wants the land."

"They'll tear down the house?"

"Wouldn't you?"

"Let's look inside."

Even before Marge opened the lockbox on the door, Corbin knew what the inside would be like. A small room on the right, a stairway straight ahead, a kitchen all the way back. There would be a rose-colored runner on the stairs, held down with brass rods. The kitchen would smell like vegetable soup. Upstairs, he didn't know. He could only imagine what the bedrooms would be like.

But he was right about the first floor.

"Do you know who lived here before?" he asked the agent.

"Two or three families that I can remember since I was a kid. The last was an old man named Mullins. As you can see, he wasn't able to keep it up. He moved to a senior citizens' home and then he passed on. An estate lawyer's handling the sale."

"Outside"—Corbin pointed—"was there ever a trellis over the driveway with wisteria vines on it?"

"There was until it fell down, yes. You know this house?"

"No." Corbin looked away. "Houses like this always seem to have them."

"Uh . . . listen. Mr. Corbin—"

"Jonathan."

"Jonathan. You're not really interested in this place are you?"

"I guess I am. Yes."

"You said you were single?"

"I'm sort of engaged."

"I hope it's more than sort of. This really isn't the kind of neighborhood a single man would be happy in. All couples, most with teenage kids or older. You might find it hard to make friends."

"Marge, you don't sound real hot to make a commission."

"I'd love the commission. I need a new car. But I'd want to make it on a house you'd like living in. You can get a good price on this place but it would cost you at least another thirty thousand to fix it up. Maybe twenty if you're a heck of a handyman. Are you?"

"Not especially."

"You want to sleep on it?"

"I suppose I should."

"I'll show you some other places tomorrow. There's a real nice one over in Riverside."

"Fine."

But at nine the next morning, Corbin handed her a check for the binder on the Mullins house.

"Tell me about Connecticut," Gwen had asked. "It began there, didn't it?"

It did and it didn't.

"I think you've really gone crackers this time," she told him. The day she returned from London he drove her to Greenwich in the secondhand Datsun he bought as a station car.

"You don't like it?" Corbin was disappointed. "But it's sort of like the Homestead. Or it will be when it's fixed up. You'll have a place to go weekends."

"You might have discussed this with me, Jonathan."

"Well, it's an investment. And it's not as if I'm going to be out here all the time. A couple of weekends a month. And I'll keep the place in New York." Corbin, in truth, had given no thought at all to the future. The apartment he'd leased had slipped his mind entirely, so mesmerized was he by this peeling, sagging pile of dry rot, which to him was a thing of joy and beauty.

He spent few nights in the city. Few nights with Gwen. Most days he would catch the earliest train he could manage and be at the Mullins house before seven. He would work there, scraping and plastering, often neglecting to eat, until midnight. Sometimes, when it was still light enough in the evening, he would take long walks through the neighboring streets. Now and then he would see another old house and stand for a long time staring at it. He did not know why.

The thought that he was behaving compulsively, or at all irrationally, never entered Corbin's mind. Nor could he understand why Gwen seemed upset with him. He did notice that she was increasingly unavailable on the occasional free nights he found time to spend with her, but he felt sure that she'd come around once she saw the finished product. Just wait until he had the house papered and furnished properly. Then every weekend would be just as happy as that one at the Homestead. As happy as he was.

Since that first time she saw his house, Gwen Leamas remembered, she had seldom seen him happy again. Thanksgiving was one exception. He was beaming like a schoolboy when she arrived to spend that holiday weekend with him in Greenwich. He was so proud of what he'd done with the house and of the Thanksgiving dinner he'd planned from a Victorian cookbook that she managed to choke down his oyster stuffing and his mashed turnips with no visible sign of distress. The dining room furnishings, which he'd found at an auction, were also authentic Victorian. So was the reproduction wallpaper. The other rooms were as yet largely unfurnished. But wait until Christmas, he said. By Christmas everything will be perfect.

It snowed several times before Christmas. An inch fell during the last week of November. Then another inch a few days later. Then two more substantial snowfalls and a few scattered flurries. And Jonathan began to change. At first Gwen made no connection between his behavior and the snow. She simply knew that he seemed to be calling in sick an awful lot. It took her a while to realize that on those occasions when Jonathan came down with the flu, or had a toothache, or couldn't get his Datsun started, it was always snowing. And his too-frequent absenteeism was beginning to wear thin with some of the network staff. When she tried to discuss it with him, Corbin brushed it off. Just a string of rotten luck, he said. Coincidence. Nothing to it.

By now he was spending nearly all his free time at the Greenwich house and paying little attention to Gwen, which Gwen increasingly resented. When he called to confirm their Christmas plans, Gwen at first declined to come, but his disappointment seemed so sincere and so innocent that she changed her mind. At the very least it would give her a chance to have a good talk with him. Christmas, as it turned out, was pleasant and even loving. She had to admit that the house was quite nicely done up and that his authentic Victorian Christmas dinner was delicious. The oysters, this time, were left on the half shell where they belonged. But as for the talk she wanted, Jonathan remained evasive as ever.

January was particularly snowy that year. Jonathan missed more days, some of them important. Whenever the skies appeared to threaten, Jonathan would either arrive very late in the morning or make a headlong rush to Grand Central for an early train home. It was Sandy Bauer who first came to Gwen's office and told her how worried she was about Jonathan. "I don't understand it," she said. "I mean, the man is standing in there right now looking scared to death. Of snow!"

He was on his way to the elevators by the time Gwen caught up with him. Jonathan foolishly tried to duck her and then tried to bluff. There was a meeting across town, he told her. He was late, he had to run. Like hell, she answered. Talk to me, Jonathan. What in God's name is happening to you?

"Nothing. I'm okay. Just a little temperature."

"Bullfeathers! Where are you going?"

"Just across town. Listen, I'll call you."

"I'm going with you."

"No."

"Then I'll follow you, damn it."

She did. Not bothering to get her coat she matched him step for step, and all the way to Park Avenue she could see the growing terror on his face. She saw him dodging obstacles that weren't there and flinching at things she couldn't see.

"What is it, Jonathan?" She grabbed the belt of his trench coat.

"Let me go. Please."

"I'll scream bloody murder if you pull away from me. Jonathan, are you on drugs? Are you hallucinating?"

"Gwen. Please." His eyes were wild, darting. Suddenly he reached for her and pulled her toward him as though guiding her out of the path of someone walking by. There was no one near, but Jonathan's eyes focused and followed as if there were.

"What do you see, Jonathan? What's frightening you so badly?" She wrapped her shivering arms around his neck and pulled his face into her wet hair and kissed his cheek. He hugged her back, tentatively at first and then fiercely. He held her for several long minutes, and she held him until his breathing became normal.

And then he said, very gently, "I must leave you now, dearest."

"What?" His tone. So strange. She tilted her head to better see his face.

"Wednesday," he whispered. "I shall visit you on Wednesday."

"Jonathan . . ." She stepped back from him.

"Be well, dearest." He brought her hand to his lips. Then he bowed slightly at the waist and tipped a hat he wasn't wearing. A stunned Gwen Leamas watched as he walked unhurriedly down Park Avenue, as if he had not a care in the world.

The man called Dancer cast his eyes around the Oyster Bar. Dour-faced commuters had quickly filled the remaining tables and were already two deep at the bar. It was clear from their manner that at least some northbound trains had already been canceled.

The thought of terminating this interview with Raymond Lesko crossed his mind but Dancer rejected it. Their conversation had taken too disquieting a turn. But aside from Lesko's acute perceptions regarding the unhappy history of the Corbin family, and his recalcitrance regarding the notebook, there was still much more to be learned from him. And more to be learned about him.

The interview would continue, Dancer decided, although he wished he could think of a more discreet place. The Yale Club and the New York Yacht Club were nearby and would offer privacy but were otherwise out of the question. Bringing Lesko to either one would be tantamount to handing him a business card. Nor would any other public place be suitable. In the more fashionable of them, Dancer would run the risk of being recognized and addressed by his real name. Any place not as fashionable would surely be just as crowded as Grand Central. Better to remain here, he supposed, and rely on the increasing levels of noise and drunkenness to dull the attention of any casual listener.

"I consider my request a reasonable one, Mr. Lesko. May I know why you are being difficult about a few scribbled pages which you can surely replicate from memory?"

"A matter of principle."

"Indeed, Mr. Lesko." Dancer almost allowed himself a smile.

"The principle is called covering my butt. If you're a lawyer, which I suspect you are because you're such a pain in the ass, you know the difference in evidentiary value between original notes and reconstructions. You also know that no reporter or policeman would ever surrender his notes."

"Defrocked policeman."

"Retired, Twinkletoes," Lesko corrected him. "Full pension."

Dancer sat back, folding his arms, debating whether to point out to this thug that his retirement was no more than two hops ahead of the Internal Affairs Division, a departmental trial, and possible indictment for drug trafficking and murder. But making Lesko defensive on the subject could be counterproductive. And his past transgressions might well have value in the immediate future.

"Your report." He leaned forward. "Please continue, Mr. Lesko."

Lesko met Dancer's eyes for a long moment, considering whether to pick up where Dancer had seemed so anxious to stop him. The subject at hand was old Hiram Corbin's widow, mother of the first Jonathan T Corbin, who was reputed to have been a very impressive old dame. Lived to be about eighty. Which might not have been all that remarkable, even for a Corbin, except that Hiram's widow didn't come to all that peaceful an end either. Lesko thumbed a few pages back, leaving Dancer to chew his lip a while longer.

He didn't really need his notes by this time. Lesko remembered. A coincidence, which had barely made an impression some two weeks earlier at the Hall of Records in Evanston, Illinois, now came back to him. Mrs. Hiram Forsythe Corbin, nee Charlotte Whitney of Baltimore, had also died in March of 1944. Another accident, it says here. Asphyxiation. Died in her sleep when the flame of her gas heater somehow blew out. No autopsy. Wartime shortage of personnel at the coroner's office. No police investigation worth the name, either. Strange. Strange because the physical evidence *could* have been consistent with deliberate suffocation. On the other hand, it *could* have been consistent with a legitimate accident or even a suicide. Still, there should have been an investigation. Particularly in view of the dates. There it was. March 19, 1944. That's just two days before March 21, 1944, when her fifty-five-year-old son had the life crushed out of him by a speeding car on Chicago's North Side. Here's old Charlotte Corbin, a woman of some standing in Chicago, whose sudden death was practically within a heartbeat of the sudden death of her son, Jonathan T Corbin the first. You'd think someone would have cared enough to wonder.

What about her grandson, Captain Whitney Corbin? Didn't he care enough to wonder? Wait a minute. March of 1944. That's when he was conceiving a son of his own. Our own Jonathan T Corbin the second.

Captain Whitney Corbin must have come home for a double funeral, following which he found consolation in the bed of young Agnes Haywood. Then he went back to England. The dates all fit. Corbin, the present Corbin, is a Christmas baby. That means conception was around March 25 or 26. So Whitney was home for at least a week. Let's just suppose that somebody really was knocking off all the Corbins. How'd they miss Whitney? There were two funerals and that meant a lot of friends around. Too many. And old Charlotte's death probably had some press coverage. Maybe they couldn't get at him, maybe they didn't want to risk going for a triple, or maybe when they looked for Whitney he was shacked up someplace with Agnes. Then when he comes home in June to marry pregnant Agnes, he's got half the Air Corps with him because of this war bond thing. They can't touch him. Maybe they sit and wait for the war to end unless Hitler does them a favor in the meantime.

"Mr. Lesko." Dancer tapped a gold pen, which he'd been nervously fingering, against the side of his glass.

As Lesko lowered his notebook to the table, he watched Dancer's eyes. He watched them fall to the page he'd been reading, the page with the dates. Then Lesko slowly peeled the pages forward to those covering the activities of the living. The relief he saw in Dancer's tight little face was unmistakable.

"The subject," he began reading, "was transferred last September from station WLAD-TV in Chicago to network headquarters in New York. Before that he'd been living for eight years in an apartment at 1500 North State Street. For at least two of those years he played house with a female street reporter from the same station. Her name is Gwendolyn Fiona Leamas. Gwen Leamas for short. English girl. She preceded the subject to New York by about six months. Her own transfer may or may not have affected Corbin's decision to move east. I'm inclined to think it didn't because except for a short-term live-in at her place when he first got here and an occasional night out since then, the word is that they're pretty much drifting apart."

"Why, then, did he come here? Any information on that?"

"Bigger job." Lesko shrugged. "Headquarters. It happens."

"No pattern of nonbusiness visits to New York? No evidence of sudden interest?"

"Nope," Lesko answered. But he would remember the intensity behind those questions. "The job opened up when the guy who had it before got sick. The Leamas girl recommended Corbin but he was probably in line for the spot anyway."

"The Leamas woman's address?"

"One forty-five East Seventy-seventh Street. Second-floor apartment facing front. Corbin's there now, probably for the weekend."

"You said they'd drifted apart."

Lesko shrugged again. "They're on and off."

"Continue, please." Dancer wet his lips. "I'm interested in Corbin's personal activities since he arrived."

Lesko told of Corbin's finding an expensive apartment in the East Sixties, putting down a large deposit, and then forfeiting it because he decided instead to buy some old dump in Greenwich.

"The broker up there gave me some real estate bullshit about the place being a handyman's dream, but I could tell even she thought he was a little bit crazy. And Corbin, as far as I know, never nailed two boards together in his whole life. But there he is, happy as a pig in shit to spend every night and weekend up there cutting back trees, painting, and prowling through junk shops to make it look like it did a hundred years ago. You talk to the neighbors, they don't know whether he's a weirdo or a fag, no offense, so they try to pretend he isn't there."

"Conclusion?"

"I don't have one."

"You see evidence of unstable behavior and you don't conclude instability?"

Raymond Lesko sipped his beer. "What instability?" he asked. "The guy found something he likes doing. Other people up there spend all their time putzing around in sailboats or collecting fake ducks."

"But Corbin, you said, had no history of an interest in restoring old homes. Such a consuming hobby, to the extent of researching authentic paints and wallpapers, usually develops over time."

"I said, as far as I know. It's possible he was into it before."

"But you don't think so."

"No, I don't." Lesko didn't recall saying anything about Corbin researching wallpaper. Someone else must be watching the guy's progress on that house.

"You did, however, mention a history of instability going back to his college years."

"I didn't say that either. I said he had some counseling. One time."

"A history of confusion then."

The ex-cop shrugged again. Confusion. It was as good a word as any for people who go to a shrink to help them sort out their worries. As for Corbin, the counseling episode in college could have been anything. Maybe the pressure of living up to his jock, war-hero father got to him. Maybe he got whacked out over some girl. On the other hand, maybe he didn't like snow in South Bend, either. Which, Raymond Lesko thought, brings us to this afternoon.

"The guy doesn't like snow."

"I beg your pardon?"

"The subject, Jonathan Corbin, hates snow. If

you're looking for emotional problems, there's at least one with handles on it. When it snows he won't even step out of his door if he can help it. I heard this a couple of weeks ago from a guy he works with. A lot of them hang out in the Warwick Bar after work and I made out like I knew Corbin from Chicago. I bought the guy a couple of drinks and he tells me that everyone likes Corbin just fine but they're starting to worry about the way he freaks out over snowflakes. If it snows even an inch, they don't see him for two days. Over a winter it adds up."

Dancer blinked, his expression still uncomprehending. Lesko was disappointed.

"Anyway, when the radio said we might get snow today, I got a room at the Warwick where I could watch Corbin through his window. It turns out it was true. The guy goes off the wall and tries to hide from it. He'd still be there now if the Leamas girl didn't drag him home with her."

"Significance?"

Lesko sighed inwardly but said nothing. Whatever the significance was, he'd hoped for a clue in Dancer's reaction. But Dancer was a blank. He was, Lesko felt sure, not pretending. It meant little to him. The message in Dancer's eyes changed slowly from incomprehension to a minor irritation, as if this latest intelligence was only one more sign of Corbin's troublesomeness.

Dancer straightened and rapped his knuckles. "Is there more to your report, Mr. Lesko?"

"That's it through today. Except I finally got some decent straight-on shots of Corbin's face through that window." Lesko placed the roll of film on the table. Dancer snatched it eagerly and slipped it into his pocket.

"Beginning tomorrow, I'd like you to concentrate on his actions in Connecticut. I want to know what he's doing there and why. If he remains in the city with Miss Leamas, as you seem to expect, you'll have an opportunity for a thorough search of his house. Look for photographs, notebooks, anything that provides evidence of his intentions."

"That's called breaking and entering, Mr. Dancer."

"It's called investigation. I rather imagine you've done this sort of thing before."

"It's also called idiocy, Mr. Dancer. You're asking me to leave tracks through two feet of virgin snow while I find a window to climb through."

"A bonus, perhaps," Dancer replied, drawing two brown envelopes from his inside pocket. "An additional five hundred dollars may help you rise to the challenge. Which brings us to the matter of your fee and expenses. Have you brought the accounting I require?"

Raymond Lesko produced a single folded sheet, which listed his out-of-pocket expenses for the preceding two weeks plus an invoice for his next two weeks' fee in advance. Receipts were attached by paper clip. These Dancer examined individually and carefully before leaning his lips closer to the attaché case.

"Expenses," he read aloud, "less a five-hundred-dollar travel advance, total four hundred eighty dollars and seventy-four cents which I will round off to four hundred eighty. These include a hotel room which Mr. Lesko will either vacate in the morning or retain at his own expense. Other receipted items include meals in amounts that are borderline reasonable, plus the rental of a telescopic camera lens. Unreceipted items include phone calls and cab fares. We also have an invoice for the agreed-upon fee of three hundred dollars per day in advance for fourteen days. The accounting is satisfactory."

Dancer did not keep the receipts. He handed the sheet back to Lesko and next withdrew several bills from the first of his two envelopes. He slid the envelope and its remaining contents across the table to the ex-cop.

"There's forty-seven hundred dollars, Mr. Lesko. Count it if you wish, but please do so under the table. You've been overpaid by almost twenty dollars, which I intend to recover at a later meeting."

"Would you like to hold my watch?" Lesko asked bloodlessly.

Dancer dismissed the suggestion, Lesko's sarcasm being lost on him, and placed his hand over the second envelope. "This envelope, Mr. Lesko, contains the sum of fifteen thousand dollars in cash." He paused and watched with satisfaction as the bigger man's lips parted.

"Go on, Mr. Dancer."

"I expect to employ you for the next two weeks at the most. Your maximum income potential from this assignment is the amount of money I've just handed you. Aside, that is, from the contents of this envelope."

"Yes?"

"There is also the prospect of the five-hundred-dollar bonus I've already mentioned. However, you might possibly earn a much more substantial bonus if you were to bring this investigation to some dramatic conclusion."

"Get to the point, Mr. Dancer," Lesko said, although he fully realized that his client had no intention of being more specific. Not while that little tape recorder was spinning in his briefcase. "How dramatic would that be?"

"I'm sure I have no idea, Mr. Lesko. Something irrevocable, I'd imagine. Would you care to hold on to this envelope while you reflect upon the matter?"

"Maybe it will give me an idea."

"Perhaps so, Mr. Lesko." The man called Dancer rose to his feet as he slid the brown envelope toward the ex-cop. Behind it he slid the bar check the waitress had left. "I'll look for you one week from today, same time, in the main hall of the New York Public Library at Forty-second Street and Fifth Avenue. I expect that you'll have earned that money."

FIVE

 WEN LEAMAS PLACED HER LAST BIRCH LOG ON THE glowing remains of the fire and blew at the coals until low flames lapped at its sides. She eased herself down beside Corbin, who was mumbling in light sleep on the thick shag rug, and rested one hand between his shoulder blades. The small pendulum clock on her mantel showed that it was not quite seven in the evening. It felt more like four in the morning, she thought.

Jonathan seemed at peace for the moment. Her prescription of a hot bath and a dose of Scotch had done its work. The fire as well. Although he couldn't spend the rest of the winter in front of one.

He stirred as her fingers brushed at the hair on his neck and she felt his left hand creeping under her cotton nightdress until it found the smooth flesh of her thigh.

"Go back to sleep." She slapped the hand lightly.

"Uh-uh."

"Behave yourself. Go to sleep."

"I don't get to lie in front of fires with beautiful naked ladies every night," he murmured, his eyes still closed.

"I'm not naked. I'm wearing a very proper gown and you are taking liberties."

"Shhh! You're naked. Not a stitch. And I'm your helpless prisoner and you're about to vent all your kinky passions on my defenseless body."

She leaned forward and kissed him lightly on one cheek.

"See?" he whispered. "You're already out of control."

Smiling, she peeled back the collar of the white terry wrap she'd lent him and touched her lips softly to a line across his shoulders. Corbin shivered and shook his arms free of the robe. She peeled it back further.

"Oh no, you mustn't," he groaned. "What decent woman will have me after this?"

"Us lusty wenches have needs too," she snarled. Gwen straddled his back once more and began tracing her fingertips over his skin until she could see goosebumps rising on his upper arms. She unlaced her nightdress and let it slide down her own arms behind her. Now she leaned forward, touching her breasts against his back and moving them from side to side before allowing her body to settle. Corbin felt her cheek nestle against his and saw her honey hair glistening in the firelight as it dropped a delicate veil across his eyes. A new warmth rose beneath him. Corbin drowsily shifted his body and with his left hand pulled at the folds of terry cloth that were bunched between his legs. That done, he allowed the hand to fall limply to his side, nearer to the fire than before, its knuckles turned toward the radiating heat.

"Gwen," he whispered.

"Ummm?"

"Thank you."

"Shhh!"

Neither spoke for several minutes, lying warm and still, until the effect of Corbin's day caught up with him again and drew him unwillingly into another light sleep. As his body became increasingly weightless and he faded in and out he became dimly aware of the tiny pinpricks of heat dancing across the nerve endings on the back of the hand that lay near the fire. Corbin didn't mind. The pain was good. The pain was satisfying. Those hot, throbbing knuckles had given far better than they got.

Corbin frowned. His unopened eyelids twitched as his semiconscious brain tried to recapture and question that last thought. But its meaning drifted into the darkness. Off in a distance he saw the fist. His fist. It was jabbing into the same darkness, against nothing at all at first, but then he began to feel what seemed like flesh and bone at the other end. Another man's face. A thin man. Yes. Oh, yes. Now he could see the face and he remembered. Corbin's brain settled back and watched.

A good caning would have done the job as well, he knew. A cane well laid against the thin man's back and thighs would have inflicted even greater humiliation without damage to himself. But in this case only fists would do. Bare knuckles were the ticket. Better even than a horsewhip.

"Jab, lad," Big John Flood had taught him. "Jab once with the left, then again, then a third time if need be till his arms are high. Now you hook that same left hand low to the ribs. That brings his arms down fast, you see, and his face tilts up like a lass waitin' for a kiss. It's then you cross with your right and it's 'Throw him down, McCloskey.' Head down now, lad. Aye. That's playin' the tune. Put your back into those belly blows but not those to the head. Let the other man, not you, come to scratch with busted knuckles."

Chin in. Yes. Corbin remembered. He'd spotted his man as he entered, picking him out among other tall men by the flash of the diamond stickpin on his cravat and another on a long, thin finger. The man's hands looked like the tools of a pickpocket. Always had. He was leaner and younger than the men who stood in a half circle around him but they were all of a piece. Pirates. Plunderers. Men not received in decent homes who had to bribe their way into clubs. Coarse and vulgar men who were strangers to breeding and manners. This one, they said, came from better stock, though Corbin never believed that. He was all shine and gloss, but there was a stink to him like a dead mackerel washed ashore in the moonlight.

The man saw Corbin. He made a show of taking a weary breath and raised his eyes toward an enormous painting of prancing nudes that covered most of the wall at his side. Next he turned to his companion and whispered mocking words, and the companion grinned and sneered. Both men held cigars between bared teeth.

Corbin stripped away his hat and ulster as he walked, placing these and his cane upon the tobacco stand in passing. At the bar, to Corbin's right and opposite the painting, a man with shoulder-length hair and wearing a Western-style hat touched the arm of the man next to him. The other man, an actor, Corbin knew, smiled his approval and clapped his hands in anticipation. "Good show!" Corbin heard him shout. Two dozen heads in the long, narrow room turned toward Corbin. Some faces showed surprise or shock, some showed excitement, even glee, and some, like the man and his companions whom Corbin approached, showed contempt. Their cigars puffed and glowed beneath hooded eyes as he closed upon them. With no words spoken, Corbin planted his feet and struck. His left fist, the jab, snaked straight at the hot tip of the taller man's cigar, splaying it across his mouth and raining glowing ash upon his chest. The man's head snapped back and his eyes blinked cockeyed wide and his hat spun a half turn upon his head. Corbin heard a cheer from the bar. He jabbed again, with a twist this time, mashing the man's lips before they could spit free the tobacco that clung to them. Then came the third blow—*Put your back into it, lad*—that crunched into the thin man's rib cage and pumped a surge of bile to his throat. Corbin held back the final blow until his man could straighten. Straighten or run, Corbin cared not which. But the man did neither. Doubled over, his face enflamed, he fell sideways and collapsed across the marble top of a small round table. He held on to its edges, sucking shallow gulps of air until he found one that his lungs could retain. Then, with a cough that loosed a spray of swallowed blood, he turned one eye up at Corbin. Corbin saw on that face, even more than pain, a humiliation that was all but unendurable. He also saw evil. And he saw hatred.

"I will ruin you," the man rasped through thickening lips. "I will destroy you and then I will mark your whore's face so she's not even fit for a cellar crib. I will have you—"

Corbin seized him by the hair before he could finish. He tore the man's face from the table and forced his head back until it was braced upon the lower frame of the huge canvas of nudes. For a long moment, Corbin held the man there, suspended. He wanted the man to look into his own eyes and see a hatred greater than his own, and he wanted the man to see the right fist that Corbin held cocked at his ear. The thin man tried to snarl or curse at Corbin, but the sound turned into the whelp of a frightened dog as he saw the fist creeping slowly back and then uncoiling, smashing flat against his nose. Blinded now, and shrieking, the man in black felt his eyes being hammered shut by the chopping blows that followed.

At last Corbin released his grip and let the torn and moaning mass slide to the floor. A tickle of hairs at the back of his neck caused him to sidestep and whirl in an upright boxer's stance. He was too late. A cane whipped downward, glancing off his temple and crashing against his collarbone. His left arm went numb. A second cane hooked over his right arm as the cane of the first man rose up to strike again. But it did not fall. It paused, quivering at the top of its arc. Its owner, his face suddenly afraid, moved his lips foolishly, first toward Corbin, then toward the man in the shoulder-length hair whose hand was clamped powerfully over his wrist.

"Now that, you see, sir," said the man who'd been watching from the bar, "is a foul." He placed his other hand over the forearm that held the cane and, with a sudden wrench, dislocated the shoulder of the man who had struck Corbin and sent him reeling, howling, across the semiconscious form of his companion. The smaller man from the bar, the actor, now stepped past the one in the Western hat and, with his thumb and forefinger, seized the nose of the one who'd hooked Corbin's arm.

"And that, sir, was another." He tweaked the nose until it bled, then underscored the point with a back-hand slap across the face.

"That will do, gentlemen." A large man, bigger and more imposing than the others and dressed in formal attire, entered the bar from what looked like a dining room. He looked at Corbin with what seemed to be a mixture of approval and rebuke.

"A fair fight, Oscar," said the long-haired man. "A thrashing well deserved."

"Be that as it may, Colonel, it cannot be permitted here. Shall we call it a day?"

The one he called Colonel turned to the bar and picked up a brandy, which he handed to Corbin, who was using his teeth to wrap a napkin around his knuckles.

"With my compliments, sir," he said. "After this settles your blood, it might be well if Nat and I watch your back until you are safely in a cab."

Jonathan Corbin loosed his fingers from their grip of Gwen's shag rug and drew the hot left hand farther back from the fire. Eyes still closed, he felt his hand brush against a soft bare calf that was almost equally warm. He stroked it tenderly and murmured with pleasure at the touch of her cheek against his and at the fragrance of her hair. One eye opened just a little. Enough to notice, to his mild surprise, that her hair seemed almost golden in the firelight. Once more he felt himself begin to swell and stiffen. He raised his body slightly to ease the pressure of her weight.

Gwen felt the movement and understood the reason for it. Easing herself off his body, she knelt at his side and turned him, unresisting, onto his back. He was nearly nude, uncovered except for the terry sleeves that now bound his lower arms loosely to his sides. He smiled as he felt her cool hands tracing over his bare chest. His body quivered at the touch of her hair, which he knew meant her lips would soon follow. Slowly, so lightly, they caressed the skin of his chest and then began their exploration of his body. Her fingers found the part that had stiffened and their touch made it leap. Corbin shuddered as her lips worked lower. His back arched in a spasm of anticipation and his wrists strained against the robe that held them. A part of him delighted in what she was about to do, yet another part could not believe that such a thing was happening. She was touching him. Kissing him. Kissing him *there*. He felt the brushing of her lips and the warm moist touch of her tongue as they moved slowly along its underside. He felt the lips part. What was she doing? He felt the hot wetness of her mouth as it closed over. "What . . . what are you doing to me?"

She raised her head and looked at him, a smile of mischief on her face. But the smile faded quickly as she saw the confusion, the discomfort, even something approaching revulsion in his eyes. She saw those eyes now darting across her features, to her mouth, to her own eyes, to her hair. Especially her hair. Something seemed to surprise him about her hair.

"Damn!" Gwen Leamas wiped the moisture from her lips and sat upright. "Damn!" she repeated more sharply. She reached for the flap of his robe and threw it roughly across his body.

Corbin tried to rise but fell back in the tangle of the bathrobe. She offered him no help. He rolled quickly onto one side and, freeing himself from the terry cloth, pushed himself into a sitting position facing her. He reached for her shoulders but she jerked away.

"Gwen, I didn't . . ." Corbin stammered, searching for words. "Gwen, I was dreaming. There was a fight, a fistfight. Then suddenly I was here with you and I—"

"Like bloody hell, you were," Gwen Leamas spat. "You were here with *her*."

"Gwen." He reached again and she slashed at his hands.

"What is it, Jonathan?" she asked. The fire danced off pools of moisture that were forming in her eyes. "Doesn't your precious Margaret go down on you? Or is she too much of a lady for anything but the fucking missionary position? To show pleasure is unseemly is what my great-grandmother used to say. Just close your eyes, dear, and think of England. Well, fuck off, Jonathan Corbin. I'll not subject you to my sluttish ways ever again. That, I promise you."

"Margaret was a whore," Corbin said quietly, his voice almost a whisper.

Gwen straightened. First confusion, then surprise, then a growing astonishment softened her features. Most of the anger and hurt drained quickly away. Because in Jonathan's eyes she saw an anguish far more profound and crushing than her own.

"Your eggs," she said, setting the tray on the floor between them. Corbin glanced at the steaming plates and mugs of coffee and then at Gwen, who had changed into an unalluring quilted robe that reached the floor. He picked up a muffin half and spread it thickly with marmalade. This he offered to Gwen as she settled facing the dying fire.

"How did you know that?" she asked, not looking at him. "About Margaret being a whore, I mean."

"It was this dream." Corbin made a helpless motion with his hands as if uncertain how to tell it. He was not even sure it was a dream.

"You were with Margaret and she was a whore?"

"No." Corbin shook his head. "I tried to tell you before. I was in a big elaborate bar. It might have been a men's club because there weren't any women, but I think the place was a hotel. There was a fight. I went there to beat up a man I know, who I think I've always known, but I just can't seem to place him. After I belted him a few times, he told me he was going to get me and my whore. He was talking about cutting up her face. I knew that he was talking about Margaret."

"The fight was over Margaret?"

"No." Corbin took a long sip of coffee. "My impression is no. She didn't enter into it until the man threatened her. I don't think I know why I hit him. But I hated the son of a bitch and could happily have blown his head off except that I wanted other people to see what a coward he was."

"Jonathan"—Gwen Leamas kept her eyes on the scrambled eggs she held—"are you in love with Margaret?"

"No." Not the way you think.

"You say that as if you're certain."

"I think the ghost is in love with her," Corbin said slowly. "The man I become when it snows, the man I was in that fight, I think he's in love with her. I know that they've had sex between them. A lot of it. But as for the kind of sex, I think what you said before was right. I think it's very basic. I also think it's all he knows. Maybe it isn't all Margaret knows, but I think he would have been shocked if she tried anything fancy with him."

"Which, it seems, is what happened." Gwen made a face. "You're telling me that I was about to give a blow job to a ghost."

Corbin winced.

"Well?"

"Not exactly."

"Then what, exactly?"

"It's true that . . ." Corbin paused, again sipping from his mug, once more searching for the words. "It's true that when I came out of the dream, I thought for an instant that you were Margaret, and I was a little shocked to see blond hair. But that was all me. It wasn't the ghost. I, Jonathan Corbin, was lying there naked with this person named Margaret and we were going to have sex. I was horrified. It's true that at first I thought it was the kind of sex that bothered me. But it wasn't. It was any kind of sex. Missionary, S and M, or hanging from a chandelier, it wouldn't have mattered. Sex between me and Margaret just seemed so terribly, awfully wrong."

Gwen leaned toward him and took his hand. "Have you any idea why?"

"None." He touched her fingers to his lips. "It's

about the way I'd feel if I woke up tomorrow morning and found myself in the buff with your sister."

"You're saying that lovemaking with Margaret is inappropriate. Even though she seems to be a prostitute."

"Yes."

"That's an interesting puzzle all by itself. And you're certain, by the way, that Margaret was not the same woman you left frozen in the snow?"

"I'm sure. They weren't anything alike."

"But you said the murdered one was young and attractive. And dark-haired."

Corbin nodded.

"What if you woke up in the buff with that one? How would you feel?"

A very good question, Corbin thought. Also an unpleasant question for some reason, though not an upsetting one. His mind wanted to fly from it. It wanted instead to replay the scene in the hotel bar where he pummeled the tall, thin man he hated so. Could the fight have been over that woman? He wasn't sure.

"Just plain disgust," he answered. "I don't like her."

"I daresay."

Corbin couldn't help but smile at the dimension of his own understatement. I don't like her. I chased her through a blizzard in the black of night and pinned her down in the driving sleet until it covered her and she was dead. I didn't like her.

"It's good," Gwen told him, "to see you getting a bit more relaxed about this."

"I guess it's a relief to be able to talk about it."

"Are you ready to talk to a professional?" She expected Corbin's hand to stiffen and pull away, but it didn't.

"You're kidding, aren't you?" he asked. But he did not seem upset by the question.

"I'm quite serious," she said evenly. "I assumed you'd want to get to the root of all this. And it strikes me that a psychiatrist might help you do so more dispassionately than you're likely to manage by yourself."

"It struck me too," he admitted. "Months ago. But can you imagine how long it would take a shrink to even get around to considering the possibility that I'm haunted? Besides, it's almost spring. If the ghost only turns up when it snows, I might spend the next eight months thinking the guy really helped me and then be right back where I started as soon as the temperature drops below freezing again."

"This ghost is in your mind, Jonathan. Surely you realize that."

"Yes, I do." Now he did let go of her hand. He pushed to his feet and wandered the several steps to Gwen's window, holding back the curtains long enough to see that the snow rushing past the streetlight had not slackened. "But it's real," he added.

"Jonathan—"

"Don't bother saying that it's only real to me. I'm dreaming things, even seeing things, that did happen. I'm seeing details I don't think I could possibly imagine unless I'd lived with them and remembered them. I know almost nothing about horse-drawn vehicles and yet right now I could name almost every kind of carriage or wagon I've seen on those streets. I can tell you how to drive a drag and I could probably show you. I could see some of those carriages in the street and be able to tell you what family owns them from a block away. The Vanderbilts, for example, always had maroon livery. The Astors' was blue. I can remember slang phrases and speech idioms I've never heard anyone use in my life. 'Throw him down, McCloskey' springs to mind."

"Who is McCloskey?"

"No one. I mean, it's a saying. It's the equivalent of

'Watch out' or 'That's all she wrote.' It's probably from a song or a popular joke of the time. I can even tell you who I heard use it. It was a big tough Irishman named John Flood who I think taught the ghost how to fight. I know other things too. I can tell you the styles of clothing people wore, I can even tell you what they drank in cold weather. And as long as you've made up your mind that I'm slipping over the edge, I'll tell you that you can also add paranoia to your diagnosis. There's a man out there who hates me and wants me dead."

"The man you thrashed in the bar?"

"As it happens, yes." Corbin's voice remained strong. "A man I, or someone, beat hell out of several lifetimes ago is still out there and he's after me. How's that for funny-farm material?"

Gwen ignored this last. "You've considered, I suppose, that you might have lived before."

"Which would make me a different kind of nuts."

"Not at all. A third of the world believes in reincarnation. Who's to say they're all wrong?"

Corbin shook his head. "This is not the same. Those people feel they've lived a lot of different lives without really knowing very much about any one of them. I don't feel like I've lived before. What's going on here is that I remember very specific events and even emotions in the life of a man who was definitely not me. But I'm seeing them through his eyes. Whatever that is, it's not like any reincarnation I've ever heard of."

"The house you bought in Connecticut. Was it his house?"

"I don't know. I don't think so. Everything about it seemed familiar except the upper floors. It's like I've been there but only as a guest. The damnedest thing about it is that I don't feel like *him* when I'm in that house. It's a very different feeling. Very happy. Like a . . ." Corbin let his voice trail off.

"Like someone else entirely?" Gwen asked. "A third person?"

"I don't know. Maybe. When I try to make sense out of that I just . . . The truth is I don't even try. I just enjoy it."

"Jonathan"—she rose to her knees—"perhaps trying to reason this out is not the way. Perhaps what you must do is go along with it and follow it where it leads."

He shook his head blankly. Gwen put down the plates she'd been gathering and stood up, stepping closer to him.

"Whatever is happening here," she told him, "is very real to you. And yet you fight against believing that it's real. At times you even feel that you are being possessed and yet it's at those very times that you are the least frightened. My suggestion, Jonathan, simple-minded though it may be, is that you make up your mind that you are not mad, that all of this is quite real, or was, and that you begin trusting and following your feelings until we are able to trace down their source."

"You believe this?" he asked. "You think it could really have happened?"

"How the hell do I know?" She threw up her hands. "But as for finding out, you're certainly not short on clues. Tomorrow, we can try to retrace this route you keep taking during the storm. We can just walk around midtown in the light of day until you see a part that strikes a chord. Or we can go over to the New York Historical Society and look at old photographs, or to the library and look at old newspapers. And if that doesn't work, we can go up to Greenwich and do the same things. And why are you grinning at me like a bloody imbecile?"

He took her to her bedroom, where they made love until the blackness outside her window had softened to a pearl gray. He made love to her, fighting sleep, until he knew that he would sleep without dreams. He made love to her in all the ways he could think of that would keep Margaret away.

Lesko had not planned to follow Dancer. Too easy to get spotted. All Dancer would have to do was turn a corner anywhere in Grand Central and wait, and he'd see Lesko, who was not easy to miss, and that would be all she wrote. What Lesko had planned to do was walk up to the Ticketron outlet in the Pan Am Building and see what Knicks tickets he could get and then maybe get a steak next door in Charley Brown's before he took the subway home to Queens. But the Ticketron window had closed down early and Charley Brown's was packed, so Lesko walked on to the newsstand past the public phones, where he could at least get a couple of Milky Ways to tide him over. He'd just passed the first phone booth when he smelled the Aramis. He kept on moving.

Could it really be Dancer? he wondered as he paid for his candy bars. What are the odds against finding two people in the same station who sponge on enough of that fruit juice to penetrate a phone booth door? Lesko eased himself down the row of telephones and peeked quickly into the last. There was the haircut. It was Dancer all right. And he was making a report.

Lesko couldn't hear the words very clearly but he heard the tone. It was respectful enough but not really deferential. As in, Don't worry, I'm handling it. This mildly surprised Lesko, who had pegged Dancer as your basic toady with whoever held the high cards. And now he was trying to end the conversation. *Sir.* Lesko heard him say *sir.* But not like he meant it. Later, sir. Something like, I'll get back to you later when I have more time. Lesko braced himself to get quickly out of sight if Dancer touched the phone booth door.

He heard Dancer break the connection, but the receiver remained in his hand, held high as if he were about to dial again. Lesko took a chance and craned his head so he could see through the glass. No coins this time. Lesko knew he'd used one before because he heard the little metallic clack of a finger checking the return slot. But this was a credit card call. Out of town. Chicago, maybe? Lesko saw a manicured finger tap a button on the top row, then on the bottom row, then back up to the top. Not Chicago. Probably the 203 area code. Connecticut. He could not make out the exchange, but Lesko would have given attractive odds that the number was in Greenwich. Lesko waited as Dancer tapped out his credit card number and settled in, somewhat nervously he felt, for a possibly long conversation.

Someone on the other end picked up. Dancer spoke about ten muffled syllables, probably his name and the person he was calling. None of the syllables sounded like Dancer. And the tone was curt. He was talking to an underling, Lesko decided, maybe a housekeeper. There was another long silence of perhaps twenty seconds, and Dancer abruptly straightened. More words, but these were different. Lesko picked out his own name twice and Corbin's three times before Dancer even took a breath. And here was the tone he was expecting. Eager but servile. Dancer, you bootlicking little shit. Lesko thought about leaving, about not pushing his luck. On the other hand, though, Dancer was now so absorbed by the sound of his master's voice that a bomb could go off or he could break a nail and it probably wouldn't have distracted him. What the hell, thought Lesko. He bit off half a Milky Way and stepped into the adjoining booth, quietly closing the door. Lesko took out his billfold and shaped it into a circle with the plastic cards inside. This he placed against the metal wall and fitted his right ear against the soft leather rim.

SIX

 P YOU GET, DUCKY." CORBIN FELT A SHOCK OF cold air across his back as Gwen stripped away the quilted comforter. She stepped to her window and threw open the bedroom drapes, flooding the room with soft filtered light. Corbin winced and covered his eyes. She was in that ugly robe again, he saw, and already freshly showered. Her wet hair lay flat and dripping against her head. Corbin faked a yawning stretch and then lunged for the comforter.

"No you don't, love." She stamped one foot over the end on the floor and snatched away his pillow. But he held fast to the quilt, clutching it tightly against his neck. Again she stripped the rest of it from his body and, leaning over him, shook her head like a wet dog. Corbin bellowed as he rolled away from the spray.

"Have more fun in b-bed," Corbin chattered the

slogan of a New York sleep shop. "Whatever happened to lazy, sexy Saturday mornings in the sack?"

"Those are for lazy, sexy people," she retorted. "We, au contraire, are energetic and coldly efficient investigators. I've made a list of what we're going to do today and left a mug of hot coffee on the washbasin next to the shower. Get cracking."

Corbin glanced toward the window and frowned. "It's still snowing, sweetheart."

"Take your shower, Jonathan," she said more gently.

"When do I see this list?" Corbin buttoned his badly wrinkled trench coat as Gwen Leamas undid the first two latches on her apartment door.

"It's in my coldly efficient head," she answered, pulling open the door and guiding him through it by the arm. Gwen followed close behind him as they descended the single flight of stairs into an old-fashioned foyer darkened by floral print wallpaper and an Oriental carpet runner on the floor. A potted palm sat near an inner door that had leaded stained glass panels. On the last step Corbin hesitated, his hand gripping the knob at the end of the mahogany banister.

"I already smell it," he whispered.

"You smell what, Jonathan?"

"The way the city smells in these . . . when I see those people."

"Jonathan"—she put a steadying hand on his shoulder—"could you be referring to horse piss, by chance?"

"I think so."

Gwen pushed him forward. "What you smell is the repulsive little boy on the third floor who occasionally urinates behind the radiator. That, and the landlord's equally disgusting cat who defecates in the potted rubber plant."

She led him through the glassed inner door and

pulled open the heavy main door, which showed evidence of delicate carving under layers of brown paint. Corbin flinched as passing flakes, sucked by the foyer's warmth, turned violently in his direction.

"It's barely snowing at all." Gwen turned him and pulled up his collar. "Most of it's being blown off trees and rooftops."

Corbin looked up. The sky, though thick and gray, had taken on a mottled appearance as the moisture content of passing clouds was reduced to random pockets. The clouds would begin to break up soon. He wished they'd slept another hour.

"Our first trial run," Gwen told him, taking his hand, "is going to be a slow and soggy walk just down to the subway station on the corner. You'll tell me what you see, if anything, and what you feel as well. If you get an impression, speak it. Don't try to reason it out first and by all means don't deny it.

"Next, we'll take a short ride on the Lex down to Fifty-first Street, where we'll start a slightly longer walk over to Saks Fifth Avenue. At Saks we'll get a bite of breakfast and then we'll buy you a pair of overshoes, a new shirt, and some socks and underthings. After you've changed in their dressing room we'll cross the street to Barnes and Noble where we'll purchase a Manhattan street map. While there, we'll browse through whatever picture books they have showing New York as it looked in the last century. Then, if you're up to it, a bracing walk over to the Burlington Building because that's where this ghostly stalk of yours seems to begin and end."

Corbin didn't know whether to feel frightened or relieved. Gwen was actually beginning to believe him. Or wanting to believe him.

"How do you expect to narrow it down?" he asked. "Nothing's the same anymore."

"Let's wait until we see a map and a few photographs." Holding his arm, Gwen started down the stone steps to the narrow packed-down path of the un-shoveled sidewalk. "You'll be fine, Jonathan," she said, not looking at him. "You'll have done so well that this afternoon I'm going to treat you to a lovely high tea at the Palm Court of the Plaza. Uncle Harry's going to meet us there."

Corbin stopped. "Um, just a second, please."

"Harry hasn't seen you since we had dinner in Chicago. He's been asking about you." Gwen offered her most blameless smile.

"When?" Corbin asked, unmoved by it.

"When what?"

"When did he ask? It wouldn't happen to have been while I was in the shower?"

"It did come up then, yes. When I called to ask if he'd have tea."

"Gwen, for Pete's sake—"

"Oh, Jonathan." She put her fingers to his lips. "What will it hurt? Harry Sturdevant comes from a very old and stinking-rich New York family. He knows this city and its history backward."

"He's also a shrink."

"Nothing of the sort. He's a doctor."

"Your uncle's field is sports medicine. His specialty is the effect of the mind on athletic performance. That makes him a shrink as far as I'm concerned. How much did you tell him?"

"Hardly a thing, Jonathan." She pulled him forward. "Now stop talking. We're halfway to the subway and you're behaving too damn normally. Conjure something."

But there was nothing. Corbin glanced around him. Just a quiet residential street on a Saturday morning. No traffic moving. In fact, no recognizable cars at all. Only an occasional mound of snow that buried clusters of garbage cans and those vehicles which had failed to find indoor parking before the storm. Blocking much of the sidewalk were a few large stone stoops he hadn't noticed before. Nothing else. A face in the window of a saloon on the far corner across Lexington Avenue. Under a sign that read O'Neill's in gilded script. Corbin ducked as several ribbons of snow blew off some overhead wires and fell toward him. When he looked up, the face and the window were gone, obscured by a sudden wind-whipped flurry.

"Watch out." Gwen tugged at his sleeve. She steered him past a thin-trunked young elm he did not appear to see and onward to the icy edge of the subway stairs.

A glorious morning, he thought happily. A bit of shopping, a brisk walk after breakfast, then perhaps by afternoon the flag would be up on the Fifth Avenue cars, indicating that the ice in the park was cleared for skating. Yes. An excellent idea. He could pick up a bird-and-bottle hamper at Delmonico's, and after a few turns around the lake they'd share it by a bonfire while the sun went down. And if we're seen together, so be it. Any arched eyebrows we encounter will be more the result of envy than of censure.

"Step carefully, dear," Corbin said as he offered his arm to Margaret.

Raymond Lesko backed away from the steaming window and placed his Styrofoam coffee cup on the glass counter. He picked up a pack of oatmeal cookies, pocketed them, and paid for them with a dollar bill. Not waiting for change, he pulled down his hat and hurried through the door toward the subway entrance on his side of Lexington Avenue.

A flash of motion caught the corner of his eye as his head dropped below street level. Lesko paused on the subway stairs, allowing the motion to register. A car door. Gray or silver. Swung partly open and then arrested. A single foot reaching out and halting there. Hesitating. As if the hand on the door knew that it had moved too soon.

Lesko continued down the steps until he was out of sight from the street. He waited, listening. A heavy car door slammed shut. He moved on toward the turnstile, a token already in his hand. He reached them as Gwen Leamas and a blinking Jonathan Corbin had just passed through and were beginning their descent to the track level. Now Lesko heard footsteps behind him, but he did not turn. He smiled as he reached for the token slot.

"Dancer, you tidy little devil," he murmured to himself. "Have you decided that this old buck needs a leash? Well, if you have, Twinkletoes, you're going to find out that leashes have two ends."

"You were with her again, weren't you?" Gwen and Corbin remained standing near the door of the almost empty car.

"No," he lied. "My mind just wandered. A slip of the tongue."

"Damn it, Jonathan! I asked you not to deny it. The last person to call me 'dear' was an aunt in her dotage."

"Okay." He dropped his eyes.

"Well, what did you see?"

Corbin's lips twitched uncertainly. "Is there a bar on the northwest corner of Seventy-seventh and Lexington?"

"A bar? No. It's a place to buy newspapers and magazines."

"Named O'Neill's?"

"No, a Greek runs it. Actually, it's a Te-Amo cigar store."

"It was a bar when I saw it. The name was in script with tiny little dots that might have been light bulbs or reflectors running through each letter. The window had a gold filigree border around it. Just inside the window there was a brass rail running at about chest height and it had red cabaret curtains hanging from it. There was a man in the window watching us."

"Do you know who?"

"Too far away. But I didn't have any sense that I should know him or even that he was a ghost. He's probably just a guy who happened to look at us because we were the only people moving on the street."

"No we weren't, Jonathan. I saw at least a half-dozen people, including the postman we passed."

Corbin's expression went blank.

"You didn't see him," she established. "Do you recall me stopping you from walking into that tree?"

"I remember you said, 'Watch out,' but I thought it was because more snow was falling off the wires." Corbin raised a hand in surrender. "I know. There weren't any wires, either."

"What about Margaret? Did she say anything?"

"No." He didn't think so. Not just then. "I was thinking about taking her ice-skating in Central Park. She might have been nervous about that for my sake. Being seen with me, I mean."

"Because you were a man of some . . . substance, and she was a known prostitute."

Corbin blanched. He wished Gwen hadn't called her that, even if he'd said it first. She was never a prostitute in the strictest sense. She was very much a lady. Good stuff in her. Educated. She could play the piano and sing. Gwen couldn't do either. And she read Henry James's novels, and Mark Twain's stories, and now she's reading Daudet's *Sappho* in the original French. She could do elaborate needlepoint faster than the eye could follow her hands, and she could make the most wonderful arrangements with flowers she dried herself. So many fine qualities. One mistake doesn't change all that. No, it was just that it was so soon, in the eyes of some, after . . . "My wife," he whispered.

"What wife? Margaret was your wife?"

"No." He made his hands into fists as if to hold on to it before it left him. "The woman in the snow. The one who just died. I think she was my wife. And before you ask, no, I didn't kill her so I could be with Margaret. One thing had nothing to do with the other."

Gwen was silent for a long moment. "My God," she said finally, a bemused smile on her face, "it really happens to you, doesn't it? This is utterly fascinating."

"I'm glad you're having a nice time."

By the time Gwen and Corbin began their crosstown walk to Saks, the snow had stopped falling entirely. The Waldorf-Astoria Hotel, the first building they saw on emerging from the subway, confused Corbin almost at once. He knew the Waldorf, he'd been in it; he and Gwen had danced in the Peacock Lounge when he first came to the city. Yet now it seemed entirely wrong. Its shape, the details of its architecture, even its location were not what they should have been. He could not explain why or describe an alternative. Gwen did not press him.

He saw nothing else that especially troubled him during the rest of their stroll toward Fifth Avenue. No phantom people or horses. No fading or materializing buildings. Only a snowbound and depopulated city digging out from more than a foot of snow. He could hear the grinding hum of plows all around him, and of dump trucks carting tons of snow to the edge of the Hudson River. He heard the hiss of air brakes on the few struggling buses and the sound of snow shovels rasping over cement sidewalks. All these sounds, modern sounds, gave Corbin comfort and a certain clarity of place. Even so, he continued to see buildings that seemed vaguely out of position, as if the city had been rearranged by some giant's hand. On these and others, Corbin, who knew almost nothing about architectural design, sensed sadly that certain stylistic adornments had been stripped away. Heavy rooftop cornices, balustrades, finials that ought to have been there, were gone, leaving an ungraceful boxy appearance to what remained. The more modern buildings, most of them, were an abomination to Corbin. Too much glass. No sense of substance. Even the streetlights, which Corbin had never particularly noticed before, now seemed a graceless triumph of function over form. Ahead of him, however, he saw the tapering spires of Saint Patrick's Cathedral and he felt, as he explained it to Gwen, something like an urge to applaud.

"Do you know why?" she asked. "Is it because Saint Patrick's hasn't changed?"

"Maybe. I don't think so."

"Try, Jonathan," she urged him. "Try to think why you'd want to clap for a church. Is it an especially religious feeling?"

"No," he said distantly. "I just like the spires. I like the way they did the spires."

"Would you like to go inside?"

Corbin looked at her. Certainly not, was what he almost said. "Here's Saks. Let's get some breakfast." He had no idea why the question annoyed him. But the spires, newly freed from their scaffolding at last, were indeed quite handsome. Roman church or no.

Gwen Leamas munched an English muffin, which, she pointed out, was neither English nor a muffin, while Corbin fortified himself with two orders of corned beef hash and eggs. He'd asked first for finnan haddie and then for kippered herring, neither of which was on the menu. Gwen tried to recall whether she'd seen him order either dish in the entire time she'd known him.

Returning to the street floor, Gwen used her credit

card at the Totes counter to buy Corbin a pair of high latex pullovers for his damp shoes, plus a pocket rain hat with a houndstooth design, and an inexpensive folding umbrella. Next, Corbin moved to the haberdashery displays where, at Gwen's insistence, he chose two new shirts, both handsomely striped, and a change of socks and underwear.

"I can pay for these," he told her. "Why don't I just write them a check?"

"Because I like dressing you. And them who buys 'em, picks 'em. You're still too young and dashing for some of the dreadfully stuffy clothing you wear."

When he went to change, she selected three colorful pocket handkerchiefs that would add a bit of spark to his boring business suits. What about an ascot, she wondered. No, he'd never wear it. In this country ascots seem to be the exclusive property of aging Hollywood types who want to hide their wattles. Her eye fell on a tubular umbrella stand, which held not umbrellas but a selection of canes and walking sticks. With no particular purpose in mind, she ran her fingers through the assortment, searching for one that was black. With a silver knob. Nothing there. Only trendy stuff such as knobbed shillelaghs made of blackthorn and assorted oak shafts with handles made of brass duck heads. Too bad. Not that he'd start carrying one even if she found it, but Jonathan did say he always seemed to be walking with a black silver-headed cane during those excursions of his. "Aha!" she said aloud. Gwen quickly returned the small folding umbrella and selected a black, tightly furled English model. No silver knob. No knob at all. Just a curved handle. But it did look like a black walking stick. Who knows? It just might possibly help speed things along.

In Barnes & Noble's, across Fifth Avenue and down a block from Saks, Gwen found a pocket-sized book of

Manhattan neighborhood maps and a small spiral-bound notebook. In the latter she began jotting notes of Corbin's random impressions while Corbin, having checked his shopping bag but still holding the thin black umbrella, wandered ahead to a section marked History. He'd noticed Gwen's switch to an umbrella more closely resembling a walking stick and at once understood the workings of her mind. He said nothing, only smiled and shook his head.

The historical section dealing with early New York contained a dozen or more books dealing with the nineteenth century alone. Most were generously illustrated. A few consisted entirely of captioned photographs and engravings. Corbin reached for one of these. The earliest photographs, dating back to a decade or so before the Civil War, had a particularly haunting quality. They were portraits of buildings, mostly, or of wider cityscapes. Their subjects tended to be immobile objects, because the plates that were used required time exposures of many seconds. The result was eerie, because even though architectural details and advertising signs were in surprisingly sharp focus, all indications of human life were blurred and ghostly. Corbin caught his breath. On a daguerreotype of a photographer's office building, probably used as a sample of his wares, he noticed a spectral horse and carriage waiting at the curb. It was precisely like the many, the hundreds, he himself had seen, except that his did not long remain blurred. His became clear and solid and they moved and made sounds. Shod hooves clacked lazily against cobblestones and iron-rimmed wheels crunched along behind them. Drivers, all of whom seemed slightly hunchbacked, made clicking sounds with their mouths to urge their horses on in spite of a monotonous cadence that seldom varied. Sometimes the drivers would wave or tip their hats to familiar faces on the sidewalk.

Corbin blinked rapidly and flipped a few decades forward.

The photographs sprang suddenly to life. Now there were people. Great crowds of them in sharp focus. Details of clothing, expressions on faces as men, women, and children on city sidewalks were frozen at a precise moment of their lives. The effect on Corbin was stunning. They were real. A derbied group of idlers stared curiously at him. A child being tugged along by a woman in a ribboned hat pointed a finger at him. Corbin snapped the book shut before they could begin moving.

"Let's get that one," he heard Gwen Leamas say behind him. "Actually, we should buy all of these that are mostly photographs."

She selected a large paperback volume entitled *Old New York in Early Photographs* and another called *New York in the Nineteenth Century*. A third was the thick *Columbia Historical Portrait of New York*. A fourth book, entitled *New York Then and Now,* caught her eye. This last was a collection of old New York street scenes with, on each facing page, a more recent photograph taken from the same vantage point.

"Jonathan, look." Gwen opened it to several pages that depicted the avenue outside, Fifth Avenue, as it had been a century before. "This really was quite a charming city once. A lot like Mayfair. Except in London we don't tear down handsome old buildings every time a megalomaniac developer feels the need to name a building after himself."

Corbin was paying less than full attention. Something, not the book she held, was making him uncomfortable. He glanced around the bookstore.

"For example," she went on, "we'd never have torn down Claridges or the Savoy just to put up an unlovely phallus like the Empire State Building." She held up two facing pages for him to see, the one on the right being the Empire State. "Imagine destroying this magnificent hotel just to give suicides a longer drop."

"Let me see that." Corbin stepped closer, his fingers involuntarily reaching to touch the print on the left-hand page. There, opposite a recent photograph of the tall Art Deco building, was an infinitely more elegant structure, which once stood on that site. It could not have been more than eighteen stories high, parts of it curiously shorter, but it gave an impression of enormous mass. Its main entrance, on the Thirty-fourth Street side, was marked by a row of tall columns. Though he could not see past them in the photograph, Corbin knew that they concealed a carriage drive that burrowed well into the building at street level. He knew at once, without reading the caption, why the Waldorf-Astoria had seemed so strange to him two hours earlier. This was the way it should have looked. This was the real one. And he'd been there. He knew that if he walked through the carriage drive toward the formal entrance, a clean-shaven doorman dressed in blue would admit him to a colonnaded hall called Peacock Alley, and farther along he would find a four-sided men's bar, which as far as he knew was the only one like it in the world. And in the dining room, with its carved pilasters and Italian Renaissance exquisitry, there would be—Oscar. The same Oscar who'd delayed in stopping the brawl in that other hotel bar long enough to see the thin man beaten senseless. Oscar. He'd be older now. He'd be . . .

Corbin shuddered. An old anger flooded back, mixing with his friend Oscar in his emotions. Anger and something else. A curious nervousness, a sense of danger that stopped well short of being fear, was now nipping at the edges of Corbin's mind. He glanced around him once more. There was no one in the sparse group of browsers who would account for the feeling. Only one elderly man who had been staring in their direction before and now was doing it again, or pretending not to.

Corbin touched Gwen's arm. "Do you know that man over there?" He gestured with a flick of his eyes toward a gaunt man of about seventy whose attention was fixed on a display of paperback gothic romances. The man wore an expensive-looking chesterfield and a black hat of a kind that was seldom seen north of Wall Street. His collar was turned up against cheeks that had a shine to them, as if the skin had been tightly stretched to cover his skull.

"The man wearing the homburg?" Gwen shook her head. "Why do you ask?"

"He keeps looking over here."

Elsewhere in the store, Raymond Lesko had settled near a dump display of hurt books under a sign that read None Over $2.99. He seldom looked at Jonathan Corbin. There was no need. Lesko had already memorized the shelf location of the books Corbin and the woman were choosing and would make a note of their titles as soon as the two of them headed for the cashier's desk. The man in the black hat was another matter. It took a conscious effort to pretend he wasn't there and to avoid letting him know that he'd been made. As a tail, Lesko had long decided, the old guy was pitiful. He wore clothing that was totally unsuited to surveillance, to subways, and even to Saturday mornings. Lesko had been studying him, a glance at a time, ever since the old man had followed them onto the Seventy-seventh Street platform for what must have been the first subway ride of his life.

Lesko remembered him staring in bafflement at the turnstile and then at the change booth before he put the two of them together. And then on the train he couldn't bring himself to sit on the soiled plastic seats, so he stood, being jerked around like he was on roller skates until he finally seized a door handle at the far end of the car. The first thing that was clear, of course, was that this old man who seemed so much out of his element did not work for Dancer. Dancer almost certainly worked for him. And whatever was going on here was important enough to the guy pulling the strings that he had to see it for himself. Which phone call was he? Lesko wondered, recalling Dancer's two telephoned reports, which were clearly to two different levels of authority. Whichever, this one was unwilling or unable to wait for Dancer to develop the roll of film Lesko had shot. He kept straining for a clear look at Corbin's full face and yet he'd duck behind a group of standing teenagers every time Corbin raised his head. Lesko, standing at the middle door where he could watch both ends through their reflections in the glass, thought he saw a certain wildness in the old man's eyes. It was a look that went well beyond fright. Lesko remembered a drug dealer named Hamsho who shot a cop during a raid and went out a back window. Lesko was back there in the shadows. He could see on Hamsho's face that he thought he had it made until he walked right into Lesko and saw his teeth smiling over the sights of the magnum that blew off first his balls and then his head. The old man had the same kind of look. Like a guy who'd thought he had it made, but now knew he was dead.

From the Fifty-first Street stop, the man in the homburg followed closely behind Corbin and Gwen Leamas on their walk across town toward Saks. Always too closely. Always stopping to gaze ridiculously at the sky every time Corbin paused. He was paying scant attention to Lesko now. Back at Seventy-seventh Street, he'd seemed visibly irritated that Lesko was on the scene, which meant for sure that he was Dancer's boss, because Dancer, now that Lesko thought of it, had been under instructions to get him out of the way by sending him on that stupid burglary errand to Connecticut. But the old man pressed on, secure in the assumption that since Lesko could not know who he was, he was invisible to Lesko.

Inside the department store, the old man, still too close, kept shifting his position, trying for the most unobstructed view of Corbin. Everything Corbin did, however artless, seemed designed to frustrate his efforts. Corbin was wearing that dumb tweed rain hat, which further concealed his features from any direction but dead-on front. Lesko watched as, again and again, the old man shook his bony fists in a sort of petulant frustration.

His face seemed vaguely familiar. Lesko couldn't place it. A politician, maybe. Or a big-shot businessman. On the other hand, maybe it's just that he was a type. He looked like all those old men who sit in the backs of limousines behind dark windows and live in big houses that have walls around them. Insular. That was the word. The kind of guy who carries the walls around with him. More than that, he had the look of a man who almost never did anything for himself and whose actions were never questioned to his face. Old money. Power. And probably a contempt for anyone who had less money and no power. It was a combination, Lesko knew from experience, that often produced a particularly stupid kind of arrogance. People like that, he thought, can spend their whole adult lives without anyone but family having balls enough to tell them when they're being a jerk.

The old man suddenly jumped. Corbin was moving. He'd turned with Gwen and was heading in the old man's direction on his way to the cashier. The old man quivered and blinked. He looked, Lesko thought, like he'd just been slapped. Corbin seemed to notice, too, but he kept on walking. Past him. Corbin did not see the old man stagger forward, snatching at the book rack for support and knocking several paperbacks to the floor. The man in the homburg held on there, his breath coming in swallows and his eyes staring wide, as if the image of Jonathan Corbin's face was still fixed on them. He was still holding on as Corbin paid for his purchases and, with a single backward glance, stepped toward the Fifth Avenue exit.

For a long moment Lesko held back, wanting time to study the stricken old man. The fear he'd seen had deepened into shock. Lesko saw recognition in his eyes. No doubt of it. Whatever Jonathan Corbin was to him, whatever compulsion forced this old man from behind the safety of his walls, whatever need he felt to see that face up close and in person, he did know Jonathan Corbin. He saw a face that, at least to Lesko, was a nice face. Friendly. Not like his own. Maybe no Robert Redford, but a good face, crooked nose and all. Yet to one man it was a face like that of the worst devil you'd see in a bad acid trip. Is that what you see, old man? A devil face? Or am I on the wrong track? Maybe an avenging angel. And if you do see an avenging angel in Jonathan Corbin, could it possibly have to do with all those dead Corbins who kept popping up in Chicago forty years ago? Of course it could. But whatever the connection is, we won't find it by standing around Barnes & Noble's all afternoon, will we?

Passing the shaken old man in a wide circle, Lesko paused at the display of historical books where Corbin and Gwen Leamas had made their selections. He made shorthand notes of their probable titles based on the spaces that were left, chose the one of them that would most easily fold into his pocket, and walked to the desk bearing the Cash Only sign. Come on, old man, he muttered inwardly. Get it in gear. Corbin would have no more than a half-block head start as long as he and the woman stayed on foot. If the old man would get moving, Lesko could keep them all in sight. Not that it mattered much now. Catch Corbin or lose him, it was all the same, because Lesko knew where he lived and would find him again tomorrow. Today, he would stick with Corbin only as long as the old man plodded along in the same direction. Lesko would go on letting him think he was invisible as long as that belief gave him peace. But before this day was finished, Lesko intended to know the location of the walls that protected this old man from the ghosts of Corbins past. He would know the name of the man who was willing to pay fifteen thousand dollars to be sure that this latest Corbin joined them. He would be a large step closer to knowing why. And he would be a giant step closer to knowing how many more thousands the corpse of Jonathan Corbin might be worth.

As Lesko had hoped, and although not wholly by choice, Corbin and Gwen Leamas were still on foot. Even by midafternoon there were few cabs to be seen on Fifth Avenue. Plows had cleared the major midtown arteries, but many of the crosstown streets remained blocked to vehicular traffic.

Corbin didn't mind walking. The sun had broken through and the city never looked so clean as it did under a bright sky that follows a snowfall, its grime and sorrows hidden, its hard edges softened.

"It's really quite glorious, isn't it." Gwen entwined her free arm into Corbin's. In her other hand she insisted on carrying the single heavy shopping bag that held their accumulated purchases. This would leave Corbin's right hand free to swing his walking stick–umbrella.

"Quite," he agreed.

She was watching him, he realized, for any sign of renewed discomfort or disorientation as they crunched northward toward Rockefeller Center. But there was nothing. If anything, he felt refreshed. Whether it was Gwen's company, the bright sky, the high atmospheric pressure that cleared it, or the memory of similar walks in Chicago, Corbin felt the way a man should while taking a healthy walk with a woman who loved him. The umbrella flicked forward.

Except for one thing, perhaps. That man in the store who kept sneaking glances in their direction. Not that it was unusual for men, even men that age, to stare at Gwen when he was with her. But Corbin didn't think admiration was what he saw under the brim of that homburg. He wasn't sure what it was. The crazy thing was that Corbin had felt an absurd impulse to walk over and knock that old man flat on his ass. There it was. The old man had presented no threat, no real offense of any kind, nor did he evoke any association in Corbin's mind that might explain the curious sense of loathing he felt. Corbin simply didn't like the son of a bitch. He tightened his grip on his walking stick.

Gwen tugged at his arm and steered him into a left turn at Fifty-second Street. Corbin shook the old man from his mind and, resisting an urge to look behind him, returned to enjoying the look of the city.

"Well?" she asked. "What do you feel?"

They'd stood for several minutes on the raised plaza of the Burlington Building between two frozen fountains that were shaped like dandelions.

"Not a thing." He shrugged. "Everything's really pretty." Some of the buildings, especially the older ones up toward the park, had begun to look like birthday cakes dripping with frosting. The tops of street lamps were like the necks of swans.

"What about the elevated railway?"

"Beg pardon?"

"The Sixth Avenue Elevated." She had a picture book open in her hands. "It did exist and it was right here. You said you saw it taking shape yesterday when we were running for the subway. And the terminus you passed under while you were chasing your . . . that woman began just up there at Fifty-eighth Street."

Corbin's lips moved involuntarily. Forming a word. A name. Damn! More names, each blurring the other, and a sudden whirlwind of memories and emotions whipped through his mind.

"Say it out loud, Jonathan. Did you feel something?"

"I think I almost had her name. I'm not sure."

"What did it sound like? Your impressions, Jonathan. Trust your impressions."

"A short name. A vowel sound. Like Anna. Emma. Something like that."

"Ava? Ula?"

"It's gone, sweetheart."

"You clenched your fists just then. Does she make you angry even thinking about her?"

Corbin squinted, trying to recall and sort out all the tiny glimpses that had buzzed past him. There was the woman, certainly. And thoughts of the man in the bar came back and they were entwined together like lovers. That notion seemed right to Corbin. That they were lovers. He must have been an avenging husband when he beat the man as he did, but that realization didn't seem to evoke any particular rage. There was something else, much greater in scope, behind his fury that evening and, if he trusted his impressions as Gwen suggested, he'd find himself believing that it had something to do with the Sixth Avenue Elevated Railroad. Not just the part that ran past here but the whole thing, and that was a trail he couldn't begin to know how to follow. Corbin shook his head.

"Let it alone then," Gwen suggested. "Perhaps it will float back when you're not trying." She closed the book of photographs and slid it into the shopping bag at her feet. Then she fished out her book of maps and her notebook and scribbled a few more items. "Now," she said finally, "this is where it could get exciting. You said that in these snowstorm visions you were following the woman in the direction of Fifth Avenue. You also said that you passed under the darkened terminus. At that point, therefore, you were clearly headed in an easterly direction across—Did you see any open sky above you? Or just tracks and terminal?"

"No tracks. The whole structure ended there."

"Then you were eastbound on Fifty-eighth Street crossing Sixth Avenue. But you also recalled crossing an earlier thoroughfare. The one on which you found her hat. And then when you crossed that street you stumbled on the body of a man named George."

"Seventh Avenue."

"What else do we know?" She held up the map for him to see. "Working further backward, you said you had turned left onto the sidewalk where you found a hat—a toque, you called it—with a Lord and Taylor label. An impressive bit of detail, by the way. You were sure she'd gone in that direction because you seemed to know that she was trying to reach a particular address. In any case, you knew that she could not have gone in the opposite direction because even you were having difficulty walking into this tremendous gale that was funneling up Seventh Avenue from the south. With the wind behind you, you followed her one block north before turning east. This means that when your dream began, you had to have been standing on the northwest corner of Fifty-seventh Street and Seventh Avenue."

Corbin glanced at the intersection on the grid where Gwen Leamas was pointing and then looked away. He saw the corner in his mind. And he felt the wind from that night chilling him, draining away all the warmth that had been building within him since he woke up that morning with Gwen at his side.

"What good is this?" he asked quietly.

"Come on, Jonathan." She took his arm. "Let's go find out."

Corbin, in the six months since he'd come to New York, could not recall ever passing the intersection of Fifty-seventh Street and Seventh Avenue. He had not avoided it. It was simply that it stood on the fringe of the midtown area and offered nothing in itself that would have attracted him in that direction. The shops and department stores he used, the expense-account restaurants, the other offices he might visit, and even Grand Central, were all in the core of midtown Manhattan. On Fifty-seventh Street itself, Sixth Avenue was a dividing line between two quite different worlds. East of Sixth Avenue, toward Fifth, was a crosstown boulevard that reminded some visitors of Paris' Rue de la Paix. It preened with some of the most exclusive shopping in the world. There were furriers offering Russian sable coats at six-figure prices, designer-original dress shops, a cluster of art galleries, and dealers in antiques and exotic home furnishings where the cost of the average purchase would feed a Third World village for a year. But in the other direction, toward Seventh Avenue, one saw a contrast that seemed almost deliberate. There, no shops were selling costly indulgences or investments in social standing, no oriflammes of financial achievement. Instead there was a sort of haute monde hippiedom. Most of the shops catered to serious practitioners of the arts. Music and dance in particular. There were stores selling instruments and sheet music, second-floor ballet studios, and lean, lithe, and ascetic women who wore their unpampered hair in tight buns. That street marked the bohemian end of a cultural axis that continued up past Carnegie Hall and curved toward its apogee at Lincoln Center in the West Sixties.

As Corbin walked with Gwen Leamas up the slight incline of Fifty-seventh Street toward Seventh Avenue, a series of odd notions began to pick at him. The first was a certain self-consciousness, as if he were in a place where he conspicuously did not belong. The feeling made no sense to him. He might have understood it if he'd been walking through Harlem, but there was hardly the same ethnic exclusivity to the sidewalk of West Fifty-seventh Street. And although no passerby looked at him with either curiosity or suspicion, the sensation of being an outsider persisted. Even that was not quite right. There were people who *thought* he did not belong there. That was it. But who those people might be, he had no idea. It seemed as if they were behind him. East of Sixth Avenue. The ones with the money.

"You're beginning to feel something, aren't you?" Gwen had been watching his brow.

"Nothing I can grab hold of," he answered. But Gwen thought she saw a certain defiance in his manner. He'd stiffened a bit and was walking with greater purpose. The umbrella-cane snapped forward.

"Do you," he asked finally, "feel any sense of being out of place here? Might anybody put you down, for example, if they knew you chose to spend time in this part of the city?"

"Of course not." She shook her head. "The fact is I do spend a fair amount of time here. I've been to Carnegie Hall three or four times, the last for a Bach festival. And I've been to the Russian Tea Room for both lunch and dinner."

"What's that?"

"A restaurant next to Carnegie Hall." She pointed up the street. "It caters to the music crowd mostly. At lunch the place maintains a sort of bohemian chic to keep the turtleneck-and-sneaker set feeling at home, but they get concertgoers in the evening. A lot of black tie."

"Like Tony Pastor's?"

"I don't know Tony Pastor's."

"Or the bar of the Hoffman House. Except that's for men only."

"You're joking."

Corbin glanced at her blankly.

"Where," Gwen asked, "would you find a public bar in this city that excludes women?"

"Well, it's . . ." Corbin stammered, his expression suddenly clouded. He was staring into the distance ahead of them. "It's not a question of exclusion. More a matter of . . ."

"Of what, Jonathan?" She tried to follow his eyes.

"Propriety." His voice was barely audible.

The corner was a quarter block ahead of them. Seventh Avenue. *That* corner. Gwen Leamas tried to make herself light and quiet so as not to disturb whatever was entrancing Jonathan Corbin.

"Tell me about the Hoffman House," she said softly.

"A hotel. Like many another."

"About the Hoffman House bar, then. It caters to gentlemen like yourself?"

"Not all those seen there are gentlemen. It is a favorite of the Tammany crowd, and of actors and professional athletes. Some good men, at least, among those. And of course every rustic who visits New York feels bound to go there and gape at the painting. No, they are not all gentlemen, dearest. There is more than one patron who might be better for having his ears . . ."

"Go on, Jonathan. His what?"

Corbin stopped. He halted in midstride, swaying, and for a moment Gwen thought he would fall. He bent and picked up a handful of snow, which he pressed hard against his face, sucking in cold air through gloved fingers. Concerned but excited, Gwen pressed him.

"Might be better for having his what, Jonathan? Don't lose your thought."

". . . his ears boxed. God damn!"

"The man you thrashed. He was in the Hoffman House bar?"

Corbin nodded, his eyes wide.

"His name, Jonathan. Quick, before you lose it."

"One of Gould's people. Corning. Carney. Something like that."

"Then who is Gould?"

"I don't know. Jay Gould, I guess. One of the old robber barons."

"You guess, you say. A moment ago you would have known." But Gwen knew she had herself to blame. She'd called him Jonathan. There he was, walking with Margaret again back in that other time and chatting away with all sorts of new clues and she, like a dolt, had to call him two or three times by a name that was almost certain to pull him back out of it. Well, she thought, I won't make that mistake again. What do we suppose Margaret called him? I assume they didn't call each other dearest all day long. How about my darling? Did they say that then? Of course. As in "Oh, my darling, Clementine." "In any event," she told him, "we've made progress. This ghost of yours beat up a man whose name sounds like Corning, who possibly worked for the financier Jay Gould, in the men's bar of a hotel called the Hoffman House."

"It's not a men's bar. Just a bar. Women didn't go there."

"Whatever." She took his hand in hers. "Now here's the important part. You saw something while we were walking that made him come out inside you. You were staring up ahead toward the corner where we think your dream starts. Was that it? Was that corner what brought him out?"

Corbin raised his head and focused on the north-

west corner, diagonally across Seventh Avenue from
Carnegie Hall. It did nothing to him. The sidewalk
there was covered for two hundred feet in either direction by a sheltered walkway of the type that protects
pedestrians at construction sites. A Chock Full O' Nuts
restaurant on the corner was barely visible under the
walkway, and a dozen or so smallish shops on either
side. On the Fifty-seventh Street side, he saw a green
awning that marked the entrance of the building that
housed the restaurant and shops. Only a portion of the
awning and its brass posts was visible under the walkway scaffolding. There was writing on it. A street address number. There were also words but they were
almost totally obscured. The letters *The Os* were all he
saw.

"Um, darling?" Gwen tugged at his sleeve.

He did not respond. His eyes, squinting, lifted and
refocused upon the massive brown structure that rose
up from the scaffolding. Corbin felt his stomach
tighten.

"Darling, what is happening?"

He'd seen the building, noticed it, as they walked
up the gentle slope of Fifty-seventh Street toward Carnegie Hall. It would have been impossible not to see it.
Even then it was familiar. So familiar, he now realized,
that it had sent no particular signal to his brain. Like
the office building he entered many times each week
without really seeing.

"I'm okay," he told her, his gaze dropping once
again to that green awning.

"Is it that big brownstone? You know it, don't
you?"

Brownstone. Yes, he nodded. One doesn't usually
think of brownstones as being that big but that's what
it was. The building was eleven stories high, a fact Corbin knew without counting, but like the old Waldorf-
Astoria it seemed half again as large. Each two-paneled

window, already oversized, had a third pane above it, a transom made of stained glass. Each stained-glass design was different. The ceilings inside must have been ten, even twelve feet high. On the outside, great ledges, bays, and cornices of stone all contributed to the feeling of immensity. Near the roof line he could see a dull mottled effect on the surface of the outer walls. The stone up there was decomposing under many decades of attack by weather and pollution. Veneerlike slivers had randomly separated and fallen away, requiring the construction of the protective walkway below.

"Jonathan!" Gwen Leamas turned his face toward her own. "*Do* you know that building?"

"I don't. I think he does."

Now Gwen squinted. "The name on the awning starts with the letters *Os*. Tell me the rest of it."

"The Osborne Apartments."

"You've seen the building before?"

"I guess."

"Damnation, Jonathan. Have you or haven't you?"

"I don't think so. I've never been over here."

"Then how could you know it says 'The Osborne'?"

"Maybe it doesn't."

"You're being exasperating, Jonathan. Let's go look."

Corbin shook his head. "Gwen, I'm not going inside that building."

"We'll get just near enough," she promised, "to read the script on the awning. And perhaps take the teeniest peek through the front door."

Corbin turned away, his jaw set.

Gwen decided not to press it. The relative calm that had sustained him through the day thus far was beginning to wear thin. Twice that she knew of, this ghost of Jonathan's had been in and out and Jonathan seemed well able to deal with it. But this building seemed much closer to home than any of the other stimuli. Very possibly it *was* home. A single glance into the lobby might bring on a flood of clear memories that would go a long way toward solving the mystery. But it might also, as Jonathan said he feared, fully bring out this strange other person while forever imprisoning Jonathan.

"Let's cross." She nudged him toward the curb. "You can wait outside that Chock Full O' Nuts while I get a closer look."

Corbin tensed but allowed himself to be led over a snow mound left by the city's plows. He was not eager to be parked by Gwen on that corner, *the* corner, of all places, and he wondered whether her choice was deliberate. But a stubbornness that was entirely Jonathan Corbin kept him from yielding fully to the sense of dread he felt.

Once there, she studied him closely, releasing him and turning away only when he reassured her with a shake of his head. Corbin did, in fact, feel surprisingly at ease and, realizing that, allowed himself to ponder why. His back was to the large brown building. That could be part of it. Or all of it. Around him, absolutely nothing was familiar. Looking back across at Carnegie Hall, a building that had to be at least as old as the Osborne Apartments, was like seeing it for the first time. It *was* the first time, of course, for Jonathan Corbin, certainly from this perspective. But if the man inside him had stood upon this corner, if this spot had made an impression so profound that it endured for perhaps a hundred years, Corbin would have expected it to trigger at least an emotion or two. But there was nothing. Only a sense of strangeness.

Looking south, in the direction from which the wind had come that dark night, he saw only office buildings of stone and glass, most with assorted retail stores at their street levels. The roadway itself, Seventh Avenue, was much wider than the dark street strewn with fallen wires that he saw in the corners of his mind. Impossibly wider. They could hardly have moved all the buildings back. It could not be the same street.

Toward the east, looking down Fifty-seventh Street toward Sixth Avenue, he again saw nothing at all that jogged his memory. He could envision the Sixth Avenue Elevated and the little signal tower that came before the terminus, but he knew he was creating these from past apparitions. As he stood there, his imagination began to fill in other details as they might have been during his grandfather's time. There would have been trees along the sidewalks. And fashionable town houses of ornate stone. There would have been a church. Down there on the left. It would have a single bell tower and it would be in a parklike setting complete with a churchyard. He could almost see Gwen and himself strolling past it on a quiet Sunday morning. Past it? Why not toward it? Into it. Corbin brushed the detail aside. Perhaps they were headed toward another church farther on. One of the Fifth Avenue churches.

Corbin turned his head and rubbed his eyes, taking a deep breath to help clear away the minor vision that had taken shape. That *was* Gwen he was with, he told himself. Long dress or no, it was Gwen. Not a hallucination. It's getting, he thought, to the point where I can't even daydream without wondering where the dreams are coming from. Knock it off, Corbin. He looked to the north. But if he had not, and if he'd strolled partway down Fifty-seventh Street, he would have come upon the remains of the church that he thought his imagination had provided. He would have seen the magnificent façade of the Calvary Baptist Church, carefully torn down some fifty years before and reinstalled as the face and motif of the Salisbury Hotel. He would have recognized it nonetheless. And as for the ghost's religious preference, if Corbin had chosen to establish it, he had now ruled out the Baptist denomination and also the Catholic faith. Admiring the exterior of Saint Patrick's was not the same as suffering to set foot inside. Corbin would have wondered at this obvious prejudice against the Roman church, particularly having attended Notre Dame, but would have recalled upon reflection that prejudices in nineteenth-century America ran deep against the Irish as well. The feelings of Corbin's ghost, who seemed obviously of an upper class, would have been ambivalent at best. And his church, the one Corbin and Gwen were peacefully ambling toward, might have been the Fifth Avenue Collegiate, which stood almost catty-corner from Saint Patrick's Cathedral. Or it might have been the very fashionable Fifth Avenue Presbyterian which, he would find, still stands or the Saint Thomas Episcopal Church, which also remains although not in its original form thanks to one of the many great fires that regularly gave impetus to the redesign of New York City.

These thoughts, however, were far from Corbin's mind as he looked northward along Seventh Avenue toward Central Park. He could not resist dropping his eyes to the spot on the sidewalk where he remembered seeing the woman's hat on that dark night. Emma's, Anna's, Ina's hat. Whatever her name, there was no imagining that hat. Not unless his imagination was so highly developed or his subconscious so teeming with unsuspected information that he could correctly name a style, the toque, and its source, Lord & Taylor's Broadway store when Lord & Taylor doesn't even have a Broadway store that anyone living remembers. But as for the spot where he'd picked up that frozen mass of cloth and feathers, not even the snow and ice looked the same. A block up and across the street he saw the corner where, according to Gwen's map, he had stumbled upon the frozen corpse of the man named George. There was another very old building there too. Talk about ornate stone, Corbin thought, from where he stood it seemed as if every square inch of it was covered with the most intricate gingerbread carvings he'd ever seen on any structure. An utterly unforgettable building once you've seen it. And he had not seen it. Not before today.

"Are you ready?" Corbin turned at the sound of Gwen's voice. She approached him, stuffing her notebook into the shopping bag and pulling out one of the books they'd purchased. She leafed through its index as they walked slowly toward Fifty-eighth Street. "Did anything happen while you were standing on the corner," she asked.

"Nothing. Nothing at all." He decided not to mention that they'd gone to church together.

"I mean in your head. At the very least, your mind must have wandered back to that night in your dream."

"Well, sure," he admitted, "but there's not a thing in this neighborhood that rings any kind of a bell."

"The Osborne certainly did."

"How could I know the Osborne and not know Carnegie Hall right across the same intersection? Or this building over here?" He pointed to the delicately carved edifice, almost the size of the Osborne, whose name he could now read over the main entrance. The building was the Alwyn Court.

"The Alwyn Court," Gwen noted, flipping forward from the index. "The Alwyn Court, designed by . . . so-and-so. Started 1907 and finished 1909. There's a lot of business here about how they made clay blocks from terra cotta molds and then plastered repetitions of the same designs all over the surface of that building. Rather looks like lace, doesn't it? It also looks as if they've sandblasted the soot off it recently. It must look just as it looked in 1909."

"I've never seen it. I'm sure."

"As for Carnegie Hall, it says here that that building was completed in 1891. There. It fits."

"What fits?"

"The Osborne was first occupied in 1885 according to the superintendent inside. He says it's the oldest building in this area except for a few small commercial lofts. If your ghost knew the Osborne during the period from 1885 to 1891, and he hadn't seen it again until today, nothing else in the vicinity would have been familiar to him. Even Seventh Avenue is much wider now."

"Wait a minute." Corbin stopped. "How do you make a street wider?"

"By slicing off some sidewalk, naturally."

Corbin glanced around doubtfully. "They don't strike me as being narrowed. They look about as wide as they ought to be."

"Many of these buildings," Gwen explained, "had stone steps or even little walled gardens extending onto the sidewalks. When the thoroughfares had to be widened, the city required that all the stoops and such had to be removed. The same thing was done in parts of London around the turn of the century."

Corbin frowned. The explanation made sense and yet it annoyed him. Images flashed through his mind of handsome façades by the thousands being defaced by crowbars and sledges. The images slowed and he began to pick out individual houses, residences, that seemed to have special meaning to him. Even a few names associated with these town houses flitted past but flew on before he could seize them. One name stayed. Tammany. The Tammany Hall Irish. Who no doubt threw themselves into the vandalizing of these homes with indecent glee. *Think of it as a kindness, yer Lordship. Y' walk about with yer nose so high in the air, yer like to trip over the dom thing anyways.*

"Let's keep moving," Corbin said.

They did not wait for the light at Fifty-eighth Street before crossing Seventh Avenue. Corbin's toes had become numb inside his unlined shoes and the dropping afternoon sun was providing less warmth than before. The comfort of the Plaza Hotel, still two long blocks distant, was becoming a welcome prospect even though it meant an hour or two of uncomfortable scrutiny by Gwen's uncle Harry. Nor did Corbin pause on the Alwyn Court's corner where the man named George had died under drifts much softer than the mounds piled there now. But a few feet from the corner, Corbin sucked in a breath.

"What is it, Jonathan?"

"Nothing."

Nothing and everything. No building, no single man-made item that caught his eye was familiar. And yet he knew this street. It was narrow, much narrower than any other side street they'd seen that day. And it was deep in shadow, almost dark. Like the street in his dream it sloped downward, several degrees more sharply, he thought, than the incline of Fifty-seventh Street.

"It *is* the same street, isn't it?" she asked.

Corbin nodded. Ahead of him he could almost see her. It was here that she turned, afraid and angry, and saw him advancing upon her. It was here that she put her hand to her mouth, the mouth he must have slapped because it had a smear of blood on it, and then cried out vainly for help at a window sealed against the storm. She turned and ran from him. Tiny steps. Her hands held wide for balance. Corbin's umbrella flicked out and he followed.

Gwen Leamas matched his steps. "You see her, don't you?"

"Sort of," he whispered.

"Are you all right?"

"Yes."

"You're remembering?"

"Yes."

She held on to him in silence.

Remembering. Yes. Impressions began to flood at him so quickly and so ill relatedly that he could scarcely seize upon a single one. There was a child. An infant. An infant he despised almost as much as the woman who ran from him. Whose child? His own? No. Not his. It was once but not now. Not ever again. The child was behind him someplace. In a crib made of woven reeds. In that building.

"She was my—" He stopped himself.

"Say it, Jonathan."

"His wife. I'm sure of it now. There was a baby, too. A son."

"What else?" she urged quietly.

"I think you might have been right about the Osborne. I think that's where they lived. The baby's asleep there in a little room with no windows. Like a dressing room. He's all alone. There was a nurse and a maid, but neither one showed up because of the storm."

"Jonathan." Gwen took a breath. "Do you feel at all that you might have been that child?"

"No," he snapped.

"Easy, Jonathan." She put a hand on his arm. "It's a possible connection, that's all."

"I'm not the child. There's no connection between me and that infant." There was still an edge to his voice.

"But the woman is your wife."

"His wife. Yes."

"So she had the child by someone else."

Put yer back into it, lad. Jab with the left, then again, then dig hard into the ribs.

Corbin raised both hands to his face and stared down and across the narrow street in the general direction of a nondescript hotel. "It's where she was going," he said quietly. "He lived down there. In another apartment house. The Flats."

"The Flats?"

"It's what the place was called. The Something Flats. Spanish Flats, I think, but there were other names, too. It's him. The same man."

"Which him? The man you beat up in the Hoffman House?"

"Yes." Corning? Carney? Car . . .

"You beat him because your wife bore his child?"

"Yes." Carling.

"And it's also why you let her die."

"Carling. Ansel Carling. That was his name."

Gwen bit her lip. Her hands trembled with excitement. "She was running to him? Away from you?"

"Twice the man I am. Twice and more, she said. But I took his measure, by God. And the whole of New York knows it now."

"Jonath—"

"She said that his child will be twice the man as well. But we'll give the lie to that boast, you and I. It's blood that counts above all the rest. Proper blood. And a proper home. You shall have a home, Margaret. You shall have a grand new life and the son you give me will grow up brave and strong."

"Yes, my darling." Gwen tried to keep her voice from breaking. "Our son will be all of that. Not like that other child."

"You can teach him the piano"—Corbin's voice became tender, affectionate—"and to converse in French. You can teach him grace and good manners and I will teach him to be manly."

Gwen's mind raced. "You can teach him the manly arts. Fisticuffs. Boxing." One of those had to be right.

"Yes," he answered. "Just as John Flood taught me. And I will show him how to play baseball. I'll teach him to cycle and swim and to drive a gig. If he wishes it, he'll go to Harvard. And one day, as I've promised, I will give him my name."

Your name. Say your name, she begged in her mind. But another question came first to her lips.

"We are not to be married then?"

He looked away. "Perhaps. One day that will be possible."

Gwen felt hurt, and more than a little irked for Margaret's sake. Did he love her or was he hiring a brood mare? "I should like that," she told him.

"No more than I," he answered sadly. "But while my father is alive, and while my business binds me to this city, we must wait. Although you deny it now, I know that the ostracism we would suffer would bring you more pain than I can bring you joy."

Well, thought Gwen, at least he didn't spell it out that she'd been irretrievably sullied and could not possibly be considered as a wife. Still, she'd like to have felt that if Margaret was good enough to carry his child, as she was now obviously doing, she ought to be more important to him than the acceptance of his blue-nosed social set. Better change the subject.

"This home I am to have. Where will it be, my darling?"

Corbin looked at her oddly. "I have told you many times."

"Yes, but I am only a woman and so many things fly from my mind."

Another odd look. It was what Gwen's grandmother might have said but she was a twit. Margaret would not have been the fluttery type.

"I'm teasing you, my darling. It's just that I so love hearing you speak of it." From the top, Gwen thought, although she knew perfectly well where this house must be.

Corbin smiled patiently, warmly. "The house is one of my prettiest properties outside New York. It was built by Tweed himself for use as a guest house, so be assured that nothing was spared. I've had a telephone installed, a new model, that will carry my voice a great distance as clearly as you hear it now. And I've spoken to Mr. Johnson about wiring for electric lights and he promised it will be done before summer is past. Have I told you about Mr. Johnson's blind horse?"

"Oh, yes." The house, Jonathan.

"The house is also steam heated, the first like it in the town, and you shall have all the hot water you need at the turn of a valve. You need never carry wood nor buckets of water for your bath. You need never again go out of doors on a cold winter morning because a bathroom with all the necessities has been built within the house. I'm assured there will be no odor or peril to your health due to some plumbing contraption that flushes away the sewer gases and keeps them from returning."

"That does sound charming," she said dryly.

"In the carriage house, there's both a surrey and a sleigh and I have my eye on a dun gelding only three years old . . ." His smile dimmed a degree or two and he touched her cheek. "You will be happy there, Margaret."

"I know."

"You will have a gentle future and you will have no past except the one we choose for you. No one need ever know. You will be a proper young widow, a very lovely young widow, and I will be first your protector and then your gentleman caller."

A new past? Gwen thought. That means a new name. "Say my new name, Jonathan." Oh, shit!

Corbin's eyes glazed and batted rapidly. He backed away from her, his eyes now darting around him with the look of a man who suddenly realizes he is lost.

"Jonathan." Gwen dropped her shopping bag and seized his lapels. "Jonathan, what's her new name? What's your name?"

"She didn't say 'children.' "

"What?" Oh, yes. The word the woman said as he pressed her into the snow. "Jonathan, say his name before you lose it."

"She said 'Tilden.' His name is Tilden."

SEVEN

AYMOND LESKO HAD CROSSED TO THE NORTH SIDE
of the narrow street. While Corbin and the
Leamas woman were involved in a particularly intense discussion on the south side,
he slid past them and went on down toward the corner
at Sixth Avenue, where he blended into a small group
awaiting taxis outside the Barbizon-Plaza Hotel. Lesko
waited there, massaging the back of his neck. It was
developing a crick from trying to watch both Corbin
and the dazed old man who still plodded along behind
them.

The look of fear and shock he'd seen on the old
man's face had, if anything, deepened since he'd left
Barnes & Noble's. Haunted was how he looked, Lesko
thought. Like a guy walking through a spook house,
trying hard to believe there were no such things as
ghosts, but afraid that any moment one would pop up
and stop his heart. Lesko would have felt sorry for him

if he hadn't instinctively disliked him. The black
homburg had been tilted off center someplace along the
way, probably one of the times he stopped to wipe the
sweat off his face. Funny about a black homburg. Wear
it straight and everybody with a flunky mentality either
sucks up to you or steps out of your way. Wear it
crooked and you look like a drunk.

Back at Seventh Avenue and Fifty-seventh Street,
Lesko had stood in a foot of snow behind a padlocked
newsstand, watching the reactions of both Corbin and
the old man as they stood on different corners, each
having been obviously and deeply affected by the sight
of the old Osborne apartment building. With Corbin,
Lesko thought, it was kind of a confusion. And a reluctance to get too close. With the black homburg, it was
more like one big moan. Lesko thought he would have
sagged to his knees if he hadn't had a corner of Carnegie Hall to hold on to. It was the Osborne that was
doing it. Lesko was fairly sure of that, thanks to the
English dame. He might not have made the connection
if she hadn't parked Corbin out on Seventh Avenue,
done a lot of gesturing toward the building, and then
run into the lobby to check out—whatever. He could
probably find out later from whoever works there. In
the meantime, he realized, she continues to be the only
one of the three of them with her head on straight.

She also, he decided, now watching as they re-
sumed their slow progress down Fifty-eighth Street,
seems to be the one who's running this show. Whatever
the hell is going on, and so far no one really seems to
know, she's the only one besides me who's working at
putting the pieces together. Uh-oh! Hold the phone.
Now all of a sudden it's Corbin who's standing straight
and it's the dame who suddenly looks shook up. It
looks like—Wait a minute. Steady, Lesko.

Raymond Lesko had been struck by a thought, an
intuition, that the pragmatist in him tried at once to

reject. What he felt was the odd notion that Jonathan Corbin was suddenly somebody else. He was standing straighter. Stiffer. Almost military. Except there wasn't any stiffness in his face or in the tone he must have been using. He looks happy, Lesko realized. And about ten years younger. Although there was nothing remotely threatening or fearful in Corbin's manner, Lesko felt an unaccountable chill and a sudden impulse to call it a day and retire to the bar of the Barbizon-Plaza. Whatever is in the air around here, he thought, it must be catching, because for absolutely no reason, he was afraid of Jonathan Corbin. Corbin *had* changed. And now he was changing again. Aging again. Lesko watched as Corbin seemed to soften and shrink into the man he was before, but more intense this time, less confused. His eyes were darting up and down, at everything and nothing, his lips moving in short, staccato bursts of sound, which Lesko couldn't hear.

"Tilden?" Gwen Leamas tugged at his arm.

Corbin shook his head, his expression telling her that Tilden was gone and that he could not call him back at will.

"Jonathan, try." She reached for his cheek and tried to turn his face toward her own. "The rest of his name. Try."

"The el station was here," he said. They had almost reached Sixth Avenue. Corbin gestured with his head. "She wanted to run for the stairs over there. But they were covered with snow and there was no one to help her there anyway." Corbin fell silent for a long moment. "There was something obscene about her looking for help in a New York elevated station. She didn't just hurt me, I mean Tilden, you know. She and Carling hurt another very good man who was connected with these elevateds. I would tell her things and she would tell Carling and people would be ruined. It was why Carling was interested in her in the first place. Information. Ammunition. If she'd reached him that night, I think he probably would have turned her away."

"Who was the good man she hurt?"

"I don't know. He built things. A lot of things."

"Like this elevated line." Gwen realized she was pointing to it as if it were there.

"Maybe. That doesn't sound wrong."

"Could you have been involved with the city's train system too?"

"Maybe."

"But you're not sure."

"It's all going away, Gwen. I knew so much a couple of minutes ago but it's all breaking up, like when you wake from a dream."

"Let's follow the woman this one last block, Jonathan. Perhaps more will come back."

"Bastard," he spat, suddenly turning his head toward the street they'd just come down.

"What is it?" Now Gwen turned. She saw nothing. Only one superintendent shoveling a sidewalk and a woman stopping to pry a piece of rock salt from the paw of a Pekingese she was walking and, off to her right, a few departing guests huddling in the doorway of the Barbizon. "Jonathan, who's back there?"

He rubbed his eyes. "No one, I guess."

"Then why did you say that?"

"I don't know." His body seemed to sag again. And now it was Gwen Leamas who felt a sudden chill.

"Let's get you indoors, Jonathan. Let's get down to the Plaza."

"There was somebody back there, Gwen."

"I know," she told him.

Lesko, sure that he'd not been seen but troubled by Corbin's apparent awareness that he was being followed, now held back until he could fall in behind the black homburg. The old man reappeared, Lesko wasn't sure from where, but from the snow on the front of his coat Lesko realized he must have thrown himself behind some trash cans when Corbin turned. The old man staggered on, his eyes hollow and fixed straight ahead. He paid no attention to Lesko, if he remembered that the ex-cop was there at all. Lesko waited until he passed and fell in behind him, but on the opposite side of the rapidly darkening street.

Farther along, he saw Gwen Leamas tug at Corbin's arm, pointing, he thought, toward the side entrance to the Plaza Hotel. But Corbin shook his head and walked on, past a small movie theater that showed arty foreign films and on almost to Fifth Avenue. At the display windows on the Fifty-eighth Street side of Bergdorf Goodman, Corbin stopped. Lesko watched as he touched the windows and the walls, as if to be sure that they were solid and real. The woman took his arm, more firmly this time. She guided him into the street and through traffic he did not appear to notice. He was gesturing as he walked, waving his umbrella first back toward Bergdorf's, then ahead toward the open expanse of Grand Army Plaza in the manner of a man recounting some event that had happened there. Lesko saw them stop, almost beyond his line of sight, and saw Corbin point the umbrella at a place on the sidewalk where there was nothing at all. He seemed to be pinning something, or stabbing something with its tip. The Leamas woman tugged again, and they were gone from view.

Lesko held back, waiting for the old man to follow. But the old man hesitated. He would lean in the direction Corbin had taken and then jerk himself back. It was the first time Lesko could recall seeing any human being actually wringing his hands in indecision. What's the problem? Lesko wondered. Had the old guy

reached his limit or was it something else? Was it the
Plaza Hotel? Betcha! Corbin and the dame must be going into the Plaza and he doesn't know whether to follow because a guy like him would be recognized in a
place like that, wouldn't he. Someone might spot him
and wonder why he looked all unwound and scared
shitless. Someone might say his name out loud within
earshot of the Corbin guy. That's it, right? Well, make
up your mind, old man. I'd just as soon see a little more
of what Corbin's doing around here, but that's up to
you. Where you go, I go.

Lesko watched with satisfaction as the man in
black straightened, brushed the snow from his coat,
tucked in his scarf, and at last centered the black
homburg. Lesko knew he'd decided.

"Way to go, Pop," he muttered. Lesko followed as
he rounded the corner and mounted the broad front
steps of the Plaza Hotel.

Harry Sturdevant, who was not actually Gwen's uncle
but who had known her since the day of her christening, had arrived twenty minutes early. The Palm Court
of the Plaza Hotel, he realized, was not an entirely ideal
place for a confidential chat with a man who might be
nearing an emotional collapse. But at least by arriving
early he could minimize interruptions by other patrons
who might know him and wish to say hello. He'd already shaken hands with several of the hotel staff, the
chairman of the Coca-Cola Company, a senior partner
at Smith Barney, and a man who'd been brakeman on
the Canadian bobsled team at Lake Placid.

Uncle Harry was a large man with intelligent blue
eyes and a generous mouth that had been molded
through use into a look of perpetual good humor. He
stood three inches over six feet and carried fifty pounds
more than his playing weight at Harvard, where he'd
lettered in eight sports two generations earlier. What

his personal physician chose to call excess lard, Sturdevant preferred to think of as appropriate substance. In any case he carried it well, with due recognition to a superb but maddeningly slow tailor he'd found during the war years on Sackville Street in London.

Sturdevant rose at Gwen's approach through a maze of tables and offered his arms for a hug whose warmth caused several nearby ladies to stop in mid-sip. Corbin waited, in a stiffness that was part politeness and part discomfort, until her uncle disengaged, then offered his hand.

"Always good to see you, Jonathan." Sturdevant gestured to two empty chairs. "You're both probably half frozen. Sit down and let's get something hot into you. Or have a drink unless you insist on being traditional." He was careful to avoid looking too deeply or clinically into Corbin's eyes, but then, Sturdevant knew that he had always done just that each of the four or five times he'd met Jonathan. There had always been something about him. Something he couldn't place.

"Coffee would be fine, thanks." Corbin, distinctly nervous, would also have preferred a Scotch. But he feared that his hold on the present was tenuous at best and he was not about to risk slipping backward again in full view of the Plaza's high tea crowd. As it was, he was troubled by the notion that he should not be sitting there except in black tie.

"Coffee for me, too." Gwen squeezed Corbin's hand reassuringly. "And some scones if they have them."

"They do indeed." Harry Sturdevant nodded to the waiter who'd been standing near enough to hear, also touching the rim of his own half-empty glass.

"Now"—he leaned closer to Corbin—"would some small talk help you to relax or would you like to get right into the business at hand?"

"I don't know how much small talk I have in me. Could I ask how much you know?"

"As in, Do I suspect you're off your rocker?"

"I suppose."

"Uncle Harry . . ."

Sturdevant put his hand on Gwen's but kept his eyes on Corbin. "I've known you, although not well, for more than two years now, Jonathan. Gwen has boasted about you to me many more times than that. She is quite a sensible young lady. I both love and respect her. I am confident that she is not one who would long remain attracted to an unstable young man. I myself have seen or heard nothing remotely troubling about you before this morning."

"I haven't been all that stable lately."

"Which brings up a point Gwen made on the telephone. Whatever difficulties you're having now, is it correct that they did not exist prior to your arrival in New York?"

"Pretty much."

"Pretty much or entirely?"

"There were some things that troubled me before coming here. They never seemed all that significant before."

"But they do now."

"Yes, I think so." Corbin leaned slowly back in his chair. His arms crept up and folded across his chest. His attention turned to a violinist at the inner end of the Palm Court.

Sturdevant raised one eyebrow at Gwen Leamas, who responded with a small uncertain shrug.

"Your body language," Sturdevant told Corbin, "suggests a considerable reluctance to say what is on your mind. I find myself wanting to ask if you'd rather have Gwen tell me, but I gather that this will be news to her as well."

Corbin's eyes were still on the musician, who was on his third chorus of "If Ever I Would Leave You."

"I once asked the violinist," he began slowly, "I think it was here, if he'd play something from Gilbert and Sullivan. From *Iolanthe,* to be exact. The violinist went and huddled with the maître d'hôtel. The maître d' came over and told me very politely that Gilbert and Sullivan was quite unsuitable in this ambience. Operetta music, as opposed to real music, was also quite unsuitable for the fine Amati violin the musician owned. However, if I had a favorite by Strauss, or Brahms, or Vivaldi or Corelli, he'd be more than pleased to oblige. I remember the conversation very clearly. I was annoyed. I thought he was an ass."

"Go on." Sturdevant was watching him intently.

"The conversation never happened. I'm not a particular fan of Gilbert and Sullivan. I don't think I've ever seen or heard *Iolanthe.* I don't know who Corelli is or what he wrote."

"But you remember the event vividly."

"That's just one example."

"Is it ever," Gwen added. "All afternoon he's been—" Sturdevant held up a hand.

"Were you never curious enough to look up Corelli or listen to *Iolanthe* to see if either evoked a special meaning for you?"

"You don't understand." Corbin leaned forward again. "I just remembered it. Just now, when I looked past those potted plants and saw the violinist. I see things, ordinary things, and some memory I could not have had comes flooding back."

"How long has this been going on, Jonathan?"

"Almost as long as I can remember."

"Often?"

"Just occasionally. They'd come in spurts maybe once or twice a year. But now it's happening often. Very often."

"You said it's troubled you in the past. Did you seek help?"

"In college, yes."

"What was your specific complaint at that time?"

"I had a feeling I was someone else. Not all the time. Sometimes."

"To whom did you go for this counseling?"

"A psychology professor at Notre Dame."

"What did he suggest, if anything?"

"He thought I might be having some trouble adjusting to college and filling my father's shoes. My father was a considerable campus hero during the early forties. They sort of enshrined him after he was killed in the war. The professor also thought I might be having some identity problems because my mother married again and her new husband got me to take his name for a while."

"If you'll forgive me," Sturdevant observed, "that seems like rather a simplistic set of answers coming from a trained psychologist."

"It wasn't his fault. I didn't give him much of a shot. You see, he asked me if I thought these memories and feelings I'd have were real. I said no. I lied."

"May I ask why?"

"I can read a psychology textbook too, Dr. Sturdevant. Believing it would make me psychotic. Not believing it just made me confused. Confused looks better on my record."

"Jonathan"—the older man idly stirred the ice cubes in his drink—"I appreciate your candor. But that was hardly what you'd call facing up to a problem."

"With due respect, you still don't get it. The memories were real. I know that now more than ever. Who was going to help me with a problem like that? As I've already asked Gwen, how many years and thousands of dollars, how many blind alleys would I have to go down, before someone even began to believe me?"

"If I were to call a friend of mine—"

"Absolutely not," Corbin interrupted. "This is as far as it goes."

"Then why are you even telling me?"

"Because Gwen asked me to try to track this thing down, with her, and she thought you might be able to help us find out whether the things I seem to remember could actually have happened. May I ask, by the way, how much she's told you?"

"That some very vivid ancestral memories seem to have surfaced in you, that you're understandably frightened by them, that they've contributed to some bizarre behavior on your part, and that a nineteenth-century strumpet named Margaret seems to have been her rival for your affections right along."

"I did not say that." Gwen reddened.

"Which part?" Sturdevant asked. "The last?"

"The personal part." She glanced at Corbin. "I don't want Jonathan to think I told you anything personal." Certainly not that they were screwing on her living room rug and Jonathan thought she was Margaret.

"It's okay." Corbin touched her hand.

"It's not okay. Some things are private and should remain so." She looked at her uncle as if for confirmation of the reasonableness of her position.

"Are you looking for me to agree with you?" Sturdevant asked her.

"I expect you to, yes. I do have a personal life and my affections have nothing to do with the problem at hand."

"I'm afraid they do, sweetheart. Margaret is why we broke up last year. I just didn't understand it then. I do now and I don't mind talking about it."

"Well I do mind, damn it. Not in front of family."

Sturdevant reached a hand to her shoulder to keep her from rising in her chair. "Jonathan," he asked, "is there a telephone call you'd like to make? Or perhaps you want to freshen up."

"Shit!" Lesko muttered. Corbin was on his feet and moving in the direction of the lobby washrooms. Black Homburg, the jerk, had picked a spot in between to watch from. Asshole! Bad enough you stand there looking like you're going to slide down the wall any minute. But when you're watching someone in a restaurant you don't watch from where he has to step over you when he feels like going to the john. It's a rule.

Lesko, standing near the fountain exit, rolled his eyes as Black Homburg raised a bony hand to the side of his face and tried to make himself small behind a pillar. Lesko held his breath as Corbin approached and then, incredibly, passed him by. The ex-cop let out a sigh. Thank God for protecting drunks and fools. Or for whatever is so heavy on the Corbin guy's mind that he hardly knows where he is. Which reminds me . . .

He sidled over to the stand of a bell captain who had smiled and waved at the big man with Corbin when he spotted him at the table.

"Excuse me."

"Sir?"

"You know how it is when you see a face and you can't place it?"

"Yes, sir."

"There's a big guy there, white hair. I think I seen him in the papers. You waved at him before."

"You're a cop, right?"

Lesko sighed again. "What is it? I give off a scent?" But he only pretended to be surprised. Cops and priests. No matter how they dress, no matter where they are, somebody always knows.

The bell captain shrugged. "After I ruled out ballet dancer and brain surgeon I kind of settled on cop. Is there a beef here?"

"Nothin' much. Anyway, it's not him. I just wondered." Lesko looked away and took a step backward to show that his interest had passed.

"Maybe you seen him in the papers," the bell captain offered. "He's into a lot of sports stuff. The Olympics. That's Dr. Sturdevant."

"Oh yeah." Lesko actually did remember. "Henry, Harry, something like that, right?"

"Harry." The bell captain looked toward Sturdevant's table and chuckled. "He was in here with Howard Cosell a couple weeks ago. People kept going over to the table to say hello and it was always to Dr. Sturdevant. You could see Cosell getting all pissed off."

"Yeah." Lesko smiled. "Speaking of sports, what did the Knicks do this afternoon?"

"Five-point favorites over the Celtics, they go down by twenty-two. You want to make a bust, go put the cuffs on Larry Bird. Shoot him, you get a medal."

"God damn it." Lesko's face turned mean.

"What's the matter? You bet the rent money?"

"God damn it." Lesko stepped farther toward the Palm Court. Black Homburg was gone.

Harry Sturdevant spread some orange preserves over a scone and handed it to Gwen Leamas. "Now," he said, "why are you behaving this way?"

"I told you. Some things are personal."

"A man whom you obviously hold in high regard comes here at your request to risk being thought a raving lunatic by a comparative stranger, and you tell me the conversation's getting too personal where you're concerned?"

"Women do take it personally, Uncle Harry, when they ask a man to marry them, are turned down, and then that rejection becomes a matter for public discussion. God knows we've discussed it enough privately."

"And you thought he was going to wash the same linen in front of me."

"He was."

"The devil he was. The man's apparently had a fixation all his life that he did not understand. It has influenced his life far more than he knows. It doubtless would have affected his choice of a marriage partner or even whether to marry at all. When you pressed him on the subject, he probably stalled as long as he could to avoid backing off entirely. Whatever reasons he might have given you had nothing to do with the real ones."

"Some of the reasons hurt," Gwen said quietly.

"He's already acknowledged they were stupid. Would you like me to tell you what some of them were?"

"Not really. No."

"That's fine, because they were irrelevant and, what's more, you knew it. You probably suggested counseling. He declined for the same reasons he won't see a psychiatrist now, which have considerable merit by the way."

Gwen was listening to his words, but her mind was replaying a montage of all the times they'd been together, especially in bed, making love, when she was sure that Jonathan was somewhere else.

"Margaret's been there all along, hasn't she?" she asked.

"Probably on and off, but yes."

"Why couldn't he have told me?"

"According to you, she never even had a name before yesterday. What could he have said that you'd have understood?"

"Going on three years now"—Gwen chewed her lip—"he's been . . . he's been with me but he's been making love to Margaret. How am I supposed to live with that?"

"You're not, because it's nonsense."

"It's not nonsense. It happened last night."

"And it was only last night, you tell me, that he

began to know anything about her. Most normal people have fantasy sex partners from time to time, yourself, Gwen dear, probably included. But this is nothing like that. Margaret has been around since Jonathan was a boy. To the boy, she was probably an idealized mother or older sister. To the man, she became a dream lover. But don't assume he revels in private sexual romps with this creature. Jonathan hates these intrusions, I promise you. They trouble him very deeply. I expect he's especially troubled by his ambivalence toward her."

Gwen nodded distantly. "He said that. He said he wanted to make love to her but that it seemed terribly wrong."

"Idealized mother to idealized lover. That's conflict enough for—" He stopped when Gwen put her hand on his.

"How do we . . . How does he get rid of her?" she asked.

"You were right the first time."

"Can we?"

"Finding out who she was should help."

"You say that as if you believe she was real."

"Don't you?"

"After today I do. Especially after today."

Corbin, having washed and rewashed his hands, and having thoroughly browsed all the shop windows lining the south wall of the Plaza lobby, paced self-consciously along the plant-lined border of the Palm Court, unsure whether to return to the table or to await a signaled invitation.

He knew that they were talking about Margaret. Twice now, no mistake, he'd seen the name form on Gwen's lips. He could also see that she was listening much more than she was talking, which meant she'd already told her uncle almost everything this morning

on the phone. Corbin didn't mind. He minded that
Gwen seemed to have been crying a minute ago, but as
for Harry Sturdevant's knowing, well, at least he
doesn't look like he's telling her to get away from this
nut case as fast as her long English legs will carry her.

Sturdevant's eyebrows arched steadily higher as he
scanned the four pages of scribbled notes Gwen had
placed in front of him.

"All this happened today?" he asked.

"Most of it in the past two hours."

"And all triggered by the sight of the Osborne
Apartments. You say that on two occasions Jonathan
was fully taken over by this other personality."

"More than twice," Gwen told him. "It happened
for a minute or so just after we left my building." She
pointed to the place in her notes.

"I see. Trees, overhead wires, and a saloon called
O'Neill's, none of which exist."

"Then there was that business about the Waldorf-
Astoria, and downing this huge breakfast after trying to
order some dishes that I'm not even sure he likes."

"Finnan haddie and kippered herring," Sturdevant
noted.

"Then all those names that kept popping into his
head."

Sturdevant traced a finger over all the underscored
proper names. "Tony Pastor's, Tammany Hall, a pugi-
list named John Flood, Ansel Carling, Jay Gould, the
Hoffman House—"

"Which is where he had that brawl."

"A woman, his wife, with a name that sounds like
Emma, a man named Johnson who electrifies houses,
the Spanish Flats, for heaven's sake, another frozen
corpse named George, an illegitimate child, two of
them, and a man named Tilden? Jonathan thinks his
ghost's name is Tilden?"

"You look like that rings a bell."

"Almost all of it does, but *Tilden*." Sturdevant chewed on the name, a faraway look passing over his eyes. He shook it off. "It'll come to me."

Gwen reached to turn a page. "We've also narrowed down the time when all this must have happened. It had to be between—"

Sturdevant held up a hand.

"Gwen, dear," he asked slowly, "do you think there could be any chance at all that Jonathan researched all this? That it's all an elaborate piece of acting?"

"What could he possibly have to gain?"

"I don't know. For some reason the thought of a very considerable gain passed through my mind. Although I can't think why he'd bother to try to fool me. And I can't imagine that he could fool you."

"Jonathan couldn't fool anybody," Gwen answered. "There's no artifice to him at all. Playing bridge with him as your partner is maddening because his face gives away his hand all the time. I've also never known him to tell a deliberate lie."

"And yet . . ."

"What?"

"Doesn't it strike you as odd that so much has happened, so much has been revealed to him, and to you, in less than a single day's time? The answer to that question might be all the various stimuli to which you exposed him. But considering that you've told me what an emotional wreck he's been these past months and especially yesterday afternoon, don't you find it striking that he's taking all these revelations and even possessions with such equanimity?"

"He's doped to the gills."

"I beg your pardon."

"I put two of those magic trancs you gave me into his coffee this morning."

"Correction." Sturdevant frowned. "If you're refer-ring to the propranolol capsules, I did not *give* them to you. I *prescribed* them for you with full knowledge of your medical history. Further, propranolol is not a tranquilizer. It is a medication used in treating cardiac conditions which has also been found useful in relieving the discomforts of stage fright without affecting perfor-mance. I prescribed them for you to help you overcome your nervousness during that series of presentations in London last fall, not to dispense willy-nilly to your friends."

"If you don't stop scowling, I'm going to climb onto your lap."

"Listen, you nasty child—"

"Oh, Uncle Harry"—Gwen reached for his hand—"they did help him. If only you'd seen the difference between Jonathan yesterday and Jonathan today. I don't think he'd have lasted half an hour without them. And look at all we've learned."

"At considerable risk to his health."

"I did dilute them in the coffee," she offered inno-cently.

"That, Gwen dear, is the single least intelligent thing I've ever heard you say. How many capsules do you have left?"

"You gave me six. I only used one myself, two for Jonathan; that leaves three."

"I would like all three returned in the morning."

"I love you, Uncle Harry."

"Yes, but did you hear me?"

"Three capsules in the morning. Scout's honor."

"Then I love you too, but perhaps not as much as that young man fidgeting over there behind the pastry cart."

"I'll call him back."

"No, dear. Go get him. While you're gone I'll look over these notes of yours."

· · ·

Raymond Lesko cursed himself as he bulled his way back toward the exit leading to Fifty-eighth Street. Sixty seconds, he thought bitterly. Sixty seconds he'd let his attention get sloppy and the old guy was gone.

It was almost dark outside. Black Homburg, he knew, would be much tougher to spot and even harder to tail. As he reached the sidewalk, Lesko had about made up his mind to forget about looking for him and get as quickly as he could up to that silver car, probably a Mercedes, the old man left up on Lexington Avenue that morning. Worse came to worst, at least he'd have the license number. Then, in a couple of hours, one way or another, Lesko would know who he was.

But the ex-cop spotted his man almost immediately. He was less than a hundred yards away, hunched over, and moving in the direction of Bergdorf's and Fifth Avenue. Thank God for the homburg, Lesko thought, whose outline showed clearly in the twilight glow of the street lamps. Staggering or not, the old man was moving fast, for him anyway. Lesko had a sense that retrieving the Mercedes was not the biggest thing on his mind. The guy ignored a couple of taxis he could have grabbed and anyway, from the tilt of his shoulders, Lesko had an idea he was heading south. The old man made his way across Fifth Avenue and continued down Fifty-eighth Street to Madison where, sure enough, he turned south for several more blocks. Approaching Fifty-third Street, he crossed Madison Avenue without even looking up, like a man on automatic pilot or guided by a homing instinct. There was another hotel on the far corner. The Beckwith Regency. Lesko saw the old man's pace quicken further as he neared the gleaming green enamel and brass of its front entrance. The doorman snapped to attention on seeing him approach and threw a salute, which the old man did not acknowledge. Lesko, ignored by the same doorman, followed him through the revolving doors.

It struck Lesko at once that the entire lobby staff also seemed to be at attention, each person following the old man's progress with smiles at the ready in case they should happen to catch his eye. Whoever the hell he was, thought Lesko, there won't be any shortage of people to ask. The man in the black homburg pressed on, still not looking up, and did not stop until a pair of elevator doors were closed behind him by an erect and smartly uniformed operator.

Lesko relaxed. Not a bad day's work, he decided. What did he know so far? He knew that the Corbin guy was hung up on something that had to have happened long before he was born. Probably even before the black homburg was born, judging by the books Corbin bought. Whatever it was, Lesko knew where it happened, or at least where Corbin and the English dame thought it happened. Both Corbin and the old guy were almost equally spooked by the Osborne and by a whole two-block stretch of Fifty-eighth Street. The money Dancer was paying him, including the fifteen-grand killing money, started out almost for sure in that old man's pocket, although given those two calls Dancer made, the old man wasn't the only horse in this race. And speaking of new entries, now we have the Olympics guy, Sturdevant, who has a few bucks of his own and probably a lot of clout and who was very likely recognized by Black Homburg. Finally, any time he wanted to, Lesko knew he could ask the name of the scared skinny old man with the fat checkbook who walked through here like he owned the place. A good day.

Also a hungry day. He hadn't eaten, he realized, since munching a package of oatmeal cookies from that Te-Amo cigar store this morning. You'd think thirty years as a detective would teach you to carry a peanut butter sandwich on a surveillance. And maybe a pair of dry socks. And maybe a goddamned tube of Ben-Gay. This is not a body that's built for long hikes. Lesko picked out a lobby chair where he could rest a while and make some notes, and leaf through *New York Then and Now*, the picture book he'd picked up at Barnes & Noble's, for what it was worth, and then reward himself with a nice expensive dinner on the fag, Dancer. He sat back, unwrapped his first cigar of the day, a mild but reeking panatela, and soon felt the tightness draining from his shoulder muscles as he gazed contemplatively into a haze of exhaled smoke.

As the small cloud thinned and dissipated, he idly noticed a row of gilt-framed portraits on the far wall across the lobby. Founder pictures, he knew. Board-room pictures. There were collections just like this one in half the city's banks, corporate headquarters, and any other old-line businesses that had a real person's name on the door. They always looked the same. The portrait on the left, the first in the series, would usually be a guy with a beard, white hair, and a stiff collar. And a glare. They always glared. It was like they knew they were going to get hung up in the next president's office or in the boardroom and they wanted that look to be a permanent no to any stupid decision. Next in line would be the guy's son, who would be pushing sixty before the guy who started the place finally keeled over and made room. This second guy would look a little smug, as in, Now that we got rid of that old fart at last we're going to do some modernizing and growing around here.

The third picture usually wouldn't even be a relative. Either the second guy always fucked everything up or else his kids turned out to be drunks or jerks who'd be out on the street if their old man didn't send them money to stay the hell away. The third-picture guy— they were always all guys—would have a Depression-era look about him. Like Herbert Hoover. A high collar and clean shaven. That guy would try to look kind and a little sad so you'd know he was really sorry about having to fire half the employees and put the rest on half salary. He would have told them how he cut his own salary, too, and you couldn't convince him that taking home half of a hundred grand a year and a whole bunch of perks was not the same as taking home half of thirty bucks a week to feed four kids.

Then would come the picture of the first one to wear a modern suit. The portrait would have a light background and brighter colors like they started using in the early forties. He'd be the first one who got painted smiling, partly because it was the war and everyone was working, and because that was when all the big executives tried to get photographed with their sleeves rolled up and their ads kept explaining how buying their products would help kill lots of Japs. But at least he was smiling. Not like the one over there. Exceptions prove the rule. The last guy over on the wall looks like he had a sharp stick up his ass—Lesko lurched to his feet.

It was him. The old guy. Maybe twenty-five years younger but it was him. Lesko moved closer, his eye on the small brass plate on the lower crosspiece of the frame.

Tilden Beckwith II, it read. Chairman of the Board, Beckwith Enterprises. Lesko whistled softly. Big bucks. Very big bucks. This hotel was only a piece of what the guy must have had. A weaselly-looking sucker. Sneaky eyes. The kind people have when they've just bullshitted you and they're looking to see if you're buying it. The kind of eyes that say, I wonder if these people know I think they're garbage. Exactly the kind of guy who would hire a little turd like Dancer. Lesko flipped open his notebook and moved one portrait to his left.

The next picture, he knew at a glance, was Tilden's father. The same gaunt bone structure. The same air of arrogance. But not sneaky or stupid arrogance like Lesko had seen on the man in black. This one looked like a snake. And there was something odd about the likeness. Lesko didn't know what it was, exactly, but something was not quite right. He looked at the nameplate. Huntington B Beckwith. Hummph! Another initial with a missing period. Chairman of Beckwith Incorporated. The Enterprises must have come later. This picture had dates, 1944–1962, it said, referring to his time in office. And beneath those, another set of dates referring to his life span, 1888–1965. Hey! Wait a minute.

Lesko felt a low hum building in his brain and a tickling at the back of his neck. Missing initials. And who else was born in 1888? Jonathan T Corbin the first, that's who. Lesko moved almost reluctantly, disbelievingly, to the next portrait of the series.

"Jesus," he whispered.

Lesko shut his eyes tightly and took a step back from the wall before he opened them again. Once more he looked into the face of this new Beckwith. Tilden Beckwith I. No middle name. No initial. Born in 1860. Died in 1944. Maybe forty-five years old when the portrait was painted. A little gray at the temples. But still trim. Athletic. A busted nose tilting a quarter inch off center and a familiar scar breaking the line of one eyebrow. Raymond Lesko was staring into the face of Jonathan Corbin.

"Friends again?" Sturdevant looked up. Corbin and Gwen had been touching and whispering over by a potted tree for a full ten minutes.

"We had a good talk," she replied, taking the chair Corbin held for her.

Harry Sturdevant tapped Gwen's notebook. "This is quite extraordinary. Shall I attempt to summarize?"

"Do you mind"—Corbin lifted a hand—"if I ask first whether you believe it?"

"Would you, sir, be reassured if I told you that this sort of thing has happened before?"

"In your experience?"

"No, but there's literature on it. I've done some research today, and I plan to do a good deal more tomorrow. May I proceed?"

"Dr. Sturdevant"—Corbin waggled the still upraised hand—"if there's literature it has a title. Or at least a subject heading."

"Naturally."

"Could I ask what it is?"

"You're concerned, I gather, that the subject heading might be schizophrenia."

"Something like that."

"It isn't. Do you mind if we come back to your question after a bit?"

"I'd really like to know the subject heading."

"I mentioned it in passing earlier. It's genetic memory. Also known as ancestral memory."

"A man named Tilden something or something Tilden lived at the Osborne Apartments sometime between 1885 and 1892." Harry Sturdevant, his head tilted back, read from Gwen's notes and his own marginal jottings through a tiny pair of reading glasses. "This Tilden had an infant son and a wife whose name sounds like Emma or Anna. One night, during a blizzard which blew in from the south, she fled the Osborne, taking a course that led her one block north and two blocks east. Tilden gave chase. At the end of the short block north, he found a frozen corpse whose name was George but whose death seems to be little more than a background detail." He glanced up at Corbin.

Corbin nodded. "I don't feel like I know much about him. Or that he was involved in the rest of it."

"You cover George up with some regret," Sturdevant continued, "and press on until you see the woman. At this point she tries to reach a building on the north side of the street. Today, with Gwen, I gather you spotted a hotel and said you thought it was the building. You called it the Spanish Flats?"

"Yes."

"Were you looking at the Navarro Hotel?"

"I didn't notice a sign."

"It was probably the Navarro. Once there was a huge complex of apartments called the Navarro Flats, also known as the Spanish Flats, running from Central Park South to Fifty-eighth Street and from Seventh Avenue halfway down toward Sixth. The Navarro Hotel is much more recent. It simply kept the name. In any case, you frustrate the woman's attempt to reach this address and you fling her hat toward one of its entrances, a gesture which I assume has significance. Lord and Taylor did have a Broadway store, by the way, I think at Twenty-third Street.

"The woman stumbled on, passing under the northern terminus of the Sixth Avenue Elevated, which you've already identified. It says here you were struck by the irony of this woman seeking sanctuary in the elevated because she'd somehow used it to betray you and some other 'good people.' Any further light on that?"

Corbin shook his head.

"Failing to find help there, and failing to attract the attention of two policemen, she pushed on toward Fifth Avenue until she reached a high iron fence which opened onto a very large home with a huge porte cochere. That would have been the home of Cornelius Vanderbilt the second, which was right across the street, where Bergdorf's is now. Cornelius, by the way, was the same Vanderbilt who built the Breakers in Newport. The woman turned away from the possible sanctuary of the Vanderbilt house, which suggests to me that she had considerable social ambition, which she was loath to damage by turning up in a state of dishabille, blizzard or no. Your notes also mention that she had blood on her mouth. It turned out to be a fatal vanity. She turned and ran across the street to a construction site, which sounds like it might have been this hotel. Is that correct, Jonathan?"

"Maybe. It doesn't seem right, though."

"It wasn't. This Plaza Hotel was erected in 1909. There was another, shorter-lived Plaza Hotel on this site before that. On our way out I'll ask when that one was built. I suspect, however, that the answer will be 1888. Everything else seems to fit the massive blizzard that hit the northeast during mid-March of that year. Including the great tangle of wires which you say were down all over the street. After that experience, the city quickly caused them all to be laid underground.

"Having settled on a probable date, and having at least partially identified two of that storm's fatalities, we should have no trouble researching their full names and therefore your own. Although it may be a bit more difficult, we can probably also find out whether a man named Ansel Carling ever lived at the Navarro Flats. You pummeled him a day or so later, I understand."

"You keep saying I did it. I'm not entirely comfortable with that. It wasn't me."

"Bear with me. You thrashed this man in the bar of the Hoffman House?"

"Yes."

"Where is the Hoffman House?"

"I don't know. Downtown someplace."

"Guess, Jonathan. Where do you think it is?"

"Near Madison Square Garden. Wait. That can't be."

"Yes, it can. It was off Madison Square. Twenty-sixth Street and Broadway. Near the original Madison Square Garden."

Corbin moved his head hopelessly.

"You're resisting, Jonathan." Sturdevant lowered the notebook. "I want you to try to see through this man's eyes."

"I'll try."

"Describe the Hoffman House bar."

"I . . . I can't. I only had that one dream last night."

"Then it's fresh in your mind," Sturdevant insisted. "Gwen's notes mention a large painting with prancing nudes."

"And a cigar stand," Gwen added. "You put your coat and cane on the cigar stand as you approached Carling. And there were two other men you knew at the bar. One had long hair."

"Actors," Corbin whispered.

"Who?"

"The two at the bar. One was with a Wild West show. I almost want to say it was Buffalo Bill."

"It could well have been Colonel Cody." Sturdevant scribbled a few more notes of his own.

"The other one was a stage actor. A smaller man. There's something about the Osborne with him too. Could he have lived there?"

"You tell me. Do you have a name?"

"No. Sometimes I almost do, but no."

"Describe him."

"Dark red hair. Not very big. Slender."

"What about facial hair?"

Corbin closed his eyes for a moment. "I don't think he had any. Now that you ask, it seems that he was the only one in the room without a beard or mustache."

"That's very good, Jonathan. A stage actor would normally be clean shaven. Give me a name."

"I can't."

"The fight was finally ended by a manager or maître d'hôtel named Oscar. What is his last name?"

"Just Oscar. He was just called Oscar."

"It was not at all common, Jonathan, to address a man by his first name in 1888, no matter what his station."

"Oscar of the Waldorf," Corbin blurted. "Later they called him Oscar of the Waldorf. The Waldorf-Astoria hired him away."

Sturdevant arched one eyebrow. "You remember that or did you read it?"

"I remember seeing him there. He was older but not old."

Sturdevant made more notes. He seemed troubled by the mention of the Waldorf. "Back to the Hoffman House," he said. "Was the cigar stand on the right or left as you entered?"

"Left."

"The bar?"

"On the right, further on."

"And the nude painting?"

"Left."

"Describe the bar."

"I don't know. A bar. Carved wood. Brass rail. The top wasn't wood. Maybe marble. What good is this?"

"Trust me. Was there a mirror behind the bar?"

"No."

"A bar without a mirror?"

"There was a painting, I think."

"Are you remembering or are you seeing? Try to see it."

"The painting's the same—wait a minute. It's a mirror. But it's high. You look up and you see those big nudes on the wall behind you."

"Excellent." Sturdevant leaned closer. "Now, Jonathan, I want you to hold it right there. Put both palms flat on the bar. What do you feel?"

"I told you. Marble."

"Keep your hands there but move them sideways until they slide off either end."

"I can't."

"Why can't you?"

"There's something big at each corner. A big lamp. With fur. A lamp with a stuffed animal holding on to it."

"What kind of animal?"

"I don't know. A dog?"

"Could it be a bear?"

"Yes. A small bear."

"What is the actor's name?"

"I don't . . ." The words faded on Corbin's lips.

Gwen reached for his arm. "Are you all right, Jonathan?"

"Yes."

"Jonathan? You are Jonathan, aren't you?"

"Oh yeah. Yeah. I'm okay."

"Did something just happen? Did you get his name?"

"Ella."

"Who's Ella?"

"Her. The woman in the snow. Her name is Ella."

"For Pete's sake, where did that come from?"

"The actor. Ella doesn't like him. He's been divorced. More than once. Ella doesn't think the Osborne should have let him in. But she doesn't like the Osborne either. Too far from everything. Too close to the Negroes. I think I'd like a drink now."

"Jesus H. Christ!" Raymond Lesko whispered, adjusting the lens of his Nikon. Tilden Beckwith I. No middle name. No initial. He took several close-ups of the face, then one each of Huntington Beckwith and Tilden II.

Wait a second, he thought. Where does Corbin's twin get off calling himself Tilden the first? Only kings and popes do that, mostly after they're dead. This guy doesn't look like the kind of jerk who'd king himself. He probably didn't. The brass plate came later. Put there by someone who wanted to make a point of the relationship. Which couldn't have been easy. Because Tilden the second who got on the elevator before doesn't look a goddamned bit like Tilden the first. Old Huntington comes a touch closer but still no cigar. And what tiny resemblance there is has a funny look to it, like—Lesko stepped back. That was it. That's what looked odd to him before. The artist had painted a portrait, and then sometime later it was touched up. Cheekbones were softened and other features were subtly altered in order to give Huntington's face at least some hint of a family resemblance to the guy who looks like Corbin. Jonathan T Corbin. No period. What does the T stand for, Corbin? Do you even know? Ask me, one will get you five it stands for Tilden.

The last portrait of the series, working backward, was that of Stanton Orestes Beckwith. Founder. First president of Beckwith & Company. There, thought Lesko, was that resemblance again. A little harder to see because of this guy's big muttonchop whiskers and a fleshier face but it was there. A lot more, at least, than with those two characters on the end. Also a middle name, the last Beckwith to use one. What did this family have against middle names all of a sudden?

A sudden flash of memory hammered that thought from his mind. Lesko quickly sidestepped back to the portrait of Tilden I and touched his finger to the brass plate—1944 again. Corbin's twin is born in 1860 and dies in 1944. Same year as half the Corbins in Chicago. What'll you bet, he asked, it was the same month, give or take? And then, also 1944, old snake-eyes Huntington Beckwith moves into the corner office.

Lesko backed away and stared up into the cadaverous face of Huntington Beckwith. It was you, you old bastard. Wasn't it? You and your jerk son over here. You knocked them all off. But you missed the one that was still in the oven.

Far to his right, Lesko heard the swish of the hotel's revolving doors. He would have paid no attention except that, from the corner of his eye, he thought he saw a pair of hotel employees snap to attention as they had when the old man entered. Once again, the hairs pricked at the back of his neck. He heard rapid footsteps brushing across the carpet behind him, but was careful to keep his face to the wall until they'd passed. Lesko turned. He watched as a small man, also in a black coat, strode distractedly into the elevator used twenty minutes earlier by Tilden the second. If Lesko had been less tired, less preoccupied with the faces on the wall, he might have realized that the man would stop and abruptly turn on entering the elevator. But more than tired, Lesko was stunned. There was no question in his mind that a massacre of some proportion had occurred in March of 1944. He had not, he was sure, found the last of the bodies, either. You don't do a job like that without finding the need to tidy up a little around the edges as well. It was as that thought percolated in Lesko's mind that the small man spun around, snapped his fingers at the elevator operator, and waited impatiently for the doors to slide shut. He stiffened as they did. Because for a full second the eyes of Mr. Dancer locked onto those of Raymond Lesko.

"Let me finish my summary," Harry Sturdevant suggested, "and if you don't mind, I'd like us to forgo anything alcoholic at least until we've had some dinner." Sturdevant was concerned about the propranolol still in Corbin's system. Although he saw no real danger to Corbin's health, the combination could easily befog what were apparently some very tenuous perceptions.

"Jonathan had a big brunch," Gwen Leamas reminded him.

"As a matter of fact, I'll get to that. First, however, let us get back to Tilden and Ella, assuming those names are correct. In mid-March of 1888, also an assumption, Tilden caused Ella's death in an act that was apparently less than premeditated. Ella, it seems, had a lover who was the father of her child. She tried to get to him at the Navarro and died trying. Tilden seems to have known that they were lovers—"

Corbin shook his head. "I think he had just figured it out."

"When? That very evening?"

"Margaret—" Corbin stopped himself and took a long breath. "I don't know whether I'm making this up or not."

"Tell me anyway, Jonathan."

"I think he had no idea how long a woman carries a baby."

"Many Victorian men and women had no idea of such things. There were one or two books on the subject, but their authors were routinely arrested for peddling smut. You mentioned Margaret. How did she come into it?"

"I think she tried to tell him. As gently as she could, she tried to drop hints that he was away, I don't know where, when the baby would have to have been conceived. I think he finally caught on and confronted Ella and that's when she told him." Corbin paused again. It struck Sturdevant that he was becoming visibly angry.

"About Ansel Carling?"

"There was more than that. I don't know exactly. Some treachery involving his business and also involving Jay Gould."

"Jay Gould was certainly no stranger to business treachery. But let's leave that for the moment and stick to the sequence of events. After you took your satisfaction from Ansel Carling at the Hoffman House, and after he threatened Margaret, do I gather that you became concerned for her safety and decided to move her out of harm's way?"

"And to have his baby," Gwen added.

"Which baby?" Sturdevant asked. "You mean another one?"

"He wanted a son of his own," she answered. "He would set Margaret up in Greenwich and give her a whole new identity if she'd bear him a child."

"How the devil would you know that? Is that all these scribblings about the house in Greenwich and teaching boxing and baseball?"

Gwen nodded. "Jonathan told me. I tried to be Margaret as long as I could."

"To Jonathan's Tilden."

"Yes."

"Jonathan," he asked, "how much of this conversation do you remember?"

"Almost none of it."

"Do you or don't you recall asking Margaret to have your child?"

"No," he answered softly. "But I know I did."

"Let me get this straight. When you're in a dream state, and you replay a recurring scene such as your pursuit of the woman Ella or apparently your brawl at the Hoffman House, you can recall it vividly afterward."

Corbin nodded. "Even during it. I mean, when it's happening, I still feel like I'm mostly still me."

"Exactly." Sturdevant leaned forward. "But when this Tilden person comes out during your waking moments and fully takes over your consciousness, you're saying that you have no recollection of that."

"I remember it for a few seconds, anyway. Then it breaks up and fades."

"As with an ordinary dream upon waking."

"I guess. Yes. Except that I've had Gwen to tell me what happened."

"Over the past twenty-four hours, according to Gwen, this takeover has been complete on several occasions and partial on several others. Is that correct?"

"Partial?" Corbin glanced questioningly at Gwen. "I don't think so."

"As an example, Gwen mentioned the large breakfast you had this morning and the unusual, for you, dishes you tried to order."

Corbin shook his head blankly.

"You've never had kippers before," Gwen reminded him. "When I've ordered them you've said 'Yuck' and told me they looked like fish mummies. And you've never had much more than coffee and toast for breakfast."

"I guess," Corbin answered. "I don't see how this matters. I was hungry. I wanted some corned beef hash and eggs."

"A large breakfast," Sturdevant explained, "was characteristic of a nineteenth-century man. Neither the large breakfast nor the initial choice of menu was at all characteristic of Jonathan Corbin. The same may be said of your desire for a bumper of mulled wine the night before or your appreciation of the spires of Saint Patrick's which, incidentally, were not completed until after 1888. The obvious suggestion is that this Tilden's tastes and therefore his consciousness are subtly intruding upon your own more often than you know. The odds are that it's happened a great many times when Gwen wasn't there to record it."

Corbin looked away. "Maybe. I have no reason to think so."

"The truth is you don't really know. Or do you?"

He shook his head.

"This could have been happening all your life."

"I've done things," Corbin said slowly, "and wondered why I've done them. But I think everybody has."

"True enough and we'll get into that later. But these complete takeovers of yours. They too could have happened all your life, could they not? Have you ever experienced blackouts or memory lapses?"

"No," Corbin lied.

"Never?"

"I was fine before I came to New York," he lied again.

"Before we go much further," Harry Sturdevant suggested to Jonathan, "I'd like access to my library and files. My home is only a ten-minute walk."

"What's happening to me?" Corbin asked. "Am I going insane?"

"No."

"Am I haunted?"

"Don't be silly."

"What does that leave, Doctor? That I've lived before?"

"In a manner of speaking, yes. Yes, Jonathan. You have."

EIGHT

T *IS* HIM," THE OLD MAN REPEATED. HE LOOKED small and frail as he sagged into a high-backed chair behind a large Sheraton desk in his suite of rooms. His hat lay on the desk before him. He had not removed his coat. "It's him and he *knows*." Tilden Beckwith II clutched his collar against his throat.

"He knows nothing, *sir*." The man Lesko knew as Mr. Dancer stood erect before the desk, his hands folded neatly at the small of his back. "The detective is another matter. I have underestimated him." Lawrence Ballanchine stepped to the desk console and picked up the telephone. He punched in the two digits of a coded number from the console's memory.

"What are you doing?" Beckwith slapped a hand over the cradle, breaking the connection before it was made.

"Ending this, I hope."

"Wait a minute. Wait. We must think this out. We must put our heads together."

"Sir." The small neat man sighed. "There is really very little to think about. You've just told me that Corbin has accurately retraced the path your grandmother took on the night she was murdered. The man is obviously acting upon information of some kind. It's only a matter of time until his knowledge is sufficient to become actionable. Especially if he recognized you."

"He didn't, you know. I was quite discreet. Quite clever."

"You may, in fact, have done the firm a great service, Mr. Beckwith." However witlessly, Ballanchine thought to himself. "Still, you took an unacceptable risk. Your connection with Corbin has surely been established by the detective. As has mine."

"Then this Lesko, don't you see, is the only link," Beckwith said eagerly. "Fix that, break the link, and the rest of the chain will fall away. Corbin and the others will wither on the vine, so to speak."

"Sir"—Ballanchine rolled his eyes inwardly—"do you wish to spend the remainder of your life wondering whether you'll turn a corner and be face to face with Jonathan Corbin or would you rather live out your days in the peace and comfort you so richly—Others? What others?"

The old man shook his head stupidly.

"Sir, there is Corbin and there is the Leamas woman. Are there others?"

"Only . . . no."

"Did you see them in the company of someone else today?"

"They just had tea . . . at the Plaza . . . with an older gentleman like myself. A doctor, I think."

"How would you know that, sir?"

"I saw them. I watched them."

"No, sir. I meant about the other man being a doctor."

"I've seen him before. At charitable functions and the like. I forget his name." Beckwith made a dismissive gesture with his fingers. "He's forever talking about swimmers and gymnasts and the like."

"But they joined this doctor at the conclusion of their walk from the Osborne building? For a prearranged meeting?"

"I suppose. But that needn't mean anything."

"The last surviving Corbin re-creates your grandmother's last hour on earth. By whatever means, he has stumbled upon the origins of an *arrangement* that affects a great many lives, not least his own. Can you really imagine that as four o'clock came, he could have put aside all that is obviously vexing him to sit down for a polite afternoon tea?"

"I don't know. I . . ."

Ballanchine picked up the phone.

Harry Sturdevant's home, also his office, took up the first and second floors of a Greek Revival town house on Sixty-ninth Street off Fifth Avenue, ten short blocks north of the Plaza. It had been built during the decade following the Civil War by a lieutenant of steel magnate Henry Clay Frick. Frick's own mansion, now an art museum, was not far away. The town house had been inherited by Sturdevant's deceased wife, Mary, and in turn passed on to him. The two upper floors had been extensively remodeled and leased to, from the top, a director of the Metropolitan Opera and a stockbroker. The basement apartment, thoroughly soundproofed, was occupied by a wide receiver for the New York Jets.

Sturdevant chose to walk to his house with Corbin and his niece for several reasons. Not least, he wanted those ten minutes to collect his thoughts and justify the utterly unscientific and unprofessional suggestions he would soon offer this troubled young man. Second, Jonathan's relative equanimity would not last much longer, assuming, of course, that it was only the pro-pranolol that was keeping him steady. But he also hoped, privately, that a walk through wintry New York at night might evoke another of the several apparent possessions his niece had already witnessed.

Corbin tensed at the prospect but he offered no resistance. Gwen had already taken his hand, which she released only to slip on her coat, and did not again let it go. Walking down the Plaza's front steps, Corbin breathed audible relief at the sight of a moon that was nearly full. No more snow would fall this evening. By the time they'd crossed the open expanse of the Grand Army Plaza, Corbin had relaxed further. At the prome-nade entrance to the Central Park Mall, where the car-riages of the wealthy had paraded a century before and where courting young couples were permitted to stroll unchaperoned, Sturdevant thought he saw a hesitation in Corbin's step and the trace of a smile on his lips. He had about made up his mind to dismiss it as the work of wishful thinking when he saw Corbin's shoulder jerk downward, as if Gwen had tugged sharply at his hand. He saw that once again as they passed the shadowy outlines of the old Central Park Arsenal, and more clearly as the Frick museum came into view. That time Gwen also reached across him and took away the um-brella he carried. Sturdevant was becoming annoyed with his niece. Each time Corbin showed signs of drift-ing off she would snap him back as if he were on a leash, and she would keep up a running chatter that was studiously irrelevant. He tried scowling her into silence, but Gwen Leamas cheerfully avoided his eyes.

Something did happen, he was sure, a few moments after the three turned onto Sixty-ninth Street. In large part, the block on which Sturdevant lived looked much as it had a century before. There were now automobiles, of course, and the graceful gas lamps were gone, and all but the shallowest stoops and sidewalk gardens had been removed. Still, Corbin would guide Gwen past each building entrance in an unnecessary arc, pausing on one occasion as if to allow the passage of a pedestrian coming down steps that weren't there. As they arrived at Sturdevant's street-level door, the doctor wondered what would happen if he were to warn Corbin that the steps, which also weren't there, were icy, but he chose to avoid the appearance of toying with the man.

Sturdevant touched a soundless buzzer and was answered at once by a woman's tinny voice coming from a speaker box. The sound caused Corbin to straighten and blink rapidly. The door soon opened and the three were greeted by Sturdevant's housekeeper, a large, pleasant-looking black woman who hugged Gwen Leamas and was then introduced to Corbin as Mrs. Starling. Corbin, the doctor thought, seemed more than a little startled. Did she seem somehow familiar to him, he wondered, or could it be that the man within him was unaccustomed to being introduced to servants. He made a mental note to explore both roads.

Sturdevant's office, more of a study actually, was as Corbin would have imagined it. Three of the ten-foot-high walls were lined with built-in bookshelves. Corbin had always felt one could tell much about a person by the books he reads, although less by the books he displays. Sturdevant seemed to read everything from current fiction to classics, some in their original languages, historical texts with particular emphasis on Renaissance Europe, a full wall of books covering every conceivable sport from ballooning to yachting, and another full wall containing medical and psychological texts, most dealing with the stresses of competitive sport. Among his well-worn reference works were a current

copy of *Who's Who* and a small bound copy of the
Social Register. Between groupings of books there were
autographed baseballs, an ancient lacquered soccer
ball, an even older football from the Harvard-Yale
game of 1924, and a score of pewter sailing trophies.
The fourth wall displayed at least two dozen photographs and framed letters covering a time span of more
than sixty years. Sturdevant, little changed except for
the color of his hair and the strategically tailored cuts
of his suits, had posed with seven different U.S. presi-
dents. There he was, smiling, chatting, or shaking
hands with an unbroken line of chief executives from
Gerald Ford back to Franklin Roosevelt, then skipping
to Woodrow Wilson, then once again back to Teddy
Roosevelt. Sturdevant could not have been more than
fifteen in that one. Also in the fading photograph was a
man Corbin took to be Sturdevant's father. With Teddy
Roosevelt. Teddy. What was it about Teddy Roosevelt?
Standing there, Corbin found it hard to think of Teddy
Roosevelt as president. Not objectionable. Not at all.
Just hard.

There were also autographed photos of a number
of Olympic legends whom Corbin recognized at once.
Jesse Owens, shy, almost apologetic. An aging Jim
Thorpe. A skinny young Cassius Clay, and several sepia
team pictures, all Harvard, all presumably including
Harry Sturdevant. In front of these sat Sturdevant's
leather-topped desk, which was equally awash with
memorabilia. Sturdevant stepped to the desk and
picked up a small pile of letters and message slips,
which he leafed through disinterestedly.

"Please sit down. Be comfortable. I'll be back in
just a minute." He gestured toward a grouping of
tufted chairs opposite his desk, then walked from the
room, closing the door behind him.

"No Jimmy Carter or Ronald Reagan." Corbin

swept a hand over the array of presidential photographs.

"Uncle Harry hasn't forgiven either one for mucking up the last two Olympics," Gwen told him. "There's also a snap in his files of him with Adolf Hitler at the 1936 games. He hasn't forgiven Hitler either. Are you all right, Jonathan?"

"I'm fine, sweetheart. Really."

"You started to get lost again on the street, didn't you."

"No." He seemed surprised. "Not at all."

"You were walking around things that weren't there again."

"Not that I remember." He shook his head. He'd stepped aside when the guy in the fur hat came down the steps but that was all. The only oddness he could recall was when he met what's-her-name, the housekeeper. Nothing else.

"Miss Gwen and her gentleman will be staying for dinner, Dr. Sturdevant?" Cora Starling looked up as he entered the kitchen.

"A light dinner in an hour or so, Cora. I think I'm also going to ask them to spend the night. I hope you don't mind at such short notice."

"Not that I mind, Doctor. I had some nice Dover sole for you, but there's not near enough for three. How about soup and sandwiches?"

"That would be fine, Cora. Whatever is the least trouble."

"Bacon, lettuce, and tomato is close to bein' a salad. It'll set the best at bedtime and not stir up bad dreams."

Sturdevant nodded. "That happens to be a very apt suggestion, Cora. Any particular reason for saying it?"

"That Corbin fella looked like he had a thing or

two messin' his head. Seems calmer though than some you've brought in here."

"He's been given something."

"Uh-huh. Seemed like."

"Cora," Sturdevant asked, "what did you think of Mr. Corbin when you were introduced? Did anything at all strike you about him?"

"Seemed nice enough." There was a touch of hesitation. "Miss Gwen knows him better than me."

"Cora, you have superb instincts about people. I'd like to know what you thought."

"He looked at me funny." Cora squinted one eye, signaling that she was offering an impression, not a confident opinion. "First I thought he doesn't care for black folks, but that wasn't it. Then maybe that he was snooty, but that wasn't it either. I think he was surprised you introduced us. Then he gave me this long look like he was tryin' to remember something."

"He thinks he's lived before, Cora. More accurately, he thinks he's carrying around another man's memories."

"From way back?"

"About a hundred years."

"Back when white people looked through black folks like they wasn't there?"

"Any servant, Cora. He wouldn't have expected to be introduced to any servant. I suspect his long stare came when he had that feeling and then tried to imagine why. You might also have reminded him of someone from a past life."

Cora nodded. "It's in the eyes. They know each other from the eyes."

"What are you talking about?"

"It's what my granny said. She believed that stuff about some folks livin' before. She said they knew each other from the eyes. The stirrin' is what she called it."

"She thought people who had past lives could recognize each other at a glance?"

"Not so much recognized. Mostly they'd see the eyes and get a stirrin'. You'd look at someone you don't know, like in a store or across a bus, and you might feel deep-down good about that person. Or deep-down bad. Sometimes even afraid. And they'd be lookin' back like they knew you too but they couldn't figure where from."

"It's not simply a matter of seeing a face that reminds you of another?"

"I suppose."

"Is it or isn't it?"

"Some of them books of yours call that denial. Denial is when you shut out the heart and listen to the head. It's what keeps folks ignorant, my granny said."

"Your granny, you say." Sturdevant smiled.

"I better fry up some bacon."

Sturdevant knocked before entering.

"Mrs. Starling will be along in a minute with some sherry." He chose a seat for himself at the small round coffee table opposite his desk and, with a gesture of his hands, invited Corbin and Gwen to sit. Sturdevant placed Gwen's notebook, his own notes added, on the table before him. "A few more questions while we're waiting."

"I'd really like to get on with it, Dr. Sturdevant," Corbin told him. "You said something about my living before."

"Actually, you said it. I said it was something like that."

"Genetic memory, ancestral memory. Whatever it is, I'd like to at least know what we're talking about."

"I have been stalling, haven't I?"

"Uncle Harry," Gwen assured him, "whatever this

is, Jonathan's hardly the type to run screaming from the room."

"It's not that." He made a wave of dismissal. "I've simply been searching for a place to begin. I'm something of a student of the phenomenon I'm about to describe but I'm hardly an expert. I'm not sure anyone is. There are several other caveats I'm inclined to lay before you by way of preface, professional ethics and competence among them, but I think you get the idea."

"You're afraid I'll say you're crazier than I am."

"Well put, Jonathan." There was a rap at the door. "Reprieved." He smiled.

Cora Starling set down a tray containing a decanted bottle of Malmsey and a small assortment of cheeses.

"Lovely, Cora. Thank you."

"Would any of you like me to dry out your shoes while you're sitting?" She was looking at Corbin.

"Jonathan?" Sturdevant asked.

"I'm fine. Thank you." He knew that he'd been staring. And he knew that his behavior had approached rudeness when he first met her as well. "Thank you, Mrs. Starling." He forced a friendly smile.

"I thought her name was Lucy," Corbin said after the large black woman had left.

"Did I say that?"

"I guess not."

"It's Cora Starling. Been with me for thirty years."

"It's nothing. My mistake."

"Speaking of women's names, does the name Bridey Murphy mean anything to you?"

"Uh-huh. There was a book." Corbin glanced toward the shelves, suspecting that a copy of it was in there someplace. "About reincarnation. A woman thought she'd lived before as a nineteenth-century Irish girl named Bridey Murphy."

"You're largely correct." Sure enough, Sturdevant

turned in his chair and reached for a volume whose
leaves contained a half-dozen paper bookmarks. "As
you see, I've been refreshing my memory since speaking
to Gwen this morning."

"We're back to my having lived before." Corbin
was disappointed.

"Bear with me, Jonathan." Don't just listen to your
head and stay ignorant, is what he felt like saying, but
it seemed unfair to steal Cora Starling's lines. "The full
title of the book is *The Search for Bridey Murphy*. It
raised quite a controversy back in the fifties and in
some measure it's still going on. It involved a Colorado
housewife and an amateur hypnotist who became the
author of the book. The hypnotist had regressed the
housewife to what seemed to be an earlier life. She was
able to describe it in detail while entranced. She knew,
for example, that she was born in Cork in 1798 and
died in Belfast sixty-six years later. She knew the names
of many relatives and neighbors, she could describe the
shops and farms, and she related all this in a quite genuine Irish peasant idiom. She provided any number of
obscure details, as you are doing, which were later veri-
fied. There doesn't seem to been any question of
fraud. None of prior conscious knowledge either. What
made the tapes of her hypnotic sessions so convincing
was the utterly prosaic nature of Bridey Murphy's life.
It was essentially insignificant. Most people who claim
to recall past lives tend to be Egyptian princes or
French countesses and such. No one ever seems to recall living a past life as a plumber."

Corbin seemed only mildly interested. "As I recall,
these memories were brushed off as the product of
books she read and stories she heard as a girl. And that
a lot of her details didn't check out at all."

"That was one argument, yes. That she was innocent of fraud but deluded. That she'd picked up her
Irish folklore from Irish relatives. Her tape-recorded ut-

terances, it was claimed, were actually a tapestry of fantasy woven from disassociated memories. But no relatives could be found who knew of any of these same details. Or who were born in Cork. Or who lived in the same little Irish village. Or who had even heard of it. The woman knew things she had no way of knowing. She knew things which were literally unknown to any living person until they were researched among long-forgotten Irish records."

"But," Gwen asked, "what about the details that were wrong?"

"Simple," he answered. "Faulty memory. She remembered them incorrectly."

"That sounds a bit pat, Uncle Harry."

"What would happen if I asked you to describe some marginally significant event in your own life five years ago and do it in detail? You would surely make mistakes substantive enough for me to argue that you probably weren't there. You learned those details secondhand somehow."

"Very well." Gwen glanced at Corbin to see how he was taking this. "The woman in the Bridey Murphy case told the truth as she knew it. Let's say it's possible she lived before. Jonathan is telling the truth as he knows it. Do you think he's lived before or don't you?"

"Not so fast," he answered. "First of all, I don't think she lived before. One school of thought, to which I subscribe, is that the Bridey Murphy phenomenon and hundreds of other cases like it have nothing to do with reincarnation and are simply illustrative of ancestral memory."

"This argument got a lot of attention in the Chicago press," Corbin recalled, "because the Colorado woman had family there. As I remember it, they established that she couldn't possibly have been related to a Bridey Murphy in Ireland and therefore she couldn't have had Bridey Murphy's memories."

"Who says so?"

"I would think she'd know. Or her mother or grandmother would."

"Not necessarily, Jonathan. Not necessarily at all. It is a rare person indeed who can confidently trace his lineage more than three generations back. The history books are loaded with illegitimate children. Da Vinci, Alexandre Dumas, William the Conqueror, Richard Wagner, to name just a few. For every acknowledged bastard there are probably hundreds more who simply have no idea. They might have been the product of adulterous affairs, they might have been adopted, they might even have been bought and sold. If a child is a result of a forcible rape, he or she is hardly likely to be told. And many women have married one man while they were already carrying the child of another. Genealogy is hardly an exact science."

"You're saying I could be a descendant of the baby Margaret had for Tilden. That I'm Tilden's great-grandson, maybe."

"I'm saying it's an avenue well worth exploring. It would certainly explain a great deal. If Margaret is your lover at one level and your great-grandmother at another, a measure of ambivalence is more than understandable."

"My great-grandmother's name was Charlotte Whitney Corbin. There really isn't much doubt about that."

"She could have adopted your grandfather," Gwen offered.

Corbin shrugged off the suggestion. "My grandfather looked too much like her. If you saw their photographs you'd think so too. But even if that's possible, it's a hell of a big step between accepting that and accepting that I'm walking around with all of Tilden's thoughts in my head. This genetic memory business is still just a theory."

"Not theory, Jonathan." Sturdevant waved a hand toward some of his psychology texts. "It's fact. Every creature, through every phase of its evolution, has stored away information from generation to generation. That's what evolution is. It's how a species adapts and develops. Memories, experiences, are also stored away in the genes. Our conscious minds prevent us from retrieving much of this information because we can't quite bring ourselves to believe that it's there. So we find other, more comfortable explanations for the odd feelings we all get. For aptitudes that are not found elsewhere in our families. For strong affinities toward particular people or places. For certain phobias that seem to have no basis in remembered experience. That's why hypnosis is often so useful in getting to the root of emotional problems. Under hypnosis, many people are enabled to recall a repressed experience and learn to deal with it."

"But not a past life experience."

"Not usually," Sturdevant explained. "Past life experiences are easily as significant as the others but now we have another problem. If a patient is being treated by a Freudian psychiatrist, whose discipline does not embrace the notion of an alternate existence, that psychiatrist will probably not pursue any suggestion that the patient is burdened with another individual's memories. A Jungian psychiatrist, who will at least consider the possibility of a subsidiary consciousness, will continue to probe for it while the other will choose a new direction. You, Jonathan, have rejected the idea of seeing a psychiatrist altogether. You're probably correct. It would be a crapshoot at best."

"You said subsidiary consciousness." Gwen Leamas frowned. "Isn't that the same as multiple personality?"

"No. One is a subcategory of the other, as middle-distance running is to track and field. There are many forms of subsidiary consciousness, not all of which need involve prior existence. Carl Jung, however, was convinced that past lives are very much a part of all of us. That the lives each of us once lived are found in the lives we're living now. Some behaviorists find proof of that statement in the so-called idiot savant who sits down at a piano and plays a Bach prelude upon hearing it once. It shouldn't happen but it does. Retarded individuals who've had no musical training whatsoever become instant virtuosos. Idiot savants just as often become math or language prodigies. Some speak foreign languages to which they've had no exposure and certainly no training. When this happens, by the way, the retarded person is not troubled by it in the least. Unlike you and me, he doesn't look for reasons. He does no conscious rejecting. He doesn't say, 'I've never learned to do this and therefore I can't do it.' He just does it. He is happily unencumbered by the intelligence the rest of us spend so much time tripping over."

"You mentioned Bach." Gwen leaned forward, fascinated. "What about people who were authentic geniuses, not idiots? What about people like Mozart, who composed a sonata at the age of four?"

"Or like Sir William Hamilton," Sturdevant added, "who learned Hebrew at the age of three. But I'm not sure it's genius. Three- and four-year-olds, remember, don't realize that they're not supposed to be able to do these things. In that respect they're like the mental defectives. They don't worry about where the ability came from."

"And you think it had to come from some remote antecedent."

"Where else, Gwen?"

"Environment?"

"There you go, tripping over your own intelligence. Genetic memory is a perfectly logical explanation of childhood prodigy and yet adults resist it because it smacks of a sort of haunting. Worse yet, fatalism. The conceit that we're all masters of our own destiny causes us to deny the simple truth that we are all products of what went before us."

"Still," Gwen answered doubtfully, "these were children. Or the mentally handicapped. Jonathan's an adult."

"An adult who admits that for most of his life he felt a vague disorientation, as if he thought he might be someone else. That's quite common, incidentally, even though most people who have such a notion keep it to themselves."

"How common?" Corbin asked softly.

"General George Patton"—Sturdevant scratched his head—"thought he'd been a warrior in many of the major battles throughout history."

"That's reincarnation again."

"Only according to Patton. I think it was something else. A better example might be T. E. Lawrence. Lawrence of Arabia. He was a product of the British upper classes and yet all his life he felt drawn to the Arabian desert. Some thought pathologically. Then there was Heinrich Schliemann, the man who located and excavated Troy at a time when everyone else believed that the city only existed in myth. Schliemann was hardly a Greek scholar, by the way. He'd been apprenticed to a German grocer when he was fourteen. And yet he could actually feel the city of Troy. He could see it. He could describe the people going about their daily lives."

"Like Bridey Murphy." Gwen nodded.

"Like Jonathan describing the Hoffman House bar. A comparatively modest vision if you don't mind my saying so and yet the principle is identical. All these people—Patton, Lawrence, the lady from Colorado, Schliemann, and our own Jonathan Corbin—have probably been carrying memories that have been recessive for many generations, perhaps hundreds of generations as in the case of Patton or Schliemann. This would not mean, however, that a Schliemann was the first of his bloodline to be affected by that particular compulsion. He may simply have been the first to do anything about it."

With a slow shake of his head, Jonathan Corbin stood up and wandered in the direction of the photographs on the far wall of the study.

"I gather you've anticipated my next thought." Sturdevant followed him with his eyes.

"You're about to suggest I do something about it."

Raymond Lesko turned off Queens Boulevard, a bag of Chinese takeout in one arm, and walked the two blocks to his small apartment in Jackson Heights. As always when returning home at night, he stayed close to the curb, avoiding doorways and alleys such as the one from which old Mr. Makowski down the street got clubbed last December. Not that he was nervous. Since the Makowski mugging and ever since Mrs. Hannigan got beaten and tied up in her apartment last summer, Lesko had been praying that some junkie kid would be hurting enough to try to take him on one of these nights. Just for the pleasure of snapping his spine and leaving him draped across the top of a parked car. His gift to the neighborhood.

But it wouldn't happen tonight. Muggers don't like it this cold. They don't like ice and snow under them where they can't move fast or run and where their hands and feet turn numb while they're waiting for the right patsy to come along. Not even if he played drunk, which he did some nights when he knew a couple of bums were looking him over back on the boulevard. One of these days, though. Some night one or two of those pieces of shit would make their move and Lesko's perfect teeth would be the last thing they saw before they went to meet Jesus.

But they'd have to wait. This, Lesko decided, would be his last night in this apartment for a while. After tonight there could be someone a little more dangerous than a strung-out Queens Boulevard schtunk waiting for him. He might even have company before morning. It would depend on how nervous Dancer is getting right now and how fast he can make another connection. Which probably wouldn't be all that fast. Dancer didn't figure to keep a card file of shooters handy. Otherwise how come he had to find Lesko's name in the newspapers. "I'm told you're a reliable sort," Dancer said that first time. "In street jargon," he told Lesko, "you're said to be a stand-up person." That's stand-up *guy,* you asshole. Stand-up *guy.* "I'm looking for a trained man in need of cash, a man who can be decisive when the need arises, and a man who is dependably discreet. The precise terminology is irrelevant."

Dancer had said the two magic words. The first being cash. The second being discreet. Lesko was discreet all right. Discreet enough not to say a damned word to a district attorney looking to find out how Lesko's partner, Dave Katz, could have a log house up in Sullivan County and a condo down in Florida on a gold shield's salary and why he got his face shot off a minute after he took his kids back to his ex-wife's house in Bayside with Harriet looking out the window. Lesko might have let it pass except for that. Dave asked for it. Lesko kept warning him that the bums he was leaning on were going to lean back one of these times and don't give me any bullshit about how you're just doing this for your kids and to climb out of a hole after your divorce because the truth is you got greedy. It wasn't like Lesko didn't warn him that there'd be a bill. He asked for it. But not like that, not right in front of Harriet and two little kids who got their father's brains all over their clothes. Lesko had explained that to both those slobs who did it. But it didn't do any good. Guys like that, they don't understand. Even the dago wise guys knew from hitting someone in front of his family, but these were Bolivians, who only know from blasting away at anything that moves and cutting out hearts like they've been doing since before Cortez. And they know from nose candy. Cocaine. A half-kilo of which the one with the sunglasses and the brown teeth held out saying take this and get lost and we call it even. Lesko's first bullet exploded the plastic bag he was holding. After that it was like shooting through a cloud.

A stand-up person. Lesko closed his apartment door and threw the deadbolt. He placed his bag of ribs and shrimp on a Formica table and reached into a cabinet for a box of Kellogg's Bran Flakes. From this he withdrew a palm-sized clump of aluminum foil. The front sight of a Smith & Wesson .38 had cut through one end. Lesko stripped away the rest of the foil and laid the revolver down next to his dinner. Only then did he remove his coat and hat.

He did not seriously expect a visitor. Not tonight. More likely there would be a telephone call. If the phone rang during the night, especially if it rang late, it would almost surely be Dancer trying to find out how much he knew. Lesko wouldn't answer it. He'd let Dancer stew a while until morning. He'd get a good night's sleep while Dancer stayed awake wondering what he knew and who he was telling. It would cross Dancer's mind to send a shooter tonight, assuming he had one handy, but he wouldn't. Not until he knew more. He would call in the morning and in his oily and tight-assed little way he would demand a meeting. He would use lawyer words like breach of faith and professional ethics and then he would try to set Lesko up. He'd have to. Dancer would have to assume that Lesko was about to put the arm on him for a hell of a lot more than the fifteen grand already in his pocket. He would also expect Lesko to cover himself by stashing his notes with someone reliable. Which meant he had to get Lesko by eight in the morning, latest, one way or the other. No phone call, on the other hand, would mean that Dancer wasn't even interested in talking first. In which case there'd be someone waiting outside his door when he opened it in the morning.

Saturday night. Lesko wondered if the Islanders were on television.

"These memories, Jonathan," Harry Sturdevant told him, "may be no less real than your own boyhood recollections. Accept that."

"I do, I guess." He moved a step closer to the framed photograph of Theodore Roosevelt grinning next to a very young Harry Sturdevant and Harry Sturdevant's father. Corbin found himself wanting to smile. He didn't quite know why.

"Is there something about Teddy Roosevelt?"

Corbin shrugged.

"Is it possible you knew him?"

"I feel as if I did, yes. But it's probably that I've read books about him."

"You're rejecting again, Jonathan. Try not to make judgments. How many books, by the way? Did you make a special effort to learn about him?"

"Not really. Now that you ask, I have picked up a book about him now and then and leafed through it. I didn't sit down and read them, though. They were too . . . I don't know."

"Superficial?"

"I guess that's the word. Yes."

"As if they were written by someone who didn't know his subject firsthand?"

"Yes." Corbin lowered himself to the edge of Sturdevant's desk.

"What was he like, Jonathan? I'd like you to try to

have fun with this question. Just let your mind flow with it as you look at his photograph."

"Very gutsy, exciting to be around." The beginnings of a shy smile twitched at Corbin's mouth. "More energy than anyone I ever—"

"Even as a child?" Sturdevant had a hunch.

"I guess." Corbin's smile dimmed and his expression became distant. "I know he was sickly. Asthma. I don't think he was out of the house all that much when he was real small."

"A bit later, then. If you were to try to see him in your mind, assuming you knew him, what would he be like as an older boy and where would that be?"

Corbin blinked once, then several times more rapidly. Sturdevant had a sense that a picture was forming but that Corbin was about to shake it away.

"Jonathan," he said quietly, "I'd like you to try to envision him. Just allow a picture, a scene, a scene to float into place. Don't force it but don't resist it either. To help it along, please sit comfortably in my chair. That desk must be getting awfully hard."

Gwen Leamas caught her uncle's eye and made a small quick nod of encouragement. Jonathan had, come to think of it, seemed somewhat bemused by that picture while Harry was out of the room.

Corbin made a face, unseen. The desk must be getting hard, yet. Next he'll be saying you feel relaxed and are getting sleepy. Corbin thought of going back and sitting with them at the little round table. But he didn't want to. It felt too much like a séance. This end of the room was more fun anyway. But the desk actually was hard and Corbin did stand up again. He turned toward Sturdevant, mild annoyance showing in his eyes.

"Does that photograph upset you in any way, Jonathan?"

"No. Not at all."

"Then perhaps it's a nice unthreatening place to

start. You did react to that photo. Was there anything in your reaction that surprised you?"

"That he was president," Corbin answered. Then his eyes clouded over as he wondered why he said that. He knew only that there was something amusing about the thought. He bit his lip to keep from smiling.

"You look as though that notion strikes you as funny and yet you're resisting it. What's happening is that you're responding to two different levels of consciousness. The two appear to be in conflict, so you reject the one that has the least tangible substance. We all do that, Jonathan. All the time. Please try not to in this instance. What surprised you about Roosevelt being president?"

"That he . . . that he pulled it off. No one in their wildest dreams ever thought he could . . ." Corbin's voice trailed off. But he let the smile happen.

"Become president?"

"Yes."

"Do you recall the circumstances?"

"No . . . yes. He was vice president. Then McKinley got shot."

"Did you know him?"

"No."

"Jonathan, do you *feel* that you knew him?"

Corbin hesitated for a moment. The answer was yes but his impulse was to deny it. He felt as though he knew Abraham Lincoln, too, but that didn't mean he did. But he also knew that wasn't what Sturdevant meant. The high-backed chair began to look good after all.

"That's good, Jonathan. Just lean back and relax. Let your body feel heavy and warm and safe and very, very relaxed."

Gwen touched her uncle's arm. "Hypnosis?" She mouthed the word.

Sturdevant smiled. "My niece sees that you're relaxing at last, Jonathan, and she asks whether you're being hypnotized like the lady from Colorado. You're not, are you? You're simply finding a little peace."

Corbin barely heard him. His mind was on a boy with skinny arms and glasses and reddish hair.

"We were talking about Teddy," Sturdevant said.

"Uh-huh."

"If you'd lived in the same city at the same time, don't you think you would have known each other?"

"I'd know his name, who he was. Our parents would have known each other better."

"But you would have had friends your own age. Wouldn't Teddy have been a friend?"

"I don't think he had many friends. Not then. Your friends are mostly boys from school. Teddy didn't go to school. He had tutors. Besides . . ."

"Besides what, young man?"

"Besides, Teddy was older. He was two years older."

"How old was he?" Sturdevant reached for Gwen's arm and squeezed it.

"Sixteen, I think."

"And you are fourteen?"

"Yes. But just as big."

"Where did you meet him? You did meet him, didn't you?"

"Yes. It was in the Rhinelanders' stable. It was just down from ours in the mews in back of our house. It's where I met John Flood, too."

Gwen flipped two pages of her spiral notebook and underscored the name Big John Flood, holding it up for her uncle to see. Sturdevant nodded.

"John Flood was the man who taught you to box?"

"Yes."

"Was that the same John Flood who once fought John L. Sullivan? I believe they called him the Bear's Head . . . no, the Bull's Head Terror."

"What?" Corbin seemed confused.

"Oh, nothing. My mistake." Sturdevant chewed his lip. "How old was John Flood, by the way?"

"Eighteen, perhaps. But he often passed much older."

Ah, Sturdevant thought, that was it. If it is the same Big John Flood who fought John L. on a barge up in Yonkers, this must be a much younger version.

"John Flood was handy with his fists all the same. Correct?"

"He was teaching Teddy. Teddy was always calling other boys out when they insulted him but he was always getting whipped. He was getting a real drubbing once from Todd Fisher and John Flood came by on a beer wagon and pulled them apart. He told Teddy he'd best either grow a few stone or learn the fancy."

"The fancy?"

"That's what the English called pugilism. He said all the young bloods were learning it. From all the best families."

"John Flood was English?"

Corbin chuckled. "You dasn't say that to John. He'll rear up on you for sure. His father still carries the cut of a British officer's saber across his back."

"I see. And Teddy Roosevelt took him up on his suggestion?"

"He went and had one lesson. How to hold his hands and to jab. How to measure your blows so you don't crack a knuckle. How to block and smother punches and how to trip up the other fellow and throw him down. Actually, Teddy's father had Teddy taking boxing lessons a full year before that. Even had a gymnasium set up at his house over on Twentieth Street. Teddy knew how to box. John Flood taught him how to fight. There's a difference, John told him. Afterward, Teddy went out looking for Todd Fisher again."

"And whipped him?"

"No. Todd drubbed him worse than before. Todd just ducked under those jabs and grabbed him in a bear hug and bit Teddy's ear near off. Then he threw Teddy down and jumped on his chest. John Flood showed Teddy how to do just that but Teddy wouldn't, don't you know. So Todd started punching up Teddy's face and I couldn't bear that so I grabbed Todd by the hair and pulled him off. I hit him too. I cut my knuckles on his teeth." Corbin held up his right fist as if to show the scar. "Then Todd went wild and started smashing me but soon Teddy was wading back into him. Todd was so crazy mad he probably would have whipped us both except that a big German woman came out of her store that we were having this grand battle in front of and began smacking all three of us with a broom. Todd backed off first. Teddy and I still wanted to have at him but the German woman between us was holding that broom like Friar Tuck's staff. Todd's mouth was bloody but what bothered him most was that his pants were split clear up the back and some of the other boys were laughing at that. He called us cowards for ganging up on him and he said he'd get us."

"Did he?"

"He tried. Teddy fought him one more time after a few more lessons from John. This time he learned slipping and dodging. And how to bite down on soft wood while you're fighting lest you get your jaw broken. That's what Teddy did to Todd at last. For good measure he put a pair of shanties on his glimmers."

"I beg your pardon."

Corbin grinned, embarrassed. "That's some slang John uses. It means black eyes."

"And that was the last of Todd Fisher."

"No, indeed." Corbin touched a finger to his once broken nose, quite proudly, Sturdevant thought. "It wasn't a fortnight before he came after me."

"With a broken jaw?"

"Yes, sir, but with a pair of knucks. He broke my nose and laid open my brow with a single jab before I tackled him and brought him down. Then I left my mark on him good and proper. John Flood says you should always finish your man and leave your mark on him. The mark on a beaten man always goes deep, he says. He'll always fear the man who gave it to him. John says it's not the same with the marks he put on me. Those are better than medals, John says. And anyway, one more good scrap could straighten out my nose as good as new."

"In any case, I gather you and Teddy Roosevelt became good friends."

"Yes, until I went back to middle school after the Easter holiday."

"What about after that?"

"Our families summer in different places. And then his family moved up to Fifty-seventh Street and we saw each other less often for a while."

Sturdevant arched an eyebrow toward Gwen to see if she'd caught Corbin's first use of the present tense. She was busy scribbling. She held a message out to Sturdevant but, preoccupied, he waved it off.

"Have you never heard the name John L. Sullivan?" he asked the boy in Corbin's mind. "Or of a prizefight between him and John Flood?"

"No, sir. John often speaks of trying his hand in the prize ring after he's saved enough of a stake to bet on himself. His father was a prizefighter, you know. Gentleman Jimmy Flood, he was called. John says his dah was never knocked off his feet by any man save John Barleycorn."

"What about John L. Sullivan, speaking of prizefighters? Or Paddy Ryan or Jake Kilrain? Ever heard of them?"

"I haven't, sir."

Gwen Leamas threw up her hands and leaned

toward Harry Sturdevant's ear. "I don't know how you managed this, but now that you have, will you stop with those damned boxers? Ask him something useful. And for heaven's sake, don't call him Jonathan."

"It's fascinating," Harry Sturdevant whispered. "Like a window into another era. Jonathan seems to have locked in on a single ancestral experience. He's never heard of Sullivan or Kilrain because no one else had either at that point. If I asked him about Ella or Margaret, he wouldn't know what I was talking about."

"You can ask him about himself. You can ask him his bloody name."

"Of course." Sturdevant banged his forehead. "Stupid of me."

"Ask him."

"Young man, does the name Tilden mean anything to you?"

Again, Corbin seemed confused. "You mean the governor, sir?"

"No, not the—" Sturdevant cleared his throat. "What governor?"

"Samuel Tilden, sir. Governor of New York."

"Um, is that the only Tilden you can think of?"

Gwen showed her teeth. "Will you please, dear Uncle Harry, simply ask him what his full name is?"

"Oh my goodness," Harry Sturdevant gasped.

"What?"

"Boxing," he whispered. "I've just realized where I've seen that face before. There's always been something familiar about Jonathan."

"Uncle Harry, I'm about to dig my nails into you."

"Young man, your given name is Tilden as well, isn't it?"

"Yes, sir."

"You're Tilden Beckwith."

"Yes, sir."

"And your father's name?"

"Stanton Beckwith, sir."

"Tilden, do you recall the name Schuyler Sturdevant?"

"Yes, sir. He's been to some of my mother's entertainments."

"What is his profession?"

"He . . . he's a gentleman, sir."

"He has no profession? How does he occupy his time?"

"Mr. Sturdevant enjoys coaching, sir. And I think he races trotters up in Harlem. On Sundays he and Father both play baseball for the Murray Hill Maroons."

"And prizefights. Does he go to prizefights?"

"Oh, I shouldn't think so, sir. Matches at his club, perhaps, but not a prizefight."

Gwen did dig her nails into Harry Sturdevant's hand. "What is going on here? Who is Schuyler?"

"My grandfather. This is incredible."

"But your grandfather was a doctor too."

"Not yet apparently. He had his fun first until he was thirty. Shhh! Now comes the tricky part." Sturdevant leaned forward on the edge of his chair. "Tilden, where are you at this moment?"

"In the park, sir."

"What park is that?"

"Gramercy Park."

"I see. And where is Jonathan?"

"You just blew it." Gwen punched him.

"Jonathan, sir?"

"Jonathan Corbin. Do you know that name?"

"No, sir."

"Oh God, Uncle Harry." Gwen felt a knotting in her stomach. "Oh God, it's what he's most afraid of. Not being able to get back."

"He seems all right. Shhh!"

"You'd better bring him out of it. Now."

"I didn't put him in it."

"You hypnotized him."

"No, Gwen. I didn't." Sturdevant was beginning to perspire.

Jonathan Corbin, the boy repeated to himself. The name did have a familiar ring to it but he was quite sure he did not know the person. The only Corbin he'd ever even heard of was the one married to President Grant's sister. That was Abel Corbin. He was one of the schemers who tried to help Jay Gould corner all the country's gold during the president's first term. Tilden didn't fully understand what they did, but he remembered that it was all his father and his father's associates talked about for quite a time because it nearly ruined some of them. Still, they seemed to admire the daring of the attempt. Though they did not admire Mr. Corbin. Father called him a covetous wretch with the morals of a slaver. And surely not Mr. Gould, whom Mother insists that neither she nor any other respectable hostess will receive.

Tilden glanced at the lengthening shadow of a Japanese maple tree and then at the western sky through its rust-colored leaves. Father would be home for supper soon. And Tilden had promised to read at least one more chapter of *Around the World in Eighty Days* and be prepared to recite at the table. He would have to ask this old gentleman to excuse him.

"Jonathan?"

Tilden blinked. He had not noticed the woman before. She was just suddenly there at the old gentleman's elbow and . . . my goodness . . . my goodness, she's wearing trousers. And a man's shirtwaist. And she's painted almost like a Sixth Avenue doxy.

"Jonathan! It's me. It's Gwen."

That name again. Now it seemed much more familiar. He wanted to tell her that he was assuredly not this

Jonathan and that he could not recall making her acquaintance but now she too began to seem familiar. And that was impossible. He had never seen a woman like her, never in his life, not even in books. A handsome woman to be sure. Quite handsome. But so bold. So direct in manner. So . . . almost manly. Oh . . . oh, my goodness. At the thought of her masculine dress and bearing, Tilden's eyes had dropped to her bosoms. They were moving. Her bosoms were jouncing as she walked toward him, rhythmically, like a carriage on its springs. Tilden felt his cheeks burst into flame, but he could not look away. Her shirtwaist was open a full four inches from the throat and he could see an expanse of flesh that was tinted almost golden, the way yachtsmen are tanned and ruddied by the sun. She was reaching for him now. Leaning down to him. Her fingertips cool and thrilling against his ears. He felt a thumping below his stomach as she drew his face closer, now touching, now pressed against a softness more wonderful than the finest goose-down pillow.

Tilden wanted to raise his hands, to touch her, to feel the firm warmth of her waist and hips, which he knew would not be bound within the bone and steel of a corset. On her breast there would be none of the wire forms resembling twin kitchen strainers such as he'd seen in his mother's room. None of the shifts and thick chemises he'd seen in the advertisements marked For the Woman of the House Only, which came in the mail from Macy's and A. T. Stewart's. But he did not raise his hands. He could not. He kept them folded tightly across his lap to contain the humiliation that would harden and rise in spite of his desperate wish that it should not. She must have seen it. She's angry. Upset. Shaking me. Oh, so embarrassing. Even the old gentleman, peering over her shoulder into my eyes. Oh, if I could die. Shaking me . . . wait . . . wait a second . . . "Gwen?"

"Thank God." She released his shoulders and straightened. Corbin brought his knuckles to his eyes.

"What's the matter? I dozed off?"

"Nothing's the matter." Sturdevant pinched Gwen's arm, unseen. "As you say, you dozed off. You looked like you were having a bad dream."

"Bad dream?" Corbin stretched and shook his head. "No. It was about Gwen, I think." That's right, he nodded to himself. Gwen and her uncle, too. But in the dream he didn't think he knew them. In the dream he'd been struck by what a sleek and sexy lady she was, just like the first time he'd ever laid eyes on her. It's funny how you can get so used to the good things in your life you almost stop seeing them sometimes. "It wasn't a bad dream at all," he said to her. "I think I was falling in love with you all over again."

"I'm going to ask you both to spend the night." Sturdevant gathered up his notes to make room for Cora Starling's sandwich tray. "There's a guest room with twin beds upstairs." He waved off any question of propriety before Corbin could express it. "Gwen knows the way. It will be well if all three of us remained in close contact for a while, especially the two of you. You, Gwen, seem to be an effective anchor for Jonathan."

Corbin was barely listening. He was near dozing again. An early night of it sounded good.

Bits of his dream were coming back to him now. A fuzzy detail here and there. The Japanese maple tree, the small park, a curious feeling of intimacy with a long-dead president, and his nose felt sore. He could even recall things that were ancillary to the dream but not part of it. He remembered, for example, that there was a book he was supposed to read, and although he forgot its title, his mind gave him a glimpse of the young man's room and the big oak table-desk on which he'd left it. There was a leather mark in place about halfway through its pages. He remembered a desk lamp that burned oil. It had a wide brass base with a slot for pencils, and it had two shades of green glass. On the wall behind it was an animal skin someone had given him. And pinned behind the animal skin were two hidden copies of the *Police Gazette,* which were the major reason why he wasn't as far along on his book as he should have been.

These memories, as they came, were not unpleasant. Not at all. He remembered that Gwen seemed troubled when she aroused him from his dream. That she was alarmed. But the dream was fine. He would not have minded staying there a while. It was a happy place and it was summer. Especially, it was summer.

"Do you want to freshen up, Jonathan?" Sturdevant's voice.

"Hmmm?"

"You'll find most of what you need in the guest room. The soup and sandwiches will keep. Actually, I'd like a few minutes to myself."

Alone in his study, Harry Sturdevant sat with both hands folded under his chin. He wished he hadn't given up his pipe, speaking of tranquilizers. Nothing like a pipe to help the mind settle and focus.

Where to start? His own bookshelves, he supposed, as long as there's no such thing as an all-night library. But what was he to look for? Was he to begin checking facts, verifying the many tidbits of detail offered voluntarily or otherwise by young Mr. Corbin? To what purpose? Did he believe Jonathan or not? He'd believed him without reservation until a few minutes ago, because he could imagine no reason why Jonathan Corbin would concoct such an elaborate and superbly researched fraud. But that was before the name of Tilden Beckwith arose. Before there was a possible motive. Money. Many millions of dollars.

A young man, let's suppose, discovers by whatever means that he bears an uncanny resemblance to a long-deceased man of wealth. He decides to claim a blood relationship. Better yet, he decides to claim that he is the only true heir. Someone switched babies, he claims. He relies on the threat of scandal and waits for his offer of hush money. But who would care nowadays? Least of all the Beckwiths, who are hardly pillars of propriety themselves. They'd laugh at such an extortion attempt. It's remotely possible that they'd pay a few dollars to avoid the nuisance of tedious meetings with attorneys, but they'd be much more likely to ignore him. Or slap him down.

Sturdevant was on his feet. No, he decided. There is simply nothing about Jonathan that would suggest deceit, especially a conspiracy this complex. Too complex to work. Murphy's Law and all that. And it would take a superb actor to pull it off. Jonathan, as far as we know, hasn't been an actor since his kindergarten Christmas pageant. It would also take a much more subtle turn of mind than Jonathan seems to have. Collegiate boxers with banged-up noses are rarely paragons of finesse. Which reminds me . . .

He stepped around the table to the bookshelves that were devoted to sports. There he found an encyclopedia of boxing and opened it to its index. Flood, John. Pages 107 to 109, photo on page 115. Sturdevant flipped forward. Ah yes, his memory had been correct. Flood, the Bull's Head Terror, fought John L. Sullivan, bare knuckles, in May of 1881 on a barge off Yonkers. Probably with a fully rigged cutter standing by in case the police had been insufficiently bribed in advance. Knocked out in eight rounds, though he did much better than anyone else who faced Sullivan that year. Sturdevant wondered whether his grandfather had seen the fight. It's possible, he supposed. But if he had gone to an illegal prizefight, as opposed to a boxing match at his club, he probably would have disguised himself and kept quiet about it afterward. They were such tawdry affairs in those days. More like a dogfight than an athletic contest. Even young Tilden of Gramercy Park seemed to know that. Biting, kicking, wrestling, even gouging. Whether a fight was allowed to finish often depended on whose supporters were better armed.

Roosevelt. There was a Roosevelt biography here someplace.

Sturdevant found a faded volume whose gilt printing had long since worn away. Roosevelt boxed. Sturdevant knew that. Boxing team at Harvard. Sparred for exercise virtually until his death. But did he ever live near Gramercy Park? Sturdevant found the reference he was looking for. Yes. Early years in his family's home on Twentieth Street, just off Fifth Avenue. That would be about five blocks from Gramercy Park. Not exactly next-door neighbors but young Tilden never said that. Only that they'd both learned to fight from John Flood in the stables back of the Rhinelander house where Flood probably worked when he wasn't driving a beer truck and fighting pass-the-hat matches in the saloons along his delivery route. As for Roosevelt, his family, Sturdevant saw, did move to a new home on Fifty-seventh Street in the summer of 1875. Number 6. And Roosevelt remained in that home until he married and returned there after the death of his first wife. That address would have him only a block from the Plaza and only two blocks from the Osborne Apartments at about the time the original Tilden Beckwith seems to have lived there. Did they remain friends? Jonathan didn't say. Or doesn't know. Not yet, at least.

Biographies.

Sturdevant ran his finger across the bottom row of books until it stopped at a red-bound copy of *Who's Who*. There it is. Tilden Beckwith II. He hadn't thought of that name in years. Chairman of Beckwith Enterprises. Which includes Beckwith Hotels, Beckwith Realty, Beckwith Land Development, and an assortment of smaller companies—probably contractors, architects, and the like. Sits on the board of the investment firm of Beckwith, Stone & Waring, which used to be Beckwith & Company, which is where the family fortune began. No other board seats, however. Unusual. A man in his position would normally have a list of a dozen or more. Certainly on that of his bank. No charitable involvement, either. No committees, no hospital boards. Not much of a listing, really, for a captain of commerce from old money. Why? Is he lazy? Stupid? On the other hand, neither has ever been a barrier to sitting on corporate boards. All one must be is a major stockholder. Attended Harvard, it says. There's another thing. Not graduated. Attended. Which probably means he didn't finish. No military service, either. No clubs listed, not even the Harvard Club. All in all an embarrassing entry for *Who's Who*. He really isn't anybody. Just a rich man's son. Yet here he is, chairman of Beckwith Enterprises. Tillie, Sturdevant mused. I believe they used to call him Tillie.

Sturdevant closed the book and returned it to its slot. His hand moved to a much smaller volume bound in blue cloth. The *Social Register* might have more, he thought, assuming the Beckwiths bothered to subscribe. Ah, yes. Beckwith, Tilden II. Homes in New York and Palm Beach. Married to the former Elvira Payson. Two children, Huntington and Barbara, then more of the same about Harvard and Beckwith Enterprises. Let's see. Huntington, named after the grandfather, would be about Jonathan's age and Barbara not much older than Gwen. Otherwise, very little information there, either. Sturdevant was about to put the blue book away when his eye drifted to a listing it had almost missed because it began at the top of the next column. Hello, look at this. Beckwith, Ella Huntington. Ella. Of Greenwich, Connecticut, of all places. Sturdevant decided to make a phone call or two.

"Uncle Harry?" The door opened following Gwen's knock. Sturdevant waved her in as he nodded a series of uh-huhs into the telephone crooked at his neck. He thanked the person on the other end, suggested lunch sometime soon, and replaced the receiver on its cradle.

"Uncle Harry," she asked, "you weren't just telling someone about Jonathan, were you?"

"His name didn't arise," he assured her. "I was refreshing my memory about the Beckwiths. How is he, by the way?"

"A bit dreamy, otherwise fine. If you don't mind, I'm going to take our sandwiches upstairs and then get him into bed. After that I might run over to my place and pick up a few things."

"Can't that wait until morning? I have everything here except a change of clothing."

"I'll see how Jonathan settles in." Gwen pushed the door until the lock clicked. "Uncle Harry," she asked, "what was all that about Tilden Beckwith? How did you come up with that name?"

"I knew him." Sturdevant brightened. "It's the most remarkable thing. Ever since you first introduced me to Jonathan I've had a feeling we've met before. He is the absolute image of a young Tilden Beckwith, including that broken nose and the scarred eyebrow, which Tilden apparently got from young Todd Fisher. How did Jonathan get his, by the way?"

"I never asked. College boxing, I suppose. Uncle Harry, don't you find it almost unbelievable that you happened to know this Tilden Beckwith?"

"Not at all. Almost everyone knew him back when I was a young man."

"He was famous?"

Sturdevant shook his head. "Everyone more or less like me," he corrected himself, reluctant to say "Everyone in my set." "He died during the war at about my age. Some sort of accidental fall in his office." Sturdevant gestured toward the telephone, as if to indicate the source of this recollection. "Which is ironic because he was always very graceful and athletic. A great sports fan too, especially of the New York Giants. His box up at the Polo Grounds wasn't far from ours. We'd also see him up at the old Saint Nicholas Arena for the Friday night fights and at just about every championship match at Madison Square Garden."

"I don't believe this, Uncle Harry."

"New York is a big city, Gwen dear, but the circles within it can be very small. Avid followers of a particular sport tend to meet and know each other. Beyond a certain income level, they tend to congregate in the same public places. The baseball and boxing crowds of today hang out at Gallagher's Steak House, among others. Go back sixty years and that crowd gathered at the Hoffman House bar."

"You're not going to tell me you saw Tilden there."

"I won't." He smiled. "I was only there a few times as a very young man and then only with my father. I did know Oscar, however, the man who stopped Jonathan's . . . Tilden's fight from turning into a Pier Six brawl. Now there's someone who was famous. He became Oscar of the Waldorf when the first Waldorf-Astoria opened back in the nineties, and he must have been a fixture there for thirty years. Not many people knew Oscar's last name. Jonathan would have known if he'd researched it, which is why I questioned him about addressing anyone by his first name in those days. He did not know it. Oscar's last name, incidentally, was Tschirky, T-s-c-h-i-r-k-y, pronounced approximately 'Jerky.' It would not do to have a maître d'hôtel at the Waldorf-Astoria, let alone the Hoffman House, who is called Mr. Jerky."

Sturdevant noted a look of mild impatience on Gwen's face with what she must have considered a bit of pointless trivia. Oscar's name, of course, was not significant in itself. However, the fact that Jonathan seemed to recall him as Oscar of the Waldorf was the single most puzzling facet of this whole bizarre episode. Genetic memory is genetic memory. One can only carry memories that an antecedent had *prior* to the conception of a descendant. The 1888 memories of the storm, the woman's death, the Hoffman House scene, were sufficiently dramatic, even traumatic, and sufficiently close to the conception of a child by Margaret that they might well have been retained in genetic imprints. But why should Jonathan remember anything that happened later? For that matter, why should he have this fixation about Connecticut if Margaret moved there only after Tilden's son was conceived? Perhaps they'd find out tomorrow.

"Speaking of names," he told Gwen, "there is not only a currently living Tilden Beckwith, of the hotel-owning Beckwiths, but he also has a sister named Ella. Care to guess where Ella lives?"

"Not Greenwich."

"Greenwich, indeed."

"We can go see her. Tomorrow."

"Not so fast, dear. If Jonathan is in fact a direct blood descendant of the original Tilden Beckwith, and if the original Ella had a child by Ansel Carling, no Beckwith from 1888 forward is legitimately a Beckwith. They will not greet that news with enthusiasm. That's assuming they don't know it already and are not keeping it a closely guarded family skeleton. Besides, the Beckwiths by all accounts are not particularly nice people."

"Your telephone call?"

Sturdevant nodded. "Tilden's son, or rather Ella's, was Huntington Beckwith. My friend thinks Huntington was Ella's family name. I remember Huntington Beckwith although I never actually met him. He was a cold, hard, taciturn man who would take anything that wasn't nailed down and pry up anything that was. A thoroughly unlovely man, no friends, belonged to no clubs, not that he didn't try to join a few. He was even blackballed by the University Club, which is about as exclusive as the state of New Jersey. In some respects he was a lot like Jay Gould, whose name also keeps popping up, although Jay Gould made no effort whatever to be accepted by polite society. Huntington, however, kept trying and was repeatedly rebuffed, which made him all the meaner."

"When was all this happening?" Gwen asked. "It would have to have been during the twenties and thirties."

"It was. Why do you ask?"

"You said Tilden, Margaret's Tilden, was very well known and liked. If Huntington was a part of New York society at the same time, how could that society have accepted one and not the other?"

"It doesn't seem to have been a problem," Sturdevant answered. "I, for example, must have seen Tilden Beckwith fifty times at one event or another. I never recall seeing Tilden with his 'son' or his 'grandson.' It appears that although he saw to Huntington's education and gave him a place in a part of the family business, their estrangement was otherwise total and one never invited Tilden and his son to the same party. No doubt an occasional hostess wondered why this seemed to be an established rule, but more likely she counted her blessings. Whatever inevitable whispers there might have been concerning the nature of their rift are now largely forgotten, but you can be sure that at least some of them focused on the physical dissimilarity between the two men."

"You mean they guessed that Huntington was a bastard."

"In more ways than one."

"How bad could he have been? He found a woman who'd marry him. And she had two kids by him, right? Another Tilden and an Ella."

Harry Sturdevant shrugged. "It's said that there's no man so mean that a woman or a dog won't love him. No offense. As for Ella the 'granddaughter,' I don't recall ever laying eyes on her or hearing anything about her. I've seen Tillie at one affair or another but never really paid much attention to him. That's sort of interesting, you know. You'd think that I'd recall having compared him unfavorably to his grandfather—he was actually just a less satanic version of Huntington—but I don't. All by itself, my mind seems to have separated the two men completely. That may be why I was so slow in making this connection unaided. By the way, there's still another generation of Beckwiths. Eric Ludlow, the friend I called, says Tillie's wife, one Elvira Payson, now lives in an alcoholic haze at the Beckwith Palm Beach home. Elvira produced two more Beckwiths, another son and daughter. The son also lives in Greenwich, where he's called Chip, if you can believe that, and is known to cheat at both yacht racing and bridge in his own sober moments, which are increasingly few. The daughter, named Barbara Beckwith, seems to have disappeared shortly after graduating from college."

Gwen folded her arms across her chest and shuddered. Sturdevant raised an eyebrow. It was the second time he'd seen her do that in the past five minutes.

"What is it, Gwen?"

"Nothing," she said. But she'd hesitated first.

"If you have an insight, I'd like to hear it."

"Nothing like that. It's just remarkable that there can be so many bad seeds growing out of anything so really lovely as the feelings between Tilden and Margaret. Or out of Jonathan." Gwen Leamas paused thoughtfully. "See what's happening? I'm beginning to think of Jonathan as almost the same man as Tilden. The nice Tilden. And I like them both very much. And I'm afraid for both of them."

"You're clear, aren't you, that the Huntington seed has no relationship whatsoever to Tilden and Margaret?"

"I understand that."

"And that Tilden and Margaret started a line that very probably ends with Jonathan. We can either fly to Chicago and try to trace it back, or go to Greenwich tomorrow and try to trace it forward."

Gwen nodded, looking away, then shivered a third time.

"Gwen, dear. What *is* it?"

"This Huntington Beckwith. He's dead, isn't he?"

"For at least twenty years, I think. Why do you ask?"

"We were being followed today. Jonathan knew it too."

"By whom?" Sturdevant frowned. "Did you see him?"

"There was a man in a black hat and coat. I think I might have seen him several times during the afternoon without it really registering. Then back on Fifty-eighth Street Jonathan suddenly turned, quite furious, as if he knew this man was there. That's when I knew it as well. But we didn't see anybody."

"Who did Jonathan think it was? Did he say?"

"No." Another long pause, her lips moving tentatively. "There is this man, who's always been after Jonathan, in his mind."

"Gwen"—Harry Sturdevant looked directly into

his niece's eyes—"who do you think was following you?"

"I know I'm wrong."

"Who, Gwen?"

"I think . . . I feel that it was Huntington Beckwith."

"Even though you know he's dead."

"His ghost, then."

"Or his hatred."

It was useless, Lesko knew, to go to bed like normal. For one thing, he had heartburn. He wasn't sure whether it was from the duck sauce he poured all over his ribs or from listening to the jarring ring of the phone while he was trying to eat his Chinese and watch the Islanders blow three power plays in a row all at the same time. Eighteen rings he counted last time. Since then it's been quiet. Too quiet. Like they say in the war movies just before the Japs charge but you already know they've been creeping up in the dark through the jungle. Lesko swallowed the last chalky quarter inch from a bottle of Pepto-Bismol, then followed it with a single Tums he found in a raincoat pocket.

How long has it been since the phone stopped? Lesko looked at his watch. A little over an hour. But now what? Would Dancer really say the hell with it and wait until morning? No, he won't. Too uptight. His choices are going to be to come over or to send someone else. If he comes over it'll be to try to make a deal that will get him the notebook before Lesko can stash it and to buy himself enough time to cover his tracks one way or the other. The best way to do that is to have no more Lesko because Dancer has got to figure old Raymond sees an annuity in here someplace. Which means he's got to send somebody over anyway so he might as well skip the first step. At least that's the way to bet. But if that happens, and Lesko is just sitting here waiting for them and if someone ends up getting shot, even assuming it's them, he's still going to have the cops and the reporters crawling all over him for the next few days. Maybe it's better I wait down in the street, Lesko decided. Maybe it's better I go sit in Mr. Makowski's car which he leaves unlocked so the junkies can see there's nothing inside worth smashing a window for.

It took Lesko thirty minutes to reach the street. The first five were gun-in-hand as he checked the stairway in the hall outside before going back and locking his door. Next he slowly climbed four flights to his roof, where he relaxed on seeing no fresh footprints in the snow. From the roof's edge he spent another ten minutes adjusting his eyes to the darkness and surveying the street below. Checking cars was easy, since only two on the entire block had clear windshields. The one alley most suitable for a potential shooter to watch and wait in was directly across the street and it was clean. Up toward Queens Boulevard, Lesko saw a single pedestrian come into view on the far sidewalk—a big man, heavyset like himself. That looks like what's-his-name, he thought, the bus driver who lives down next to Mrs. Hannigan. But in the dark he could have been Lesko to anyone down there who was looking for Lesko. The ex-cop held his service revolver in both hands and with it tracked the bus driver's progress down the street. No one, nothing, stirred. No one stepped out of a doorway for a closer look or pointed a finger. Lesko waited until the man was safely inside his front door, then crossed over to the adjoining building and made his way down to the street. At the end of thirty minutes he was cursing Mr. Makowski, who had locked his car after all. At the end of an hour, now on numbing feet in the alley across from his building, it began to dawn on Lesko that this was a very stupid idea. No one, he realized, was coming after him. He wasn't the problem. In Dancer's mind, he knew, Raymond Lesko was an annoyance and a potential expense, but he was not really the priority problem. The priority was Corbin. Lesko half ran toward the subway on Queens Boulevard.

NINE

TWIN BEDS.

"Twin beds are the latest thing."

Corbin had never liked them much. Now he hated them. The beds had made no particular impression on him when he entered Harry Sturdevant's guest room and when Cora Starling, who now seemed to be watching him closely, turned them down at one corner and fluffed the pillows. If anything, he appreciated that twin beds would probably make Gwen's uncle more comfortable about their sharing a room together in his house.

"Everyone is talking about twin beds and I intend to be among the first to have them."

All the other furnishings, Corbin noted dimly, had a turn-of-the-century look. Not Victorian, really, like the Homestead, but almost as old and probably more valuable. Had Gwen told her uncle about the Homestead, he wondered, and about some of the peculiar

thoughts and memories it stirred up? He didn't know.
Maybe Dr. Sturdevant got the idea all by himself of
putting them together into a room whose furnishings
could help to send him back in time or to bring someone else forward. Corbin didn't know that, either. But
it wasn't going to work. He was just too beat. He
waited patiently until Mrs. Starling finished her fussing
with the towels and washcloths, and when she closed
the door he kicked off his shoes and settled back
against the cool pillow.

*"I will not be denied this, Tilden. I've made quite
enough sacrifices as a good little wife and I've seen far
too little consideration in return."*

Corbin jerked his head off the pillow and brought
his hand to his eyes. Get up, he told himself. Do a few
push-ups or splash cold water on your face. He knew
what was happening to him. Half-dreams, he called
them. The kind that come when you're not fully asleep
and you're not fully awake. The trouble is you can
never get yourself to wake up all the way. Four in the
morning is when these usually come. What time is it
now? It can't even be nine o'clock.

*"To think that I gave up Philadelphia, where I
would probably be the wife of a Drexel by now, for the
excitement and glamour of New York society only to
find I've wed a man who prefers a baseball game to a
cotillion and who has no greater goal in life than to see
to the construction of an appallingly ugly railroad for
the convenience of a lot of smelly factory workers."*

He did warn me, Corbin thought. He did say we
might have different views concerning what constitutes
worthwhile achievement and, for that matter, who constitutes a worthwhile acquaintance. Wait a minute.
Who warned me? Teddy. Teddy Roosevelt? That can't
be right.

"But thank you. I'm grateful for a friend's concern.
However, she's actually quite excited about the ele-

vated project and the development of the West Side. And she loves to hear me talk about athletics. And as for my acquaintances, the most appealing thing of all about New York to Miss Ella is its social democracy. You know the saying. In Boston they ask how much you know, in New York they ask how much you have, and in Philadelphia they ask who your grandfather was. She is more than eager to meet new and vital people who've made their own mark, people who would never be received in Philadelphia. Men like Cyrus Field and Jim Brady. Even pariahs like Gould and Russell Sage."

"These men are all rich and powerful, Tilden. Not all of your friends are either. Even you and I have had to learn to look for a man's worth in his heart and in the honesty of his gaze. Ella will not easily overcome a lifetime of Philadelphia insularity and a congenital contempt for any man whose hand is not soft and any woman who owns less than a dozen gowns from Paris."

"I think that you do not know her, Teddy."

"And I think that I've probably said too much."

"She's quite beautiful."

"She is that. Yes."

"And she has a lot of fire. I know that there have been whispers about her. I am aware that there are some who consider her to be headstrong and willful and selfish. I know also that she has a worrying habit of running about unchaperoned and yet no real misconduct has ever been linked with her name. These are youthful high spirits, Teddy. If she were other than high-spirited she would have remained entombed on Philadelphia's Main Line forever. Good Lord, if only you could have seen some of the wispy, swooning dullards my father has dragooned me into meeting, I believe you'd look a good deal more favorably upon my choice of Ella Huntington."

"Hah!" Roosevelt flashed a grin so huge it seemed there were more teeth than face. "I believe I would, my friend. By George, I believe I would."

"You'll stand up with me then."

"Saint Thomas's on the eighth. Depend on it, sir." Teddy Roosevelt offered his hand. "Depend on it."

"Ella, you didn't actually believe that babies were born in cabbage patches, did you?"

"No. Not actually. But this? This simply can't be how it's done."

"Adam and Eve were the first. Married couples have deviated very little since then."

"Do not mock me, sir."

"Have you never seen a servant throw water upon two dogs, one dog seeming to climb upon the back of the other?"

"Yes. It was because they were being filthy."

"They were mating, Ella. It is how little puppies come into being. Is it possible that no one has ever explained such things to you?"

"I do not know about New York, but it is hardly a fit subject in Philadelphia."

"I believe that. Sad to say, I believe that."

Several nights and one visit from a doctor passed before Ella became persuaded that Tilden's disgusting suggestion might have some legitimacy. She yielded, rigidly at first, biting hard as if she were being flogged and trying not to breathe or make a sound. Soon, however, she became tolerant, almost willing. The martyred protests decreased in length if not in frequency and her expressions of disgust subtly shifted from the act itself to Tilden's apparent incapacity to control his animal urges. Ella, though it would never do to let Tilden know, not Tilden or anyone, was beginning to like it. She was discovering that for all her revulsion toward the messy physical act, it sometimes produced a most remarkable inner thrill. She kept this secret strictly to herself, quite sure that no other woman could possibly experience such a sensation.

Tilden, for his part, was thoroughly confused by her behavior. The same woman who began as a block of stone had progressed to being critical of the way he deported himself in the bedchamber. After dismissing him to his own twin bed, which he minded less and less, she would make the most maddeningly obscure references to the quality of the act that had just taken place between them. Tilden had no idea what she was talking about, nor would she express herself plainly on so delicate a subject. She would simply and aggravatingly point out that it was not the business of a woman to instruct a man on the business of being manly. As for Tilden, it was only a matter of months before marital congress with Ella became an altogether unpleasurable experience.

Unlike the ladies at the fancy houses he'd sometimes visited as an unmarried blade, though with considerable trepidation because he'd heard stories of diseases that led to insanity, Ella showed no interest at all in pleasing him. The ladies at Georgiana Hastings's house at least pretended to be pleased by him. And interested in his conversation. Which was another thing. Ella's interest in any of Tilden's activities, any at all, seemed to have evaporated the moment the wedding vows were spoken. She now considered many of his recreational activities to be loutish. His business activities were dull and tedious, to say the least. His reluctance to ingratiate himself within the correct social circles, circles in which his family was already well established, was both selfish and stupid. She was quick to notice other men who knew how to seize opportunity and wring full advantage from it. Some of Gould's associates, for example, to say nothing of Gould himself. Imagine a man being denied a box at the Academy of

Music, then determining to destroy the Academy of Music by organizing and building the new Metropolitan Opera House in competition with it. Imagine a man being denied membership in the New York Yacht Club, then promptly founding the American Yacht Club up in Westchester. There was a man. A powerful man. Gould himself had neither the time nor the eye for ladies, more's the pity, but there was no shortage of men in his circle who did. Strong, daring men. Buccaneer types like the heroes of Robert Louis Stevenson. Polished men like Stevenson's Dr. Jekyll and dangerous men like his Mr. Hyde. Men like Ansel Carling. What was Tilden to a man like Ansel Carling?

Although Ella now found room for improvement in every aspect of Tilden's being, she resented most of all his decision to choose as their residence that ridiculous apartment. An apartment, heaven save us! Not a home on Fifth Avenue, not even a home off Fifth Avenue, but an apartment. An apartment on the West Side in the bargain. So far to the west she might as well have stayed in Philadelphia. A scant two blocks from the Ninth Avenue niggertown, so close one must either close one's windows when the breeze came from the west or endure the scent of musk all day.

It wasn't, after all, as if Tilden could not afford a proper home. He and his father owned several excellent properties in and out of the city and Tilden has earned enough on his New York Elevated stock alone to buy a house at least as grand as the one that silly cowboy Roosevelt has down the way, practically right on Fifth Avenue. But instead, mouthing some nonsense about the air being cleaner this close to the park and the two of us having more time together if we kept some distance between ourselves and the "social straitjacket" as he so coarsely refers to the communion of everyone worth knowing, he entombs us in this stone warren filled to its seams with nobodies. There is even an *actor* in residence on the fourth floor, that Nat Goodwin man who compounds his disreputability by being divorced every second or third year and Tilden actually *speaks* to him in that steam elevator which, by the way, is certain to blow us all into eternity at any moment. As if the actor were not enough, Tilden had the temerity to invite a prize-ring ruffian, an Irishman no less, into our parlor and sit him down with a brandy in my fine crystal until I made it clear that he might be more comfortable in other surroundings. And on the subject of other surroundings, if it is my penance to live, however temporarily, in an apartment, the apartment building chosen might at least have been one with a modicum of cachet such as the Navarro Flats, where Ansel Carling keeps his suite of bachelor rooms. Speaking of manliness. Speaking of breeding. Speaking, not least, of power. It radiates from him. I see it in his eyes when he looks at me and I feel it on my cheeks and I feel it here, deep inside me.

At about this time, Ella had begun to come upon Ansel Carling while abroad shopping or on calling day, which was Tuesday in her part of the city. Calling day was another social ritual that Tilden, in his ignorance, considered an absurd waste of time. One day each week, several hours were set aside during which a household would receive callers, mostly women and children, the men being occupied in business or bastioned at their clubs. A call would last fifteen minutes, little more and little less and regulated by some inner clock since it was considered unmannerly to glance at a timepiece. Mrs. Sherwood's book of etiquette also prescribed those topics of conversation which were acceptable, ruling out all that might possibly give offense, and effectively leaving only the weather. During the first months of their marriage, Tilden gamely made these rounds in order to help establish Ella but, like most men, found it exhausting to mouth expressions of appreciation of the charms of each season at one stiff parlor after another and was glad when he could consider his duty done.

"It is *not* done," Ella told him. "If one is to remain *en évidence,* one must call. If one is to appear on the better guest lists, one must be known at the better homes."

"But I *am* known, Ella," Tilden pointed out. "We have not gone a single week in the past year without at least two stultifying dinner parties at which everyone expresses restrained enthusiasm for the wines and the sauces and inquires about my day while having not the slightest interest in my reply."

"That is another thing. At the Whiteheads' the other night, your five-minute account of having your shoes polished was not at all amusing."

"You complain, madam, when I speak of business and when I speak of athletics. If I am to be boring, I might as well try to make an art of it."

"You are quite hopeless, sir."

"What has happened to you, Ella?" he asked quietly. "You were once so gay. Could two years in New York have taken the joy out of you or is the love of life something you put on and take off with the rest of your wardrobe as it suits your purpose?"

"I have no idea what you mean, sir."

"No, I don't suppose you have."

"It is late, Tilden." Ella allowed her face to soften. "I suppose you'll be wanting to share my bed tonight."

"No, Ella," he answered, "as a matter of fact, I will not."

I dare say Ansel Carling would, she thought, angrily at first, and then quivering inwardly at the daring of that notion. There is also a man who understands the need to call and to cultivate. It may be true, as they say, that Mr. Carling has received more than his share of cards sealed in envelopes. But these are from weaklings. Anyone who uses the language of calling cards to discontinue a relationship with a man like Mr. Carling is simply less of a person than he. They fear his strength. They fear those eyes. Those marvelous jungle-cat eyes.

It was not long before coincidence found Ella and Carling calling at the homes of mutual acquaintances at very nearly the same hour, and not long after that before they were discreetly lunching together at a café in Greenwich Village where waiters sang Italian opera. Soon he was walking with her around his building, explaining the several Spanish architectural styles of the Navarro Flats and the motifs of its various lobbies. Soon after that, she was in Carling's library viewing his small but quite exquisite collection of illuminated manuscripts, one of which he'd snatched practically from the hand of J. P. Morgan, whose agent was late to an auction, and his not inconsiderable collection of diamond studs, which were no less polished than Ansel himself. And no less hard.

In this way, ever more boldly and recklessly, in only the second year of her marriage to Tilden, Ella's ultimate destruction set its roots. Tilden suspected nothing, noting only that ever less about him seemed attractive or even tolerable to Ella. The announcement to her that he must voyage to London for ten weeks on a business matter brought an unexpected flicker of excitement to her eyes. For the briefest moment he thought that she would beg to accompany him, and, in fact, he had prepared himself to argue any such request by citing the dangers and discomforts of a two-week crossing in March. These reasons, in any case, would not be true ones. Business aside, a solitary crossing aboard a packet steamer in the company of rough-hewn men seemed a welcome tonic for a soul that found little peace of late. But Ella denied him the scene and speech he'd rehearsed for this occasion. Her interest, far from being in going with him, seemed to be more in the fact of his prolonged absence. Tilden, perversely, found himself both annoyed and disappointed. On the day of his departure there was only his father to see him off.

Ten weeks later, the trip a modest success, Tilden returned to a New York that had sprung miraculously to life with the flowers of May, although winter held fast inside his flat at the Osborne. He plunged back into his work. On a pretty afternoon a week later, he chose to leave his office at five, two hours short of his usual time, and to forsake the Sixth Avenue Elevated in favor of a long and invigorating walk up Fifth Avenue with perhaps a stop along the way for a sherry at one of his clubs. The nearer his stroll brought him toward Ella, however, the more doleful Tilden became. On the corner of Thirty-sixth Street, he paused for no reason that he knew. Georgiana Hastings's parlor house, he realized fully, was only a few doors down, but to stop in there now that he was married would be quite inappropriate. But perhaps not, he argued. Georgiana's sherry was as good as could be found elsewhere and the conversation a good deal more cheerful. An hour at most.

"Good evening, sir." A butler named Wilkins brightened with recognition. "Mrs. Hastings will be very pleased to see you again."

"Thank you, Wilkins." Tilden, warmed at once by the welcome, held out his walking stick and hat. "I was just passing by and I thought—"

"Is that Tilden Beckwith?" A soft Southern accent flowed like honey down the stairway past the butler's shoulder. The glint of silver shoes and the skirt of a brocade gown from Worth of Paris came into view, then the narrow waist and bosom and welcoming smile of the proprietress of New York's finest sporting house. Georgiana was perhaps thirty-five years old, though she'd aged not at all since last he'd seen her, and from

Charleston, it was said. Her hair, piled high, was the color of chestnuts before roasting, and her skin was like risen cream to which a drop or two of coffee had been added.

"Georgiana." Tilden grinned, stepping forward and taking the ungloved hand she offered. "How wonderfully well you look." More than well, she was quite lovely. She was also the first woman ever to have taken Tilden to her bed. He remembered gratefully how patient she'd been, how kind and encouraging, with the clumsy and painfully bashful young man soon to be graduated from Harvard.

"Are you here as a client," she asked, "or dare I hope that you've come to see an old friend?"

"In truth I was rather tugged here in passing," he told her. "It is a gentle place, Georgiana. A happy place. But not as a client, I think. Perhaps for a glass of your very fine Malmsey."

"A happier place than some others, I gather. Come"—she took his arm in hers—"sit with me."

She steered him toward the quietest of three sitting rooms on the first floor of her handsome town house. In one of the others Tilden caught a glimpse of a very wealthy yachtsman he knew, and a city official with Boss Croker's Tammany machine, and another man he thought might have been a judge. The latter was playing whist with a petite blond girl in a middy costume who seemed no more than thirteen. Annie, he recalled. Yes. Little Annie. She had looked thirteen when last he saw her as well, on the occasion of the bachelor party forced upon him by his friends, but he'd learned at that time that she was easily past twenty. Great heavens, he thought, does no one age in this place? Does no one frown?

"I see an uncommon weariness in your eyes, Tilden." Georgiana led him across a velvet carpet to a small sofa that sat beneath two excellent paintings and an expensive gilt-framed mirror. A grand piano filled one corner of the room. "You are well, I hope? Your father is well?"

"His vigor isn't what it might be. He's been fighting the effects of cholera for twenty years now. But he speaks of retiring to the Carolinas soon."

"Cholera." She nodded. "It was aboard one of Cyrus Field's cable ships, was it not?"

"What a memory you have, Georgiana. When must I have told you that? Five years ago, at least."

"A young man's pride in his father becomes him, Tilden. The laying of a telegraph cable all the way to Liverpool is a feat that dizzies one even to think on it."

"The feat was Mr. Field's," Tilden corrected her.

"But your father did assist; he secured the necessary funds when others thought the notion to be lunacy, and he did it at great peril to his health. Let that be our toast to him, Tilden. To that and to a rest in the Carolinas, well earned."

A tray had appeared, brought by Wilkins, although Tilden had seen no signal. He waited while the butler poured the garnet-colored liquid and then picked up both glasses, handing one to Georgiana Hastings.

"And what of you, Tilden?" she asked, barely touching the sherry to her lips. "Now that you are here, how can I please you?"

"You have already with your kindness, dear lady."

Georgiana reached for his hand and squeezed it. "It has been a long time since we've had a good talk. There is more than one way to find comfort in my house." That remark was as near as Georgiana thought proper to asking him outright about Ella. One did not ask a client, not even an affectionate friend such as Tilden, about his wife or about his other personal baggage unless the client first showed a wish to unburden himself. But Tilden had come to her, more than a year ago, for her advice in understanding the mysteries of womanhood, and of the art of pleasing his new wife in their bedchamber, and of the sullen moods that overtake her every fourth week. And then, not two weeks past in this very house, Georgiana had overheard Ella's name and Tilden's mentioned amid sneering laughter. She heard boasting of the ease with which Ella had been seduced, and of her contempt for the man she married, who was at that time abroad. They were Jay Gould's people. Something else was said, which Georgiana did not quite catch. It was about business. Business secrets, she thought. Cyrus Field's name had been mentioned. Could Ella possibly have been betraying her husband's business affairs as well? Georgiana did not know. In any case, the men were told that their patronage would not be welcomed in future.

"A bite of supper then," she offered. "What would you say to a plate of cold roast beef?"

"Nothing for me, thank you." He snapped open his watch. "Actually, I should be getting home."

"I will not permit it." The young madam held fast to his hand. "No friend of mine may leave my house with any weight, however small, upon his heart. Perhaps some soothing music." She gestured toward the Steinway. "You are partial to Bach, as I remember."

"You've learned to play?" he enthused, glad of a suggestion that did not require conversation.

"No new tricks for this old dog, I fear. Although I'll tell you in confidence that I've been plucking away at a harp when no one is listening. No, there is a young lady who has come to stay with me. She plays quite beautifully."

Once again, Tilden saw no nod or glance in Wilkins' direction, but in the foyer outside the parlor door he saw the butler's arm reach for a bell cord and give it a silent tug.

.   .   .

She was wonderful. She sat shyly, nervously, at the piano at first, never once meeting Tilden's eyes, forcing a small but pretty smile in answer to Georgiana's encouraging cough. But when her fingers caressed the keyboard and the melodic whisper of a Bach cantata caused even the chatter in the other room to cease, a look of dreamy contentment came over her. Tilden could see Wilkins at the door, thrilling to each exquisite counterpoint, his right hand twitching as if it held a baton. Little Annie, the childlike whore, appeared at the butler's elbow, beaming and shaking her fist in a soundless cheer. The slender girl at the piano looked up at her with a generous blushing smile, which to Tilden seemed to brighten the room by the light of another dozen mirrors. She completed the piece and, not waiting for applause, moved smoothly into a medley from the "Well-tempered Clavier" and several fugues, which heretofore Tilden had heard only in concert halls.

"Where did you find her?" he whispered.

"Wait." Georgiana patted his hand. She brought her fingertips together under her chin and made a slight bow in the Oriental manner toward the young woman who was playing. Wilkins grinned in apparent anticipation, and Annie clapped her hands excitedly. A new sound filled the room, a delicate and haunting tune that called up images of a Japanese garden.

"What is that piece?" Tilden asked softly. "It isn't Bach."

"It's Gilbert and Sullivan. Their new operetta. Have you never heard *The Mikado?*"

"No."

"She loves Gilbert and Sullivan. One day we'll coax her to sing for you as well."

"Ask her now."

"She's too shy. Shhh!"

"But it's her job, isn't it? She's one of your girls."

"Not exactly. Be still, Tilden."

A maid brought in a tray of cheeses and set them before Tilden, where they sat unnoticed. He could not take his eyes from the delicate dark-haired girl in the green high-necked dress whose heart was now adrift in the distant court of the Japanese emperor. When at last she finished and her heart returned, Tilden rose to his feet, clapping loudly, startling her as one might a forest deer.

"Thank you, sir," she managed. Her enormous brown eyes met his for a fleeting moment and her soft smile caused a curious thumping in his chest.

"Margaret, dear," Georgiana Hastings said, "this is Mr. Tilden Beckwith. He is here as a friend. Though he may look the part of a brawler, he is a very kindly young man."

"How do you do, sir." Something happened to the young woman's expression. The shyness remained but now she appeared to be studying Tilden, appraising him.

"Tilden Beckwith, this is Margaret Barrie. She lives in my house, she assists me, she plays music as you've heard, and she sometimes makes conversation with my guests. She has no other duties."

"I am delighted, Miss Barrie." Not to say relieved, he thought to himself.

"Thank you, sir." She answered his bow with a curtsy. "Perhaps you'll visit again one day soon."

"I believe I shall, miss. I believe I shall indeed."

"Margaret," Georgiana told her, "you may stay with us or go, as you prefer."

"I have some of your correspondence to finish." She gestured toward the stairs.

"Another time then. We'll talk tomorrow."

"What was that all about?" Tilden asked when they were alone.

"I don't know your meaning, Tilden."

"If this were a home of another sort, I would swear that a possible match was being arranged. She was evaluating me as if I were a prospective suitor."

"Nonsense. She simply found you interesting."

"I would never dream of contradicting a lady," he said pleasantly, "not even a shameless schemer such as you. But you *were* matchmaking, were you not?"

"Discovered!" She laughed.

"Is Margaret one of your girls or is she not?"

"She is deciding, Tilden." Georgiana stepped to the door and closed it. "And yes, I am matchmaking. I promised Margaret that she and I would choose her first guest together and in her own good time."

"And I am being considered for the honor?" Tilden's smile faded.

"If you wish it, yes."

Tilden found that he was appalled. He searched for a way of responding that would not insult Georgiana.

"I do not think I could bear that," he said at last.

"May I ask why?"

"Well"—he threw up his hands as if the answer should be obvious—"romping with a girl who has already chosen that path is one thing. Deflowering virgins to make whores of them is quite another."

"Margaret is hardly a virgin, Tilden." Georgiana took his arm and forced him into his seat. "What she is is a quite charming young lady whose prospects have been limited by circumstance. I have offered her this alternative and suggested others. The decision will be her own."

Tilden felt his cheeks becoming hot. While he had never considered that any girl within these walls might possibly be unspoiled, it upset him to hear that Margaret was not the pure young thing she gave every outward appearance of being. Nor, though he was not unworldly at the age of twenty-seven, had it ever occurred to him that the decision to become a *fille de joie* must be consciously made at some point and with no small amount of consideration. He rose again and stepped to the piano, where he touched his fingers to the keys she'd played for him. Her warmth was still upon them.

"She could teach piano," he said quietly. "Why can she not teach piano?"

"She can," Georgiana answered. "She might also teach French, in which she is fluent. But to earn a proper living at it she must teach in the better homes. Those homes will require references. Margaret cannot provide them."

"Cannot?"

"Margaret's story is like many another, Tilden," she said gently. "It is not unlike my own. She was well raised in an upright home, she met a young man, was betrayed by her own heart and by the young man as well, and once the whispers began she found herself without prospects for a decent marriage and probably without a roof over her head if her parents chose not to share her disgrace."

"You say 'probably.' I assume you know her history perfectly well."

"I know what she's chosen to tell me."

"Who are her people? Where is she from?"

"I never ask that, Tilden."

"I would like to know."

"You have no such right."

"Then I would like to know how a decent young girl, compromised or not, spurned by her family or not, heads straightaway to the front door of Georgiana Hastings's house and enrolls herself as an apprentice prostitute." Tilden was becoming angry and did not quite know why. "It is a ridiculous story, Georgiana. It is the stuff of those melodramas which the Eagle Theater plays to weeping audiences. Surely a girl like Margaret could not have been without a friend or protector."

"I am her friend," the madam said evenly.

"You are her—" Tilden stopped himself.

"You were about to say that I am her ruin." Georgiana withdrew her hand and folded it with the other across her lap. "Tilden," she asked, "how do you suppose I find my girls? It is said that they are the handsomest and most cultivated young ladies of any house in New York. It is also said that there are twenty thousand prostitutes working their trade in this city. How do you suppose I find the best of them?"

"I have not considered it."

"Of course you haven't. They are here, they are available for your pleasure, they are to be forgotten or denied when you leave, and that is that. What is it to you how they came here?"

Tilden sighed deeply. "I stop in here for a quiet sherry and now I am an unfeeling beast. Since your business appears to be thriving, can I assume that not all your patrons receive this lecture? If I go to buy a new shirtwaist, am I hardhearted if I fail to consider the immigrant seamstress who ruins her eyes in the stitching of it for fifty cents a day?"

"You asked," Georgiana reminded him. "You asked where she came from. You were also making judgments and you have no right to do so."

Tilden threw up his arms in a gesture of surrender. "How *did* she come here, Georgiana?"

"I found her."

"Poised to leap from a ledge, I presume."

"Tilden—"

"I'm sorry."

"Margaret has been in New York for a year," she went on, "from someplace near Boston, I think. She tried, as you suggested, to teach piano. She then applied that same dexterity toward learning to be a typewriter. Margaret next secured a position with the *New York World* where a senior editor forced his attentions upon her and then fired her when she rebuffed him. I know a reporter there who told me the story. After she'd gone several months without employment, speaking of melodramas, her landlord offered to forgive her the back rent she owed in return for her favors. She refused and she was evicted. Margaret was on the street with her belongings when I went for her with my carriage."

"How could you have known?" he asked. "I mean, how did it happen that you came to her rescue in the nick of time? Speaking of melodramas."

"The reporter, whom I pay to keep his eyes open, recommended her as a prospect."

"A pimp."

"A talent scout, Tilden."

"And you seduced her."

"I befriended her, Tilden." A flash of her eyes showed that she was controlling her temper. "Margaret was and is free to leave at any time. I pay her a small salary to do my typewriting and to keep my books. My hope is that the money she can earn here as one of my girls will encourage her to embrace this life just long enough to accumulate the means to begin a new life elsewhere."

"I'm sorry, Georgiana." He turned away. "I still think this is terrible."

"Twenty thousand girls, Tilden. Most with a choice between starving virtue and a few years of selling those same bodies which men take and discard so freely. I was not, I'll tell you, the first of my calling to approach Margaret. I would not have been the last. She is so beautiful, you see, and so alone. And the fact that you think it terrible, Tilden, is one of the most endearing things about you. Most men would leap at the chance without a care in the world for her. And as for me, remembering, Tilden, that she is alone and friendless and easy prey to those who would take advantage of her, tell me in whose hands you would rather have found Margaret. I will bank her money for her, invest it safely, and when I send her off at the age of twenty-five, she need never depend on anyone else again."

"If she does indeed retire. And if you do indeed send her off."

"Do not insult me, Tilden."

"What guarantee do you offer that she will not simply move on to another such house?"

"If she does, she forfeits her money and she signs a paper to that effect at the start. No girl of mine, Tilden, has ever ended up in some Irish or German crib on Sixth Avenue. No girl of mine will ever walk the streets. Least of all a girl like Margaret."

"Assuming she accepts your proposition."

"Assuming that, yes."

"How do you know I won't try to dissuade her?"

"You are free to try." Georgiana smiled.

But you won't try, Tilden, she thought. Not very hard. There is scarcely a young man alive who would be content to maintain Margaret Barrie's virtue at its present imperfect level when the alternative is a night of pleasure with that wonderfully firm body and gentle face.

"I must consider this, Georgiana," Tilden said slowly. "It is not an arrangement one is offered every day."

"Not overlong, Tilden. I have been offered a thousand dollars for the first night with her. And by quite an important man, though older and rougher than you."

Now Tilden smiled, albeit uncertainly. "I have read in the newspaper that the Brooklyn Bridge has been sold more than once by a persuasive bunco steerer. I think it might have been you."

"I don't know what you mean, sir," she said innocently. "I do not lie about the thousand dollars. There are some who would pay ten."

"Still older and still rougher, I presume."

"Richer, Tilden."

"Very well," he said. "What, by the way, is my price to be?"

"With my compliments." Georgiana leaned forward to kiss his cheek. "Plus whatever generous gift you choose to have me invest for her. Through your firm, of course."

"Of course." Tilden grinned helplessly. "I will consider it, Georgiana. May I pay you a call tomorrow at this hour?"

"You are always welcome here, Tilden."

He walked north along Fifth Avenue more slowly than before. Many feelings had to be sorted out. The first of these, the one that kept the smile upon his face all the way past the towering fortresslike walls of the Croton Reservoir and on across Forty-second Street, was the fantasy vision of knowing the sweet body of that marvelous woman who played so beautifully and who had eyes like a wounded bird. The next, as the scaffolded and skeletal spires of Saint Patrick's came into view, was the sickening thought that that same body was being bid upon by fat and balding old men with cigar-stained teeth. Tilden dashed away that image. There it was. His conscience could hardly bear his being the one to take her, yet he could not stand the thought of her body being pressed against some other. Georgiana, the witch, well knew that he would be thus confused. A thousand dollars, someone had bid. Another might bid ten. Was this an invention, one of Georgiana's celebrated wiles, or was it true? In Tilden's heart he knew it was. Or must be. He would pay that much himself to relieve the ache his heart felt for her.

He walked on. Approaching Forty-seventh Street his eye drifted to the northeast corner where stood the four-story brownstone of Jay Gould. Tilden frowned.

There was a man who could buy and sell Margaret a thousand times over. Georgiana's entire house, for that matter. But of course he would not. Gould was a money-getter, not a woman-getter. A destroyer of men and their dreams. The destroyer of that good man Cyrus Field. Tilden looked at the sidewalk outside Gould's house where, it was well known, the consumptive little insomniac would pace away the night, alone with his thoughts except for armed guards who stood watchfully along his path. It was a wonder, armed guards or no, that someone did not manage to put a ball through his black heart one night. If someone did there would doubtless be a monument proposed to honor the deed. Tilden would be among the first to reach deep into his pockets for its subscription.

He quickened his pace for a half block or so. Gentler vistas ahead were more suited to reveries of young Margaret Barrie. There were green trees here and there, sprung to life in the time he was away. There were the wonderful new homes of the Vanderbilt sons and their ambitious wives, homes as fine as any château in Europe. There were the twin Italianate palazzos directly across from Saint Patrick's, built by William Henry Vanderbilt for himself and his daughters, the most elegant in New York until they were outdone by the turreted fancy commissioned by William Kissam Vanderbilt. Actually by Alva, his wife. Decent enough sort, that Willie K. Spends most of his time aboard his yacht these days to avoid the tedious entertainments given by Alva, to which Ella would give her soul to be invited more often.

Ella. God, that there can be an Ella and there can be a Margaret. That an Ella can have had every advantage and be so mean of spirit and so impoverished of accomplishment and that a Margaret, who must be the most gentle girl in the world, could have suffered such pain as Georgiana described.

A building on his right, across from Alva's house, drew his eye. It was taller than most, all of six stories, and fairly new. Tilden's glance fell not so much upon that building as upon the ghost of the dwelling it had replaced by popular demand just a few years before. Madame Restell had lived on that site. Madame Restell, the abortionist, who had built her fortune on the blood of a thousand unwanted babies and who would proudly and defiantly go coaching along Fifth Avenue and through the park, indifferent to taunts and protected by those whose secrets she knew until that lunatic vice crusader, Anthony Comstock, entrapped her at last and drove her to cut her throat rather than suffer her remaining years in a cell on Riker's Island. But how did it all begin? How, in heaven's name, does one enter such an atrocious life? Was she not once a charming young girl who ran and played games and sat in her mother's lap? And if such a girl could become such a monster by degrees, could not such a fate be in Margaret's stars as well? No. Tilden shook his head. It is impossible. Madame Restell was never a charming little girl. She was a grasping little sneak who probably tortured frogs with burning sticks and then cried her innocence when accused. She was probably not unlike Ella must have been. Ella surely did not blossom in her adulthood into the petulant, selfish, and fundamentally useless creature she is now. She must always have been so except she would have had the guile to conceal her true character lest the discovery of it interfere with her designs.

But I will not think upon that, he decided. One cannot condemn Ella without damning oneself for marrying so foolishly. And that done, there is nothing left but to make the best of it. I will think upon Margaret. But that is all that I will do. If I could put aside my conscience and be the first to have her, the first since the swine who ruined her, what then? Could I walk away and leave her to an endless line of panting old men? Could I return to her knowing how many sweating bellies have been pressed down upon hers since the time I first knew her sweetness? Could I watch her become hard?

Tilden had made up his mind. He turned the corner at Fifty-seventh Street, passing the home of dear Teddy Roosevelt at number 6, and continued on toward the looming mass of the Osborne two blocks in the distance past the signal tower of the elevated. Dear Teddy. My small joys and sorrows have been nothing to his, have they? There could have been no finer wife than Alice when he married her, no more blissful life together for the four short years until her unhappy death. What is it? Three years ago now. And since then a year of desperate distraction at his ranch in the Dakotas, a return to New York, a defeat in his effort to become mayor, a new marriage to his lovely Edith, and the publishing of another book which, by the way, I must have him inscribe for me. An eventful enough life for a man of fifty but a remarkable one for a man not yet twenty-nine.

Dear Teddy. I used to be younger than you and now I feel ten years older. Or ten years more tired. But it's my own stupid doing, and you did try to warn me. Here I'm going home to a woman who will barely raise her head when I enter my apartment and who will soon retire, with hardly a word, to her damnable twin bed. Damn the twin beds. Damn her. And damn Margaret for stirring all this up inside me.

"Jonathan?"

He was standing on the far side of the bed nearer the window when Gwen entered her uncle's guest room. His chest rose and fell as if he'd just been startled awake from a nap. But the turned-down bed he was staring at had not been disturbed. Corbin blinked at the sound of his name.

"Jonathan? Are you all right?"

His head lifted in her direction, and his eyes flitted over her features, her form, and the clothing she wore for the briefest moment until recognition came to them.

He rubbed them. "I'm fine, sweetheart," he said. "Just tired."

She gestured with the tray she carried. "Do you want your sandwich?"

"No. No, thank you." He looked at the soup, now cold, and the sandwiches. For some reason he expected cheese and sherry but he didn't want that either. It was odd. He could actually taste the sherry. Had he had some? Oh yes. Downstairs. A while ago in the study. Listening to piano music? No. Just talking. About Bridey Murphy and some things.

"You look exhausted," she told him. "Why don't you get out of your things."

He looked at the twin beds.

"Jonathan?"

He blinked again. "Do you mind if we move these up against each other?"

"No," she said. "Of course I don't."

Raymond Lesko's mood was not improving.

He'd made one slow pass on foot down the south side of Seventy-seventh Street, enough to determine that the old man's car had either been removed from Lexington Avenue by some flunky or towed away by the city, that no lights burned in Gwen Leamas's second-floor apartment, and that a man wearing a knitted ski hat, probably the kind that pulls down over the face, was sitting low in a dark car double-parked just down the street from her door.

For an hour now, he'd been waiting for something to happen. For Corbin and the dame to show up. For the guy in the car to make a move toward the foyer of her building. Lesko's feet were getting more numb by the minute. The time, he guessed, his eyes being too tired to focus on his watch in the dim light of the doorway he'd chosen, was about ten o'clock.

He was sure that the guy in the ski hat had not seen him except when he made that first pass. His head never turned to see where Lesko was going, which meant, of course, that the guy probably didn't know from Lesko. It was always possible that the guy didn't know from Corbin, either, but there were not many reasons Lesko could think of why a guy would sit in an unheated car on a night that would freeze a witch's tit with his head facing number 145 and being careful to keep it no higher than the headrest of his seat.

How about that he's not a shooter but he's just muscle out to put a scare into Corbin and maybe slap him around a while. Not likely. You never send muscle in numbers smaller than two against anyone, least of all against Corbin, who could probably do some slapping around of his own.

Silly me, Lesko thought. There *are* two of them. The one who won the coin toss went and worked the lock of 145's front door and is waiting warm and cozy inside, maybe even up in the apartment.

Lesko could not very well go in and find out, even if he were so inclined, because by the time he finished messing with the front door himself he would surely hear a tap of the horn from the car warning whoever was inside that something funny was happening. His other choice, then, was to wait until the guy inside came out. That wasn't any good because he would only come out when he decided to give up on Corbin for the night and that could be hours from now. Lesko would be too stiff by then to do anything but watch them drive away. Maybe there was a better idea. Maybe he should just leave a message and go home.

. . .

Ed Garvey made his way through the darkened apartment to Gwen Leamas's kitchen. There, he opened her refrigerator and with a gloved hand drew out a quart of milk and took several swallows from the plastic bottle. He replaced it and retraced his steps to his position in the living room near the entrance hall. He sat there, adjusting the small steel crowbar that was tucked in his belt. He was a big man, almost Lesko's size but with several inches less girth. The ladder-back chair creaked as he moved. Garvey had already paced the floor of the hallway and part of the living room, testing it for squeaks as he put his weight on it and making a mental note of those spots to avoid when he knew that Corbin and his woman were coming up the stairs. With any luck it would be quick and quiet. He had already located Gwen Leamas's valuables, such as they were. He would take them when it was done and make just enough of a mess so the burglary would look kosher to the cops when they found those two with their heads bashed in. Given the time, he would jimmy the door whose single lock he had already picked, thanking the woman in his heart for being a limey and for not living in New York long enough to know that four locks are better than two. Used to be everyone had just one lock. Now, with the way things are going, people are going to start laying minefields in their hallways before long. Got to get out of this town. Go out to Colorado. To Aspen, where there's lots of money and where the only thing they lock up is their skis. Or to Los Angeles, where the real big houses all have television cameras and Dobermans so Charles Manson shouldn't come back but where all the littler houses just have Lhasa apsos and Shih Tzus which you just throw into the fridge while you pick up some walking-around money.

Three short horn blasts outside.

Three?

What the hell is three supposed to mean?

Ed Garvey listened for sounds on the hallway stairs, heard nothing, then crossed to a window facing the street and looked down without disturbing the curtains. He could see the car but nothing in it past the steamed-up windshield. Jerk! How are you supposed to see anything, you let the windshield get like that?

Three more quick taps of the horn. And now a white handkerchief wiping a twelve-inch circle in front of the driver's face. The sound of an engine starting and a belch of white smoke from the exhaust.

Garvey let his face show, questioningly, at the second-floor window. In answer, he saw an arm at the driver's side waving him to the street.

Raymond Lesko rolled up the window, then eased himself into the back seat while pulling erect the unconscious body of the man in the ski hat. His name was Coletti, he'd acknowledged, along with a few other particulars. That was between the time Coletti told this clown asking directions to get lost and the time Lesko slammed his elbow several times against Coletti's jaw and temple. The gun muzzle Lesko stuck against his ear had also encouraged him to start his motor both for the sake of Lesko's comfort and to communicate some urgency to his friend upstairs. Lesko sat low in the seat and waited. In less than a minute, Ed Garvey's shadow appeared in the doorway of number 145. He hesitated there for a few seconds, surveying the street, before shaking his head in confused annoyance and stepping quickly to the passenger-side door of Coletti's car and opening it to slide in. Halfway he stiffened, almost levitating, as his peripheral vision took in the fist and the black metal cylinder in it that were extended toward his face.

"Shut the door," Lesko told him. "You grow up in a barn?"

Garvey hesitated, weighing his chances of rolling back out to the sidewalk and out of the line of fire.

"Go for it." Lesko shrugged. "But make up your mind."

Garvey sagged slightly and took a breath. Then he pulled his remaining leg inside and closed the door. He peered at Coletti, noticing for the first time that Coletti's eyes were closed.

"What'd you do to him?" he asked.

"Nap time," Lesko told him. "I want to see both your hands flat on the dash."

"Who are you?"

Lesko pressed the .38 into his neck. "You don't want to show me your hands? You want to make me nervous?"

Garvey stretched both arms forward.

"What I'm going to do now, Ed, is I'm going to reach over and frisk you. You're not even going to twitch, right?"

Garvey nodded. Lesko, his gun barrel still pressing into Garvey's flesh, used his left hand to pat the other man down, removing first the small heavy crowbar, then a set of lock picks in a vinyl case, then a long thin screwdriver he carried in his inside coat pocket.

"Now lean forward, Ed," Lesko suggested. "I'm going to see what you got in back. Then you take your right hand and you pull out your wallet and you just hold it where I can reach for it."

Garvey complied silently.

"No weapon, Ed?" Lesko did not really expect to find a gun or knife. Not on Garvey as long as he was working a burglary. You can plea-bargain a burglary. But not if you're carrying. Anyway, Coletti had already surrendered the small automatic he carried in an ankle holster and the one under his seat that he was holding for Garvey.

"No," Garvey answered.

Lesko twisted his front sight painfully into the soft flesh under Garvey's ear. "That was already a fib, Ed. This here screwdriver's a weapon. This here jimmy is a weapon. Here. I'll show you." Lesko slammed its hard edge down across Garvey's left collarbone. Garvey screamed and lurched forward. Lesko could see his right hand grasping the injured part. Lesko could not see Garvey's left hand but he knew its fingers were frantically searching for the pistol under Coletti's seat.

"Any time you're ready, Ed. You want to sit up straight please?"

"What do you want?" Garvey gasped.

"I think you were going to hit somebody up there, Ed. I think you were either going to hit two people with this jimmy or you were going to stick them with this screwdriver."

"You're crazy."

"Do I have to get your attention again, Ed?"

"No." Garvey flinched.

"I mean, here I am calling you by your name, which means Coletti here told me a couple of things, right?"

Garvey said nothing. But he crossed his left arm up to protect his other shoulder.

"Then you're up there for at least a fucking hour. I honk the horn and you come down but you come down empty. The lady didn't have at least a couple of rings you could stick in your pocket?"

Garvey shook his head.

"Your wallet here says you work for Beckwith Realty. It says you're in Security. Coletti says he's in Security too. Someday maybe we'll all get together and have a good laugh about that."

"We were checking out something, that's all. We heard there's a dame lives here and she and her boyfriend been working one of our hotels."

"Oh, I see, Ed. That explains everything."

Garvey winced again.

"Here's what I want you to do, Ed. I want you to open your window about four inches and then I want you to stick both your hands out through it just past the wrists." Lesko jabbed him. "Do that right now, Ed."

Garvey complied. Lesko shifted the .38 to his left hand and with his right he reached over and rolled up the window, pulling hard on the crank until Ed Garvey squealed in pain. Coletti stirred, moaned, and jerked into a low level of consciousness. Lesko relaxed him with another elbow to the temple. He then picked up the crowbar once more and tapped Ed Garvey with it.

"Do you know who I am, Ed?"

"No."

Lesko tapped harder. "For true?"

"I swear. What's to lie about that?"

"How about Mr. Dancer? You know a fellow named Dancer?"

"No."

"That's another fib, Ed."

"I swear. No. Give me a name I know and I'll tell you."

Okay, Lesko thought. Maybe he's just Dancer to me. "He's a little guy, Ed. Wears black suits. He looks and talks like a wind-up toy and he never sweats or gets dirty. He's also a honcho with the Beckwiths."

"That's Ballanchine. Lawrence Ballanchine."

Ballanchine? Lesko squinted. Ballanchine. Dancer. There was a guy who ran the New York Ballet. Forever. He's dead now. George Balanchine? Yeah. Probably no relation. Lawrence Ballanchine, the sly little rascal, takes Dancer as his code name, probably thinking that was very intellectual. Ballanchine-Dancer. Oh, I get it. You devil, you got a sense of humor after all, don't you.

"Who sent you here, Ed? Him or someone else?"

"Head of Security. Tom Burke."

"Burke reports to who?"

"Ballanchine."

"And Ballanchine reports to who?"

"The old man, I guess. Beckwith. Maybe the family. There's a lot of Beckwiths."

"This guy, Tom Burke. How old do you think he was back in 1944?"

"Huh?"

"Okay, how old is he now?"

"I dunno. Maybe fifty."

"You can tell Ballanchine I asked that. Tell him I was wondering whether Burke might be old enough to have been hanging around dark apartments or driving on dark streets in Chicago back in 1944. You know what I'm talking about, don't you, Ed."

"Chicago, 1944? What am I supposed to know about that? I never been there. I wasn't even born then."

"That was just a little trick question, Ed. I believe you."

"Listen, my hands are killing me."

"I'm going to fix that." Lesko slipped the two small automatics into his overcoat pocket. He took Ed Garvey's driver's license out of the wallet and tossed the wallet into the front seat. He held the license for Garvey to see. "So I know where to find you," he told him. Next, Lesko holstered his .38 and, picking up the crowbar, slid toward the rear right door and stepped out. Slamming the door behind him, he turned and peered through the slit between Garvey's swelling hands, now scarcely two inches deep.

"Here's a message for Ballanchine," Lesko told him. "Tell him he deals with me. Tell him he leaves Corbin and the dame alone until I give a green light. Tell him I get very upset when sneaky bastards like you and him try to hurt us decent people. Tell him when that happens, I get even. Show him your hands and he'll believe you."

Garvey did not appear to understand that last part. But the first glimmer reached him as he saw the big man with the teeth step back away from the car and rear one shoulder back in the manner of a man chopping wood with an ax. Garvey's eyes went wide as the crowbar whistled down against the back of one hand and he felt a spear of pain that felt like it splintered his entire arm to the shoulder. Garvey's already injured collarbone split and separated and its jagged ends tried to burrow through his body. The scream rising up in his throat turned into a choke as the crowbar came down upon the second hand, this time sending a spray of blood through the narrow slit into his face. He made an odd hooting sound as he threw his body back from the window, tearing loose the safety glass whose laminated shards cruelly shredded his wrists and palms.

Lesko was halfway to Lexington Avenue, casually walking, before he heard the first scream Dancer's killer could manage. Near the top of the subway stairs, Lesko found a sewer and dropped the glistening crowbar through the grating. The two pistols followed. Then he walked down the stairs and waited for the first subway to Queens Boulevard.

TEN

OW DID YOU SLEEP, JONATHAN?" HARRY
Sturdevant looked up from the breakfast
table overlooking the small garden area at
the rear of his house. Cora Starling, who
also smiled a greeting, had poured his coffee when she
heard him on the stairs and set it down at his place near
a glass of fresh orange juice and a basket of warm
croissants.

"Very well, sir," Corbin answered, although it
seemed he'd spent the entire night going from one frag-
mented dream to another. "Gwen's just putting on her
face. Good morning, Mrs. Starling."

"Mr. Corbin." She nodded. He saw her eyes flick
over to Sturdevant, which told him they'd probably
been talking about him. He didn't mind. Corbin wished
he could place her though. He thought she might have
been in one of his dreams. Maybe not. Maybe someone
a lot like her whose name he kept wanting to say was

Lucy. Lots of dreams. Margaret was in most of them. And a woman he didn't know at all, named Georgia. No. Georgiana. Then there was a fight dream; there's always at least one, except this time Corbin didn't think he was involved in it. A man, a big guy, had hands that were terribly smashed and torn and there was broken glass. He was screaming. It was awful. But Corbin didn't seem to feel particularly sorry for him.

"Some of these croissants have chocolate centers, Jonathan." Harry Sturdevant passed the basket. "I'd have another except Cora is watching me."

Cora sniffed and said nothing, although she did crane her neck to count the remaining pastries. Then, hearing a creak on the stairs, Cora picked up the coffee-pot and poured at Gwen Leamas's table setting.

"Don't anyone look at me." She entered the breakfast room palms forward. "Not until I can get my own stuff and paint it on."

Corbin looked anyway. He thought she looked fresh and clean and healthy, and it was one of the enduring mysteries of his life why women always thought they looked like hags in the morning but thought an unshaven man looked cute and rumply.

He'd dreamed about Gwen too, he thought. Sure he did. As a matter of fact, sure, there was one dream about Gwen and Margaret at the same time, maybe finally meeting each other and Margaret saying how happy she was for him that he had found such a lovely woman and how she hoped they would squeeze every moment of joy out of the time they had and try never to be apart. A nice dream. A real nice one. And if it happened the way he sort of remembered it now, that was the first time ever that he saw Margaret while he was Jonathan Corbin and not Tilden Beckwith. There was another nice little dream in which he was teaching Margaret how to ride a bicycle and she was laughing because he wasn't a whole lot better at it than she was.

He was Tilden there. Nice to know Tilden had some good times.

"When you've finished your coffee"—Harry Sturdevant took a final sip—"my car is garaged just down the street. Gwen, I gather you'll want to change at your flat before we drive up to Greenwich?"

"Take me ten minutes."

Cora Starling approached the table with three small cups holding an assortment of tablets and capsules. "These are all vitamins. The way you people eat it's a wonder you're alive. I also fixed up some fruit and some granola bars in a cake box. Remember you got them when Dr. Sturdevant here starts sniffin' for an anchovy pizza around noontime."

The phone rang on the kitchen wall. Cora crossed to the receiver.

"Sturdevant residence."

She listened.

"May I say who's calling, please?"

Cora frowned.

"Will you tell me who this is, please?"

She listened again, glancing across the room at Harry Sturdevant.

"No, we're not interested just now. Thank you kindly." She replaced the phone. "Just some folks lookin' to clean our carpets," she said. "Dr. Sturdevant, you got some checks to sign in your office before you go."

Sturdevant joined her there while Gwen Leamas was pulling on her boots.

"What was that about, Cora?"

"Second time this morning someone called to ask if Mr. Corbin was here. Two different people. First time, he was in the shower and I asked the man to leave a message but he said it's not important and he hung up. That time just now I tried to make that man give a name before I'd say Mr. Corbin was here but he hung up too."

"You said it was a carpet cleaning service not to alarm Mr. Corbin?"

She nodded.

"Cora, I'm not sure there's a need for alarm," he told her, "but can you avoid going out today or opening the door to anyone you don't know?"

"I just might have someone in to visit with me."

"That would be fine. I'll be calling in several times."

Sturdevant waited in the double-parked car outside 145 East Seventy-seventh Street while Gwen, Corbin with her, ran up to pack an overnight bag. Corbin might have waited with Sturdevant, but he felt a vague uneasiness about letting her enter the empty flat alone. And then a crunch of broken glass underfoot as he stepped from the car called back the now-distant dream of the man with the torn and shattered hands. It had no meaning to him but it troubled him distantly. Once inside her door he paced the living room as she spent her allotted ten minutes, a promise in which he had no trust whatever, selecting cosmetics from her bathroom and applying certain of them to her cheeks and eyes. As he paced, his own eye kept falling on a single chair that sat just inside her entrance hall and which seemed to him out of place by several inches. At last he straightened it. While he'd been pacing, Corbin had also found himself identifying and avoiding two spots on the floor, which squeaked when stepped upon. A remote anger stirred within him as he did this and his hands tightened into fists. Corbin looked at them, shook his head, then made them relax, disinclined to dwell on what was just one more of the many peculiar thoughts and emotions that whispered within him these days. Besides, soon he would be in Greenwich. No such thoughts ever annoyed him there. Nothing annoyed him there.

As Gwen Leamas changed into a bulky sweater and a blue suede skirt, Corbin wandered into her kitchen, idly touching the appliances and countertops there. His fingers brushed across her refrigerator door, then its chromium handle, and then the anger simmered in him once again. He opened the door.

"Still hungry?" she called from the other room. "I'm afraid there's not much."

"I guess not," he answered. "Thanks."

There was a tub of cottage cheese, inverted for a better seal, the remains of a chicken, a partial bottle of good Chablis, a few eggs, and a six-pack of Molson's from which one can had been removed. Also a jar of peanut butter—Corbin did not understand people who ate peanut butter cold—a pint of half-and-half, and a plastic bottle of milk, which was empty save for a quarter inch. He took out the bottle and allowed the door to swing closed as he examined it in his hand. Corbin saw his fingers tremble for an instant and then curl in against the plastic bottle, crushing it, spitting off its top, which fell to the floor and rolled. Someone had been here. The man with the ruined hands had been here. Corbin no sooner had that thought than his mind began at once to deny it. He'd seen nothing. Nothing wrong. An almost empty milk bottle in Gwen's refrigerator meant that Gwen had put an almost empty milk bottle in her refrigerator. Period. There was no man with ruined hands. Corbin knew that. But he also knew that there was and that the man had held this milk bottle. He dropped the crumpled plastic into her trash.

"Do you mind if we go up the West Side Highway?" he asked Harry Sturdevant once he settled into the back seat, where Gwen joined him.

"If you wish. The Triborough's much more direct."

"The West Side Drive is prettier. Anyway, we're facing that direction."

"We are indeed," Sturdevant answered. He put the car in drive and started across town, toward the roadway through Central Park, glancing into his rearview mirror several times each block to see whether by chance a strange car might have fallen in behind them. He saw none.

"Gwen, dear. Did you bring me that medication I asked you for?"

"I'm sorry, Uncle Harry. It slipped my mind," she lied.

As the tires of Sturdevant's Mercedes hissed along the park transverse road at Seventy-second Street, Corbin settled back, Gwen's hand in his, and felt himself relaxing. The park was beautiful. The morning sun had not yet melted the snow, which turned each tree and bush into fragile shimmering glass. Tilden and Margaret. He wondered how often they came here in winter. They'd come ice-skating, he was pretty sure. On the big lake up near the Dakota Apartments. Maybe just Tilden skated. Yes. Margaret was pregnant, wasn't she. She would sit by one of the bonfires, munching on a capon and watching Tilden try to show off and laughing each time he went *splat*. And they brought a carriage up here in the summer. Several times. They would either just go riding or tie up down near the Mall and listen to band music from inside the carriage because they were still being careful about being seen together then. And Margaret's belly was just beginning to show.

The Mercedes left the park and continued across Seventy-second Street to the West Side Highway. There, turning north along the Hudson River, which was dotted with slow-moving floes of ice, Corbin leaned forward in his seat to better see the view ahead of him. The concrete highway stretched out before him in an almost straight line leading to the George Washington Bridge, but Corbin's mind erased both of these. He focused instead on the gentler, slower roadway of Riverside Drive and on the lovely old homes that lined it, each with fine vistas of the river and the green cliffs of New Jersey. There were now high rises on those distant cliffs, but Corbin's mind erased those as well. This mental purging of the landscape was a deliberate act on Corbin's part. It involved no ghost; none, at least, that Corbin feared this morning.

The elevated had done all this. All that was up here before the elevated were tiny farms and squatters' shacks and pigs and sheep roaming freely. And rocks. Rocks and boulders everywhere. These had to be cleared. And broad avenues laid out. And trees planted. At first fast-growing evergreens, which would shoot up fifteen feet in a mere three seasons and then pause to wait for the slower elms and pin oaks. Cyrus Field had done this. His Ninth Avenue Elevated curling up beyond Morningside Heights meant that all those office workers who'd been forced to live in New Jersey or Brooklyn and rely on uncertain ferries could now live an hour or more closer to their jobs. A horsecar from Central Park to City Hall could take an hour and a half, but Field's elevated line could cover that distance in just twenty-eight minutes. Even from Morningside Heights and the country lanes of Harlem, the ride lasted no more than three quarters of an hour. And for only five cents. For ten cents, of course, one could choose to ride in one of the elevated's apple-green parlor cars with mahogany paneling on the walls, real Axminster carpets on the floor, and seats of red leather. For pleasant viewing, each car had seven high-arched windows a side. Instead of the slat blinds of ordinary cars, the windows had tapestry curtains trimmed in red leather to match the seat coverings and mounted on spring rollers whose mechanisms were concealed by cornices. All Field's doing. Other men may claim credit but it was Field. That such a man should be ensnared and broken . . .

Corbin folded his arms across the top of the empty front seat and rested his chin upon them. More fine old homes drifted past. Some of them, more than a few, he felt as if he knew. Ahead lay a wide stretch of Riverside Drive, where he—where Tilden and Margaret—had cycled. And an inn, the Claremont Inn, where they'd dined. More than dined. They'd stayed there, had they not? Yes, Margaret had taken a room there until the house was ready. And right across there, at the foot of that hill, was the stable where he'd rented the rig in which he took her to see her first baseball game over at the Polo Grounds. They'd tethered their horse to a cast-iron weight right in the outfield of the New York Mets —he must learn to stop calling them that, the public fancy these days being to call them the Giants although he was at a loss to explain why when Margaret asked. The biggest player on the team was Roger Connor, at three inches over six feet, followed by Del Gillespie, who was the same height as Tilden. None of the other players, to his knowledge, was over six feet. Not Buck Ewing or Monte Ward or the outfielder Silent Mike Tiernan, whose back was to them all afternoon as they lunched from the picnic hamper assembled by the Claremont Inn. But who can explain the public fancy where nicknames are concerned. The Boston team is called the Beaneaters and that makes sense enough. And the Brooklyn players are the Trolley Dodgers, although of late they are being called the Bridegrooms, four members having been wed in as many weeks this past spring.

"Would anyone like some grapes?" Gwen Leamas opened the cake box Cora Starling had handed her.

"Not just now, dearest," Corbin murmured.

Gwen quietly put the box aside and touched Harry

Sturdevant's shoulder. Sturdevant nodded, indicating that he'd heard.

"Nice day," he said to Corbin.

"It certainly is." Corbin did not move his chin from its resting place on his arms. The roadway, the river, the buildings of the West Side, had faded. Before him, Corbin saw only a broad green field dotted with men dressed in white except for their caps and he wished he'd brought a pair of opera glasses because Buck Ewing was at bat as the potential winning run and Hank O'Day was on second with two out. Brooklyn's Adonis Terry had the full count on Ewing who seemed baffled by Terry's underhand curve ball which Terry would change to an overhand fastball every time Buck thought he had figured Terry's number. Corbin didn't know how he could since even from his distant vantage point he could see that a considerable flap had been torn in the ball's hide and a new ball wouldn't be allowed unless there was another inning. Every time Adonis Terry got his hands on the ball he would tear the flap a little more and in a different direction so that with each pitch the ball would do ever-crazier things.

"You're Tilden Beckwith, aren't you?"

"Hmmm?"

"I say, you are Tilden Beckwith, are you not?"

Corbin made a please-wait motion with his fingertips. That was Harry Sturdevant. He knew that. And he knew what Gwen's uncle was trying to do, but the fact is he was not Tilden Beckwith at the moment. But he *was* trying to watch a game. And even if he were Tilden Beckwith it should have been clear to Harry that if he wished for social intercourse during the game he would have sat in the grandstand and not out here at the outfield's perimeter. Besides, he was in the company of a lady and it was just possible that he might not care to be put in the position of having to introduce her. In any case, there's the pitch and—oh no, Bucky, not a fly ball—oh, oh, look out. A sigh rose from the grandstand because Ewing, having choked up on his bat for a hard ground ball through the infield, had caught the pitch low and fat and the result was a looping fly to right field. But the crowd's dismay turned to astonishment, then glee as the mischief Adonis Terry had worked upon the ball being pitched had a similar effect on the ball in flight. There was the right fielder waiting for an easy catch but the ball played him false and died like a bird shot on the wing and the right fielder made his desperate lunge too late. The crowd was screaming as Hank O'Day headed home and Buck Ewing had rounded second and against their advice was dashing toward third. Slide, Ewing, slide, they screamed and this he heeded but he threw his body high in the air in a broad jumper's attitude, hurtling toward the aghast third baseman and diverting his eye from the ball which now whizzed past him and into a crowd of onlookers, one of whom promptly pocketed it. Giants, Giants, the fans chanted as Buck Ewing crossed home plate and as the Brooklyn players threw their hats and gloves to the ground in frustration.

"Giants."

"What?" Gwen asked.

Corbin sat upright, embarrassed. "I'm sorry, sweetheart. What did you say?"

"I didn't say anything. You said 'Giants.' "

"Just daydreaming." He wiped his eyes. "I was thinking about a baseball game." But the details of it were receding as fast as the passing landscape.

"As yourself or as Tilden Beckwith?" Sturdevant turned his head but kept his attention on the road ahead of him.

"I don't know." He stretched. "It was nothing. Just a daydream."

Gwen did not press the question of where he'd been nor, more surprisingly, did Harry Sturdevant.

Corbin pretended not to notice the eye contact between them in the rearview mirror nor did he react, other than to smile inwardly, when Sturdevant announced that some music would be nice and made a production out of selecting an appropriate tape cassette. He was fairly sure that Sturdevant would not be so obvious as to pop in a Gilbert and Sullivan tape of *Iolanthe*, but he might play something by Corelli, the composer Corbin said he'd never heard of before he told that story about asking the Palm Court's violinist to play a more lively piece. But no, the label he chose said Gustav Mahler. Corbin was not really familiar with Mahler's work, but he would have bet anything that the piece he was about to hear was a hot ticket back around 1888.

Choral music. Against an orchestral background. German words and voices. That, he guessed, was as close as Sturdevant dared come to playing an operetta. This was fine, but Corbin would have preferred Bach. He sat back to enjoy the ride.

Out the window, on both sides, he could see straight up and down the Harlem River as the car left Manhattan and crossed into the Bronx. Just ahead of him and to his right he saw Yankee Stadium, and that made him turn in his seat to see if he could spot the Polo Grounds. There was nothing. Just a housing project. It didn't matter. The more or less modern stadium that had been there wasn't the way it used to be anyway. It used to be wonderful. The first Polo Grounds, the one where he'd taken Margaret, was much farther downtown, right at the upper corner of Central Park but not part of the park. He hated to see it move but the city needed the land and for the last five years the owners had let it go to seed. Peeling paint. Rotted benches. More dirt than grass on the field. But the new field was magnificent. Big new grandstands, with two tiers, and then bleacher seats along the third-base line. You could take the elevated right to the gate and, in fact, some special trains would park there and you could remain inside and watch the game if you wanted. The best way to watch the game was still from the upper deck of the grandstands, where everybody had hampers and pails of beer, but the most comfortable way, especially if you wanted a little privacy, was, as before, from a surrey in the outfield, where they staked off a carriage area maybe three hundred feet from home plate which meant that during any given game you'd still see an outfielder scrambling under a horse to retrieve a ball and sometimes even playing one he'd hidden in the outfield grass against an emergency.

Margaret.

He had not exactly lied in not telling Gwen that Margaret was there. It was just that it wasn't any of her business. There. It sounds harsh, doesn't it, when you put it into words. But there were some things about Margaret that Gwen just didn't have any right to know, and some feelings neither he nor Margaret had any obligation to share, and, come to that, some of it seemed even too personal for him, Corbin, to know about.

Is it possible, he wondered, that Tilden's ghost, if that's what it is, or Jonathan Corbin's ancestral memory, if that's what it is, is capable of picking and choosing what Jonathan Corbin is permitted to know. And *know* is the right word, isn't it? It's not the same as remembering. It's not the same as revelation or discovery either. It makes you wonder if everybody has a Tilden Beckwith. Sturdevant sure thinks they do. Maybe dozens. Hundreds. Hearing from them is just a matter of the right stimulus coming along and the right switches being thrown.

Talk to me, Tilden. Am I your great-grandson? Talk to me. I mean, you let me stand there watching while old Ella gets frozen stiff, you take me to bars, you take me to ball games that happened a hundred years ago. I think you took me to a whorehouse in New York, but it's as though you made me stand facing the corner in that one. Okay, how about just answering yes or no. That whorehouse was—Tilden, why did I just get the feeling you don't like it when I call it a whorehouse? How about seraglio? Bagnio? You can't be crazy about bawdy-house either. Establishment? You want establishment. Okay, You met Margaret for the first time in that establishment, right? She was one of the—Let's not go through that again. Whatever she was doing there, that's where you met her. I think she played music for you and I think there was something about how she could be exclusively yours if you—if you what? If you bought a season ticket? What?

Suddenly Corbin winced. Something, somehow, had made him feel deeply ashamed of himself. He felt as if his face had just been slapped.

I'm sorry.

I really am.

She was special to you. I understand that because I've felt it and because she's special to me, too. One way or the other you got her out of there. You didn't plan to. You didn't intend to go back there even though you were very attracted to her. Something about the whole thing was making you sick. But you did go back and you—what? You paid some woman, and you took her out of that life. Right? Tilden?

That's wrong, isn't it. It didn't happen quite that way. I know that because I'm beginning to feel ashamed again except it isn't really me who's feeling ashamed.

It's okay.

It's enough that you got her out of there.

Tilden had. But not right away. The twin beds had done it. The cold wall of frigid air that persisted between himself and Ella had done it. And a sleepless night spent staring into the blackness at the slender form of Margaret Barrie and into the lost and frightened sadness of her eyes. And feeling his manhood rise against his sheet and becoming disgusted with himself because of the animal lust it signaled and because he was finding that he had little will after all to resist the cold logic of Georgiana's proposal. He needed time to think. But there was only until tomorrow evening. Then, if Georgiana is to be believed, Margaret goes on the block to the highest acceptable bidder. Impossible. That cannot be allowed. And Georgiana, that witch, knows full well that Tilden Beckwith will not permit it.

"Margaret"—Georgiana Hastings's manner had a special gladness to it—"you remember Mr. Beckwith, do you not?"

"Of course." She offered her hand.

"In the room upstairs just past the Greek urn," Georgiana said to Tilden, "you will find a bottle of champagne on ice. A light supper will be brought up shortly. I suggest that the two of you go there now and take all the time you like to become better acquainted."

Tilden rubbed a nervous hand across his chin, freshly shaven at his office for the occasion. He wished he'd bathed a second time as well; he had not counted on perspiring so.

"Now, Tilden. You may go now if you wish."

"Yes. Yes, of course." He offered a solemn arm to Margaret, who was waging an equally losing battle to appear at ease.

"I want to know about you." Tilden refilled her glass, his hand somewhat steadier than when first he poured. "Will you tell me about yourself?"

"It isn't really done, I'm told." Her honest eyes did not avoid his. "To speak of personal things, I mean."

"On the contrary," he answered. "Not that I am

greatly experienced here, but several of the girls have told me their entire histories."

"They made them up, I think," she replied uncertainly. "They will answer such questions if it pleases a patron to want to know more about them. But these histories are rehearsed, sometimes invented upon the moment. Do you know the girl called Little Annie?"

"The one who dresses like a child, yes."

"She helped me make one up for myself. I will tell it to you if you wish."

"But, dear Margaret," he asked, "what would be the point if it isn't true?"

"I think it is to satisfy your curiosity without troubling you unduly."

"And possibly to let your patron feel he's more a friend than a cash customer?"

"I expect so. Yes."

"Is it your intention to so delude me, Margaret?"

"Oh no, Mr. Beckwith." She seemed genuinely upset that she had given that impression. "My intention is only to please you. I would have told you my story straightaway, but I am not yet artful enough at it."

"At what? Lying?"

"Entertaining." Tears were forming in her eyes. She knew, Tilden could see, that she was making a bad job of this.

"Margaret"—Tilden paused, searching for words —"how artful are you at pleasing a man?"

"The girls have told me some things. And they've shown me drawings in books."

"But you are not, as you say, artful at it."

A single tear cut a shiny ribbon on her cheek. "I will try to please you, Mr. Beckwith."

There was a rap at the door. Margaret rose to open it, taking that opportunity to blot her eyes as a tray was pushed into the room by a maid in uniform. Margaret waited until she retired, then, putting a mask of cheer upon her face, began preparing a plate for Tilden.

"Margaret—"

"These oysters are excellent. The sauce is coriander and honey."

"Margaret." Tilden stepped to her and took the plate from her hands. "Margaret, why in God's name are you doing this?"

The young woman swallowed hard. "Mrs. Hastings assured me that she explained my situation to you."

"Only in the vaguest terms. She told me that you were considering, only considering, a life of—this sort of life."

"I have made my decision." She dropped her eyes. "I would like to try to please you now."

"Margaret"—he touched her cheek—"can we not just visit a while?"

Her lower lip trembled. She bit it. Then, having steeled herself, she reached for the lapels of his coat.

"Margaret." He threw up his hands and backed away. "This entire affair is absolutely ridiculous. You have no business whatever in a place like this."

"I can do it." The tears came again. "I *can* please you. Oh sir, must we talk so much?"

"No," he told her. Tilden reached for her shoulders and drew her against his chest, very lightly, as he might comfort a daughter or niece. He could feel a heaving at her bosom and a quivering along the muscles of her back. She wore no corset. She was all softness. "I would very much like to try the oysters," he said.

Tilden barely tasted them, or the slices of cold woodcock on toast points, or the small dish of lemon sorbet. Margaret quickly regained her composure and was making amiable conversation, no doubt rehearsed, on subjects in which he was known to have a special interest. Tilden's mind, however, was in turmoil. On the one hand, there he was in the presence of one of the most charming and lovely young ladies he had ever seen, who was perfectly prepared to offer her body to him in any way he chose to use it. It was all he could do to keep his eyes from lingering upon her breasts and her waist and on her gentle hands, whose marvelous dexterity he had already witnessed. On the other hand, though he wanted her beyond his powers of forbearance, his head swam with reasons why an act of such lasting consequences should be avoided or at least postponed. It simply could not be that no other alternatives existed for her. Women everywhere were becoming teachers, bookkeepers, journalists, even doctors and lawyers. Margaret already knew how to be a typewriter and how to keep ledgers. These were enviable skills for a woman, and Tilden was certain that he could help her find a situation in which she could earn at least a thousand a year and possibly half again that much until a suitable husband came along. As for making a good marriage, it was true that she had dim prospects in any stratum of society which would insist upon a blameless reputation and a well-defined lineage, but there were any number of good and honest fellows who were making their own way in life and who lived in worlds where few such questions would be asked. Such a charming young lady would find no shortage of proposals of the decent sort.

But here she was. Seduced by Georgiana Hastings with a promise of having independent means and the freedom from relying upon the whims of any man in return for two years of selling a body which a husband, whether chosen well or recklessly, could use as he sees fit anyway. That, Tilden was sure, was the hub of Georgiana's argument. She doubtless told Margaret of the many who've retired to respectable lives but not of those who have been unmasked by a chance encounter with a former patron or an anonymous letter to a husband. Or of those who retire not soon enough, who waste their money or are cheated of it and who, as age overtakes them, desperately seek employment in an ever-more-disreputable sort of house until at last they are like those pathetic disease-ridden hags who prowl past hotels, smiling through rotted teeth at every passerby.

"I will undress now if you wish." Margaret folded her napkin and placed it on the tray.

I do not wish it, Tilden shouted in his mind. I wish you to leave this place with me at once and then I wish you to learn to care for me and I wish you to love me and only me because you are, by heaven, every beautiful thing I could have hoped for in Ella but have been denied.

"Yes," he choked. "If you are quite ready."

He watched as Margaret rose from the table and walked slowly to the side of the canopied bed, her back to him and her fingers working the buttons of her bodice. He saw her shiver but she did not pause. One bare shoulder appeared, then another. Her back was wonderfully straight and its unmarked skin was naturally tan like that of some French women he'd seen. She stepped out of the bottle-green dress she wore and folded it neatly over a bedside chair. Her fingers moved to the straps of a lacy chemise.

"Might we turn down the lamps?" she asked, her face still turned from him.

"If that pleases you," he answered hoarsely. He reached under one Tiffany shade and extinguished it altogether. On the other he left only a tiny crescent of blue flame. When he looked at her again, the chemise and other silken things had fallen. She stood naked in the semidarkness, her arms folded across her breasts. She looked small. Tilden crossed to her and placed his hands upon her shoulders, turning her, feeling the thrill of her skin as he held her. Slowly, she made herself relax, allowing her head to lean against his lapel and bringing her hands tentatively to his hips. He could smell the scent of almonds in her hair.

"Margaret . . ."

Please do not speak, she begged silently. Just let it be done. She reached for his lapels and peeled them back, draping his jacket across her gown. She unbuttoned his waistcoat and then her fingers worked to solve the knot of his cravat. It both pleased and saddened him that she was inexpert at loosing it. Tilden did it for her, then quickly removed his shoes and trousers and held up the comforter for Margaret to slip beneath it.

"Margaret . . ."

She kissed him and put her fingers to his lips.

She traced the fingers of her other hand down his chest and stomach and, pausing only for a heartbeat, lowered them further until they took him and caressed him in a way that Ella had done only when the wine was in her. Tilden shuddered and his breath came more quickly. Her free hand reached to his neck and she gently guided his body over hers and in the same motion eased him into her. He could feel that she was tight, yet he entered smoothly. She must have prepared herself, he realized. Georgiana must have shown her how.

"Margaret, you are so tender. So beautiful." His body began its slow and delicious motion. His hands sank deep into the soft down mattress on either side of her. Even holding his elbows straight, he feared that he was pressing too hard against her. He raised himself up further.

"Is that better?" he whispered.

In answer, she placed both arms around him and drew him down to her.

"That is better, Tilden," she said gently. "Enjoy me now. Just enjoy me."

He tried.

He did.

The end, when it came, was too soon. But he stayed inside her, moving with a rhythm that matched her own as long as he was able.

"You have honored me," he said at last. The words, though odd in choice, seemed appropriate.

"And you have pleased me greatly," Margaret told him.

Tilden frowned. "There is no need to tell me that. I had almost forgotten that I am a patron here."

Margaret took his hand and kissed it. "It is true, Tilden." Then, more sadly, "I suppose I too had forgotten."

He chose to believe that. She'd said, he recalled, that she was not yet artful at this trade. Tilden was glad that she was pleased. He remembered a time when it would have shocked him to learn that a woman took any satisfaction from this act beyond that of performing her duty to her man. After all, everyone knew of Dr. Otis Willard's statement that to suppose that a woman takes animal pleasure in the performance of the reproductive act is the most damnable calumny upon the soul of this noble creature.

But some of his friends had told him of women who actually invited the act and who laughed and talked during it and to whom it seemed great fun, but he had supposed such women must be whores at heart. And he'd heard that there were other women who cried out, not in pain but in pleasure, and some who moaned in the same way he did when his back was being scratched. These too, he felt, must be depraved at heart. A friend, at last, had given him a book written for women by a woman doctor and there it all was, in cold print: the affirmation that nature's design had made the act pleasurable for the females of all species and especially pleasurable for the one species possessed of an imagination, and to deny this any longer could lead to nervousness and even madness.

"I wish I could stay here with you," he told her. "I wish I could stay here always."

"Stay a while, Tilden. Hold me a while." Margaret closed her eyes. It was done at last. After all the urging from the other girls. *Just once, Margaret dearie, to show your appreciation to Georgiana.* She did not know whether the urging was done at Georgiana's request, but it did not truly matter. She had to know whether she could do this. *They all wash off, dear. After they leave you're as good as new and a little richer.* Could she do it for the two years Georgiana promised in a place where she would be protected and where all the men were well behaved and where she would have companions who were, after all, not unlike herself? She still did not know. Not all would be as tender as this battered warrior who knew Bach when he heard it and who tried, at least, to make love slowly, and who lingered with her when other men she'd heard about would turn and snore or even begin to smoke. She did know, however, how much she'd wanted to be held by a man she trusted.

"Margaret," he asked softly, "what happens now? After tonight?"

"I don't know."

"Perhaps . . ." He searched for the words. "Perhaps, until you've made a decision, that is if I can arrange it, you would care to see only me."

She raised her head.

"I mean, not just this way. Not at all if that's what you'd like. We can visit. And talk. And you can play the piano. And perhaps we could slip away and hear one of those operettas by Herbert and Sullivan."

"Gilbert."

"Exactly, yes. Do you play cards? We could play cards as well."

"That would be lovely, Tilden."

"What? Which part?"

"All of it, Tilden. If you mean it, it would all be lovely." Yes, it would, she thought. But Margaret could not allow herself to hope that the ardor he felt tonight would survive into tomorrow, let alone to days beyond.

"Of course I mean it."

"Dear Tilden."

"You say 'dear Tilden' as if I am a little boy who doesn't know his mind."

"No, Tilden," she told him, "I say it as if I am a woman who would rather not be hurt if I can help it."

"I will not hurt you, Margaret."

She kissed him.

"I would die first."

After a while, they made love again.

"This *is* a business, Tilden," Georgiana Hastings reminded him as she poured his brandy. "I charge three times the normal rate for the exclusive use of a girl. Seventy-five dollars a night, every night, would put a considerable strain upon your pocket."

"I too am a businessman," he answered. "And Margaret is not yet one of your girls. Let us negotiate seriously, Georgiana."

"Make your offer."

"Make yours."

"I'm afraid it's a seller's market, Tilden. Whether we reach agreement or not is all the same to me."

"Nonsense. At the moment, you have no income from her at all. I'll pay you twenty-five, but you must keep paying her the salary she earns as your secretary."

"How is your brandy, Tilden?"

"Not good enough to derail me."

"Seventy-five."

"Georgiana, we both know that you are fully prepared to split the difference at fifty dollars and still be satisfied that you have bested me. Let us get on with it."

"Fifty then," she agreed, "plus five hundred for to-night."

"Ridiculous."

"Most of the five hundred is for Margaret. I'll keep less than a hundred of it."

"Fair enough. What is her share of the fifty?"

"None. I'd make more than that on the average girl."

"Georgiana—"

"It's true, Tilden."

"Then I will pay you seventy-five on condition that you bank twenty-five of it for Margaret. Can I rely on you for that?"

"It is we whores"—Georgiana winked—"who are supposed to have hearts of gold, Tilden."

"Do we have a bargain, you barracuda?"

"Pay me fifty, Tilden. I shall bank half of it for Margaret."

"Of course," Tilden said, "some barracudas are quite nice."

"And I'd like you to look over my investments. Your advice will be without charge, naturally."

"Of course. Would you like a dollar for the brandy?"

"That won't be necessary, Tilden."

"It looks like Berlin at the end of the war, doesn't it," Gwen observed. She was looking out the car windows at row after row of gutted tenement buildings along the Cross Bronx Expressway. Most did not seem like slum dwellings at all. There were red brick apartment houses, which looked perfectly middle class, and one in particular, on a parklike knoll, was faced with yellow brick and had pleasant terraces at its corners. It must have been quite nice at one time, she thought. But now it sits there looking back at you rather like a dog who's been left at home and doesn't understand why he's being abandoned.

"This is the South Bronx," Harry Sturdevant announced. "It's becoming a ghost town. Thousands of buildings like these, many of them burned out."

"What happened?"

Sturdevant shrugged. "These were mostly rent-controlled apartments. When oil heat and electricity shot up, their owners couldn't operate them at a profit and they couldn't sell them because the area was deteriorating anyway, so they just abandoned them."

Corbin, irritable, tried to shut out their voices. He'd dozed off for a minute there and he'd had some kind of dream, which he was losing now, but he knew it was about something very exciting. He'd pulled off some great coup or had a terrific idea that made him happy and excited.

"Now it's New York's dumping ground," Sturdevant continued. "You'll see whole streets lined with abandoned wrecks of cars. And massive brick piles where the city has leveled rows of buildings because they've been dangerously weakened by fires. You watch, though. Ten years from now this could be a garden spot. You'll see developers flattening all this and starting from scratch because it's wonderfully convenient to the city. But the first two or three will be like fortresses, I'm afraid. This area has one of the highest crime rates in the world."

Corbin squinted, trying to remember who that was. The one who was talking about developers. It didn't matter. What was that about crime, though? What's there to steal out here? Chickens? That fellow was right about the future, though. Some day soon all these little farms will be gone and the main roads paved and the elevated will reach all the way out here from New York to create whole new villages in this great empty space between Vanderbilt's railroad lines.

Jonathan, Gwen realized, had not said a word since they turned off the West Side Drive. She leaned forward until she could see his eyes. They were open, not glazed, just a bit dreamy. She sat back, placing one hand on his shoulder and idly massaged it. He grunted appreciatively. His left hand reached back and gave her thigh an affectionate squeeze.

"You are a magician with those fingers," Tilden murmured. He lay facedown upon the canopied bed, fully dressed but for his coat and tie, which he'd replaced with a red floor-length robe of Japanese silk. Margaret sat at his side, upright, her long legs tucked under a white summer dress that made her look like a bride. "They do wondrous things with piano keys; they turn stiff muscles into jelly, not all muscles, of course, and they—"

"Why, Tilden Beckwith"—Margaret playfully slapped his head—"that is the first racy remark I've ever heard you make."

"I can't be blamed for it. I am bewitched. I am not the man I was."

"As long as you're a happier man." Her hands returned to his shoulders.

"I am," he said after the smallest pause. "I am indeed."

Margaret knew perfectly well why Tilden hesitated. She knew that as water rises in one place it must fall in another. So it must be with Tilden's happiness. And her own. These past two weeks, almost three, she had been living each day only to pass the hours until the call finally came from Wilkins that Tilden had arrived.

"I did not ask if you were content, sir." She poked him lightly. "A pig having his back scratched with a stick is content." She brought her fingertips down until they touched his ribs. "I asked if you were happy. You must reply in a happy manner or I will tickle it out of you."

"I warn you, woman . . ." His left hand snaked free and found her waist. "In all that time you spent practicing the piano, I was learning to tickle. At the age of eight I bested Fat Fannie Bumpus in two tickles flat and before I was ten I—ouch."

Margaret easily broke his grip and threw herself across his back, at once burrowing both her middle fingers under his rib cage.

"It is no use," he said, his face purpling. "See? I am like stone. Job himself would envy my self-command."

Her lips brushed against his ear and parted. "Fat Fannie Bumpus is one thing. Mad Meg Barrie is quite another." A warm wet tongue darted into his ear as both fingers found hidden nerves. Tilden screamed.

"Yield," she demanded.

"That's a foul!" he roared. "An absolutely shocking foul!"

"Yield, I say."

"This won't be forgiven."

"Last chance, Tilden."

"I yield."

"On your word? No revenge?"

"On my word, Margaret."

She released him slowly, in steps. Then, satisfied that he would not spring at her, she turned her attention to the straightening of her dress. It was a fatal error. "You promised," she squealed as Tilden's mass rose up like a wrathful bear and rolled across her body until both crashed loudly to the floor. They wrestled desperately, each thrusting and parrying with index fingers until they suddenly froze at a sharp rapping on the door. Margaret struggled to her feet and, patting her hair in place, ran to answer.

"All is well, I take it." Tilden heard Georgiana's

voice. He imagined that both her hands were behind her back and that there would be a blackjack or bung-starter in one of them.

"Yes, Georgiana," he called, "just a bit of giddi-ness."

"It was a tickling fight." Margaret laughed, breathing hard. "I won and he said there would be no reprisal but he broke his word."

"No such thing." Tilden came to her side. "I gave my word to Margaret. I gave nothing to Mad Meg Bar-rie."

"Deceiver," Margaret charged.

"Torturer!"

"Um." Georgiana smiled helplessly and turned down the hall. "I can remember when this was such a quiet house. So restful. I shall not miss either of you. Not a bit of it."

Margaret, giggling, eased the door shut. She turned toward Tilden. A curious expression on his face caused Georgiana'a last remark to register anew.

"What did she mean, Tilden? That she would not miss us?"

"I was going to speak to you."

Her good humor faded. "Have you made some de-cision for me?"

"Not at all," he answered quickly. "But I have pre-pared the way for you to make a decision. I have taken that liberty. Yes."

"What have you done?"

"Come"—he reached for her hand—"sit and hear me out."

"Tilden, what have you done?"

"I have asked Georgiana to release you from any obligation she might consider that you have toward her. I had to do that before I could ask you to leave here with me and move into a proper set of rooms."

"As your mistress?"

"As my friend, Margaret. All affection between us grows out of that."

"The answer is no, Tilden." Margaret turned from him. "I will not be a kept woman."

"Please hear me." He stepped closer but did not touch her. "I am prepared that you may refuse me, but please hear me first."

Margaret said nothing.

"You have an account, in your name, at the firm of Beckwith and Company. It consists of several hundred shares in each of three very safe businesses. Properly managed, it will provide you with an income which, while not large, should keep you from ever being in doubt of food or shelter. That stock transfer is irrevocable, Margaret. It is done. You need do nothing in return for it."

"Nothing?" There was doubt in her tone.

"Nothing. You can tell me to step out of your life this minute and I will be bound to do it. I have no power over you."

"But you are confident I will not do so."

"It is my earnest hope."

"I can sell these shares and say *that*"—she snapped her fingers—"for you?"

"I'd advise that you keep them. But yes."

"What other arrangements have you made, Tilden?"

"None."

"You have not prepared a love nest someplace? You have not chosen where I am to live?"

"No. I knew that would insult you."

"When am I to leave here?"

"When and if you choose." Tilden took her by the shoulders and guided her into a chair near the window. Tilden had expected some amount of hesitancy. He was, after all, proposing a major alteration in the way she lived her life, but he was at a loss to understand the logic of resisting the prospect of being a mistress when Margaret had come within a hair's breadth of entering a life of prostitution. He'd taken Georgiana at her word that Margaret would not leap at his proposal—she said one thing has nothing to do with the other—but he did not understand it. He did, however, accept Georgiana's advice that he guarantee Margaret's independence and that he impose no conditions. Expensive advice. Five thousand worth of Eastman shares for Georgiana's blessing and another ten of Eastman, New York Elevated, and Sears and Roebuck for Margaret's account.

"What are you thinking, dear Margaret?"

"I don't know." She dabbed at her eyes. "My head is whirling."

"God knows I wish I were free to—" He stopped himself. He was about to suggest that he might ask her to be his wife were it not for Ella. He would want to marry her. Truly. But in the end it would be impossible. "Although I have made no arrangements concerning your—our—future, I have had an idea or two."

She looked up at him, silently.

"The first thing we must do is find you some respectable lodgings. Sunday. We'll do that Sunday. I'll get some listings and we'll go look at them together until we find a place that suits you just so. For the sake of discretion I thought I might represent myself as your lawyer and you as the young widow of an influenza victim. If I am your lawyer, it would not be taken amiss when I begin to call on you often. If you wish, you can change your name as well. You will begin an entirely respectable new life."

"Until you begin spending the night," she said quietly.

"No, that would not do. You're quite right. We could meet whenever we wished but we'd meet elsewhere. We could meet at—Do you know what a house of assignation is?"

"A love nest?"

"Not precisely." Tilden had a notion that he was talking too much but he did not seem able to help himself. "It is somewhat like this house, Georgiana's house, except there are no girls there. There are only rooms where men and women can meet privately. There is a household staff, of course, including a butler who admits only those known to him or those with proper letters of introduction. No woman's name is used or even known by the staff. One guest never sees another, and meals and even baths can be taken in private quarters. Such places are much more comfortable than hotels, Margaret. One can relax in them and shut out the whole world."

"It's gladdening," she said dryly, "that you are so experienced in these matters."

"Oh! Oh no." He knelt at her side. "Georgiana told me about them. I had no idea. I mean, I knew men went to places like this but it never occurred to me that there might be places where women went. The fact that houses of assignation exist came as a shock to me. If they exist they must have clients. If they have clients"—he smiled—"a great many respectable women in New York must be a good deal less respectable than I imagined."

Margaret rose to her feet and paced thoughtfully to the foot of the bed, where she stopped and steadied herself on one of the canopy posts. "So many lies, Tilden," she said at last. "It is so much more simple, more honest, when you come to visit me here."

"But it is a brothel, Margaret. I cannot have you in a brothel."

"Perhaps . . ." She chewed her lip. "Perhaps because of what it is, I expect less from you here, Tilden. Here it is natural for men to come and go according to the demands upon their time. And in between your visits I have the company of Georgiana and Annie and the other girls. Being your mistress sounds so terribly lonely."

"Little Annie is leaving, by the way. Georgiana told me."

"Oh?"

"Georgiana says Annie has saved enough to start a new life. You can be sure she won't call herself Little Annie anymore either."

"I'm so selfish. I should be glad for her."

"Eureka!" Tilden shouted. He jumped to his feet and took Margaret in his arms. "You want it simple? It *is* simple. I've been a fool."

"What are you talking about?" Margaret shook her head, blinking.

"Do you not imagine that Annie, once settled in her new life, will soon attract a male admirer or two?"

"More than likely." She nodded.

"That's it, then. Your problem is solved."

"Tilden, might I have some small clue to what you're thinking?"

"You, dear Margaret, are retiring. Exactly like Annie, you are taking your ill-gotten gains, changing your name, and beginning a respectable new life. During your days you will pursue whatever activities may please you. Or excite you. You might teach piano, or open a dress shop, or continue your education. But as for the evenings, you must not be surprised if a male admirer or two should begin turning up at your door, flowers and bonbons in hand. He will ask you to dinner at Delmonico's in order to turn your head. He will ask you to walk with him, ride with him, skate with him, and dance with him. Thoroughly smitten, he will flood you with attention. And who knows? Perhaps one day you might so far forget yourself as to consent to a glorious weekend with him at some country inn."

"I might even let him kiss me." She smiled.

"That is too much to hope for."

"You *are* a lunatic, Tilden."

"Your answer, woman," he demanded.

"Yes, Tilden. Yes. As soon as I've saved some money."

Tilden looked confused. "How much more could you need?"

"You said that I should not sell those shares. And I have only sixty dollars saved from my salary here. And no, I'll take no more money from you, Tilden."

"But you have nearly a thousand dollars on account with Georgiana."

Margaret shook her head slowly, not certain that she understood him. "The working girls have accounts, not I. I get only the twenty dollars a week I'm paid in salary."

"Well"—he shrugged—"the money is there and it's yours. It must be some sort of dividend." Idiot, he berated himself. There was no doubt about the money. Georgiana had quoted the figure not five minutes before he climbed the stairs to see Margaret. She must have put off mentioning it to her so that Margaret would not realize that he was paying for her company and so that Margaret could persuade herself a while longer that she had not actually begun to sell her body. Well, it didn't matter. She was not a prostitute. Her first night with him was a different matter entirely. He must be sure, however, to alert Georgiana on the way out that questions will be asked.

New Rochelle, Larchmont, Mamaroneck, Rye, Port Chester. The towns along Interstate 95 all ran together across Corbin's field of vision as if the ride past them had taken only seconds. Welcome to Connecticut. Use of Radar Detection Devices Prohibited. Buckle Up for Safety. 55 Saves Lives. Greenwich Next Exit. Corbin, as always, suddenly felt himself being very glad about something. Before just now, he'd never actually known what it was. Now he knew a part of it. Right around the Greenwich Tolls he'd found himself expecting that Margaret would be waiting for him. He'd be walking up the road from the station on a hot summer day and she'd be waiting on the porch, her hair freshly brushed, a smile whose glow he could see a block away, and she'd be pouring a cold lemonade to tempt him into walking faster. As if the lemonade were needed.

Anyway, Margaret would not be there. And it was not a summer day even if this morning was just as bright. Still, he felt good. Gwen was here and at least that was something. More than something. He loved Gwen, he reminded himself. He loved her more than any human being alive and more than anyone he'd ever known. And yet, Margaret, even now, still got in the way of that feeling.

"Which way after I get off, Jonathan?" Sturdevant clicked on his turn signal.

"Pardon me?"

"Here's Exit Three. Where do I go then?"

"Left at the bottom of the ramp. That street winds up to the Post Road."

Corbin settled back and took Gwen's hand. He kissed it. That action, which she took as a show of affection, was more in the nature of an apology for those times during the ride up there when he realized that the woman touching him, rubbing his back, was Gwen and not Margaret, and he'd felt a mild resentment. As if Gwen were intruding. He hoped it hadn't shown. There was nothing in her eyes, no hurt, that would suggest that it had, but who knows? Gwen was so perceptive. And besides, he'd been half dozing most of the way up from New York. Daydreaming. Highway hypnosis. Who knows what you say or do when you're half asleep. He found himself wondering what he'd say to her if she ever asked. What if she asked, What would you do if you had to make a choice between me and

Margaret? But she wouldn't. If she asked anything at all, Gwen's questions would be much more pointed. Such as, Jonathan, isn't it time you separated your feelings once and for all between this living woman who loves you and a woman whom you loved a century ago? Fair enough. But where am I supposed to go to get away from Margaret? Out of New York? Somehow it doesn't seem as though that would do it, especially if Sturdevant is right and this woman I'm half in love with turns out to be my great-grandmother. Out of Greenwich? No. Greenwich is my home.

"Where now?" Sturdevant had climbed a hill to a Stop sign, which required a turn left or right.

"Go right, then bear left, and you'll come to the Greenwich Library on the Post Road. Go right at that light. My house is on Maple Avenue, down another half mile."

"I know where I am now. You said the library was open on Sunday?"

"Until one, I think."

"Do you mind if we stop there first? I'd like to check a few things, particularly if they have newspaper microfilms going back far enough. Do they?"

"Let's take a look."

The main branch of the Greenwich Public Library, a large building of gray stone, was originally a Franklin Simon store, with ample parking in the rear. The store had failed as a business, never quite grasping that old money tends to dress down rather than up, and the property was bought by the town of Greenwich for one of several potential uses. The library won out, but that raised another question. The Franklin Simon building, with four floors including the former bargain basement, was much larger than anything the library could envision needing. However, since all activities tend to expand to fill the time and space available to them, the

Greenwich Public Library soon grew to be one of the largest in the state, complete with a theater that was the largest in all of Greenwich.

Harry Sturdevant found the microfilm section by following signs. Four projection machines and several cabinets contained back issues of the local newspaper, *Greenwich Time,* its ancestor, the *Greenwich Graphic,* and the *New York Times* dated back before the Civil War. Each file tray held microfilm spools covering a period of two to five years. He opened the drawer marked New York Times—Nov. 1887 thru Feb. 1890 and drew out the spool that would contain the month of March 1888. This he handed to Corbin.

"Would you rack this up for me, please, Jonathan, while I locate one or two others?"

Corbin looked at the spool and then at the nearest viewer, which he stared at for a long moment before noticing the set of instructions taped to its lid. Sturdevant pretended not to be watching him. Corbin began by inserting the spool upside down, then backward, then eventually finding the correct track by process of elimination. It pleased Sturdevant to see that the machine had baffled Jonathan. He was now more certain than ever that Jonathan was about to see these pages for the first time. The first, at least, as Jonathan Corbin. Sturdevant took a seat at the viewer and advanced the fast-forward lever until he reached the masthead for March 10, 1888. A Saturday.

The famous blizzard, he already knew, would not actually begin until the evening of the eleventh, but Sturdevant decided that knowing a bit about its context might be useful. A glance at the front page reminded him that Grover Cleveland was in the White House and that Abram Hewitt, the man who'd defeated Teddy Roosevelt for mayor in 1886, was in City Hall. Otherwise, the paper seemed filled with thoughts of spring. The past winter, one column noted, had been the mildest in seventeen years. Robins had already been sighted, trees were budding, crocuses were up. The forecast for the day: again unseasonably warm, temperature in the fifties. The Barnum, Bailey, and Hutchinson Circus arrived in New York that day from its winter headquarters and a torchlight parade through two miles of lower Manhattan was planned for that evening. A bit of entertainment news caught Sturdevant's eye. Ada Rehan was appearing in *A Midsummer Night's Dream,* and the legendary Ellen Terry was starring with Henry Irving in *Faust* at the Star Theater down on Thirteenth Street. He checked the forecast for Sunday. Cloudy. Light rain. Temperatures still above normal. Sturdevant advanced the spool to March 11.

Sunday. Still no indication of anything really amiss. Except that the forecast was calling for heavy rain. Into the evening. Several department stores were announcing spring sales. Sturdevant found himself wondering how Tilden Beckwith had spent that day of rest. At home with his wife and her infant, of whom he must surely have been suspicious by then? Off with Margaret in some cozy hideaway? He didn't know. But their final confrontation certainly did not happen on Sunday.

Monday's edition, the day on which the storm had broken in full fury, was quite thin and generally unenlightening. It had a patchwork look, as if it had been put together by a skeleton staff. Sturdevant wondered how many copies, if any, had actually managed to find their way to the public. On to Tuesday.

There it was. The full magnitude of the disastrous storm screamed from the front page of the *New York Times* dated Tuesday, March 13. Sunday's heavy rains had changed to snow shortly after midnight. By six o'clock Monday morning, when the *Times*'s staff and all other city residents were preparing to go to work, the temperature had dropped to twenty-three degrees and was still falling. Winds were averaging thirty-six miles an hour and gusting as high as eighty-six. These extraordinary winds began piling the driven snow in freakish fashion. One side of a street would be buried in drifts while the other might be swept clean except for an icy coating. By noon, the temperature had dropped to five degrees above zero and the winds had climbed to an average of forty-eight miles an hour. Wires were down everywhere. Even poles. One item mentioned 150 telephone poles down on Tenth Avenue alone. Not that it mattered in terms of service. The Metropolitan Telephone Company, which had sixty-nine hundred subscribers at the time, had asked the electric company not to turn on its dynamos for fear of setting live wires dancing all over the city's streets. All electricity was shut off shortly after noon. Transportation in New York had come to a virtual halt. Elevated trains, their small engines unable to make the slightest grade, stalled high above the streets. Entrepreneurs down below secured ladders and began charging passengers a dollar a head for their use, the alternative being to remain where they were until they froze or until their bladders gave them cause to rethink their options.

On the surface, the streets were clogged with abandoned wagons, horsecars, and dead horses. Hack drivers were collecting appalling fees, in advance, for the attempt to reach destinations that might normally be fifteen minutes away. Some made it hours later, some not at all. Sturdevant could almost see the desperation on the faces of clerks and factory workers as they struggled on toward jobs in which job security was unknown. A day's pay was the least an absence might cost them. Even the owners of businesses felt compelled to appear, partly as an example to their employees, partly as an obligation to those who might otherwise arrive and find the doors locked, and because they knew no other way.

Tuesday's entire issue was dotted with tales of futility, venality, heroism, and tragedy. B. Altman's department store had opened Monday and had one customer all day. A woman bought a spool of thread. R. H. Macy's on Fourteenth Street closed early, brought in food, and turned its furniture department into a dormitory for the staff. Four patrons turned up for the dinner show at Tony Pastor's. Pastor put the show on anyway and treated the cast and the loyal four to a champagne and sandwich party afterward. Several well-dressed men appeared at the city jail, confessing that they were vagrants who ought to be incarcerated, at a time when the understaffed jail was offering to release legitimate vagrants, all of whom declined with thanks. A policeman found a wagon driver who was coated with ice and appeared frozen stiff. Upon being roused, the driver was shocked to learn where he was. He had thought he was home in bed in Brooklyn.

Others never woke up at all. Bodies, either dead or nearly so, were being found everywhere. The old woman who sold flowers in front of the New York Herald Building died of exposure on her wooden box before anyone noticed that she was no longer moving. Some of the poor who huddled for warmth near the sidewalk steam grates of office buildings succumbed there. Several children were discovered. Two of them had been given baskets and sent out to beg by their fathers. One man had been observed trying for a full hour just to cross Seventy-second Street near the Hudson River. At each attempt the wind would slam him down or drive him back. He finally crawled across only to disappear in a whirl of snow out of which the helpless witness knew he would never rise. In the fifties, an asthmatic malts and hops merchant tried to reach his office and sank exhausted into a drift not a block from his home—Hello! Sturdevant looked up at Corbin, who was helping Gwen thread a spool of the *Greenwich Graphic*.

"Jonathan," he asked, "does the name George Baremore mean anything to you?"

"Baremore?" Corbin narrowed his eyes. "Was that the George found dead in the snowbank?"

"You tell me."

"I'm not sure. Baremore sounds like it could be right."

"How well did you know him?"

Corbin shrugged. "The best I can tell you, I sort of see myself saying hello to him at the elevator and making polite conversation. He was in the beer business, I think."

"Malts and hops. What did he look like?"

"A big man. Bigger than me. About my age."

Sturdevant rubbed his hands. The newspaper account gave Baremore's age as thirty-seven and noted that even a two-hundred-pounder was helpless against this storm. "Did you know he had asthma?"

Corbin shook his head, a touch impatiently.

"Yes, Jonathan," Gwen reminded him. "You said he looked as though he was gasping for breath."

"Never mind Baremore." Corbin moved to Sturdevant's shoulder. "If you're looking at a list of the dead, look for Ella."

"There's no list." Sturdevant gestured toward the page. "Only random anecdotes. The storm is still going strong as this is written. But I'll move ahead."

Wednesday's paper. March 14. The *New York Times* described a city that was entirely cut off from the outside and eerily stilled. No trains ran anywhere. All supplies, especially coal, were rapidly being depleted, and profiteers were selling eggs for as much as forty cents each. In the harbor, nine of New York's pilot boats were sunk. Authorities feared the loss of up to two hundred other ships of every description. Searches at sea were impossible because Tuesday's winds still averaged forty-five miles an hour and the snow kept fall-

ing, although temperatures had risen from one degree
below zero at dawn to twenty-three by midafternoon.
More people were found. Many of those who survived
would lose one or more limbs to frostbite. Sturdevant
reached for the fast-forward switch and was about to
advance the reel to the next day's edition when he felt
Corbin's hand on his.

"No," Jonathan whispered. "Next page."

Sturdevant brought it into frame. Before he could
scan it, Corbin's hand moved slowly into view and his
finger pointed at a column in the top right corner next
to an ad for Scott's Emulsion. Sturdevant saw the name
at once, although it was only one of a dozen names.
Missing. Mrs. Tilden Beckwith. Age 24.

Ella.

Reported by her husband.

Last seen the evening of March 12th. Heading east
on 58th street. Destination unknown to Mr. Beckwith.

"How dare you accuse me?"

"Answer me, Ella." His voice was quiet, controlled. "How is it possible that the child can be mine?"

"By the usual method, I suppose. There are books
on the subject if human reproduction remains a mystery to you."

He realized now that Margaret had tried to tell
him. Margaret, whom he'd taken out of Georgiana
Hastings's house only to neglect most cruelly when a
month later Ella told him she was with child. Ella, who
for the first and only time in her life had actually
pleaded with him to come to her bed during his second
night home from his trip abroad. Ella, who had never
again shown such appetites after that one night. Margaret, in whom he again sought comfort and compan-
ionship, although not without guilt as before because of
the child who was swelling his wife's belly. Margaret,
who had been all his joy these past eight months. She

had tried to tell him. In her gentle way, she had tried to make him count the months. She would never have said, "Tilden, an infant born in mid-January had to have been conceived in mid-April of the year preceding. You were in London then, Tilden. All that month and parts of March and May as well. You have been cuckolded, Tilden." No. Instead, Margaret spoke of mother cats and the number of days in which their kittens would invariably be born after the encounter that ultimately produced them. Only sixty-three. So much faster than for cows and women, both of whom take a full nine months. But Margaret would not mind. That, she told him. She would take pleasure in every single day of the nine-month term as long as she had the child of a man she loved growing inside her. Margaret would speak of these things and Tilden would notice an odd sorrow in her eyes. He had never questioned it. He felt sure that her sorrow was no more than an unspoken regret that it was Ella who carried his baby and not she.

In the end it was Georgiana who told him. On a Saturday two days past when she came to his office to discuss her investments, Georgiana inquired of the child. She asked, innocently enough, with what name he had been christened. Ella's choice was Huntington, he told her, after her family name, but the christening would not be until Sunday a week. Describe him, she then asked. What is his coloring? And from there on her questions became even more pointed until at last he demanded their purpose. It was then she told him of the laughter she'd heard in her house that past April from men who spoke of the absent Tilden and the available Ella with equal contempt. Men who chortled about Ella's loose tongue in matters of Tilden's business and who made reference, however unclear to Georgiana, to a relationship between Ella's infidelity and the financial destruction of Cyrus Field at Jay Gould's hand. Men to whom she had thereafter barred her doors. Men named Albert Hacker and Ansel Carling and another whose name she could not recall.

"There are books," Ella had sneered.

"I need no books, Ella," he answered her, "only a calendar. The child, as all but the blind could see, is not mine. Whose child is it, Ella?"

"You are such a fool, Tilden."

"We can rule out Albert Hacker. Hacker is fat, has bad teeth, and does not clean his fingernails. It is hard for me to imagine you tumbling with a man so unfastidious. There's another in that crowd, I forget his name, but he chews cigars and leaves brown spittle to dry on his vest. Enough said of him. That would seem to leave Ansel Carling, Ella."

She stiffened but quickly recovered. "A long rest in an asylum would do you a world of good, sir. Consider it."

"Tell me about Ansel Carling, Ella. He is quite the cultivated gentleman, isn't he? And a lion of commerce on top of it. A latter-day Ivanhoe."

"It is unbecoming, Tilden," she said icily, "to mock that to which you cannot aspire."

"Hardly the sort of man," Tilden continued, "who would bandy a lady's name about in a Thirty-sixth Street whorehouse. Hardly the type to boast of his conquest to friends without even being discreet enough to do so behind closed doors."

Ella paled by several shades. "What are you talking about?" she asked.

"He laughed at you, Ella."

"You are a liar."

"Oh, he laughed at me as well. He laughed at me for being blind, which was true enough. But he laughed at you because you were so easy for him, Ella. And because he finds you silly, Ella."

"Liar!" she screamed.

"Aside from that unaccountably dark and sallow infant in there"—Tilden gestured toward the nursery—"what else did you easily give him? Did you give him the knowledge of Cyrus Field's business affairs? Did you give him the means, from my private records, to destroy a man who is worth a thousand of you, Ella?"

Her eyes went wide. She stared at him for several long moments, her face first a mask of fear, then of contempt, then fear again. "I will hear no more of this." She turned away from him, passing an iced-over window that crackled under the assault of driven sleet.

"I want you gone, Ella," he said coolly. "Tomorrow, if the trains are running, I want you to take your child and go home to Philadelphia. Take your twin beds as well. I intend to divorce you on a bill of adultery."

"Do you indeed, sir?" She stopped and faced him.

"With all possible haste. If you do not go of your own accord, by the way, I will put you and your belongings on the sidewalk."

"To make room for your slut, I presume."

Now Tilden paled.

"Hypocrite," she spat.

Tilden held his tongue, though alarmed by her use of the word *slut*. It troubled him less that Ella seemed to know of Margaret than that she might know of Margaret's origins and could use that knowledge to do her harm. And if Ella knew, so, by deduction, did Carling. And therefore Jay Gould as well.

"There will be no divorce, Tilden"—she smirked—"except at a time and on conditions of my choosing. Press me on this and I swear I will leave your life in tatters."

"As with Cyrus Field, for example," he hissed.

"He's as great a fool as you. Though not so great as to have bought himself a private whore."

Tilden took two steps closer to her and paused, an

expression almost of sorrow on his face. Then he slapped her hard across the mouth.

"Tomorrow, Ella," he told her. "Tomorrow I want you gone."

She'd almost fallen, not from the force of the blow but out of shock. She had never dreamed that Tilden might strike her. No one had hit her, ever, not in her entire life. He is a madman. An animal. Ansel. I must get to Ansel. He will protect me. Gathering herself, Ella crossed to their entrance hall and fought the knob of the clothes closet there. When I tell him what has been done to me here, when I show him, he will rush back here and give Tilden the caning of his life. He will avenge me. And oh, how he'll laugh at Tilden's childish lies. Easy, indeed. Silly! We shall see who is silly.

Ella snatched the first coat she found and struggled into it. She reached for a hatbox, knocking several to the floor, and plucked from the debris a small feathered toque that would be useless for the conditions outside. She ignored three pairs of boots that sat in the rear of the closet.

Tilden considered stopping her. She was dangerously out of her senses. If her intention was to cool her fury she might find more coolness than she bargained for. But let her go, he decided. He was sure that she would go no more than a few steps once she saw that the storm was slapping her with a force much greater than he had used.

His back was to the door when he heard it slam. In the hallway outside he heard a single squeal of rage and then a series of smacks, which he imagined were the sounds of her hand pounding the call button of the elevator. He regretted that the night operator must see her condition. He heard the sound of sliding doors and the clatter of metal gates.

"Tilden." He jumped at the echoing sound of his name. "You are not a man, Tilden." Oh no. He closed his eyes. The operator. The neighbors. *"I know what a real man is like. Sleep well, Tilden. But do not be surprised if Ansel pays you a visit and whips the life out of you."* The elevator doors rolled shut.

"My God! Is it possible?" he gasped through his embarrassment. Would she actually go there? At night? Unescorted? He could not permit it. Tilden walked quickly to the closet and found a gray lamb's-wool coat and hat. But what of the infant, he thought as he pulled on his gloves. Neither Bess, the housekeeper, nor Mrs. Vickers, the nurse, had come because of the storm. In the whole building, hardly any servants and few staff had made it through. Could he leave the infant alone? Tilden crossed to the nursery door and looked inside. All was quiet. The infant would be fine for the few minutes it would take to remind Ella of her duties and to drag her back if necessary.

Tilden chose a stout walking stick from the hallway stand and stepped through the door, closing it quietly behind him. He headed toward the stairs. A visit from Ansel Carling, he muttered to himself as he descended them. I dare not even pray for such a blessing. But there will be a visit. Depend on it, Carling. And it is I who will do the visiting.

Tilden reached the lobby and went quickly into the storm. No one saw him leave.

Sturdevant moved his chair aside to afford Corbin and Gwen Leamas a better view of the projected microfilm page. He glanced up at their faces. Gwen's expression was animated, excited. She caught her breath when she saw the name Tilden Beckwith on a printed page and repeated it aloud. Corbin, fascinated at first, now seemed confused, dazed. But a bit angry as well, Sturdevant decided.

He watched as Corbin's hand reached slowly forward and his thumb began brushing over the glass at one edge. Gwen stiffened. She knew at once what the hand was doing. It was attempting to turn the page. Sturdevant touched a finger to his lips and advanced the reel, slowly, one page at a time, moving on only when Corbin's thumb began to move. On page 2 of the newspaper dated Thursday, March 15, Corbin's hand went flat.

There it was. Storm victim. Ella Huntington Beckwith. Age 24. The wife of Tilden Beckwith of the Osborne Apartments. Reported missing on March 12th. Found between stacks of bricks on the construction site of the new Plaza Hotel. Police were investigating.

Investigating? Why? Ah, yes, Sturdevant realized. Statistical probabilities. How is it that two unrelated neighbors from the same apartment house perished in the same storm in the same general area? It might be possible to dig up the record of that investigation for what it might be worth. Probably not much. Once the police established that no relationship existed between Ella Beckwith and George Baremore, the coincidence would have been accepted and Ella would be just one more person who fatally underestimated the storm that first night.

"Can we talk in private, sir?" The policeman, a hulking figure who introduced himself as Inspector Williams, cocked his head toward John Flood, who had visited Tilden daily since Ella was first reported missing.

Flood rose to his feet. "I'll just use that fancy bathroom of yours a while, lad. Sing out if you need me." He met the inspector's eyes and held them. Neither man blinked until Flood had passed.

"That's John Flood, ain't it? The Bull's Head Terror?"

"Yes."

"I seen him fight Sullivan up in Yonkers. I don't

guess a gent like you would have been there." His voice was curiously high-pitched.

"I was there, Inspector."

"Tough man." He raised a fist. "Went eight rounds against John L. No one but Paddy Ryan has lasted longer."

Tilden nodded, waiting.

"Appertainin' to that, sir," he asked, "how is it that a society feller like yourself is pals with the likes of John Flood? You wouldn't be feelin' no need for a bodyguard, would you?"

"John's been a friend since I was twelve." He ignored the last part of the policeman's question.

"Though by the look of you, sir, you've mixed it up once or twice yourself."

"Can we get on with this, Inspector?"

"We can, sir. We can indeed."

Tilden waited again.

"You can understand, sir, how the Baremore feller and Missus Beckwith both bein' from the same address caught the eye of the department. Could there have been a connection, sir?"

"No." Tilden shook his head. "They scarcely knew each other on sight."

"I thought as much myself." Williams spread his hands. "Mr. Baremore left for work that morning. Your wife a full ten hours later. Odd thing, though. She must have practically stepped right over his body to get to where they found her."

Tilden said nothing.

"Have you a notion where she was goin', sir, that was worth bein' out on a night like that?"

"No."

"Well, this is real embarrassin' for me, sir, but I have to point out I know different. I know you and her had some strong words, maybe even a blow was struck, and I know she said something about a feller named Ansel comin' to fix your hash."

Color rose on Tilden's neck. He did not know what infuriated him more, whether the fact that his striking a woman for the only time in his life was now public knowledge, or that a linkage of her name to Carling's was as well, or that this thug of a policeman could even consider the notion of Ansel Carling surviving two minutes with him.

"Would this Ansel feller be livin' over at the Navarro Flats?"

"He would. Why do you ask?"

Williams pulled an object wrapped in paper from his coat pocket. "Your wife had no hat when she was found, sir. We found this along the way, right in front of where a man named Ansel Carling lives." He showed the crushed lump of cloth and feathers to Tilden. "Looks like a dead bird, don't it. Would it be her hat, by chance?"

"It would." Tilden took a breath.

Williams examined it curiously. "A poor excuse for a head covering, ain't it, all things considered. It's a damn sight short of a nor'easter."

"Will there be anything else, Inspector?"

"No, sir." Williams rose to his feet, placing the hat on a table beside his chair. "I'll leave you to your grief now."

He stepped toward the door and paused. "By the way, sir, did you leave this house at all that night?"

"No."

"You're certain, sir?"

"Yes." He decided to risk it. "There's the baby."

"The baby. Yes, of course."

"May I ask you a question?"

"Yes, indeed."

"Why is an officer of your rank conducting this investigation?"

"Well, sir"—Williams made a sweeping gesture, which took in Tilden and the apartment's furnishings—"not all the men in the lower ranks are as tactful as me in dealin' with people like yourself. Some of them might even have asked if you, by the slightest chance, might have a lady friend you want to keep quiet about and they might have asked you for a little gift appertainin' to them keepin' mum on it." He held up a hand before Tilden could start toward him. "The real truth is, I'm lookin' in on you as a favor to a mutual friend. That's Mr. Gould, by the way."

"Jay Gould?" Tilden's eyes widened.

"There ain't but one. And he has nothin' but kindly thoughts for you, sir. I know he hopes you feel as kindly toward him."

"Good afternoon, Inspector."

John Flood pulled the chain of the carved oak toilet tank, causing a pipe-banging rush of water that would allow Tilden to believe he'd not been listening in case that was the way his friend wanted it. But Flood had left the door ajar, not so much to eavesdrop as to be within quick reach if Tilden's interview with Williams turned ugly. The stare-down he'd given that copper promised as much. Tilden was a handy enough man with his fists, fair to say, but he'd be no match for Clubber Williams if it came to that, even if the Clubber was twenty years his elder.

Flood himself was just a boy of fifteen when he saw Williams lay out some of the toughest men in New York. John had been working as a swamper in the old Florence Saloon down on Houston Street near Broadway and taking a pass-the-hat fight in the alley out back four or five times a week. Clubber, though they did not yet call him that, was the new patrolman assigned to that little section of the Fourth Ward where the worst of the city's gangs had their hangouts. There was a chalkboard on the wall of the Florence where the

Whyos and the Plug-Uglies kept a sporting record of
the policemen each gang had killed or maimed. The
gang that let two weeks pass without having a copper's
hat or ear to show as a trophy had to stand drinks for
the other. But taking souvenirs was becoming harder
work those days because the coppers were learning
never to walk in groups of less than three. Over in Five
Points, coppers had learned not to walk at all. Except
Clubber Williams. Williams saw things different. His
first day on the beat he walked right up outside the
Florence and commenced to pick a fight with the two
toughest men he saw there—Hoggy Walsh and Dandy
Johnny Dolan of the Whyos—and he smashed both of
them to the ground with his stick. Dandy Johnny Dolan
got up and tried to use this eye-gouger he had special
made for his thumb—it was carryin' eyes around in his
pockets that finally got him hung—but old Clubber
smashed his hand and then his knee and threw him
through the Florence's window. Four more Whyos and
two Plug-Uglies came runnin' out to teach him a lesson,
includin' Skinner Meehan with his hash knife, and
Clubber laid 'em out to a man. It's said he cracked a
skull a day for three years after that till they jumped
him to captain and put him where the money was. Now
there ain't a whorehouse or gaming joint in all the Ten-
derloin, well named by Williams himself, that don't
ante up to him the first of every month.

"Did you hear?" Tilden asked as John Flood reentered the living room.

"Not a word, lad," he answered, "unless you want
I did."

Tilden nodded, sighing deeply, then walked slowly
to a window looking out upon New York. "Is there
anyone in this city," he asked sadly, "who does not
know that Ella was . . . deceiving me with Ansel Carling?"

"Not so many, lad. Not so many at all."

"And of that number," he added, "how many will always believe it was I who killed her?"

"I did not hear that either, Tilden," John Flood said firmly. "And I don't ever want to hear it again." Flood had made up his mind it was an accident at worst, a suicide at best. "If you'd choked the life out of her with your own hands, I would not have blamed you. But you didn't. 'Twas she who fell; you did not knock her down. 'Twas she who mocked you and spited you to the end when a single word of repentance would have saved her. What else could you have done? Could the man I know have stepped aside and let her run on up to Ansel Carling's kip?"

"I should have. I should have just walked away and gone home."

"She'd be dead as Kelsey's goat all the same. Forget it, lad. It was no murder. You had no murder in your heart."

Tilden said nothing for a long moment. He looked out across the city he now despised. It was five days since the snow had stopped, and it remained in great mounds on every street corner and along every curb. Ella's body, not much colder dead than alive, was being kept on ice in a Ninth Avenue mortuary until the gravediggers could catch up with their backlog or until her family answered his wire asking if they'd rather she lie among her own in Philadelphia. He hoped they would take her. It would save him the agony of a service and it would place her all the farther from his thoughts. The Reverend Bellwood from Saint Thomas had come to comfort him and during his visit had inquired of his plans to have the child christened before his soul went much longer without that protection. Saturday next, Tilden decided. Be done with it. What name, sir, the Reverend Bellwood asked. Her name, not mine. Call him Huntington.

"Huntington Beckwith." The minister wrote it down. "And the middle name?"

"Sir?"

"Have you chosen a middle name? It is customary to bestow one or more family names upon a child in addition to his Christian name so that he may carry his heritage with him always."

"His heritage, you say?"

"That is the custom, Mr. Beckwith."

"Give him the initial *B*. Nothing more."

"*B*, sir? What does it stand for?"

"It stands alone. It is his heritage."

"It will be so, sir." Though he was doubtful, the Reverend Bellwood agreed.

And may God forgive me this as well, thought Tilden. But if bastardy is his heritage, let him carry it. May God forgive me that I cannot love this unlovely child. True enough that the child cannot be blamed for his mother's sin, but even if this were a pretty and well-tempered infant, which it is not, how could I ever look upon its features except to be reminded every day of his life of Ella Huntington and Ansel Carling.

Through the window, on down Fifty-seventh Street, his eye fell upon the signal tower of the Sixth Avenue Elevated. Cyrus Field's elevated. Even that had now turned ugly where once the sight of it had never failed to thrill him. Tilden's father had helped to build it just as he'd helped Cyrus Field ten years before that in the stupendous accomplishment of laying the Atlantic cable. Beckwith & Company had financed or secured loans for both and had issued the shares. The Sixth Avenue Elevated was a wonderful success. The fulfillment of one dream and the beginning of another. Crawling, congested traffic in the city's streets would be a thing of the past. And Cyrus's New York Elevated Company was turning a solid profit. It was much more successful, much better managed, than the rival Metropolitan Railway Company, which ran the Second Avenue Elevated under the rapacious ownership of Jay Gould and Russell Sage. Yet Cyrus Field had agreed to a merger of the two companies. Tilden and his father were against it. But Field was adamant. A centrally managed cooperative system was essential to well-ordered growth, he said. Just so, Stanton Beckwith argued, but not with these two brigands. They would surely raise the fares until the people are squeezed dry, and they will work every possible mischief with the company's shares.

They did, of course. Gould quickly moved to double all fares and Field, though resisting at first, finally yielded to Jay Gould's argument that the resulting windfall would permit expansion all the way to the borders of Westchester. But when the *New York Times* loudly condemned the action, pointing out that the new Manhattan Company would be picking the average worker's pockets of one full dollar a week out of the mere eight that he probably earned, and when that paper began tarring Field with the same brush as Gould and Sage, Cyrus, Tilden believed, began to fear for the place in history his Atlantic cable accomplishment had already secured for him. He forced the restoration of the five-cent fare, threatening to take his case to the public if Gould did not yield on the matter. Gould did yield, agreeably on the surface but deeply resentful of Field's sentimentality and poor business sense. More, that Cyrus Field had defied him. Gould was not a man to forget such a thing. It was said of Gould that he ate his revenge cold. He would wait. In the meantime, he would content himself with the ten-cent fare being charged for the specially decorated parlor cars. But even these revenues soon fell beneath his expectations. Too few men and women were willing to pay the extra fare, the novelty of Axminster carpets having worn off, for so short a ride as a shopping excursion to the department stores of Fourteenth or Twenty-third Street or the daily half-hour ride to a Wall Street office.

By this time, Ansel Carling had become one of Gould's most trusted agents, to the extent Gould trusted anyone at all. Carling had first surfaced ten years earlier in San Francisco, where he appeared at the offices of the Central Pacific Railway bearing a letter of introduction from the governor general of the British East India Company. The letter said that after serving in the British army with great distinction, Carling, third son of England's reclusive Sir Andrew Carling, had joined the company and soon became one of the driving forces in the completion of the railway between Lucknow and Calcutta, slapping aside governmental interference and Sikh attacks with equal vigor. The Central Pacific's president, Collis P. Huntington, no relation to Ella, put him to work extorting bribes from towns along the railroad's right-of-way, offering them a choice between paying for a line or spur to be laid through them or withering into ghost towns as the spurs were granted, legally or not, to the higher bidder elsewhere.

After Collis Huntington moved his family to New York, built a Fifth Avenue mansion across from that of Cornelius Vanderbilt, Jr., and settled into the pursuit of his wife's social ambitions, Ansel Carling developed similar, if more modest, tastes. He now had the Central Pacific Railway's letter of introduction to add to that of the British East India Company, and these he brought to Jay Gould, who at that time owned the Metropolitan Railway Company, parts of several other lines, plus the Western Union Telegraph Company and the *New York World* newspaper as well. Gould was much impressed by Carling's buccaneer spirit and even more so by his lineage, Gould himself being a former grocery clerk from upstate New York. Gould hired him and eventually made Carling his executive assistant. The two men, being equally unencumbered by business scruples or compassion, understood each other well.

In 1885, Cyrus Field secretly began buying up shares in the Manhattan Elevated Company in an effort to gain full control and to squeeze out Gould and Sage. As before, he did this through Beckwith & Company. By early 1886, Gould realized what Field was doing but bided his time, waiting month by month as the stock price was slowly driven up by Field's purchases. As the share price climbed higher, Field was obliged to buy on margin. Gould rubbed his hands. When the moment was right, and Field was believed extended to the breaking point, Gould and Sage dumped their stock on the market, forcing the share price down sixty points below the one Field was obliged to pay. Field was bankrupted. Utterly ruined.

Both Tilden and his father had been aware that their friend was playing an extremely dangerous game. If Gould knew what Field was up to, and they had to assume he did, Gould would certainly do all in his power to learn precisely the right moment to strike. Through bribery or blackmail he would doubtlessly try to subvert some clerk at Beckwith & Company into telling him which transactions in Manhattan Elevated stock were those of Cyrus Field in disguise. To safeguard against this, Tilden chose to keep all such records at his home. He knew that Gould would learn about this as well, but he was not greatly concerned. Short of commissioning a burglary, Gould would have no access to them. Tilden never imagined, of course, that Jay Gould would simply commission Ansel Carling to seduce his wife.

A loud jarring ring cleared Tilden's eyes and startled John Flood into a defensive stance. It rang again and Flood touched his palms to his ears. "Jesus," he shouted over the sound, "I'll never get used to those things." Tilden crossed to the telephone, whose clumsy box of oak and brass hung on the living room wall near its entrance.

"Hello, who is there?" He spoke loudly into the funneled mouthpiece. "Yes, Nat, I hear you. Yes."

That would be Nat Goodwin, the actor from downstairs, Flood decided, although if he was in his apartment Flood couldn't imagine why he'd use that contraption when he could as well open a window. But wherever he was, whatever he was saying, Tilden's face was turning black as thunder as he listened.

"How many men are there," Tilden asked, "and how many with him?"

He nodded, satisfied.

"I'm grateful, Nat. Thirty minutes at the most. Stand them a round if you must but try to hold them there. I'm breaking off now so I can dress." Tilden replaced the earpiece on its hook.

"Carling?" Flood asked quietly.

"Yes." Tilden stepped past him toward his bedroom. "He is at the Hoffman House with some of his friends."

"I'll be going with you."

"No, John." Tilden pulled off his shirt and slipped out of his trousers. From an armoire he'd already cleared of Ella's clothing he selected a suit of evening dress. "Nat Goodwin will watch my back if there's a need. He also has that *Wild West Show* fellow, Cody, with him at the bar."

Tilden fumbled with his studs and John Flood moved to help him. "Goodwin's no brawler, lad, and he's a bantamweight at best. I'd better work your corner."

"No." Tilden shook his head. "When this is over, I do not want it said that I needed the man who gave John L. Sullivan all that he could handle to deal with the likes of Ansel Carling. There's more pride in that than I intend to leave him with."

Flood grunted doubtfully. "See that he doesn't leave you with your head stove in from behind or with a sword cane's blade between your ribs."

"You're a good friend, John." He turned to receive the jacket Flood was holding for him.

"Good enough," the fighter asked, "to say aloud it's cruel of you to have had no thought for Margaret in all that's happened?"

"I've ached for her, John." Flood saw his face soften at her name. "Whatever thoughts I've had, she's there beneath them."

"How would she know that, lad?" he asked gently.

Corbin, his hand still flat against the projected image of the newspaper page, nodded sadly.

"Jonathan?"

Corbin jerked.

"Jonathan," Gwen asked, "is something happening?"

"I'd better go," he whispered. He straightened and turned, then suddenly winced at the shock of bright fluorescent lights. Harry Sturdevant pushed back his chair and reached for his arm.

"Wait." Corbin waved him off. "Wait. It's all right." The maelstrom of his mind began to slow and his inner eye watched as unconnected thoughts and fleeting memories settled one by one into sequence. Corbin knew where he was. The library. And there was no need to go after Carling. He'd done that. It was over.

Nor was there a need to berate himself for his neglect of Margaret. He'd dealt with that as well. He must have. Because he remembered walking with Margaret when the child, his own child, was almost full grown in her and she was asking him to tell her again about the house that would be hers in Greenwich and about the grand new life they would begin there together. They were walking down Fifty-eighth Street in the snow and he was saying how her house would be the second in all Greenwich with electric lights inside, and she laughed when he told her about Mr. Johnson, the president of the Edison Electric Company, who not only had the first electric house but who even had an electrified carriage with battery-powered light bulbs on it including one that hung on a long pole in front of the horse and made him cockeyed.

No. No, hold it. That conversation wasn't on Fifty-eighth Street. It was up at the Claremont Inn where he'd moved her once her belly began to swell, and gave her a new name, and waited for the house to be ready. A new name. Yes.

"I think I will choose the name Charlotte. It is a name I have always admired. There is a certain gaiety to it, do you not think so, Tilden?"

"Then may I suggest Whitney for a surname. It smacks of wealth and substance. I will be Harry Whitney while we stay at the Claremont. Men named Harry are always good fellows. I will be a salesman. Of baseball equipment. That will explain why I am not there most nights and, selfishly I confess, it will give us an excuse to spend more time at the Polo Grounds."

Charlotte Whitney. Corbin nodded, his fingers rubbing his eyes. Grandmother Corbin's name. Charlotte Whitney Corbin. He'd accepted last night, in Sturdevant's den, that Margaret Barrie and Charlotte Corbin were probably the same woman. But accepting it was not the same as knowing it.

"Come on, Jonathan." Gwen took his elbow. "Let's get some air."

"No." He leaned against the microfilm cabinet. "Just let me stand here for a minute."

A few pieces were still floating down. Like leaves. Or more like snowflakes because some seemed to melt in the air. And there remained a great open space between the time Tilden left for the Hoffman House and the time he and Margaret sat around deciding what names they'd put on the Claremont Inn register. But he knew most of it, he supposed. He certainly knew what he'd done to Ansel Carling, and he remembered Carling's threat to ruin him and to cut up Margaret's face. Was that why he hid her at the Claremont? To keep her safe from Carling?

Fights. More fights. Not with Carling this time. But with whom? There were two thugs, maybe hired by Carling, and he was fighting them on a dark street at night, and losing, going down, and then he's fighting one of them again and it's daylight but indoors with many other men watching. In a prize ring? Some back room? Corbin couldn't tell. He would try to see it and then there would be still another brawl, involving different men, sort of superimposed on top of it, and during this new fight broken glass was falling all around him.

Corbin shook his head. He almost whistled. That was at least three major fights, all with fists. He found himself hoping that Tilden had one hell of a cut man or at least was smart enough to carry something inside his hands.

Corbin shut his eyes, the better to see and sort out all these different people Tilden was hammering, and being hammered by. But when he did, another part of his brain threw still more fight scenes on the screen. Here's one where they're all in business suits. And Tilden's older, much older, but still popping away. Didn't they ever leave him alone?

Then, on top of all the others, Corbin saw himself. He was younger, about twenty, and he was in another dark place and there were two other men. Tough men, although they could have been his father's age. He didn't know them, but he hated them and was enjoying what he was doing to them. He was hurt and bleeding, but not as badly as he was hurting them.

Corbin knew this dream. He'd had it before. And he also knew it wasn't real. It was a revenge fantasy he'd created years before to help him deal with a beating he took from two men who attacked him for no reason in the parking garage under Chicago's Drake Hotel when he was home on Christmas break. It wasn't even a mugging. They took nothing.

Corbin shook that vision away. It embarrassed him. That vision had him winning, methodically shattering the knees and elbows and finally the heads of those two men, but he knew it hadn't happened that way. He'd barely had a glimpse of them before it was he himself who was helpless on the cold concrete floor.

Think about Margaret. Why the name change? And why the move to the Claremont? Corbin knew he'd gone to her, maybe right from the Hoffman House, because he was afraid for her after Carling said what he'd do, and because Williams seemed to know about her, too—Williams. Oh, Christ! Now who the hell is Williams? Someone connected with Jay Gould. Right. Anyway, Tilden went to Margaret and either that same night or soon after he asked her if she'd have his child. Let's see. Christmas. Grandfather Jonathan was born on Christmas Day of 1888. That means conception was the end of March. Yes. It fits. Margaret must have agreed. She must have stopped using those little vinegar sponges of hers right away. It's funny that old Tilden lets me see some things and not others.

Corbin glanced at Sturdevant. Good fellow. All men named Harry are good fellows. Sturdevant was saying something to Gwen about wanting to look at some more microfilms but you and Jonathan go ahead. He'll walk to Maple Avenue. Corbin wondered whether he should say anything to Harry about the way Tilden picks and chooses what he'll let him see. Better not.

Sturdevant would only start looking at him as though he was a laboratory slide again, because he would have just taken one hell of a leap from Sturdevant's benign concept of genetic memory into a whole new ball game in which Tilden is real, a real person who thinks and makes decisions and even smacks ancestors across the face when they make wisecracks about whorehouse season tickets.

Get back to Margaret. She was working. Tilden had set her up in a place in the East Sixties, but she'd found a job. Something to do with a newspaper. Women were starting to make a stir as journalists. Nelly Bly. Around the world in eighty days. But Margaret did want Tilden's child. And she couldn't stay at any newspaper or even in her rooms if she was unmarried and beginning to show. So, the Claremont Inn. As Charlotte and Harry. A long, peaceful autumn of sitting on the Claremont's porch, watching the Hudson River drift by, going to baseball games with picnic hampers, and taking the train up to Greenwich to see how the carpenters and the electrical linesmen were progressing.

How am I doing, Tilden?

Batting about .500, right? Because that's when most of those fights were happening, wasn't it. Someone was leaning on you. Carling, Gould, somebody. And there was a new guy, I don't know his name but I can see him, Colonel something-or-other, sounds like Colonel Dan, and he had a newspaper, not Margaret's newspaper, and he was trying to hit you for a payoff to keep your name and Margaret's out of it, and you told him to buzz off, and then he tried to sell you something else, something about Carling.

"Dr. Sturdevant," Corbin asked, with a firmness of voice that surprised Gwen's uncle, "have you ever heard of a newspaper publisher with a name like Colonel Dan?"

"From the late nineteenth century?"

"Yes."

"Could you possibly mean Colonel Mann? He published a scandal sheet called *Town Topics*. Full name was William D'Alton Mann."

"Looked like Santa Claus?"

"Now that you mention it"—Sturdevant nodded—"he always carried sugar cubes for horses and rock candy for children. But he was a notorious blackmailer. Why do you ask?"

"It's nothing." Jonathan shook his head.

It's none of your business.

ELEVEN

 OT A SOUL DOWN ON THE CORNER . . . IT'S A very certain sign . . . Those wedding bells are breaking up that old gang of mine."

Raymond Lesko turned on his shower hot and full, then sat fully clothed on the edge of his toilet, facing out toward his apartment door. His service revolver hung from his right hand. With his left hand he held a washcloth in front of his lips to lightly muffle the sound of his singing voice. He turned the wrist of that hand to look at his watch. Ten after eight. No call from Dancer.

He had to assume that Dancer had decided against negotiating. If that was correct, he'd have to further assume that Dancer would be sending shooters. Or Beckwith security people. Whatever. And if the shooters happened to be already waiting outside the door, and they heard the shower going and his voice lifted in carefree song, that would seem like a very good time to kick in the door and start blasting away through the shower curtain. So, just in case, Lesko had decided, he'd give about ten minutes of sound effects for the benefit of anyone who might be hanging around out in the hall. You can't be too careful. If nobody comes, at least the steam is getting rid of some of the wrinkles in his suit so it shouldn't be a total loss.

Lesko chose "The Marines' Hymn" as his final selection, then waited another minute. Nothing. No sounds from the hall. No slowly turning doorknob like in the movies. It's safe enough, he guessed, to take a real shower. Just make it quick. He jammed a chair under his front doorknob and adjusted his bathroom door so that he could watch through the dressing mirror that hung on its outside.

Lesko was dried and dressed fifteen minutes later. He poured a second cup of coffee. Eight twenty-five. A little while now and he'd hear the Tomasi family upstairs heading out for the nine o'clock Mass at Saint Agnes down the street, and the McCaffreys in 3C would be doing the same. Lesko would fall in with them at least as far as the sidewalk. Lesko had made up his mind that if he happened to see a strange male face anyplace in between, he would take the guy out real fast and apologize for any mistakes afterward.

Another fifteen minutes. What the hell, he thought, reaching for the phone. Let's see if I can ruin the little bastard's breakfast. He dialed the Beckwith Regency and asked to speak to Mr. Ballanchine.

"May I tell him who's calling, sir?" Lesko remembered the guy at the front desk who snapped to attention every time a Beckwith walked through the lobby.

"Sam Babcock. Field agent, Internal Revenue."

"One moment, sir."

Lesko wondered, come to think of it, what kind of breakfast Dancer would eat. Ham and eggs? No. Dancer would be a three-minute-egg type. Out of a porcelain egg cup. With one of those little tools that slices off the top of the shell. And either orange juice or prune juice, probably prune juice, and probably laced with Metamucil.

"He doesn't seem to be answering, Mr. Babcock."

"Mr. Ballanchine wouldn't be ducking Uncle Sam, would he?"

"Oh, I'm sure not, sir. Hold on and I'll inquire."

Lesko waited.

The voice came back on. "Mr. Babcock, it seems Mr. Ballanchine and Mr. Beckwith have gone up to Connecticut for the day. They left just before I came on at eight. Did Mr. Ballanchine have an appointment with you, sir?"

"He was trying to reach me last night. We keep missing each other. Give me a number and I'll try him up there."

The desk man hesitated.

"And in case I still miss him, I want to leave him a message."

"Go ahead, sir."

"Tell him Uncle Sam hopes he won't have to rap his knuckles. He'll know what it means."

"Perhaps you'd better tell him that yourself, sir. I imagine you can reach him at the Beckwith residence on Round Hill Road in Greenwich. It's in the book."

Lesko knew that the desk man would have a phone number. He also knew that he was trying to involve himself as little as possible. Fine. "Which Beckwith lives in Greenwich, by the way?"

"I believe that would be Tilden Beckwith's sister, sir. Miss Ella Beckwith."

Lesko wished him a nice day.

The old guy's sister! Lesko wondered whether she was as big a turkey as he was. He suspected not. Not if it was her Dancer was talking to when he made that second call Friday night from Grand Central. The one to Connecticut. But for now, he decided, let's see if we know where the rest of the players are.

He flipped open his notebook and dialed the number of Gwen Leamas's apartment. No answer. He expected that. Next he punched information and asked for a Harry or Harold Sturdevant. How about H. E. Sturdevant at 12 East Sixty-ninth? That's him. Lesko tried the number.

"Sturdevant residence." A woman's voice, the housekeeper.

"Yeah, I'm looking for Jonathan Corbin."

"May I say who's calling, please?"

Lesko nodded. Corbin was there. He started to hang up without answering.

"Will you tell me who this is, please?" The woman's voice was strong, almost angry, more so than a rude silence should have made her. Lesko brought the phone back to his ear. He was tempted to ask Sturdevant's housekeeper what had her in such a testy mood so early in the morning. Was it possible, for example, that this was not today's first phone call from someone who asked for Corbin and then hung up. Not that she'd tell him, the way she sounded. Lesko broke the connection.

He made one more phone call, to Mr. Makowski, who said yes, he could borrow the car, which is open except you have to kick the door, and the spare key is in the back seat ashtray under a gum wrapper, which reminds me, please don't smoke those cheap cigars because the smell was there for a month last time. Lesko promised. Upstairs, Mr. Tomasi yelled, "Let's go. I'm not waiting all day," as he did every Sunday. Lesko threw on his coat and eased the chair from under his doorknob. Gun in hand, he waited until the Tomasi family had almost reached his landing, then poked his head into the hall.

Empty. Lesko tucked the gun out of sight and closed the door.

Below him the McCaffreys were already on the stairs, taking them slowly as they had since Mrs. McCaffrey hurt her hip. Lesko started down. He realized it was not altogether neighborly to use other churchgoing tenants as shields, but he was betting the Beckwith security people were not psychos like the Bolivians and would not make any bigger mess than they had to.

Lesko reached the sidewalk without incident and followed the McCaffreys as far as Mr. Makowski's Chevrolet. Mrs. Tomasi, following close behind, scowled at Lesko as he swept the snow from the windshield and opened the car door. She'd allowed herself to hope that he was actually going to Mass. Once inside, Lesko's gun was back in his hand as he fished for the hidden key, that being a good time for anyone so inclined to make a move. But there was nothing, not even the sound of another engine starting. As much surprised as relieved, Lesko rocked the car free of the curb and crunched out toward Queens Boulevard, then climbed on the expressway entrance leading to the Queens-Midtown Tunnel. The sparse Sunday morning traffic had him in the city in just over ten minutes. It took less than another ten to reach East Sixty-ninth Street. Sturdevant's address, number 12, would be on the south side, about halfway between Madison and Fifth. Lesko decided he'd better circle the block. It was hardly necessary.

He spotted the other car so easily that at first Lesko wondered if he was wrong. It was a blue BMW, parked in an ideal position for watching Sturdevant's front door a hundred feet farther down and across the street. But the driver was doing almost nothing else right. He was sitting low in his seat, too obviously low, his window was open all the way, and he'd left his engine running to keep warm. Lesko had seen the exhaust as soon as he turned off Madison. Worse, Lesko saw as he passed, the BMW was parked at a curb cut between two No Parking signs. Someone wants to take a car out, he has to move. Or a passing cop tells him to move. If he'd just double-parked he might have been more visible, but the same passing cop would have assumed he was waiting to pick someone up and not bothered him. And double-parked, the guy also would have been harder to block in.

Lesko continued around the block. There was no back-up car, no crash car, nothing. He considered pulling up behind the BMW and waiting, but if the other driver looked back through his side mirror, they could end up sitting there all morning staring at each other. What the hell, he decided. Let's get something going here. He pulled up close against the BMW's door, immobilizing the BMW and its driver, then reached across and rolled down his passenger-side window.

"Good morning." He showed his teeth. "I'm Raymond Lesko."

The face looking back at him reminded Lesko of Marine top sergeants he'd known. It was square-jawed, deeply weathered, and topped with a stiff brush of hair gone mostly gray. The eyes were blue and rock-steady except for a brief light of recognition that the man was not quite able to control.

"I beg your pardon?" Lesko saw a movement of the man's shoulder as he spoke.

"And your name is Tom Burke, I betcha. A guy named Ed Garvey works for you, but I think he's on sick leave now."

"Move your car, buddy," the man said quietly.

Lesko leaned closer, dropping his voice to a confidential tone. "I don't want to embarrass you or anything, but a guy who's head of Security shouldn't get blocked in when he's doing a tail. You *are* just doing a tail, aren't you, Tom?"

"Move it now"—the shoulder did something else—"or I'll get out and move it for you."

Lesko held up one finger and slid back behind the wheel. He made a show of putting Mr. Makowski's car in park, then shutting off the engine. He held up the ignition key for the other man to see, stuck out his tongue, and placed the key on its center. Tom Burke blinked at him.

"Here's another thing," Lesko slurred wetly, gesturing toward the windshield of the BMW, "doing a job like this, I'm a little surprised you'd drive around with a Beckwith Hotels parking sticker on your car. How about your gun? Can I see it? Do you at least have the right kind of weapon?"

The square jaw reddened at its jowls but the hard blue eyes went slack. What kind of dingo is this, Lesko could see him wondering. That was good. Lesko stuck out his tongue, showing the key again, then tucked it back between his teeth. "Except, whatever you got, don't shoot me with it." He felt for the left door lock behind him and snapped it down. "You shoot me, then first you have to come over here and smash this window to get the door open, then you have to pry the key out of my mouth so you can move the car, but by then I'll probably have swallowed the damned thing. First thing you know we'll both have parking tickets."

Tom Burke's eyes darted up and down the street. Lesko saw angry frustration in them rather than any hope of aid from a third party. But on Burke's last glance to his right, Lesko saw his eyes widen slightly. That was the direction of Sturdevant's front door. Lesko shot a look of his own, no longer than the click of a camera shutter, but enough to know that more than one person had appeared on the sidewalk and that they'd started to move more or less in his direction.

"Look what's in my hand, Tom." Lesko brought his right hand into view and tapped the barrel of his .38

against the doorpost. "See? I'm showing you my weapon. Now you have to show me yours."

Burke showed no sign of fear, only calculation and controlled fury. His chances, he knew, were next to none in terms of advantage. The best he could hope for was a standoff. He could simply sit still. This Lesko character would not shoot. Not with witnesses on the street.

Suddenly Lesko screamed. It was a gagging, rasping scream that made Tom Burke jump. It came again, high-pitched this time. Lesko's face was purple, his eyes bulged. Burke saw the face and then the gun hand thrusting across the narrow space between their cars, and he felt Lesko's gun stab painfully into his armpit. "Gimme it," Lesko choked, saliva dripping from his mouth. "Gimme the gun." Burke froze. It was a face and voice from an exorcist movie. His chest tightened and his mouth went dry. Lesko was going to kill him. The armpit was to muffle the shot. This fucking loony was going to kill him.

"Okay," Burke piped. "Easy. Just take it easy." Slowly, carefully, he lifted the wooden pistol grip of a cut-down shotgun into Lesko's view. Lesko snatched it with his left hand and pulled it into his car, where he dropped it into the floor well. His hand came back into the other man's face, snapping its fingers and showing an empty palm.

"Your piece, you holdout," he hissed. "Let's have it."

Carefully, as before, Tom Burke produced a gleaming Beretta automatic. For a moment he held it beyond Lesko's reach. "Take the clip," he begged. "It's enough you just take the clip." Lesko's eyes bulged again and he took the breath for another scream. Burke slapped the gun into his palm. He winced as Lesko threw it clattering against the other. Lesko leaned back into his car. With his own gun held out of sight but ready, he looked over his right shoulder. Corbin, Gwen Leamas, and Harry Sturdevant had reached the parking garage down toward Madison and were pausing at its entrance ramp. He saw the Leamas woman looking around, upward, as if for the source of the peculiar shout she'd heard. She seemed more curious than alarmed. But not Sturdevant. Sturdevant looked nervous. He touched her arm, and all three disappeared down the ramp.

"That coat!" Lesko pointed to a folded trench coat on Tom Burke's passenger seat. "Take out your wallet, put it in the coat pocket. Do it now." Burke obeyed. "Now your keys." Burke freed a large ring from the steering column and moved to disconnect his ignition key. "All of 'em. In the pocket. Now. Then gimme the coat." White with silent rage, Burke did so. He thought of arguing for all the keys Lesko had no business having, all the new locks that would be needed on so many Beckwith properties, of the punishment he'd face for surrendering them, but he looked at Lesko's insane face and at Lesko's fingers, which were pressed hard against his temple as if in an effort to control a building madness, and he handed the weighted coat through the window. Lesko threw it on the floor.

Lesko listened. From behind his car he heard the whine of another engine climbing a ramp in low gear. Once more he glanced over his right shoulder to see Sturdevant's Mercedes pause at the curb cut, its turn signal flashing. Two heads, Corbin's and Leamas's, were visible in the back seat.

"Shhhh!" he whispered across to the BMW. "Shut your eyes real tight so they won't see you. Shut them now." Burke's eyes glazed at the lunacy of Lesko's order, but he shut them. "I'll count ten," Lesko told him. "When I say ten you can peek. If you cheat, though, that's very bad."

Lesko began counting as the Mercedes hummed past his back. At five he spat the key from his mouth and started his engine. He was at eight when Sturdevant reached the corner traffic light and disappeared left onto Fifth Avenue. At ten, Lesko squealed away, leaving the Beckwith security chief blinking in helpless disbelief.

"You putz!" Lesko muttered as he caught a last glimpse of Tom Burke through his rearview mirror. But he was smiling, pleased with himself for guessing right. Some people you can outtough, some you can't. Some people, like old Crew Cut back there, there's just no way you're going to scare them or bluff them except for one thing. You make them think you're out of your fucking mind. It also helps if they're a little stupid.

He saw Sturdevant's car. It was signaling left again, about to turn east on Sixty-fourth Street. Lesko crept closer so the light would not hang him up.

Burke might be a putz, but he's a dangerous putz. A guy like that has probably punched out more people than most other people have even had bad thoughts about. And no doubt he's dusted a few, too. And that shotgun there says he was about to notch three more unless it happens to be fucking quail season in Central Park.

Lesko reached for the trench coat, which he'd taken solely to cover the gun collection on Mr. Makowski's floor, and groped for the wallet in its pocket. He found it and flipped it open. Burke. Yeah. Chief of Security, Beckwith Hotels. That was another good guess. When he had time to look through the wallet more carefully, Lesko was betting he'd find out the guy was maybe ex-military police or shore patrol, or maybe one of those psycho'd-out Feds which the CIA turns loose and leaves alone as long as they don't write books. For sure, he was no ex-cop.

The thing was, though, that all those guys always worked with a partner or a back-up. Burke was alone.

One man, one car. Lesko looked up at his rearview mirror. Nothing. No one behind him all the way back to Central Park. Which might explain, he realized, why the company he expected this morning never showed up. I mean, Beckwith Enterprises is a big company and all that, but it's not like the Mafia, which has whole clam houses full of killers they can call when they need them. With Ed Garvey on the disabled list, and Coletti probably still on queer street, maybe old Tom Burke is all they got left until they can run an ad.

A block ahead, Harry Sturdevant's Mercedes signaled left onto Second Avenue. Lesko followed, staying well behind until Sturdevant signaled again at Seventy-seventh Street. The English girl's place, he knew. Let's hope they're not going to hang around there too long. A BMW's a bitch to hot-wire, but Burke could have a spare key stashed. Let's also hope Ed Garvey didn't leave a mess so we don't have a call to the cops slowing down the action here.

He waited as Corbin and Gwen Leamas left Sturdevant with the double-parked car and climbed over a snow mound toward her door. As on Sixty-ninth Street, there were no parking spots except where curb cuts had been cleared. A half dozen other cars were double-parked. Lesko pulled in behind a station wagon. Sturdevant, who'd seemed a bit uneasy when he left his house, showed no sign that he was concerned about being followed. But he was drumming his fingers on the dash. Probably a little antsy about those two calls this morning. Lesko leaned over and lifted a corner of Tom Burke's raincoat. The shotgun, he recognized, was a Remington 1100, a five-shot automatic. At least a foot and a half of barrel, as well as most of the stock from the pistol grip on back, had been cut away. He whistled. If he'd been five minutes later, just a few more cars on the road or the Midtown Tunnel Tolls down to one lane, he would have arrived just in time to see the three of them splattered all over Sixty-ninth Street.

Someone isn't fooling around. Someone also has to be a little crazy to order a slaughter like that. Sturdevant's a prominent guy. And that part of town is all money. The mayor and the police commissioner would be there even before the TV cameras. Lesko leaned over for a closer look at Burke's Beretta. "Oh, Mama," he said aloud. A model 92. Fifteen shots if it doesn't jam, which this gun won't do very often. Also six hundred bucks retail. Thank you, Tommy Burke. I don't blame you for trying to hold on to it. Lesko sat back and patted Dancer's fifteen thousand dollars, which he still carried in his inside pocket. The rich get richer.

Gwen Leamas, carrying a small canvas tote, emerged ten minutes later. Corbin was close behind. Lesko lowered himself in his seat. Looking at the woman, he saw no sign that she was agitated by anything she might have seen upstairs, but Corbin was a different story. He was looking around. Sniffing the air. He had that same funny look, Lesko saw, that he'd had the day before when he suddenly seemed to realize the old guy was following him. When Corbin all of a sudden looked taller. When just for a few seconds the thought hit Lesko that Corbin was somebody else. Lesko wanted to shake it away. But this was twice. What the hell. He shrugged. With all the other weirdness going on around here, I should decide what's too crazy?

Lesko gave the Mercedes a block's head start.

At the Greenwich Public Library, Lesko picked up a large book entitled *Mainstreams of Modern Art,* a subject that bore no risk of absorbing his attention, and chose a chair that gave him a partially obstructed view of Corbin's group. He'd suspected Greenwich as their destination from the start, especially when he saw

Gwen Leamas's tote bag, although the detour up the West Side Drive had temporarily confused him.

They'd gone directly to the microfilm section. Lesko made a mental note of the file tray from which they'd chosen a reel. He would check it later, but he had little doubt its dates would correspond to the books Corbin bought at Barnes & Noble's and to a time when the Osborne Apartments were not so old. Lesko wished he'd thought to bring a pocket recorder. If he had one, he could just wander along those nearby bookshelves until he found a place to leave it running, then go back and sit with his art book until they were through.

What would he hear? Lesko asked himself. Ghosts? Raymond Lesko does not believe in ghosts.

That's fine, Raymond. Then tell me what you think is going on over there. Do you think it's just three reasonable people doing some just-the-facts kind of research in old newspaper files?

No. What you got is Jonathan Corbin, who sees things no one else sees, who is a ringer for a guy who died the same year he was born, and who keeps looking like he's changing into somebody else. You saw it on Fifty-eighth Street, and coming out of the subway, and when he came back out of the girl's apartment looking like he picked up Ed Garvey's scent, and you're seeing it now. And if he is changing into someone else, who is it? Tilden Beckwith, right? I know you don't want to believe that. But stay with it anyway because what you got, at the very least, is what those people over there already believe.

Lesko thought of the time when the cops on Staten Island brought in this psychic to help them find some missing little girls. They gave the psychic, this Dutchman, clothes that belonged to one of the kids and right away the psychic tells them where to search for the body and about a guy who made these girls write compositions before he killed them. Turned out to be a substitute teacher who later hung himself in his cell although the cops probably gave him a hand. Why is this weirder than that? Lesko shrugged. If a psychic can get into the head of a murdered little girl just by touching her things, why can't Corbin get into the head of the original Tilden, someone who's already in his blood, by seeing the same things Tilden saw?

Lesko ducked his head. Corbin was leaving. He was putting on his coat, and so was Gwen Leamas, but Harry Sturdevant looked like he was staying with the microfilms. From where Lesko sat it did not seem that Sturdevant wanted them to leave. Neither did Lesko. These people were enough trouble when they were all in one place. Now Sturdevant was trying to hand his car keys to Corbin, suggesting in a voice loud enough for Lesko to hear that they'd be better off driving. He'd follow them on foot later; Maple Avenue was not that far. But Corbin refused the car, saying it was only a ten-minute walk for them, too. They'd put the coffee on and whenever Sturdevant got there they'd eat some of Mrs. Starling's lunch. Whoever that is.

Lesko didn't like this at all. He did not want Corbin waltzing unprotected up to his house, but he did want to know what other digging Harry Sturdevant planned on doing. He decided to split the difference. Lesko waited until Corbin and Gwen Leamas had reached the information desk and turned right toward the automatic doors before he moved to follow. He watched them cut through the parking lot, with no other eyes on them that Lesko could see, and onto the sidewalk of Putnam Avenue, then he walked quickly to Mr. Makowski's car and pulled out in the direction of Maple Avenue. He was there within two minutes. Corbin's house was a few blocks up the hill past the kind of stone church that's built mostly for debutante weddings and past an equestrian statue of a Revolutionary War general named Israel Putnam. His car made the hill with difficulty although the road surface had been sanded. Lesko made a note to explain about snow tires to Mr. Makowski. He continued on past Corbin's Victorian without slowing, his immediate interest being cars, especially BMWs with New York plates, that might be parked within a few hundred feet of the house. There were no cars at all except those in driveways. Lesko turned around. He passed Corbin's house once more, this time slowing to be sure that the snow cover on the walk and driveway was not unduly disturbed. It was not. He saw only the tracks of a single dog across Corbin's front lawn and the tire marks made by Saturday's mail truck when it cut within arm's reach of Corbin's box. A ridge of lumpy snow had also been plowed across his driveway entrance. That was the good news, that no one had been here. The bad news was that now Corbin might decide to get out there with a shovel so that Harry Sturdevant could get the car in. Lesko stopped. He shifted into reverse and backed across the foothigh mound, penetrating half a car length into the driveway, then cut his wheels and pulled out in the other direction. There. It would look like someone had just turned around. And it might keep Corbin off the streets. Lesko swung back down the hill onto Putnam Avenue and began looking for him.

He spotted the pair halfway back toward the library. They seemed fine. Still no one behind them. Corbin was gesturing as he walked, telling some kind of story that the Leamas dame found fascinating, but his manner was calm enough and he appeared to be himself. Go make the coffee.

As Lesko reentered the Greenwich Library, he saw Harry Sturdevant standing at the information desk. Lesko hesitated. Let's see how long he's going to be there, Lesko decided. Maybe I can do a quick pass at the microfilm machine and see what kind of notes he's taking.

Two women were seated at the desk, which was more of a U-shaped counter. The older of the two, the one looking up at Sturdevant, struck Lesko as being out of place. He knew what it was. Expensive clothes, hair done just right, a single strand of real pearls. Lesko imagined her husband was a company president she only saw on weekends and her kids were moved out or away at school and her shrink told her to get a job like this to keep her out of the Stolichnaya. He noticed the way she worked. She dithered. That was the word. A lot of rich ladies who do volunteer work cultivate a certain incompetence so no one should mistake them for somebody who actually needs the job. The other girl, younger, sort of pretty, was more clearly there to make a living. She was moving crisply through a pile of paperwork and taking all telephone inquiries more complicated than what time the place closes.

Lesko was about to pass on when a curious change in the older one's expression stopped him. A few seconds ago her face was saying to Sturdevant, How do you do, you're my kind, aren't you, just tell me what you're looking for and I'll do my best to help you. Now she looked like he asked whether the library had any good animal porn. Whatever he asked, it made the young girl look up from her telephone and she was trying not to smile. Lesko edged closer. He stepped past Sturdevant to a rack of oversized atlases and opened one at random to a map of Peru.

"Are you a journalist, by chance?" he heard the rich lady ask. "A writer?"

"No." Sturdevant looked slightly bemused. He'd noticed the sudden chill. "My interest is entirely personal."

"Well, I'm sure we have nothing like that at all."

"In a library this size? The *Greenwich* Library?"

"Nothing. I'm sorry."

Lesko saw the younger woman's eyebrows arch.

"Is there someone else I could ask?" Sturdevant persisted. "I know you have old newspaper accounts at the very least because I've been reading them. And, this being the Greenwich Library, I'm confident that you have a section dealing with the history of Greenwich. I'd hoped that you could save me some time by telling me where there's a single source dealing with this Anthony Comstock episode."

The younger woman was scribbling as he spoke. She tore a sheet off a yellow pad and held it out to Sturdevant. "Aisle seven, sir. The far end, lower right-hand shelves."

Sturdevant glanced at the titles she listed. "Thank *you*," he said. He walked away shaking his head. Lesko decided to study Peru for another minute or so.

"I don't know why you did that," the older one snapped.

"Because this is a library, Barbara," she answered patiently. "The man wanted library information."

"How do you know he doesn't write for one of those trashy little newspapers they sell at supermarket check-outs? How do you know he's even from Greenwich?"

"This is also a *public* library, Barbara."

"Whose purpose is to *serve* this town," Barbara Blackthorne added, "not to embarrass it."

The younger woman winced but said nothing.

Barbara stood up. "Well, I'm going to have a talk with Mr. Hoagland."

Lesko watched her go, heading toward the elevator across the library floor.

' The lady's upset," he said.

"Excuse me?" Carol Oakes looked up from her index cards.

"I didn't mean to eavesdrop. Couldn't help hearing. But now that I have, who's Anthony Comstock?"

Carol continued sorting. "Oh, he was a nineteenth-century vice crusader. A fanatic, actually, and a thundering ass. Have you ever seen *September Morn*, the painting?"

"Sure. My mother hung a copy in the upstairs bathroom. Kind of a polite nude. With folded arms."

Carol squinted, remembering. "A French artist did it, I forget who or when. But a New York art dealer bought a bunch of prints and they weren't selling. The dealer had a brainstorm. He put a copy in his gallery window, then made an anonymous call to this nut, Comstock, saying that a lewd painting was being displayed where passing schoolchildren could see it. Comstock rushed down, brought a reporter, and tried to have the dealer arrested for peddling smut if he didn't take it out of his window. A crowd gathered, the paper ran the story, and within a few weeks this ordinary little nude was one of the best-known paintings in America."

Lesko laughed. He'd tell his mother next time he called Florida. "Yeah, but what's the connection with Greenwich?" he asked.

She shook her head. "I really don't know. Some scandal about prostitutes back then who moved up here from New York and married locals."

"What happened? The guy struck out on *September Morn*, so he decides to bother retired hookers? Every town in the country must have at least a couple."

"I suppose," Carol guessed, "but this is Greenwich. Most of us could care less, but some of the older families are sensitive. Mrs. Blackthorne's people have been here forever. After a while they make a hobby out of being very Greenwich. Ancestor worship is part of the hobby. Some of these people don't even want you to know they go to the bathroom, so you can imagine how they get if you start poking around their family trees with anything less than admiration."

Lesko closed his atlas. He liked this girl and was enjoying the conversation, but he wasn't sure if it was heading anywhere useful. But Sturdevant, on the other hand, must think he's on to something. A guy named Anthony Comstock comes here a hundred years ago and starts rooting out ex-hookers. There's got to be a connection with the Tilden Beckwith who was a ringer for Corbin, but what's the connection between Beckwith and a hooker? Did he stash one here? Way out here? Why would he go to the trouble?

"Thank you, miss." He tipped an imaginary hat to Carol Oakes. "Nice talking to you."

Lesko wandered past the card files to a point where he could see down aisle seven. Sturdevant was at the far end on one knee, one book under his arm and another in his hands. He was checking its index. Lesko guessed he could count on at least a minute to go back and see what Sturdevant had on the microfilm machine. He walked quickly in that direction.

Sturdevant had left the machine on and a fuzzy front page was projected onto the reading surface. Lesko touched the focus knob. The *Greenwich Graphic,* the masthead said, August 1890. Comstock's name jumped up from a two-column headline. COM-STOCK BEATEN, it said. Then underneath in bold type, "Thrown Down Stairs." Then in smaller type, "Vows to Press On Fearlessly." Who threw him down the stairs? Beckwith? No. Some doctor named Palmer. Way to go, Doc.

Sturdevant's note pad was lying open on the projector. His notes were spotty. Cryptically written. A lot of names.

Comstock. Margaret/Charlotte fearful?
Dr. Miles Palmer. Delivered J's grandfather?
Carrie Todd and Belle Walker. Retired prosts? Pos-

sibly Laura Hemmings too. Did they recognize Margaret?

Charlotte. Lesko raised one eyebrow. Charlotte Whitney Corbin, right? Corbin's great-grandmother. She lived here in Greenwich? Sturdevant sure thinks so. And she had a kid here. Corbin's grandfather. His namesake.

All the other names, except for the doctor, seemed to be known or suspected ex-hookers. Charlotte Corbin too? Otherwise, why should she be afraid of Comstock? Margaret. Margaret slash Charlotte.

Wait a minute.

Holy shit!

Lesko backed away from the machine and looked to see if Sturdevant was on his way. He was but someone stopped him. Up near the information desk, a tweedy-looking man of about sixty had just intercepted Sturdevant. Mrs. Blackthorne was returning to her seat and Carol Oakes was giving her a "you're such a twit" look. The man in the tweeds had to be Mr. Hoagland who, Lesko assumed, had to be the head guy around here. He was questioning Sturdevant and Sturdevant was not loving it. But Sturdevant at least was not telling him to buzz off as Lesko would have. He was opening one of the books he carried and asking a question in return. Lesko decided he had another minute at least. He hurried back to the machine and flipped Sturdevant's notebook to its preceding page.

More names and notes, most of which meant nothing to him. *Colonel Mann. Town Topics.* Something about the colonel blackmailing Tilden. And a lot of stuff about a blizzard. Someone named *George Baremore. Baremore found first, then Ella.* Lesko moved back one more page.

There it was. *Margaret Barrie and Charlotte Corbin—same woman.* Lesko scanned the rest of the page. There were references to a Hiram Corbin who had died in a train wreck, leaving Charlotte a widow. But the tone of Sturdevant's notes seemed to doubt that Hiram Corbin ever existed, or at least that Charlotte was ever married to him. Sturdevant thought she'd been carefully set up here by Tilden, probably with a full but concocted life history. Lesko put the note pad back the way he found it.

So, Lesko asked himself, what do we have? Tilden has a mistress, probably a hooker, who gets pregnant. The pregnancy is probably deliberate because hookers don't have that kind of accident. He moves her up here with a new name so she can have the kid in peace. But then along comes Anthony Comstock a year or so later and makes everybody so nervous that they're still touchy about it. But why, come to think of it, did he come? Did someone blow the whistle?

Lesko shifted his attention back to the projected page of the *Greenwich Graphic*. The story about Comstock being thrown down the stairs offered little more information except that he'd broken three ribs. It contained almost no background detail, which suggested to Lesko that Comstock's activities were being reported on a continuing basis and that this was just the latest episode. The rest of the page contained routine local news, a few ads and social notes, an argument over whether the main street should be electrified. The name Laura Hemmings caught his eye. It was one of the names in Sturdevant's notes. The item was a report on the weekly meeting of the Women's Christian Temperance Union of Greenwich. They were going to have a tea dance in September. Laura Hemmings would head the dance committee and—aha!—in charge of decorations would be Mrs. Charlotte Corbin. The item went on to say that this inseparable pair was the same duo that organized the famously successful July 4 pageant and the uproarious roller-skating party of last May. Lesko sniffed. Reformed bimbos are as bad as reformed drunks. But this group didn't sound like the Carrie Nation types who used to go around smashing up perfectly good saloons with hatchets. It seemed more like a social club than a bunch of pain-in-the-ass teetotalers.

"I'm afraid I'm using that machine." Lesko heard the voice behind him.

Shit!

"Oh, sorry." Lesko moved aside. "Those old ads just caught my eye." He saw an expression of annoyance on Sturdevant's face, more than his being there should have justified but Lesko understood. After being bugged by Mr. Hoagland and Mrs. Blackthorne, Sturdevant didn't need another nosy local taking an interest in what he was doing.

Lesko touched a finger to the projected page. "Dr. King's New Discovery for Consumption." He smiled. "Says here it contains chloroform and opium. A couple of shots of that and you wouldn't know whether you were sick or not. I didn't know they could sell opium like that."

"Oh yes." Sturdevant relaxed a notch. "Opium and cocaine. There were millions of addicts in this country at the turn of the century because of patent medicines like that one. Even Bayer's aspirin used to contain cocaine."

"No kidding." Lesko raised his eyebrows. "I knew about booze in these old medicines but I didn't realize about the drugs. A drugstore I was in once had this old poster for Hostetter's Celebrated Stomach Bitters. Whatever you got, this stuff would fix it. A little card underneath the poster said it was forty-four percent alcohol, which is a fairly decent shot." Come on, Lesko said in his mind, smile at that. I'm just a harmless guy who hangs out in libraries. No smile? Okay. We'll try something else.

"My grandmother wouldn't touch a drop," Lesko lied. "I mean, she was one of these temperance ladies, but if she was feeling down she'd swig some stuff called Lydia Pinkham's Extract right from the bottle and it was as good as a martini, I find out later."

"Temperance ladies?" He had Sturdevant's attention. "You mean in Greenwich?"

"Yeah."

"Your family's been here a long time?"

"Since just after the Civil War. They had the butcher shop in town."

"Does the name Charlotte Corbin mean anything to you?" Sturdevant asked. "Your grandmother might possibly have known her."

Lesko shook his head. "Doesn't ring a bell."

"Or Laura Hemmings?"

Lesko shrugged. "Sorry. She told a lot of stories about the old days but I don't remember those names coming up." Come on. Ask.

"Did she ever mention a man named Anthony Comstock? He caused a stir in town back around 1890 by trying to root out some former prostitutes who'd come here to live."

"The religious nut. Yeah." Lesko brightened. He told Sturdevant the story of *September Morn*. "Some people around here still get touchy about all that hooker stuff he did."

"So I've learned." Sturdevant gestured in the general direction of Mr. Hoagland while hefting the two volumes he was carrying. "And these Greenwich histories don't shed much light on it either. There's barely a mention."

No shit, Lesko thought. Who do you think would bother writing a history of Greenwich except someone with two last names, like Carter Woodruff the third, who lives back in the four-acre zoning and who wants all his friends to have something nice for their coffee tables? One of those types is going to write about ex-bimbos? He's going to say, Guess what, some of our grandmothers screwed half the U.S. Navy before they moved up here and picked out a Yalie to settle down with?

"I guess those newspaper files are your best bet." Lesko pointed. "You're trying to track down those two women you mentioned? What were they, hookers or temperance?"

"I'm not really sure. They were both certainly members of the Women's Christian Temperance Union."

"You could try Chicago," Lesko said offhandedly. As he expected, Sturdevant's eyes widened in surprise.

"Chicago? How could you know?" He stopped.

"The WCTU," Lesko explained. "They got their national headquarters out there. Up in Evanston. My grandmother, if she wanted to look up a member she lost track of, she'd write to Evanston and if they had the address they'd forward the letter."

"That's an excellent suggestion, Mr. . . ."

Lesko pretended not to notice he was being asked his name. "The next thing you do is check with the county tax assessor's office. It's easiest if you have a street but a name is enough. They'll have a record of how many times the house has been bought and sold and who owned it. Another good bet most people don't think of is the Water Department. They'll know when they first turned on the water for a particular house. If they had electricity, it's even easier."

"You'd make a good detective," Sturdevant observed.

"Yeah. Well, look, I gotta run." He turned away toward the chair on which he'd left his coat. "Good luck finding those ladies."

Lesko waved off Sturdevant's call of thanks and headed back toward the information desk. At a pay phone nearby he opened the Greenwich directory to Beckwith. There were two listings, only one of which showed a Round Hill Road address. Lesko made a note of both. Returning to the rack of atlases, he found a Hagstrom street map of Fairfield County and, fishing out a dime, made a Xerox copy of the page showing both Round Hill Road and Maple Avenue. He then blew a kiss toward Carol Oakes. Lesko stepped through the automatic doors.

Letting Sturdevant see him might not have been ideal, he knew. But maybe it helped move things along. Harry Sturdevant seemed like one of those very deliberate types, aside from being an amateur. He'd be in that library forever, getting all bogged down in the historical romance of what he was trying to find out instead of zeroing in on who, what, when, and where. And who did what to who. Whom. Maybe now he'd make a couple of those connections quicker. Lesko had, for sure. He knew, for example, that Sturdevant was already aware of the connection between Tilden Beckwith and Jonathan Corbin. Sturdevant also seemed aware that a woman named Margaret was in the picture, but it apparently came as news to him that this Margaret and Corbin's great-grandmother were the same person. It might even be news to Corbin, although Lesko somehow doubted that. It sure wasn't news to Dancer and the Beckwiths.

Lesko looked up at the sky as he unlocked Mr. Makowski's car. It was still mostly clear. But far to the west he could see what looked like a misty mountain range. More snow maybe. He hoped so. The Corbin guy always gets so much more interesting when it snows. But for now, speaking of interesting, maybe it's time we had a chat with those nice folks up on Round Hill Road.

"I think you're being silly," Gwen Leamas said to him as they walked slowly past shop windows toward Maple Avenue.

"Your uncle doesn't have to know everything," he told her. "Like you said yesterday, some things are private."

"But you're talking about one obscure gossip item this Colonel Mann printed almost a hundred years ago."

"It hurt her," he said quietly. "And it frightened her."

She took his hand. "Jonathan, should I start worrying about you all over again?"

"What do you mean?"

"You do understand she's long dead, don't you? You're talking as if she isn't."

"I know she's dead." Most of the time, I know that. "Gwen"—he gave her a squeeze—"there's so much buzzing through my head that I couldn't possibly know except through Tilden Beckwith. When I talk about these things out loud, and you get that worried look like now, and your uncle looks at me like I'm a laboratory rat, you can understand if I get self-conscious. I'm also tired of people scribbling every time I open my mouth. That's another reason I didn't want to talk about Colonel Mann."

"Will you tell me if I don't scribble?"

"It's not that big a deal."

"What if I look blithely unworried? How's this?" Gwen twisted her face into a wide-eyed simper, her front teeth protruding over her lower lip.

Corbin tried not to laugh. He turned his head away toward the street. A car went by. Something about that car. Oh, shit. Cut it out. He turned back toward Gwen Leamas, whose face was determinedly frozen into that same idiotic expression. Corbin surrendered.

"There really isn't much to it."

"Tell me anyway. Just tell me a story and this time don't give a thought to how you know it."

"There was a newspaper called *Town Topics*. He

ran it. Like your uncle said, he was a very pleasant-looking man who used to carry sugar for horses, but he was a real bastard underneath."

"A blackmailer." Gwen nodded.

"He'd pay household servants, for example, for tidbits about their employers. If the information was juicy enough, he'd go to the people involved and extort a lifetime subscription out of them for thousands of dollars. The problem got so bad that employers would deliberately drop little made-up stories in the hearing of their servants. If one appeared in print, the servant would be fired."

"And one of Tilden's servants sold him out?"

"I think it was Ansel Carling. But remember, this Colonel Mann was also a double-crosser."

"Go on." Gwen walked with him.

"Tilden and Margaret went to the World Series that year—1888, I guess. It seems to me it was the Giants against the Saint Louis Browns and the first four games were in New York. Anyway, after the fourth game an issue of *Town Topics* came out with a blind item that said—see, I even remember this—'What scion of a respected Wall Street firm, lately and suspiciously widowed, has been attending the world championship series of baseball in the company of a lovely but soiled dove who is very much in a delicate condition?' There was never much doubt who he was talking about because whenever he'd run one of these blind items, all you had to do was look over at the adjacent column and you'd see a harmless and legitimate reference to the same person by name. Margaret used to read *Town Topics*. Everybody did. So she opens the paper and there in one sentence she not only sees herself identified as a prostitute but she sees doubt expressed openly about the circumstances of Ella's death."

"What happened then?"

"They just laid low. They were already staying at the Claremont Inn."

"But you said she was hurt and frightened. Was she frightened of Tilden?"

"No." Corbin shook his head. "The soiled-dove reference hurt her, mostly because of the child she was carrying. I can see her crying and taking Tilden's hands and putting them on her belly, and I can see him holding her and promising that everything would be fine once they got her to Greenwich and that he'd take care of Colonel Mann. That's the part that frightened her. I'm not sure they ever talked about whether he killed Ella, but she was afraid he was going to kill this Colonel Mann. But he wasn't. Mann was easy to fix because all you had to do was pay him and he'd never mention your name again. That was a point of honor with the colonel, ridiculous as it sounds. The real problem was Carling."

"I gather Tilden then had at him a second time."

Corbin shook his head and was silent for a long moment. "It gets mixed up here. There seem to have been a whole series of violent fights. After the one in the Hoffman House, maybe two weeks later . . . now, see, this is also after Tilden went to see Margaret and asked her to have his child, but that had to have been a very personal meeting because Tilden doesn't let me see it, except I can see where John Flood is urging him to go to her—"

"Whoa!" Gwen Leamas stopped him. "What do you mean, 'Tilden doesn't let me see it'? You sound as if you think Tilden's still around."

"I think he's part of me." Corbin met her eyes.

"But do you think he's a living person? Living inside you right now, I mean."

"I don't know," Corbin answered. "Your uncle seems to think he is."

"Correction, Jonathan." Gwen Leamas frowned.

"Uncle Harry believes, and I believe it too, that you're carrying an unusual number of your great-grandfather's genes and therefore his memories. That's not the same as believing that he's still alive."

"You keep telling me that I've become Tilden when I've been with you."

"You've become *like* him. It's those memory genes, nothing more."

"Fine." He shrugged.

"Do you *believe* that, Jonathan?"

"Sweetheart"—he touched her cheek—"I'll believe whatever helps me handle all this. But for the record, no. No, I do not believe Tilden Beckwith is still alive inside of me."

Corbin gestured with his head toward Maple Avenue, still a half block ahead, and started Gwen walking again.

How'd I do? he asked himself.

Fine, he answered.

TWELVE

WEN TOOK CORBIN'S HAND AND TUGGED IT TO break the thoughtful silence of the last half block.

"I'm sorry I lectured you, Jonathan," she said. "I guess I'm getting a bit spooked."

"It's okay, hon." He squeezed back and let her see a smile. "Glad to have you in the club."

"Where were we, anyway?"

"I kind of hoped we were getting ready to change the subject."

"Just one more loose end." She made a kissing sound to appease him. "You said Tilden was going to confront Colonel Mann, or perhaps Ansel Carling, but you thought there was some other violence in the meantime."

"There's a lot. But it all runs together."

"Well, who else did he beat up on?"

Corbin was silent for a long moment. Gwen saw

that he was wincing. "Nobody always wins, sweet-heart," he said at last.

"Good evenin' to you, sir."

Gwen felt his hand crushing hers as it tightened into a fist.

"You look like a gent what'd have a match to spare."

Two men. One in a grimy pea jacket. The one speaking wore a heavy fleece-lined coat.

Tilden had just stepped into the glow of the Osborne's electric lights when he heard the voice and hesitated. Had it not been so late, had he not still been wrapped in the warmth of these last few hours spent with Margaret, he would have tightened his grip on his cane and passed them with a shake of his head. They would, he knew, have expected no more for their impertinence. Had it not been for the memory of Margaret's tears, her tender solicitude in answer to his neglect of her, he would have wondered why two such men should be abroad at night in this part of town. Coarse and common men. White men, yet coming from the direction of the Negro section to the west where no white men ever went, save policemen and rent collectors. Had Margaret not asked him for a week's grace in deciding upon his proposition, a week without contact, a condition which weighed heavily upon his heart, he would not have paused and fumbled absently at his pockets for matches he did not carry.

"A fifty-center, that is." The man in the fleece jacket held the cigar up high, inspecting it in the glow of the Osborne's lights. *"I can remember when a full day bent over a shovel would fetch me little more than the cost of this one good Havana."*

Tilden looked up in spite of himself. The fist came low and hard to his stomach. There was no avoiding the blow; he took it full beneath his rib cage though he crouched to smother it as best he could. The cane in his right hand slashed forward by reflex, but it was poorly aimed. The man in the peacoat parried it and countered with a lead slung sap that tore away Tilden's hat and a flap of his scalp. He saw an explosion of white fire and felt his knee crash painfully against the pavement. He knew that he was down. Down and blind. Cover your head, Tilden. Bring your knees against your chest and your arms against your head. But the arms had gone flaccid; they could not obey the command of his brain. Then roll, for God's sake. Don't give their boots a target. Again, his body did not answer.

A hand gripped his hair. A voice, soft and calm, was speaking to him through the diffusing light. *"You've been a bad boy, you see. You've been fighting. 'Fess up, now. You've been fighting, have you not?"* He felt an open palm smash across his cheek. *" 'Fess up, I said. The way we hear it, a feller can't even have a quiet drink these days without you comin' in and busting up the place."*

Carling.

Another hard slap shocked him. Its sound blew through the glistening cloud inside his head, dispersing more of it. Yes, he thought. Talk to me. Keep talking to me.

"Bad boys get punished, don't cher know." A third blow. The same cheek. *"First bad boys and then bad little girls."* The hand came again. But softly this time. Its fingers were caressing the side of his face. *"And the way we punish 'em is we mark 'em. We mark 'em so there's always a lookin' glass to remind them o' the error of their wicked ways."* Tilden felt a thumb slide gently across his cheekbone until it came to rest at the corner of his left eye. Gougers. They were going to gouge his eyes and bring them back for Ansel Carling to see. Now. Now or never.

A scream. The hand was snatched away from his cheek, and the man who owned it screamed. One hand, the other man's, still gripped Tilden's hair, but the hand of the gouger was now tearing at Tilden's forearm, then at Tilden's fingers, searching for a hold that would loose the desperate grip Tilden had on his genitals. Even the hold on his hair eased as the other man, the peacoat, wondered through ponderous wits about the source of his companion's agony. Tilden, from his knees, brought up the spike of his cane, ramming it with all his gathering strength into the armpit of the peacoat. That arm, too, snapped back, tearing his hair as it went. Tilden swung the cane once more, its silver knob finding Peacoat's ear and staggering the man. He brought back the cane to strike at the one in the fleece jacket, but the cane's shaft struck the edge of a low iron fence and it snapped in two. Before Tilden could think to use the jagged edge as a thrusting weapon, the writhing thug in the fleece jacket wrenched himself free and, enraged, began a dance with heavy boots upon Tilden's body.

"It's a pepperbox I'm holding, boys. Stand off." The voice seemed to come from far away. It had a melodic flourish to it, a resonance. Tilden knew that voice. *"Back 'way nicely or, by God, I'll spray you both."*

Nat. Nat Goodwin.

"Tilden, can you stand?"

Tilden nodded that he could, but his legs would not serve him. A hand took his arm and helped him rise.

"Careful with that thing, Nat," the one in the fleece jacket said. *"We'll be calling it a day now."*

"You'll stand where you are," the actor ordered.

Tilden could see them backing off toward the darkness. The peacoat had one hand to his ear and blood was streaming from it down into his collar. The eyes of both men were locked upon the eight small barrels of Nat Goodwin's pistol.

"Nothin' personal, Nat. Just a job of work with us.

Nothin' we'd deal you into." They continued backing away.

"*Move, Tilden,*" he barked. "*Get inside.*" Goodwin shoved him up the steps. It could be, he knew, that those two bummers had enough. But it could also be that they carried longer guns than his little pepperbox and were backing into an advantageous range. Nat Goodwin held his ground until he saw the outer glass doors swing open and the frightened night manager ran down for Tilden and took his weight. Goodwin followed them, backing in, his pistol still trained on the two retreating toughs.

He was wearing a dressing gown, Corbin remembered. Nat Goodwin. The actor. It was made of silk brocade and it reached to his ankles. It was red. The collar was of velvet and Corbin could see dull spots on it where spilled makeup had been imperfectly scrubbed away.

"Thank you, Nat. I owe you." Tilden rested on a lobby bench.

"Thank Mr. Peebles here. He came and woke me when he saw those two closing on you."

"Yes. Thank you." Tilden nodded gratefully. "But please, no word of this."

"Come along, my friend." Nat Goodwin helped him to his feet. "Let's see if I can piece you together."

"Nat, you knew them," Tilden whispered when he was out of the night man's hearing.

"Just another pair of toughs, Tilden. New York's full of them."

"Who were they?" Tilden allowed himself to be led into the elevator. Neither man spoke during the short ride to Goodwin's floor. Then Tilden asked the question again.

"It's no good calling the police, Tilden," the actor told him. "The fellow you nearly gelded is thick with Captain Devery and Clubber Williams." Goodwin pushed open his apartment door and guided Tilden through to a large mirrored dressing table he kept in his bathroom.

"Williams?" Tilden repeated the name as Nat Goodwin took a wet sponge to his scalp. "They were sent by Ansel Carling, Nat. Why should Williams have a hand in it?"

"I don't know that he does. Except that Carling works for Jay Gould and so does Williams when he's needed. You're sure Carling is behind this?"

"The man as much as said it." Tilden winced at the touch of a chloroform swab to his cut. "Nat, he meant to take my eye."

Goodwin frowned.

"That doesn't sound like the Clubber's style. It's his stick that got him his reputation and got him hob-nobbing with his betters. He wants people to fear him well enough but not to turn from him in disgust as they would a gouger. Ask me, Williams knew nothing of it except perhaps to pass on a name or two."

"I'll have that name, Nat."

"There are a thousand like him." Goodwin stepped to his tub and turned on both taps. "As he said, it's just a job of work with him. Why go after a hireling if you know who's paying the freight?"

"Because he talked like he was paid to hurt Margaret as well. 'Bad girls get marked,' he said. Carling made the same threat."

Nat Goodwin chewed his lip.

"What do you mean to do, Tilden, given the man's name?"

"He spoke of me, and Margaret, looking in a mirror always and remembering what he'd done to us. I mean to have him remember me."

"You'd go after him alone? If that's your plan, my friend, you'll get no name from me."

"Perhaps John Flood will back me."

Goodwin sighed deeply. "And perhaps my pepper-box as well," he said.

Pepperbox . . . Big John Flood.

It was done the next day, Corbin knew. It seemed to him that Tilden should have waited longer, until he was healed or at least not slowed by the bruises on his back and thighs. But Corbin could smell a foul yellow mixture, which Nat Goodwin had plastered upon his welts after another soaking in a tub of salts. And he could see in his mind the gloves that John Flood had brought for him. Tight, fingerless gloves of thick piled leather. They had little pockets sewn into their palms to hold either sand or birdshot, and there were strips of rough canvas stitched across the knuckles. Have you seen to Margaret? Tilden asked him. Give her no thought, John Flood answered. She's safer by half than you will be if you don't keep your wits full about you. And John Flood gave a nod and wink to Nat Goodwin, which Tilden saw but did not question.

The saloon was O'Gorman's, and Tilden's man was Billy O'Gorman himself. He'd be in the back, Nat Goodwin had learned, playing poker with two fat cats from Tammany and a pair of rubes down from Buffalo who'd be nearly blind on O'Gorman's liquor within the hour. Goodwin entered first and took a place at the end of the bar where he could watch the two bartenders. John Flood entered just behind Tilden, a handkerchief at his nose, and quietly took a stool near a pool table where two rough-looking men with short cropped hair were intent on a game of nine-ball. Stay cool, lad, he urged to himself. A cool head keeps 'em off balance.

Tilden walked to the center of the bar and stood surveying the half dozen tables and the score of men who were lounging there, some hard, some more like ferrets. He stepped to the nearest table and pushed it several feet farther from the bar. Next he moved the chairs, lifting one of them with a ferret still seated in it. The two bartenders exchanged glances. The larger one took a step closer to his bungstarter. Nat Goodwin rested a hand upon the butt of his pistol. Tilden moved another table, its two patrons looking at him more with curiosity than annoyance. They noticed his hands, which were covered with wool knit gloves stretched tight over outsized palms. He would not be the first man to come in doing songs and tap dances for free drinks and a sandwich, or to do a juggling act, or to take on the toughest man in the house for a pass of the hat. This last seemed the more likely given the look of the man's nose, except he wore the clothes of a swell. At a far table, a man with a bandaged ear reached from his seat and took a pool cue from its rack on the wall.

"What's your pleasure, sir?" the larger bartender asked.

"Mr. Billy O'Gorman, please. Tell him Mr. Beckwith is here to see him."

The bartender, Joe McArdle, gestured toward the space Tilden had cleared. "You figurin' to mix it up with Mr. O'Gorman? You got ambition."

Tilden pointed to the mirror and row of bottles behind McArdle. "I'm going to ask for him one more time and then I'm going to throw a chair through that."

The bartender shrugged. He brought up his hands, showing a long-handled wooden hammer. "I guess you must be holding some good cards. I got this here mallet. You mind showin' me what else you got before I go botherin' Mr. O'Gorman?"

"Right here." The sound came from John Flood's mouth. All eyes except Tilden's followed as John Flood rose from his stool and walked toward the man with the bandaged ear. The man seemed to know what was coming. He pushed back his chair and waited, the pool cue held low at his side. Flood, without breaking stride, feinted with a shoulder and easily ducked the tapered stick as it whistled past his head. A crushing right hand slammed downward to a point below the bandage, making the sodden snapping sound that told of a jawbone separated from a skull. John Flood's left hand seized the man's shirt and steadied him, unconscious, in his chair.

Joe McArdle's expression, save for an understanding nod, changed not at all.

"Would your name be John Flood, by chance?" he asked.

"Yours truly." Big John bowed at the waist.

"Another time, I'd admire to shake your hand. Will you be asking Billy to take you both on, can I ask?"

"It's Mr. Beckwith's show. I'm here to keep it square."

The two men playing nine-ball stopped their game and took seats at the edge of their table. McArdle studied their faces. They, too, seemed familiar.

"Fair and square you say. On your word?"

"On my word," Flood called back.

McArdle turned to the smaller bartender. "Would you tell Mr. O'Gorman that there's a fine gentleman here to dispute him. Tell him it's my opinion he'll be back at his table before the next raise."

The bartender walked quickly to a door at the rear of the room, rapped twice, and entered. He was gone a full minute, Nat Goodwin noted. When the white-aproned man reappeared, he announced in a nervous mumble that Mr. O'Gorman would be joining them shortly. He glanced once at Tilden and then, Nat saw, once more toward the doors leading to the street.

"On your toes, Tilden," he said softly. "O'Gorman will be coming at your back."

The words were barely out before Nat Goodwin felt a draft on his cheek, then a fuller rush of air. He turned, almost casually, his right arm extended and his pepperbox pointed full in the startled face of Billy

O'Gorman. O'Gorman had come in at a runner's crouch, a baseball bat held low in front of him. His surprise ruined, O'Gorman straightened and spat.

"I'm getting very tired of staring into that thing, Goodwin. Next time I'll make you eat it."

"Drop the club, Billy. Please."

O'Gorman lowered it but kept his grip. "I don't think so. I also don't think you'll go to Sing Sing for shootin' a man who only has a stick."

"Try to remember, Billy, that I don't like you very much."

"You'll put that away if I drop this? No matter how rough it gets?"

"If I see no guns or knives."

"Your word?"

"We've been through that."

"Then *done,*" O'Gorman shouted. He whipped the baseball bat at Tilden's feet and charged as Tilden leaped aside. A running kick glanced off Tilden's hip inches from his crotch, and a backhand fist caught him high on the temple. Tilden spun away, both hands up, and shot three quick jabs at O'Gorman's mouth, snapping his front teeth and sending him reeling against the bar.

O'Gorman shook his head. He brought a hand to his mouth and spat into it. Blood and bits of teeth. Next he stared hard at Tilden's hands.

"What have you got there?" he demanded.

Tilden advanced on him, saying nothing.

"Those are weighted gloves." He pointed, looking accusingly at Nat Goodwin. He backed along the bar away from Tilden. "You said a fair fight."

Tilden cut him off. He faked another jab and dug a snarling right hand into O'Gorman's ribs. The bigger man gagged and buckled. Tilden straightened him and threw two hard rights at his eye, slicing open the brow. O'Gorman crashed to his knees. His hand found the rim of a heavy brass cuspidor, but Tilden kicked it away before he could grip it. Tilden seized O'Gorman's hair as his own had been seized and aimed a tattoo of chopping lefts at O'Gorman's other eye.

"Help me," O'Gorman screamed, sinking to the floor. "Fifty dollars a man. Get him."

Three men exchanged glances, shot a measuring look at John Flood, and reached for pool cues. At another table four men rose, one slipping on a pair of studded knucks. The two who had been playing nine-ball smiled.

"So everybody understands"—Nat Goodwin projected his best stage voice—"those two gentlemen by the pool table are Paddy Ryan and Alf Greenfield. With John Flood there, you're looking at three of the best bare-knuckle heavyweights in the world. On the other hand, fifty dollars is fifty dollars. So don't back off on my account."

Goodwin watched with satisfaction, and the three fighters with disappointment, as one pair of hands after another disappeared deep into trouser pockets. Tilden took Billy O'Gorman's hair once more and rolled him onto his back. He sat across the bar owner's chest, pinning his arms at his sides.

"I'm done," O'Gorman pleaded. "No more, for God's sake."

Tilden stripped off his wool knit gloves and laid them aside. He placed his thumbnails against the edges of O'Gorman's eyes and leaned forward, pressing.

"Oh, Jesus. No. No, Mr. Beckwith," he bawled.

"Nothing personal," Tilden whispered. "Your employer wants a pair of eyes and I'm going to bring them to him."

"Oh, please. My mother. My babies."

"And you were hired to hurt a woman as well. What were you going to do to her, Mr. O'Gorman?

Were you going to take one of her sweet eyes, sir? Or the tip of her nose?"

"Oh, I'd never. Oh, please God, believe me." He was blubbering. "Jocko will tell you. Jocko was the one whose ear you done last night. Jocko will tell you I said no, not for all his millions would I put my hand to a lady."

"Millions?" Tilden glanced up at Nat Goodwin, then back to O'Gorman. "Whose millions?"

"Mr. Gould's. Not for every dime of his would I have done that."

"Who hired you? Was it Gould himself?"

"It was his man. Carling his name was. But he said he spoke for Gould and for the Clubber."

Tilden pressed harder.

"Jesus. Jesus."

"Would you like to keep your eyes, Mr. O'Gorman?"

"Oh, yes. Yes."

"Then pass a message for me to all your kind. From this moment on, you are to be that lady's protector. Should any harm come to her, even any fright, through whatever agency and even if you be innocent, I will come for you. I will claim your eyes and your hands as well. Do you doubt that, Mr. O'Gorman?"

"No," he croaked. "It will be like you say. I swear it."

Tilden felt John Flood's hand upon his shoulder. "It's enough, lad," he said softly. "Let's take a walk." He lifted Tilden onto legs now drained of strength and, signaling for Nat Goodwin to watch their backs, led him toward the door. Behind him, he could hear Joe McArdle climbing over the bar and helping Billy O'Gorman to his feet. The smaller bartender rinsed a bar towel in clear water and handed it across. McArdle held the towel to O'Gorman's face.

"Beckwith," the beaten man called.

Tilden looked over his shoulder. The saloonkeeper was blinking through his own blood at Tilden and at some of the barroom idlers who had witnessed his defeat.

"I'll want to try you again. Without them damned gloves."

"You know where I live," Tilden answered wearily.

"I'd have took your eye well enough, but I'd have left you the other. And I told you true about the woman."

Tilden took another step toward the door but John Flood stopped him. "Don't do that, lad," he whispered. "Hear the man out."

"Beckwith?" O'Gorman assumed a fighting stance though he could barely make out which form was Tilden's. "I'll have you again right now."

"Say you've had enough," John Flood said softly. "Say he's the toughest man you ever faced. Say that out loud, lad."

Tilden sighed. "Twice is enough, Mr. O'Gorman. I might not be so lucky a third time."

"If it was only one eye you had your thumb against, I'd have spit in your face and said pluck and be damned."

"I know that, Billy." Tilden nodded. "Two eyes made it different. A man who'd lose both his eyes for want of asking to keep them is a fool."

"Damned true," came Paddy Ryan's voice in agreement. O'Gorman could see others nodding.

"You caught me off balance."

"I said I was lucky."

"I ain't an altar boy. But I ain't the worst, either."

"Worst or not, I'd hate to see anyone tougher. Good day, sir."

Corbin had his eyes on the sidewalk as he climbed with Gwen up the narrow shoveled path on Maple Avenue.

It was strange. He'd always understood that. That you should never take it all. Leave the other person some room. It was not a thing he remembered learning in his life so much as a thing he'd always known. But now he remembered.

He could almost hear John Flood's voice, which would have been a whiskey tenor but for one punch too many at his throat. "Three hundred men. I've licked three hundred men in my time," he said, "from mining camps, to farm and cow town saloons, to the prize rings of London. I've clubbed men to the dirt who became fast friends, men like Paddy and Alf, and Joe Goss and Tommy Chandler. Some were bummers, sure enough, who it gave me pleasure to cosh. But I never took all a man had, Tilden. I never shamed him. I never put a man where he had to piss on my grave before he could lift his own eyes. That O'Gorman's a bad one, but you left him proud. Ansel Carling's a bad one but you left him nothin', lad. Nothin' but gettin' even."

"I know."

"It's goin' to be him or you. Or Margaret in the bargain."

"You're certain that she's safe?"

"Goss and Chandler have been sittin' outside her house in a meat wagon all day. They seen her at the window a few times. Nat's arranged for two Pinkertons to take over the watch till the danger's past."

"It won't be past. Not while Carling's alive."

"Don't do it yourself, Tilden. Leave it to me. This city's full o' men who'll do the job for just what they find in Carling's pockets. You don't have the stuff for it."

"You can say that?" Tilden arched. "You just saw me about to tear out a man's eyes."

"You wouldn't have done that either."

"You cannot know that."

The big man put an arm around Tilden's shoulder. "You're handy enough with your fists. And you're a hard man to keep down. But this just ain't your game. And as for O'Gorman, don't go tellin' yourself you were a match for him just because you put him down. Without Nat Goodwin at your back and me and my mates ready to tear the place apart, you would have been in a sack by now."

"Thank you for such confidence." Tilden tried to pull away.

"Right now, lad, you got hate in you sure enough," John Flood told him. "But you got no schemin'. You got no sneak. Everything in your life you do head-on and face to face. That's well and good in the prize ring, but even there you got a referee and cornermen. Outside the prize ring, it's goin' to get you hurt one day, Tilden. Truly it will."

Up ahead, past a snowcapped juniper hedge, Corbin caught his first glimpse of the house on Maple Avenue since Friday morning. Just a moment before, he almost thought that the sidewalk he was on was outside a row of Sixth Avenue dives, but now all that was washing away in the clean whiteness of the Greenwich landscape. Faces and names were fading as well, some quicker than others. Nat Goodwin. Corbin knew that Goodwin was an actor, that he had reddish hair, and that his friendship once meant a great deal to Tilden Beckwith, but he could remember little else. The lumpy Irish face of big John Flood was more clear in his mind, and the face of Ansel Carling the most vivid of all. He saw Carling's face as he left it that night at the Hoffman House bar. Badly battered. Even more so than . . . than whom? There was another man in another bar. Another fight. It was leaving him.

He tried to think what happened with Carling later on. Carling had tried to get even, tried to hurt Tilden and Margaret. Corbin was sure of that much. So Tilden almost surely would have gone looking for Carling again. But when Corbin tried to envision that second encounter he saw nothing at all. Maybe, Corbin thought, he never found him. Try that. Try just looking. He'd go over to the Navarro and hammer at the door of Carling's apartment. Or he'd wait for him in the shadows outside. At that thought, Corbin could feel a small surge of annoyance coming from deep within himself, an emotion he knew was not entirely his own. No. Right. That wouldn't have been Tilden's style. What, then, would Tilden have done? Try to look at it sort of sideways, sort of from the corner of your eye the way you have to look at certain dim stars in order to see them at all. Corbin tried it. It did not do to look to his left because Gwen was there, walking at his side and slightly ahead. Try the right. Yes. There. It looks like a man over there. Corbin had to blink several times and settle his focus to keep the image from washing away like a piece of corneal lint.

It was a man in a black suit, a fat man, not Carling, and he was in an office someplace very high up above the street. See? Let it happen and it seems to come. The trick, like Gwen has been saying for two days, is not to deny it. Maybe Sturdevant is right, too. Maybe there isn't all that much difference between daydreaming and ancestral memory. Now, fill in the background. It is an office. There are old-fashioned oak desks all around, two of which are in glass enclosures. There are paintings on the wall. They all have telegraph poles in them. Western Union. This is the old Western Union Building down on Madison Square. That's more than a guess, isn't it, Tilden? Especially considering that I've never been to Madison Square and the only thing I know about it is that's where the Flatiron Building is, except the Flatiron wasn't even built at the time this fat guy in the black suit is pointing toward the door behind you and saying get out before he has you thrown out.

Hacker.

Albert Hacker.

The one in the Hoffman House bar that night. He hit Tilden from behind with his cane.

And there's Tilden stepping over this low oak railing and walking toward Hacker, whose expression is changing very quickly, and now Tilden has him by his shirt and is forcing him back toward an open window. The fat man has his hands up in a pathetic attempt at defense, but Tilden easily spins him around and bends him so that his head and shoulders are sticking out the window five or six floors above the street and Hacker is screaming something about New Jersey.

"That will do, Mr. Beckwith."

A small, sad-faced man is in the room. A black beard, long and narrow.

"I want Ansel Carling." Tilden turned his head while holding the terrified fat man in place. "Where is he?"

"Out of harm's way, Mr. Beckwith. As you and a score of pedestrians have just heard, he is in New Jersey."

"At Taylor's Hotel, I suppose."

Taylor's Hotel. Corbin knew of it. In Jersey City, right on the river. Less a hotel than a fortress these past twenty years. Guarded by twelve armed men and two six-pounders against occasional mobs of vengeance-minded investors who'd been skinned by this little man with the face of a disappointed poet.

"That would seem a prudent address," Jay Gould answered, "all things considered."

Two more men, both in derby hats, had appeared, each carrying a repeating rifle across his chest. They stood on either side of the man who owned the Western

Union Company and several railroads, including most of the New York elevateds, and who had ruined Cyrus Field with the help of Ella Beckwith. Tilden released his hold on Albert Hacker.

"You cannot protect him forever, Mr. Gould," Tilden said quietly. "Short of having your bravos there put a bullet in my head or try for *both* my eyes this time, I will get my hands around Carling's neck sooner or later."

The bearded man blinked. "Am I to understand the reference to your eyes?"

"I think you do." Tilden took a step forward. "And I'll tell you what I told your man O'Gorman. If any harm comes to a certain woman merely to get at me . . ."

Jay Gould held up a delicate hand. He touched the other to his brow as if to relieve the confusion that was evident on his face. "Mr. Hacker," he called softly, "a word with you, please."

The perspiring Hacker was already edging in Jay Gould's direction. He now broke into what would have been a run but for the furniture in his path. Tilden could do little else but watch, arms folded, as the two men conferred in whispers. Although nothing at all, as usual, could be read upon the melancholy countenance of Jay Gould, Albert Hacker was at once clearly explaining himself, denying an active role in these events, and proclaiming himself innocent of their consequence. Tilden saw one of the guards roll his eyes at the other. "Please wait in my office," he heard Jay Gould say. And when Hacker hesitated, still furiously shaking his head with his fingers pointed to his breast, Gould glanced at the nearest guard, who then put a firm hand upon the fat man's shoulder. Albert Hacker left at once by the door Gould had entered.

"Will you accept my oath, sir"—Jay Gould looked

across at Tilden—"that I had no knowledge whatsoever of intended violence?"

"Of course." Tilden nodded. "Why would you break a man's body when you can break his heart as you did with Cyrus Field."

"A simple reply in the affirmative would have been sufficient, sir."

"If it's true, then give me Carling."

Gould waved off the suggestion. "I will give him cause to redirect his energies. You will not be troubled further."

"And you think that ends it."

"Mr. Hacker informs me that you have a friend who has also been in peril of Mr. Carling's vengeance. Surely you would like to see that peril ended. Surely you would also wish our relationship to be restored to one in which there is some profit."

Tilden was stunned. Here was a man so singularly directed toward the getting of money that he could not imagine why the threat of plucking out Margaret Barrie's eye should be unduly brooded upon. Here was a man who at worst authored and at least condoned the seduction of Ella for the purpose of getting the records of Cyrus Field's stock transactions, and he seems to be saying what's past is past and let us not let it stand in our way if there is another dollar to be turned. Tilden could only shake his head in wonder.

"The policeman," he said finally, "Inspector Williams. You did send him to me, did you not?"

"I suggested certain avenues of investigation to him."

"To what end, sir?" Tilden's jaw tightened.

"To determine, sir, whether a man in my employ might possibly be caught up in a public scandal. That is the long and the short of it."

"And to convey your feelings of friendship toward me."

Gould almost smiled. "I did ask him, if the occasion arose, to communicate my sympathy. And to make it clear, as I hope he did, that no other suspicions concerning your wife's unhappy end would be pursued unless—"

"Unless what, sir?"

"Let us regard that matter, too, as closed."

"Unless what, sir?" Tilden stepped toward him. One guard's thumb touched the hammer of his Winchester.

"I spoke of redirecting Mr. Carling's energies. It is possible that your energies of late, sir, nearly all of them, have been misdirected as well. I do not expect that you would take my advice where your private affairs are concerned, but I have some hope of persuading you that your continued efforts on Mr. Field's behalf are inappropriate."

"My God!"

Gould closed his eyes. "Do not be pigheaded in this instance, sir." He clipped off the words. "Do me the goodness to hear me out. In my office. With no ears but ours."

"My God, are you not finished with that good man yet? What else can you do to him?"

"That good man betrayed me. Or tried to."

"Betrayal!" Tilden sputtered. He was moved to dispute Gould's choice of that word, but he knew it would be of no use. "In any case, the man is beaten. Whatever his designs or mine might be toward the restoration of a decent station for himself and his family, I am willing to assure you that they involve no threat to you whatsoever."

"He remains a bad example to others, Mr. Beckwith."

"You can go straight to hell, Mr. Gould."

.   .   .

Another fortnight passed before Tilden would consider dismissing the Pinkertons who were guarding Margaret's brownstone. It was in that time that Margaret agreed to his proposal. She would bear him a child if she could, and she would remain with him and be his wife in her heart as long as he wished. But if that should end, if he should choose to take a wife who was more suited to his station, let it be understood now that she would not hand over the child as if she were nothing more than a cow whose purpose had been served. Tilden was horrified that she had seriously entertained such a concern. He tore a piece of foolscap from a tablet on which she'd been writing and sat at once to compose a promise of his affection and his love, his most joyous acknowledgment of any child that might come of their union, of his eternal support from his heart as well as his purse, and that, on all his honor, the subject of one or the other giving up the child would never be raised. On that Friday, with the Pinkertons following for the first mile only, Tilden and Margaret drove to the Claremont Inn, where they registered as Mr. and Mrs. Harry Whitney. There and under that name the child was conceived.

It was June of that year before the last traces of the great blizzard melted from deeply shaded nooks and with them at least some of the pain Tilden bore from the night of Ella's death. Nothing more had been heard from Carling or Jay Gould. Not directly. As for Carling, it was said that Gould had sent him first to a surgeon for the repair of his face and then to Texas to do penance supervising the construction of cattle pens along the decaying Southwestern Pacific Railroad. He would forever be useless to Jay Gould in New York, where nearly everyone had heard of his humiliation at the hands of Tilden Beckwith and had marked him a cur and a coward. A good many held the whispered belief that his attentions, which some said were welcomed and some said were not, had somehow been responsible for the death of Tilden's wife. Those who wondered why Gould kept a man like that on his payroll at all were told it was a question of which had more on the other, but not to worry, for Jay Gould would always let a man hang himself in the end. As for Gould himself, Tilden's firm soon felt the consequences of his displeasure. One account, then another, then several more were withdrawn by sweating men who would not meet Tilden's eyes. But luckily for Beckwith & Company, Jay Gould had more enemies than friends. A few of these came forward, providing Tilden with sufficient business that his income was approximately maintained and that no employees were discharged in consequence.

In midsummer, Tilden took permanent rooms at the Claremont Inn and spent all his weekends there with Margaret, plus as many weekdays as he could manage. John Flood joined them on an August Saturday for one of their outings to the Polo Grounds. Flood had sworn to Tilden's lie that the bruises he showed these few months before were the result of a friendly rough-and-tumble between them and, no, true enough, there had been no new trouble with the Carling fellow. Margaret remained doubtful, but now it seemed forgotten. It was a fine summer day. A good day for baseball. Although John Flood did not fully share Tilden's passion for the sport, and although a day in Margaret's company was inducement enough for him, this day was a banner one because none other than John L. Sullivan, lately back from Europe, was scheduled to pitch three exhibition innings before the regular game against the Providence team. Sullivan, Flood pointed out, had played the game for Boston College and had considered a professional career before his fight on a dare against Cockey Woods, the toughest man in Boston, and his shocking fifth-round knockout persuaded him that a career of swatting heads instead of baseballs might be worth a further look. You could count on your fingers, said Flood, the number of men who've lasted five rounds with him since, yours truly among them, and not counting the shameful thirty-nine-round draw Sullivan just fought in France against the limey Charley Mitchell, who kept running and falling down until his friends saw it was dark enough to claim a draw.

Margaret, watching through opera glasses from their carriage parked beyond the outfield stakes, could not believe the man she saw was the great John L. He looked ten years older than Tilden, not the two that Tilden claimed. His face was soft and puffy, and he carried what must have been thirty pounds of excess above his belt. The crowd in the grandstand noticed as well, because there was more murmur than cheer when he took the field and doffed his hat. "It's the bottle," John Flood said sadly. "Too many saloons and too many rounds stood by him and by those who'd say they drank with John L. hisself and shook his hand. Maybe a draw against the likes of Charley Mitchell was not such mischief after all."

Sullivan pitched well enough in the exhibition innings, throwing underhand as even many professionals still did. The grandstand crowd forgot its first surprise at his appearance and was cheering every called strike and miss. A two-base hit in his first at bat brought them screaming to their feet. But John Flood continued to be grim. Near the end of the final exhibition inning, he excused himself and walked down the left field foul line toward the Giants' dugout. A policeman moved to stop him, but then several in the grandstand recognized the Bull's Head Terror and began chanting his name. John L. Sullivan was in mid-windup when he heard the sound. He stopped and turned, searching the faces on the sidelines until he found John Flood, then bowed with a flourish in his direction.

"I didn't know they were friends," Margaret said excitedly.

"Oh yes." Tilden nodded. "John says after he fought Sullivan they drank their way through half the bars and clubs in New York. They did the same in Philadelphia and Chicago. John went with him on the road and worked his corner for several fights while picking up a few of his own along the way."

Margaret watched as the inning ended on a grounder to third. Sullivan bowed like an actor taking curtain calls; then, before the cheers could thin, he strode off to the sideline, where he pounded the shoulders of the waiting John Flood.

"My goodness," she exclaimed, "John Flood is a full head taller than Mr. Sullivan. How on earth could he have been beaten?"

"It's mostly in the hands. Sullivan's are lightning fast and he's able to hit much harder than other men."

"How could he hit harder," she asked, "than a bear of a man like John Flood?"

"Most bare-knuckle prizefighters," Tilden explained, "don't hit nearly as hard as you'd think. Heads, jaws, and elbows are much tougher than knuckles. A fighter must protect his hands and wear the other man down with body blows and by slamming him to the ground, but most blows to the head must be pulled. Sullivan is different. Through some freak of creation his hands are much stronger than those of other men, so he's never reluctant to try for the knockout punch."

"Oh look." She peered through the glasses. "I think they're quarreling."

Tilden saw. John Flood had put an arm around Sullivan's back and was walking him in the general direction of their carriage. Annoyance was plain in the champion's manner. "I suspect John L. is being told of the evils of demon rum. Though I think it's demon champagne in this case."

"John Flood doesn't drink at all, does he."

Tilden shook his head. "He took the pledge four years ago. John will tell anyone who'll listen that it was alcohol more than Sullivan's fists that denied him the heavyweight belt. Now he's afraid that alcohol will take that belt away from Sullivan. Sullivan just went thirty-nine rounds with a man he easily knocked out in three, five years ago. And he's about to be challenged by Jake Kilrain, a hard man who takes his training seriously. I for one would have trouble betting on Sullivan."

"Oh." Margaret touched her hair. "They're coming here. They're coming to the carriage."

John Flood's frown and John L. Sullivan's scowl turned to pleasant smiles as if on signal as they approached Tilden's hired landau. Sullivan doffed his cap with a glance toward Margaret and extended a hand to Tilden. "Ah, young Mr. Beckwith. You are looking well and fit, sir. I have become expert on the subject of fitness these last few minutes."

John Flood cleared his throat. "May I present Mrs. Charlotte Whitney," he said, sparing Tilden the need to lie to an old acquaintance.

"Your most bedazzled servant, madam." He bowed. "May I say that you are the loveliest flower I've seen this summer."

A smile split Margaret's face. "Are all pugilists so gallant, Mr. Sullivan?"

"Only champions, madam. It comes with the job. Certain others, as a rule, remain tiresome nags for the rest of their lives." He turned to Tilden, throwing an elbow into John Flood's stomach in the process. "Your father, Tilden. I trust he is well?"

"He is retired to Charleston and he writes that the sea air is having good effect. A better tonic, of course, would be the news that you've beaten Jake Kilrain."

"Then I shall make a point of it, sir."

"Can you picnic with us, Mr. Sullivan?" Margaret asked. "We have fried chicken, orange juice, and some wonderful canned peaches in syrup."

John Flood coughed again.

"I can imagine no finer lunch, Mrs. Whitney, and no grander company with one oversized exception. I have people waiting for me who will not make faces with every bite I take. Another time perhaps."

"We must make a point of that as well, sir."

"Your servant, madam."

John Flood spent much of the regulation game deep in thought as Tilden attempted to follow the action while responding to Margaret's frequent questions about the champion. She was thrilled that he and Tilden knew each other in spite of Tilden's insistence that Sullivan probably would not have remembered his name but for John Flood reminding him as they approached the carriage. At the seventh-inning stretch, a new custom unique to the Polo Grounds, John Flood asked if he might excuse himself and return downtown by other means. There were a few more things he wished to say to Sullivan about his ruinous habits. It was time, he said, that someone not in awe of him stepped forward to take him in hand.

A few days later, Tilden noticed an item in the sports pages of the *New York World* which read uncannily like the exchange that had occurred with Sullivan, right down to the record of his two fights with Mitchell and his reluctance to partake of peaches in heavy syrup, having promised a return to form and a victory over Jake Kilrain, a hard man who took his training seriously. The article carried no byline. But Tilden recalled that Margaret had been briefly in the *World's* employ, and he recalled the tablet from which he'd torn the page to record his promise of fidelity. Many of the pages had been filled in her fine hand with what seemed like random notes. "Is it possible, my dearest Margaret," he asked when they dined that night at the Claremont, "that I am acquainted with the author of this piece?"

"I'm sure I have no idea, Tilden," she replied innocently. "Do you think, by the way, that my figure is beginning to resemble a toad's?"

"Madam, I will not be diverted." He tried to be firm. "Nor will I be manipulated into telling you that you are all the lovelier in your condition, nor will I allow you to fluster me by inviting me to feel the child's movements as we sup in a public place. Did you write this item?"

"I thought you would never ask."

"How is it that Margaret Barrie, piano teacher, bookkeeper, and tutor of French, is now revealed to be a newspaper correspondent?"

"Well, Tilden," she reminded him, "we did discuss my need to earn my own way. In the short time that I was employed by Mr. Pulitzer's newspaper, I became quite excited by all the bold new things he was doing. I had never realized what a telling instrument a newspaper could be in the cause of social justice, as Mr. Pulitzer put it, or of the many worthwhile issues that needed to be faced and fought."

"Such as John L. Sullivan's capacity to lose his paunch."

"Tilden!"

"Forgive me."

"And Mr. Pulitzer," she went on, "was also the first publisher in New York to hire a female correspondent. She is only the smallest slip of a girl named Elizabeth Cochrane and yet she quickly became his star reporter. I went to see her. Elizabeth writes under the name of Nelly Bly, you know, and she is a marvelous young woman of enormous pluck. Just this year she had herself committed to the lunatic asylum at Blackwell's Island for ten whole days and then wrote an exposé of conditions there which—"

"I read it, dearest." Tilden touched her hand. "Pray do not tell me that you intend being convicted of a capital crime so that you may write firsthand of Sing Sing's new electric chair."

Margaret closed one eye. "Elizabeth told me I should expect to be patronized by men."

"Again, I apologize." Tilden raised his hands. "What is it you intend doing in this new career, and how will it be possible from the Claremont Inn?"

"Stories are everywhere"—Margaret made a gesture embracing the world around her—"and you seem to know everyone. All I need do is be attentive as with Mr. Sullivan, compose a little story, and send it in to Elizabeth by telegram."

"Hmmm." Tilden took a bite of his bluefish. "I do applaud your resourcefulness, Margaret."

"But you're about to ask me to curtail it."

Tilden shook his head. "Not at all, my dear. The Sullivan story is harmless enough, but you did meet him through me. Now you speak of my knowing a great many other people. In future, if you intend submitting an item in which I am in any way involved, might I ask that you show it to me first?"

"Done." She clapped her hands. "Oh, Tilden, I'm so pleased that you don't mind."

"You're going to do it anyway, so I might as well get credit for supporting the proposition."

"I have so many exciting ideas. Would you like to hear them?"

"I am breathless."

"What if I were the first woman to report firsthand on a championship fight?"

Tilden winced. Aside from the Blackwell's Island asylum, he could imagine no worse assemblage of human dross. After an hour in that company, she'll want to burn her clothing.

"Exciting, yes." He tried not to stammer. "That is an exciting one." But not while I have a breath in my body.

"My other thought," she enthused, "one that you could assist with, Tilden, was that I could write some wonderful inside scoops based upon the stories you've told me about Jay Gould."

Tilden choked. A bit of bluefish sprayed from his lips.

"Are you all right, Tilden?"

"Yes." He touched his napkin to his mouth and held it there. "Yes. A bit of bone in the fillet."

"You don't like that idea, do you?"

"It's just, umm, I can't imagine what good it would do. There's hardly a newspaper in the country, including the *World,* which Gould, in fact, used to own before Pulitzer bought it, which has not attacked Gould at one time or another. The man is absolutely impervious to criticism or rejection. When the Academy of Music refused to sell him a box, he simply gathered some other rich outcasts and founded the Metropolitan Opera. When the New York Yacht Club rejected his membership application, he founded the American Yacht Club up in Rye. Here is a man who publicly said that he could hire any half of a striking work force to kill the other half. Do you understand what I'm saying, Margaret?"

"You're telling me, I think, that you find this proposal even more appalling than the first."

"The first was better." He shook his head. "Not by a great deal, but better."

"And where Mr. Gould is concerned, you're saying you'd prefer to let sleeping dogs lie."

"Exactly so. Yes."

"As always, Tilden"—Margaret lowered her eyes demurely—"it shall be as you wish."

Looking back upon that conversation over the next several weeks, Tilden could not escape the suspicion that he had been shamelessly manipulated by Margaret and, further, that Margaret had been coached by Miss Elizabeth Cochrane in the technique of getting a man to agree to the lesser of two evils. That business about exposing Jay Gould was a stratagem, he was sure. He could only hope that the one of watching two men pound each other's faces into liver was a tactic as well. In any case, he had already given Margaret his blessing to write as she pleased within reasonable limits, and he resolved to give Jay Gould as little thought as he could manage.

That resolution, however, was more easily made than kept. In late September, Tilden went with Margaret to the first four games of the 1888 World Series against the St. Louis Browns. A week later, after the series had moved on to St. Louis, where the Giants sewed up the championship by winning six out of the first eight games of the ten-game series, that first dismaying item appeared in *Town Topics*. Tilden waited for a second item to be brought to his attention before he swallowed both his anger and his pride and sent a message to Colonel William D'Alton Mann to the effect that he was prepared to offer a donation in the cause of future anonymity. To Tilden's surprise, the message went unacknowledged.

After waiting several days, and having seen the hurt in Margaret's eyes, Tilden met first with his attorney, Mr. Andrew Smithberg, to inquire as to hastening the availability of the Greenwich house and also as to the progress Mr. Smithberg was making in the construction of a fictitious personal history for Margaret. Tilden had confided in the attorney because he reasoned that if Margaret were to live under an assumed name, she ought to be armed with satisfactory answers to any questions that might normally arise, whether they be casual or official. Smithberg assured Tilden that he was diligently at work on both projects and hoped to have a resolution shortly. Tilden did not bother questioning the Beckwith & Company lawyer regarding any legal recourse against Colonel Mann. There had been no provable libel against him personally, not even in Mann's use of the word *suspicious* in reference to Ella's death. And the "soiled dove" euphemism as it applied to Margaret was not one he chose to challenge in open court.

Upon completing his interview with Mr. Smithberg, Tilden left his office early and walked to Park Row, where he waited on the sidewalk outside the editorial offices of *Town Topics*. It was useless, he knew, to request an appointment with Colonel Mann and even more so to attempt a confrontation in Mann's office. Prudence had long ago dictated to the publisher that he keep his stout office door locked at all times and that all visitors be well screened. A male receptionist behind a barred bank teller's desk kept an updated list naming a hundred or more possible visitors of hostile disposition. A silent alarm would be touched if any of these were to appear. Colonel Mann's hack—he owned no carriage—was met by a guard each morning, and he was escorted to it at the curb each evening. Tilden's intention was to loiter until the colonel left for the day and follow the hack on foot until an opportunity arose to leap aboard. He waited less than an hour before the genial snow-bearded man appeared, paused on the sidewalk to admire a passing babe in a wicker perambulator, gave a cube of sugar to the hack driver's horse, and bade good evening to his guard. Tilden mingled with the homebound crowd at the first uptown intersection. As the hack slowed to allow their crossing, Tilden slipped to its blind side and was aboard in a single leap.

"Hey," the driver snapped. "What do you think you're up to?"

"It's all right." The colonel raised a hand, noting no threat of immediate harm in Tilden's manner. Tilden, in fact, had clasped his hands over his knees and was affecting a posture of carefree relaxation. "My young friend will not be staying long." Colonel Mann met Tilden's eyes and directed them to the small two-shot Derringer that peeked from beneath his lap robe.

"Don't be ridiculous," Tilden whispered, his tone good-natured. "The thing isn't even cocked and for heaven's sake don't do it now. I'm here to talk business."

"Hmmph!" The older man looked down at the weapon. "Another day, another lesson learned. You're quite sure I'll have no occasion for this?"

"The fact is I'd break your arm, you rascal, if I thought it would help. But I know it would not. Now, how can we reach an accommodation?"

"That's a problem, sir." He sighed. "Care for some rock candy?"

"Tell me the problem, Colonel."

"I would very much like you to pay me the compliment of buying a lifetime subscription. But the dilemma I find myself in is that the person supplying the information I've used is probably more interested in having it in than you are in having it out."

"Ansel Carling?" Tilden held his smile.

"Oh, goodness no," the colonel laughed. "Oh, dear me. That's a good one. Ansel Carling, indeed."

Tilden stared at him.

"I am sorry, Mr. Beckwith. It's rude of me. I know you don't get the joke. The person I refer to is Mr. Gould, of course."

"You admit that?"

"Yes, indeed. Mr. Gould himself insisted that there be no duplicity. He divined, you see, that you would be paying me a visit, although he did not predict it in this fashion. Dear me. I hope others won't be making a habit of leaping into my cab."

"Did Mr. Gould predict the outcome of this meeting?" Tilden asked.

Colonel Mann shook his head. "He suggested that I tell you as soon as possible, so that no unpleasantness happens first, that it is he whom you must ask for an accommodation. I am asked to remind you that Mr. Gould cherishes nothing more than the hope that you will be his friend."

"And my alternative is to read about myself in your newspaper."

"You have two weeks' grace, young Tilden, before another eye is cast upon your activities."

"I see." Tilden rubbed his hands. "Can you and I make some arrangement in the meantime that would restrict your reportage to me exclusively?"

"I'm afraid not. Mr. Gould was quite specific. I do have something else to sell you, however. It is beyond the scope of my understanding with Gould, and you are sure to find it useful. The price is two thousand."

"Might I have some clue as to the subject matter?"

"Ansel Carling."

Tilden snorted. "Nothing that man might have done would surprise anyone."

"It's worth the money, I promise. It will surely give you a card to play against Gould."

Tilden thought for a long moment, finally concluding that one card might be better than none at all.

"Two thousand, you say?"

"And a bargain."

"Done. Unless it's a thing I already know, or unless it's something I find to be false, you will have your money by close of business tomorrow."

"He's a Jew."

"I beg your pardon?"

"He's a Jew. Named Asa Koenig. Never been closer to India than an inkwell. He grew up in England, true enough, but as the son of a valet who came from Germany with one of Prince Albert's retainers. Arrested for forgery and deported to Botany Bay. Learned his railroading there, first in a work gang and then apprenticed to the surveyors. Letters of recommendation are forgeries, of course." The colonel looked with satisfaction at the dazed expression on Tilden Beckwith's face. "It's a honey, isn't it."

"Does Jay Gould know this?"

"He's known for some time," Mann said cheerfully. "It was your doing, indirectly. Back when everyone was talking about what a coward you made Carling to be, and talking about Carling himself, the talk eventually reached another Englishman who knew the family Carling was supposed to come from, except this fellow said the only Ansel Carling he could recall went to India sure enough but he died there of the cholera. That got back to Gould and Gould commenced checking up and in time he found out the truth. He never confronted Carling, or Koenig, with it, just got him far away out of his sight."

"What use is this to me?" Tilden asked coldly.

"Why, for trading, of course."

"Trading?"

"Gould is not a man who wants it known he's been fooled. He's also a man who's gone out of his way to convince people with whom he does business that he's not a Jew himself."

"You are suggesting that I blackmail him. I will keep quiet about this if he will keep quiet about me. May I ask why an accomplished blackmailer such as yourself has not taken more direct advantage of this intelligence?"

"No one gets his name in Jay Gould's book if he can help it."

The hack turned left onto Canal Street. Ahead of him, Tilden saw the Sixth Avenue Elevated, which could have him at the Osborne in twenty-five minutes or the Claremont in forty-five. He had not planned on seeing Margaret tonight. Charlotte. It would be well if he got into the habit of saying Charlotte, although the name had not the same music for him that it had for her. He had intended to see to certain affairs at home and to dutifully look in upon the child and his nurse. But now that prospect seemed less attractive than ever. Bad enough that he was raising the son of Ansel Carling, the sneak and coward. It now seems, given that this other devil's story is true, that he has given his name to the son of a confidence man and convict. The business of his being a Jew meant little to Tilden. The Jews in his acquaintance shared a sense of tradition and of family and of industry. Would that Carling, or Koenig, shared any of these qualities. He was more like an Irish Catholic.

"I'll get off here," Tilden said.

"I can expect your draft tomorrow?"

Tilden nodded, stepping to the street at the foot of the station stairs. "I will pray, Colonel Mann, that a special corner of hell is being prepared for you. Good day, sir."

At Central Park, he found a flower stall where he bought a bouquet of yellow asters. With these he boarded the Ninth Avenue train and carried them to the warm and welcome smile of Margaret Barrie. He spent the night in her arms.

It was scarcely a week later that Tilden's lawyer, Mr. Smithberg, in a state of considerable excitement, tracked Tilden down at the Athletic Club. Taking Tilden to a private room, he spread out several papers, one of which was an issue of the *New York Times*, then six days old. Its masthead date was October 11. He directed Tilden's attention to an item on the first page which described a terrible train wreck that had occurred on the Lehigh Valley Railroad at a place called Mud Run in Pennsylvania. Tilden, like many New Yorkers, had seen the article, but Smithberg brushed aside his attempt to say so. An excursion train, Smithberg recounted, had been carrying members of the Total Abstinence Union to a rally in the town of Hazleton. It seemed, however, that neither the union's members nor the train's crew were totally abstemious. Their intake of beverages led to an unplanned relief stop, and in the course of it the train was struck from behind by another. The last two cars were telescoped, and sixty-four men, women, and children were killed outright. Smithberg read aloud an account by a local correspondent. "Oh, what tongue could tell," the anonymous author had written, "or what pen picture this most dreadful calamity? The roasting, scalding engine under which were crushed those poor young children, and the car ahead being ground to splinters and the lives crushed out of those who but a few moments since were full of life. Oh, God, why visit upon your unhappy children such a death."

The breast-beating tone of that selection carried over into a listing of the dead, continued on page 12. On that list, Tilden saw, a number of names had been underscored. One of them, Hiram Forsythe Corbin of Wilkes-Barre, said to have left a wife heavy with child, was followed by two check marks.

"There you have it, sir." The lawyer slapped the newspaper with his palm.

"There I have what, Mr. Smithberg?"

"It was a mistake. There is no wife, no child, no known relatives in point of fact. The man's body was unclaimed. The city of Wilkes-Barre interred him this morning."

"He had no friends? No position in the community?"

Andrew Smithberg beamed. "Young Hiram had only just arrived in town two months before. The story is that he'd been a second mate aboard a China clipper these past four years and had a yen to settle on land. He was drifting west from Baltimore with a wagonload of Chinese silks when he passed through Wilkes-Barre and saw a dry goods store up for lease. The papers he signed list no next of kin. The attorney who drew them up tells me that Hiram Corbin was hardly a teetotaler, but he went on that excursion in the hope of meeting the townspeople a bit more quickly."

"You are about to suggest," Tilden mused, "that he would serve nicely as Margaret's late husband and that Margaret would serve equally well as the wife left heavy with child."

"Not Margaret." Smithberg shook his head. "Charlotte. The name Charlotte Whitney Corbin gives her one more remove from Margaret Barrie. It is perfect, Mr. Beckwith."

Tilden hesitated. He was finding, to his mild surprise, that he did not care for the notion of another man's name attached to Margaret's, even a man she'd never known, even at one more remove, as Smithberg put it. An invented ghost would have been more to his liking. Still, Smithberg was right. It did seem ideal.

"You can provide any other documents she might need?" he asked.

"A simple matter. She'll already have the *New York Times* clipping. And I can create a paper past dating all the way back to her birth. She'll have been born on a farm. Or in a town whose records are no longer extant for one reason or another. Thousands of people are living without evidence of their existence because a church or a town hall has burned to the ground. As for evidence of Hiram Corbin, photographs of young seamen are obtainable among the samples of any waterfront studio. A few yards of Chinese silk, an ivory fan, a piece or two of carved ebony furniture, and she'll have all the artifacts necessary to satisfy the curious who might visit her Greenwich home."

"The stage props will not be necessary." Tilden made a face. "Only the papers."

"They would lend great credibility. It would be very natural for a young wife to keep mementos of her dear departed husband."

"Only the papers, Mr. Smithberg."

"Corbin," Margaret repeated, trying on the name as she would a gown. "It has an honest sound, Tilden. Charlotte Whitney Corbin."

It crossed Tilden's mind, not for the first time, that Margaret Barrie might not have been the name she was born with, either. But it did not much matter to him. The name of any girl had always seemed to him a temporary thing, having little significance as an identity if it were so easily surrendered upon an exchange of wedding vows. Wedding vows.

"Tilden, dearest, you seem troubled," she said to him.

"No." He shook his head. "Not at all. Just some office business I have neglected."

If she had said, *I despise this new name, Tilden.* If she had said, *I feel as you, Tilden. It seems like another man's body against mine and I want no body but yours and no name but yours.* If she had said, *Be not fearful for me or fearful of Gould and Carling and Colonel Mann or of the women who whisper sly stories over cups of tea, but let me and our child be an adornment to you and to the name of Beckwith,* he might have swept her into his arms and driven her to the nearest magistrate. But she did not because she had made a bargain. And he did not, as he was beginning to know, because he was a fool.

Two more weeks passed, as did another scurrilous mention in *Town Topics,* which Tilden kept from her, before Andrew Smithberg appeared with all the papers needed for the purchase of a Greenwich property by a young widow named Charlotte Corbin. The furnishings were now in place, and true to Tilden's word, the house had been electrified and a telephone installed and a glistening bathroom was inside the house and a shiny new carriage and sled awaited in the barn. Everyone knew there was profit in the China trade. Margaret moved in just before Thanksgiving.

Two neighbors appeared on the very first day, bearing casseroles and fresh-baked bread. Mr. Smithberg was there, as was Tilden, who was obviously nervous and awkwardly solicitous of the very pregnant and very lovely young widow. The neighbors, ladies of early middle age with large families of their own, understood Mr. Beckwith to be the owner of this property before selling it to Mrs. Corbin, and they understood his behavior to be that of a man suddenly smitten upon coming face to face with a woman he had heretofore met only through Mr. Smithberg. Andrew Smithberg assisted them in coming to this conclusion. It would not surprise him at all, he told Mrs. Gannon and Mrs. Redway in confidence, if young Mr. Beckwith, a tragic widower himself, begged the honor of calling upon Mrs. Corbin in future. Confidence notwithstanding, the two ladies lost little time in encouraging Margaret to receive him.

The child was born, to the delight of all, on Christmas morning. A healthy son, delivered there in the house and without great distress by Dr. Miles Palmer with the assistance of a young and very large black nurse named Lucy Stone. Mrs. Redway had been with Margaret since before dawn, having been alerted by the prearranged signal of flashing electric lights that the pains of labor had begun. Mrs. Redway called first Dr. Palmer and then Tilden Beckwith, who had taken a room in the Indian Harbor Hotel. She spent much of the morning calming him and pouring coffee for him even after the first cry of life sounded from the room upstairs. A body would think he was an anxious father if she didn't know perfectly well that they'd been acquainted barely a month. Mrs. Redway was charmed. Perhaps the dear baby would not long be denied a father after all.

The noon church bells sounded before Tilden was allowed a short private visit. Margaret was pale but without much discomfort, even though she had refused Dr. Palmer's offer of laudanum.

"Oh, Tilden, look," she said upon returning his kiss, "he is the image of you. I'm afraid a tongue or two is going to wag."

Tilden, who thought all newborns resembled halibuts as much as anything, pretended nonetheless to share her conviction of their resemblance.

"He is a Beckwith, to be sure." Tilden squeezed her hand. "Though on the inside I'd be proud if he's more of a Barrie."

Margaret smiled, then was silent for a long moment.

"Sometimes, Tilden," she said to him, "when I see a person I have not met, I try to guess his name. It's a little game I play."

Tilden waited.

"When I first saw you at Georgiana's house, I decided that your name should be Jonathan. You look like a Jonathan."

"Because all Jonathans are noble and handsome, I take it."

"I have decided to call our son Jonathan," she told

him. "It is not my first choice. But it is fitting and I will be pleased with it."

"I, too, am pleased." His eyes moistened. "Most pleased."

"He will be christened Jonathan T Corbin. You and I will both know that the *T* is for Tilden. That is enough."

Tilden's face clouded. His mind went back to the initial, similarly incomplete, which he'd given Ella's child in a moment of hurt and anguish.

"What is wrong, Tilden?" She asked. "Please do not forbid it."

"Oh." He kissed her. "Nothing of the sort. I was just wondering if it would be so reckless to give him Tilden as his second name and be done with it. After all, the whole town knows we've become good friends. And women have been known to name babies after people they hardly knew, such as the doctor who delivered them, or after famous people they did not know at all."

"This way is best for now. I have a fear of you feeling too much bound to me and the child."

"Bound," he stammered. "I will not hear of such a thing. You might as well say I fear being bound to my own arms and legs."

"Later, Tilden." She touched his lips. "Let us have one day at a time for now and be thankful for each of them."

Now Tilden fell into a brooding silence.

"Tilden?"

He raised an eyebrow.

"Merry Christmas," she whispered sleepily.

"Merry Christmas, my one great love."

Gwen Leamas carried a tray of coffee and some toasted pound cake into the living room. Corbin was on the floor, cross-legged, his back against a window seat. His face, she saw, was oddly tranquil, although no less lost in thought than he'd been all morning.

"Are we about to play Indian?" It was something to say. She was tired of asking if he was all right.

"Does it feel like Christmas to you?" He looked up.

"Hmm!" She set down the tray in front of him. "We could do with some chestnuts roasting. Or at least an open fire."

"I'll build one in a minute." He took a cup and sipped from it. "You know something, Gwen? I think I know where I am now."

"Where you are? You mean this house?"

Corbin nodded. "It always seemed as if I've been here before. But you know when it's most familiar? It's most familiar from down here on the floor."

"Tilden Beckwith had no chairs?"

Corbin grimaced. "Gwen, honey, do you want me to start thinking twice before I say something to you?"

"I'm sorry," she said. So much for trying to keep it light. "Go ahead, Jonathan."

Corbin pointed to the doorway through which she'd come with the tray. "Tilden Beckwith walked right through that door. He came over here and picked up a ball that was rolling around between my legs. He put it in his pocket and then he picked me up. He looked at me, down here, as if to see if I was wet, and then he kissed me on the head and tucked me in one arm. If I turned my head, and I did, it was because his whiskers scratched. I could see Margaret coming from up high through the same doorway. She was fixing her hat in place with a pin and talking to a much smaller woman with straight blond hair. And the blond woman, she's very pretty, she sees me and she waggles her index finger and aims it like she's going to tickle my ribs and I start to laugh and squirm. Then Tilden growls and pretends to bite my neck."

"Jonathan."

"Um?"

"Nothing. Please go on."

"That's really all. Just some messing around with a baby. From where I sat, I was the baby."

"Can you get it back, this vision you were having?"

"It wasn't a vision, sweetheart. I was remembering."

"As Tilden and Margaret's child?"

Corbin nodded, smiling at the still fresh images.

"And you see nothing absolutely cockeyed weird about that?"

"You mean about going from Tilden's head into his son's? Into my grandfather's?" Corbin shrugged, still smiling gently. "You and your uncle just spent two days trying to put me at ease about what's happening to me. Now you want me to start thinking I'm crazy again?"

Good point, she told herself. Bite your tongue. But Gwen did not like this at all. Especially not that contented smile. She had liked it better yesterday and the day before. Although it scared her half out of her wits, she liked it better when Tilden would break through Jonathan's fear. And she could talk to him.

"No. No, you're quite right." She glanced toward the doorway where he'd said Margaret and the blond woman stood. "You were saying that Tilden bit your neck and—Jonathan, I can't help it. Why do you look so damn pleased with yourself?"

"You like me better hiding behind office curtains or screaming in bathtubs? Talk about weird." He pushed to his feet and selected two logs and a handful of kindling from a wrought iron rack by the fireplace. He tested the flue. "Listen, Gwen, I've told you right along I feel good up here. Among the things that make me feel good right now, aside from you being here with me, is that I now understand why this house was so familiar. But only the lower part and especially when I sit on the floor. I've *been* here, Gwen. I've visited. I didn't know what the upstairs looked like because I never had a reason to go there. I was here in this lady's house with both my parents and I was very small and very happy. We all were. Everything was . . ." His voice trailed off.

"Everything was what, Jonathan?"

"Fine." The pleasure was fading.

"Talk to me. What did you just see?"

"It's nothing." He shook it off. "Really. It just seemed that the blond woman was telling Margaret everything would be fine. But she wasn't saying it. It was with the eyes, you know? And with a squeezed arm. So Tilden wouldn't hear."

"Who was she?"

"And I'll tell you something else." He brightened again. "Do you remember when I met Mrs. Starling? And she seemed familiar and I had an idea her name should be Lucy? Lucy was the baby's nurse. She was a big black woman who looked just like Cora Starling."

Gwen Leamas set down her cup. "Who was the blond woman, Jonathan?"

"I don't know. Some friend of Margaret's." He dismissed the question. "Do you know"—his eyes narrowed—"that I have no bad dreams when I'm in Greenwich? I mean, not one. All my life I've had a feeling that something wasn't right or that someone had it in for me. All my life I've had dreams of me beating up on people or people beating up on me. I mean, that Hoffman House thing was just the beginning. It was like a whole tournament I had to go through. All the time I was boxing in college I'd stare hard at whatever opponent I drew, trying to figure out if it was him, whoever the hell *him* was, and I'd do my damnedest to clobber the guy just in case. Then when I finally did get beat up in real life it was by these two men in Chicago, and I kept dreaming about that for years afterward, except in the dreams it was me beating them, I mean really totaling them. But none of this, none of it, ever happens here in Greenwich."

"Jonathan." He was talking so fast. Babbling. She stood up and reached to touch him. He backed away.

"Don't ruin this for me, Gwen."

She blinked. "The blond woman, Jonathan? Is all this because I asked about the blond woman?"

"Don't ruin this for us. I mean it." His eyes were burning.

A car drove by outside. For an instant Gwen hoped desperately that it was her uncle Harry, but the tires she heard had chains. What's keeping him? Gwen wandered to the window, trying not to show that she was frightened. They should have cleared the driveway for him. But he'll get in. Someone had flattened down the driveway entrance. Gwen stiffened as she heard the floorboards creak behind her. She jumped as a hand touched her hair.

"I'm sorry." Corbin stepped back. He raised both palms as if to promise that he would not touch her again.

She crossed her arms. "I've never seen you like that."

"Neither have I," he murmured. He knelt and picked up the tray. It was something to do. When he stood again she saw tears in his eyes.

"Jonathan"—her shoulders trembled—"I don't know what to do. I'm afraid to ask you anything."

"It wasn't . . ." He looked around helplessly. "That wasn't me."

Uncle Harry, where are you?

"Gwen, honey. Please." He threw up his arms. "I don't even know what I'm saying."

"Jonathan, how about if I made you a Bloody Mary?"

"You asked me . . . I don't know that woman's name. I mean, I almost do. If I heard it, I'd know it. And it wasn't because you asked. She was Margaret's best friend. She was fine. She was telling Margaret not to worry."

"About *what*, for Pete's sake?"

"Everything was so terrific here. God! Here I am . . . I know, I really know, that it's dumb for me to be living up here. It's expensive, it's inconvenient, it's lonely because I don't have any friends, and even with all that, here I am still thinking how terrific it is and damn near willing to kill anybody who screws it up."

"And you thought I was going to do that."

"No."

"Let me make that drink, Jonathan."

"Gwen, I'm trying. Don't you think I know how this sounds?"

"Okay." Gwen crossed to him. She took his hand and steered him to a wing chair by the fireplace. "I'm going to get you a Bloody Mary and one for myself." Except the white stuff floating in yours is going to be two of Uncle Harry's magic pills instead of horseradish. "Then we'll see if we can figure this out, okay?"

"Laura. Aunt Laura was the blond lady."

"Your aunt Laura." Gwen stopped.

"There was somebody trying to ruin everything for Tilden and Margaret. Laura was trying to help. When I try to think who wanted to hurt them my mind starts churning with faces and names. There's Gould, there's . . . No, Carling's not there, I think he's dead. There's Ella, except she's still alive. There's this fat man a lot of people in Greenwich are afraid of . . . There's Bigelow . . . Oh, shit. Oh, God damn it."

"Jonathan?" She squeezed his hand. "What's wrong now?"

"Bigelow." He looked up at her. "He's one of the men in Chicago."

"So?"

"He never had a name before. I had no idea who those men were."

"I'll have your drink in two minutes."

THIRTEEN

"IS THAT YOUR DETECTIVE?" HUNTINGTON BECK-with's daughter took her eye from the antique brass telescope that was trained on her main gate. She was a slender woman, erect in carriage but for a tilt toward the cane that supported one arthritic hip. Her hair, certainly dyed, was a dark reddish brown, and she wore it cut close to her head. From behind, where Lawrence Ballanchine stood, she might have been forty years younger than her true age, the evidence of which was substantially hidden by a long-sleeved dress with black lace at her wrists and throat.

"I'm afraid it is, yes." Ballanchine needed no glass. The distant shape squeezing out from the unwashed car was unmistakably Raymond Lesko.

"What was it you called yourself during your intrigues with him? Dancer, was it not?"

"Yes, Miss Beckwith."

"That name implies a certain nimbleness. Do you feel that you were altogether nimble, Lawrence?"

"I did misjudge him," Ballanchine admitted.

"You did indeed, sir." She put her eye once more to the lens, studying the man who was searching the gateposts for a bell or voicebox.

"It's him. It's Lesko." Tom Burke's voice rasped over an intercom on her desk. "Do I open the gate or not?"

Ella Beckwith turned toward the speaker. "I hardly think he'll go away if we ignore him. Mr. Ballanchine and I will hear what he has to say. Is your car out of sight?"

"Yes, ma'am."

"You stay hidden as well. Remain in the kitchen unless I buzz you."

"Yes, ma'am. What about your brother?"

"Where is he at this moment?"

"Back in the trophy room. I better tell you he doesn't look so good. He's had a couple of drinks."

"Leave him with his bottle and tell him I said to remain there. Have you rearmed yourself, Mr. Burke?"

"No, ma'am. I drove straight out here."

"There is a weapons case in the trophy room. Please choose something inexpensive."

Ella released the speaker switch and looked out the window past the telescope. Lesko was standing, hands in his overcoat pockets, watching the electric gates as they slowly swung away from him. He hesitated for a long moment. Then, brazenly, Lesko reached back into his car for what appeared to be the belt of a trench coat and proceeded to tie the open gate to the trunk of a small evergreen. He slid back behind the wheel and started up the long straight driveway.

"Wasn't something to have been done about that man by now, Lawrence?"

"Not yet, no." Ballanchine shook his head. "In any

case, not before I had his notes. Corbin was the main priority. My expectation was that Lesko would accept the commission to handle Corbin himself, which would have been the best of all worlds. We could have disposed of Lesko at our convenience."

"But instead he chose to pocket fifteen thousand dollars of my money." Her face grew dark. "Worse, he set about unraveling this terribly clever web you've woven."

"Lesko knew nothing." Ballanchine lifted his chin. "Nothing at all that could lead him to the Beckwith name. He wouldn't have even laid eyes upon the Osborne if he'd gone to Greenwich yesterday as I instructed. My mistake, if I made one, was in briefing your brother, never dreaming that he'd decide to follow Corbin around town and allow Lesko in turn to follow him back to the hotel."

"You were aware, sir," she said quietly, "that my brother is unstable. You were aware that your Mr. Lesko is insubordinate. And yet you expected cheerful obedience?"

"I don't deserve sarcasm, Miss Beckwith." Ballanchine pulled out a handkerchief and touched it to his mouth. "If I may say so, I believe I'm due some credit for trying to act decisively in your interest. You agreed, after all, that we should put the problem in Mr. Burke's hands for his immediate attention. With any sort of luck at all, Corbin would be dead and disfigured by now, and the Leamas woman with him."

"And if I may say so," Ella Beckwith hissed, "the measure I agreed to was a good deal more subtle than your alternate plan, which involved no less than a massacre on the doorstep of an internationally known figure. Had you hoped, sir, that it would somehow escape the notice of the media?"

"That was Burke's idea. I'd only told him the matter was urgent."

Ella Beckwith closed her eyes and sighed. She stepped behind a Duncan Phyfe desk and sat down within reach of the intercom call button. "Would that Mr. Bigelow were still alive," she said, shaking her head. "Your detective rather looks like him, you know. He seems equally efficient as well."

"Bigelow would be nearly ninety by now," Ballanchine said sourly. "In any case, he made his share of mistakes, as I understand it. Corbin should have been long dead."

Ella Beckwith arched her brow. "You are saying that he should have divined the existence of a Chicago college girl who might be carrying a Corbin heir? A pathetic defense, sir."

"He had a second chance," Ballanchine said stubbornly. "He had his hands on Corbin twenty years ago, according to your brother, and he made a hash of it."

Ella glanced over her shoulder at Lesko's car, which had slowed and stopped outside her front door. "Tilden told you that?" she asked.

"He told me weeks ago, when you first saw Corbin standing out on the road looking up at your house. He told me Bigelow's dying words as well. That the man who did that to him, to him and his partner, was the man in the lobby portrait."

Ella could hear the knocking of Lesko's engine. He seemed in no great hurry to shut it off or leave the comparative safety of his automobile. She looked up at Ballanchine.

"Is Tilden yet persuaded that the man Bigelow saw was not an avenging ghost?"

"On the contrary, he believes it more than ever. He claims that on the street yesterday, Jonathan Corbin became Tilden Beckwith before his very eyes."

Ella nodded slowly. Behind a sudden weariness in her expression, Ballanchine thought he saw the briefest glaze of fear. But she blinked it away and sat erect, her hands clasped in front of her. Ella's face became hard again.

"I have three concerns, Lawrence," she said quietly, "aside from Mr. Corbin and his entourage. One is a brother who is a coward, a fool, and unbalanced in the bargain. The second is Mr. Lesko, who is clearly not a fool and who, due to Tilden's stupidity and your own, knows far more than he should."

"If you are about to say that I am the third—"

"Heavens no, Lawrence." She glared at him. "You are far too greedy to risk the considerable rewards of your position and far too indictable to be anything but loyal. The third is Mr. Burke, who seems considerably less competent than you represented him to be. He has also seen Jonathan Corbin's face, both in the photograph you gave him and in person."

Ballanchine did not understand. "He was sent to destroy Corbin. How was he to do that without seeing him?"

"The point, dear Lawrence, is that he's probably made the connection. If your Raymond Lesko made it during one chance visit to the Beckwith Regency's lobby, do you not think that Mr. Burke, who has passed that portrait hundreds of times, might also have noticed?"

"You don't even know that Lesko saw the portrait," Ballanchine argued. "All you know is that he followed your brother and he saw me when I came in. As for Burke, I gave him a photograph which Lesko had taken through falling snow and through a pane of wet glass. He never even got a good look at Corbin outside the Sturdevant town house because Lesko got in between. And his man Garvey, incidentally, never had more than the Leamas woman's address."

"Where was Lesko standing, Lawrence, when you looked out from the elevator? Was it in front of Tilden Beckwith's portrait?"

"You still can't be sure."

"Then why don't we ask him, Lawrence? Please go let him in."

"I certainly will not. Not until you tell me what you intend."

"To reduce my concerns, Lawrence," she told him.

"And why, by the way, did you tell Burke to arm himself and wait? You can't possibly mean to shoot Lesko in this house. There are servants just out over the garage."

"The house is quite soundproof, Lawrence. But never fear. I will try to avoid any extravagant behavior in your presence."

"What then?"

"The man is clearly here to bargain. I intend bargaining with him. He does so resemble Mr. Bigelow."

The Bloody Mary was good. Just the right thing. As a rule, Corbin didn't like drinking before evening, let alone before lunch, not even drinks that were invented for the purpose. They tended to put his afternoons in soft focus. But at least, he noted, he felt no preference for any more arcane drink such as hot buttered rum or peppered ale. Maybe that meant he was back in full control. Maybe it meant only that the Victorians hadn't figured out any excuses for boozing in the morning yet. Whichever. There were better things to think about.

Bigelow.

So now he had a name. And it seemed to Corbin that he'd known it all along. But he didn't really want to think about Bigelow, either. Or why Bigelow and Bigelow's still nameless friend jumped him in the Drake garage and did what they did to him. Corbin would only start fantasizing, as always, about what he would do to them—what he *did* do to them—but those fantasies would not make him feel better for very long. He'd just end up ashamed that he couldn't give as good an account of himself in real life as he does in his dream world.

Tilden could have handled them.

Tilden would have ground them into hamburger.

"I'm sorry, sweetheart." Corbin touched Gwen Leamas's hair.

She was sitting at his feet in front of the Morris chair where she had sat him down. Her cheek rested against his knee as she watched the fire.

"Forget it." She squeezed his leg. "You didn't mean it."

"You could never ruin anything for me," he told her. "If anything, you could make it even better."

"How is that?"

"You could live here with me. You could marry me."

She looked up at him.

"I'm serious." Corbin forced a smile.

"You mean live here? In this house?"

"For a while, I guess, until we find a place we both like better."

Gwen took a long sip of her drink. She'd added no vodka to hers. "Are you sure there is such a place, Jonathan?"

"I don't get you."

"If this is a place where you feel so at peace . . ."

Corbin shook his head. "I told you. This is just a house I visited. One of Margaret's friends lived here."

"You've tried to find the house where Tilden and Margaret actually lived?"

"That's not what I had in mind. For us, I mean."

"But what if you find it?"

"It's gone, sweetheart." Corbin was certain of that. If it still stood, he would have found it. "I've spent all kinds of hours just walking the roads. I'd see a house that seemed familiar, or that stirred some kind of feeling in me, and I'd stand there staring at it, trying to see through the walls." Corbin chuckled. "I think a couple of those people got nervous and called the police. Police cars have stopped me twice to make sure I live around here."

"It could have been remodeled."

Corbin shrugged. "There's not a whole lot you can do to remodel a turreted Victorian. Anyway, for every Victorian still standing, there must be five that have burned down or been bulldozed down to make room for Cape Cods and colonials. The fact is, I think I know where it was. Right up the road here"—he used his thumb—"on North Street. There's a split ranch there now and all the landscaping has changed, so it doesn't even begin to move me. But from the street outside, the shape of the land and the view down the hill toward town were so right that I could look back and actually see the house the way it was. I'd see it in summer when everything was green. Summers were the best times."

"Finish your drink, Jonathan." Gwen touched his glass. "I'll make you a fresh one." He was getting into that dreamy and talkative state. Which was better than dreamy and silent, as he'd been all morning.

"You know when all this started, don't you?" he asked. "I mean, looking at houses and getting good feelings? It started with the Homestead. I knew that house from the front. The inside didn't really do anything for me, maybe because of all the changes to make it a restaurant, but when you and I played croquet on the lawn it seemed as though I'd done that there before. I could taste pink lemonade and little finger sandwiches with watercress and minced ham. It might have been at a lawn party there back when it was a private house. I can't envision the owners. When I try I just see them as shapes way up on a dark porch while Margaret and I—Margaret and Tilden—are"—Corbin paused to clear his throat—"passing it on the road."

He'd almost said *sneaking* past it. Corbin had had

a glimpse of a hot summer night, and felt there were more than one, when Tilden and Margaret would make their way down to a little sandy cove where they'd swim Indian style. Gwen didn't need to hear about Margaret and him being nude. Nor was Tilden giving Corbin much of a look anyway, it seemed. But it must have been delightful. To reach the end of an August day, the kind you spend trying not to move except in slow motion, sitting on a porch in a rattan rocker, the only breeze coming from the fan you keep in front of your face, waiting till the sun was almost down and then getting a cold bird and a bottle from the cooler and wrapping them in a blanket and driving down to a little wooded area where you hide the horse and rig before going the rest of the way on foot. It wouldn't do to drive all the way. People like the Culbertsons, the family that lived in the Homestead, would be out on their sleeping porch and know where you were headed and the children would follow you down there and peek. Or the adults might see you and tongues would wag. Better to play Union spy and slip down there through the gathering darkness with Tilden trying to get Margaret to step quietly and to stop giggling. Then to peel off all those layers of cotton and hold each other's hand as they waded out neck-deep in cool salt water that had a layer of mist across its surface. They'd just sit there, soaking, Margaret at first trying to keep her hair dry and then not caring, making more mist as the steam rose from their bodies, cooling until they knew that the night air would chill their skin deliciously, and then wading back ashore to wrap themselves in their blanket and sip their wine as they watched the moon and the distant flickering lights of Long Island.

The dark mass a few hundred yards offshore was Great Captain's Island, another favorite place for Indian bathing. But not at night. Too many other young blades had rowboats. The island was best on foggy days when no summer visitors were abroad, when you could barely see your rowboat's wake, and Tilden and Margaret would grope their way to a stretch of empty beach and pretend they were Adam and Eve. Tilden would never quite pretend all the way. He would talk in whispers or in hand signals, but Margaret would run laughing through the surf, sometimes chasing crabs, sometimes picking them up and chasing Tilden with them. It was such fun. So much better than going to the beach in daytime and dressing up in those ghastly bathing costumes which, for the women at least, had nearly the fabric they wore on land and in which it was impossible to swim freely and gracefully. Women who tried looked like bobbing corks for all the air their baggy costumes trapped. Thick, shapeless corks because now there were no corsets to hide a soft or spreading waist. Margaret could swim like a seal as long as she was equally unencumbered. And she was pleased with her own waist, returned or nearly so to the size it was before young Jonathan swelled it and hardly marked at all save for a few shining lines where her skin had been stretched beyond the limits of its elasticity. These saddened her at first, and she tried to hide them from Tilden until he told her of his relief that she finally had a woman's body and not that of a silly girl and that he loved her all the more for them.

At the end of such an outing to their fog-shrouded Eden, Tilden would hand Margaret his compass and she would pilot as he rowed back through the fog to his waiting buggy and then they would drive back to her house where they would play in the freshwater shower a while longer. The shower was a godsend in summer, especially for bodies crusted with salt, and a convenience to be envied at all other times. Tilden was sure there were no more than a half dozen showers, indoors at least, in all of Greenwich. Still, for all its pleasures, it could not compare with the forbidden delights of sneaking off on one of their bathing adventures.

Lucy Stone, the large and laughing black nurse who had assisted in Jonathan's delivery, was there almost full time now except when Dr. Palmer needed her for special assistance. More, she was fast becoming Margaret's friend. And she seemed to have an almost mystical talent, Tilden noted appreciatively, of making herself invisible and unheard whenever Tilden and Margaret wished to be quietly alone, or of discovering some urgent errand whenever Tilden looked into Margaret's eyes in a certain way and then Margaret took Tilden's hand and led him to the stairs.

Corbin rubbed a hand across Gwen's shoulders. "You know, I don't think Tilden ever spent the night there."

She arched catlike at his touch. "Never?" she asked. "You don't mean they stopped being lovers after the baby was born."

"No, they were very definitely lovers. But you had to be very careful of a woman's reputation in those days. Given Margaret's background, Tilden was probably more sensitive than most." Corbin tickled his fingers down her back. "While I think of it, how about taking a shower together before your uncle gets here?"

"What?" she laughed.

"It just seemed like a nice idea."

"Well, I have my own reputation to think about. At least until after dinner." She put her mouth to his knee and bit it. "Where would he stay?"

"Who? Tilden?"

"He didn't go back to New York every evening, did he?"

"He usually stayed down at the Lenox House. Or sometimes at the Indian Harbor Hotel." Corbin grinned on saying that and shook his head. The feel of Gwen's cheek against his knee told him she was smiling, too, with the same degree of bemusement. Odd, how they were both getting so used to it. A question would come out of the blue whose answer he should not have known, but the question was asked and the answer was there. Corbin could see both hotels in his mind. The Indian Harbor Hotel was a rambling mansard-roofed affair down on the water near where the Indian Harbor Yacht Club is now. And the Lenox House was on the Post Road at the top of Greenwich Avenue. Funny. Now that he thought of it, the red brick office building standing there had always seemed out of place and here, suddenly, is the reason.

There were hops at the Lenox House every Saturday night. And tea dances on Sunday afternoons. And Margaret's club met there Wednesdays. Margaret's club. There was something, Corbin thought, something troubling about Margaret's club that he wished she'd told him about before the damage was done, but Corbin couldn't think what that damage was. Anyway, he didn't want to dwell on troubling thoughts. He wanted to remember roller-skating down at Ray's Hall for the first time in his life. Margaret coaxing him onto the polished skating surface, swearing she'd stay at his arm to steady him, and then treacherously shoving him and sending him flailing the length of the rink. He wanted to remember walking barefoot with her along the beach, digging for clams and collecting fresh mussels by the bucket. And canoeing with her down the Mianus River. And band concerts under the stars. And yachting on the Sound, carrying Jonathan along in a hamper if the seas were calm enough. There was so much to do.

Greenwich was booming like a frontier mining town that year. A number of New York families had long kept summer homes there, but now, with reliable train or packet boat service that could have them in the city within an hour and a half, many were staying in Greenwich year round, and they began telling their friends about the many advantages of life in Connecticut. Almost no crime, no street ruffians, no foul-smelling mixture of soot and powdered horse droppings coating every garment, to say nothing of every throat. And the friends came. By the dozen, it seemed, every summer month. Building fine homes within easy reach of the station or of the pier at the Indian Harbor Hotel. Forming clubs to replace those they'd left in New York. Athletic clubs, yacht clubs, riding clubs, shooting clubs, and, of course, the full assortment of gardening, sewing, literary, and civic betterment clubs for the ladies. Tilden considered joining a new tennis and archery club, mostly for Margaret's sake, because these sports were now considered suitable exercise for ladies of fashion. At a luncheon given for prospective members, all went well enough until one of the founders rose to assure Tilden that he could safely embrace the sport of tennis because it, unlike baseball and boxing, for example, was not a game that would offer any attractions to the lower orders. Tilden glanced across the table at Margaret, who was crossing her eyes at him, a certain sign that a giggling fit would soon follow. His own face aching, he made his excuses and tried to get her to the carriage park before she erupted. Neither of them made it.

The Riverside Yacht Club and the Indian Harbor Yacht Club had each opened during their first summer in Greenwich. Members of both clubs, men well known to Tilden in New York business and social circles, had invited him to join their number. He chose the Riverside. It was a bit farther away, closer to the original Greenwich settlement now called Sound Beach, but the charming little clubhouse was on the mainland while that of the Indian Harbor Club was on an island offshore, the better, he'd heard it said, to discourage women from hanging about. That was enough for Tilden. He surprised Margaret with the purchase of a twenty-foot naphtha launch, which he named Mad Meg in honor of an infamous tickler he once knew. In his mind, Corbin could see Margaret at the helm of that launch, its throttle turned on full, slashing through waves, her clothing soaked through, her face split in a happy grin as Tilden muttered silent prayers that rocks and lobster buoys would have the good sense to stay out of her way.

Corbin smiled for Tilden. He was having a good time. He deserved it. They both did. Gwen Leamas, who was hearing a bit more than the usual bits and pieces this time, smiled with him.

"You'd think he would have been nervous," Corbin said to her, "about all these new people coming out from New York at the same time."

"What new people?"

"People like him. Businessmen. Men who might have been clients at Georgiana Hastings's house and who might have seen Margaret there."

"I suppose." She shrugged. "But according to you, she didn't sleep with any of them."

"She just played the piano, I'm pretty sure."

"Then she probably wouldn't be recognized. Remembering a woman from a profile bent over a keyboard is not the same as seeing a face you've slobbered over while pumping away at her body."

Corbin frowned.

"Sorry. That was a bit tacky."

"What's wrong, sweetheart?" He touched her.

"It's nothing to do with Margaret, I guess. It's just that lying under boozy rich men for money is not my favorite vision of a woman."

"Well, I wouldn't like to think of you that way, either. But you could have done it, for all I know. You could be just as terrific as you are and still have spent two or three years as a hooker building a bank account before you came over from England to start fresh."

"That doesn't happen to be a male fantasy of yours, does it?" she asked.

Corbin let out a sigh. "I'm just saying it wouldn't necessarily have changed you. If those pilots who spent six or seven years in North Vietnamese prison camps could get through all the beatings and degradation by managing to put their minds in neutral, I don't know why a prostitute couldn't do the same thing and then put it all behind her. Everyone has something that they have to try to put behind them."

Like Bigelow, Corbin thought darkly, and what Bigelow had done to him.

"Okay, so I've been a high-class London whore. What are your black secrets?"

"I didn't say high class. That's your story."

"Don't be a smart-ass." She took his drink. "While I'm refilling this you can prepare to make a full confession and it better be juicy."

Corbin watched her leave the room by the door where Laura Hemmings had stood. And hugged Margaret. And was her friend. But was ruining everything. What was it about Laura Hemmings? High-class whore. Those words popped into Corbin's mind when he thought about Aunt Laura, but that was impossible. Out of the question. She was so small and dainty. And nice. She would sit on this floor rolling a rubber ball to him, a white one with red stars, or she would crawl after him, making buzzing sounds like a bee, and try to sting him on his leg with her finger, or she would sit him on her lap at her piano and help him pick out tunes. No, Aunt Laura could never have been a whore. But she must have known about Margaret because she was trying to protect her. From what, though? Exposure, maybe, or the fear of it. Yet Margaret had been happily out in public with Tilden all that spring and summer. What happened?

More names.

Gould.

Colonel Mann and his scandal sheet. Carling. The cop, Clubber Williams. And Bigelow. Always Bigelow. A name that has nothing to do with any of this.

Wait a minute. Except for Bigelow, these people were the reason for Margaret's new name in the first place. They wouldn't just have gone away. But as many as three years must have gone by since those items first began turning up in *Town Topics*. Corbin knew that because he had a clear memory of himself, out on the front lawn, trying to swing a cut-down bat at that same white rubber ball. There's Tilden, lobbing it. He's wearing a striped shirt, no collar, and an open vest. See? I've got to be at least two in that scene, but much younger when I'm looking up at Aunt Laura. All these scenes, all these names, keep jumping around.

Sequence.

Maybe the problem is sequence.

You try to see things out of order and they get all messed up. They come in disconnected flashes. Random sparks, Sturdevant says, from genetic imprints. Everybody gets them. But they come so out of context that almost everybody brushes them off and decides they don't mean anything.

Go back. Pick up with Colonel Mann. Or with Jay Gould. Tilden wouldn't just have let that lie. Gould wouldn't have, either.

Sequence. Try Mann first.

Corbin closed his eyes and called up the Santa Claus face of William D'Alton Mann as he'd seen it that day in the publisher's hack. It came, but it would not focus. Just bits and pieces. Words and facial expressions. Corbin tried to concentrate harder, but a part of him became impatient with the effort and said it didn't matter. The colonel was a minor player. Gould, then. Try Jay Gould. Corbin erased the scene in the hack and replaced it with the melancholy face of Mephistopheles.

That's what they called him—the Mephistopheles of Wall Street. And he heard Gould's high-pitched voice . . . Hold it. Gould didn't have a high voice. It was low and soft, very measured, because if he took in too much air he'd risk a coughing fit. The high voice sounded more like Teddy. Teddy Roosevelt. Corbin wiped Gould aside to look for Teddy's face, but all he could see was a door with smoked glass. The voice seemed to be behind it, shouting, not angry but shouting. Don't waste time trying to make sense of this. Teddy's always shouting about something. It seems like his normal voice some days.

Talk about fragments!

Let's try this one more time, he decided. Chronologically.

What do we know?

We know that Tilden went to see Colonel Mann. We know that Mann would not agree to lay off in return for a mere lifetime subscription because it was Jay Gould's wish that the heat be kept on. Mann was very open about that. But a dollar was a dollar, and he did sell Tilden that information about Carling. What would Tilden have done with it? Wouldn't he have gone to Gould to make some kind of a deal? If Gould stayed out of his personal life, Tilden would not reveal what he knew about Carling. Gould just might have folded, at least until he had some new cards. The last thing Gould needed, as Mann pointed out, was for his business enemies to know he'd been plucked. That he'd hired a total fraud, a confidence man, a convict. Worse, he'd hired a Jew who had denied his Jewishness, just as Gould was suspected of adding an extra vowel to his name in order to grease his way into the Protestant business community.

Yes indeed. His enemies would have a grand time with this Carling affair. They'd have him in the laughing stock. A few would start getting bold ideas. They'd start trotting a little closer to him like one of those coyote-dogs Teddy wrote about in *The Hunting Trail* who amble alongside a sick buffalo for a while, taking its measure and then testing it with a nip at its hind-quarters to see whether it could run and did it have a fighting heart.

The Hunting Trail?

Don't stop. Don't ask. It's Teddy's book. It came out the year it snowed and you know that so don't worry about how. And there was a party at Delmonico's to celebrate its publication and you should have gone but you didn't because you knew he would have heard these whispers about your "soiled dove" and you didn't know what you'd say to this good and moral man if he asked you outright about Margaret and God forbid that he, not knowing the depth of your feelings for her, would characterize her with words that could not be forgiven.

Have him read the inscription.

The shouted words came from the outer office, from beyond the smoked glass of Tilden's office door.

Have him read it aloud.

Tilden winced at the shrill nasal voice that put him in mind of a dentist's drill fast pedaled.

"Have him read, 'For my great and good though absent friend, Tilden,' but let him know that it is a singularly insincere sentiment motivated solely by past affections and that I can no longer regard him as such because of his shocking abandonment of me."

The door opened following a timid knock. Tilden's head clerk, a Mr. Levi Scoggins, stepped through it bearing a volume held open in his hands.

"Sir, I'm afraid it is . . . I mean, I am to tell you . . ."

"It's all right, Mr. Scoggins." Tilden smiled. "I heard."

"This is terribly embarrassing, sir. I had no notion that he'd begin carrying on so."

Tilden stood at his desk and took the autographed book from Levi Scoggins.

"Ask Mr. Roosevelt, please, if I dare ask him into my office without first calling the riot police to stand by."

"Lord, where have you been?" Sturdevant heard Cora Starling's agitated voice through the pay telephone at the Greenwich Library. "You said you'd call in regular."

Harry Sturdevant checked his watch. It was barely past noon, not as if he'd been out all night. "Sorry," he said. "I lost track of the hour. I'm doing some research in the library up here."

"Well listen, Dr. S, I don't think the three of you is all there is up there. I think you been followed."

Sturdevant chewed his lip. "Have there been more mystery phone calls?"

"It's not the calls now. It's people. There's a man, maybe two of them, who followed you when you drove off out of here."

"You're certain, Cora?"

"I can just tell you how it looked. You remember you went by a beat-up car double-parked across the street? Well, there was this white man in it and he was blockin' in another white man in a blue car. I wasn't watching them real close but all of a sudden the double-parked man starts screamin' at the other like a maniac, and the man in the blue car starts handin' stuff through his window like he was bein' robbed and one of the first things he hands through looked to me like a sawed-off shotgun. I been half out of my mind not knowin' whether to call the police."

"It's just as well you didn't, Cora." It's also possible you've been watching too much television. "You said you thought we were followed?"

"The first man, the double-parked one, he took right off after you went by. The second man, he messed around under his dashboard for maybe five minutes, but then he took off too, lookin' real mad."

"That one couldn't very well have followed us, Cora. What did the first one look like?"

"You know some of them old football players who come over here, they're not fat exactly but they have to go sideways through a door? The first one was like that. And mean lookin'."

"Thank you, Cora. I'll keep an eye open." But Sturdevant had an idea he'd already met the man with the mean face.

"When are you coming back, Dr. S?"

"I imagine I'll have dinner here with Gwen and Jonathan and then drive home after that. I'll call you if there's a change."

"You call me change or no, Dr. S," Cora Starling insisted. "I don't have a real good feelin' about today. Is Mr. Corbin still gettin' his stirrin's?"

"I think so, yes."

"Well, when he gets them, you listen. Don't go thinkin' what I said was just granny talk."

"I won't, Cora."

I promise you.

Sturdevant gathered up his papers, his mind now on the thickset man with the mean face but friendly manner who knew so much about Greenwich. The man he said would make a good detective. The man who was probably going through his notebook while he was away from the viewing machine.

As he walked toward his car, Sturdevant carefully noted the other automobiles parked both in the library lot and on the nearby streets. He saw nothing that resembled the double-parked car he recalled from that morning. He did notice, however, that the morning's brightness had gone. A dark gray quilt of clouds had been drawn over Greenwich; only a narrow band of blue remained far to the east. Sturdevant smelled snow in the air.

Lesko did not have a good feeling about entering that house. Not alone. All the time he was a New York gold shield he always had a back-up. He'd never even been in a house like this except for once when this Wall Street big shot who was a closet fag killed a male prostitute who was putting the arm on him. And Lesko had blown that one, he knew. Big shot, big house, a shit-load of money, and he hangs around with senators. You get intimidated. You get polite. And by the time you tell yourself you got to lean on the guy, he's got six lawyers around him. The papers say rich guys get away with murder because they can hire all those lawyers. That's not why. It's polite cops. How can you expect a cop whose idea of luxury is a rinkside ticket to the Islanders games and sneaking in a six-pack of imported beer to treat a guy whose house looks like an art museum the same as he'd treat some pimp who sliced up one of his whores. Polite cops, polite assistant district attorneys. Cops shouldn't have to come to houses like this. Crimes in houses like this are for Nick and Nora Charles.

Tap. Tap. Tap.

Lesko looked up and saw Dancer at the window, hitting it with his ring, motioning impatiently toward the front door. He relaxed a bit. Politeness wasn't going to be a problem with Dancer.

"We don't have all day, Mr. Lesko." Dancer had opened one of the white double doors and stood waiting. Lesko, with Tom Burke's trench coat draped over one arm, climbed the portico steps and entered.

"You can leave your coat on that chair"—Dancer pointed—"and any weapons you're carrying as well."

"Behave yourself, Dancer." Lesko looked past him. "Where's your boss?"

"Leave your weapon or get out." Dancer folded his arms and stepped into Lesko's path.

Lesko leaned over and kissed his forehead. Dancer leaped back, sputtering. An open right hand raised to shoulder height and for a moment Lesko thought he was actually going to get slapped.

"For heaven's sake," came the woman's voice, "bring that man in here."

"I'll keep the coat." Lesko winked. "Thanks anyway." He smoothed it over his left hand and over the Beretta model 92 he held in its folds. Lesko stepped past toward the sound of the voice.

"Some sherry, Mr. Lesko?" She was seated behind a desk, her hands in her lap. Dancer followed and remained standing to one side, his arms folded.

"Nothing for me, thanks."

"I'd offer you some coffee but I'm afraid there's no one here to serve it."

Lesko made a face. "I'm supposed to think the three of us are alone in this big house?"

She read his eyes. "My brother is here but he's quite indisposed. He is asleep in another part of the house. There will be no servants until late afternoon."

Not bad, Lesko thought. She's quick. If I knew Dancer was here, I knew who he came with. Lesko looked past her, down the hill toward the gate and then at the area surrounding the window for some evidence of a switch that might have opened it. There was nothing. The question became, If he was standing down at the gate looking up at the old dame and Dancer standing in this window looking back at him, who opened the gate?

"You're full of shit, lady." Lesko showed the Beretta. Politeness. Politeness can kill you.

"But *where*," Roosevelt bellowed, "was Tilden?"

Arms flailing the air, he paced the oriental carpet in front of Tilden's desk. Tilden could only sit in helpless silence. Teddy, he fully realized, was intent upon a monologue performance. To offer an excuse or apology before its crescendo was reached would verge on rudeness.

"There I was"—he pointed stiff-armed in the general direction of Delmonico's—"dutifully ensconced behind a great mound of books—would that I might *sell* as many as were given away that evening—enduring the literary pretensions of the following." An index finger shot up, trembling. "First there was the Tammany crowd, for whom cuspidors were invented, and who to a man have not cracked a book since *McGuffey's Reader,* if then, and certainly not the Constitution of the United States, telling me how breathlessly eager they are to devour my book, and one of whom, God as my witness, actually saying that he's 'hoid of dis *Hunting Trail*' and thinks his wife has a cousin who lives there." A second finger joined the other. "Next we have the fur-draped dowagers who are stunned to learn that animals actually suffer death in the process of making a coat and that they do not, like New York's poor, merely pawn their pelts every spring." A third finger snapped into place. "Next we have my editor, a worthy who without consulting the author changed 'leg of venison' to 'limb of venison,' so as not to offend the sensibilities of refined lady venison, and who hovered at my elbow suggesting appropriate flyleaf sentiments until I stabbed him in the hand with my pen. Which, of course, was entirely Tilden Beckwith's fault."

Roosevelt paused but Tilden chose not to rise to the bait. He would only hear that he, not the editor, should have been at Teddy's side and that he, by his absence, was responsible for the editor's impalement.

"Sam Clemens!" Teddy tried another hand, another finger. "Samuel Clemens had the grace to drop in and wish my humble effort well. As did Henry James and Ida Tarbell and little Nelly Bly who, by the way, inquired after a friend of yours."

A second pause. A second lure left untaken.

"But no Tilden Beckwith." Roosevelt pounded a fist into his palm. "The loss, however, was his own. For if he'd been there he would have seen Maurice Barrymore reciting *Hamlet* while attempting, on a wager, to juggle four live lobsters. He would have heard his friend Nat Goodwin cornering the aforementioned dowagers and regaling them with the proper technique of disemboweling a jackrabbit, and our friend John Flood who tried for the knockout punch with tales of biting the heads off chickens as a lad in County Sligo."

"Ireland?" Tilden could not help himself. "John was born right here."

"A detail of no consequence to a lady sliding down the wall in an attack of the vapors." Roosevelt's face softened just a fraction. "I missed you, Tilden."

"I am sorry, Teddy." Tilden rose from his chair, his hand extended. "Life has been complex this past year."

Roosevelt took the hand and held it. He looked into Tilden's eyes through his spectacles. "And the widow Corbin, is she quite the rose by whatever name that John and Nelly claim she is?"

"John told you?"

"I threatened to go a round or two with him if he didn't."

"She is a very good woman, Teddy," Tilden said solemnly. "She fills all the corners of my heart and I honor her."

"Then may God bless you both." He released the

hand. "But may I curse you first for thinking that your friend is such a prig?"

"There were private things I could not tell you, Teddy. With what remained, I did not think I could make you understand."

Teddy leaned closer. "May I also curse you for thinking that your friend would be your friend only as long as you thought as he did?"

"Accepted." Tilden bowed. "And deserved."

Roosevelt clasped his hands behind his back. "You have other friends, you know, who think differently from either of us. Have you noticed that your name is nowhere to be found in the pages of *Town Topics* these past weeks?"

Tilden had noticed, as much with apprehension as relief. He shook his head to show that Roosevelt's meaning eluded him.

"John Flood and Nat Goodwin are your friends," Teddy said quietly. "And they in turn have a friend who seems to have visited Colonel Mann and told him, after clubbing his bodyguard to the ground, that the next mention of any Beckwith in his paper would be at the cost of both his eyes. I am to tell you that Billy O'Gorman sends his compliments."

"O'Gorman?" Tilden blinked. "O'Gorman acted for me?"

"I don't know the man. John said you'd understand if I reminded you that you left O'Gorman with his pride."

Tilden remembered. *I never took all a man had . . . I never shamed him . . . That O'Gorman's a bad one, but you left him proud. Ansel Carling's a bad one, but you left him nothin', lad. Nothin' but gettin' even.* Tilden pushed Carling out of his mind, but he made a mental note that he'd have to give Billy O'Gorman another crack one of these days. He owed him that. "Where is John, by the way?" he asked. "I've tried several times to reach him."

"He's gone back upstate with John L. Sullivan. Chopping trees and running mountain roads. It seems he's taken up the mission of keeping Sullivan out of saloons and pastry shops so he's fit to defend his title against Jake Kilrain next summer."

Tilden shook his head doubtfully. "He'll need every week he's got from the look of Sullivan last time I saw him."

Roosevelt's expression said that while the subject interested him, his mind was on more troubling matters. "Back to this chap O'Gorman, Tilden. There is a thing I'd like to ask you."

"Ask." Tilden waited.

"His report to John Flood was that when Colonel Mann was in fear of blindness or worse, Mann whimpered some tale about having given you some valuable evidence on Jay Gould's man, Carling. The implication was that it is sufficiently damning that you might blackmail Gould with it."

"It might have been if I had chosen to use it. I did not so choose."

"Not even to protect your friend? To say nothing of what I hear Gould is doing to your business accounts?"

Tilden straightened. "My friend has a name, Teddy. I hope you will be pleased to meet her one day."

"One day soon, I hope. No offense meant, Tilden."

"As for the business, we are holding our own. We've lost the accounts of a few timid men, but I will not win them back at the cost of becoming a blackmailer."

"Even at the cost of failing in your father's trust?"

"Honor *is* my father's trust."

"And yet you paid for the information."

"My intention was and is," Tilden said slowly,

clearly annoyed that his friend would doubt his course, "precisely what yours would have been. I intended to take Carling by the scruff of the neck when next I found him, whisper in his ear the things I know, and suggest that Australia might be a more suitable address for him."

"Will you tell me what it is you know?" Roosevelt asked.

"It is a private matter."

"Hah!" Roosevelt grinned suddenly and hugely. "It is as I'd hoped. Now it's time for me to confess that I've been meddling in your affairs. I've been to see Morgan about you. He wants you in his office tomorrow at ten."

Tilden stared uncomprehendingly. He knew who Morgan was, of course. There was only one Morgan.

"What could he want with me?"

"He wants to help you. I knew of some of the losses you'd suffered, and when I mentioned them to Morgan the man snorted and said he'd replace that pittance before lunch."

Tilden shook his head. "Teddy"—he searched for words—"I may be slow on the uptake . . . I am his competitor. It's true that Beckwith and Company is a mere gnat against the House of Pierpont Morgan, but all the same, why would he possibly want to assist me?"

"He likes you."

"Nonsense. J. P. Morgan doesn't like anyone. The man has looked at me exactly three times in my life. The first time he scowled, the second he grunted, the third he nodded."

"You see," Roosevelt said brightly. "He's been warming up to you. For Pierpont Morgan, a grunt is the equal of a soliloquy."

Tilden sat on the edge of his desk and folded his

arms. "Teddy, do you or do you not intend revealing why Morgan would be interested in me?"

"He hates Gould, of course. Despises the man. To sweeten matters even further, he also believes he's been cheated by Ansel Carling, who once sold him a leaf from an illuminated Bible. It was supposed to be a rare Septuagint, I think, and it turned out to be a sixteenth-century copy."

Tilden felt a weight in his stomach. He knew that Carling had a small collection of illuminated manuscripts. Ella had pointed it out as evidence that some men of business were more cultivated than others. Knowing Carling, Tilden thought the entire collection was probably made up of copies or fakes, yet was adequate to its purpose of creating the illusion of both piety and culture, plus an occasional sale to the unwary. Still, Tilden remained doubtful.

"That seems a poor reason," he said. "The whole of Europe has been cheating Morgan and half the other moneyed men in America for the past ten years, Gould included."

"Naturally." Roosevelt clapped his hands. "The combination of unlimited funds, unlimited pretensions, and profound ignorance of art has served to tidy up many a French or Dutch attic. Morgan, however, is no fool. He knows that the value of a work of art is what someone else will pay for it, and he knows there are many who'll pay handsomely for a piece that was once in the Morgan collection. There are many forms of cheating, you see. But being cheated by a dealer and being bested by Gould or one of Gould's people are not the same thing. Go see him, Tilden. It is a rare opportunity."

"Ten o'clock, you say? Tomorrow?"

"At Twenty-three Wall Street. He says he plans to take a walk with you."

. . .

"Your father is well?" John Pierpont Morgan did not otherwise greet Tilden, nor look up from his desk, as an assistant in a swallowtail coat ushered Tilden into the great man's office. Tilden made a conscious effort, as Teddy had warned, not to let his eyes rest upon Morgan's veined and swollen nose.

"Quite well, sir. Improving."

Morgan was sifting through a pile of correspondence, lingering, it seemed, no more than five seconds on a given page, then either making a note across the top or dismissing some earnest proposal with a contemptuous sweep of his pen. Tilden glanced around the office, waiting. It was smaller than he would have imagined, and crowded. A few more items and it would have resembled an auction gallery. There was not a square foot of wall space left uncovered by a painting or tapestry, most having religious themes. Tiny miniatures set in little jeweled frames competed at a disadvantage against gaudy church ornaments. A built-in bookcase fairly bulged with faded manuscripts, which seemed insignificant alongside gilded special editions in red and brown leather. Yet among those cracked and shabby manuscripts, Teddy had said, were almost the complete original works of Sir Walter Scott and many of the poems of Keats and Lord Byron. Byron's poem "The Corsair" hung framed in glass beneath a photograph of Morgan's yacht, which bore the same name.

"You are a yachtsman?" He still had not looked up.

"I own a small launch at the moment," Tilden told him, "but I enjoy racing under sail. And an occasional pleasure cruise."

"*Corsair* is steam, not sail."

"I know, sir."

"You prefer sail?"

"Yes, sir."

"I don't."

"Yes, sir. Shall I sit down?"

"We're not staying."

Tilden examined the ceiling. He knew better than to be offended by Morgan's curtness. The man's reputation was that he had almost no capacity for polite conversation and none at all for a democratic view of his fellow man. He considered people, including women, according to function and their level of competence. He was a compulsive, self-driven man, quite aware that he stood supreme among men of business and that he wielded more power than many a head of state. Here was a man to whom more than one United States president had come as supplicant, who lent money to his nation's treasury, and who attached strict conditions to its use. Here was also a man who had been known to throw food or clothing at servants who failed to anticipate his wishes and to likewise throw ledgers at the heads of his executives when he thought their decisions shortsighted, but who would be astonished to learn that either took offense. They were there to serve his needs and that was that.

"Buy a boat," he said.

"I beg your pardon?"

"Sail it. You'll live longer. 'The gods do not . . .' " Morgan cocked his head. What was the rest of it? " 'The gods do not subtract . . .' " He drummed his knuckles impatiently, then jabbed a finger in the air toward Tilden.

" 'The gods do not subtract from a man's allotted span the time he spends in boats.' "

"Just so. Yes." Morgan nodded. It may have been a trick of the light but Tilden thought he almost saw a smile. "Let's take our walk."

Morgan rose from his desk and strolled past Tilden. A door opened by some unseen signal, and the clerk in the cutaway appeared with a topcoat, which Morgan stepped into without breaking stride. A gesture of Morgan's right hand told Tilden he was to follow close upon that side. He did so through a series of other doors that were held open for them and onto Wall Street, where they turned left up the hill toward Trinity Church. Tilden had not a clue where they were going, if anywhere, or what was to transpire in the course of this constitutional. One question, at least, was answered within a hundred paces when, at a tilt of Morgan's head, the doors of the New York Stock Exchange were opened for them by two armed guards.

The floor of the exchange was in its customary chaos. A full two hundred voices, one of which should normally be that of Tilden Beckwith, shouted their calls one against the other with each quote that appeared upon an enormous chalkboard. The sound hushed noticeably upon J. P. Morgan's entrance. Tilden felt a hand on his shoulder. Morgan's hand. And with it Morgan urged him forward, across the widest portion of the floor, past men he knew in business, powerful men, men of influence, some of them builders and doers whom Tilden admired, too many of them predators and tearers-down, all of them, to a man, eager adherents to Spencer's law of survival of the fittest, a most convenient theory which allowed them to believe that exploiting the other fellow was nature's way, and an imperative that rendered fair play as superfluous as it was in the forests and the seas. Still, some were more cynically rapacious than others, and Tilden found himself wanting to break away from Morgan long enough to slap a smirking face or two in a small knot of Jay Gould's people. But Morgan held fast and, anyway, what he thought was a smirk now looked more like consternation. At the far end of the floor near where the House of Morgan had its seat, Pierpont Morgan stopped and turned to face Tilden.

"Good day, sir." He offered his hand. "Buy that boat."

"Uh, thank you, Mr. Morgan." Tilden took the hand in utter bafflement. Morgan's free hand loudly slapped Tilden's upper arm as if in a gesture of filial affection. Morgan leaned closer.

"I vacation three months the year on mine," he said quietly. "For years I took no holidays at all. I have learned that although I can do a year's work in nine months, I cannot do a year's work in twelve months. Take your holidays, young man. You will be all the richer for them."

"Yes, sir."

"When you leave, leave smartly. See that there's a hop in your step and a light in your eye."

Tilden did his best though he felt like an idiot. The hairs on his neck were hot from all the eyes that he knew were upon them. His step slowed once he reached the street. He wandered in a daze all the way back to his office, where he sat for an hour, undisturbed at his request, puzzling over the morning's odd events. Mr. Scoggins knocked and entered.

"Mr. Roosevelt is on the telephone, sir. He is quite insistent."

"Very well, Mr. Scoggins." Tilden rose. He probably should have called Teddy straightaway.

"And there are some other matters that need your attention. All quite pleasant matters, I think."

Tilden was too distracted to question this last. He followed Mr. Scoggins through the outer office, where the level of activity seemed unusually frenetic for this hour, and into the mail room, where he took the earpiece from a waiting clerk.

"Yes? Can you hear me?" He covered his other ear against the sound of telegraph keys.

"I just heard from him, Tilden. It went splendidly. Bully for you, sir," the voice crackled.

"Just heard from whom? What went splendidly?"

"Morgan. He said you had a good long talk about

art, literature, sail versus steam, and the proper admixture of work and play. And on his advice you're going to purchase a boat, I understand."

Tilden paused, touching his fingertips to his temples. "Teddy, I'm afraid one of us has gone quite mad. Art and literature?"

"Did you have your talk or not?"

"Well yes, but not for a fraction of the time you seem to think. And my glancing around Morgan's office and reading the title of a framed poem hardly constitutes a discussion of art and literature."

"To Morgan it does. You must have looked appreciative. And in any case you've certainly advanced beyond the nodding and grunting stage. What about your walk through the exchange? I'd give anything to have witnessed that."

"Witnessed what, for heaven's sake?" Tilden shouted. "The man walked me through as if I were a little boy being shown where his father works, and then he as much as patted me on the cheek and told me to skip along home."

"How can you be so dense, Tilden? Can you be unaware that you've just been knighted?"

Tilden closed his eyes. Of course. The flurry of activity in his outer office. Pierpont Morgan choosing the most visible spot on the entire exchange floor to stop, to shake his hand, to give for the world to see the appearance of affectionate advice.

"Why, Teddy? Why did he do it?"

"I told you. He likes you. He also respects your father."

"And?"

"And he is also a man of gargantuan conceits. The suggestion was made that such is his power that a mere handshake, properly witnessed, was the equivalent of his handing a man a million-dollar letter of credit. The suggestion was made that a pat on the arm by J. Pierpont Morgan has greater weight in the financial community than all the schemes of all the Jay Goulds put together."

"You are a shameless man, Teddy."

"Thoroughly."

"A manipulator."

"To a fault."

"You should run for mayor again. Your plots deserve a larger stage than the New York State Legislature."

"Perhaps I'll get Morgan to shake my hand as well one day."

It was going to be fine, Corbin thought dreamily. He could have protected her. Just as he had friends, such good friends, who protected him. Nat . . . John . . . Ted. Especially Ted. "You never met Teddy, did you?" he asked.

Gwen was at the window, her back to him, watching the first flakes of snow and wishing her uncle would hurry.

"Teddy?" She turned. "Teddy Roosevelt?"

"Yes." He was staring at nothing, a wistful near smile on his face.

"I've . . ." What to say? "I've never had that pleasure."

"You should have it. I should see to it. But you never go into the city any more, do you." It sounded, to Gwen, more an observation than a question. An odd observation. Wouldn't Tilden know? And wouldn't he know whether Margaret had met Roosevelt? Maybe he wasn't talking to Margaret.

"Hardly ever . . . no."

"Perhaps we'll get him out here next summer for a day's sail. He's quite a good helmsman, you know. One wouldn't expect it the way he jerks about at all other times, but he has a very soft and steady touch on the tiller." He turned to her, his face lighting up as if he'd just recalled an anecdote, but his expression suddenly clouded and his lips moved soundlessly.

"Tilden?"

He shook his head.

"Is something wrong, Tilden?"

"Don't . . ." He waved a hand. "Don't do that. It's me." He rubbed his eyes.

"Wait a moment. It's *who?*"

"It's okay. It's me. Jonathan." He stood up and stretched, then bent and touched his toes several times to get his blood flowing. "I was only daydreaming."

"Was I Laura Hemmings just then?"

"I guess so."

"Why not Margaret?"

"It's no big deal, sweetheart." He shrugged. "This used to be Laura's house, that's all."

There was more to it than that, he knew. He wasn't sure how often Tilden visited Laura by himself, but it seemed like a lot of times over a long period. It was a way of being close to Margaret. Why not Margaret? Gwen had asked. Because Margaret was gone. And Tilden was very sad. And so, as a matter of fact, was he.

"Honey," he said, "I'm going to take a little walk by myself." If he stayed, Gwen would keep asking questions about Laura. And there were things about her that were no one else's business.

"It's starting to snow, Jonathan."

He looked past her through the window. He felt nothing. Not fear, not even relief that he felt no fear. "You know what?" He followed the course of a few single flakes. "I think it's gone."

Gwen understood at once. She could see it. "No sweaty palms? No ghosts?"

Corbin shook his head. He could see in his mind all the scenes, the people, the fading or materializing places he had seen before, but they no longer frightened him. They'd become part of him. Like memories. He could think of the woman running from him in the storm, but now he knew who she was and that scene held no terror for him. Only a dim anger that she could not manage to stay dead and forgotten.

"All the more reason to take a walk," he told Gwen. "I've got to try this out."

"I'll go with you." She started toward the closet.

Corbin reached for her, putting his arms around her. "Gwen, honey, you've been holding me by the hand for three days. Let me just give this a shot."

"Will you stay in sight of the house?"

He forced a smile. "That would be a little wimpish, don't you think?"

"It would be a lot more sensible, don't *you* think?"

Corbin tried to reassure her with a hug. "My car's been down at the station since Friday morning. I'll have to dig it out sooner or later." He released her and reached for his coat.

"Why can't you wait for Uncle Harry? He can drive you."

The answer, which he could not give her, was that the dim anger he felt was not so dim anymore. At Ella. At questions concerning Laura Hemmings, because there were things a gentleman simply did not discuss. At Margaret for going away. At all the people who would not leave them in peace. At Bigelow. Even him. Especially him. At whoever was ruining the peace he'd felt in this house, in this town, for so long.

"Just give me an hour." He kissed her lightly and squeezed her hand as he moved toward the door. "I need an hour."

Then, remembering, he stepped back to the closet for his umbrella. "It could change to rain," he said.

Or the snow could get heavy.

FOURTEEN

OU'RE FULL OF SHIT, LADY."

Raymond Lesko crossed Ella Beckwith's drawing room and stood with his back to a display case of Limoges figurines, facing the door he'd entered. Another door was on his left, and Ella's desk was to his right. Lesko let his coat fall to the floor and stood with the Beretta held low in both hands. "Why don't we get old Tom Burke in here where I can see him?"

If the gun frightened Ella, she gave no sign. Dancer's eyes were locked on it. "Whatever are you talking about, Mr. Lesko?" she asked.

Lesko gestured toward the window behind her. "Who opened that front gate for me?"

"I did, of course."

"You want to walk back over to that window and show me how you did it with you and Dancer both standing there watching me?"

"It is done by remote control. Certainly." She moved her thin fingers toward the buttons of the telephone console as if to demonstrate.

"Suit yourself, lady." The ex-cop raised his weapon and trained it on the closed door opposite him. "Go ahead. Push."

She looked up at him with an expression meant to convey utter bewilderment. But her eyes met his a bit too long, and she seemed to realize it. Slowly, she brought her hands together and leaned forward over the desk.

"Very well, Mr. Lesko." She drew in a breath that bared her teeth ever so slightly. "Mr. Burke is indeed here. He is in the kitchen, some distance away. I would prefer not to summon him because I intend this to be a private interview."

"Yeah." Lesko made a face. He had not lowered his gun. "Well, I don't want to stand like this all day, lady. How do I know he's not right outside the door?"

"You have my word."

"Right." Lesko showed his own teeth. He crossed the room once more and dragged a heavy chair in front of the door. It was intended to delay, not stop, anyone who might suddenly enter. Next he snapped his fingers at Dancer and pointed to the second door. "Throw the latch on that one," he ordered.

Dancer looked helplessly at the old woman, hesitating. Ella Beckwith snapped her own fingers and motioned him on. Dancer's hands went to his heart. "You can't intend locking us in here with *him?*"

"Mr. Lesko is merely being prudent, Lawrence dear." Lesko thought he saw a glimmer of appreciation as she spoke. "In any case, Mr. Lesko is not here to harm us. He is here to attempt an extortion."

Dancer shivered but stepped to the bolt of the remaining door, which he clicked three or four times, as if it were stubborn. Lesko made another pained face at Ella Beckwith. She smiled and nodded in return.

"Lawrence, dear."

"There!" Dancer turned and straightened.

"Lock it, Lawrence," she said. "Actually lock it."

Dancer hesitated, then glanced at Lesko, who was patiently drumming his fingers on the Beretta. He turned back, his face flushed, and slid the bolt easily into place.

"Lawrence," the old woman asked, "can that be your last attempt to outwit Mr. Lesko?"

"Well, I only . . ."

"Sit down, Lawrence." She looked up at Lesko. "I know, sir, that you are not a fool. I flatter myself that I am not a fool. May we begin on that assumption?"

"It depends." Lesko made a final check of the room. He could have locked the hallway door as well, but then he'd still have to worry about where Burke was when he was ready to leave. This way, Burke has a chance to bust in if he's going to. But as soon as the door hits that chair, anyone behind it is going to get a hole in him. "What about your brother?" Lesko asked. "What does 'indisposed' mean?"

"He is alone with his bottle and his fears. He is in no way a danger to you." She rapped her desk top to indicate dismissal of that subject. "Would you care to show your cards, Mr. Lesko?"

"For openers," he said nonchalantly, "how about 1944?"

"A card or two more, sir, if you don't mind."

"You would have been what? Twenty-five or thirty? Were you part of it or did you just stick around to pick up the marbles?"

"I see we must fence for a while," she sighed. "Very well." Ella affected the look of an aged Scarlett O'Hara, the role she'd played when he first entered the room. "Whatever could you mean by that, sir?"

Lesko studied her. She was old and thin, and so pale that he wondered if she ever stepped outside this house. And every now and then there was just a flicker of that funny little light you see in the eyes of people in psycho wards. But psycho or not, like she said, she wasn't any dummy. And she was used to a lifetime of getting her way. Of never being pushed too hard. So, let's see how she handles a press.

"You people killed Charlotte Corbin." His tone was matter-of-fact, not accusing. "Or you had it done. You also killed Charlotte's son, who turned out to be the Corbin guy's grandfather. You would have killed Corbin's father too if the krauts didn't get him first."

She didn't even blink. "And why, please, would this be done?"

Lesko waved off the question. "The same year the original Tilden Beckwith has this accident in his office. If I had to bet, I'd say he went first and the accident had a little help. I'd also bet that if I looked real close I'd find a couple of other stiffs along the way because things like this never go as clean as you'd like."

"I repeat." She folded her hands under her chin. "Why, Mr. Lesko?"

"Money. What else?"

"I have more than I could possibly spend. That was almost equally true in 1944."

Lesko nodded. "If the Corbins let you keep it."

"I see." She smiled. Lesko thought she seemed relieved. "At last, we have a motive. Tilden Beckwith sired a bastard son. The legitimate Beckwiths, fearing a pretender to the family fortune, eventually took up arms against the pretender and his entire line, slaying all but one who was hidden like Moses among the reeds. Is that approximately what you believe, Mr. Lesko?"

"It's in the ballpark."

Ella Beckwith laughed aloud. "Can you imagine,

sir"—she lowered her voice as if sharing a secret—"the number of illegitimate children produced by rich men who dally with cocktail waitresses? Or the number of alleged relatives who surface every time a rich person dies?"

Dancer smirked. "I'm sure, Mr. Lesko, that any competent attorney would advise Corbin not to waste his time without documentation."

"Who says he doesn't have paper?" Lesko asked offhandedly. Then he watched Dancer's eyes to see if they would widen and glance toward Ella Beckwith. They did.

"Such as what?" Dancer tried to affect a scornful disbelief.

Lesko waved off the question with a wink. He had no idea what Corbin might have had, but he knew at least that there could be something. "What do you say we speed this up? Next you're going to tell me that whatever the guy has, it doesn't matter because you got more lawyers than he does and you'll tie him up in the courts for years until he's ready to take any bone you throw him. Then I say yeah, but how come you tried to kill the guy twice? Then you, lady, you say that's news to you and if it's true, old Tom Burke must have been acting on his own for some reason, right?"

Ella's smile flickered but remained.

"Once we get past that," Lesko went on, "you're going to tell me there's no evidence of attempted murder, especially since I screwed up both attempts."

"You are peeking at my hand, Mr. Lesko. Play your own cards, please."

"Oh, sorry." Lesko scratched his head. "We were talking motive. If you don't like money, how about blood?"

"Blood, sir?"

She turned a shade more pale. Lesko would not have thought it possible.

"Blood," he repeated. "As in, Corbin and the first Tilden Beckwith look like twins because they got the same blood. The rest of the Beckwiths, you included, all look like each other because you all got the same blood too, except it's not Beckwith blood. You got as much Beckwith in you as my cat, lady."

Ella's smile became a mask.

"No arguments?" Lesko spread his hands.

"He could be recording this," Dancer warned.

"Recording what?" The detective shrugged. "So far I'm doing a solo."

Ella Beckwith raised a hand to stay Dancer's concern. That funny little light blinked on. "Were you approaching a conclusion, Mr. Lesko?"

"Tilden's wife, she was your grandmother, right? She screwed around a little."

Dancer emitted a horrified moan at Lesko's crudeness. Ella didn't even blink.

"Anyway," Lesko continued, "she gets pregnant. I have a feeling that the guy was not a class act. I have a feeling you're not real anxious for people to know you came out of him and not out of uptown types like the Beckwiths." Lesko watched her for some sign that the pecker who started all this could be identified if you dug deep enough and got lucky. He saw it on her temple. A vein there had begun to throb.

"What was he," he pressed, "part nigger, maybe? Or maybe he got hung up by his balls for molesting little boys."

Now a tic appeared at the corner of Ella Beckwith's eye. Lesko knew that he'd hit. If not the ten ring, then something very close. He decided to let it cook by itself for a while.

The detective began to pace. "Next thing you know, your grandma has this baby. Tilden probably takes one look and says you gotta be kidding. No way that came out of me. He'd like to throw the wife and kid out but maybe he keeps them for appearances. But then, I figure, Tilden decides he wants a kid of his own and he sure as hell isn't going to ask your grandma for it. He goes to this girl who's maybe a young hooker. He gets her to have a kid for him. He sets her up right here in Greenwich, maybe in that same house Corbin came back here and bought. She stays here a few years, she raises the kid, then something spooks her and she splits for Chicago. Fifty years later there comes a space of maybe six weeks in which Tilden dies, she dies, her kid dies, and I think her kid's kid would have died too if you could get a clean shot at him while he was in town for the funerals."

"You are traveling in circles, Mr. Lesko." Her voice was cool but he heard a tremor in it. "Furthermore you know nothing, sir. Nothing."

"Corbin won't think so," he said pleasantly. "Put what I know with what he knows, mix in what the Sturdevant guy is digging up, I think we'll pretty much dope out what happened. If you want me to guess right now, I'd say some time around January of 1944, your old man, the one who looks like a snake, got a look at Tilden's will. I think old snake-face was going to get cut out, and you and your indisposed brother right along with him."

Lesko noted with satisfaction that Ella had stopped breathing again.

"That is absolutely absurd," Dancer sputtered.

"Lawrence," Ella hissed, "shut up."

"How could you permit this cretin—"

"*Shut up!*" she shrieked.

Dancer flinched at her sudden vehemence. Even Lesko was startled. And on the other side of the door that Dancer had latched, the wild-eyed old man who had followed Tilden's ghost through the streets of New York sank to his knees with a silent wail. He pressed both palms against his mouth and held them there to stop the bile he felt rising in his throat. *Shut up*. The words echoed in his head. Always shut up. *Shut up, Tillie. Go away, Tillie. Grow up, Tillie. Don't be a fool, Tillie. The man is dead. He can't hurt you.* Bigelow must have been wrong, you say. But you found out, didn't you, Ella? You're always so smart. Ella always knows everything. *There are no ghosts, Tillie.* And yet it's you who stays up on this hill with your doors and windows locked and the drapes pulled tight when it's dark. You knew. You knew all the time. You knew one day you would look out your window and you would see him standing there looking back at you and you finally did. I told you.

Ella's brother climbed to his feet with the aid of a chair and leaned against the door frame until his breathing had slowed and he was sure he would not sob aloud. The voices inside were softer now. Hard to hear. It didn't matter because he knew what they would be saying in the end. Kill this one, kill that one, and everything will be fine. We are protecting what is ours by right. He deserved what he got. They all deserved it for what he did to your poor grandmother. For all the shame and humiliation he tried to bring upon us. Never a smile for you or me or your father. Everything for that slut and her bastard. He deserved to die. He still deserves to die. Ah, yes, Ella, but don't you see? He can't die. He keeps coming back. Now he's found us the way he found Bigelow. He will do to us what he did to him. You can't kill him. But you can talk to him. No. You can't. But I can. I can explain. None of it was my fault. I couldn't help it that they gave me his name.

Tilden Beckwith II straightened until he could stand without the aid of the door frame. He tried to remember where he had set down his drink. The trophy room. He lurched in that direction, his movements silent on the thick blue carpeting. The spring of the carpet and the lightness of his head gave him a floating feeling. He felt weightless. Free. It was such a good idea and it was he, not Ella, who had thought of it. Of course, she couldn't though, could she? He would never listen to her. But the two Tildens could have a talk. They could have a drink together and thrash this out like gentlemen. He does enjoy a drink, you know. Scotch. Glenlivet. The Plaza always had a bottle for him. All his clubs as well. There was probably a bottle in the trophy room bar. Bring it. Show him you mean him no harm. Even bring one of the guns from that cabinet the Burke fellow was rummaging through. An excellent idea.

Ella Beckwith's right hand had begun to convulse. She reached to quiet it with the other, then raised both hands toward Lesko as if to say Never mind that outburst, stay where you are, I am collecting my thoughts. I am fine now.

"You speak of . . ." She paused and swallowed. "You speak of sharing your theories with Mr. Corbin. May I ask how that would be to your advantage?"

Lesko shrugged. "It might be worth a piece of the action when you and Corbin settle up."

She looked like she was going to explode again. To scream Never. But she swallowed the word before it could get out and took a breath. "It seems to me, sir," Ella said quietly, "that you've already been given a substantial sum for services not yet rendered."

Dancer waved at her across the room. He cupped a finger to his ear, reminding her of the possibility that Lesko might be wired.

The ex-cop smiled, patting his inside coat pocket, which still held the envelope of fifteen thousand dollars. "All Dancer here said was I should do something dramatic for it. I figure I qualified when I put two of your security guys in the hospital instead of in the lock-up."

Ella stared at him, at the bulge on his chest. She

had that snake look, he realized, that they all seem to have. Not that he was worried, but Lesko knew he would have been smarter not to let her know he had it on him.

"So be it." Ella dismissed the fifteen thousand dollars with a flip of her fingers. She glanced at Dancer, then back at Lesko. "Is Lawrence's concern legitimate, sir? Are you recording this interview?"

Lesko shook his head. "Scout's honor. Dancer here can pat me down as long as he doesn't get affectionate."

Ella nodded to Dancer who, his face reddened, crossed to Lesko and ran his fingers lightly over his body. He turned to her as he stepped away and shook his head. Ella held his gaze. That look again. She seemed to be asking Dancer some other question with her eyes.

She cleared her throat and looked again toward Lesko. "You speak of casting your lot with Mr. Corbin and company. That seems rather a long-term investment, Mr. Lesko."

"On the other hand, they're a nicer class of people and they probably won't be looking to kill me first chance they get."

Ella snorted. Lesko wasn't sure at what. She chewed her lip. "Mr. Lesko," she asked slowly, "if you were to withhold your theories . . . and otherwise protect me against further annoyance in these matters . . . what would you regard as a fair consideration?"

"Fifty grand a year, every year," he answered at once.

"An ambitious proposal."

"Not really." He shook his head. "It's not even blackmail. What I want is a lifetime contract as a security consultant with Beckwith Enterprises. That's a hell of a lot less than you pay either Burke or Dancer here, and they're both mutts."

"And you'll want it in cash, I presume."

"Nope. On the payroll. All legal."

"And your contribution to the firm's security will be what, exactly?"

"I discourage Corbin but I don't kill him." Lesko took a step closer to the desk. "The main thing is, you don't either. Anything happens to him, I go to the cops and the papers. Anything happens to me, my notes and a deposition go to the cops, the papers, and to Harry Sturdevant. Beyond this Corbin thing, which you leave strictly to me, I'll do as much or as little for my keep as you want. Within reason, of course."

An unsettling smile pulled at the dried-out corners of Ella Beckwith's mouth. "And this deposition you mention, sir," she asked innocently, "do I assume that it is in safe hands, as they say in the mystery films, with instructions that it go to the authorities should anything happen to you?"

"You got the picture, lady."

"Since you assure me that this is not blackmail, Mr. Lesko"—the smile brightened—"it must be a question of competitive bidding. What is it exactly that you have to sell this Mr. Corbin? Since you can prove nothing of a criminal nature against any of us, you must have it in mind to help him draw up some sort of family tree."

A buzz sounded on her telephone. Ella Beckwith ignored it.

"Do you propose, sir, to endear yourself to Jonathan Corbin by establishing that his sainted great-grandmother was a former prostitute? And if that does not sour him on the worth of your services, imagine when he learns that his very upright great-grandfather was in fact a murderer. He was, you know. He murdered the woman whose name I bear."

"Lady . . ." Lesko shook his head wearily. The buzzer sounded twice more. She glanced at it and then at Dancer, who crossed to take the call. Ella rose to her feet and, propped up on her cane, leaned into Lesko's face. The smile now had a wildness to it.

"Oh, bear with me, Mr. Lesko. I have saved the best for last. Do you believe in ghosts, sir?"

Lesko closed his eyes. "You're going to tell me your brother does. I've already seen that, lady." He looked past her at Dancer. Whatever he was hearing on the other end was making him blink.

"My brother, that wreck of a man whom you saw following Corbin through the streets of New York yesterday, has believed for twenty years that he is being stalked by the ghost of his namesake. He had never seen him, mind you. He had only the word of a dying man that the ghost of Tilden Beckwith had become flesh. That he was not only alive, but alive in his full, youthful, saloon-brawling and homicidal vigor." She bit off and spat these last words.

"Miss Beckwith!" Dancer cupped a hand over the phone. Lesko saw that his face was flushed. His head kept pivoting between Ella's back and the window looking down on the driveway. She flicked a hand, waving him off.

Lesko could see at once where this was heading. Someone had run into Jonathan Corbin twenty years before. Someone who knew what Tilden looked like when he wasn't a whole lot older than Corbin must have been at the time. But she said the guy was dying when he told the story. Saloon-brawling and homicidal?

"Dying from what?" he asked. "Corbin did a number on him?"

"Corbin beat him to death. Jonathan Corbin murdered a man named George Bigelow and another man named Howard Flack. Flack died at once, Bigelow a day later." Her voice was rising into a snarl. She was beginning to spray spittle. "He stomped them, clubbed them, broke their knees and elbows—"

"Ella!" Dancer snapped. "We have a problem."

Go solve it, Lesko wished in his mind. This is getting too interesting to stop. He could see from Dancer's expression, however, that the problem at hand was even more urgent than getting his boss to stop shooting off her mouth. Ella began backing in his direction.

"A nicer class of people, you say," she hooted. "If we have killed, sir, as you claim we have, it has been to defend what is ours. To survive. To see justice done. But how do your nice people kill, Mr. Lesko? They will murder a beautiful young mother out of injured pride and leave her poor body to freeze on a dark New York street. They will sadistically and systematically crush the bones of two men—not young men, by the way, men approaching their sixties—and leave them for dead in a hotel garage—*What is it?*" She spun on Dancer, who was trying to seize her arm.

"Talk to Burke." He thrust the phone into her hand and practically forced it to her ear.

"*Yes!*" she shouted into the mouthpiece.

Lesko watched her eyes grow wide, then narrow. "And you allowed this?" she asked. "You let him go?" She peered out her window as Dancer had done. Lesko noticed for the first time that it was snowing. Heavily. A half inch must have fallen just since he'd arrived. He could barely see his car where he'd left it, but a fresh set of tire tracks was clearly visible on the upper driveway. They came from behind the house at its far end and headed weavingly down toward Round Hill Road.

"That fool!" Ella hissed through her teeth. Uh-oh, Lesko thought. Her spooked-out brother must be thinking for himself again. "Get in here at once," she barked into the phone and then slammed it down. Ella did a double take at Lesko almost as if she'd forgotten he was there. "You may wait in the kitchen, Mr. Lesko, while I consider your offer. Mr. Ballanchine will show you the way."

Lesko wondered if he was hearing right. "Uh, listen, lady—"

"That will be *all,* sir." Then, another funny little eye message to Dancer.

"Yeah, well, I got some questions." As he said this, Lesko held up the Beretta in the flat palm of his right hand and pointed to it as if asking, Does anybody here remember that I got this thing? "Like, who was Bigelow and was he, by any chance, the guy who knocked off Tilden and the Corbins for you back in 1944?"

Lesko heard a sound at the door he'd entered. Dancer heard it as well and suddenly remembered the chair that blocked it. Dancer moved toward it, but Lesko stepped forward and grabbed the collar of his suit coat, holding the smaller man fast between himself and the door. "Easy does it, Twinkletoes," he said quietly. "How about an answer before we let old Tom come in."

He almost knew it already. George Bigelow then was probably what Tom Burke was now. Bigelow would have done the killing. The guy Flack probably helped him do it. But twenty years later he runs into Corbin? And Corbin wastes him? Corbin was just a college kid then.

"Miss Beckwith?" The voice came from the hall outside. The door had hit the heavy chair. "Are you all right?"

No answer.

Lesko snapped a look at Ella, who was just out of his line of sight over his right shoulder. She was just standing there. Behind her desk. Standing with her hands folded over the knob of her cane and staring at him with that snake look they all had.

"She's fine, Tom," he answered for her. "We're just

finishing up a little talk." Lesko twisted Dancer's collar to get his attention. "Just so I can sleep tonight," he said into Dancer's ear, "did these guys find Corbin or was it the other way around?"

"I don't know," Dancer choked. "It's true. No one knows what happened."

"So Corbin found them, right? Because no one knew there was a Corbin left until you hired me to verify it another twenty years later."

Dancer could only shake his head. Lesko was sure that he knew more than he'd admit to, but maybe not a whole lot more. Twenty years. Twenty years they've been looking over their shoulders because a dying man, Bigelow, says that the guy who done him was the same guy hanging in the lobby of the Beckwith Regency. If he's dying, it figures he's a little out of it, right? But still, even if you believe that a college kid could have dismantled two grown men who had to be pros, would a pro like Bigelow have said it was Tilden who did it? He might have said it was some kid who maybe looked like him. Wouldn't he? But then, how do we explain that Corbin knew Bigelow? If it *was* him.

"It was him." The words came labored through crushed and crusted lips.

Huntington Beckwith leaned closer over the dying man's bed. Both legs were suspended in traction. Both arms were splinted upon raised wooden boards. Ella and her brother stood together on the bed's far side. "It was who, George? Who did this to you?"

"Old Mr. Beckwith. He's alive."

"No." Ella's father shook his head. "No, George. He is not alive. Think hard who really hurt you so that we may find him."

"He is alive." The man named Bigelow choked. "He's alive and he's young and strong again."

Huntington looked up at his daughter, his expres-

sion a mixture of frustration and annoyance. "He is hallucinating. It's the drugs they gave him for the pain."

"It was him," Bigelow shouted, but the effort brought a surge of agony that almost made him faint.

"No, George. He's dead and gone. They are all dead and gone."

Ella stepped closer. "Could one have been missed, Father?" she asked in a whisper. "Could the one who was a flyer have left a son?"

The dying man turned his face to Ella. "He came out of a bookstore. Flack and I were passing on the street. I didn't get a real good look at first because the snow was in my face. He was just a kid who looked familiar. He barely looked at Flack and me. Then when we passed him, I remembered who he looked like. I turned around, even though he was walking the other way. But he wasn't, you know? It was like he knew us too. He stopped on the sidewalk after we passed him, and when I turned around he's just standing there, real straight, and he's looking at us. And his eyes were different. They were like a wolf looks. I says to Flack we ought to find out who this kid is for sure, but Flack says let's just get out of here because he's starting to feel funny just like me because the kid was all of a sudden different. He wasn't the same."

Ella heard a whimper behind her. Her brother, Tilden, had crowded back against the wall. She shook her head in disgust. "What then, Mr. Bigelow?" she asked. "You followed him, did you not?"

"He followed us," George Bigelow rasped. "We went to the garage under the Drake where Flack's car was and we hid behind this post and we waited for him. Then he comes walking in like he doesn't care if we know he's coming or not. Then he just stands there, real straight like before, listening. I figure enough is enough so I step out from the post but I tell Flack to *stay where he is. This kid walks right up to me and he's squinting and then nodding like now he's sure he knows me and now I see his nose is bent just like the old man's was. I say, 'Who are you?' He just smiles and he says, 'Hello, George.' And I get scared and I yell for Flack and Flack comes around and grabs this kid around the neck from behind. But he's still got this smile and there's a look on his face that says, Oh, Jeez, I'm really gonna love this. So I throw a punch because I'm going to wipe off that smile, see? And I split open his eyebrow. It was an accident, exactly where I hit him, I mean, but now he's got this cut exactly where the old man had it and now he looks even more like the old man than he did before and this smile is still there. Next thing, real fast, he kicks Flack in the shin with his heel and he spins and gives Flack three hard shots and they knock him on his ass between some parked cars. Flack gets up holding his mouth and I think he's running away but he runs to his car and he gets this billy he keeps under the seat. Then this kid comes at me except now it's him. It's Tilden. And he brings up his fists like the old-time fighters. I get a few shots in but he's too fast. He's too strong. I went down and he comes down right on top of me. Then I see Flack with his billy and I know Flack nailed him. And I say, 'Good, get him off me,' and Flack pulls him up by the hair and starts ramming the billy into his kidneys. But he doesn't feel it. I look at those eyes and I know he doesn't feel it."*

Huntington Beckwith shot a withering stare at Ella's brother, who had the look of a frightened child. Bigelow sucked in a deep, whistling breath and Huntington could hear the bubbling of mucus and blood that would fill his lungs and kill him during the coming night.

"I hit him." Tears formed in Bigelow's eyes. "Flack hit him. It didn't do no good."

Huntington Beckwith shook his head. "I don't understand, George."

"The eyes. They never changed. It was like he couldn't feel nothing. It's like we were hitting someone else."

At the far wall, Tilden Beckwith II had turned his face away and was sobbing, one hand over his mouth.

"Ella," her father whispered sharply, nodding in his direction.

Ella turned and slapped her brother's face. "Not another sound, Tillie," she warned him.

"He told you," Tilden wailed.

She slapped him again.

"He said we would have to answer to him. He said there's no hole deep enough—"

The third slap, backhanded, drew blood from his mouth. Tilden squealed at the taste of it and, shoulders hunched, he slid down the hospital wall. He made no further sound.

"Mr. Beckwith," George Bigelow whispered.

"Yes, George."

"How did he know?"

"I don't think he could have known, George. There's some mistake here. We'll sort it out, I promise."

"He did know. He knew everything."

"I don't understand, George." Huntington's eyes narrowed.

"He took Howie Flack's billy. He went for our knees first so we couldn't get away. He smashes my knee. He says 'Margaret.' He smashes the other knee, he says 'Jonathan.' Maybe twenty times before I pass out, he says 'Margaret' and 'Jonathan.' When I can't even feel the billy anymore, I hear 'Margaret' and 'Jonathan.' Ask Flack. Flack will tell you."

Huntington said nothing.

Bigelow tried to raise his head. "Howie? Howie's not dead, is he?"

"We're going to see to his family very handsomely, George. And you yourself are going to be in quite comfortable circumstances once you get well. I'll take care of everything here, of course. A few months," he lied, "you're going to be better than new."

"Sure." Bigelow closed his eyes.

"The police will want to question you," Ella said softly.

"Don't worry."

"Of course not, George." Her father patted his arm.

"I want a priest."

"You don't need one, George. Truly."

"Look. I want a priest. A priest can't tell no one what I say."

"Of course, George. Of course."

In the hallway outside, out of her brother's hearing, Huntington Beckwith asked Ella to stay with George Bigelow until the end. It came that night, hastened by the drain in his chest that had unaccountably become pinched. A priest came at sunset. Ella managed to persuade him that a general confession before last rites would be sufficient, given Mr. Bigelow's weakened state. The priest, one Father Desmond O'Conner, unknowingly prolonged his own life by accepting Ella's suggestion.

Ella returned to Greenwich, where she spent the next year peering into every young male face she encountered. Her visits beyond her front gate, which she'd quickly had installed, became increasingly infrequent, then rare, then not at all. Her brother, Tilden II, took up residence on his yacht, rarely setting foot ashore until his father's death in 1965. Tilden, by this time, lived in an almost constant haze of alcohol and barbiturates. His wife, Elvira, moved with the children to the Palm Beach house, where she discovered vodka and orange juice was a balm to her loneliness. On Huntington Beckwith's death, Ella sold Tilden's yacht from under him, effectively forcing him to accept the titular leadership of Beckwith Enterprises in the office of chairman. With the job came a very large and well-guarded suite on the penthouse floor of the Beckwith Regency Hotel. In the more than twenty years since George Bigelow had drowned in his own fluids, Ella and Tilden's predawn thoughts were haunted gradually less by the vision of the ghost who mouthed the words *Margaret* and *Jonathan* with each advancing step. The part of Ella's brain into which that image was etched had almost healed over. Then came the day when she looked down across her sloping lawn to Round Hill Road and saw the long-dead face of Tilden Beckwith staring up at her.

A slamming thump sounded on Lesko's left. That would be Tom Burke, trying to kick in the other door for a shot at his blind side. He yanked Dancer's squirming body toward the sound and heard a rustle of fabric behind him as Ella Beckwith scurried out of the line of fire.

There goes fifty grand a year, was his first thought. The foot against the bolted door had instantly multiplied his doubts about any good-faith bargaining with old Ella. The question now was how to get out of here. But then, there was also a question of professional pride.

"Hey, lady," he said over his shoulder. He beckoned her closer with the Beretta, which he waggled over the mussed-up top of Dancer's head.

Ella hesitated, but she took two steps nearer.

"I mean"—Lesko showed her the pained expression on his face—"if this guy is the best you got, don't you get a little embarrassed sometimes?"

Ella blinked. Her eyes still glistened with malice, but Lesko's patient self-possession seemed to slow her heartbeat.

"Counting letting your shit-faced brother drive off, that's at least three times today old Tom out there fucked up, excuse the expression."

The door slammed once more.

"Look at this." He gestured toward it with the blue automatic. "The guy thinks maybe I didn't notice the first kick. Right now he's ducked back away from the door because he also thinks bullets don't go through plaster." Lesko dropped his sights to the right of the door, about where he judged Burke's buttocks to be, and fired twice. Dancer shrieked and flailed like a puppet at muzzle blasts that sounded like thunderclaps in the confined room. Beyond the fist-sized holes that appeared in the wall, Lesko heard a frantic tattoo of feet but no sound of a falling body. He'd missed, he knew, but not by much. Burke might be picking wood lath out of his ass for the rest of the afternoon.

"Ah, Mr. Lesko"—he heard Ella's voice behind him—"you do know how to drive home a point."

"Yeah." He scowled. "Well, Dancer and me are going to take a walk down to my car now. Sorry we can't do business."

"Truth be told, Mr. Lesko, so am I," Ella said wearily. "Indeed, sir, so am I."

Lesko heard her inflection changing on the last three words she spoke. Their sound was strained in the manner of a person lifting a heavy weight as he spoke. Or swinging an ax. Or a cane. It is amazing, he'd often thought, how much faster the brain works than the body. He knew that it was a cane. And that it was whistling toward his head. He had time to curse himself for being stupid, for leaving her behind him, for playing games. But his body had no time to even wince. The room exploded into light. Then more light, then darkness. And through the darkness there were smaller silent flashes of light coming from where his right hand should be. He heard shrieks and screams, but they were more distant. Then the flashes from his right hand stopped as his body fell upon it, dousing them.

FIFTEEN

ARRY STURDEVANT CHECKED HIS WATCH AT THE strike of Corbin's mantel clock. Half past two. Jonathan had been gone for nearly an hour. Sturdevant didn't like this at all. Not a bit of it.

He couldn't have missed Jonathan by much more than ten minutes. And at that, he should have passed him on the Post Road, unless Jonathan crossed it and took the back streets down to the railway station. If Cora was right, if they were being followed by that wrestler type who was so helpful in the library, Jonathan could be very easy pickings walking alone through a heavy snow that darkened the day into twilight.

Nor was Sturdevant entirely pleased that Jonathan's fear of the snow seemed to have left him. It did not necessarily mean, as Gwen seemed to think, that his snowstorm hallucinations would leave him as well. It might mean only that he was becoming comfortable with them. Worse yet, that he was beginning to accept them as his reality. All this business he'd told Gwen about being a child here, and playing ball with Laura Hemmings, a name, by the way, that he should not have known, and his anger at Gwen when he seemed to think she was threatening some sort of fairyland existence, and new memories, conscious this time, of a continuing friendship with Teddy Roosevelt, and a mysterious but obviously related enmity toward a man named Bigelow—these hardly add up to a man who should have been allowed to walk off into a snowstorm by himself.

"How do I look?" He heard his niece's voice on the stairway behind him. Sturdevant turned from the window where he'd been waiting.

He watched, one eyebrow raised, as she paused at the foot of the stairs to smooth the heavy velvet skirt she'd been holding during her descent. It was a full-length white dress with braided trim across the bodice and at her wrists. Its high collar made her neck look twice its length and all the more graceful. Her honey blond hair was piled high and held in place with black and yellow tortoiseshell combs.

"Where on earth did you get that?" he asked.

"Upstairs in Jonathan's bedroom closet," she answered offhandedly. "It doesn't really fit right without a corset. And Jonathan doesn't have any underthings up there."

"Thank heaven for small favors." Sturdevant didn't like this, either. "Why do we suppose Jonathan is stocking his closets with nineteenth-century women's clothing?"

"It's not that at all." She smiled. "I went to an auction with him last November, and these came as part of a lot he was bidding on. Jonathan didn't even want them, but I said it would be a crime to throw them out."

Sturdevant softened only a shade. "Does he ask you to dress up like this when you spend time with him here?"

"Will you please relax?" She crossed to him and reached to kiss his cheek, then turned her back to him. "I can't get those buttons."

"Does he, Gwen?" He started awkwardly at the lowest one, wishing he had one of those hooks his mother had used.

"Nope." She shook her head. "He bought me one gown last Christmas because it was beautiful and I loved it. Stop looking for new ways for Jonathan to be crazy, Uncle Harry."

Her back was bare beneath the dress. She wore no halter or foundation garment, not even the petticoats that would have given the dress its proper fullness below the hips. That bothered him. Harry would admit that he was sufficiently old-fashioned to dislike thinking of his best friend's daughter in any state approximating nudity. If that was overprotectiveness, or a reluctance to accept that Gwen was a grown-up woman, so be it. But there was also a certain vulnerability to an improperly clothed woman which, especially today, made him all the more anxious for her in view of all the hostility that seemed to be bubbling up in this supposedly idyllic community of Jonathan's. Antagonistic librarians. Thugs with guns if Cora was correct. And Jonathan himself practically threatening Gwen, even though she makes light of it and says he was merely confused about who she was, as if that explanation even began to be adequate. Sorry I shot my wife, your honor; I thought she was a girl who turned me down for a date once. Or, He didn't mean to throttle me, officer; he just thought I was another one of his ghosts. Which reminds me . . .

"Gwen, dearest." He turned her to face him. "May I ask, by the way, why you are in this dress?" He'd allowed himself to assume that it was only some girlish puttering to pass the time.

She smiled prettily. "I just wanted to see how it looks on me."

"Hmmph!" She looked entirely too innocent. "Well, now that we know it's lovely, why don't you change back into your own things."

"I will." She patted his chest. "After I show Jonathan."

Sturdevant raised his eyebrow again and held it there until she had to look away. He folded his arms. "All right. What do you think you're doing?"

"Nothing" she answered, wide-eyed.

"If you're toying with Jonathan . . ."

"I'm hardly *toying*, Uncle Harry. I'm trying to help him."

"You helped him yesterday," he reminded her, "by giving him a drug whose effect you could not possibly predict."

Gwen swallowed but did not otherwise react.

"And today, here you are in what was apparently Laura Hemmings's house and you are dressed, I presume, to resemble Laura Hemmings, a woman who seems to have antagonized Jonathan in some way."

"I *did* help him," she said stubbornly. "He knows those things he saw were real now. He knows he's not crazy. And he's not afraid of the snow anymore."

Sturdevant waved that off. "You are playing a very reckless game with a man who, whether you choose to face it or not, may still be dangerously deluded."

"He is not deluded," she said sharply.

"Did you see his face just before you left the library?" he asked. "I won't pretend I know why, but he looked for all the world like a man who had a few scores to settle."

"How would *you* feel, for Pete's sake? In less than twenty-four hours he found out that Tilden Beckwith was practically his father and that the woman who was practically his mother was badgered out of New York and eventually even out of Greenwich by people who simply would not allow them to be happy."

"Happiness!" Sturdevant snorted. "I have a feeling there's far more at stake than that. This is not an episode of 'As the World Turns.'"

His niece's eyes went flat. "That was patronizing, Uncle Harry."

Harry Sturdevant turned toward the window, staring out at nothing in particular. A plow rattled by, its blade still up. But no sign of the car Cora described or of his friend from the library.

"I think I'd better clear the driveway entrance before it gets much worse or freezes." He picked up his coat.

"You shouldn't be shoveling snow."

"At my age, you mean?"

"Gotcha." She punched him.

Harry Sturdevant shook his head in surrender as he crossed to the door. He stopped there and turned.

"These old scores I mentioned," he said gently, "if I'm right about them, and Jonathan intends to settle up with the Beckwiths, he is going to find himself in serious trouble." He waited for a long moment before finishing his thought. "But if, God forbid, he intends to settle with people who are no longer living, I assume it's clear to you that Jonathan is in deeper trouble than either of us imagined."

Maple Avenue, once it crossed the Post Road, became Milbank Avenue. Corbin chose that route down a long, curving hill toward the railroad station. It was the way Tilden would have gone. Milbank Avenue was a good carriage road then, kept well combed and swept because several merchants who had built new houses

along it were also members of the Greenwich town
council.

Corbin was pleased with himself. It was snowing
hard and he was walking in it. The houses, although
the newer ones seemed dimmer than the older buildings, remained solid. Cars remained cars; they did not
fade into sleighs and wagons. If he looked along the
street in a certain way he could still see it as it probably
once was, but he felt content that these were Tilden's
memories and not his own. At one point, a few blocks
down, he answered a friendly wave from a man who
was no longer there by the time Corbin raised his arm.
He felt none of the old terror. Corbin fully understood
now that the things he saw were real, or had been once
to Tilden. They could not hurt him. They could not
entrap him in another time. It was not altogether unlike
going back to the places of his own boyhood and seeing
in his mind, but almost with his eye, the events that
happened then. There I am hitting a three-run homer in
my first Little League game. There I am walking that
high tree limb on a dare. There I am in my fistfight with
Mike McConnell and him being the first to quit but
both of us getting suspended for it. See? he thought.
Anyone can see the past. It seemed almost natural.
Even if Corbin had known about the tranquilizing drug
Gwen had twice slipped into his drinks, he would not
have given the drug full credit. He was in Greenwich,
and he was walking in the snow without fear. Why
shouldn't he feel good?

If he allowed himself to dwell on them, there were
indeed thoughts of scores that should have been settled.
But again, these were Tilden's thoughts. And they were
old scores. Too old to matter now. Corbin pushed them
far back in his mind. Some were already more distant
than others. The hated Ansel Carling was barely a
shadow, far away. Except that the effect of Carling's
seedy little seduction seemed to go on no end, the man

himself no longer mattered. Anyway, Corbin had an idea that he'd come to some terrible end down in Texas. He wasn't sure what. Tilden probably knew, but Corbin was not inclined to start anything by asking. Carling was done with and that was enough. So was Colonel Mann, at least in terms of any future mischief he might have done. Thanks to Billy O'Gorman. And to Tilden's friends.

As he neared the bottom of Milbank Avenue, Corbin found himself thinking how lucky Tilden was to have such friends. Corbin really didn't have any, at least at the moment. There was Gwen, of course. But that was different. Gwen was as good a friend as anyone could have, and very much more, but that wasn't the same as having buddies like John Flood and Nat Goodwin, and especially Teddy Roosevelt, and even Georgiana Hastings, who would stand up with you no matter how the breaks were going. Yeah. But wait a minute. The fact is you have just as many friends. Good ones. Come to think of it, several are athletes like Flood, one is an actor, and another one ran for Congress last year. Offhand, there isn't anyone who runs a brothel, but three out of four isn't bad. The real difference between you and Tilden is that Tilden wouldn't have gone the past five or six months as you have, not returning calls, not even Christmas cards, and burying yourself in your office all week and out here every weekend. And being so sullen and distant all the time. You're getting like Gould.

Anger.

Corbin felt the surge.

Tilden's anger.

He tried to push it away.

Then he saw Margaret's face, her eyes shining with held-back tears, and he saw little Laura Hemmings reaching up to dab them with a handkerchief and telling her to smile and not let Tilden see her this way.

Corbin stopped. He bent to pick up a handful of snow and rubbed it across his face. "What good is this?" he asked aloud.

Now Laura Hemmings was gone and there was Margaret, holding a little boy's hand, an embroidered carpetbag at her feet, and they both looked so terribly sad, and as the picture was receding, Margaret was mouthing the words *I love you*.

"I'm sorry, Tilden," Corbin said softly. "I care about you both and I feel almost as bad about that as you do. I don't know what you think I can do about it."

A woman, walking a police dog on a leash, rounded the corner of Railroad Avenue onto Milbank. She blinked at Corbin, then quickly changed direction and tugged the dog toward the other side of the street.

Corbin watched her, first embarrassed and then alarmed because she was not watching where she was going and was about to collide with a large, whiskered man who was coming in the other direction. The man was not watching, either. He was busily winding what looked like a small box camera and Corbin noticed that he was not wearing winter clothing.

The two passed through each other.

Corbin felt another surge of anger, but this time he raised a patient hand as if to stop it. "That's Comstock, right?" He nodded with resignation. "Is that Anthony Comstock?"

No answer came. Corbin didn't need one. He knew.

"Look," he dropped his voice, "I don't even understand this part." He watched as the fat man passed him and continued down Railroad Avenue toward the depot area. There he saw a wagon piled high with vegetables. And another whose sign said Walker & Sons Fresh Fish and it had a striped awning that shaded several wooden tubs of mussels and lobsters. Corbin suddenly realized that the snow was gone. The trees were the dark green of late summer. He saw two women coming his way. Both wore dresses that swept the ground and carried fishnet shopping bags. One held a black parasol against the sun. The fat man spotted them and scurried to intercept them on the wooden sidewalk. The older of the two women spoke sharply to him, but he ignored her. He was looking down, searching for her in the viewfinder of his camera. The woman took one step and swung her parasol at his head. He ducked, then tipped his hat, then took another blow across his arms. He circled round them, having spied still another woman farther down.

"Comstock is the vice crusader, right?"

Right. Corbin knew that as well.

"Gwen and I talked about this," Corbin said. "We don't know why Margaret should have been worried."

He listened for his own feelings. He would have been furious if he had lived here then. Just on general principles. Here's a man taking pictures of every halfway-decent-looking female he meets and you know he's going to show them around someplace to try to nail any who might once have been prostitutes. Corbin would have walked down and kicked his fat ass. Tilden would have, too. Unless Tilden was afraid to call attention to himself and therefore to Margaret.

"Then why didn't you just get her out of town? A vacation. Sail up to Newport or go back down to the Claremont Inn for a week or so. See a couple of ball games."

"You cannot." Laura Hemmings took Margaret's hands in hers. "You will stay here, you will smile sweetly, and you will go about your blameless life as if that idiot does not even exist."

"Oh, Annie."

"My name is Laura. And your name is Charlotte. Even when we're by ourselves, Comstock or no."

"He arrested Carrie Todd this morning," Margaret said miserably, "and he claims to have his eye on three others."

"You are not one of them, dear. I promise you that."

"And it's not just Anthony Comstock." Margaret twisted a lace napkin in her fingers. "Inspector Williams bought a house in Cos Cob. Everyone's talking about the grand new dock he's adding to it and all the fine English furniture he's bringing in. It appears that he's planning to live here, Laura."

"Clubber Williams must spend his graft someplace," Laura Hemmings said, shrugging. "In any case, what is that to you? He's never seen you, has he?"

"No." She shook her head. "But he is Jay Gould's man. And Tilden has had trouble with both of them although he never speaks of it. John Flood told me. What if Williams should see Tilden and me together at the yacht club or in a restaurant? What if he begins wondering who I am?"

"What if, what if, what if." Laura Hemmings flitted her fingers. "Charlotte, are you turning into one of those tiresome women who cannot bear to be happy because they are convinced that the world is and should be a vale of tears?"

"We have a great deal to lose, Laura," she said evenly. "I am not just being silly."

"We're going to lose nothing." Laura reached for her friend's hat. "Come. I won't let you become a recluse. Dr. Palmer has asked me to a picnic lunch, and you and little Jonathan are joining us."

It had been two full years, back to the spring of 1889, since Margaret had serious cause to feel that her happiness was threatened. Her life for the most part was one of great contentment. She dearly wished, of course, that she could see more of Tilden than just on weekends, but in that respect their relationship was not unlike that of many Greenwich families. A good number of husbands spent their weekdays in the city. Her fondest wish was that she and Tilden could fall asleep in each other's arms and wake up together in the morning without having to slip away to the Claremont Inn for that purpose. But in spite of the lack of that sweet convenience, or perhaps because of it, their lovemaking retained all its early excitement and more. They enjoyed each other when and wherever they could, on long Saturday afternoons in Margaret's bedchamber, on starlit beaches, even in carriages. A dash of mischief and intrigue, Margaret found, made their intimate moments all the more delicious.

The worry that came those two years back was one of short duration, but so unexpected that the shock of it almost stopped her heart. It involved the Greenwich chapter of the Women's Christian Temperance Union. Several of the ladies of that organization had come to visit Margaret within the very week that she moved into her new electric home. They were fully aware of the tragedy that had befallen the Total Abstinence Union of Wilkes-Barre and had heard that the Mud Run calamity had also claimed the life of Margaret's husband. The good women offered their most profound sympathy and their fullest support, reminding her that the Greenwich chapter of the WCTU would not permit a distressed member of a sister organization to want for anything. They'd heard and they could see that she was large with child. Once the baby is born, they told Margaret, and when she felt up to it, they would be honored to see her at one of their Wednesday afternoon teas, especially those on the first Wednesday of every month, because that is when new members are officially received. Margaret was quite moved by their kindness and more than a little saddened at the need to deceive them, one of her deceptions being that she was something less than a total abstainer. Perhaps, she decided, she had better abstain after all. She could not very well accept the ladies' invitation and then be seen in the village spirits shop, or have them call and see a decanter of sherry on her sideboard. She would abstain. Mostly. She could keep the sherry out of sight in the kitchen cabinet, along with Tilden's Scotch whisky, and Tilden could replenish the cellar wine supply from New York each weekend. As for dining out with him, well, she could always sneak a sip from his glass when no one was looking. Perhaps a bit of intrigue could do for a glass of wine what it did for making love. She would soon find out. She would also soon learn that she was by no means the only lady of the WCTU who practiced this small artifice.

It was almost the beginning of May and several recruitment visits later when Margaret agreed to attend the tea for new members on the first Wednesday of that month. There was one other candidate, a dark fortress of a woman named Phoebe Peterkin, whose husband had lately bought a pig farm upwind of town. It was the custom for the new candidates to pour for the other members and, while doing so, give a brief oral biography of themselves and perhaps a word or two of their convictions on the matter of temperance. The presence of another candidate cut Margaret's pouring duties by half, and that was good, because she was becoming quite anxious about giving a speech, that requirement having come as a revelation to her when it was too late to withdraw gracefully. Mendacity did not come easily to her. It was bad enough that she had to mislead these ladies about her origins, but to do so about her principles was more than she would permit of herself.

Phoebe Peterkin was the first to pour for the dozen or so members who fell as her share as Margaret waited nervously, her eyes on her fidgeting hands. The Peterkin woman began her discourse by announcing that she spoke to them through lips that had never touched alcohol in any form and she held aloft a hand which she said had dashed the cup from many a man who had so far forgotten himself that he was about to pour a thief into his mouth to steal his brain. Margaret heard a moan. She wasn't sure whether it came from one of the ladies who sat facing her or from within herself. Mrs. Peterkin went on to say that although it had not pleased the Almighty to bless her with children, she did have a good upstanding husband although, truth be told, he had not always been so. As a young man he was seduced into an evil fellowship with rum by none other than the Union army, whose custom it was to give each man a daily ration of that horrid stew. He was drunk when we met and drunker still when we married, so much so that I had to hold him straight with one arm around his waist or he would have bolted from the salvation that was to become his once I took him in hand.

There came another moan and then a snort that had the sound of stifled laughter. Margaret lifted her eyes toward its source. Several women were smiling, others squirming. She saw one woman, very tiny, blond, whose hands were covering her face and whose shoulders were shaking convulsively. Something about her seemed familiar. Margaret dropped her eyes once more and wished desperately that she could be almost anyplace else on earth.

"Thank you, Mrs. Peterkin," she heard the voice of the chapter's secretary, Mrs. Gannon, saying. "I am sure we are all the stronger for having shared your story. Perhaps we might hear from Mrs. Corbin now."

Margaret rose to her feet and began pouring from the heavy service, getting as much in the saucers and on the tea table, she feared, as she managed to get into the blue china cups.

"I think most of you know of my background," she told them, her voice near breaking. "It is painful to repeat . . . for several reasons . . . and if you will allow it, I would prefer to speak no more of what is past." She took a long breath, relieved to see that several heads were nodding their understanding.

"On the matter of temperance"—she threw back her head—"I fear, from what has just been said, that I do not belong in this company. The truth is that I do enjoy a glass of wine or a sherry from time to time."

Phoebe Peterkin gasped audibly, then folded her arms and glowered at Margaret.

"I believe as you do," Margaret continued, "that alcohol when taken to excess is one of the greatest evils of our time, and I would gladly support any effort you might make to prevent its ravages and to ease the suffering of those afflicted. But I also believe, with Voltaire, that neither abstinence nor excess ever renders one happy. I do take wine in strict moderation and I expect that I will continue to do so. I am sorry to have misled you." Margaret sat down, her cheeks burning, and wished with all her might that the floor would open under her.

Mrs. Gannon coughed and then stood to face the meeting. "We have somehow left Mrs. Corbin with the impression that we have achieved perfection in our ideals. Conversely, we seem to have persuaded the good Mrs. Peterkin that we are a group of fanatics whose idea of a pleasant outing is to smash a saloon."

The tiny blond woman, the one so amused by Mrs. Peterkin, also rose and quickly turned her back to Margaret. "I for one," she said, "applaud Mrs. Corbin's candor and would very much like to see more of her."

That voice. Margaret narrowed her eyes. Something about that voice. And that slender little form.

"I stand with Laura on that score," Mrs. Gannon added.

Laura?

"And as for Mrs. Peterkin"—Laura Hemmings turned toward the pig farmer's formidable wife—"since we have confessed to being less perfect than she, perhaps she should consider whether her excellent qualities would blossom more fully in some other sodality."

My God! Margaret's mouth fell open. She barely heard the applause that followed Laura Hemmings's remarks or the ensuing fury of Phoebe Peterkin as she railed against slackers, backsliders, and compromisers. *My God, it's Little Annie.*

Laura Hemmings winked and smiled. *Hello, Margaret Barrie,* she said with just her lips. Then the two women stepped toward each other and touched their cheeks in a polite manner that was not nearly the unrestrained hug which Margaret had given her two years earlier when Little Annie left Georgiana Hastings's house for the last time in her life.

She could still pass for fifteen, Margaret thought admiringly. Given the right clothing, a young girl's clothing. At Georgiana's house she favored middy blouses and straw sailor hats and she wore her hair long and straight and brushed down so that it hid much of her face. The hair did not conceal the wide, full mouth for which Little Annie was famous most of all, for Annie's specialty was making love in the French manner, a prospect made all the more erotic to some by her apparent youth and innocence. She was also possessed of a legendary talent for muscular control by which she could constrict and release her inner parts in such a way that her maidenhead seemed to be rupturing under the thrusts of each first-time customer who was willing to pay double to deflower a tender virgin. For added effect, Little Annie often kept a tiny bladder of beef blood concealed in her palm.

Annie, Margaret recalled, was almost equally adept at saving and investing her money. She did so with

Beckwith & Company through the agency of Georgiana Hastings. And she was at least as well educated as Margaret. She had told Margaret what was apparently the true story of her upbringing and downfall. Her father, still living, was a minister who had taught in mission schools all around the world. In her eighteenth year he was given a parish in Providence, Rhode Island, so that he might finish his ministry in his native country. It was in Annie's nineteenth year that she fell into disgrace and was forced by public and family pressure to remove that stain from the community. Her experience in other cultures had left Annie a worldlier girl than most, and she knew at the outset that a term of prostitution in the right sort of house and with the right sort of act offered her the greatest promise of early recovery from this personal disaster. She no sooner entered "the life" than she began planning her retirement from it. Annie's little-girl role and its attendant disguises was intended as much to assure future anonymity as it was to maximize her income. Her ultimate ambition, she told Margaret, was to open a school for refined young ladies. She had often taught in her father's mission schools and was well acquainted with the essential domestic and social arts. She was fluent in French, of course, that being the nearest thing to an international language and, also like Margaret, she played the piano with sufficient facility to be able to teach it.

Another less practical but potentially satisfying part of her plan was that upon her retirement from Georgiana's house, she would make one last visit to the community from which she'd been driven in shame. She would go there in the company of a titled European husband, hired for the occasion. She would stay in the finest hotel, give evidence of being annoyingly rich and happy for a few days, then confront both her father and the young man, now married, who had turned his back on her, announce publicly that she had forgiven him so that everyone would know that there was something to forgive, and announce that she and her husband would now and forever take their leave to his ancestral home in the south of France.

It pleased Margaret to learn, once she and Laura Hemmings had a chance to talk, that Little Annie had elected in the end to forgo the triumphant return to Providence. Instead, Annie took the name Laura Hemmings, the legitimacy of which Margaret did not bother to question, and moved directly to Greenwich, where she tested the waters for a year, laid her historical groundwork, and then announced the opening of Miss Hemmings's School for Young Ladies in a six-bedroom house on Maple Avenue, just a few hundred feet from Margaret's famous electric house.

"Does Tilden know?" was one of Margaret's excited questions when they spoke in the ladies' convenience at the Lenox House Hotel. "Or did Tilden suggest Greenwich to you as well?"

"Tilden has no idea," Laura Hemmings answered. "I've passed him twice while shopping on Main Street and he hasn't shown a glimmer of recognition. As long as I keep my hair out of my face and avoid middy blouses he'll be none the wiser. Tilden was never one of my Johnnies in any case."

"Oh, then we mustn't tell him," Margaret agreed. "You will be my great new friend from the Temperance Union—you *will* be my friend, won't you, Annie?"

"I will if you can stop calling me that."

"Yes, of course. And I'm Charlotte, although that name will sound especially strange when you say it. How long have you known I was here, for heaven's sake?"

"Almost since you arrived," Laura said, smiling. "I saw Tilden first. Remember, you can't get to that beacon of a house you live in without driving past mine.

John Flood tramped by a few times as well. Actually, I still wasn't sure it was you until you came to the door one evening to greet Dr. Palmer. I was waiting for him in his carriage." Laura's smile widened. "Dr. Palmer and I have been keeping company this past year."

"I remember the visit," Margaret said. "I asked him to bring the lady inside, but he said he'd only stay a minute. You must have been terrified that I'd blurt out your name."

Laura Hemmings took her hands. "Either that or I'd have shocked you into childbirth right then and there."

"I hope I'd have been glad. You were always so kind to me. I'd have been more worried about discomforting you."

"I was used to it." Laura's smile dimmed, but her eyes held their shine. "Yours is not the only familiar face I've seen in Greenwich."

Laura confided to Margaret, as she could have done with no one else, that they were not the only Greenwich ladies who were not entirely what they seemed. Carrie Todd, a dressmaker in the Sound Beach section, had probably been there longest. She was a prostitute turned abortionist, having learned that trade under Madame Restell some fifteen years earlier in New York. Upon Madame Restell's entrapment and subsequent suicide she fled the city. Laura wouldn't have known her at all but for a chance encounter when she and Georgiana were shopping for bolts of fabric at Macy's, and there was Carrie, in the city on a buying trip for her new business.

Next came Belle Walker, known simply as Spanky in her New York days because of her skill in satisfying a particular desire some men have. Spanky had married a former client, the eldest unwed son of the owner of Greenwich's largest oyster fleet. He was at least five years younger than Spanky, although he probably didn't know it. Spanky—Mrs. Walker—had been there three years and produced two children. She, too, recognized Carrie Todd, who might well have prevented several more during Spanky's early career. Belle Walker had no great fear of exposure or blackmail because Carrie had at least as much to hide, nor did Carrie wish anything more than to work quietly at her dressmaker's trade. But Belle, who was socially ambitious, had invented a past much grander than that of Laura or Margaret and despised Carrie Todd for knowing a different truth. She took every opportunity to belittle Carrie's dressmaking skills and her fashion sense in the hope of forcing her to seek customers elsewhere.

Belle recognized neither Margaret nor Laura. She was before Margaret's time at Georgiana's and she and Laura had overlapped only briefly, a matter of days. Georgiana had suggested that Belle might be better suited to a house whose standards were less exacting. It was then that she allowed young Frank Walker to save her.

It surprised as much as troubled Margaret that there were at least three former prostitutes, to say nothing of one near miss, in such a little town. But Laura, who had a head for mathematics, pointed out that if the statistics cited by various reformers were correct, there were twenty thousand prostitutes in New York and at least one in ten of these left the life each year or attempted to do so. Where did they go? Practically none, Margaret agreed, would return to their places of origin. Only a few would have gone abroad or headed west. Most would have chosen among the many quiet villages on the periphery of New York City. Laura postulated that the population density of former whores was probably greatest in the lower reaches of Westchester County, in northern New Jersey, and on the north shore of Long Island, gradually diminishing with distance. Further, the more polished among them would surely apply their arts to attracting the best of the local young gentry. That being the case, and with another two thousand retiring each year, Laura saw a day not more than a generation hence when the entire matriarchal leadership of suburban society would be composed of superannuated strumpets. The laws of statistics and of algebra seemed to require that this be so.

Margaret found the idea most amusing. Tilden laughed loudest of all when Margaret, speaking hypothetically and not mentioning Laura, outlined her theory for him.

In the end it was Belle Walker who made the smiles vanish. Belle Walker and Anthony Comstock. And Tilden would have cause to wonder whether Jay Gould himself didn't have a hand in it.

The newspapers, it seemed to Tilden, had been full of Anthony Comstock all his life. As a boy, and like many his age, he eagerly followed the often bizarre adventures of the curious figure who dedicated his being to a one-man war against smut in all its forms. And because Comstock found smut everywhere, there was always much for Tilden to read, whether in his clandestine copies of the *Police Gazette* or in his father's *New York Times*.

The *Times* called Comstock the Paladin of Purity but not, Tilden thought, without a touch of mockery. But Comstock made good and frequent copy with his indiscriminate raids. He seemed to see little difference between libraries, art galleries, and the pornography shops along Ann and Nassau streets. Publishers of popular fiction were also among his targets. He admitted to a reporter that he had once wasted half a day reading a novel. But he never picked up another, he said, except to explore it for its content of smut.

This portly, muttonchopped figure also crusaded against abortion, birth control, and the publication of any information concerning either. He decried any form of nudity in works of art and any painted scene that seemed to hint at impropriety, including those which showed a man and a woman with no chaperone in sight. That was smut. One had only to look deeply and he would see it. Comstock was also the enemy of alcohol, betting parlors, punchboards, and scented stationery in sealed envelopes. He caused the arrest of a woman who had used a mildly salacious expression in a perfumed letter sent to her own husband through the mails. Tilden remembered this well because accounts of it so outraged his father that it was one of the rare times Comstock was discussed at the dinner table. What most incensed Stanton Beckwith was that Comstock's "disgraceful peeping" was legal. Comstock had been almost single-handedly responsible for the passage by Congress of a bill prohibiting the mailing of any lewd, obscene, lascivious, or filthy matter. He asked for and got an appointment as special postal officer to enforce the new law. The problem of defining obscenity was left entirely up to Comstock, who knew it when he saw it. Now even a serious article describing the physical dangers of abortion could not be sent through the mails except at risk of a jail term.

The most sensational of Comstock's forays against abortion came when Tilden was about seventeen. There was a particular mansion on Fifth Avenue, on the northeast corner of Fifty-second Street, which he had never heard discussed in any voice louder than a whisper. It was a place where heavily draped carriages, and sometimes hearses, pulled up to a side door in the darkest part of night. It was where terrified daughters of wealthy men went to be rid of their shame and where even married women went to be free of unwanted or embarrassing babies. Although Tilden did not fully understand how this was accomplished, there was clearly great profit in it. The house was an ornate brownstone far larger than his father's and, although rather far to the north, it was in an area rapidly becoming fashionable. And the owner of that house, a certain Madame Restell, had the habit of taking the air each day in a most elegant barouche attended by two liveried footmen. Tilden had often seen her while coaching in Central Park. Though her hair was still black, she was an older woman, thin, with sharp features. She would smile and nod at passing coaches and that was strange, because the occupants of those coaches would almost always turn their faces away. Far from taking offense, she seemed to find a curious pleasure in that.

By this time, the year being 1878, Madame Restell was essentially in retirement. But Anthony Comstock had vowed that she would not escape temporal punishment for her crimes. He went to her, disguised, wearing a rich man's clothing and having shaved off his muttonchops for the occasion, and begged an interview. Tears streaming down his cheeks, he said that his dear wife was with child but her health was so frail that she could not survive the torment of another birthing. Even now she waited, pale and weak, in a carriage nearby, for word that she might live through the mercy and artistry of Madame Restell. Comstock collapsed into sobs and Madame Restell, cautious at first, relented. Comstock promptly arrested her. To her great surprise, she was indicted solely on the strength of Comstock's testimony. Several newspapers, under pressure from the YMCA, which largely funded Comstock's activities, began trumpeting the end of her nefarious career. These same newspapers, which had willingly accepted transparent advertisements for her discreet midwifery and her Infallible French Female Pills, now seemed bent on being rid of her. Her greatest crime, Tilden heard it observed, was that she lived in a part of town where the Vanderbilts were planning fine homes, but she was not an acceptable neighbor. Sixty-seven years old, and facing the certain prospect of a long jail sentence, Madame Restell retired to her marble bathroom and opened a vein at her throat. Thousands of women of good family breathed silent relief that their secrets were at last safe. Madame Restell's assistants, Carrie Todd among them, scattered with the wind. Comstock, however, received little praise. The *Times* and the *Sun* roundly condemned him for driving her to suicide by means of fraud. He was unabashed. Madame Restell's was one of fifteen suicides he would boast of causing.

As Tilden grew older, what was once titillating became tiresome. And Comstock became so indiscriminate in his assaults that newspaper editors and cartoonists now saw him as a buffoon. In 1887, Comstock took it into his head to declare war on the living French artists of the Barbizon school. He raided the respected art gallery of Herman Knoedler and confiscated all the works of Henner, Perrault, and Bougereau, including prints of the huge Bougereau that hung in the Hoffman House bar. He tried to get that taken down as well but was heaved into the street by patrons.

But Anthony Comstock had not otherwise touched Tilden's life until one June day in 1891, when he thundered into the office of the *Greenwich Graphic*. Comstock announced to the startled editor that the town of Greenwich had a cancer festering within its borders. A blood-soaked abortionist, a butcher of sweethearts, had disguised herself as a dressmaker, and if the editor would accompany him to her place of business, they would doubtless discover instruments suited to a purpose far more evil than the stitching of feminine adornment. The two men went but found nothing incriminating, Carrie Todd having fully abandoned her past. There were, in fact, at least two other abortionists in the vicinity who did a substantial business, abortion being the most common method of birth control and in the end usually cheaper than the accumulated cost of

those rolled rubber skins, which sold for a full dollar
each.

Carrie, as it happened, had a common "female
problem" and was being treated for it by Dr. Miles
Palmer. Among her private records, Comstock found
references to frequent visits to his office but no indication in her ledgers that she had paid him for his services. Having secured the distraught dressmaker's
arrest on the promise of evidence to come, Comstock
went to confront Miles Palmer. He had vaulted to the
conclusion that the two must be in business together.
Miles Palmer held his temper. Carrie was a patient, no
more, no less, her complaint being none of Comstock's
business. Like many of his patients, she paid for her
treatment by the barter of goods. When Comstock demanded an examination of his records, Miles Palmer
suggested that he leave while he still could under his
own power. Comstock persisted, asking why the doctor
should wish to be paid in ladies' dresses and demanding
a list of their final recipients. Miles Palmer, without a
word, then dragged Comstock to the second-floor landing and threw him down the stairs, breaking a banister
and three of Comstock's ribs.

Comstock was not discouraged. He announced
that by the time his injuries healed he would have
rooted out all that was putrescent in the town. He
claimed to have new information charging that more
than one notorious prostitute from the New York flesh
pits had sought to deny her past and was living in
Greenwich under the guise of respectability. Modern
invention, he announced, would help him drive the
guilty from their hiding places. With one of the new
Kodak Detective cameras he would range through
Greenwich taking photographs of any woman who
might conceivably have been attractive enough that a
certain type of man might have paid for her entertainments. These photographs would be shown to the New

York City Police for identification of the tainted. Comstock could not be discouraged. He was knocked down or canned at least three more times by outraged husbands or fathers, was slapped or otherwise belabored by a score of women, and had two cameras smashed, one directly over his head. Far more men and women, however, meekly submitted, fearful that any show of reluctance would be wrongly interpreted.

Tilden, in the beginning at least, was more annoyed than concerned. Comstock had done this sort of thing before and not much ever came of it. He'd once made a show of purifying nearby New Canaan, presumably because he was born there and still owned the family farm, except in that case his focus had been more on the public library, a small brewery, and a dance class. Nor was Laura Hemmings at all worried. Her past, she felt sure, was known only to Margaret. If Tilden did recognize her he was being a gentleman about it. And she was sure no one in New York would know her likeness the way she looked and dressed now. Nevertheless, when Comstock first approached her as she roller-skated with her pupils at Ray's Hall, she slapped his face on general principles.

Nor was Margaret particularly concerned at the start, except for poor Carrie Todd. Margaret, as Laura pointed out, had hardly been in the mainstream of New York's flesh industry. But the more Margaret saw of Comstock in the streets of Greenwich, and the more she saw other women scurry to avoid him, the more her mind began to work. She thought not so much in terms of discovery but of the devastation that would result. She would lose her lovely home. She could never remain in Greenwich. All the friends she'd made would turn away. Even Laura might not dare stand by her. She would lose Tilden. If he would not take her as his honest wife even after she bore his child and was respected in the eyes of all who knew her, what could she expect if she were publicly branded? The life of her son, Jonathan, might be shattered and shamed almost before it began. What would he think of her once he was old enough to understand the taunts of schoolmates? Would he draw away at her touch?

This was Margaret's state of mind on the day when Anthony Comstock brought his Detective camera to the regular Wednesday meeting of the Women's Christian Temperance Union.

It was also the day on which Tilden, who had been watching a growing anxiety in Margaret, was seen whipping a horse on the Post Road in the direction of Westchester, an expression of black rage upon his face. Unseen, crushed in his pocket, was a letter in Jay Gould's hand.

SIXTEEN

 HE TREES OF RAILROAD AVENUE WERE BARE AGAIN and laced with snow. Corbin rubbed his face. For a brief moment he thought he was caught in some netherworld between then and now, because the sweep of the town landscape was the same and even the Walkers' seafood store remained where he'd seen it, although the awning and tubs were gone. He felt a dim urge to hurl a brick through the Walkers' window. He did not quite know why. Nor did he dwell on it or speak again to Tilden. Just get the car, he told himself. Get the car and get back home.

His secondhand Datsun was one of only a handful left in the station lot. Corbin used his hands to sweep the snow from his trunk and then extracted a small folding shovel, which he used to clear a path behind the rear tires. The Datsun started without great protest.

Corbin sat for a while, letting the engine warm. He could feel heat building within himself as well. A low level of anger. He was not having much difficulty now separating Tilden's thoughts from his own. Tilden's part had to do with the heavyset man with the whiskers and the camera, Comstock, and with one of the Walker women, Belle by name. Corbin wasn't really sure what she'd done. And Gould. Tilden always seemed to be stewing about Gould. Corbin wondered whether Gould could actually have done even half the things Tilden seemed to blame him for. Gould must have had better things to do than spend his life hounding Tilden and the other man, Cyrus Field. Anyway, they were all long dead. Everyone was dead. So what did it matter? There was no more use in brooding over those old hurts than there was in chewing on the bitter moments of your own life. They were just as dead, although you wouldn't think so the way they keep bubbling up to the surface at odd moments. Corbin wondered if his own grandson, if he ever had one, would someday feel the vague sting of one of the ordinary minor humiliations of Corbin's life. Maybe he'd wake up in the middle of the night feeling crushed because his grandfather was left off an invitation list fifty years earlier. Maybe he'd have nightmares about getting beaten up by two aging thugs in an underground garage. Genetic memory. Corbin put the car in gear. Genetic memory is a pain in the ass.

Sorry, Tilden. It's all over. You and Margaret have taken up enough of my life, and I'm finished with you. God, I can't believe what a twerp I've been. Like a puppet with you pulling the strings. If I think any more about this I'm going to feel about you the way you feel about Gould, and it isn't worth the effort.

Gould. Anger.

"No dice." Corbin shook his head, then cut the Datsun out of its parking space. "I'm going to drive straight up to Maple Avenue, I'm going to go inside, and I'm going to tell Gwen that I'm unloading that house and everything in it. I'll tell that terrific lady that I can't believe she stuck with me this long and why don't we see how fast we can get on a plane to Barbados where we'll lie in the sun and cook all this right out of me. I'll teach her to scuba dive and to wind surf. I'll dance her feet off and bring her breakfast in bed. While she's eating it I'll think up new ways to show her that five minutes with her is worth all the Christmas mornings of my life."

Corbin was saying these things aloud as he pulled out of the station lot and made the two right turns that would wind him back toward Milbank Avenue. But then he made a third right turn and found himself on the Greenwich entrance ramp to the Connecticut Turnpike. Corbin cursed. He slowed and stopped, checking his rearview mirror, then allowed the car to coast backward down the ramp.

Gould. Please. Corbin heard it. Or felt it.

"Uh-uh." He shook his head. "Not Gould. Gwen."

Please.

"Oh, nuts!" A pickup truck was turning into the ramp behind him. Corbin angled over to the side to let it pass.

Please, Jonathan.

"Shut up!" Corbin said sharply. "Jay Gould is dead, and even if he wasn't I just told you I'm . . ." He took a long breath. "Look at this. I just decided I'm through being crazy and here I am sitting around arguing with you."

He'll hurt Margaret.

Corbin sighed again and sat back. Barbados was looking better by the second. Yet for the first time since he realized who Tilden was and what he was, Corbin began to feel sorry for him. If Tilden was real, right now, even if he was a real ghost, which seemed to make more sense than to believe he was just a collection of stored memories, he seemed stuck in time. Whether or not Jay Gould hurt Margaret, it's done. It's over. And Tilden and Margaret both survived. If Sturdevant's right, Tilden lived about another fifty years, which isn't all bad, and Margaret—Grandma Corbin—lived at least that long.

Then there's Anthony Comstock. Tilden wants me to share his anger at Comstock, and at Belle Walker for some reason, and even at Laura Hemmings, because they all had something to do with Margaret's packing off to Chicago. But so what? In the next fifty years, nothing good happened? There must have been a whole sequence of . . .

"Sequence," Corbin whispered. Everything so far was in sequence. Tilden's memories. Or the memories that are Tilden. All the little scenes that played in Corbin's mind. They were all in sequence. Sitting with Gwen before and having all those buzzing thoughts, like about Teddy Roosevelt's new book and taking a walk with J. P. Morgan—none of it made any sense until he got it in some kind of order. Maybe that's Tilden's problem. He can't just put this thing on fast forward and leap ahead. Maybe it's what keeps him around.

"Look." Corbin turned to the passenger seat as if Tilden were sitting there, then realized what he was doing and slapped himself on the head. He closed his eyes. "Look, Tilden," he said quietly, "Gould's house is maybe twenty minutes from here if the roads are decent. It's over on the Hudson." Which you know damn well, but we're not even going to think about how *I* know it. "You know it's a museum now, right? There aren't any Goulds there." In reply, Corbin felt only a distant feeling of profound relief. "All I'm going to do is a flyby because I want to get back before Gwen worries more than she has already. If that gets you off the dime, fine. But whether it does or not, I have to tell you"—Corbin depressed his clutch and put the car in first—"I'm out of here and headed south. If I were you I'd head for Chicago, which you should have done in the first place."

"You called it real good, Miss Beckwith." Tom Burke reentered the shambles of Ella Beckwith's oversized study. Snow crystals clung to his hair and shoulders, and his trousers were stained white on one side with pulverized plaster. He held out a blue spiral notebook in his hand. "It was stuck behind the backseat in his car."

Ella tilted her head distractedly, but her eyes remained locked on the crumpled pile that was Raymond Lesko. She knew the notebook would be close by, if not on his person then in his car. He'd as much as said so when she mentioned the fifteen thousand dollars he'd already been paid and his hand went involuntarily to his breast pocket. He would have left the money in a safe place if he'd had the chance. And if he'd thought to conceal anything at all, it would have been his notes. If he still carried one, he carried the other.

Lawrence Ballanchine limped forward and snatched the notebook from Tom Burke's hand. "You still took a terrible risk," he muttered toward Ella. "You can't be sure he didn't have this photocopied." The little man still managed to sound peevish, although his clothing was limp with perspiration and his right leg was bloodied below the knee where one of Lesko's wild shots had grazed it.

"He didn't copy it." Burke walked to Lesko's side and kicked it. There was no response. "If he made a copy"—he looked up at Ella as if for approval—"that's what he would have brought. You stash the original, not the copy. Miss Beckwith knew that right away."

"He is ruining my carpet." Ella's voice was small and distant.

Ballanchine leaned over with difficulty and picked

up a copy of *Architectural Digest* that lay amid the
shattered glass of a collapsed coffee table. He slid it
under Lesko's head, then wiped his hands against his
lapels. "I don't know what we're going to do about this
mess," he said, scanning the room. He counted seven
ragged holes in the plaster walls, including the two
Lesko had aimed at Burke earlier when Burke tried to
force the door. One shot had also smashed a banjo
clock and another tore the stuffing from an upholstered
chair. And one, he noticed with a shudder, was ac-
cented by a tiny spray of his own flesh and blood. Ballanchine was afraid to think of what the adjoining
rooms might look like.

"Is he dead?" Ella asked.

"I don't think so," Burke told her. "Not yet, anyway."

"Well, what are we supposed to do with him?" Ballanchine asked with distaste.

Tom Burke rubbed his hands. "I figure we load him
in his trunk. We leave him there until he's stiff. Then
tonight we drive him down to Rye or some other hick
Westchester town and we dump him one place and the
car in another. Maybe we pour some vodka into him so
the cops figure he got drunk and took a fall before he
could remember where he parked." Burke waited for
Ella Beckwith's approval, but she did not seem to be
listening. Ballanchine had turned pale, appalled at the
prospect of touching Lesko's body at least two more
times and keeping him refrigerated in between. "Unless," Tom Burke spoke the alternative, "you want to
just give him another good rap on the head for insurance and then call the local cops. You tell him he came
in here and threatened you; you can say he claimed he
had something on your brother, maybe, then you show
them how he shot up the place, and we say it's me or
Mr. Ballanchine here who whacked him first chance
we got."

"No." Ella blinked. "No police."

"You're better off," Burke agreed. It pleased him that she saw him and not Ballanchine to be in control of the situation. "You probably have some paint and plaster down in the basement. Me and Mr. Ballanchine can clean up this place before any of the help sees it."

"Paint and plaster?" Ella's head jerked.

"There's usually some left over. The same color. I've done this before."

"Paint and plaster," she repeated aloud. The absurdity of discussing cosmetic repairs while this possibly dying detective lay at their feet hastened her recovery from whatever had seized her thoughts. "Does either of you recall that my brother has left this house in a drunken state, carrying a rifle?"

"I was going to go look for him," Tom Burke said lamely. In fact, like nearly everyone else, Burke had become accustomed to ignoring Tillie Beckwith.

Ella's expression turned wistful as she looked down once more at the blood-caked head of Raymond Lesko, a part of her wishing that an accommodation might have been possible. You were so right, sir, she thought. The man is an ass.

"Lawrence"—she closed her eyes—"tell Mr. Burke where my brother can be found."

"At Corbin's house," Ballanchine replied.

"Tell him why he went there, please."

"With the gun? He went to try to shoot a ghost."

"That being established, would you both kindly go and retrieve him? Do so at once, please."

Burke reached for his trench coat, which was on the floor where Lesko had dropped it.

"Use this man's car," she said, pointing to Lesko. "Be good enough to take him with you."

Burke caught Ballanchine's eye and indicated with a gesture that Lesko's feet would be his portion of the load. Ballanchine looked ill, but he hobbled forward.

"Mr. Burke"—Ella raised a hand after they'd lifted Lesko—"I want this ended. If you fail to intercept my brother before he speaks to any of those people, I want it ended tonight. Do nothing, however, without Mr. Ballanchine's expressed approval."

"Yes, ma'am."

"Lawrence?"

"Yes, Ella."

"My brother has been a great source of worry and embarrassment all my life."

"I know."

"End that as well, Lawrence."

Overlooking the Hudson River, twenty minutes from Greenwich "if the roads are decent," there is a spectacular stretch of rolling hills which so reminded the early Dutch traders of the upper Rhine Valley that they began building great manor houses there as they prospered in the fur trade. Stone castles, many with keeps and turrets, rose on commanding sweeps of land that resembled Old World baronies. Jay Gould, it was said, chose this place to build what he hoped would become an ancestral home because Newport had been closed to him. But it was also argued that the choice was Gould's. The lonely grandeur of the place was much more suited to a solitary man who'd shown not the slightest interest in the lavish ritual entertainments and the stultifying dinner conversations that were a way of life in the colonies of the very rich. Lyndhurst—the patrician name he gave to the brooding Gothic castle he commissioned—had other advantages. It was private. Once the pine forest closed around Gould upon entering his estate, he could as well have been in Europe, yet he was always only an hour from New York by steam launch. Should the sudden need to cross a state line arise, he was an even shorter time away from the friendly protection of the New Jersey authorities.

Corbin remembered how he'd known of Lyndhurst. Photographs of it as it looked when it was built and as it looked today, which were virtually the same, appeared in several of the picture books Gwen had found in Barnes & Noble's. Was that only yesterday? And did it explain how, as he drew nearer the Hudson River, he began to see the plan of Gould's landscape in his mind, and the interiors of certain rooms, and to hear the sounds of one of those ghostly brawls, the one with so much smashing of glass.

Corbin began to curse himself for doing this. The roads were not decent. Fifteen minutes had passed and he hadn't even reached White Plains. It was stupid. Worse, it was dangerous. He was beginning to see things. If he allowed his attention to wander, if he did not concentrate fully on who and where he was and on keeping the Datsun under tight control, he would begin to imagine that he saw the rhythmic jouncing of a horse's head and rump just beyond his hood. Twice he blinked that image away and twice it returned. When it appeared the second time he also felt that the steering wheel he held was softening into a pair of leather reins.

"This is all I need." He raised his voice. "All I need is to have to hit my brakes because I see a truck up ahead and all I get is you pulling on some goddamned straps that aren't there."

The bobbing horse faded. Corbin heard the word *sorry*. He grimaced on realizing that his own lips had formed it.

A few minutes later, Corbin wasn't all that sure he was better off without the horse. At least it wasn't snowing so hard when the horse was there. It was hardly snowing at all. And the grass along the side of the road was green and tall, not matted and dead under a foot of wet snow, and there were apple trees hanging heavy with fruit. But the gentler season brought no gentler thoughts. There was only worry, and anger, and the determination to look into the eye of the man who was at its source, to finish with him, and then get back to Margaret and be able to tell her she was safe, that she had nothing more to fear, to be there waiting for her when she came home from the meeting she'd so dreaded attending and to take her in his arms . . .

"Cut that out," Corbin snapped.

Sorry. Yes.

"I also have to keep this car on the road. I can only do one thing at a time."

Yes.

Corbin saw the sign for Tarrytown. *Off here, go left on Route 9 to Irvington.*

"What meeting, by the way?"

No answer came. Only a jumble of impressions and images. There was the Temperance Union. And Comstock with his dumb camera. That must have been it. Comstock's taking pictures of whole groups now. And there was Laura Hemmings saying something about smiling sweetly and looking righteous. And Tilden wondering what Margaret and her friend, whom he knew perfectly well was not always named Laura but he would go along with the game if that is what she wished, seemed to be whispering about all the time. And wishing Laura would leave so that he could sit Margaret down and tell her what a blockhead he'd been for not asking her with the greatest of pride to be his wife and to show her the papers he'd already drawn up, not just the letter acknowledging Jonathan as his son, and the free and clear deed to the Greenwich house, but see, an affidavit affirming that Jonathan is in fact my only son, and the names of witnesses who have sworn to hearing Ansel Carling boast that it was he who fathered Ella's child, and here, a statement of your account at the bank in Greenwich—you'll see that a handsome sum has been deposited so that you need never feel bound to me. Do not answer now, dear Margaret, but later. Go to your meeting with your head held high while I do one errand that is required of me. We will talk later. We'll open one of your forbidden bottles and plan the day. Who should be my best man? Teddy, do you think, or should I ask John Flood? John Flood in stripes and swallowtail—wouldn't that be a sight? Or the wedding can be small if you prefer, small and private, though for myself I'd want the whole world watching. Oh, Margaret, Margaret, please be there.

"Tilden?" Corbin saw the gates of Lyndhurst ahead of him. "Tilden, why are we doing this?" He felt a growing agony, which he knew was not his own.

Gould.

"He's not here. The man's dead. If you're worried about Margaret, why don't we just turn around and go back?" Corbin was aware of the logical inconsistency within that question, but it seemed to fit the situation.

Your harlot mistress . . . your hidden son . . . Corbin saw the words in his mind. Saw them. They were written in ink.

"What's that? A letter?"

. . . that it might be in your interest, therefore, to accommodate me in this matter.

"From Gould. He's trying to blackmail you? What for?"

. . . an interview at your earliest convenience . . . I trust in the meantime that Mr. Comstock's activities are causing you no great distress.

"Gould." Corbin knew. He felt Tilden's growing rage. "Gould sent Comstock." But even as he said those words, Corbin doubted them. He couldn't imagine why Jay Gould would bother. Or what he'd want from Tilden. Unless it was that old business about Cyrus Field. "Listen, why do you let him get to you like this? You decided to marry Margaret no matter what, so marry her."

Gwen is a slut. A whore.

The words shocked Corbin. He could not believe they were coming from Tilden.

To hurt Jonathan, hurt Gwen. He married a whore. His children will be whoresons.

"Tilden"—the anger was now Corbin's own—"what are you trying to do?"

Do as I wish. Now. Always. Or I will point and say slut, whore.

"I guess I get your point." Corbin chewed his lip. "But fuck off, Tilden."

"Tilden?"

Corbin turned into the long driveway. There was an immense greenhouse on his right. Ahead of him he could make out the gray silhouette of Lyndhurst. He peered through his windshield in search of a parking area. He saw no signs. There should have been signs.

He heard a crunching sound under his wheels that sounded like gravel. Gravel. He shouldn't hear gravel. And now the horse was trying to form again and the snow on the ground was turning into a greenish smoke and the trees were thickening.

"No you don't." Corbin wiped the horse away. "I'm heading back right now."

He felt a brief moment of panic when he could not find the gearshift. But it was there. His hand found it. He'd just lost it for a moment in the dim light inside his car.

"And I'll tell you something else." Corbin groped for his clutch pedal with his foot. Where the hell was his clutch pedal? "If you think I'm going to walk through the whole rest of your life with you step by step, you're nuts. This is as far as I go."

Corbin looked up.

And when he did, he had only a quickly fading memory of the words he'd just spoken. A puzzled memory. He had no idea now what they meant, nor what it was that he was searching for on the floorboards of his carriage. He dismissed it from his mind. His attention was fixed upon the massive oak door in front of him and the consumptive little weasel who would be waiting behind it.

Tilden had withdrawn a card from his case and out of habit began to bend up its right end to indicate that he was there in person and wished to be received. He crumpled it in his fist and gave a violent pull to the door chime. This was not a day for social niceties. He would push past the butler if he must, but he would damn well be received.

There was no butler. The door opened upon a large, hard-eyed man who wore a jacket that could not close across his chest. Tilden hesitated, measuring him, then took a step forward. The man only smiled and beckoned him inside.

"Good afternoon to you, Mr. Beckwith." He attempted an unpracticed bow. "Himself will be down in just a minute when he gets some clothes on. He seen you comin' up the road."

"We've met before." Tilden paused at the threshold. "The last time, you were holding a Winchester across your chest."

"You got a good eye, sir." The man's smile seemed good-natured. "And you was holdin' old Mr. Hacker out a top-floor window down to the Western Union Building. There was them who was sorta hopin' you'd get the dropsy, Mr. Gould among 'em the way it turned out."

The big man moved to close the door, but Tilden put a hand on it. No butler. No downstairs maid polishing and dusting. No kitchen smells. He began to wish he'd thought to bring John Flood to stand at his back. "Why don't I see any household staff?" Tilden asked. His left hand curled into a fist.

The big man, his name was Charley Murtree, understood. "The boss, he told us you might get spooked. He said I should tell you right off we ain't startin' nothin' if you don't. You got my word on that, but to tell you true, I'd sorta like to try you. I mean that friendly, now."

Tilden forced a smile. "I'd pay to see that myself." There were two Winchesters that day, he recalled, and this one had just said the boss told *us*. He braced himself to throw a short left hook. If he was in trouble, the time to cut the odds was now. But the bigger man, his smile faded and his gray eyes flat, held up a hand.

"I said you got my word, Hoss."

Murtree stomped a heel twice against the floor and another man, the second Winchester, stepped from a room off the entrance hall. "I'm Murtree, this fella's name is Calicoon." The good humor crept back. "Me, I'm Mr. Gould's bodyguard and old Calicoon here, he's mine. That quick left hand of yours would have got you a knot on the head and there wouldn't have been no call for it."

Tilden nodded to the one called Calicoon, who winked back at him. But Tilden stayed within the arc of the open door.

"Mr. Gould asked me to tell you some things"— Murtree began rolling a smoke—"to sort of pack them out of the way before you and him talk. Now this first thing, I'm to tell you I don't know what it means but you will. He says that what Ansel Carling set out to do for Mr. Gould was one thing, how he went about it was something else. I think that means whatever else Carling did along the way, Mr. Gould didn't know until he bragged on it and Mr. Gould didn't like it one bit because it wudn't his style."

Tilden drew a contemptuous breath.

"Ask me," Murtree said, "he's tellin' it true. Anyway, you won't see Ansel Carling no more. Some Texas Comanch' hung him upside down from a fence and cooked his brains. Old Mr. Hacker, he got off with just drawin' his pay."

Tilden blinked. "Cooked his brains?"

"Fella like that"—Murtree shrugged—"it's only a question of time till he gets shot, cut, or hung. He's a slippin' and slidin' sort of fella. Must of had a real careless upbringin'. I don't know why Mr. Gould didn't fire him outright instead of packin' him off down to the Texas Pacific line. I figure Carling had a hold-out ace or two, but that Mr. Gould, he's real smart about givin' people enough rope to do themselves. One day he's out ridin' track, shootin' antelope to pass the time, and he comes on this water tower with two Comanch' boys playin' in it. He shot 'em both. Next day the Comanch' send word there ain't no trains movin' till they get the man what done it and any man or Chinee who goes out from camp is goin' to lose his hair. The track boss, he's Calicoon here's daddy, he gives Carling a gun with one load in it and throws him off a track layer. Damn fool should have used that load. Feller died hard."

Tilden felt sickened in spite of himself. He also found himself wondering how Jay Gould could have orchestrated a minor Indian uprising or whether the Comanche episode was a chance occurrence that saved him the trouble of executing some other plan. He had the feeling that Calicoon's "daddy" would have terminated the Gould-Carling relationship one way or the other.

"Mr. Murtree"—Tilden cleared his throat—"do you by chance know why I've been called here?"

Murtree shook his head and spit a shred of tobacco through the open door. "He's got somethin' in his craw, for sure. I don't think it's against you, though. I got so I could tell when he respects a man and when he don't. Likely he means to tell you soon enough."

"And when will that be, sir?"

Murtree gestured toward a bell cord. "Soon as I pull that there rope which tells him you gave your word you and him can have a talk without me and Calicoon havin' to tag along. Mr. Gould ain't no coward but he ain't no fool. He knows about that left hand."

"You think I'd strike that sick little man?"

"I don't. But I'll need your word."

"You have it."

Charley Murtree pulled the cord.

"Walk with me, Mr. Beckwith." Gould's soft voice came from the carriage drive outside. He'd gone out some other way. A secret passage would not have surprised Tilden. The small man gathered his lapels across his thin chest although the day was mild. He stifled a cough, then gestured toward his greenhouse, indicating it as their direction. He did not offer his hand when Tilden joined him. He kept both behind his back.

"That business with Morgan"—Gould almost smiled—"walking through the exchange with his arm around you. Neatly done, Mr. Beckwith. Very neatly done indeed."

Tilden saw no point in admitting that he scarcely knew what was happening at the time.

"Has it occurred to you, sir," Gould asked, "that your maneuver with Morgan had an element of fraud to it? You were, after all, implying a close tie with him for the purpose of improving your income."

"Mr. Gould." Tilden stopped. "If you hope to establish that your standards and mine are the same at bottom, it's going to be a long afternoon."

"Ah yes, my standards." Gould began walking again, shook his head, then stopped once more. "I am trying, Mr. Beckwith, to communicate with you. Clumsily, perhaps, I am trying to find common ground. Please do not be so arrogant as to reduce our relationship to good versus evil."

Gould had a point and Tilden knew it. He was playing the white knight against Gould's dark angel. With another man, Tilden might have apologized for being tiresome.

"You once purchased some intelligence from Colonel Mann. Correctly used, it could have caused me some embarrassment. I am told you declined to use it at all. Why was that, Mr. Beckwith?"

"That intelligence concerned Carling, not you."

"But still you did not use it."

Tilden drew a breath. "All I wanted of Carling was that he leave New York before I killed him. As it happened, he left of his own accord."

Gould did not dispute on whose account Carling had left. "You could have hurt me with it. The fact that he duped me with a false history could have cost me the confidence of some men and encouraged boldness in others. The fact that he was actually a Jew named Koenig would have been delicious to those who insist I am a denied Jew myself."

"Extortion is Colonel Mann's field, Mr. Gould," Tilden answered. "I do not care to compete in it. In any event, I'm sure it would not have bothered you in the slightest."

"If you prick us, sir, do we not bleed?"

Tilden sighed. "I know that you are not a Jew, sir. Not that I care a damn one way or the other."

"How do you know?"

"My father told me."

"He told you what?" Gould raised a hand upon seeing Tilden's impatience with this irrelevancy. "Please. Indulge my curiosity on this and I will satisfy any of yours."

"He said," Tilden answered with strained patience,

"that you come from Yankee Protestant stock. He said that this Jewish business persists only because there is so little else that is vulnerable about you and because you encourage it. He remarked that you are wise enough not to reward such people with even a denial. Better to let them chew on it, be distracted by it, he said."

"While I do what, exactly?"

"My father's words or mine?"

"I have an idea I'd like your father's better."

"He . . . appreciates you," Tilden admitted, "though with reservations. He has approximately the same attitude toward Genghis Khan, Attila the Hun, and the entire British nation."

"That I am a plunderer, you mean." Gould seemed disappointed.

"No." Tilden softened. "He does admire your tenacity. It is a quality I have observed in you myself."

Gould suddenly bent forward. A coughing fit swelled and then burst from his chest. Tilden saw a spray of blood in the handkerchief he held. Gould did not have the look of a man who had time for much more mischief.

"And you, Mr. Beckwith," he gasped as he recovered, "what do you think of me? I ask, not to invite an insult, but to understand the mind of a man who would choose me as an enemy without hope of gain."

"There actually are men who act out of decency, sir. My father is one of them. I do my best to follow his example."

"Not in all things, it seems. He did not condemn me so roundly as you do."

"No," Tilden had to acknowledge. "In truth he did not."

"He is quite a remarkable man," Tilden's father had said to him. "He has built a great fortune upon the single premise that most other men are thieves at heart.

He is not at all like the other money-getters and manipulators. They are opportunists for the most part. They are raiders and profiteers. They attack and they withdraw. But Jay Gould keeps coming with a dreadful and unshakable singleness of purpose, for he always has a plan that looks several moves ahead, in the manner of a chess champion. The tenacity of this feared and silent little man is his power, you see.

"Imagine if the devil himself appeared in New York and stood on the sidewalk outside the exchange, staring at it by the hour, then at last letting his eyes grow narrow and permitting a smile to pull at the corners of his mouth. Why, you'd have traders scrambling out the windows and running for their lives up the hill toward Trinity Church. Jay Gould has nearly the same effect. He has but to cast an interested eye upon a business firm and its shareholders fall over each other getting out of harm's way. When the timid have sold enough shares and the price of the rest is low enough, Gould buys control. Now it is the investors who sit and watch like vultures. Did Gould buy this company because it is an inconvenience to his larger schemes and is therefore to be destroyed? Or is it essential to his schemes and therefore to be raised up? They watch the stock prices. If they begin rising, those who would ride on Jay Gould's coattails leap aboard and force them quickly higher. The prudent ones take a decent profit and get out. The reckless ones stay, confident that they can scurry for cover at the first sign that Gould is setting another ambuscade for them.

"Gould, of course, is watching them as well. At the first sign of caution he will lull them with good news through some newspaper or politician he controls. When their guard is down, when they begin buying all the more heavily, he will knock out the pins and catch them all. I see little evil in this, Tilden, because the victims all know the game they are in and are most often defeated by their own greed. And yet they groan and tear their hair and rail against this 'silent little Jew' and his trickery."

"It is said of me"—Jay Gould stopped at the door of his immense greenhouse—"that I see all men and their works as my lawful prey. It is said that I see good in no one. That kindness, loyalty, honesty, and all the other virtues are foreign to me. In my heart, Tilden Beckwith, I believe this not to be true. But I have chosen, upon hard lessons, to live my life with the certain knowledge that any man I trust will turn and feed on me sooner or later. I am not often disappointed. This Ansel Carling business came as no great disillusionment."

"It is true that he's dead, by the way?"

Gould nodded. "We are both well rid of him. But I'm afraid he will haunt you far longer than me. If you had used that intelligence of Colonel Mann's, you are quite correct that it would not have bothered me. But I would have turned it on you. I would have caused it to be widely known that your little boy, the one you named Huntington, is not a Beckwith at all but the son of a Jewish former convict, swindler, and assassin named Asa Koenig."

Tilden's eyes flared but Gould raised both hands. "Mann lied to you, of course. He tried to sell it to me first. I'd have no part of it."

"What is it you want, then?"

"Come." He opened the door at one end of the greenhouse. "I will show you something very beautiful."

The greenhouse, which Tilden had seen upon entering Lyndhurst, was fully three times the size of the largest he had ever seen before. It was warmed to a tropical climate by a series of copper stoves upon which kettles of water simmered, causing a mist of fine rain to hang in the air. There were orchids everywhere. Thousands of them.

"It is where I find peace," Gould whispered as if in a church. "When the sun is right, you can see a rainbow in here." He pinched a withered leaf off a nearby plant and touched the wound gently with his fingertips. "I have developed several new varieties, you know. The Horticultural Society has given my name to two thus far, and to a new rose as well."

Tilden wondered if his family received such affection. "Where is your family, by the way?" he asked, remembering the empty house, which had seemed so ominous.

"On my yacht," Gould answered absently, "taking the sea air." He saw an ant on the labellum of one of his prize lady's slippers. He brushed it off.

"And your servants? I saw no butler."

Gould looked up. "You suspect a snare, don't you." He smiled. "There is no butler here, Mr. Beckwith. Nor are there liveried footmen standing at every door with doubtful coats of arms etched on their buttons. I have no interest in that foolishness. There are two cooks and two maids here at Lyndhurst, and perhaps a dozen groundskeepers and gardeners. That is all."

"And your bodyguards."

"And my bodyguards," Gould acknowledged. "They are also companions. Have you ever tried to converse with a butler? Men of business are even worse. They choose their words so carefully, even on superficial matters. Ask one of them the time of day and he'll wonder what design is behind your question."

Probably with good reason, Tilden thought. Gould was attempting to relax him, he knew, although he did not know how the man could hope for it in view of the language of the note he'd sent. *Your harlot mistress. Your hidden son. Comstock.*

Jay Gould seemed to read his mind. "I wanted you to come see me," he said slowly. "I thought it best to use language you could not ignore. There was a reference to the lady, Margaret—Charlotte, if you prefer—for which I apologize most abjectly now that you are here."

"But Comstock *is* in Greenwich by your hand?" Tilden asked darkly.

Gould shook his head. "That too was an artifice. The culprit is a retired tart named Belle Walker. It seems the presence of another like her caused her some discomfort and she wrote a letter which I think will be her own undoing. Your Margaret has no serious cause for concern in this instance. In any case, Mr. Comstock will soon be taking his leave. I happen to know that his crusade is about to be energetically discouraged by your old friend, Inspector Williams."

Tilden waited, mildly stunned at the extent of Gould's knowledge and all the more doubtful of his claimed disassociation.

"No," Gould said, smiling, "nor am I the agent of Comstock's departure. You have none other than Mrs. Williams to thank for that."

"Clubber's wife?" Tilden nearly returned the smile.

"She's not another tart, if that's what you're wondering. Comstock made the mistake of accosting her on the street and taking her photograph."

Tilden could no longer prevent a grin. He longed to rush home and share this news with Margaret. She would be greatly relieved, Laura Hemmings as well, although both of them feigned unconcern in his presence. But the grin faded as he considered that Jay Gould had not learned so much without purpose.

"Are you about to say what you want of me, Mr. Gould?"

"It is as before," he said directly. "I want you to withdraw your support from Cyrus Field."

Tilden closed his eyes. "As my father said, you do keep coming, don't you, Mr. Gould?"

"This is important to me."

"For God's sake, how? Haven't you found enough joy in knowing that a piss ant like you could utterly shatter the health and fortune of a giant like Cyrus Field?"

"I took no joy in that. It was business."

"Mr. Field is a businessman. You are a pirate. Mr. Field builds up. You tear down. The laying of the Atlantic cable made him wealthy, but there was a much greater risk that it would have broken him. You would not have taken that risk. You would have bought your way in when the terms were most favorable and then you would have plundered it just as you sought to plunder his New York Elevated."

"*His* New York Elevated," Jay Gould sighed. "His Atlantic cable. These are businesses, Mr. Beckwith. Not monuments. Cyrus Field was defeated in the end by his own vanity. And I pray you, sir, do not be so naive as to conclude that Mr. Field is exempt from greed or is above deceit. He tried to force me out of a business that was essential to other designs of mine. He tried it secretly and through guile. He bought shares under any name but his own in his effort to wrest control from myself and Russell Sage."

"But you knew what he was doing. And you bushwhacked him."

"Naturally."

Tilden could only stammer.

"Is it possible that shocks you?" Jay Gould asked calmly. "The man had his agents buy seventy thousand shares in less than a year. His purchases alone, nearly all on margin by the way, drove the price from ninety-five dollars to a hundred and seventy-five. Sage and I dumped our shares on the market because their value had been inflated far beyond their worth and the profit was there to be taken. Is this not a first principle of investing, Mr. Beckwith?"

Tilden could have argued. But he knew it was pointless. He could have noted that Gould picked the time when Cyrus Field was recklessly overextended and when the crash Gould engineered would have left him a literal pauper, but Gould would simply have asked, "What other time was there?" He could have argued that greed played no part in Field's actions, although vanity certainly did to some degree. But never greed. The shares he'd bought would never have stayed at the value to which he'd forced them. Nevertheless, he would have his elevated and the working classes would have cheap transport to their jobs and the city would expand marvelously because fully another third of Manhattan Island was now practical as a place of residence for them. Planners would come from all the great cities of the world to study this newest miracle he'd created and there would be no Jay Gould, no Russell Sage, to shake it and wring it dry. Oh, Mr. Field. If only you had been a bit less thoughtful of your place in history and a bit less innocent. But I will have to grant him it was as much suicide as murder.

"Fair enough, then." Tilden withdrew on that issue. "But I admire him nonetheless and will not see him reduced further."

"I admired him as well. I trusted him."

"You trust no one."

"I trusted him. He was the only one. He broke my heart."

Once more, Tilden was dumbstruck. Had anyone, he wondered, even Jay Gould's wife, ever heard such words from him. And they seemed honest words. He saw the pain in the little man's eyes.

"I will tell you how Cyrus Field affected me." Gould stepped closer to Tilden. "For twenty years I watched him as he did great things in apparent defiance of the laws of nature. How, I wondered, could a man who was trusting, loyal, and patient as a country parson not only survive in business but prosper. Here was a man who could walk through the valley of death happily sniffing a carnation. Here was a man who could trust in the protection of the Almighty and actually receive it. When I allied myself with him in the elevated business, I will admit to you, sir, that my first thought was to share in that protection. But I grew to admire the man and even love him. He had no great head for business and he was too much ambitious of sainthood but I held him in great esteem nonetheless." A fire was growing behind the pain.

"Even when he fought me," Gould continued, "on the matter of doubling the fares, which of course is what fares are for, I yielded to his pleas that the higher fares would do great harm to people who were nothing to me, who would thank me not at all, and who would soon be fleeced out of the extra nickel I left in their pockets regardless. By that time I was so accustomed to Field's apparent altruism that it never occurred to me he might have some other design, that he might be secretly scheming with you and your father."

Tilden, who had been following this with difficulty, was now lost. "What on earth are you talking about?"

"I bear you no grudge for it. If I did, I'd have long since built a tannery next to each of your properties."

"No grudge for what, sir?"

"He did not want the fares increased because he feared that the higher tariff would make your northern real estate holdings less attractive. He was in them with you. He was a money-getter no less than the rest of us."

Tilden felt dizzy. There was not a word of truth to it. Field had no interest at all in real estate, financial or otherwise. His interest was in systems. Communications. Shrinking the globe. But now Tilden was beginning to realize with growing horror that Cyrus Field's destruction was based upon a mistake. And worse, that Tilden's own persecution these past three years, the damage to his business, the violence to Margaret's peace of mind, even Ansel Carling's disastrous seduction of Ella and Ella's betrayal of him and of Cyrus Field, all followed from a single wrong suspicion in the dark little mind of this sick little man.

"Did you ever ask him if this was so?" Tilden's voice was suddenly hoarse.

"There was no need. Sage had good intelligence of it."

"And you simply took the word of a grasping miser who won't spend more than ten dollars for a suit of clothing, and you began baiting traps for Mr. Field."

"He set his own trap. When he knew I would not again yield on the matter of the fares, he began his attempt to force us out."

Tilden turned his back and walked a few steps away from Gould, his hands pressed over his ears whether to keep out further evil or to comprehend the enormity of what he was hearing. "And you are still not finished with him." Tilden closed his eyes. "He is a bad example to others, you said. I am not to help him. He is to be ground down further."

"On the contrary," Gould said softly, "I wish to raise him up. But it must be me who does it. He must come to me."

It was too much.

"To be humiliated."

"To apologize."

"Apologize."

"I will not make him grovel, Mr. Beckwith, if that is what you fear. The act of coming to me will be sufficient. I will offer him my hand and I will raise him up."

"He won't come. I pray that he won't. I will give all that I have to prevent it."

"Then you will lose all that you have. All that you

value. Your house in Greenwich is made of glass no less than this one."

Tilden's mind, as he recalled it later, seemed to shut down when this was said. He'd been pacing Gould's greenhouse like an animal, he thought, but he felt as if he were floating. He remembered his hand coming down upon a large metal watering can and he remembered the can spinning once around him before sailing through the air and smashing a four-foot hole in the glass greenhouse wall. The shock of it caused other panes to crack and fall. The place seemed to be raining glass. He remembered seeing Jay Gould choking and coughing at the end of an arm that held him by his shirtfront, and he thought that it was only Margaret's hand upon his other arm that kept him from smashing a fist into that red and frothing face. Then he remembered that his mind had cleared at the sound of Charley Murtree's voice saying, "Ah, now you done it," and seeing Murtree and the other man, Calicoon, the silent one, advancing toward him between rows of flats, each man with a rifle in his hand, and he let Jay Gould fall to one side and then raised both hands to show that they were empty before he made them into fists and smiled an invitation to Charley Murtree who smiled back nodding and laid his rifle down and so did Calicoon.

If rounds had been counted, Tilden won the first, he thought. Both men went down, one to his knee and the other into a trough of seedlings. Tilden was sorry about the flowers. And more glass fell. So much glass. The second round might have been a draw. There must have been a third, but Tilden could not remember it.

Laura Hemmings took a long sip from her cup, peering over its rim at the faces of the women in the room. Everyone was there. The entire membership. It was the first chapter meeting she could recall at which there were no absentees. Even Belle Walker, who had not attended in weeks, and who'd seemed to want nothing more of her membership than her name upon the roster, had dared not miss this meeting. Belle looked ill. Old Spanky. Take care it's not you who goes bottoms up this time.

Of the other faces Laura saw, some seemed to be enjoying this. Some were titillated by the very idea that they might once have had bodies and skills for which men would pay hard cash. Others were fascinated by Anthony Comstock's tales of vice avenged. Many thought the whole affair tedious, yet they had taken the trouble to primp very prettily, thank you, for their moment in front of Comstock's camera. A few, only two or three, were enthusiastic. And, oh, so righteous. They testified loudly of their feelings toward women who had betrayed their sex and brought shame to the noble temple that is the female body. Laura made a mental note to cross them off her list. After she'd cut them dead, of course. She also made a mental note to see more of Peggy Gannon, on whom fell the duty of introducing today's guest speaker and who, when asked by him why she did not join in the restrained applause that followed his message, replied, "Because you are an ass, sir." Peggy was the first to be photographed.

Poor Margaret. Now third in line, the regular members being taken alphabetically. Smile, Margaret. Look at ease. And for heaven's sake, put down that cup and saucer before it starts shaking like a roundsman's rattle.

Laura crossed quickly, her own cup in hand, to the place where Margaret stood trembling, babbling something about Margaret's lovely dress while being careless of the hem of her own. "Oh!" the two women cried at once. Laura's cup skidded from its saucer well and dashed its contents over the fine ecru linen of Margaret's skirts.

"Oh, I've ruined it, dear Charlotte." Laura seemed

close to tears. "Oh, come, let us soak it quickly. You there." She stepped past the first two women and waggled a finger at the fat man who was sorting through a valise full of Kodak cameras. "You there. Comstock. Make your photograph of this girl at once or not at all. I will not be bound to replace her dress because you took overlong in your foolish business." She sat Margaret down in the chair that Comstock had placed facing a sunlit window, first turning it slightly so that the light would be less favorable.

The vice crusader made a dithering effort to restore the orderly system he'd intended, but a half dozen more women now surged forward, some attempting to blot the stain and others calling advice for its removal. It was a bad job, he realized, best to give it up. Comstock took two exposures of Margaret. The first was of her face looking down upon the stain and half hidden by the brim of her hat. With all that, Laura also brushed the big man's elbow as he pressed the shutter release. For the second, he demanded that Margaret look up. She did, but the camera captured a face writhing in discomfort from the hot staining liquid, a face that imitated the expression pantomimed by Laura from her position behind the photographer. Laura then took the next place in line, alphabet or no, and gazed sternly into the lens with an expression never seen on Little Annie. She next took Margaret quickly to a Post Road cab and had the linen dress soaking in milk and soda ten minutes later. Laura poured a sherry down Margaret's throat even before the stays were loosened and another down her own. By their second glass she had Margaret smiling at her imitations of Anthony Comstock and of the several women who joined him in ringing testimony.

Back at the meeting room, meanwhile, left behind in a terror that was at least the equal of Margaret's and with far more cause, was Mrs. Belle Walker. Belle didn't even try to blink. She stared transfixed, not at the camera lens but at Anthony Comstock himself. He saw the fear and a curious pleading in her eyes. The picture taken, he watched her as her knees went soft, and she sought the support of a wall as she made her way back to the tea service. As soon as she could decently leave, Belle rushed to the Oyster Pier, where she told her husband of her fear that the life from which he'd rescued her might today have been discovered. Frank Walker, who was normally not allowed within a yard of her unless he first bathed in lye soap and hot water, took her in his arms without protest from Belle. He knew of her background, of course, having been a most enthusiastic patron during his oat-sowing visits to New York. Although the Spanky of later years was a bit more sharp tongued than he would have liked, and a good deal more righteous, Frank had no great cause to regret making her his wife. The whippings and paddlings she could be induced to give him at least once a week, and the soaring sexual arousal that came out of them, to say nothing of two children, seemed well worth the price.

Frank Walker told his wife not to worry her head about all this and proceeded to make the first of two cardinal errors. He found Comstock at the post office, where the crusader was preparing to mail his cameras back to the Kodak company for developing and refilling. It was his honor, he said, to be the husband of Mrs. Belle Walker, a woman whose character has been an adornment to Greenwich since the day of her arrival. Comstock asked if she could possibly have adorned New York in a different manner before attaining the happy state of being his wife. Whatever her past, Frank answered, admitting nothing, you understand, Belle Walker had more than proved herself to be a foe of all that is iniquitous. It was she, he announced proudly, who wrote the letter advising Comstock of the lurid past of the unfortunate Carrie Todd. Comstock lifted his nose. He pointed out to Frank Walker that informers, however salubrious their result, do not stand high before the Almighty and went on to cite several examples, notably Judas Iscariot and the accusers of Mary Magdalene.

Then Frank Walker made his second error. He attempted to bribe Anthony Comstock. Comstock replied that if anyone should pay it should be he, and if Frank would wait while the postmaster made change, the Society for the Suppression of Vice would gladly pay thirty silver dimes for the information Belle Walker provided and then call their accounts even before God and man. That insult, and the realization that he'd made a catastrophic mistake, moved Frank Walker to violence. He threw a looping right hand at Comstock's jaw but managed only to fracture his hand against the top of Comstock's ducking head.

Belle Walker was exposed in the next week's issue of the *Graphic*. The story cited highlights of her arrest record together with a woodcut of a photograph from the files of the New York City Police. It also gave the date of her birth, which preceded by eight years the one she'd claimed to those who knew her. Belle, by that time, was in seclusion, having spent one night in the Stamford town jail awaiting the bondsman. She had been charged, not with any unexpiated vice offense, but by Comstock himself with sending lewd, lascivious, and obscene matter through the mails. The evidence Comstock offered was the very letter in which Belle used illegally vivid detail to describe the past activities of Carrie Todd.

By the time that issue appeared, Margaret was nearing the end of her tether. The continuing presence of Anthony Comstock, the leering stares of other boorish townsmen who took to wondering which pretty bird might next be flushed, the thought of some oily New York policeman even now putting a glass to her likeness, all paled before the greatest worry of all. *Tilden had disappeared*. Nine days had passed since he'd said he had an errand to run. Nine days since the day of the tea-stained dress. Nine days since Tilden told her he'd been a fool and a blockhead, though he would not say how, promising only that he'd tell her when the moment was right and wine poured and they sat before a fire with their son on Tilden's lap.

"If you were to ask me"—Laura Hemmings took her hand—"I'd say he intends to marry you."

"No." Her eyes filled with tears as she shook her head. "He will not do that. He never speaks of it, but Tilden could never forget where he found me. What would he say to his family, his friends?"

"Ask me again," Laura insisted, "and I'd say it is on that score he knows he has been a blockhead. Two of his closest friends already know and they, both John and Nat, would be the first to give their blessing."

Margaret would not be consoled. She would not be encouraged with a hope that could be dashed so soon and cruelly. What if her worst fears about Tilden lying broken and delirious in a hospital somewhere, even dead in a roadside ditch or lying unknown and unclaimed in some mortician's ice house, what if these were not the worst fears at all? What if the state she'd been in these past weeks had driven him to seek a respite of laughter and gaity? What if he had noticed the tiny lines that were beginning at her mouth and eyes, or was repulsed by the shiny ribbons that the birthing of Jonathan left on her belly? What if he had found another woman, just as he found one more amiable than Ella, and was even now lying with her?

"I know that look." Laura Hemmings frowned. "I should slap your face for it."

"I don't know what you—"

"Every woman thinks in terms of rivals the minute

a man's behavior becomes in any way odd. Tilden would never betray you."

Margaret wanted to believe Laura.

"Is there any word from John Flood?"

"He has his friends looking for Tilden. Even Teddy Roosevelt, he says, is coming down from Albany to join the search. John tells me to buck up, but I know that he too fears the worst."

"All will be well, my friend. I promise."

"I cannot bear this, Laura."

"It will pass."

"And if it does, then what?" Margaret slipped her hand out of Laura's and turned away. "Shall we live as before? The people in this town are not blind or stupid, Laura. They have only to look at Jonathan to know that he is Tilden's son. And that I am his mistress. And am therefore a liar. And possibly one of Comstock's whores. Even now, everywhere I go, men stare at me, wondering."

"They stare at me as well," Laura answered. "I flatter myself that it is because I'm pretty, though not nearly so pretty as you."

"They don't look at you the same way," Margaret said stubbornly.

Laura stuck a finger in her ear as if to clear it. "I beg your pardon?"

"They admire you. They don't wonder about you."

Laura Hemmings considered pointing out to Margaret that she'd had more men in more different ways than Margaret had logs in her winter woodpile, and that was counting bark chips. If anyone should be sensitive to stares, look-agains, and don't-I-know-you questions, it was she and not some doe-eyed apprentice who to this day would scarcely know a dildo if she tripped over it. But she chose not to say it. Margaret's fears, she realized, had far more shadow than substance, and a reasoned approach to them would accomplish nothing at all. What Margaret needed was Tilden's gold band upon her finger and his arms around her body, preferably in a place a thousand miles from New York. That is if there is indeed a Tilden anymore. No one simply falls into a hole for nine days. Certainly not a Tilden Beckwith. A thousand miles. My God, that's it. Evanston. Margaret, and little Jonathan with her. Evanston. But how to manage it?

"Margaret." Laura Hemmings tugged at her. "You need a holiday and I need a favor. I am going to insist that you do it for me."

SEVENTEEN

ARRY STURDEVANT CHOPPED AT THE LAST SHOVEL-ful of hard-packed snow that had threat-ened to block Corbin's driveway entrance and tossed it into a dormant azalea bush. He rested for a minute, his arms folded across the shovel handle, deciding whether to attack the driveway itself as long as he was there. When he was a boy he'd have gotten as much as fifty cents for the whole job. But he doubted whether he'd get anything from Jona-than except a lecture about heart attacks. That did it. Let the ingrate clear his own blasted driveway.

As he turned back toward the house, his eye caught a movement fifty feet up Maple Avenue and on the other side. Sturdevant peered through the slanting gray veil. He saw a man there. Not a young one, judging from his posture. Not the one he'd seen in the library, either. This one was dressed in dark clothing, to the extent that Sturdevant could see fabric under the film of clinging snow. He could easily have passed for a shadow, or a small juniper, if he hadn't shifted his position. He wore a homburg, which looked rather silly on him because a snow cone had formed on its crown. Against one leg he held what Sturdevant assumed to be a uselessly furled umbrella. Sturdevant wondered how long he'd been standing there. It surprised him that he felt no particular alarm. On the contrary, he had a sense that it was the man in black who seemed scared half to death. Sturdevant lifted his chin and gave a questioning shrug. The man stiffened, then snatched up the thing he was holding and held it across his chest. Now Sturdevant *was* alarmed. Unless his eyes had tricked him, he'd caught a glimpse of the outline of a rifle stock.

There didn't seem to be much to do but wait. If the man was content to stand there with the snow in his face and a rifle in his hands, Sturdevant decided he'd rather hope for a car to come along than to make a sudden dash for cover. That spry he was not. But the man suddenly lurched forward as if he'd read his mind. He moved almost drunkenly. A part of Sturdevant knew who the man was as soon as he saw him move. By the time half the distance between them had been covered, Sturdevant was sure.

"Hello, Tillie," he greeted the man who was now peering stupidly into his face. "You want to be careful with that thing."

There were times when Raymond Lesko was sure he was dead, and others when he thought he was probably home asleep. The sickening pain in his head and the woolly dryness of his mouth were not altogether unfamiliar to him. Too much garlic in the clam sauce and too many beers topped off with a bottle of Ginney red had done it in the past. Too drunk to wake up and too thirsty to fall asleep, so you lie there in the dark with crazy thoughts going through your head. It's the time when everyone finds out what it's like to be insane.

The part where he thought he was dead came when he saw this batty old lady put a big long spike against his temple and then pound it with a mallet until the spike went through and nailed him to the rug. That's what it felt like, too. His body could still move—he could feel it being jerked and tugged—but not his head. Hands were going through his coat pockets and patting down his belt and his legs all the way to his ankles. Then someone kicked him. Lesko wasn't sure who because there were so many people floating around all of a sudden.

Is he dead? He heard a woman's voice.

I don't think so. Not yet, anyway.

Asshole. That's the guy Burke. Shows how much you know. The old dame had a good question because one of the faces floating around looked like Corbin until Lesko noticed he was dressed like the guy in the hotel picture. He was drifting in real close and looking worried, then he looks up at the old lady and he shows his teeth—he got good teeth too—then he looks back down and reaches for Lesko's head like he's trying to fix it. But right there behind him is Lesko's ex-partner, Dave Katz, speaking of holes in the head, and he was saying to the Tilden guy how he shouldn't worry because Polacks got heads like truck tires and they're just as empty inside. Yeah. Right. But that's better than being full of dog shit like yours is, you stupid Hebe. You could have talked to me. You should have trusted your partner. I would have helped you fix it then instead of later. I did fix it, you know. Did you know that? Two less fucking Bolivians. You run into them there where you are, give 'em another kick in the balls for good measure.

Ohhh, Jesus. His head. They picked it up and stuck something cold and slippery under it. A magazine. She's worried about her rug. Sorry, lady. I'd have made it to your bathroom if I could. At least I'd be closer to a drink of water.

There was more talk but Lesko could only get pieces of it from far away. His fifteen thousand. He could kiss that off. Then something about his notes, and something else about the old dame's brother and a gun. A while later, Lesko wasn't sure how long, it struck him again that he might be dead because now it was him who was floating. He was flying. He was flapping his arms and he was hovering right in front of Dancer, who was grunting and gasping like he was trying to move a couch up a flight of stairs. Wait. They were moving him outside. It must be because Lesko felt cold and snow was hitting him in the face. He opened his mouth to get some of it on his tongue, but they twisted him away and threw him into a thing that smelled like oil and rust and old rubber—a trunk. Mr. Makowski's trunk. It had to be. Who else's car would stink like this.

Lesko knew for sure when he heard the ignition and felt the whole car quiver with effort until a blast from its exhaust exploded under his head like a firecracker in a metal drum. He felt his body press forward as the car hissed down the long driveway, and he banged his head once more as it braked at the gate before turning left onto Round Hill Road. It was so cold. He heard voices through the ringing in his ears. Arguing voices. Dancer. Lesko groped in the darkness, feeling for something he could use, a jack handle maybe, if his fingers were still working when they opened up the trunk again.

The drive back toward Greenwich from Lyndhurst was agonizingly slow, but Jonathan Corbin would never remember it. He would not remember the two accident scenes he'd come upon, or the spin-out of another car, which he'd caused in avoiding it, or the state policeman who'd tried to flag him down and had to leap for his life across a guardrail. The storm through which he was burrowing was nothing compared to the one inside his head. Both Tilden's emotions and his own whipped and twisted in a maelstrom of visions. On Tilden's part, though it was hard to separate them fully, Corbin felt the same sting of torn knuckles, the burning face and ribs, the numbness of forearms and kidneys that he'd felt that day in the garage under the Drake Hotel. He understood that Tilden was with him then as well, but he did not know why nor did he dwell on it.

Through one set of eyes he saw only darkness, but if he extended both his arms he could feel cold brick walls on three sides and a door of steel and planking on the fourth. He knew it was a jail cell because his ankle was attached to an iron bed by a length of chain just long enough to let him reach the wooden bowl of some kind of stew and the small pail of water that were shoved through a trap door once each day. How many bowls had there been? Ten, at least. Perhaps twice that number. The scabs on his cuts had fallen off, their healing work done, but his voice was gone from the screaming and raging he had done at the sound of other distant voices and at the opening and slamming of other doors. Gould had done this to him. There had been no trial, no judge, probably no charges, either. Gould had called some friendly constable or deputy and had him buried alive.

Margaret. What could she be thinking? She, and perhaps Laura as well, afraid to go abroad in Greenwich and just as afraid to remain unseen by that idiot with his camera. What fears must be working upon her mind? That I am dead as well as buried? That I have abandoned her? Go to her, Jonathan. Tell her I am safe and well. Tell her that I will come home again.

Corbin tried to shake away this pleading voice. The

memories were one thing, the voice another. He could accept that since his birth he'd carried visions of the things Tilden Beckwith had seen and felt, but the soul he carried was his own, not Tilden's, and the voice must therefore be the invention of his mind. He was having his own visions, and they troubled him more than Tilden's ancient memories. The frightened woman he was seeing was Gwen Leamas, not Margaret Barrie, except that she wore a dress that made her look like Margaret but for the color of her hair. She was standing in the doorway of his house, of Laura Hemmings's house, and she was peering into the night at two men who stood in the driveway—Harry Sturdevant and the one from yesterday, the one in black who seemed to keep appearing everywhere they walked; he was back again and he had a rifle in his hands and he was staring back at her with a terror that only the face of death should have caused. Get to her, Jonathan. Get there quickly.

Corbin cleared his eyes and focused once more on the road, but then other faces drifted up into his field of vision. One man, rough-looking, like the one called Bigelow. And just like Bigelow in Corbin's last memory of him, this one was lying with his face against the floor and he had crooked little streams of blood running across it. Corbin bent closer. He knew that face. He'd seen it yesterday, Saturday. When he and Gwen had just left her apartment building and a corner cigar store changed into a saloon called O'Neill's and this man was watching them through its window. Then he'd seen him again this morning, he thought. No. He'd felt him. When he and Gwen left her apartment the second time after picking up her things and he felt that this face was still watching them, but Corbin shrugged it off because he seemed to know that this man was not a threat. Maybe it was Tilden who knew that.

But he knew differently about these other faces.

There was another Bigelow type. This one had gray hair worn in a crew cut and a face that was both cruel and stupid. And there was a little miniature of a man who was perspiring sort of awkwardly, as if sweat was a new experience for him, and he had a bloodstain on his trouser leg. And a woman. An old woman. Corbin blinked and looked closer. If he didn't know better, if he took away fifty years of lines and wrinkles and put her on a New York street in a snowstorm a hundred years ago . . . Never mind. It couldn't be the same woman.

Except there was Tilden, not in his cell anymore, standing in the middle of the room next to the man on the floor and looking straight at her, his eyes very cold, and she was acting as if she could feel him there. She'd stare back, not directly at Tilden but around him, as if she were searching the room for him. Then her eyes dropped to the knob of the cane she was holding and she touched the blood on it. The blood must have belonged to the man on the floor, but she seemed confused about that. She looked up again at the space that Tilden occupied and her eyes grew wider. She could not see him, Corbin was sure, but she seemed to feel that he was there. And now Tilden, too, was bleeding from the head. Her eyes opened wider still. She remained standing this way long after the other faces were gone from the room.

To New England, the road sign said.

Corbin tested his brakes before entering the ramp that curved down onto the Connecticut Turnpike. A part of him wished that his mind could bring summer again so the road would be faster. He quickly shook off the thought. If the wish made it happen, he'd find himself with neither the road nor the Datsun under him. Just keep moving. Just get back to Gwen. He realized, with a faraway sadness, that it was too late for Margaret. Margaret was gone. She'd been gone two full days before Teddy Roosevelt knocked on her door.

"I cannot just leave," Margaret answered Laura Hemmings, "not knowing whether Tilden is dead or alive."

"You cannot stay," Laura insisted. "Look at you. You're becoming a wreck and you stand a very good chance of giving yourself away in your condition. All I am proposing is a vacation far enough away that you will feel out of danger, far enough that no one could possibly know you, where your fears can mend, and most of all where your mind will be kept busy."

"But Chicago is so far."

"Minutes away by telegraph. I will wire you the moment there is news of him." The suggestion Laura made, which she'd couched as a needed favor, was that Margaret and the child, Jonathan, make a pilgrimage in her stead to the national headquarters of the Women's Christian Temperance Union at Evanston, a village just north of Chicago. Laura had been scheduled to go there as a delegate to a committee that was advocating legislation by Congress prohibiting the on-the-job consumption of spirits by railroad employees. It was an important mission, she argued, but one that cut dreadfully into her preparations for the opening of her school that coming fall. Further, Margaret would be the more suitable delegate. Had she not, after all, lost a husband in a train wreck caused by drunkenness? Who could think it amiss if she departed from Greenwich for such a purpose?

Lucy Stone, the housekeeper, lent her own voice to the argument that the change would do Margaret good. And Peggy Gannon shared Laura's view that Margaret should have been elected their delegate in the first place. Margaret hesitated two more days, even as Laura began packing for her. Her depression steadily deepened. Nearly a fortnight had passed without word from

Tilden, and Anthony Comstock was now railing on street corners about the hidden pustules that still marred the shining face of Greenwich. Margaret, in turning to avoid him the day before, had nearly collided with Inspector Williams and his wife, who were walking up Main Street. She felt a burning on her neck, as if he had turned and was staring after her. By the day that followed, Margaret had not so much agreed to make the journey as she'd allowed herself and young Jonathan to be put aboard the train. Laura gave the conductor a half dollar, asking him to take care of the poor woman and keep a special eye on the boy if she dozed. Margaret would do more than doze, Laura knew. She made her swallow two full ounces of Dr. King's New Discovery for Pain. By the time the train reached Albany before turning west, Margaret could probably have had a tooth extracted without complaint.

Another two days passed, time enough for Margaret and Jonathan to be met at Union Station and escorted to Evanston, before Teddy Roosevelt appeared at the Maple Avenue address and encountered a very startled Lucy Stone. There were few men living who could intimidate Lucy Stone, least of all a man half her size, but she was not prepared for the arrival of a well-known political figure with a most forceful personality who also had the reputation of being slightly mad. He asked politely enough for an interview with Margaret, then quickly became agitated upon Lucy's nervous insistence that she knew nothing of Mrs. Corbin's whereabouts. It was a foolish lie but a protective one. She had no knowledge of Roosevelt's relationship with Tilden and even less confidence in the motives of any politician. For his part, Roosevelt began to imagine still another sinister disappearance and began shouting his demand that she tell him all she knew at once. Thoroughly frightened, Lucy pointed down the road in the direction of Laura Hemmings's house and indicated, before slamming the door, that the white woman who lived there might have more time to talk to him.

Teddy's interview with Laura was even less fruitful. Laura, unlike Lucy, was aware that Tilden and Roosevelt were friends of long standing, but she did not know how much he knew of Tilden's relationship with Margaret or of Margaret's history. In any case, after working so hard to get Margaret out of harm's way, she was not about to undo it all on the very day Margaret was unpacking in Evanston. She told Teddy that Margaret had been suffering from melancholy of late and had gone, she believed, to Wilkes-Barre, where she and her child were visiting the family of her late husband. Roosevelt, this time, saw the lie in her eyes. But he also realized that Margaret was clearly being protected and was probably in no danger at all. As for her true location, Wilkes-Barre or elsewhere, he imagined he'd learn it soon enough. He did not know why she'd gone but, in his heart, he could not dismiss the notion that a permanent estrangement might be for the best all around. It was a relationship, as it stood, that promised more pain than pleasure. Teddy thanked Laura Hemmings for her time and returned to the station, where he entrained for New York.

Wherever Tilden was, whatever harm had befallen him, Roosevelt had no doubt in the world that Jay Gould was behind it. But he could not risk confronting Gould without evidence. Gould would simply answer him with silence and then cover his tracks all the more. He was grinding his teeth over this dilemma as he stepped through the front door of his house at 6 West Fifty-seventh Street and was met by a wide-eyed housekeeper who told him that three plug-uglies were waiting in the parlor. She had told them that they must wait out on the sidewalk, but the biggest one had simply picked her up and kissed her forehead and told her that a cup of tea would be very nice indeed, especially if she was to pour a nip of good whiskey into it.

"Who are they?" he whispered, stepping to his umbrella stand and choosing a sword cane from the instruments there.

"I don't know, sir," she said in a hushed tone. "But they are Irishmen. The one called Sullivan says his name prouder than Christ himself would say his own."

Teddy was still grinning hugely as he stepped into his parlor and offered his hand to John L. Sullivan, to his dear old friend John Flood, and to a third battered-looking tough who was introduced to him as Mr. William O'Gorman.

Roosevelt had seen nothing of the champion since his seventy-five-round drubbing of Jake Kilrain nearly two years before and not a great deal more of John Flood, who had helped get him in shape for that fight and would soon begin drying him out again if the much-talked-about challenge by young James Corbett was taken. At another time, they would have sat and talked boxing right through supper, but Teddy knew that this was not a social visit no matter how welcome.

"I think maybe we found him," John Flood said after all hands were shaken. "Mr. O'Gorman here posted a hundred dollars for the man who found Tilden's trail. It was claimed yesterday by one of Jay Gould's groundskeepers who saw what he thought was a dead man of Tilden's description being hauled away from Gould's place up on the Hudson a fortnight ago. Billy then sent six men up to Westchester to scout the hospitals and the jails. Two of them went to a lockup in a town called Ardsley. One went in, the other waited outside. The first never came out. The second ran for his life when he saw a constable with a bleedin' nose come outa the jail house and come at him with a cosh in his hand. This was this mornin'. He told Mr. O'Gorman here and Mr. O'Gorman found me at the gym with John. John says he's throwin' in with us because he's been wantin' to take apart a jail house since they put him in one down in Mississippi after the Kilrain fight, especially if Tilden's inside it. I figured we better have a little law on our side too and you're the closest thing to it we know."

"I'll have my carriage brought around." Teddy squeezed the sword cane in his fist.

Tilden was indeed in the Ardsley jail. Teddy knew it the moment their carriage stopped outside and he heard a bolt being thrown on the door of the constable's office. Billy O'Gorman touched John Flood's arm and pointed to a single black wire, which ran through a hole drilled in the brick at one end of the small building and on up to the crossbars of a utility pole. Flood gave a sign, and Billy O'Gorman severed the phone wire with a knife cut so fast as to be almost unseen. If that were a man's throat, John Flood knew, he'd still be standing there wondering why he couldn't talk no more. Flood was less subtle. He took one long step and smashed a shoe against the point where he guessed the bolt to be. The entire door fell in, held only by its bottom hinge. Flood caught a glimpse of two armed men ducking down behind a desk before he slid sideways out of the line of fire. He also saw a telephone set on the wall, its ear horn dangling uselessly.

"This is Theodore Roosevelt of the state legislature," Teddy called. "I am coming in and you will hold your fire."

"You come through that door," came a voice from inside, "and you'll never go through another."

"And this, God damn it, is John L. Sullivan himself," the champion roared. His voice made even Roosevelt flinch.

"The hell you say."

Sullivan held up a fist in the open doorway. "Don't

try my patience, boys. Unless you have a cannon bigger than this, put down those things and start behaving like goddamned gentlemen."

"Next you'll tell me that's Jake Kilrain out there with you."

"It's a better man than that, by God. That was John Flood who stove in your door."

"John Flood? The Bull's Head Terror?"

"The same."

"Is that so? Is that you, John?"

"It is."

"Then show yourself."

Flood stepped full into the door.

"It's him, by God," the deputy inside said to the other. "It's John Flood himself."

John Flood cocked his head toward Sullivan and shrugged an apology. Teddy Roosevelt sighed. The basically simple process of breaking into a jail now required a vote on the personal popularity of the men breaking in. Sullivan's expression was just on the edge of a sulk.

"I seen you fight." The deputy stood up. "I seen you fight Joe Goss."

John Flood entered the office, followed by Teddy and O'Gorman. Sullivan followed, muttering something about how Goss would have fared against his maiden aunt.

The deputy lowered his shotgun but held it ready. "Keep your distance, boys. Even you, John Flood. I ought to arrest you for what you done. I'd admire the company for a few days."

Flood pointed to a barred steel door behind the other deputy. "Who you got back there, lad?"

"I can't tell you that, John."

Billy O'Gorman cupped his hands to his mouth. "Larry Donovan? Are you in there?"

"Who's that?" came a distant and filtered voice. "Is that you, Billy?"

"It's me and some friends. Is Beckwith in there with you?"

"He's down the cellar. They got a bleedin' dungeon here just like bleedin' Newgate."

The deputy swung his shotgun onto Billy O'Gorman's chest. Sullivan, who had drifted to one side in apparent disinterest, made a lightning slash at the shotgun's breech, his little finger jamming under the twin hammers, then snatched away the weapon as the hammers slammed down harmlessly. Within the same instant, Billy O'Gorman's knife came up under the younger deputy's chin as Teddy's hand snaked forward to relieve him of his weapon.

Sullivan glowered at the man whose shotgun hammers still pinched his little finger. "Did you hear who I said I was just before? Did you hear me say I was champion of the world?"

"You'll be champion of Sing Sing if you don't give back that gun. Anyways, you're a damned liar. You're both too small and too sober to be John L. Sullivan."

"Hmm . . . Gentlemen . . ." Teddy stepped forward but Sullivan waved him off.

Sullivan recocked the shotgun and offered it back to the deputy. "That's a champion's speed that stopped those hammers." He leaned his face close into the other man's. "Would you like to try me again? Except this time, by God, I'll show you a champion's right fist as well."

"I'll take his keys first if you don't mind." Teddy reached for a ring on the deputy's belt.

"Won't do you no good for the cellar. The chief constable carries those and right now he's fishin' for shad up by Poughkeepsie."

"You've kept the man in a basement cell for two weeks?" Roosevelt asked quietly as he opened the cell block door. "We're told he was hurt. Has he received any care?"

"This ain't my doin'."

"Answer my question, sir."

"He gets fed. Most days he eats what we push through the trap."

"When did you last see him?" Teddy handed the keys to O'Gorman, who disappeared toward Larry Donovan's cell.

"When they toted him in here."

Teddy reached for the deputy's arm with a gentleness that brought a scowl to Sullivan's face. "Come. Show me the way to the cellar," he said. John Flood did not scowl. He knew what the soft voice meant. He knew that Teddy's touch would not long be gentle.

Charley Murtree groaned to his feet at the sound of the door chime. The color around his left eye had faded to a light mustard shade and the swelling had gone down around the cuts on his knuckles, but his ribs would need two more weeks before he could hope for a decent night's sleep on them. Still, he was better off than old Calicoon. Calicoon, he got rocked back into one of them hot water kettles and it just rolled over on him like a fat lady on a rope bunk. Never heard Calicoon make so many different sounds in his whole life.

Murtree shuffled to a bay window and peered out at the two men who waited at Jay Gould's front door. Just two. Both of them dressed proper. All four of their hands showing. The little one carrying what looked like a coil of chain. He glanced at the brougham they'd arrived in. Weren't no station hack, that's for sure. A rich man's carriage. Had a curly little gold *R* on the side but no livery on the driver. They're probably all right. That little one looks awful familiar. Roosevelt. That's who it is. It's that Roosevelt feller. And the other one—

damn . . . damn if he ain't a ringer for . . . naw . . . naw, it couldn't be.

He picked up his Winchester and checked that a round was chambered before setting the hammer on half cock. That done, he approached the front door and shifted the rifle into his left hand so that the door would conceal it when opened.

"Good afternoon, sirs." He raised a hand, indicating that they should remain outside the threshold. "Would you say your business, please."

Teddy held out the coil of chain. "Give this to Mr. Gould, if you will, and tell him that Mr. Theodore Roosevelt would like five minutes of his time."

"He ain't in today, sir. If you want to leave that thing and your card, I'll see he gets 'em."

"He is in residence today, is he not?"

"Maybe." Charley Murtree never liked this part. A man's in or he ain't. "The word I have is he ain't receivin' for anything short of the second comin' and that's where it sits."

"This manacle is from the Ardsley jail. He may change his mind when he notices it's empty."

Charley understood. One way or another they busted out that Tilden feller. Couldn't say he was sorry, but it wouldn't brighten Mr. Gould's day any. "Like I said, I'll give it to him soon as he decides he's here. Ain't no polite way to do this but I got to close the door on you now."

Sullivan, who had been eyeing this man oddly, stepped past Teddy Roosevelt and thrust his face forward. "Do you know who I am, sir?"

Feller sure did look like John L. Sullivan. Except . . . "I keep repeatin' myself. If you ain't Jesus, you ain't on the list."

"I am not Jesus," the champion snarled, "and I am not the king of England, but I am no more accustomed to having doors closed on me than they are. I am John

L. Sullivan and I am the heavyweight champion of the world."

"Damn." Murtree smiled. "I would have thunk you'd be bigger."

It wasn't that Murtree saw the punch coming because he never did. But someplace in there, between saying what he did and seeing that front door zooming away from him like the view off the back of a train, and feeling the floor bounce under him, the little bit of daylight left in Charley Murtree's brain told him he'd picked exactly the wrong thing to say. He never would figure out why.

Teddy Roosevelt threw the leg manacles on Jay Gould's library desk, scarring it badly. Gould barely looked up. He lifted the chains onto a leather desk mat and touched his fingers sadly to the wounds they had made.

"It would seem, Mr. Roosevelt, that you and Mr. Beckwith both take pleasure in destroying beautiful things. He wrecked my greenhouse, you know."

Roosevelt glanced back at Sullivan, who waited just outside the library door, and nodded. Sullivan quietly closed it and, arms folded, took a sentry's position outside. From where he stood he could see Billy O'Gorman through a tall, leaded window. O'Gorman remained on the driver's seat of the brougham, the deputy's shotgun hidden beneath the duster he'd borrowed from Teddy's driver.

"Whatever he's done, whatever you've done, Gould, it ends today."

Gould's eyebrows shot up. "Are you quite serious, sir?"

"Dead serious, I promise you."

Jay Gould fingered the chains. "Do you mind my asking how you accomplished this? I dare say no judge in the county would have written a release order without consulting me."

"We kicked in the door. Some friends and I."

"But not the door of the isolation cell, I think. My question, sir, is not asked without admiration."

"We were fortunate in that another prisoner was gifted in the locksmith's art."

Gould nodded slowly. "The one who came by the jail this morning. Asking questions. You do move with vigor, don't you, Mr. Roosevelt. Can I assume that Mr. Murtree has been incapacitated by that bruiser outside my library door?"

"You can." Roosevelt noticed the bell cord behind Gould's right shoulder. "The man who bested him is another of Tilden's friends who also happens to be the heavyweight boxing champion of the world. I tell you this so that in all fairness you will not find your man deficient. Another of Tilden's friends waits on my carriage with a shotgun. I tell you this lest you endanger more of your people by pulling that cord before we have completed our business."

"What business is that, sir?"

"I told you. This ends today."

Jay Gould gazed at Roosevelt in a long look of amused disbelief. He rubbed his eyes, then clasped his hands and rested his chin upon them. "Let me test my grasp of this situation, sir. A member of the New York State Legislature, in the company of various hoodlums, has broken into a proper jail and released two prisoners who were in the custody of legally constituted authority. From the look of your knuckles, I gather there was a physical assault as well."

Roosevelt said nothing. But he had, true enough, asked to be left alone with the deputy once he saw Tilden's desperate condition. He resisted an urge to check his watch. John Flood and the safecracker Donovan should have him over the county line by now and within an hour of Bellevue Hospital.

"You then come to my house, you add trespassing

and another assault to your growing list of indictable offenses. I suspect that threatening comes next and extortion not far behind. And you tell me that all this ends today as if by a mere act of your aristocratic will."

"Add theft, Mr. Gould. I stole the jail's log."

"The jail's log," Gould repeated.

"The one that records arrests and incarcerations, sir. I could find no entry of any kind for Mr. Beckwith. Or for the man arrested this morning, for that matter. I would recommend that you spend a quiet hour one day reading the Constitution of the United States except that I think I prefer your ignorance of it."

"Mr. Beckwith was awaiting my decision on how I would prosecute the matter."

"*Your* decision." Roosevelt brought both fists down upon the desk. "This is a nation of laws, you arrogant ass. You detained Tilden Beckwith illegally on at least three particulars. That was not an arrest, sir. That was a kidnapping."

"That rather depends," Gould said dryly, "on whose judge hears the argument, does it not, Mr. Roosevelt."

Teddy closed his eyes. "I bring you three messages, sir. The first is from Tilden. You will be relieved to know that he has no intention of prosecuting you on the charge of kidnapping."

"That does lift a great weight from my heart."

"Tilden, in fact, invites you to do your worst as far as he himself is concerned. But if you in any way harm Mrs. Corbin or her son, Jonathan, or if they are even made sorrowful by any act that is traceable to you, or if harm or sorrow come to them through any unknown agency or suspicious accident, Tilden will be left with nothing but the satisfaction of putting a bullet between your eyes."

Gould answered with only a weary smile. A bullet.

How many times had he heard such a threat. How many hundreds of times.

Teddy returned the smile, acknowledging Gould as if saying, I know, the delirious ravings of a sick and beaten man. A man with no heart for such an act no matter how the cards were played.

"In all candor, Mr. Gould, I find myself wanting to share your skepticism. There is, however, the second message. It comes from a rather disreputable fellow who, for reasons unknown to me, has chosen to admire Tilden greatly. I can tell you that he has been arrested six times on suspicion of murder and eleven times on a charge of atrocious assault, the specific atrocity being the gouging of human eyes. He intends to have yours as well, sir. I'm afraid he intends to have them regardless of the outcome of this interview."

"Would that be the same fellow who called upon Colonel Mann a year or two ago? If it is, you might tell him that threats, like sauces, carry greater effect when used sparingly."

Teddy had resolved that he would not pass on the second part of Billy O'Gorman's threat. That what happens to Tilden's own will happen to Jay Gould's own as well. That Jay Gould's wife and children have eyes as well. Teddy kept that resolution with more difficulty than he'd expected.

"The third message, sir, is from me." Roosevelt leaned forward until his face was no more than a foot from Gould's. "Do any further harm to Tilden Beckwith or to those dear to him, or to those he chooses to befriend, and I will fight you. With all the resources at my disposal, with all the laws, with all my friends in business or government who will unite in their common contempt of you, I will by fair means or foul hound you for all your remaining days."

Gould blinked. "What part of that is new, sir? By all accounts, you have hardly been my friend in the legislature. Or in the financial community for that matter."

"Fair means or foul, Mr. Gould. I have been fair thus far. I have not, for example, dashed a glass in your face whenever we have encountered each other at Delmonico's or Rector's or in the home of an undiscriminating host. I have not bribed any employee of yours to keep me informed of your activities. And when information has come my way I have not passed it on to Morgan or Harriman or any of the others who would take pleasure in thwarting your designs."

The dark little financier rose from his chair and stepped toward one of several orchid-bearing plant stands that were placed about the room. He stopped and studied the largest of the blossoms, first thoughtfully, then touched it with a tenderness that surprised Teddy Roosevelt.

"The glass has been replaced," he said distantly. "The damaged plants will grow again. Tilden Beckwith will heal."

Teddy waited.

"I will see that no charges are placed against you. I will, however, place charges against Mr. Beckwith but only within the jurisdictions of Irvington and Ardsley. He can avoid arrest by staying away from my house."

"Fair enough. I'm sure you'll do him the same kindness."

"I will also yield on the matter of his child and his whore. They are nothing to me."

"You will take that back, sir." Roosevelt took a step toward him.

"His child and his lady, then." Gould waved him off, then touched his fingers to his temples. This conversation was becoming annoyingly familiar.

"And the affairs of Beckwith and Company?"

"That, sir, is a matter of business. I will yield nothing. From Mr. Beckwith's own mouth I am invited to do my worst. If it pleases me to do so, I shall take him at his word. In any event, I will not have you calling me to account every time some ordinary transaction of mine happens to affect the fortunes of Tilden Beckwith."

"Fair as well," Roosevelt answered. "And he will, of course, continue to support Cyrus Field if it pleases him to do so."

Gould was silent for a very long moment. Then, as Roosevelt watched, the smaller man's shoulders began to quiver. A hand groped at his trousers pocket, finally producing a handkerchief too late to stay the spasm of coughing that was overcoming him. The cough had a terrible, desperate sound. It put Teddy in mind of the dry sucking of a pump whose hose did not quite reach the drowning fluids. Gould turned away from him and stayed hunched against one of his tapestried walls until he was sure the fit had subsided. When at last he righted himself and dabbed at the tears on his cheeks, Teddy saw a pair of eyes that seemed reddened by much more than the pain of his chest. The eyes seemed haunted.

"Cyrus lives in Ardsley," Gould said in a choked whisper. "You have agreed that Beckwith will stay away from Ardsley."

Teddy agreed that it was so.

"He never comes here."

"Who never comes here? Field?"

"It is nothing."

Teddy narrowed his eyes. "What in heaven's name is it between you and Cyrus Field? I know Tilden tried to ask you this, but why can you not just leave the man alone?"

Jay Gould's head jerked curiously. An unmuscled arm waggled at a plant stand at the far side of the room. "That variety," he said. "It is named for me, you know."

Immortality. The word formed from nowhere in Teddy Roosevelt's mind. Ask about Cyrus Field and you learn about orchids. Talk about orchids and you soon begin to find, as others have observed, that Jay Gould sees his very soul in them. His soul as he wishes it could be. It is said that there is a certain fine madness in every man. Gould's own madness, and certainly his obsession, seemed to be his orchids. But where was the tie with a sick old man named Cyrus Field? He must come to me, Gould had said to Tilden. He must come to me and I will raise him up. Redemption? Redemption was the word Tilden used as they bathed him at the jail in Ardsley. Teddy had barely listened at the time, putting it down as the raving of a fevered brain. But perhaps Tilden had seen a great truth in his two weeks of darkness. Perhaps he saw that in a frightened dying corner of his own fevered brain, Jay Gould believed the raising up of Cyrus Field, a builder, a giver, a better man by leagues, would bring about his own redemption.

"Did Tilden ask you . . ." Teddy's voice was kindly in spite of himself. "Did Tilden ask why you don't simply go to Field and offer your hand?"

If there was an answer to that question, Jay Gould could not bring himself to give it. The haunted look was again in Jay Gould's eyes. If he turns me away, they seemed to be saying, then what is left for me? Teddy had no way of knowing what thought, that or another, was in this man's mind at that moment. But he thought he knew nonetheless. And he knew a madness, more desperate than fine, brought on by a lifetime of denied humanity, was there.

"Good day, sir," Gould whispered.

Teddy hesitated. It seemed that more should be said. Or that pity once felt should be spoken.

"Good day, sir," Gould repeated. The blood-sprayed linen square remained in a hand made anxious by the knowledge that another seizure was building inside him. The eyes were becoming wet again, but harder as well.

"Good day," Teddy answered. He turned and strode toward the library door.

"I'm bound . . ." Gould swallowed a cough. "I'm bound to say that your interest in this matter baffles me."

Teddy stopped. "Tilden is my friend."

"Your friend, indeed. Is he a true friend? One who would never play you false?"

Roosevelt opened the door without bothering to answer.

"Ask him this, then. Ask your true friend to look you in the eye and tell you plainly that he did not murder his wife."

EIGHTEEN

ES," THE MAN IN THE HOMBURG WHISPERED. "YES, I know you, don't I?" A measure of the old man's fear fell away as he peered closely at the face of Harry Sturdevant. Harry saw relief in his eyes as well. And, he thought, perhaps a hint of disappointment.

"I'm Harry Sturdevant, Tillie. It's been a few years." He pulled the glove from his hand and offered it, hoping to lure the other man within grasp of the large bored rifle he carried. But the old man scurried three steps backward. On the last, his heel found a shard of ice Harry had chopped from the driveway and he slipped, falling heavily on his hip.

"Stay back," he croaked as Sturdevant reached toward him. The man who bore Tilden Beckwith's name struggled to his knees, the Weatherby's bore waving in Sturdevant's general direction. Sturdevant straightened and relaxed. A look of sudden horror returned to the old man's face. Frantically, he patted one hand against the pocket of his coat, then reached inside and pulled free a bottle of Glenlivet Scotch, whole and unbroken. He waggled it at Sturdevant. The horror vanished. He looked pleased with himself.

"This is for him," he said. "It's his brand, you know."

"For *him*," Sturdevant repeated blankly.

"For Tilden Beckwith. Glenlivet is his favorite. I never in my life heard him have to ask for it because everyone knew. Other people would have to say what drink they wanted, but not Grandfather Tilden."

"Yes," Sturdevant answered, staring. "Yes, I remember." He turned and glanced up toward the house. A shadow moved behind the living-room curtains. When he turned again he saw the hollow-eyed old man squinting past him through dim late-afternoon light and the falling snow.

"He's in there, isn't he?" The voice fell again to a whisper. "He's come back."

"Tillie—"

"I saw you with him, you know. I saw you yesterday at the Plaza. You were having drinks and talking, and I bet his drink was Glenlivet. You were so much older than he was. When you knew him before, you were younger. Now you're older. But he didn't change at all."

Sturdevant shook his head. "Tillie, that was not—" He stopped himself. There didn't seem to be much use in explaining the truth of it. If this man had been following Jonathan, which was the way it sounded, he must have known perfectly well that Jonathan had a name and that name was Corbin. Another thought struck him. "Tillie, have you had other people following us? Did you have someone waiting for us outside my house this morning?"

"Not me. That wasn't my doing."

"I see."

"It was always Ella. I would say, Don't do this, or, I don't want to do that, and she would just slap me and go and do it anyway."

"What sort of things would she do, Tillie?"

"Lots of things. Is he in there?"

"No. He's gone out. And you are not going to walk into that house with a loaded gun."

"It's not to hurt him. It's just to keep him from hurting me until we have a drink and talk. None of it was my fault."

"What, Tillie? What wasn't your fault?"

"Ella hit him. He struck Father and Ella hit him with her cane. And then they told me to go away, to go to Florida, and they sent Bigelow to Chicago after the others. But he came back for Bigelow and now he's back for Ella."

Sturdevant suddenly felt cold. Deathly cold. The storm reached beneath his coat as if it had fingers. "Ella," he repeated softly. "Ella killed him." He did not phrase it as a question.

"He knows that, doesn't he." There was that relief again. "He told you."

Sturdevant nodded slowly, almost afraid to speak. His mind fought against accepting the words he was hearing and the monstrous truth to which they were giving shape. "The Corbins," he whispered finally. "They tried to kill all the Corbins."

The old man nodded distantly. He stared into a space beyond Sturdevant's shoulder as if watching a scene that was being played there. "He came back for my father too, you know. He was waiting for him when he died. Right there at the bed. Father saw him. Ella tried to tell him it was only the minister. He didn't even hear her. He started screaming and crying and trying to crawl up the headboard and then suddenly he just sort of melted there. They couldn't close his eyes, did you know that? They had to use thread or they wouldn't stay shut."

"And Bigelow"—Sturdevant tried to form a question that would not betray his ignorance of that person's existence—"The man Ella sent to kill the Corbins . . . he too saw Tilden when he died?"

The old man shook his head slowly. "Tilden didn't have to wait for Bigelow. He was alive again then. He was young again."

"He didn't tell me about that," Sturdevant said carefully. "He said only that he found Bigelow. He did not say when or where."

Sturdevant had no clear idea why he was pursuing this Bigelow business, nor why he lied about having heard the name before, except that the words *alive again* and *young again* called up the picture of a living though not so young man who was the image of Tilden Beckwith down to the last fine detail of his face. A response formed on the old man's lips, but it froze there. His mouth fell slowly open, and his eyes stared past Sturdevant with the expression of a silent moan.

"Uncle Harry?" He heard Gwen's voice calling behind him.

"Ohhh!" The old man backed away, tears spilling on his cheeks.

"Are you okay?" He heard her voice again. Sturdevant raised a hand in reply, but he did not take his eyes from Tilden Beckwith II or from the trembling finger that was tightening over the rifle's trigger. He knew without turning what this wreck of a man was seeing. He was seeing another dead person made newly young. He was looking at Gwen Leamas standing framed in the doorway of a Victorian house and wearing a long, white Victorian gown. But he was seeing Charlotte Corbin, a graceful old woman who was murdered in Chicago forty years before. He was seeing Margaret Barrie.

. . .

It had never entered Margaret's mind that she might not return to Greenwich. If Laura Hemmings had told Teddy where she was when he came back to her house with news of finding Tilden, if Tilden could have wired her directly and not used Laura as an intermediary, she would almost surely have been on the first train east. She would have come quickly, even though it was Tilden's wish that she stay, stay until his fever was broken and his cruel injuries had healed, stay until it was known that all outside threats to their happiness were gone from them. She would have come back even if she did not yet know that it was in Tilden's mind to ask her to be his wife.

But Tilden's message to Margaret was not at all direct. It was filtered first through Teddy, a friend deeply concerned for him, and again through Laura, a friend just as well intentioned where Margaret's welfare was involved. It is best that you stay away, was the meaning Margaret saw in the language of the message she received. The second message, the one which broke her heart, was one which had lost even more in translation. It had occurred to Tilden near the end of his first week at Bellevue that Margaret might find herself in need of cash. He arranged, through Teddy, for the bank in Greenwich to send her a draft in the amount of five hundred dollars and to advise her of the much larger amount which was on deposit in her name. He scribbled a loving note that was meant to accompany the draft.

The draft and the intelligence of the larger deposit were forwarded by wire once Laura Hemmings provided the bank with her address, but Tilden's note did not go with it. If he had been less befogged by laudanum and less distracted by the pain of his wired jaw, he would have known that the banker, J. H. Hinckley, would not have opened a sealed envelope in order to add its message to the wire bearing the draft, nor would he have considered that Hinckley, having placed the letter in his rolltop desk to await a forwarding address, would have forgotten it entirely. What Margaret received, then, was simply the five-hundred-dollar draft and a statement of the balance of her account. The transaction being complete in and of itself, Mr. Hinckley added, as was his custom in such matters, that no further communication was required from her. Margaret was crushed. It appeared to her that she had been paid in full for services rendered.

The two weeks that followed brought no relief to this tragic misunderstanding. Margaret promptly mailed the draft back to Laura Hemmings, together with her interpretation of its meaning. Laura presumed that interpretation to be accurate because she presumed it to be based upon a clear communication from Tilden and not upon a banker's routine addendum. Furious, Laura forwarded the draft to Tilden's office with the advice that Margaret did not want his goddamned money and that no further communication would be required of him, either, if she had her way. A full five weeks had passed since he left Margaret to do his "errand" at Lyndhurst and three weeks since Margaret had departed for her Evanston visit when Tilden felt well enough to ask his head clerk, Mr. Levi Scoggins, to bring his accumulated correspondence to his room at Bellevue. It was then, to his horror, when he realized that either a terrible mistake had somehow been made or that Margaret had simply decided that she'd had enough of Greenwich, of living with her fears and in an indefinite relationship, and of Tilden Beckwith himself. He leaped into his clothes and rushed from Bellevue without the leave of any doctor. Cursing the wired jaw that prevented him from telephoning Laura Hemmings, he caught the first available train from Grand Central to Greenwich and was pounding upon Laura Hemmings's door within three hours of opening her letter. Three hours after that, he was aboard a train to Chicago.

For the rest of his life, Tilden would mourn what might have been save for those three drugged weeks and a misplaced letter. He would never fully understand all the things which contributed to Margaret's decision that she would not return with him. There were times when he thought that the soaring ecstasy of their reunion was, in its own odd way, as responsible as any other factor for what would follow. "I almost think," she told him, "that it is better to be melancholy all the time, or happy all the time, than it is to swing so greatly and so often between those two ends of the same frayed rope." She had refused to see him at first, though her resolution lasted not a quarter hour, and that was well because the ladies of the WCTU were becoming certain that their stoutest doors and Evanston's burliest policemen would not long keep him at bay. After sending down word that she would consent to a brief interview, she steeled herself and descended the stairs toward the building foyer where he waited, pacing, and she dissolved into tears at her first sight of the sutures on his face and his bandaged hands and at his first words through jaws that would not open. It took a half hour more before he could scribble all that was in his heart, all the news of the past five weeks, on the backs of every scrap of paper he could find. And all the while he cried as hard as she.

They spent that night together, appearances be damned, and all the next day as well. There was scarcely a moment when Tilden's arms were not around Margaret, or around Jonathan, or around both of them together.

It was at the end of the second day, at dinner, when Margaret told Tilden that she'd been asked to consider moving permanently to Evanston. She confessed that she'd told the ladies there that she and Jonathan were quite alone in the world and without ties to Greenwich or any other place. And they spoke to her of the wonderful opportunities that existed for women in this fine new Chicago which had risen from the great fire of 1871. Women were a great force here, they'd told her. There had been too much work to do, too much need for women's energies, to waste time perpetuating silly myths about the proper role of that sex. A newspaper, the *Chicago Sun,* had already printed a piece she'd written on the work of the Temperance Union and had asked her to do another on—"Do not laugh at this, Tilden"—the high-priced sporting houses of South Dearborn Street from a decent woman's perspective.

Tilden had been listening attentively enough, and he was indeed amused, but he listened as if the topic had no real significance because she and Jonathan would, after all, be returning with him as soon as she could complete the task for which she'd come.

At dinner on the third night, Margaret asked Tilden why he did not consider moving to Chicago as well. He could surely begin a new brokerage business there, or else open a new office. Tilden answered that he, in fact, had considered starting a branch office or two, and Chicago was certainly a candidate for one of them, what with all the new building still going on and most of the nation's cattle and grain wealth being funneled through that city. But such a move was at least a year or two in the future. If and when it happened, he promised Margaret, they would visit Chicago often. These words spoken, it was Margaret's silence that made him all the more attentive. And this time he did not smile.

"My heart stopped beating just now." Tilden placed his hand against it. "I had the strangest notion and it turned me cold."

"Your heart is listening to mine, I think," she said softly.

"Do not say it, Margaret." He forced these words through his wired jaw. "Please don't say you'll not return with me."

"I will not go back to Greenwich."

"But you love it there. You said so."

"I love its beauty. I love our home there. Our friends. Our little cove where we slip off to swim. I do not love all the new people who are moving there from New York, like that Inspector Williams of yours. I do not love living so close to a man who hates you that I can almost feel his breath. I do not love Anthony Comstock."

"Gould has pulled in his claws and Comstock is gone. You have nothing to fear."

"Gould only waits. You said yourself that he's a man who eats his revenge cold. As for Comstock, he left a stain on that town, Tilden, which will never wash away."

"New York, then," he said urgently. "We'll be married and we'll live in New York."

"The fate of Carrie Todd and Belle Walker can find me there just as easily, Tilden. Marry me and it will find you at the same time."

"In which case we'll have a perfectly good reason to move to Chicago."

Margaret took his hands. "Do you mean that, my darling?"

"To Chicago, to London, or in a hut among the heathen Chinee. It is all the same if you are with me. If you are not, there is no life for me at all."

"Then move here now. Move to Chicago."

"I cannot." He touched his lips to her fingertips. "Not now. The business has been given to me by my father. It is a sacred trust. Even more sacred is my responsibility to those employees and friends who stood by me through time of great difficulty and who made sacrifices on my behalf. Please say you understand that, Margaret."

"I do, Tilden," she answered gently. "If I had no child, I would be on the train with you tomorrow. But I have no right to risk Jonathan's name. And I will not risk his good opinion of me if I can help it."

He squeezed her hands until he realized that the tears he saw were from pain as well as sorrow. "Do not leave me, Margaret." Tilden's jaw trembled. "I will die."

"I will never leave you, Tilden," she whispered.

"Does that mean you will—"

Margaret touched her fingers to his mouth. "It means I will wait for you, Tilden."

Nothing between them changed very much from the day Margaret made that promise. The house in Greenwich was sold within the year and Tilden sent some of the money to Margaret and invested the rest in her name. Tilden traveled to Chicago twice more that summer. On the second trip he brought Lucy Stone who, having heard on Margaret's authority that the coloreds of Evanston lived in houses as nice as the whites, had elected to join Margaret. The press of business kept Tilden in New York through the early fall, but he came for a long Thanksgiving holiday and again over Christmas of 1891.

Between visits and well into 1892, Tilden and Margaret exchanged letters every week without fail. A planned visit for July of 1892 was delayed by the death of Cyrus Field. Tilden was chosen as a pallbearer and as one of the eulogizers at Field's service. As he looked down from the pulpit and saw that Jay Gould had taken a preeminent place among the mourners, Tilden was sorely tempted to depart from his prepared text and heap public scorn upon Gould and those like him.

But he chose to honor Cyrus Field by doing no such thing. Gould called enough attention to himself by coughing away a little more of his life at intervals throughout the service.

The following month, Tilden wrote to Margaret, suggesting an excursion by riverboat to New Orleans, where in September they would watch John L. Sullivan defend his title against the San Francisco Dancing Master, James J. Corbett. Margaret was thrilled. She quickly wheedled a reporter's assignment from the *Chicago Sun* so there would be no question of her being allowed inside the arena. Even then it took Sullivan's intercession to get her past the gatemen. John Flood was there, of course, and to Tilden's delight Nat Goodwin as well, along with Bat Masterson, once a famous frontier lawman, now a sportswriter. These men toasted Sullivan's chances before the fight, then his grace in defeat after he lost it, all with equal enthusiasm.

Tilden needed all of the three-day riverboat ride up the Mississippi to recover. Once they were back in Chicago, their sorrow over the champion's defeat turned immediately to gladness because they were to attend the wedding of Lucy Stone to a roofing contractor named Amos Tuttle who'd been called in one day to repair a leak in the shingles of Margaret's house. Lucy moved into her own home in the colored part of Evanston but still spent her days with Margaret and Jonathan. Jonathan had begun calling Tilden Uncle Tilden. Tilden told Margaret he'd much rather be called Father but could offer no practical suggestion unless of course Margaret stopped all this foolishness and came back to New York and married him. Margaret would smile and kiss him and say, once again, "I will wait for you, Tilden."

Jay Gould's end finally came in December of that year, not five months after Cyrus Field's passing. It was said that he declined all the more rapidly from the day of Field's service, that he seemed a man for whom there was no hope and no consolation. Tilden had told no one but Margaret of his curious conversation with a man who saw no evil in the harm he did to those he did not admire, but who seemed to see damnation in the harm he did to a better man and who saw his only hope of salvation to be in restoring the good man he'd broken. It was an obsession that Tilden never quite understood. But, as Margaret pointed out, many dark workings of the mind are beyond all reason and understanding. What of Collis P. Huntington, who built his great house on the corner of Fifth Avenue and Fifty-seventh Street and then refused to live in it upon hearing a chance remark that rich men build fine homes only to die in them? What of A. T. Stewart, who spent millions on a gallery of fine paintings and then allowed not a single human being to see them, not even a servant with a feather duster? What of Russell Sage, who will inquire into the cost of a man's suit upon meeting him and will eat no meal costing more than a dollar though he's worth fifty million? Tilden agreed. He could think of none among the very rich men he'd known who'd been spared some sort of madness. Perhaps madness is what is required of one who aspires to be rich. Madness and an essential unattractiveness, because Tilden could also think of none he'd care to meet again in this world or the next if the choice were his.

"Move to Chicago, Tilden," she said. "Be with me and Jonathan."

"Come back to New York," he replied. "You'll find greater peace there with Jay Gould gone."

"In my mind," she answered, "I see Jay Gould's fallen body. And I see a circle of dogs closing on it. The dogs will always be there, Tilden. They'll be there for you, too, in the end."

"You could watch my back, dear Margaret, as John Flood used to do."

"I will watch sunsets with you, I will watch our child's face on Christmas mornings, I will watch your naked body on a moonlit beach. But I will not watch your back, Tilden. No one with a choice should live that way."

So quickly did the years go by. It seemed no time at all before Margaret, who was then to the *Chicago Sun* very nearly what her friend Nelly Bly had been to the *New York World,* saw on the wire service reports that Teddy Roosevelt had been commissioned a lieutenant colonel of the First United States Volunteer Cavalry soon after the opening of hostilities with Spain. A phone call to his office on the new Chicago-New York telephone connection confirmed an appalling intuition that Tilden Beckwith, heaven save us, had dashed on down to enlist as one of Teddy's cowboys.

"The Rough Riders are not cowboys, dear Margaret. They might just be the finest light cavalry in the world short of the Ogalala Sioux."

"Whatever. Tell me that you have not enlisted."

"What choice have I? Our nation is at war. As long as I have no wife to mourn me, I must do my duty. Of course, if I were married, it would be another matter."

"I *am* your wife, Tilden. License or no, I have been your wife for ten years. Have you enlisted or have you not?"

"I have just enough time to rush to Chicago and marry you before the troopship leaves. Then you can come back with me and wave tearfully from the pier."

"Tilden, you didn't!"

"Not yet. I thought I'd give you a chance to prevent it."

"I see."

"You see what?"

"Teddy turned you down."

"That's not exactly true at all."

Margaret howled with glee. "He said you're too old, didn't he?"

"Thirty-eight is not old. Teddy's forty, for God's sake."

"He did. He wouldn't take you," she whooped.

"This is not a laughing matter, Margaret."

"Get out here, Tilden. Let's see how old thirty-eight really is."

"What an absolutely shocking thing to suggest on a public telephone."

"When, Tilden?"

"Friday next. My wife, you say."

"If you need proof, wait till you see me box your ears for upsetting me."

The war with Spain vaulted Teddy into a limelight he never relinquished and of which he took full advantage. He no sooner returned a hero than he announced himself a candidate for governor of New York and won the election handily. Margaret and Tilden traveled to Albany to attend his swearing in. Tilden met privately with Teddy over breakfast during his second day in office. It amused Teddy to tell him that there was already talk of his running for vice president in another two years just on the strength of a single hill climb in Cuba, not that he had any interest in that office. In any case, there was enough to do as reform governor of the state of New York. There was a civil service to be restructured, a wilderness to be conserved, Indian children to be educated, and Negro children to be integrated into New York's schools. On the matter of civil service, he asked, would Tilden believe that there are those who resist the notion that a policeman ought to be able to read and write or be able to approximately identify the president of the United States?

"Clubber Williams, by the way, is finished." Teddy rapped the table. "I've told him I'll have his resignation in January or I'll have him in prison by June. It might interest you that his house in Greenwich, Cos Cob actually, contributed as much as anything to his downfall. He had trouble recalling how he could buy a Connecticut estate, buy a yacht, and spend thirty-nine thousand dollars on a dock for it, all on a salary of thirty-five hundred a year."

"Careful budgeting, perhaps," Tilden suggested dryly. He recalled the Lexow Committee of the previous year, which had established that the opportunities for acquiring wealth as a New York City police officer were so great that an appointment as a $1200-a-year patrolman sold for as much as $300 on a sliding scale that brought an average of $15,000 for a captaincy.

"One must admire the man's boldness, however. I've always liked audacity in a fellow, no matter what his other sins. I've admired your audacity, Tilden."

There was something about the way Teddy left that last sentence hanging, as if incomplete. Tilden decided to let it go.

"Has he ever bothered you again, Tilden?"

"Who? You mean Williams?"

"Yes. Did he ever put any further pressure on you, either in Gould's interest or his own?"

"No." Tilden's eyes narrowed. "I've never even seen him again except from a distance around town. Teddy, why are you asking?"

"No particular reason."

"Hogwash."

Teddy squirmed in his seat. "I thought you and Charlotte would have married by now."

"I thought we would as well. One day we will."

"I wondered if there is perhaps something in your past, some secret, some regret, the exposure of which by Williams or Gould or someone else might possibly bring tragedy to a marriage once undertaken."

"In *my* past, you say."

"Yes."

"Teddy, what on earth are you talking about?"

His friend looked away. "Gould asked me a question once. He asked me if you could look me in the eye and tell me you did not murder Ella."

"Look at me, Teddy."

Roosevelt met his eyes.

"Ella ran from me into a blizzard. I went after her to keep her from going to Ansel Carling. She fell in the snow and I stood over her for what now seems no more than a minute or two. It must have been a great deal longer."

"And she died there?"

"If I had not gone after her, if I had not stood over her, she would probably not have died. That much is true, Teddy. There is no way around it."

"Was it in your heart to cause her death?"

"I do not think so."

"When you left her . . . when you turned away, what were your thoughts?"

"To be rid of her. To send her and the child back to Philadelphia. To present Ansel Carling with a bill." Tilden indicated his fist.

"To divorce her, you mean."

"Teddy"—Tilden leaned forward—"you are about to tell me that if divorce was on my mind, then I could not have believed that she was dead or dying. I have tried to believe that as well. It is not always easy. I have satisfied myself that I can do little but go on with my life and await God's judgment at the end of it."

"Well"—Teddy folded his napkin—"when that happens, perhaps it wouldn't be a bad idea to have a pardon from the governor of New York in your pocket."

. . .

More years peeled by. Teddy did accept the vice-presidential nomination, he was elected on William McKinley's ticket, and nine months later a stunned nation learned that McKinley had been mortally wounded and that this "damned cowboy" would inevitably be president of the United States. Tilden was a frequent visitor to Washington, once staying for six months as an adviser on the abuses of an unregulated securities industry, and for another four months as a member of Roosevelt's reelection committee. Teddy's first six years in office effectively ended the days of the great robber barons. They were men whom Teddy and Tilden despised as individuals, yet there could be no denying that this relative handful of men had literally built this country. Whether they did so out of personal greed was academic. The government could not have done what they did. It had neither the competence nor the imagination nor the freedom of action. But the government under Roosevelt did learn to put reins on them and to use them, even to learn from them.

Near the end of Teddy's second term, Tilden traveled to Chicago to witness Jonathan's graduation from New Trier High School in Evanston. Jonathan would be attending Northwestern University in the fall on, to Tilden's soaring delight, a full four-year baseball scholarship. For the next two years he saw Jonathan play as often as his schedule permitted and read with pride the occasional reports that the Chicago White Sox had a covetous eye on him. That pride turned mixed in 1907, when Jonathan announced he was quitting school to pitch for the White Sox at $3000 a year. That was twice, he told his mother, what he was likely to earn at any other livelihood upon graduation. Margaret was unimpressed by that argument, as was Tilden. But Tilden did recognize that athletic careers can be cruelly short and that the opportunity might not come along again. He extracted a promise that Jonathan would keep up with his studies even while traveling with the team and that he would eventually return for his degree.

Jonathan's career was even briefer than Tilden anticipated, lasting not quite two seasons. The pitch on which he'd built his reputation was the spitball, followed by two variations of his own design called the scuffball and the greaseball. By the end of the very year he'd signed, both leagues outlawed the spitball and all other creative uses of foreign matter. Jonathan spent the intervening winter trying to develop an alternate repertoire, but his efforts, particularly on his fastball, brought on a worsening tendinitis in his shoulder. The White Sox kept him on for the better part of the 1909 season, but the shoulder failed to improve. He was retired in time to register for the fall term at Northwestern. Jonathan graduated the next year, stayed on as a graduate instructor and baseball coach, and eventually became an associate professor of English literature.

In 1916, the Great War in Europe erupted in full fury. Jonathan tried to enlist as a flyer but was rejected because of his age, twenty-seven. A relieved Margaret then prevailed upon him to wait out the current school year before trying any other branch of the service. During that year, Jonathan began keeping serious company with a former repertory actress who was the drama coach at Northwestern, Barbara Holman. Sweetheart or no, there was a war on and many of Jonathan's friends were already in France. Jonathan volunteered for the American Expeditionary Force in June of 1917. He passed the physical and was as good as in uniform when he was asked to raise his right hand for the oath. An officer, one he recognized as an acquaintance of his mother's, asked him to please raise his hand higher. Jonathan complied but with obvious pain and difficulty. The officer asked him to step out of ranks and report to another room for further examination by a doctor. The doctor concluded that Jonathan's chronic shoulder problem was such that he could neither salute nor sight a rifle satisfactorily. Jonathan was sent home. When he asked his mother whether she'd seen a certain officer lately, she could not imagine, she insisted, what he could be talking about. This near miss, however, became the impetus for Barbara Holman to press her intentions. They were married at the end of 1917.

To Margaret's astonishment, Tilden arrived for the wedding in a private railway car. He had advised her that he might bring another guest or two. Margaret let out a shriek as Laura Hemmings stepped from the car behind him, towing Dr. Miles Palmer, whom she'd long since married, and their two blond daughters, both in their early teens. Next came Big John Flood in one of his wildly checked suits that never quite fit him, Nat Goodwin with the latest and last of his seven wives, and a waving, shouting Peggy Gannon, who was in her fourth term in the Connecticut State Legislature. Last off, his bellowing voice preceding him, was all three hundred pounds of the former heavyweight champion of the world, "Yours truly, John L. Sullivan," as he announced his presence to the city of Chicago. Teddy Roosevelt, who'd been ill for some time, was represented by five dozen hothouse roses for Margaret and an autographed photo of himself for the newlyweds, framed in the claws of a bear he'd shot in Wyoming.

The next two years, however, brought more sorrow than joy. Most of the joy attended the birth of Tilden's grandson, Whitney Corbin. Margaret had hoped that the boy would be named for Tilden, but Jonathan had chosen to honor his mother with his first-born by giving the baby her unsuspectedly false maiden name. At the christening, Margaret could only shrug helplessly at Tilden, who crossed his eyes in return.

The first sorrow came with the passing of John L.

Sullivan not long after the wedding. A heart attack took him at his small Massachusetts farm the following February. Tilden was a pallbearer, as was Jake Kilrain. Margaret missed the funeral because she was traveling on assignment from her newspaper but came later and spent several days with Kate Sullivan, John's widow.

Less than a year later came the numbing news that Teddy Roosevelt had died in his sleep of a blocked artery in his chest. Margaret rushed to New York when word came over the wire service. It was her first return to that city, except to change trains, in nearly thirty years. She attended the funeral at Sagamore Hill with Tilden and John Flood, both of whom were honorary pallbearers. Tilden did not speak at the service nor could he have done so if he'd been asked. He was crushed. Most of that winter passed before Tilden was able to accept a world in which there was no more Teddy. Margaret stayed a month with him, then forced him to spend another month with her in Evanston. They had no sooner recovered from that loss when the influenza epidemic, which was killing millions worldwide, reached into Evanston and took Barbara Holman Corbin. She was carrying Jonathan's second child at the time. Margaret and Lucy Stone Tuttle undertook to raise young Whitney just as they'd raised his father.

In the meantime, Huntington Beckwith, the false son sired by Ansel Carling, grew up, was sent to Yale, and then to Columbia Law School. He was sent anywhere he had the slightest interest in going as long as it kept him away from Beckwith & Company. Margaret reminded Tilden on several occasions, the latest being on one of their stays at a charming Wisconsin inn they'd discovered, that Huntington could hardly be blamed for the circumstances of his birth. Truth be told, his life thus far seemed more blameless than either of theirs.

"But that's just it," Tilden said, agreeing. "There's

no blame to him but there's little else, either. No passion, no joy, no friends to speak of, no interest in athletics, and above all he's extremely neat. I detest neat people. He doesn't even perspire. His body somehow repels dust. He speaks only when he is spoken to, and while he's waiting to be addressed he sits there and watches. Like cats watch. I detest cats and neat people with equal feeling."

"He resembles Ansel Carling, doesn't he," Margaret said softly.

"I suppose he must. My right fist develops a twitch whenever I stand close to him."

"You have not been kind to him, Tilden."

"I am not kind to cats, either. But they go away and he doesn't."

"You cannot punish him for Ella's sin, Tilden. That is wrong. It is also unworthy of you. Can there be no place for him in your business if not in your heart?"

"As for my heart, it has been filled to overflowing for more than thirty years. It has been broken again and again by a great lady whom I seem doomed never to possess. Even the spaces between my heartbeats are filled with you. It's a wonder that I find room to love Jonathan as well."

"And Whitney? Not Whitney?" She smiled.

"Whitney, too. He fills the cracks where my heart has broken in the knowledge that he will never call me Grandfather."

"He'll know one day. I promise."

"Yet one more uncertain treasure."

"What is that?"

"It's from a poem I read. I regularly torture myself by reflecting on it. It goes, 'Margaret's love, uncertain treasure, hast thou more of pain or pleasure? Endless torments dwell about thee. But who would live, and live without thee?' "

"*Margaret's* love?"

"I made a change or two. The fact remains, I would not live without you, Margaret."

"Nor I without you, Tilden, my bent-nosed gladiator."

"Who knows perfectly well when he's being buttered up. What do you hope to extort from me?"

"It would lighten my heart if you would soften yours toward Ella's child."

"Already done. He will have a place in my business because he's studied for it and there seems to be no help for it. He also plans to marry soon. All things considered, I cannot decently deny him a situation."

Margaret seemed pleased though startled by the news. "This is already decided? That you'll take him in?"

"It was done three months ago. He'll have his chance to earn a partnership and possibly even my esteem, although it's a long way from my ledgers to my affections. I'm afraid, though, that his chosen wife will make it doubly hard for him. She's another of those cat people. Stares silently all the time. They doubtless spend their evenings hunting mice together."

Tilden assured Margaret that young Huntington would be treated fairly and even receive some consideration in Tilden's will. But she, Margaret, and their son, Jonathan, would be the major beneficiaries. He would also hold her to her promise that Jonathan would one day be told that Tilden was his father.

"The young man is not a dunce, you know." This conversation took place several years before Jonathan married Barbara. "All his life he's been hearing people remark on how closely he and I resemble each other. I bet he's just too polite to bring it up."

"I know." She looked away.

"Then why don't we tell him together and get it over with?"

Margaret sighed. "It would mean admitting that

I've lied to him all his life. I've had to tell him that Wilkes-Barre train-wreck story. Then, of course, it's also on my official WCTU biography, one result of which is that it's also turned up in nearly every other piece that's been written about me. Talk about tangled webs."

"Telling Jonathan and telling the whole world are not the same thing."

"Let's wait a while, Tilden. Please."

Huntington Beckwith did marry his cat-woman wife and quickly produced two children. The first was a daughter, whom he named Ella to Tilden's unspoken displeasure. The second was a son, whom he named Tilden Beckwith II to Tilden's even greater annoyance. Tilden had refused to consider himself a grandfather until Barbara and Jonathan produced Whitney.

When Huntington entered the business, although Tilden silently begrudged him the place he'd like Jonathan to have taken, he could not deny that Huntington was resourceful and industrious. The Great War, like all wars, brought good business to those who were far from the battlefields. Beckwith & Company expanded as never before. Where the firm's real estate subsidiary had previously been a builder or improver of property, under Huntington's management its emphasis shifted more toward speculation. Real estate speculation could certainly be profitable under boom conditions but still, Tilden found it distasteful. It smacked too much of money changing and profiteering as opposed to adding value to a thing and helping it grow. Nonetheless, he gave Huntington his head because the profits allowed him to buy a fine old hotel he'd long had his eye on, the Regency, plus a once-elegant brownstone house on Thirty-sixth Street just off Fifth Avenue, which he gave to the city on condition that it be used as a hospice for homeless young girls. He enjoyed thinking that Georgiana Hastings would be pleased, wherever she was.

The 1920s were one long sporting event for Tilden Beckwith. Jack Dempsey, Babe Ruth, the Four Horsemen of Notre Dame, and his divided loyalties between the Chicago White Sox and the New York Giants all vied with Margaret for his attention. Whatever time was left, after an additional deduction to watch young Whitney grow, went to the affairs of Beckwith & Company. When the twenties ended with Wall Street's collapse, heralding the sad gray years of the Great Depression, Tilden was forced to pay more attention to his affairs. Though his losses were considerable in terms of reduced market value, they were not catastrophic. Cyrus Field's disaster had taught him the folly of buying on a ten percent margin. Huntington Beckwith, however, had not had the advantage of that lesson. Many of his land speculations, especially those made on his own initiative, turned largely to dust. It would take another war to restore their value to the prices he had paid. It became a point of honor with Tilden that no employee be laid off or have to take a reduction in salary or suffer in any way at all because of the folly of their management. Tilden punished himself for his own neglect by cutting his salary in half for the first five years of the new decade. Huntington resisted a similar reduction until Tilden informed him of the alternative.

By the second half of that decade, the firm's fortunes had recovered their full vigor. The rest of the world, Tilden noted ruefully, could not say the same. He smelled war. Just as armed robbery is an inevitable condition as men tire of being poor when a neighbor is not, armed conflict is the same result among nations. He watched newsreel films of that strutting little Hitler fellow in Germany. Half the men behind him seemed to look like Huntington. The other half, discounting the fat one, Göring, looked like Huntington's son.

In the year 1937, Tilden Beckwith II entered Yale for all of three months. He was most often called Tillie for short, other variations being Silly or Dilly. These nicknames were a great relief for Tilden, who wanted as little room for confusion as possible between himself and Huntington's son. After Tillie failed out of Yale, Huntington approached Tilden with a request that he use his influence to get Tillie accepted by Harvard. Tilden was aghast. The thought of Tillie Beckwith walking halls once trod by Teddy Roosevelt seemed an insult to Teddy's memory. It was bad enough that the daughter, Ella, was at Radcliffe and within hissing distance of Harvard. Tilden suggested Boston College. That way, he thought to himself, they could be let out together at night. Cat people!

Whitney Corbin, meanwhile, set about breaking many of his father's records at New Trier High School and, in 1938, announced his intention of attending Notre Dame University. It was best, he thought, not to play baseball at Northwestern under his father. Besides, Notre Dame had a better boxing program—his grandfather's influence—was more demanding academically, and had many more advantages once you overlooked the fact that the place was overrun with Catholics. Whitney also had a private dream of playing football under Frank Leahy and passing into that school's book of legends. Sadly, however, he did not survive the final cut in either his freshman or sophomore year. But by his third year he was a baseball star and he'd won his first intercollegiate boxing title. He gave no more thought to football. Only to baseball, to boxing, to his studies, and to those wonderful vapor trails made by high-flying airplanes when the weather is right.

Tilden's friends seemed to die in clusters. In June of 1943, he received a letter postmarked Los Angeles, California, from a legal firm. Under a one-line cover note from a faceless lawyer, there was a typewritten letter on scented stationery. It read:

Dearest Tilden:

If you are reading this, I was more ill than I'd hoped. I am ninety years old. I can scarcely believe it but I'm afraid you would if you could see what's become of my fine Spencerian handwriting. Thank God for typewriters.

I have been out here in Hollywood since 1922, living quite as respectably as this mad little town permits. I was invited here by one of the studio heads who thought his actresses needed instruction in how to behave like great ladies or stars or top-flight whores and was wise enough to know that the three do not differ in their fundamentals. They have paid me outrageous amounts of money and I don't even have to give half of it to the local constabulary. If only I'd known.

A friend has told me what you've done with a certain address on 36th Street in New York. I love you for that, Tilden. I also love you for what you have been to a certain lady of our mutual acquaintance. I want you both to know that you have always been in my thoughts. Perhaps, from time to time, you'll find room for me in yours. Bon chance . . .

                                        Georgiana

In a postscript, she listed the names of several very well-known actresses under contract to Metro-Goldwyn-Mayer. Instead of sending flowers, she said, go to the movies and watch one or two of these ladies. You'll see and hear more than a little bit of Georgiana Hastings.

Tilden resolved to do that, but he sent flowers anyway after calling the lawyer for the name of the cemetery where Georgiana rested. On the following Sunday, he was sitting in his box at the Polo Grounds, not really watching the game but gazing dreamily out toward the left field bleachers, where there was once only an open field and a place for carriages to park and picnic. An acquaintance, a man near his own age, stopped to say hello. As he was about to move on he paused, then said to Tilden that he was sorry to read about John Flood. "Oh . . . I'm sorry, Tilden. I thought you knew." It had been a very small item in the *New York Daily Mirror,* which Tilden seldom read. BARE-KNUCKLER DIES was the headline. Like Georgiana, he had passed away three weeks earlier. In Saratoga, New York. A heart attack while watching a new young heavyweight train.

On the Monday after that, having made a note to call a writer he knew at the *New York Times* to see if he could arrange a more fitting obituary, Tilden returned to his office and learned that Andrew Smithberg, who had joined the firm as a very new lawyer and had been active in it for almost sixty years, the last twenty as executive vice president and chief counsel, had suffered a fatal stroke the evening before. Late that same morning, Tilden wandered sadly into Andrew Smithberg's office and found Huntington browsing through Andrew's files as another of the firm's lawyers, Chester Wax, stood uncomfortably by.

"What are you doing there?" he asked quietly.

Huntington's head snapped up a bit too quickly. "Just seeing what's where," he answered. "The business must go on after all."

The open file drawer began to resemble a coffin and Huntington a graveyard ghoul feeding on its contents. Tilden blinked the image away.

"The business will go on perfectly well after a decent interval of mourning. Would you both leave this office, please, and do not return until invited."

"I meant no disrespect, sir." Wax stepped forward. "On the contrary, there are personal papers belonging to Mr. Smithberg that I'll need to help his family make the proper arrangements."

"They would be in the safe, Mr. Wax." Tilden's tone softened. "I will sort them out and deliver what you need to your desk."

Left alone in the office, Tilden stood for a while, his eyes drifting over the many mementos of the past six decades. Eighty-one. It was impossible to believe that he was eighty-one years old. And that Margaret was what? Seventy-seven? That's ridiculous. The woman is no more than thirty-five. Never mind that Jonathan is well into his fifties. An irrelevancy. Perhaps Margaret is thirty-nine. Whatever she is, she still can turn a head when we're walking together, can't she. There is a proudness to her, a grace, that no amount of time can wither.

Tilden, at last, stepped to Andrew Smithberg's safe and, lowering himself to one knee, worked the combination. He found two folders, both marked Personal, one bearing Smithberg's name and the other his own. Margaret's papers. Copies of the originals, rather. We'll hope that she keeps hers secure, not that she seems to intend ever using them. He took a quick look through the folder to assure himself that all was intact, then slid them into his pocket. The safe in his own office would probably be a better place for them now. Next he sorted through Andrew's papers—birth and baptismal record, his will, that sort of thing. These he would deliver to Mr. Wax.

Tilden spun the dial one more time and swung the safe door shut. Its sound masked another door that was quietly closing behind him.

Huntington Beckwith stepped softly down the corridor to the office of Chester Wax, who, five years before, had been detected by Huntington diverting relatively minor amounts of cash from the company accounts. Realizing that a cooperative attorney in the hand was worth two disbarred lawyers in prison, Huntington reached an ongoing understanding with him.

"I want to see that will," he whispered. "The will, and whatever else is in that folder. It's probably going into his own safe."

"But I don't have that combination either," Wax told him.

"I want to see that folder." Cat's eyes.

"Does Mr. Beckwith have another attorney?" the lawyer asked.

"He's only used Smithberg."

"Then why don't we wait just a while? He'll probably ask me to handle some routine affair before long."

Huntington nodded. "Don't wait. Make yourself useful to him. Win his confidence." He turned to walk out, then stopped. "There is a way that you look at me, Mr. Wax, whenever I leave a room or my back is turned. Make sure Tilden Beckwith sees it."

Chester Wax was right. And so was Huntington. Only a few days passed before Tilden began to notice a polite but definite cautiousness on the lawyer's part in virtually any matter that concerned Huntington. Wax seemed neither to like nor trust him. In that particular at least, he was very much like Andrew Smithberg. He was taking up several of Andrew's more urgent duties without needing to be asked, and he was assisting in the ordering of Andrew's estate with apparent sensitivity. By the end of the second week, Tilden was assigning certain of his personal affairs to Chester Wax. Within the month, Wax had seen Tilden open his safe a half dozen times or more. He was almost sure he had the combination memorized.

A day came soon after when Chester Wax was called into the Board Room to sit in on that portion of a directors' meeting that concerned the disposition of Smithberg's shares in the firm. Huntington offered to buy them at a figure well below their true value. Tilden ignored the offer, then announced that he himself would buy them at a premium. Wax, Tilden noticed, seemed to give a silent cheer. Wax lingered until all the directors save Tilden had filed out. Tilden now saw a look of concern on Wax's face.

"You have something on your mind, Chester?" Tilden asked.

"It's really none of my business, sir."

"Try me. I assume it concerns the company."

"It's just that Mr. Smithberg's passing was so sudden, sir. It has led to some worried water-cooler talk about what might happen to the company if Tilden Beckwith was to . . . be incapacitated."

"If I kick the bucket, you mean."

"Yes, sir."

"There is an order of succession. Each of the directors has a sealed envelope outlining my wishes. It amounts to a posthumous proxy vote."

Wax's concern appeared to deepen. "But by then, sir, your legal heir will be the majority stockholder. Your instructions will carry no weight if Mr. Hunt—if your heir chooses to ignore them." The lawyer's slip was deliberate.

"You presume a great deal, Chester. Mr. Huntington is a salaried executive. Nothing more. That has been made clear to him at least annually for the past thirty years."

"He *said* that?" Huntington's sallow skin was stretched even tighter across his face. "He actually *said* that I am not named?"

"He implied it very strongly."

"I must see his will. You must get into that safe."

"I believe I know the combination." Chester Wax looked smug.

"You know the—" Huntington's black pupils opened wide. "Well then, write it down for me."

"I'll take five thousand dollars for it. Cash."

"What you'll get is a jail cell if you're not careful."

"It's now *six* thousand. Cash."

"Six thousand, you say?" The voice came back over Huntington's private line.

"Yes. What do you think?"

"Wax handles a few trust accounts, does he not?"

"Yes. The only sizable one is Tilden's endowment for that hospice of his."

"Can you get at the funds?"

"There is a way, yes."

"Get the six thousand there, if you can. The more Wax is compromised, the better. But waste no time on this. Even if you must beg or borrow the money, get into that safe before this week is out. Do you understand me?"

"I understand you, Ella. And kindly reserve that tone for your brother."

Corbin.

Mrs. Charlotte Whitney Corbin. Huntington stared disbelieving at the name.

He knew who she was. He'd known for almost a quarter century. He'd seen her with him at the service for Theodore Roosevelt. She was that Chicago woman he was forever traveling to visit. That she might receive some consideration, some remembrance, would not have surprised him. But his heir? To almost everything? Cash accounts, real estate, insurance policies, personal mementos . . . everything. To Charlotte Corbin and to Jonathan T Corbin, who appears to be her son, and who is named as executor of the estate with absolute discretion over the affairs and the disposition of Beckwith & Company. Huntington turned to a number of codicils that had been added over a period of years. Another Corbin. Whitney. And somebody named Lucy Stone Tuttle. Lesser bequests but still quite substantial. And here. Huntington Beckwith. Huntington Beckwith is to receive an income of $45,000 per year for ten years, whether or not he remains active in the affairs of the firm. If Huntington Beckwith should challenge this will, that bequest is to be withdrawn from him and added to the endowment fund for Hastings House.

Huntington had to restrain himself from crumpling the document in his fist. Forty-five thousand. And a codicil. Not even mentioned in the will proper. Ella and Tilden II not mentioned at all, not even a provision for the continuance of their present income.

Do not challenge it, he says. You'll get nothing, he says. We'll see about that. No probate court in the world would uphold such a will. Huntington checked his wristwatch: 4:15 A.M. He was not likely to be disturbed. Huntington set out a note pad and began reading the will more carefully. He would get to the other documents soon enough.

Tilden's will made no direct reference to Jonathan being his son. This omission was deliberate and out of sensitivity to Margaret's concern about Jonathan learning from strangers that he was an illegitimate child. But it did not take Huntington long to begin to suspect the truth. Next in the portfolio were photographs of the woman, some quite old and worn, as if they'd been handled often, and several of a man who had to be this Jonathan. He was the image of Tilden Beckwith. Tilden's bastard. Huntington stared long and hard at that face, and as he did a part of him knew that what he had long suspected was true. He, Huntington Beckwith, was not Tilden's son. It would explain much. It would explain why there was so little resemblance.

Why they were so little alike in all ways. Why the old man had had so little regard for him all his life and why he was effectively disinheriting him at the end of it.

Whose son was he, then? And what of these dates? Birth dates. And what of the coincidence of his mother's death so soon after his birth? Let's see. That was March when she died. March of 1888. And here is this Jonathan born in December of the same year. So he must have been conceived almost immediately after Mother's death. Clearly, a relationship existed between Tilden and Charlotte at the time of his, Huntington's, birth. What happened to Mother? Did she learn about that relationship and confront him? Did she rush distraught into the night only to be killed by that storm? A most convenient storm for Tilden, it seems. No. More likely it was he who did the confronting—about the birth of a child who looked so little like him. And very possibly, though it could never be proved, Tilden was the cause of Mother's death. And for that he would be punished. For that, and for all the cold looks, all the perfunctory greetings, all the distant schools, all the insults. Tilden would be punished.

Letters. Notarized and witnessed by Andrew Smithberg. Jonathan Corbin is hereby acknowledged to be . . . et cetera, et cetera . . . the *only* true son and heir of Tilden Beckwith . . . born 25 December 1888 in Greenwich, Connecticut, to the woman then and subsequently known as Charlotte Whitney Corbin . . . now residing Evanston, Illinois . . . her address. *Then and subsequently known* . . . Peculiar language.

Affidavits. Ansel Carling. Who was Ansel Carling? Ohhh, damn. Oh, God damn it to hell.

It was all there. Three affidavits. One by a man, another by a woman named Hastings—Hastings?— who attested to hearing Ansel Carling boast that he had fathered Ella Beckwith's child. The third by Tilden himself, in his own hand. It amounted to a diary of the events of 1888. He could not, Tilden had realized, be this child's father. His travels to London the year before had ruled out that possibility. The human gestation period of nine months seemed to come as a revelation to him sometime in March of 1888. He did confront her. She ran from him. Toward this Carling person. The next paragraph was very nearly a confession of murder. The one after that confessed an assault upon this Carling, in unnecessary but prideful detail, Huntington thought, down at the old Hoffman House. Carling dead later that same year . . . Texas . . . his death possibly arranged by Jay Gould "before I could get my own hands on him one more time." Then several clippings attached and what seemed to be a handwritten biography, a hand not Tilden's, of Ansel Carling, formerly Asa Koenig. A Jew? A former convict? A confidence man?

It was too much. He and his daughter, and young Tillie as well, were being stripped of everything. There would be no money, no lineage, no position. A Jew! Jews are people they tell jokes about and keep out of clubs. His own clubs. They would have nothing. Only humiliation if this became known.

"Be calm," Ella told him. "These papers. Are they originals or copies?"

"All copies. And the will is legal enough, but I can find no evidence that it's been filed."

"If you ask me, I think it's because this Jonathan Corbin has never been told. You notice the relationship is never specified in the language of the will. That might end up saving our bacon."

"A Jew."

"What?"

"I am the son of a Jew."

"Oh, don't be a fool, Father. We're talking about millions here. Do you know a reliable detective?"

"I suppose."

"Do you or don't you?"

"There's a man we've used named Bigelow. I thought he was very efficient, but Tilden said we are no longer to use him because he was discharged from the Chicago Police Force on corruption charges."

"Chicago, you say?"

"He keeps a furnished room in New York as well."

"Retain him, Father. I want him to try to trace Charlotte Corbin all the way back to her first involvement with Tilden. Who is she? Where did she come from? Why the 'then and subsequently known' language? What is there in her past that we can use as leverage?"

"Wait. I'm writing this down."

"Father."

"Yes?"

"Just tell Mr. Bigelow to come see me, please."

Bigelow's report raised as many questions as it answered. It took him only a week to compile a basic biography on Charlotte Whitney Corbin, which worked backward from Chicago to Greenwich to Wilkes-Barre. But he could find no real evidence of her existence prior to the train wreck that supposedly killed her husband. Bigelow went to the New York Public Library, which had several illustrated books on the subject of rail disasters. All of them told about Mud Run. The author of the latest and most detailed book lived in New York City. Bigelow called on him and offered him a hundred dollars if he could find anything in his source material about a Charlotte Whitney or a Charlotte Whitney Corbin. The author, an obsessive little man whose apartment was littered with railroad furnishings and memorabilia, called back the next day. The only Corbin, he said, was a fatality named Hiram who was new to town and certainly not married. There was no other Corbin connected with that train wreck or even mentioned in the Wilkes-Barre census. Yes, he was sure of it. He listed all the sources he'd checked in the hope that Bigelow would still pay him the hundred dollars.

If the name Charlotte Corbin was fictitious, and Bigelow felt sure it was, someone had gone to considerable trouble to conceal her true identity. It struck him that she seemed to have left Greenwich rather suddenly at about the same time several retired whores were being run out of town. Maybe there was something there, maybe not. Nor could he make anything at all out of the name Margaret, with which Mrs. Corbin had signed several of the letters found in Tilden Beckwith's safe. Chances are it was Charlotte's real name but it dead-ended right there.

"You don't really have much except bluff," he told Ella Beckwith. "I have this notion, it won't go away, that Charlotte might have been a hooker once named Margaret. You could try laying that on him and watch his face. You'll get a pretty good idea if it's true or not. Even if it isn't true, you got a woman out there in Chicago who's made a pretty good name for herself, and who has a son who's a college professor and a grandson just getting out of Notre Dame, but whose whole life has been this big lie. Ask me, that's not such bad leverage."

"How are you at burglary, Mr. Bigelow?"

"I worked five years in Safe and Loft."

"Charlotte Corbin has some papers I want. One is the original of Tilden Beckwith's will. Then there are certain affidavits, correspondence, and the like."

"The fee's a grand for trying it, three grand if I deliver the goods. If they turn out to be in a bank vault someplace, I don't want to come up empty."

"How expensive is arson?"

"What do you mean?"

"If you find these papers, I want you to burn her house down behind you."

· · ·

Tilden flew almost directly to Evanston as soon as he heard the news. He used his influence to hitch a ride aboard a DC-3 flying into the naval air station in nearby Skokie. Jonathan met him at the hangar with a limousine and driver, which Tilden had arranged by telephone. It was three days before Christmas. They drove past the tidy affluent homes of Winnetka, most of them decorated with lights and cutout Santas. Many had service stars hanging in their windows and war bond stickers on their doors.

"How is your mother holding up?" Tilden asked gently.

"She's pretty depressed. All her scrapbooks, letters, all the gifts we've given her over the years. It's just gone. I shouldn't tell you, but she made you a cardigan sweater and a quilted smoking jacket for Christmas. They're gone, too."

"Jonathan?"

"Yes, Uncle Tilden."

"Stop calling me that."

"Yes, sir."

"Jonathan."

"We're starting over?"

"Jonathan, I am not going to leave here this time until your mother marries me."

"No kidding."

"What do you think about that?"

"I think it's great. What kept you?"

"She did, actually. I did in the beginning. Then she did. The whole business has been very—"

"Dumb?"

"I was about to say complex. There have been other considerations. I . . . your mother and I . . . are going to have to have a long talk with you, Jonathan."

"Neat. Is this where I find out I'm really your son?"

Tilden choked.

"And have been all the time?"

"Uh, that is more or less the case, yes."

"Uncle—" Jonathan stopped himself. "Would Dad be all right?"

"Ahh . . . Dad would be . . . ahhh . . . perhaps we'd better wait and decide with your mother."

"How about Tilden as an intermediate step?"

Tilden nodded his thankful agreement. "I'm afraid your mother is going to be very cross with me for blurting this out like I have."

"Could I ask you something?"

"Certainly. Yes. You may indeed."

"I've been looking in mirrors for a long time. Do you think I haven't noticed that there's something very familiar about me?"

"I have been told there's a resemblance. There is. Yes."

"Is it possible that . . . I know there are probably many good reasons . . . but is it possible you and Mother haven't married because you couldn't figure out how to break it to me and Whitney?"

"It's been a factor. No denying it, Jonathan."

"You do know that I love Mother very much. And that I love you, and admire you and respect you, and that I think you're an absolute gas?"

"That's very kind of you indeed . . . son."

"Then you won't mind my saying that I think you've both been a couple of prize jerks."

They were married three days later. On Christmas Day. On Tilden's eighty-third birthday. On Jonathan Corbin's fifty-fifth birthday. They honeymooned at the little inn on the shores of Lake Geneva, Wisconsin, where they'd gone so many times. Tilden signed the register as he always had, Mr. & Mrs. Tilden Beckwith. His new bride took the pen from his hand and crossed out what he had written. She wrote, in its place, Tilden and Margaret Barrie Beckwith.

"Margaret," he said as tears came to his eyes.

"Tilden?" She stepped closer to him.

"Yes, my dearest."

"I don't suppose you know a place where we can swim naked this time of year."

Three short weeks later, Margaret and Jonathan saw Tilden off for New York on the Twentieth Century Limited. He would need a month at most, he'd told her, to convene the directors, announce his retirement, set up an orderly transition, and then come back forever. Jonathan had made it clear that he had no interest whatever in trying to learn, at his age, how to run the company. But yes, as majority-stockholder-to-be, he would attend all directors' meetings to see that the company continued to be managed with a sense of responsibility to its past, its place in the community, and its employees. Perhaps Whitney will want to share the task once this war in Europe is over, and if he doesn't try for a baseball career. And don't worry about Mother. The furnished apartment she's renting will be fine until you get back. Either Lucy or I will see her every day. And don't worry, Margaret told him, about those papers and your will. They don't really matter anymore, do they. Hurry back, Tilden. But not too fast. I need time to knit you a new cardigan.

It was late on a cold afternoon when Tilden, still beaming, walked into the offices of Beckwith & Company. His grin changed to puzzlement when he realized that the offices were empty. Perhaps there was snow in the forecast. Perhaps the staff had been sent home early. There was a light inside his office. He hesitated for a moment, wondering whether he should go out again and call the police. But then he thought he heard Huntington's voice coming from inside. Huntington? What was Huntington doing inside his office? Tilden stripped off his hat and coat and laid them across his secretary's unattended desk. "No, stay there, Tillie," he heard Huntington say. "Stay right where you are." Tilden pushed open the door.

Huntington was facing him as he entered. He was standing, arms folded, in front of Tilden's desk as if he'd just been sitting on the edge of it. Behind him, in Tilden's chair and looking, as usual, as if he'd been caught at something, was Huntington's son. Ella, the daughter, sat erect and forward on a leather tufted chair to the left of the desk. She wore a full-length dark coat and a fedora-style hat. Her hands were folded over the knob of the walking stick she affected. And she, as usual, for all her slender build, managed to look a good deal more manly than her brother, whom Tilden was going to swipe out of that chair in about three seconds. To Tilden's right, almost out of his field of vision, stood Chester Wax, nervous, his eyes getting moist, snapping shut a briefcase and murmuring something about excusing himself. A thickset man seated near Wax completed the tableau. He was rising slowly, stretching, indicating to Huntington that he would be outside if needed. Tilden thought he knew that one. Was he not the detective whose further employment he had forbidden?

"It's time we had a family conference," Huntington said as Tilden heard the door click shut behind him.

"Is it really?" Using just his eyes and the tip of a pointing index finger, Tilden raised Huntington's draft-dodger son from his chair and deposited him near a small fireplace behind his silent sister's chair.

"Twenty-one right," Huntington said to him, "seven left, nine right past seven, fifteen left." Smiling, he gestured toward the cabinet that concealed Tilden's safe. "We know everything."

"You are referring, I assume, to the stipulations of my will and to the circumstances of your birth." Now Tilden used his eyes to hold Huntington in place.

"I am. Among other things."

"You've just lost your job, Huntington."

"In fact, I no longer want it. I've decided I would prefer to be a full partner."

"And you are about to tell me why the son of a man named Ansel Carling should lay claim to that."

The smile stayed frozen. "I take pride in having his blood, by the way. He was a bold and daring man, much like myself."

Tilden gagged, then held a hand to his mouth until he was sure he would not laugh aloud. "I could name several things that are wrong with that sentence, Huntington. But I'll simply point out that you've made one anti-Semitic remark too many in your mean little life for me to take you altogether seriously."

"Get on with this," he heard Ella's voice. She had not moved.

Huntington Beckwith straightened. "I told you that we know everything. We have all your papers and we've learned a good deal more. You are quite right that the three of us would prefer not to have our ancestry gossiped about for the rest of our lives, but we are resolved that that is nothing compared to what else is at stake here. The real questions, Tilden Beckwith, are these. Does the noble and respected head of Beckwith and Company wish to be known and forever remembered as a man who probably murdered his wife in a fit of jealousy?"

Tilden only shook his head wearily.

"Do you want it known"—Huntington's voice rose a notch—"that you gave your name to a convict's child and pretended he was your own only to divert suspicion, treating that child most bitterly in the process?"

Tilden's eyes flickered. The last part was true. And

he knew there was shame in it. It was all that had made him keep Huntington in his employ and provide an allowance to the others this long. It was all that kept him now from taking Huntington by the collar and throwing him out the door, age difference or no.

"Do you want it known that the noble and blameless Tilden Beckwith was a hypocrite who sired a bastard child of his own and supported that child all his life and yet would not give that child the Beckwith name? Even more, do you want the why of it known?"

Tilden took a step forward. "The why of it, sir?"

"That she was a whore, sir. A tart. A doxy. That the equally noble and blameless and beloved columnist known as Charlotte Corbin is in fact a prostitute named Margaret who was once driven from Greenwich, Connecticut, by fear of exposure."

Huntington's head seemed to be floating in space. The desk, the office, the young woman in the chair, and the nervous young man who stood by the fireplace had faded into a dark gray vapor.

"A prostitute . . . Margaret . . . you will see her reputation go up in smoke just like—"

"Father, shut up."

"Just like her house . . . and all she had . . . except for the things we've saved to use as evidence if you do not—"

"Shut up, Father."

Out of the corner of his eye, Tilden saw Nat Goodwin's elbow nudge the ribs of Colonel Cody, but his attention snapped back to the sneering face that floated near the base of the large painting of nudes on the wall. The face was leaner, darker, younger. It was Carling's face, and it was Huntington's. It was the pinched and watchful face of Huntington's daughter, and the cowardly, mewling face of Huntington's son. And the expression was turning as Carling's had turned from contempt, to disbelief, to fear.

Jab, lad. Jab once with the left, then again . . .

The face rocked backward.

Now the left to the ribs, lad . . . then cross with the right as his arms come down . . . Put yer back into it, lad.

The face sprayed blood and fell away across the desk.

He heard movement behind him and half turned toward the cane, Albert Hacker's cane, that he knew was being raised to strike him. Tilden was not alarmed. He knew that the cane would not fall. It would be stopped in its descent by the strong arm of the man wearing long hair and a Western hat. Yet he felt a blow across his temple. What was it? Where is Colonel Cody? Nat? Nat? He tried to find their faces within the white light that was blinding him. But the face that came through was Ella's face—the dead Ella, and her teeth were bare and snarling her hatred, just as they were that night. Her arms were pinned behind her in the snow, but somehow she got one of them free and with a great heave she swung it in a wide arc toward his head. Now it was he who was on his back. Or was he still standing? He couldn't tell because now they were both floating in a great cold darkness among a million snowflakes and she was hissing at him, saying, *Twice the man you are, Tilden. He is twice and more.* The last face he saw was Margaret's. Young Margaret's. She was running to him, reaching for him, her face twisted in anguish. But he was falling too quickly.

The funeral was five days later. Ella Beckwith delivered the eulogy. Tilden II led the first hymn. Huntington Beckwith, sending word that he admired his father as he did no man living, was too distraught to attend. He was under a doctor's care for painful injuries as well as grief, having fainted full on his face when he learned the news that his beloved father had apparently suffered an accidental fall in his office.

No Corbins were there. They were, of course, not notified. Nor did the news of Tilden's death appear in the Chicago newspapers. It was during the following week that Margaret, concerned because she had heard nothing from him, called his office. She came to New York with Jonathan the following day. Whitney, in England, was denied leave for the death of a nonrelative. Jonathan took his mother to the cemetery on Long Island, where they laid flowers on Tilden's grave. He left her alone with him for an hour.

He drove her from there to Greenwich, where she visited an ailing Laura Hemmings. They spent another solitary hour in each other's arms. She tried the next morning to visit Huntington, but he would not see her. She wrote to him upon returning to Chicago. He did not answer. She tried calling, but he would not come to the phone. She wrote again without reply. Most of February passed. Margaret wrote him one more time, expressing the hope that she would not be forced to involve an attorney in family business of a delicate nature.

Within a month of posting that letter, Margaret was dead. Perhaps of natural causes, perhaps asphyxiated by a defective heater in her rented apartment. There were no signs of forced entry, no reason to suspect foul play. Just another old woman living alone. Two days later, Jonathan Corbin, perhaps distracted by his grief, stepped into the path of a speeding car as he crossed Evanston's main street on his way to a consultation with a local lawyer. The driver sped off, a hit-and-run. George Bigelow drove the car to Chicago's South Side, where he abandoned it to the first passerby who noticed that the key was in the ignition.

Two months after that, a burglar strangled an aged black woman, another widow named Lucy Stone Tuttle. Captain Whitney Corbin missed that funeral as well, although he'd been flown home for those of his father and grandmother. Before the snows came again, he, too, was dead. The only surviving Corbin, the only surviving Beckwith, was growing, unsuspected, in the womb of the former Agnes Ann Haywood of Wilmette, Illinois.

NINETEEN

 HERE IS A BEND ON MAPLE AVENUE THAT ONE must pass before the former Laura Hemmings house comes into view. Tom Burke spotted the old man's car there. He had parked it out of sight from the house. Burke rolled down his window and signaled to Dancer that he was stopping. Dancer pulled in behind him. Burke stepped from his BMW and made a throat-cutting motion toward Dancer, who then shut off the ignition of Mr. Makowski's dented blue car. It dieseled loudly, then died.

Burke walked toward the bend and stopped there. He motioned Dancer forward, telling him with hand gestures to move carefully and to stay concealed. Dancer reached his side. He held a fur cap firmly on his head with one hand and peered through the wind and the gathering darkness. In the golden light of a doorway he saw a slender woman in an old-fashioned gown. Still within the doorway's light, she stepped to the edge of the porch and, picking up her skirts, walked toward two shadows at the foot of the driveway. The larger of the two shadows moved toward her, into her path, before half turning. He seemed to be shielding her with his body. The second shadow moved. Burke and Dancer could see the rifle now. Ella's brother was either forcing them or following them inside.

"Go get 'em, Mr. Beckwith," Tom Burke muttered. "Way to go."

"What are you talking about?"

"Maybe he'll save us all a lot of trouble. He shoots them all, he gets put in a funny farm. Scratch four problems."

"I saw no sign of Corbin."

"He's either inside or he'll be along. How's Lesko?"

"No sound or movement."

"We might have to thaw him to get him back out of that trunk." Tom Burke chuckled as a memory came to him. "In Korea, sometimes they had to break a guy's arms to get a body bag around him."

Dancer closed his eyes. He could feel a migraine coming on. "Listen, Burke," he said quietly, "you're not taking what Miss Beckwith said literally, are you?"

"I don't get you."

"She seemed to be saying she wanted all these people killed tonight."

"It's what she said." He shrugged. "Especially if her brother gets to them, and he did."

"I keep trying to persuade you that massacres attract attention, Mr. Burke. In any case, she also said you're to do nothing without my expressed approval."

"Well, make up your mind then, Mr. Ballanchine. It's almost dark, you got all this snow and wind, you're not ever going to have a better chance."

Dancer wished he'd taken a Valium. The thought

of several murders was not what unnerved him. Burke, in his limited way, had made a point. Lesko could be disposed of across the state line and, in all likelihood, no connection with the rest of them would ever be made. As for Corbin and those other two, it might very easily be made to look like a double murder and suicide. No one who looked into his recent behavior would be terribly surprised. The antique costume that girl is wearing might even help make it seem like some sort of ritual killing. But Ella's brother would not fit into that scenario at all. Worse, he'd be an immediate link back to Ella, and neither she nor her bullet-riddled house was in a state to receive visitors for the next day or so. He and Burke would, after all, have to spend the rest of the night plastering and painting. Then it would probably fall on him to dispose of Mr. Burke. All this with his leg throbbing so badly. But then it would be over and he would be rich. The new chairman of Beckwith Enterprises. Perhaps even Ella's heir. None of this, however, might happen if they just stood here in the snow while Tillie was down there botching it.

"Two things are essential," he said to Tom Burke. "We get Tillie out of there and keep him quiet even if we have to fill up another trunk. The second is that it must appear as if Corbin killed the other two and then himself. Do you understand that, Mr. Burke?"

"You got it," Burke replied. "I need that scarf and hat you're wearing."

Dancer did not quite understand but he surrendered them. Burke placed the thick fur cap loosely over the muzzle of his Beretta and tied it in place with a dozen wraps of the wool scarf.

"Neat, huh?" Burke smiled. "It'll make it a little quieter."

"That's wonderful, Mr. Burke," Dancer said dryly. "Let's go have a look."

·   ·   ·

"You're her, aren't you?" Ella's brother had not taken his eyes off Gwen Leamas. He followed them across the porch and through Corbin's front door, which he closed behind him and pressed his back tight up against it. "I saw you with him yesterday." His voice quaked badly. "You were showing him the way the city is changed. You were showing him the things that were still the same."

"Just . . . just one moment." Harry Sturdevant stepped between them again, both hands upraised and open. "We'd better start with some introductions." He looked at Gwen, gesturing back to the man with the rifle, who seemed older than he even though he was fifteen years Sturdevant's junior. "This is Tilden Beckwith the second. He is the . . . nominal grandson of the Tilden you know, and he is very upset at the moment. Tillie"—he turned—"this young lady is—"

"I am Margaret," Gwen Leamas said calmly.

Sturdevant moaned aloud. He spread his hands further as if separating the two people. "Don't do that, dear. You don't know what you're into here."

"I can see that Mr. Beckwith is frightened and there's no need. May I offer you some tea, Mr. Beckwith?"

"How . . . how . . . how come there's no need?" His eyes blinked rapidly.

Sturdevant could see no way out. "What he's asking, dear, is how come you're not upset with him if you know he was there when Tilden was murdered"—he stared hard at her, giving her a moment to absorb that part—"and that his family also arranged for the murders of every living Corbin. This gentleman assures me, however, that none of it was his fault. I believe him, and I know that Jonathan . . . that Tilden . . . will believe him too when he gets here."

Gwen never batted an eye. But inside she felt like throwing up. One knee began to quiver beneath her long white dress. "I do wish you'd put down that rifle and have some tea, Mr. Beckwith."

His features twitched indecisively. Then, his face lighting up, he patted his coat pocket and pulled free the quart bottle of Glenlivet.

"That's *your* Tilden's brand, you will recall," Harry Sturdevant told her. "Tillie here intends to have a friendly drink with him."

"Yes," she agreed. "That's a very nice idea." She crossed to him and held out her hand for the bottle. He tensed as the outstretched hand came within reach, then suddenly cradled the bottle against his chest and shook off the glove that had been holding it.

"May I touch you?" he asked.

Gwen did not know what to do. She moved her hand closer, suspended. Ella's brother touched the back of it lightly, then her fingertips, then snatched his own hand away.

"Your skin is cold," he whispered, wide-eyed. "It's very cold."

Gwen blinked. She knew exactly what he meant, but she had no idea where to go with it. She was not about to point out that her extremities, which were cold to the touch at the best of times, had just been outside in a blizzard. On the other hand, she wasn't sure what letting him believe she was a walking corpse would do to his already tenuous state of mind.

"That rifle," she said, pointing. "It really won't do you much good, you know."

"Yes it can. It can help you. I'll be on your side when they come."

"When who comes, Tillie?" Sturdevant asked.

"If I'm on your side, will he let me keep my position?"

"Your position," Sturdevant repeated blankly. "You mean as chairman of Beckwith Enterprises?"

"I work hard. I go to all the meetings. I don't always just do what Ella says."

"We'll work something out, Tillie." Sturdevant glanced toward the undraped windows. "Did you say someone's coming here? Are we in danger?"

"They're the ones who are in danger." Ella's brother patted his Weatherby. "Anyway, trying to kill you never works. They tried this morning in the city and Lesko stopped them. They tried last night and he stopped them then, too."

"Wait a minute, Tillie." Sturdevant made a time-out sign with his hands. "Who is Lesko, exactly?"

"He's like Bigelow."

Sturdevant made another hand signal, as if to put him on hold. "Bigelow"—he turned to Gwen—"is apparently the hired killer who killed . . . um, you . . . and the others. But then Tilden came back"—Sturdevant cocked an eye at Ella's brother for confirmation—"but he came back much younger, and he killed this man, Bigelow."

"And Flack. He got even with Flack as well."

Sturdevant shook his head to clear it. "And when did you say this happened, Tillie?"

"Twenty . . . It was 1964. In Chicago."

"Chicago," he repeated. "And a very young Tilden Beckwith killed the man who killed . . . you, Margaret . . ."

"And Flack."

"Yes. And Flack. Margaret, do you know anything about—I mean, has Jonathan ever mentioned—" Sturdevant stopped. He waved his hands to erase the question. It was hardly a discussion they should be having now. But he could see by Gwen's expression that she knew what he was driving at. Rule out a ghost and it had to have been Jonathan. Or a ghost inside of Jonathan. Gwen was recalling a long-ago mugging he had told her about. A mugging that had troubled him, even shamed him, deeply.

Sturdevant stepped to the nearest window and pulled the drapes closed over it. "Let me pour you some of that Scotch, Tillie," he said as he moved to the next window. "While I'm doing it, you can tell me who this Lesko is."

The backseat was loose. Lesko could feel it through a hole in the composition board that lined the trunk. He could get one hand through and he could move it.

Burke. He said the name to himself. Burke, you asshole. It would have been Burke, he knew, who searched the car for his notebook. Burke who pulled out the seats. Burke who didn't think to snap them back even after he piled Lesko in the trunk and wasn't even bright enough to tie Lesko's hands. Those right there are rules one and two. And it's about your fifth mistake. I get out of here, I guarantee this'll be the one that kills you.

If I get out.

Lesko's legs were gone. Twisting them under him in an effort to get at the jack handle had brought on such an agony of cramping that it was a relief to feel them slowly die. One of his shoes was off, he remembered. Kicked loose by the squirming. On, off, it almost didn't matter. He couldn't feel either foot.

His hands weren't much better. He could no longer use them to pry at the composition board, even with the jack handle, but he could poke at it, ram it, try to break it down. Come on, you sucker. Break. Goddamned Makowski. Everything in his fucking car is falling apart except the one thing I need to be falling apart.

He heard a loud crack. Come on, baby. That's it. He ran the back of one hand along the surface until he found a curving fracture that ran almost top to bottom just off center. He pressed one side of the break. It gave. It was ripping. He could get his hand into the break, and if he could only get enough leverage . . . How much time? Dancer's gone what? Ten minutes? Fifteen? Where the hell are we? They had to get the old guy. That's right. The dame said that. She said he was going to go shoot ghosts. So we're parked around Corbin's house, right? Yeah, well, stupid, who gives a shit where we are if Burke and Twinkletoes come back and they find you with your fat head stuck in the springs of the backseat here.

The door. Oh, shit. Lesko heard the door.

The backseat fell forward into the car. It slammed forward. It wasn't Dancer who did that. Lesko gripped the jack handle as best he could with the pointed end up. Maybe one last shot at Burke. Come on, Tommy. Get nice and close and be your normal dumb. I'll ram this thing right through your face. More of the composition board tore away.

"You have no key, I suppose."

If the voice startled him, its tone confused him. It sounded like the doctor at his last physical who said, "You haven't been exercising, I take it."

"Do you have a key? It would be easier from the back." The voice was calm and polite, but a bit impatient, Lesko thought, like a guy passing by who'd be happy to help as long as it didn't take all night.

"I look like I was driving this thing?" Lesko gasped. Schmuck.

Lesko saw a hand grip the loosened seat and pull it through the open left rear door. A moment later he heard a crackling thump off to his right. The man had thrown the seat across the car roof into someone's pine trees. Now a shadow filled his field of vision. He felt strong hands gripping the shoulder padding of his coat. Lesko's head reached the foot well. He felt a hand searching for his belt, finding it through his coat, and using it as a handle to pry loose the rest of his body. Lesko raised himself on one elbow. He could make out the face now. Enough of it. The bent nose and the square jaw. If there was a little more light he'd see the split eyebrow as well.

"Corbin. You're Corbin."

The face turned away in the direction of the steering wheel. "If we could start this motor in some way, you could warm yourself."

"Give me a hand. Get me into the front seat."

Lesko had to be dragged. Corbin was strong, he realized, stronger even than he looked. He pulled Lesko free of the backseat and held him erect with one arm while his other hand fumbled at the recessed handle of the front door, as if its workings were unfamiliar to him. Lesko moaned as blood began swelling his feet. The door finally opened.

"Wait," Lesko gasped as he was lowered behind the wheel. "Wait. We don't have time for this."

"You have time," was the calm reply. He was studying the dashboard. "There are wires to the starter button which one crosses to start a car. Do you know which ones they are?"

Lesko reached under the steering column. Starter button? He joined his middle and index fingers together, using them as hooks to tear loose the wires running to and from the starter switch. These he touched while pressing on the accelerator with his screaming foot. The engine coughed and caught.

"I'm going now," Lesko heard him say. "When you can walk or use these pedals, go down the street to Laura Hemmings's house. There is a doctor there."

"Laura Hemmings's house? You talking about that Charles Addams house you bought?"

"It's a white house. Number one ten."

"Yeah, well, let me tell you something. There's also

a shooter named Tom Burke and a little pansy named Ballanchine down around there someplace."

"The doctor will clean your head." He touched his fingertips to the thick mat of clotted blood and hair above Lesko's left ear. "Your friend is right." He dropped his left hand to the nearest heating vent. Warm air was beginning to come. "Goodbye," he said, and turned up Maple Avenue in a direction away from the Hemmings house.

"What friend?" Lesko called after him. "Right about what?"

". . . head . . . tire," was all Lesko could hear in the wind.

"Wait a minute. What?"

He saw Corbin half turn as he walked. "He said the Poles have heads like truck tires."

Then the storm swallowed him.

Lesko didn't wait. His hands were good enough to turn a wheel, and his feet had enough touch to stamp on a pedal. He was not about to sit there getting toasty warm just on Corbin's word and all of a sudden feel Burke's Beretta stuck in his ear. He cut the steering wheel left and put Mr. Makowski's car in gear, taking out one of Burke's taillights as he swung onto the hill of Maple Avenue. He left his own lights off.

Lesko rounded the bend and stiffened as Corbin's house came into view. One porch light. Drapes over the windows. No sign of Burke or Ballanchine. No sign of anyone. He coasted by, his foot ready on the accelerator. Two houses past Corbin's, he switched on his headlights. They lit up a small red Datsun parked on the road, its hood only beginning to accumulate snow, as if it had recently been driven a substantial distance. Corbin's car, he was sure. The one he uses to putz around town and get to the station. He's got a car, why's he walking? Lesko continued on almost to the Post Road.

Putnam Avenue. And the statue of General Israel Putnam on his horse, escaping from the British who almost
captured him because they heard he was in town shack-
ing up with one of the townies. So everything around
here is Putnam. Putnam Travel, Putnam Trust, even
Putnam Liquors.

Fucking Greenwich.

Wouldn't you know they'd pick a patron saint who
the one damned thing he was best known for was not
getting caught.

Lesko swung into a U-turn back up Maple Avenue.
Driving was easier. His feet were working well enough
that he remembered there was no shoe on one of them.
Pull in behind Corbin's car, he decided. If I have to dig
back into that trunk, better do it down the hill here.

Lesko found the shoe among the oil cans. But he
was sweating when he scrambled back out because he
remembered how near he'd been to being dead there.
He wondered how long it would be before he could
enjoy riding in someone's trunk again.

Right.

What other things can we think about that will let
us stall going up to that front door without at least a
flack jacket and a riot gun? We can kill a little more
time wondering why Corbin was acting so weird, but
what else is new? We can always—Wait, wait a second.
Poles—Polacks—have heads like truck tires? That's
what Dave Katz said. Dave Katz's ghost said that to the
Tilden guy when I was on queer street on old lady
Beckwith's floor.

Ohhhh, shit.

Lesko laced his shoe. All this, he thought. All this
and I bet I come up empty. Not another dime out of it.
He took a long breath, then reached for the tire iron
he'd left in the well behind him.

· · · ·

On the left-hand edge of Corbin's property there is a long high privet hedge that separates it from the lot of his nearest neighbor. Corbin's driveway is along the right-hand edge, its entrance softly lit after dark by a street lamp just up and across the road. If you were sneaking up on the house, Lesko knew, you would pick the hedge side and stay in its shadow. He looked for tracks. There were two sets. One continued on toward the backyard, where he could see an oddly shaped tree through the snow. The other crossed the lawn on a bias. This second set headed up the front steps but crossed older tracks already there and then seemed to angle off along the porch. Lesko stayed with the hedge.

He was abreast of the house, cut off even from the dim light of the distant street lamp, and deciding whether to try a window or to first circle the house as Burke and Dancer must have done. His coat snagged on a broken branch of the hedge. His foot came down on another. Several more were on top of the snow, and a portion of the hedge was bent inward as if someone had crashed through it. The snow was trampled. He saw a small, dark lump that might have been a dead animal. Lesko squatted and picked it up. A fur hat. The Russian kind with flaps on four sides. He could tell by feel it was made for a small head. Dancer's hat? But what happened here? Maybe he slipped in the snow and grabbed the hedge to break his fall. Lesko moved on.

He almost didn't look at the tree he'd noticed. As he reached the rear of the house, his intention was to follow its perimeter. But the shape became more peculiar as he passed it. Its upper trunk seemed to be separating. Lesko dropped into a crouch. He held that position until his mind could confirm what his senses chose to doubt. There was a man in that tree. And he was part of it.

Lesko stepped closer, his tire iron held ready. The

legs were the first part he saw clearly. They were swaying toward him, pushed by each gust of wind, their shoe tips barely brushing over the surface of the snow. Then he saw arms hanging limp. Lesko patted his pockets for the penlight he carried. It was worth the risk. He found the light and aimed it, before switching it on, at the shape of a head that seemed welded to a branch at a height not much taller than himself. He thumbed the switch.

Burke.

Burke's swollen face stared back at him.

He had been lifted bodily, Lesko saw, and jammed into a crook between one stout bough and a smaller branch, the smaller one across his throat. A wool scarf, wound once around his neck and then cleated through the branches, held him there. Lesko saw a Brooks Brothers label on the scarf's loose end. He raised the beam once more to the face. It was turning black. One side, the right, was strangely shaped, as if the cheekbones had been moved. Lesko flicked off his light. In deeper darkness than before he ran his hands over Tom Burke's body, searching for his weapon. There was none. He retraced his steps back along the hedge toward where he'd found the cap, once more using his penlight. There he found an L-shaped depression near the spot where Tom Burke must have begun to die. Lesko reached down and pulled the Beretta free.

"Jesus." He shook his head. Old Tom Burke, he said to himself, could fuck up a two-car funeral. He could also find more ways to get killed than any two men Lesko had ever met. The Beretta's safety was on and locked.

Lesko turned back past Tom Burke's dangling body and continued on his path around Corbin's house. He walked more confidently now. It wasn't just the gun. He was walking in tracks made by another man who, he knew, had to be Jonathan Corbin or whoever Jonathan Corbin turned into when it snowed. He also knew pretty much what he'd find on the other side of the house. Besides, his feet were getting numb again. And he would kill for a handful of aspirin and a very large belt of Seagram's.

"What are you doing, Harry?" Ella's brother called from his chair, a drink in one hand and the Weatherby lying carelessly across his lap. He'd been crying. The tears came when he asked Gwen Leamas whether it hurt to die, and she answered that it hurts most, she thought, to leave those you love. She'd answered with feeling. Gwen didn't know whether she could stay with Jonathan, and whether anything could ever be sane, simple, and happy between them again. But as the liquor further loosened this sad old man's tongue, she also found herself wondering, with a deep thumping dread, whether she would even see him again. Oh, let him be alive. Let him, please God, show up at that door. Then we'll see. We'll see.

"Harry? What are you doing out there?"

Sturdevant had been in the kitchen, standing with one hand on the earpiece of a reproduction antique wall phone. At last he lifted it from its hook.

"I'm getting us some reinforcements, Tillie. I'm calling the police."

"That's a good idea, Harry." He nodded stupidly. "Have them bring some bullets."

"Bullets, Tillie?"

"I forgot to take some."

"Good grief," Sturdevant muttered.

He gave his name and the address of Corbin's house to the sergeant who answered and told him he had reason to think that there were prowlers outside. Harry, in fact, had heard a sound while he was on the phone. But it came from in the house, not outside. He dismissed it and completed the call. The receiver back in place, he felt a coldness on his neck. Whether it was a chill or a draft he was not sure. His eye fell on a block of carving knives. His hand moved toward it.

"Easy." He heard the voice behind him. "The porch door wasn't locked."

Harry Sturdevant turned slowly. He saw a thickset man whose legs wore a crust of snow up to the knees. A second, smaller set of legs draped down from his shoulder. Several lines of dried blood crossed the rough-looking face he'd first seen at the Greenwich Library.

"You would be Mr. Lesko, I take it."

"Uncle Harry?" Gwen Leamas came rushing down the short hall from the living room. Ella's brother, rifle in hand, reeled behind her. Sturdevant, who now saw the automatic in Lesko's free hand, neatly plucked the rifle from Tillie's hands as he came within reach and laid it atop the refrigerator.

"I'm Lesko." One eyebrow raised at the sight of Gwen's long dress and the other at the appearance of the batty old man, Black Homburg, he'd followed most of Saturday. "This here"—he cocked his head toward the pair of legs—"is Lawrence Ballanchine. He's been looking to kill all of you." Lesko hitched his shoulder and let Dancer slide to the kitchen floor. Sturdevant could see at a glance that his jaw was shattered and his nose cartilage crushed. From the bubbly sound of his breathing, he guessed that his throat was damaged as well.

"If you're still in the mood," Lesko said wearily, "he could use a doctor. Tell you the truth, I'm not feelin' so hot myself."

"Tilden," Ella's brother whispered, staring at Dancer's face.

Lesko looked at him.

"You did this?" Sturdevant asked.

"Tilden did it," the old man answered for him.

Now Gwen Leamas looked at him, her head slowly shaking as if trying to deny the thought that was forming in it. "Do you know Jonathan Corbin?" she asked Lesko. "Have you seen him?"

"I seen him."

"He didn't . . . he didn't do this." She shook her head.

Lesko didn't answer. *If you like this, wait till you see what's hanging from your tree outside.*

"I have to go." He picked up the Glenlivet bottle from the kitchen counter and took a long swallow. "I got one more stop. Tell the cops I'll be back."

"Tilden did it." Ella's brother's head was nodding.

"Where is Jonathan now?" Gwen's voice had fear in it. "You said you saw him. Is Jonathan where you're going?"

Lesko jammed the Beretta into his belt and stepped past her to Sturdevant. "This guy's gun is out on your porch with his prints on it. Also tell the cops to take a walk around the back yard."

"Was it Jonathan?" Sturdevant asked quietly.

"Ask me"—Lesko walked through toward the front door—"the old guy called it right."

"I'm going with you." Gwen ran after him.

The telephone on the kitchen wall rang.

Ella Beckwith slammed down the receiver and bit at the knuckles of her fist. A mature voice had answered, almost certainly Sturdevant. She had hoped for no answer at all. Neither Lawrence nor Burke, she knew, would have picked up the phone if they were there and, if they were, or if they'd finished and gone, no one else could have, either.

Imbeciles.

Ella returned to her front window and stared into the full darkness. She could see nothing at all. Just the snowflakes nearest the Thermopane and the dim yellow glow from the coach lamps atop the stone gate columns at the foot of her driveway.

Ella caught her breath. The gates. She'd forgotten them entirely. The gates were still wide open, tied that way by the detective, Lesko. She rushed back to her desk and poised a hand over her intercom, then hesitated. She could call one of the servants in their quarters over the garage, but she knew that whichever one walked down through a blizzard to remove a trenchcoat belt from her gate would wonder about it and remember it. Better to leave them out of it. Better to leave the gate—No, no, the gate could *not* be left open for anyone who pleased to come through it and—Ella closed her eyes and shivered. She was remembering the day when her heart had almost stopped. The day when she looked down on the road and saw a face that could not have been there gazing back up at her. She remembered being so badly shaken that she'd knocked over the telescope in reaching for it and then, once it was righted, she could barely hold it in focus on the old man made young again who seemed to be looking directly into the lens. A face that a part of her had been expecting for more than twenty years. Perhaps for more than forty years.

The gate. The gate had to be closed. Ella yanked open her desk drawer and found a pair of scissors. These in one hand and her cane in the other, Ella struggled with the bolt of the door that was still whole and passed into her entrance hall. At a closet there she snatched a long, hooded coat, which she hadn't worn in almost a quarter century. There were no boots. There had been at one time but some servant had removed them over the years. They were never used. Miss Beckwith never went out in weather. Miss Beckwith hardly went out at all.

The storm stung her cheeks. And the snow on the driveway seemed to bite at her ankles and try to crawl up her legs, and the cold went through her coat as if contemptuous of it. But she was managing. She could move quickly and without great peril of falling if she stayed to the ruts pressed into the snow by the cars and if she watched where she was stepping. She pressed on stiffly, like an awkward novice skier, her eyes locked on the ground immediately before her, daring only once to glance up and measure the distance remaining to Raymond Lesko's knotted belt. Another fifty feet. Good. Keep moving.

Some things are seen by the eye and others by the mind. Ella's eye saw the strip of snow-covered cloth that bound her electric gate to a bush. It was all her eye sought. But as she looked down again to the snowy surface at her feet and her brain calculated the decreasing distance to it, her brain also began filling in the surrounding detail that her glance had also photographed. There was the gate itself, then the nearest column crowned by a steaming brass lamp, then the other stone column, and between them, set back several feet just at the farthest reach of their light, her brain replayed the image of a man. Standing there. Not moving.

Ella denied this last. She would not look up again. She would take her scissors, she would cut that belt, the gate would swing shut and locked, and anything that might possibly be standing there would be shut out in any case.

She reached the belt. Ella lowered herself on her cane and fumbled with the scissors, twice dropping them from icy fingers before their jaws at last closed on the stiff fabric and began chewing through it. The belt parted with a snap. Like a frozen snake it began unwinding. The gate creaked forward. Ella felt a joy that approached hysteria.

"Good evening, Ella."

Close. Keep going. That's good. Yes.

"It won't close, Ella. The snow will stop it."

Ella denied the voice as well. And what it said. The gate will close. It is a heavy gate. And the snow is not so high. It will need a little push, perhaps. But it will close.

A shadow moved. The man who was not there stepped closer.

"*No!*" Ella shrieked. But still she would not look up. With one bare hand she clawed at the blocking snow while the other held the scissors stiff-armed toward the shadow. It moved closer. It crossed the line between her columns where her locked gates should have been.

"*Stay out of here! Stay out!*" She drew back the scissors and hurled them at him, backhanded. They sailed harmlessly by, but it seemed to Ella they passed through him. Ella squealed. Her cane. Where was her cane? She groped for it in the snow and, finding it, tottered to her feet. Once erect, she gripped the cane at its tapered base and swung it wildly at the night. "*Burke!*" she screamed. "*Burke!*"

"Burke is gone now, Ella." The voice was almost gentle. "Burke, Bigelow, Flack, your father. They're all gone."

Ella's thin chest was heaving. Her head remained cocked to one side in a desperate hope that what was vague in her vision would remain vague in form. Her mouth began to froth at its corners. Her eyes were wide and unblinking in spite of the snow.

"It's time, Ella," the voice said softly.

"I'll kill you," she hissed.

He smiled. It was a sad smile, as if she'd made a very poor joke.

"It's time to answer for Margaret, and for Jonathan, and for poor Lucy. There was never a need to harm Lucy."

A low, growling wail started deep in her throat.

She slashed viciously with her cane, although his shape remained ten feet distant, between her pillars. Now she hurled the cane as she had the scissors. The cane struck his chest, but lengthwise and without force. He snatched it before it could fall and held it for a long moment. He seemed to study it. At last he brought it down to his side. Something in his pose brought another wail from Ella. She spun drunkenly toward the house, her arms reaching for it. She fell facedown in the snow. She lay there gasping, staring at it, waiting in terror for the shadow to cross over her.

But instead there was light. Headlights. Their glow grew bright on the snow and—she twisted her head—on her columns and the shape between them. She heard the sound of a motor, first loud, then purring. She heard a car door. And another. Lawrence. Lawrence and Burke. See? They are not gone. Liar. Kill him, Lawrence. Kill him now and you'll be rich.

"Jonathan!" Gwen ran to him, one hand gripping her white skirts. She'd brought no coat. Raymond Lesko approached more slowly. He held the pistol ready in his pocket as he scanned the darkness. He saw Ella. She was kicking her legs, crablike, trying to back away, but she was making no progress. *"Kill him,"* she was screeching.

Corbin stared at Gwen. It seemed to her at first that he did not know her. His eyes were odd. Then recognition showed in them, then affection, then something like appreciation. But it was more the look Jonathan might have given her the second or third time they met.

"You must be cold," he said.

If she was, she was not conscious of it. She stood, looking hard into his eyes as he peeled off his coat and wrapped it around her shoulders.

"Are you Jonathan?" she asked.

His eyes took a sort of hitch, like that made by a film when it jumps to another scene.

"Yes, sweetheart." He closed his lapels across her throat. "I'm Jonathan." He gestured with his head toward the woman who was shouting into the storm. "That's Ella Beckwith."

"I know. Mr. Lesko told me."

"She killed them all. Or had it done. She was going to kill us."

"I know that, too. Jonathan, let's get away from here."

"In just a minute, sweetheart." He touched her cheek tenderly. But his eyes changed again as they turned and locked on Ella Beckwith. "In just another minute."

He was coming for her. Ella hooded her eyes against the coach-light's glare and she saw him moving toward her. Where was Lawrence? Where was Burke? She could not have imagined that they'd come. She'd seen them. Two of them, rushing from the car. Now there was no one. Only him. Except for just an instant she'd imagined she saw his Chicago whore standing at his side, but now she, too, was gone.

Get a grip on yourself. Think. If you can just get to . . . where? Get to where?

She tried to remember. There was a building, she knew, that she wanted to reach. A place with light and warmth and stout doors. But the snow was piling high and her feet were numb and the hem of her coat was heavy with ice. She would never reach it. He would be there first.

Ella looked back.

He was coming. Steadily. Unhurried. The cane swinging in his right hand. There was hardly any snow. Why was there so little snow for him and so much for her? Everything seemed turned around somehow. She was even moving downhill now. How could that be when her driveway climbed steeply upward?

At last Ella reached a broad, open space that was flat. It should have been where her front terrace and her wisteria trellis were, but it was all so different. The trellis was so high, so much bigger, and its posts seemed more like steel pillars. She heard a scream. An odd scream, not like a woman's. It came again. From a distance. She stared past the pillars and saw it. It was a horse. A horse was screaming because it had fallen and could not rise and there were two men, policemen. Oh, glory. Yes. Policemen.

"Police," she croaked. "I need you. Police!"

But the wind shredded her words and drove them back into her face.

A Greenwich patrol car, its blue lights strobing, skidded to a stop in front of the car Lesko had driven. Two policemen stepped out. Both had hands over holstered guns. One drew his weapon at the sound of Ella's screams.

"Don't get nervous." Lesko held up a hand. "I got ID."

He showed his wallet and flipped it open to a small gold shield. "New York Detectives," he said. "Retired last year."

"Are you armed, Mr. Lesko?" a tall sergeant named Gorby asked. The second policeman, the one who'd drawn his gun, stepped past Lesko. He quickly appraised Corbin, who stood quietly, his arms around Gwen, then turned and blinked at the old woman who was on her hands and knees, screaming at him from some fifteen feet inside her gate.

Lesko produced the Beretta, butt first. "This belongs to a guy named Burke. Maybe you seen him hung up in a tree."

The sergeant nodded. "This man did it?" He looked at Corbin.

"Not exactly. I'll tell you later."

Sergeant Gorby blinked through the snow at the screaming woman. "That's Miss Beckwith, isn't it? What have you been doing to her?"

"Nothing, sergeant. Not a damn thing."

She ran on, stumbling, her ice-laden coat slapping at her legs, tripping her. And still he came. Closer now. Suddenly she came upon another large building, its front door lit as bright as day. She could find safety there. They would take her in. But for a reason she did not know, Ella turned from that grand house and staggered toward a place where there was darkness and great mounds of snow. The mounds had a maze of alleys between them. She could hide. She could escape. But the spaces had filled in too much. They trapped her legs. They tripped her. She felt herself turning, then stumbling backward. Her arms plunged deep into the snow behind her. And he was there. She could not rise and run again. She could not even claw at his face because her arms were held fast. She spat. And when she did she felt the hard tip of his cane, though it did not hurt her, pressing at a spot between her breasts.

Nothing hurt.

She no longer even felt the cold.

"I do not feel anything." She was tired. She would rest.

"I know that, Ella."

"You cannot keep me here, you know."

"Stay there, Ella. It's where you belong."

"No."

"Goodbye, Ella."

Ella screamed.

.   .   .

"I do not feel anything."

Sergeant Gorby wrapped his emergency blanket around her head and shoulders. He placed another over her feet.

"I know. But you're going to be fine," he told her.

"You cannot keep me here, you know."

"An ambulance is coming, Ella. It won't be long."

"No."

"Just sit tight, Ella."

Sergeant Gorby stood and turned toward Corbin, who had not moved from his place between the gate columns. His policeman's eye saw that no footsteps but his own had crossed Ella Beckwith's property line. Looking back, he saw the dim traces of the path the old woman had followed from her house, and a wider flattened area no more than ten feet across where she alone had flailed and tamped the snow. He took two steps toward Corbin, and Ella began screaming again. Screams so loud and long that he feared for her heart. He turned once more to quiet her. But she looked past him as if he did not exist. She saw only Corbin. And when Corbin slowly turned away, the screams, impossibly, grew all the more shrill until her vocal cords gave way and there were only silent clouds of steam.

But Ella would never stop screaming in her mind.

EPILOGUE

ONDAY WAS CHAOS. JUST AT DAYBREAK, THE Greenwich detectives came back for the second time. A New York lawyer, summoned by Sturdevant for Jonathan's sake, arrived, chauffeur-driven, an hour before that.

As word leaked out of police headquarters concerning the magnitude of Sunday evening's events, the press began to arrive in force. A uniformed policeman kept most of them at bay, but two stringers for the *New York Post* found the unlocked porch door and strolled into the kitchen while Jonathan and Gwen were making breakfast for themselves, Harry Sturdevant, and Raymond Lesko. None of them had eaten since breakfast the day before, except for some Dunkin' Donuts at the Greenwich police station. The two stringers left quickly after Lesko showed his perfect teeth and wrapped a friendly arm around each of their necks.

At nine o'clock, Gwen Leamas called the Network

to explain why neither she nor Mr. Corbin would be in the office for a few days at least. A Network news executive called back ten minutes later, astonished at his good luck to have two Network staffers in the middle of a major story, and announced that he would have a live remote crew there within the hour for an exclusive interview. There would be no interviews, Gwen told him firmly and hung up, though she knew that her refusal would not deter these news types in the slightest.

The next call was for Lesko. Sergeant Gorby had agreed to let him know when Dancer showed signs of regaining consciousness at Greenwich Hospital. It was Lesko's idea that his presence at Dancer's bedside might do much to loosen his tongue. He further suggested that a Polaroid of Tom Burke's blackened face might also make a nice conversation starter, but Gorby felt that Lesko's face had enough heart attack potential as it was. He would pick up Lesko in ten minutes.

Ella's brother, who had been arrested and booked on the convenient charge of threatening with a gun, had talked freely to detectives for much of the night, ignoring the pleas of a lawyer whom the police had called in on his behalf. He admitted that he had seen his sister murder Tilden Beckwith in 1944 and that, although she soon made him go away to Palm Beach, he knew perfectly well that she was already arranging the eradication of Tilden's entire blood line. An explanation of the Corbin line versus the Beckwith line, to the extent that he fully understood it, took two hours by itself. He would also doze when asked a question he found difficult.

He admitted, after a fashion, that he, and Ella, and Ballanchine had also conspired to murder Jonathan Corbin, Gwen Leamas, and Harry Sturdevant, and that two attempts, which were foiled by Mr. Lesko, had been made, and that a third was in process when it was foiled by Tilden Beckwith himself. It was at this point that the confession began to lose what small measure of clarity it had had. Its usefulness was further compromised, to the lawyer's relief, by Tilden's insistence on explaining that Jonathan was in fact Tilden and the one called Gwen Leamas was in fact Charlotte Corbin whose name was really Margaret, all of whom, most of whom, were, in any case, dead. Ella's brother dozed again. When he awoke shortly, the only topic that interested him was his continuance as the chairman of Beckwith Enterprises. The detectives promised that he would certainly get their vote and agreed among themselves that there was little point in continuing the interrogation until they'd spoken further with Harry Sturdevant, who seemed best able to make sense out of this.

Sturdevant and Raymond Lesko had already agreed on a simplified version of events. Jonathan Corbin had very likely been drawn to Greenwich as a result of some forgotten stories he'd heard as a child. Ella Beckwith spotted him one day. His striking resemblance to the murdered Tilden Beckwith and her own fears did the rest. She had had Lesko hired to find out who he was and where he came from. When Lesko learned too much, and began to realize that the Corbins were blood relatives of Tilden Beckwith and all the other Beckwiths were not, and that the Chicago Corbins had probably been murdered as well, Ella Beckwith decided to try once more for a clean sweep. There would be no mention of Charlotte Corbin's ever being anyone else. If the name Margaret arose at all, it would be dismissed as a pet name, nothing more. There would certainly be no mention of Corbin's hallucinations or waking dreams, whatever they were. In any event they were gone. Just as his fear of the snow had gone. And Tilden, Jonathan had assured Harry Sturdevant during a quiet moment late last night, was gone as well. Jonathan had felt him go. It was early last evening. Just before Ella Beckwith started screaming.

There was still a chance, Sturdevant's chauffeur-driven lawyer advised him, that Jonathan Corbin could be charged with a felony. True, there seemed to be ample evidence that this Tom Burke entered Corbin's property with violent intent and that Corbin defended himself. But hanging the man in the crook of a tree with his own scarf after he was disarmed and disabled could be regarded as excessive force under the law.

"Horseshit," said Lesko on returning from Greenwich Hospital. "I would have made sure his clock was stopped myself if I knew there was still another guy with a gun on the other side of the house. This is the only town where they'd think about indicting a guy not for what he did but because he did it untidy."

"I assume Mr. Ballanchine confessed to his role in this."

"Dancer?" Lesko shook his head. "Guys like him don't confess. They try to deal. He's not awake ten minutes before he's trying to give away the store in return for immunity on the conspiracy and attempted-murder raps. He wants me to come back and see him alone, but he's got nothing to sell. The cops got his gun, they got that crazy old man's testimony, and they got mine. If they get around to searching Dancer's office they'll probably find a recording of him offering me fifteen grand to knock off Corbin." Lesko almost patted his chest again for emphasis. He'd retrieved the money from Dancer's pocket when he found him on the porch. Last time he patted his chest it got him twelve stitches plus a ride in an icebox. Lesko figured he'd earned it.

"Did he say anything about . . ." Sturdevant hesitated. "About what happened to him?"

Lesko nodded. "The guy who bashed him talked to

him first. He says it wasn't Corbin. He changed his mind later, but that's where he started."

"It was Tilden?"

Lesko shrugged.

"What do you think, Mr. Lesko?"

"I don't think anything. If you think I'm going to go around saying I believe in ghosts, you're crazier than old lady Beckwith."

"I don't suppose you'd make an exception, just between us."

The ex-cop shrugged again. After a thoughtful pause, he shook his head firmly.

"But you've already acknowledged," Sturdevant persisted, "that it was a very different person who helped you out of that car and who then walked over to Ella Beckwith's house. And once he was there, you and Gwen both saw him change right before your eyes."

"Sorry, Doc. It's as far as I go." It had taken him this much of his life, he decided, to learn that the simpler you look at things, the less you screw them up. Ghosts, he didn't need. Lesko was already working very hard on forgetting that someone who was dressed like him *could* be Tilden Beckwith bent down next to Dave Katz and looked at him back when he was laying on Ella Beckwith's rug with his brains scrambled. The scrambled brains would have been all the explanation Lesko needed if Corbin—if whoever pulled him out of his car hadn't remembered the wisecrack Katz made about his head, but Lesko had almost convinced himself that he hadn't really heard that, either. You can't let yourself start with that stuff. He had all of that he needed back when he was a kid going to Our Lady of Sorrows and the nuns taught them that they all had guardian angels watching them all the time and after that it was a year before most of them could even jerk off in peace.

Lesko knew what Sturdevant wanted to hear.

Gwen Leamas had explained it to him. Sort of. Sturdevant had this theory about genetic memory where everybody's brain taps into some ancestor's passed-on genes from time to time, which makes a lot of sense when you think about it, except she says the theory started falling apart where Corbin was concerned because the way the theory is supposed to work is you can only inherit memories that happened before you were conceived. Corbin remembered the Tilden guy's whole life, Gwen Leamas says, by the time he had it out with the old lady. Now Sturdevant has to come up with another theory because he doesn't have the sense to forget about it. He keeps pushing me about ghosts, Lesko decided, I'll tell him about guardian angels and let *him* see how it feels not to be able to even take a private shit for the next year or so. Anyway, we got more important things to think about.

"Listen, Doc"—Lesko gestured up the stairs where Corbin and Gwen had gone to be alone—"with this Beckwith Enterprises thing, Corbin's going to be rich now, right? But it's going to be a battle."

"I don't know that he wants any part of it. But if he does, yes, it will surely be a battle."

"He'll want it. If not for the money, then to keep any more fake Beckwiths from living off it."

Sturdevant nodded. "I've already told my lawyer to file for a freeze on Beckwith assets."

"What lawyer? That other black suit who thinks only poor people drive cars? I bet he hits you for two hundred grand a year, five years minimum."

Sturdevant tried not to wince, but he knew that Lesko was not far wrong. Any lawyer worth the name would get the testimony of Ella's brother thrown out on grounds of incompetence. The evidence Ballanchine might give will be labeled hearsay where events of forty years ago are concerned. From all reports, Ella's mind has snapped completely, so there won't be much help there. Nor will Jonathan be welcomed by the Beckwith Enterprises major stockholders and directors, or by Tilden II's wastrel son, Chip, who is at this moment probably lolling on a sailboat somewhere off Antigua, being served Mount Gay rum and tonics by some bare-breasted rental. Then there's the daughter, Barbara, the white sheep of the family by most accounts, who walked away from it and vanished shortly after graduating from Cornell University with a degree in veterinary medicine. She would have to be found, if only to offset Chip and, unlike him, she might even be persuaded to do the decent thing. Yes. The law firm would have to hire a good private detective to—Aha! We now leap ahead to whatever is behind Mr. Lesko's question.

"If you're about to suggest that you stay on this case"—Sturdevant shrugged as if it were a nonissue—"I would be crazy to let a law firm start over with a new investigator."

"I don't want to work for a lawyer at all. You hire me direct, Doc. It'll save you time and money."

Sturdevant had to agree. "But to do what, exactly?"

"Dancer says there was a will, and some other legal papers showing that the Corbins are the real heirs. I don't think they found all the copies. He says when those guys went out and burned down Charlotte Corbin's house, all they found was a third, maybe a fourth carbon. He says that's why they went out a few months later and burglarized Lucy Stone Tuttle's house and ended up killing her, too. He thinks she told them to buzz off before they strangled her, which means they came up empty. It's also why they didn't push Corbin in front of a train as soon as they knew who he was. They wanted to know if he had any idea who he was and if maybe he had those papers."

"Where would you begin looking?"

"Lots of places." He'd start with Dancer one more

time, he'd already decided. Dancer did say he wanted to see him, and there was always the chance that Dancer had found those papers and stashed them. But he didn't think so. If Dancer had that kind of leverage he'd have been living like a king years ago. Then he'd head back out to Chicago and track down Lucy Tuttle's grandchildren and the family of Whitney Corbin's widow and ask them to go through their attics in return for an eventual piece of the action. But first he thought he'd hang around Greenwich for a while. Especially around this house. Charlotte had come back here one more time after Tilden died. Corbin was as sure about that as if he'd been here to see it. She came back to see her best friend, Laura Hemmings. And Corbin himself had come here. He was pulled here. Like he had no choice. Maybe we'll have to tear up a few floorboards before we're through.

"Listen," Lesko said to Sturdevant, "I also got my old age to think about, and you're going to want someone who can keep an eye on things at Beckwith Enterprises. Tom Burke is now a vacancy. I want to be the new chief of Security at whatever they were paying him plus a bonus if I find the papers."

"A bonus, certainly," Sturdevant granted. "But I have no influence over whom that company hires."

"You will. Just have your lawyer file that freeze and then put me in a room alone with the board of directors. Some of them will resign anyway as soon as they read today's papers. The rest will be falling all over themselves trying to make their hands look clean."

Late that afternoon, Lesko made one more visit to the isolation wing at Greenwich Hospital. A don't-fuck-with-me expression, plus the bandage on his scalp and a flash of his gold shield got him past the guard with no questions asked. When he entered Lawrence Ballanchine's room, Ballanchine had to turn his head to see him. The whole left side of his face was packed with a heavy compress. Another wrapping of gauze held his jaw in place until surgery could be scheduled. For all his pain, Dancer seemed relieved that Lesko had come back.

"Shut the door," he slurred by way of greeting.

"You got two minutes." Lesko left it open.

"We can help each other, Lesko." He spoke with difficulty through thickened lips. "I have something you want. And you're going to help me walk away from this."

"Fat chance." Lesko shook his head. People like Dancer never failed to amaze him. Suck up to everyone who has money, treat everyone else like shit. Even here, like this.

Dancer ignored his response.

"The conspiracy and attempted-murder charges will never go to trial without your testimony. Agree to withdraw it, and I'll give you something you can sell for a lot of money."

"You got the will and those other papers?"

"Something better."

Lesko looked at his watch. "Now it's a minute. Then I'm out of here and your tight little ass is on its way to a Sing Sing gang rape."

Dancer closed his one eye. "Must you be such a pig, Mr. Lesko?"

"What do you want from me? A bedside manner? I get snippy with people who stuff me in trunks."

"They were married, Lesko."

Dancer waited for a reaction. He seemed troubled that there was none.

"Did you hear what I said? Tilden Beckwith and Charlotte Corbin were married. I know when and I know where."

"That's not such big news," Lesko lied. "It was just before they killed him, right?" He watched Dancer's face for the beginnings of a nod and he saw it. It was true. He'd felt right along that there had to be a better reason for killing the Corbins. A will, they could have fought. A will and a legal wife was something else.

"It was quite some time before." Now Dancer lied. But it was too late. He hadn't stopped the nod in time. "I'll give you the place and date after you've had a satisfactory meeting with my lawyer."

"No deal, Twinkletoes. See you around." Lesko turned toward the door. He wanted to get to the hallway so he could let the excitement show on his face.

"You couldn't have known this." Dancer's voice was desperate.

"Not for sure." Lesko couldn't resist. "But then you gave it to me when you said you had something better than a will. You even gave me *when* before you tried to take it back. The *where* part figures to be someplace around Chicago."

"Well, it isn't."

"Bullshit." Lesko turned again.

"You don't even know where to start looking. I know where the records are."

"That's what you're offering? You'll save me a little legwork if I let you walk without paying the tab?"

"It could take you months. You might never find it."

"I get paid by the day, pal."

Lesko stepped through the door.

"Jonathan?" She said his name softly.

He didn't stir. He lay facedown on the bed, fully clothed, the way she'd left him when she went to take her hot soaking bath in the big tub that had feet like claws. Gwen gathered the loose folds of Jonathan's terry robe and eased herself down onto the bed, her back against two pillows. She wished she still smoked cigarettes. This was one of those perfect times for a cigarette.

She reached to touch the white Victorian dress, which she'd draped over a high-backed bedside chair. It was dry. Soiled at the hem, but dry. Not ruined. She let her eyes drift lazily around the room, taking it in, feeling it. She began to understand how it was possible for Jonathan to drift back into another time. It had almost happened to her as she sat in the tub watching the steam rise. It was almost happening now.

Laura Hemmings had used that tub. And she'd slept in this room. Perhaps in this very bed, which had come with the house because it was too heavy to move. And Margaret had surely been up here. Visiting. Chatting. Looking at a new dress Laura bought. Maybe they cried together here.

Maybe it was here where she decided she didn't want to live with fear and hurt and uncertainty anymore. Gwen could understand that. God knows, she'd almost bolted herself.

She touched a hand very lightly to Jonathan's back. Such a gentle man. A good man. So full of life and fun and good ideas. At least he *was* like that, and perhaps will be again. His eyes were clearer, last night and this morning, than they'd been in—a year? A year at least.

A good and gentle man.

Who has killed three other not so gentle men. With his bare hands. Or Tilden has. Oh, that *is* going to take some getting used to.

"Tilden! Tilden Beckwith, old buddy!" She called him in her mind.

She imagined a curl of smoke from the cigarette she didn't have. She made it drift over the bed to its footposts, and she caused it to form into Tilden. There. There he was. Standing there with that same little-boy smile Jonathan has when he's pleased with himself.

"If I decide to stay here for a while, you're not

going to be hanging about all the time, are you? I mean . . ."

Wait.

You go away, Tilden.

I want to talk to Margaret.

Gwen started another curl of smoke.

Margaret was there. She gave Tilden's hand a squeeze and smiled up at him. Tilden bowed once to Gwen, and then he was gone.

Gwen's Margaret was smaller than she expected. She wore a green embroidered dressing gown with a high oriental collar. She had brown hair, shiny and all brushed out, and her eyes were almost the color of her gown. She was wearing slippers. That's why she looked smaller. She was grinning at Gwen.

"Hi!" Gwen grinned back at her and waved.

Now what?

"Margaret, you're really very lovely, by the way."

Gwen's Margaret blushed and returned the compliment with a gesture of her hands.

"Margaret." Gwen stopped. It suddenly struck her that she had taken the last of Uncle Harry's propranolol tablets last night after she saw that man hanging from the tree. Was the pill doing this? No. She was doing it. She was making it up. And there was nothing wrong with that.

"Margaret? Are you and Tilden together now? For good, I mean."

Margaret nodded happily.

"I'm glad."

Margaret made another gesture that took in both Gwen and Jonathan. It was the same question.

"I think so. It depends a little bit on what I was going to ask Tilden. Are you and he going to be living . . . um . . . staying here in this house?"

"Oh, no." Margaret's lips formed the words. Then she said something else that looked like "This is . . .

this is Laura's house." Margaret made a quick erasing motion with her hands, as if she were playing charades, and pointed to the bathroom door. A very tiny blond woman came through it, carrying a bundle of soiled towels.

"Oh, now wait," Gwen Leamas laughed. She made an erasure motion of her own, and Laura Hemmings was gone.

"She wasn't really there, was she? Tell me this house isn't haunted."

Margaret winked a reassurance and shook her head.

"Margaret?"

She waited, still smiling pleasantly.

"Margaret, where do you go? I mean, what happens afterward?"

Margaret's reply, although Gwen could not hear it, was untroubled and without hesitation, but she seemed to stumble after she'd formed the first few words. She paused thoughtfully and tried again. She reminded Gwen of someone who'd been stopped on the street and asked for directions to a place that person knew perfectly well but could not for the life of her explain how to get there. Margaret at last gave up. She shrugged helplessly at Gwen.

"Gwen, honey?"

She felt Jonathan's hand touch her cheek.

"Hi!" She took the hand and squeezed it.

"Were you asleep?"

Gwen stretched and looked around the bedroom. "I don't think so."

"You were talking."

"Oh." She hesitated. "Then maybe I did drop off." She thought about asking him to describe Margaret again. And Laura Hemmings. Perhaps some other time.

"You smell terrific." His fingers probed for an opening in the terry robe at her waist.

"Well, you don't." She slapped his hand. "The bathtub's free now."

"Will you wait right here?"

"You betcha."

Yes. I'll wait. And I'll be glad when you come out all clean and shaved and naked. But take your time.

"Jonathan?"

"Yes, sweetheart."

"You were talking about us flying down to a warm beach someplace."

"Just as soon as they let us."

"Would you care if we went someplace else?"

"Wherever you'd like."

"I'd like to go to Lake Geneva."

"Wisconsin? In the winter?"

"They have some really cozy inns up there. With rooms looking out over the lake where we can go skating and iceboating. And the rooms each have their own fireplaces."

"Where did this come from?"

"I don't know. It's what I'd like."

"Gwen?"

"Uh-huh?"

"Would you marry me, please?"

"In Lake Geneva? I will in Lake Geneva."

"Um, sure."

"That's a lovely idea, Jonathan."

ABOUT THE AUTHOR

JOHN R. MAXIM lives in Westport, Connecticut, except when he's in places like Moscow and Zurich. He won't tell us what he does there.

The author has written seven previous books, including *Abel Baker Charley* and *A Matter of Honor*, and is currently at work on a new novel.

JOHN R. MAXIM

A MATTER OF HONOR ──────────

Paul Bannerman thought he had finally left the world of contract assassins and spies behind. With the fall of communism and the triumph of democracy, he was ready to forget his bloody past and start a new life as a private citizen. Then he gets an urgent call from Vienna that shatters his false sense of security.

Carla Benedict is Bannerman's most ruthless agent—but she's also a woman in love. And she's just had to eliminate her lover, a smooth, lethal spy. Meanwhile, in Russia, a retired American police detective is invited on a honeymoon trip that is far less innocent than it seems. Soon they will all become unwitting pawns in an underground civil war involving hard-line Communists, devious reformers, drug smugglers, and a new and brutal Russian mafia. And Bannerman, with a very unlikely ally, will blast his way out of retirement.
❏ 29920-4 $5.99/$6.99 in Canada